LADY of QUALITY

TWO NOVELS IN ONE

CHARITY GIRL

# LADY of QUALITY

**TWO NOVELS IN ONE**

# CHARITY GIRL

## GEORGETTE HEYER

FALL RIVER PRESS

*Lady of Quality* © 1972 by Georgette Heyer
*Charity Girl* © 1970 by Georgette Heyer
Internal design © 2006 by Sourcebooks, Inc.
Sourcebooks and the colophon are registered trademarks of Sourcebooks, Inc.

This 2010 edition published by Fall River Press,
by arrangement with Sourcebooks, Inc.

Fall River Press
122 Fifth Avenue
New York, NY 10011

ISBN: 978-1-4351-2396-0

Printed in the United States of America
1 3 5 7 9 10 8 6 4 2

The characters and events portrayed in this book are fictitious
or are used fictitiously. Any similarity to real persons, living or dead,
is purely coincidental and is not intended by the author.

# Contents

# Lady of
# Quality

# One

THE ELEGANT TRAVELLING CARRIAGE WHICH BORE MISS Wychwood from her birthplace, on the border of Somerset and Wiltshire, to her home in Bath, proceeded on its way at a decorous pace. This was dictated by her coachman, an elderly autocrat, who, having known her from the day of her birth, almost thirty years before, drove her at the pace he considered proper, and turned a deaf ear to her requests to him to 'put 'em along!' If she didn't know what was due to her consequence, as Miss Wychwood of Twynham Park, he did; and even if she was an old maid—in fact, almost an ape-leader, though he would never call her one, and had turned off the impudent stable-boy who had dared to do so, after giving him a rare box on the ear— he knew very well how his late master would have wished his only daughter to be driven about the country. He had a pretty good idea, too, of what Sir Thomas would have felt had he known that Miss Wychwood had set up her own establishment in Bath, a few months after his death, with only a squinny old Tough to lend her countenance. A mean bit, Miss Farlow, if ever he saw one: more like a skinned rabbit than a woman, and a regular gabble-grinder into the bargain. It was a marvel to him that Miss Wychwood was able to endure her bibble-babble, for she wasn't short of a sheet, not by any means she wasn't!

The lady thus stigmatized was seated beside Miss Wychwood in the carriage, beguiling the tedium of the journey with a stream of small talk. She was of uncertain age, but it was unkind to describe her as an old Tough; and although she was certainly very thin it was unjust to liken her to a skinned rabbit. She was a distant relation of Miss Wychwood, left by an improvident parent in indigent circumstances; and when she had received a visit from Sir Geoffrey Wychwood, and had grasped that she owed this unprecedented honour to his urgent wish to procure her services as chaperon to his sister she had seen in his unromantically stout person a Paladin sent by Providence to rescue her from a drab lodging, mean fare, and the constant dread of finding herself in debt. She was not to know that her prospective charge had fought strenuously against having her, or any other female, foisted on to her; but when she had presented herself at Twynham Park, nervously clutching her oldfashioned reticule, desperately anxious to please, and staring up into Miss Wychwood's face with frightened, pleading eyes, Miss Wychwood's heart had overcome her judgement, and she had had no other thought than to make the poor little creature welcome. Lady Wychwood, quite unable to picture meek little Miss Farlow as a companion, and far less as a chaperon, to the lively Miss Wychwood, took the earliest opportunity that offered to beg her sister-in-law not to accept Miss Farlow's services without careful consideration. 'I am persuaded, dearest, that you will find her a dreadful bore!' she said earnestly.

'Yes, very likely, but I should find any chaperon a dreadful bore,' said Annis. 'So, if I must have a chaperon—not that I see the least need of one, at my age!—I'd as lief have her as any other. At least she won't try to rule my house, or to dictate to me! Besides, I'm sorry for her!' She laughed suddenly, perceiving the doubtful look in Lady Wychwood's mild blue eyes. 'Ah, you are afraid she won't exercise any control over me! You are perfectly right: she won't! But nor would anyone else, you know.'

'But, Annis, Geoffrey says—'

'I know exactly what Geoffrey says,' interrupted Annis. 'I've known what he would say any time these twenty years, and I find him far more of a bore than poor Maria Farlow. No, no, don't try to look shocked! I daresay no one knows better than you that he and I *cannot* deal together. The only time when we have been in perfect agreement was when he assured me that I should love his wife!'

'Oh, Annis!' protested Lady Wychwood, blushing, and turning away her head. 'You shouldn't say such things! Besides, I can't believe you mean it, when you won't continue living with me!'

'What a rapper!' commented Annis, the laughter still dancing in her eyes. 'I could live happily with you for the rest of my days, as well you know! It's my very worthy, starched-up, and consequential brother with whom I can't and won't live. Yes, isn't it unnatural of me?'

'So *sad!*' mourned her ladyship.

'Oh, no, why? You would have cause to say so if I did remain here. You must surely own that life would be very much more peaceful without me provoking Geoffrey a dozen times a day!'

Lady Wychwood did not deny this, but she sighed and said: 'But you are far too young to be setting up your own establishment, dearest! I *quite* agree with dear Geoffrey about that!'

'You always do agree with him, Amabel: indeed, you are the perfect wife for him!' interjected Annis irrepressibly.

'I am sure I'm no such thing, though I do try to be. And as for agreeing with him, gentlemen are so much wiser than we are, and so much better able to *judge* of—of worldly matters— don't you think?'

'Emphatically, No!'

'But indeed Geoffrey is right when he says it will present a very odd appearance if you go to live in Bath all by yourself!'

'Well, I shan't be all by myself, for I shall have Maria Farlow with me.'

'Annis, I *cannot* persuade myself that she is the right person for you!'

'No, but the beauty of it is that having chosen her, and foisted her on to me, Geoffrey will never acknowledge that he was in error. Depend upon it, he will soon be discovering all manner of virtues in her, and telling you that her meek disposition will have an excellent influence over me.'

Since Sir Geoffrey had already said something very like this to her, Lady Wychwood was obliged to laugh; but she shook her head as well, and said: 'It's all very well for you to turn everything to a joke, but it won't be funny for Geoffrey—or for me either!—when we have people thinking that you left home because we were unkind to you!'

'My dear, they won't think any such thing when they see that we are on terms of perfect amity. I hope you don't mean to cut my acquaintance? I expect to entertain you frequently in Camden Place, and give you fair warning that I shall always look on Twynham as my second home, and am likely to descend upon you without ceremony for long visits. You will be wishing me at Jericho, I daresay!' She saw that Lady Wychwood was looking melancholy still, and went to sit beside her, taking her hand, and saying: 'Try to understand, Amabel! It isn't only because Geoffrey and I rub against one another that I am going to set up a home for myself. I want—I want a life of my own!'

'Oh, I do understand that!' said Lady Wychwood, in quick sympathy. 'From the moment I set eyes on you I have felt that it was positively wicked that such a lovely girl as you should be wasting her life! If only you would accept Lord Beckenham's offer, or Mr Kilbride's—well, no, perhaps not his! Geoffrey says he's a here-and-thereian, and a gamester, and I suppose that would hardly do for you, though I must confess that I thought he was excessively charming! Well, if you couldn't like Beckenham, what did you find to dislike in young Gaydon? Or—'

'Stop, stop!' begged Annis laughingly. 'I found nothing to dislike in any of them, but I couldn't discover in myself the smallest wish to marry any of them either. Indeed, I haven't any wish to marry anyone at all.'

'But, Annis, *every* woman must wish to be married!' cried Lady Wychwood, quite shocked.

'Now *that* provides the answer to what people will think when they see me living in my own house instead of at Twynham!' exclaimed Annis. 'They will think me an Eccentric! Ten to one, I shall become one of the Sights of Bath, like old General Preston or that weird creature who goes about in a hoop, and feathers! I shall be pointed out as—'

'If you don't stop talking such nonsense I shall be strongly tempted to slap you!' interrupted Lady Wychwood. 'I don't doubt you'll be pointed out, but it won't be as an Eccentric!'

In the event, both were proved to be right. Annis had acquaintances amongst the Bath residents, and several close friends living in the vicinity of Bath, with whom she had frequently stayed, so that she did not come to Bath as a stranger. It was thought to be a trifle eccentric of her to leave the shelter of her brother's house, but she was well-known to be a very independent young woman, and as she was, at that date, six and twenty years of age, long past her girlhood, only the stiffest and most censorious persons saw anything to condemn in her conduct. She was possessed of a considerable independence, and it was not to be wondered at that she should avail herself of its advantages. The only wonder was that she hadn't been snapped up in her first London Season by some gentleman on the look out for a bride in whom birth and beauty were accompanied by a handsome fortune.

No one knew the size of her fortune, but it was obviously large: her family had owned Twynham Park for generations; and her beauty was remarkable. If there were those who considered her too tall, and others who could only see beauty in brunettes, these critics were few in number. Her admirers—and she had a host of them—declared her to be a piece of perfection, and from the top of her guinea-gold curls to the soles of her slender feet they could detect no flaw in her. Her eyes were particularly fine, being of a deep blue, and so full of light that one infatuated gentleman, of a poetic turn of mind, said that their brilliance put the stars to shame. They were smiling eyes, set under delicate, arched brows; and her generous mouth seemed to be made for laughter. For the rest, she had an elegant figure, moved grace-fully, dressed herself with exquisite taste, and had charming manners, which endeared her to such elderly sticklers as old Mrs Mandeville, who pronounced her to be 'a very nice gal: none of your simpering misses! I can't think why she ain't married!'

Those who had been acquainted with her father knew that he had been dotingly fond of her, and supposed that that might have been why she had accepted none of the offers made her. No doubt, said the wiseacres, that was also why she had come to live in Bath now that he was dead: she meant to marry at last, and what chance of meeting an eligible gentleman could there be in the wilds of the country? Only one lady saw any impropriety in it, and as she was notoriously spiteful, and had two rather plain daughters of marriageable age on her hands, no one paid any heed to her. Besides, Miss Wychwood had an elderly cousin living with her, and what could be more proper than that?

So Sir Geoffrey was right too, and was able to plume himself on his wisdom. He very soon became reconciled to the situa-tion, and found himself more in charity with his sister than he had ever been before. As for Miss Farlow, she had never been so happy in all her life, or enjoyed so much comfort, and she felt that she could never be sufficiently grateful to dear Annis, who not only paid her a very generous wage, but who showered every sort of luxury on her, from a fire in her bedroom to the right to order the carriage whenever she wished to go beyond walking-distance. Not that she ever did avail herself of this permission, for that, in her opinion, would be a sadly encroaching thing to do. Unfortunately, her overflowing gratitude caused her to irritate Miss Wychwood almost beyond bearing by fussing over her incessantly, running quite unnecessary errands for her (much to the jealous wrath of Miss Jurby, Annis's devoted dresser), and entertaining her (she hoped) with an inexhaustible flow of what Annis called nothing-sayings.

She was doing that on the journey back to Bath from Twynham Park. The fact that she received only mechanical responses from Miss Wychwood did not offend her, or cause her to abate her cheerful chatter. Rather she increased it, for she could see that her dear Miss Wychwood was a trifle in the dumps, and considered it to be her duty to divert her mind. No doubt she was sad to be leaving Twynham: Miss Farlow could well understand that, for she was feeling rather sad herself: it had been such an agreeable week!

'So very kind as Lady Wychwood is!' she said brightly. 'I declare it makes one sorry to be going away, not but what home is best, isn't it? We must look forward now to Easter, when we shall have them all to stay in Camden Place. We shan't know how to make enough of those sweet children, shall we, Annis?'

'I don't think I shall find it difficult,' said Annis, with a faint smile. 'And I fancy Jurby won't either!' she added, twinkling across at her dresser, who was sitting on the forward seat, holding her mistress's jewel-box on her angular knees. 'Little Tom's last encounter with Jurby was a very near-run thing, I promise you, Maria! Indeed, I am persuaded that had I not chanced to come into the room at that moment she'd have spanked him—as well he deserved! Wouldn't you, Jurby?'

Her dresser replied austerely: 'Tempted I may have been, Miss Annis, but the Lord gave me strength to resist the promptings of the Evil One.'

'Oh, no, was it the Lord who gave you that strength?' said Annis, quizzing her. 'I had thought it was *my* intervention that saved him!'

'Poor little fellow!' said Miss Farlow charitably. 'So high-spirited! Such quaint things as he says! I'm sure I never saw such a forward child. Your sweet little goddaughter, too, Annis!'

'I fear it's useless to ask me to go into raptures over infants in arms,' said Annis apologetically. 'I daresay I shall like both children well enough when they are older. In the meantime I must leave it to their mama, and to you, to dote on them.'

Miss Farlow realized that dear Annis had the headache, which was the only possible explanation for her want of enthusiasm over her nephew and niece. She said: 'Now, why do you let me rattle on when I am persuaded you have the headache? *That* is not treating me as you should, or as I wish you to! There is nothing so irritating to the nerves as being obliged to attend to fireside chatter—not that this is the fireside, of course, though the hot brick I have under my feet keeps me as warm as toast—when one is not feeling in good point. And it wouldn't surprise me, my love, if it is the weather which has made your head ache, for a cold wind frequently gives *me* a sort of tic, and the wind is very sharp today—not that we are conscious of it in the carriage, which I am sure is the most comfortable one imaginable, but there is bound to be a draught, and we mustn't forget that you stood talking to Sir Geoffrey for several minutes before you got into it. That was what started the mischief depend upon it! I expect it will go off when you are safely home again, and in the meantime I shan't tease you by talking to you. Are you sure you are warm enough? Let me give you my shawl, to put round your head! Jurby will hold your hat, or I will. Now, where did I put my smelling-salts? They *should* be in my reticule, for I always put them there when I go on a journey, because one never knows when one may need them, does one? But they don't seem to be—Oh, yes, here they are! They had slipped down to the bottom, and were under my handkerchief, though goodness knows how they can have *got* under it, for I distinctly recall putting them on top of everything else, so that they would be handy. I often think how extraordinary it is that things move by themselves, which no one can deny they *do!*'

She continued in this way for several minutes, and when Annis declined the shawl and the smelling-salts, wished that they had thought to bring a pillow to put behind Annis's head, or that it were possible to make her a tisane. In desperation, Annis shut her eyes, and after drawing Miss Jurby's attention to this, and telling her that they must be as quiet as mice, because Miss Annis was just dropping off to sleep, she at last subsided.

Annis had no headache, nor was she depressed at leaving Twynham Park. She was bored. Possibly the bleak weather, though it hadn't made her head ache, had affected her spirits, making her feel, most unusually, that the future was as gray and as unpromising as the sky. Lady Wychwood had tried to keep her at Twynham for a few more days, prophesying that it was going to snow, but Annis could not be persuaded to extend her visit, even if it was going to snow, which she thought extremely unlikely. Appealed to, Sir Geoffrey said: 'Snow? Pooh! Nonsense, my love! Far too much wind for that, and nothing like cold enough! Naturally we should be happy to keep Annis with us, but if she has engagements in Bath we should neither of us wish to deter her from keeping them. What's more, if it *did* snow she will be perfectly safe with Twitcham on the box.'

So Annis had been allowed to set forth without further hindrance from her anxious sister-in-law, privately thinking that if it really did snow she would be better off in her own house in Bath than immured at Twynham Park. No snow fell, but no gleam of sunlight broke through the clouds to enliven the gloom of a sodden landscape; and a north-easterly wind did nothing to alleviate the discomforts of a March day. Her spirits were understandably depressed, and she was only roused from a melancholy vision of her probable future when, some eight miles short of Bath, Miss Farlow cried: 'Oh, goodness me, has there been an accident? Ought we to stop? Do look, dear Annis!'

Jerked out of her unprofitable meditations, Miss Wychwood opened her eyes. No sooner did they alight on the cause of Miss Farlow's sudden exclamation that she tugged the check-string, and, as Twitcham pulled up his horses, said: 'Oh, poor things! Of course we must stop, Maria, and try what we can do to rescue them from such a horrid plight!'

While her footman jumped down to open the carriage-door, and to let down the steps, she had time to assimilate the details of the mishap which had befallen two fellow-travellers. A gig, with one wheel missing, was lying at a drunken angle at the side of the road, and beside it were standing two people: a female, huddled in a cloak, and a fair young man, who was feeling the knees of the sturdy cob which he had drawn out from between the shafts of the gig, and who said, just as James, the footman, pulled open the door of Miss Wychwood's carriage: 'Well, thank God, at least this bone-setter is none the worse!'

His companion, whom Miss Wychwood perceived to be a very young, and a very pretty girl, replied, with some asperity: 'I don't see much to be thankful for in that!'

'I daresay you don't!' retorted the young gentleman. '*You* won't be called upon to pay for—' He broke off, as he became aware that the slap-up equipage which had just swept round a bend in the road had come to a halt, and that its occupant, a dazzlingly lovely lady, was preparing to descend from it. He gave a gasp, pulled off his modish beaver, and stammered: 'Oh! I didn't see—I mean, I didn't think—that is to say—'

Miss Wychwood laughed, and relieved him from his embarrassment, saying, as she alighted from her carriage: 'Did you suppose anyone could be so odiously selfish as *not* to stop? Not I, I promise you! The same thing happened to me once, and I know just how helpless it makes one feel when one loses a wheel! Now, what can I do to rescue you from this horrid predicament?'

The girl, eyeing her warily, said nothing; but the gentleman bowed, and said: 'Thank you! It is excessively good of you, ma'am! I shall be very much obliged to you if you will direct them, at the next posting-house, to send a chaise here, to carry us to Bath. I am not familiar with this part of the country, so I don't know—And then there is the horse! I can't leave him here, can I? Perhaps—Only I don't like to ask you to find a wheelwright, ma'am, though I think a wheelwright is what is chiefly needed!'

At this, his companion intervened, announcing that a wheelwright was not what she needed. 'Ten to one he wouldn't come at all, and even if he did come, whoever heard of a wheelwright mending a wheel on the road? Particularly a wheel that has two broken spokes! It would be *hours* before we reached Bath, and you must *know* that it is of the first importance that I should be there not a moment later than five o'clock! I might have known how it would be when you meddled in what is quite my own affair, for of all the mutton-headed people I ever was acquainted with you are the *most* mutton-headed, Ninian!' she said indignantly.

'Let me remind you, Lucy,' retorted the gentleman, flushing up to the roots of his fair hair, 'that the accident was no fault of mine! And, further, that if I had not meddled, as you choose to call it, in your affair you would have found yourself at this moment stranded miles from Bath! And if we are to talk of *muttonheads*—!' He broke off, controlling himself with a visible effort, set his teeth, and said in the icy voice of one determined not to allow his anger to get the better of him: '*I* shall not do so, however!'

'No, don't!' said Annis, considerably amused by this interchange. 'You really have no time to indulge in recriminations at just this moment, have you? If it is a matter of importance to you to reach Bath before five o'clock, Miss—?'

She left a pause, her brows raised questioningly, but the youthful lady before her did not seem to be very willing to fill it. After hesitating for a few moments, she stammered: 'If you please, ma'am, will you just call me Lucilla? I—I have a very particular reason for not wishing anyone to know my surname—in case they come in search of me!'

'They?' enquired Miss Wychwood, wondering what kind of an adventure she had stumbled on.

'My aunt, and *his* father,' said Lucilla, nodding towards her escort. 'And very likely my uncle too, if he can be persuaded to bestir himself!' she added.

'Good God!' exclaimed Miss Wychwood, her eyes dancing. 'Can it be that I am assisting in an elopement?'

The haste with which both the lady and the gentleman repudiated this suggestion was attended by so much vehemence, and with so much loathing, that Miss Wychwood was hard put to it not to burst out laughing. She managed to keep her countenance, and said, with only a tiny tremor in her voice: 'I beg your pardon! Indeed, I can't think how I came to say anything so shatter-brained, for something seemed to tell me at the outset that it was not an elopement!'

Lucilla said, with dignity: 'I may be a sad romp, I may be a little gypsy, and my want of conduct may give people a disgust of me, but I am *not* lost to all sense of propriety, whatever my aunt says, and nothing could prevail on me to elope with *anyone*! Not even if I were madly in love, which I'm not! As for eloping with Ninian, that would be a nonsensical thing to do, because—'

'I wish you will keep your tongue, Lucy!' interrupted Ninian, looking very much vexed. 'You rattle on like a regular bagpipe, and see what comes of it!' He turned towards Annis, saying stiffly: 'I cannot wonder at it that you were misled into supposing that we are eloping. The case is far otherwise.'

'Yes, it is,' corroborated Lucilla. 'Far, *far* otherwise! The truth is that I am *escaping* from Ninian!'

'*I see!*' said Annis sympathetically. 'And he is helping you to do it!'

'Well, yes—in a way he is,' Lucilla admitted. 'Not that I wished him to help me, but—but the circumstances made it very difficult for me to stop him. It—it is all rather complicated, I'm afraid.'

'It does seem to be,' agreed Annis. 'And if you are going to explain it to me—not that I wish to be vulgarly inquisitive!— how would it be if you were to get into my carriage, and allow me to convey you to wherever it is in Bath that you wish to go?'

Lucilla cast a somewhat longing look at the carriage, but shook a resolute head. 'No. It is very kind of you, but it would be too shabby of me to leave Ninian behind, and I won't do it!'

'Yes, you will!' said Ninian. 'I have been wondering how to get you to Bath before you are quite frozen, and if this lady will take you there I shall be very much obliged to her.'

'I will certainly take her there,' said Annis, smiling at him. 'My name, by the way, is Wychwood—Miss Annis Wychwood.'

'And mine, ma'am, is Elmore—Ninian Elmore, entirely at your service!' he responded, with great gallantry, 'And this is—'

'Ninian, *no!*' cried Lucilla, much flustered. 'If she were to tell my aunt where I am—'

'Oh, don't be afraid of that!' said Annis cheerfully. 'Never shall it be said of me that I'm an addle-plot, I promise you! I collect that you are going to visit a friend, or perhaps a relation?'

'Well,—well not *precisely!* In fact, I haven't met her yet!' disclosed Lucilla, in a rush of confidence. 'The thing is, ma'am,

I am going to apply for the post of companion to her. She says—I have brought the notice I saw in the *Morning Post* with me, but most foolishly packed it in my portmanteau, so that I can't immediately show it to you—but she says she requires an active and genteel young lady of willing disposition, and that applicants must call at her residence in North Parade between the hours of—'

'North Parade!' exclaimed Annis. 'My poor child, can it be that you are going to visit *Mrs Nibley?*'

'Yes,' faltered Lucilla, dismayed by Miss Wychwood's very obvious pity. 'The *Honourable* Mrs Nibley, which made me think she must be a perfectly respectable person. *Isn't* she, ma'am?'

'Oh, yes! A pattern-card of respectability!' answered Annis. 'Renowned in Bath as the town's worst archwife! She has had I don't know how many active and genteel ladies to wait on her hand and foot during the three years I've been acquainted with her. Either they leave her house in strong hysterics, or she turns them off because they have not been *sufficiently* active or willing! My dear, do believe me when I tell you that the post she offers would not do for you!'

'I guessed as much!' interpolated Mr Elmore, not without satisfaction.

Lucilla bore all the appearance of having sustained a stunning blow, but at this her spirit flickered up in a brief revival, and she said: 'No, you didn't! Pray, how could you have guessed anything of the sort?'

'Well, at all events, I guessed no good would come of such a bird-witted start, and I said so at the time! You can't deny that! *Now* what do you mean to do?'

'I don't know,' said Lucilla, her lips trembling. 'I shall have to think of something.'

'There's only one thing you *can* do, and that is to return to Mrs Amber,' he said.

'Oh, no, no, no!' she cried passionately. 'I would rather hire myself out as a *cook-maid* than go back to be scolded, and reproached, and told I had made my aunt ill, and *forced* to marry you, which is what would happen, on account of my having run away with you! And it wouldn't be the least use to tell my aunt, or your papa, that I didn't run away with you, but away *from* you, because even if they believed me they would think it *worse*, and say we *must* be married!'

He blenched visibly, and ejaculated: 'Oh, my God, that's just what they would do! What a hobble we're in! It almost makes me wish I hadn't caught you creeping out of the house, and thought it my duty to see you came to no harm!'

'Forgive me!' interposed Miss Wychwood. 'May I offer a suggestion?' She smiled at Lucilla, and held out her hand. 'If you are set on being a companion, come and be a companion to me!' She heard Miss Farlow within the carriage utter a faint, outraged clucking, and made haste to add: 'It won't do, you know, to be putting up at an hotel, all by yourself; and it's not to be expected that Mrs Nibley—even if she engaged you, which I think extremely unlikely—would be prepared to do so immediately. She will require you to furnish her with the name and direction of some respectable person willing to vouch for you.'

'Oh, goodness!' exclaimed Lucilla, dismayed. 'I never thought of that!'

'*Most* understandable that you should not!' said Annis. 'One can't think of everything, after all! But I do feel that it is a matter which ought to be considered, and I also feel that it is quite impossible to consider anything when one is standing in the open road, with a perfectly horrid wind positively freezing one's wits! So do, pray, get into my carriage! Mr Elmore will follow us in due course, and we can discuss the matter when we have dined, and are sitting snugly beside the fire.'

'Thank you!' Lucilla said unsteadily. 'You are *very* kind, Miss Wychwood! Only—only how is Ninian to manage, when he can't leave the horse?'

'There is no need for you to fret about me,' said Mr Elmore nobly. 'I shall lead the horse to the next hostelry, and trust to being able to hire some sort of a carriage to carry me to Bath.'

'You might even ride the horse,' suggested Annis.

'But I am not dressed for riding!' he said, staring at her. 'And—and even if I were, it is not a saddle-horse!'

Annis now perceived that Mr Elmore was a very correct young gentleman. She was a good deal amused, but although the ready laughter sprang to her eyes she said, with perfect gravity: 'Very true! We must leave you to do as you think best, but I should perhaps warn you that since this is not a post-road you may find it difficult to hire a chaise at the—the "next hostelry", and may even be reduced to contenting yourself with some vehicle *quite* beneath your touch! However, I shan't despair of seeing you in Upper Camden Place in time for dinner!' She then furnished him with her exact direction, smiled benignly upon him and pushed Lucilla to the steps of her carriage.

Propelled irresistibly by a firm hand in the small of her back, Lucilla mounted them, but paused at the top, to say, over her shoulder: 'If I could be of the least use to you, Ninian, I wouldn't leave you in this fix, even though you wouldn't have been in it if you hadn't meddled in my affairs!'

'You may make yourself easy on that head!' responded Mr Elmore. 'Far from being of use to me, your presence would make everything worse! If it could be!' he added.

'Well, of all the unjust things to say!' gasped Lucilla indignantly. She would have said more, but Miss Wychwood cut short her recriminations by thrusting her into the carriage. She then directed her interested footman to transfer her unexpected guest's baggage from the gig to the carriage, and, when this was done, herself mounted into the carriage, briskly desired Miss Farlow to make room for a third person on the back seat, pushed her own hot brick under Lucilla's feet, tucked a generous share of the fur-lined carriage-rug round her, and nodded to her footman to put up the steps. In a very few minutes the coachman had set his horses in motion, and Lucilla, snuggling between her hostess and Miss Farlow, heaved a small sigh, and, stealing a cold hand into Miss Wychwood's, whispered: 'Oh, I *do* thank you, ma'am!'

Miss Wychwood chafed the little hand, saying: 'You poor child! You are quite frozen! Never mind! We shall soon be in Bath, and we shan't discuss your problems until you are warm, and have dined, and—er—have the benefit of Mr Elmore's advice!'

Lucilla gave an involuntary choke of laughter, but refrained from comment. Very little conversation was exchanged during the rest of the journey, Lucilla, worn-out by the day's adventures, being on the brink of sleep, and Miss Wychwood confining her remarks to a few commonplaces addressed to Miss Farlow. For her part, Miss Farlow's usual flow of chit-chat was dried up, because (as she would presently tell her employer) her feelings had been wounded by the imputation that her own companionship did not suffice Miss Wychwood. Miss Jurby preserved a rigid silence, as befitted her position, but she too had every intention of favouring Miss Wychwood with her opinion of her latest, ill-judged start, as soon as she was alone with her—and in far more forthright terms than would be used by Miss Farlow.

Lucilla awoke when the carriage drew up in Upper Camden Place, and was insensibly cheered by the welcoming candlelight coming through the open door of the house, and by the benevolent aspect of the elderly butler, who beamed upon his mistress, and accepted, without a blink, the unheralded arrival of a stranger in her company.

Annis handed Lucilla over to Mrs Wardlow, her housekeeper, with instructions to bestow her in the Pink bedchamber, and to direct one of the maids to wait on her; and prepared herself to deal with her affronted companion.

Waiting only until Lucilla, meekly following Mrs Wardlow up the stairs, was out of earshot, Miss Farlow said that while she trusted it would always be far from her intention to criticize any of her dear cousin's actions she felt herself bound to say that had she known that her companionship no longer satisfied dear Annis she would instantly have resigned her post.

'Whatever the exigencies of my circumstances,' she said tearfully, 'I should prefer to live in utter penury than to remain where I am not wanted, however comfortable this house may be, which indeed it is, not to say luxurious, for *Better a dinner of herbs where love is than a stalled ox and hatred therewith*! Even though I am not at all partial to herbs, except for a little parsley in a sauce, and I have never been able to understand how anyone, even a Biblical person, could possibly *live* on herbs. However, times change, and when one thinks of all the *most* peculiar things that happened in the Bible, well, it makes one positively thankful one didn't live in those days! Bushes catching fire, and ladders coming down out of the sky, and people being swallowed up by whales, and not being a penny the worse for it well, I should find that sort of thing most disconcerting! Manna, too! I've never been able to discover what kind of food that was, but I am persuaded I shouldn't like it, even if I were starving, and it was suddenly dropped on me, which I think extremely unlikely. *But*,' she continued, fixing Miss Wychwood with a reproachful gaze, 'I would make a push to like it if you wish to set Another in my place!'

'Don't be such a goosecap, Maria!' replied Miss Wychwood, in a rallying tone. 'I haven't the least desire to set Another in your place!' Always appreciative of the ridiculous, she could not resist the impulse to say: 'I can vouch for it that there is no hatred in this house—unless Jurby hates you, but you wouldn't care for that, because you must know that she wouldn't do so if she didn't fear that you were ousting her in my regard!—but the stalled ox has me in a puzzle! Where, cousin, do you suspect me of stalling an ox?'

'I was speaking metaphorically,' answered Miss Farlow, in outraged accents. 'It is not to be supposed that you could stall an ox anywhere in Bath, for you may depend upon it that it would contravene the regulations. I daresay you wouldn't be permitted to stall a *cow*, and that would be of far more use to you!'

'So it would!' agreed Miss Wychwood, much struck.

'Oxen and cows have nothing to do with the case!' said Miss Farlow, dissolving into tears. 'My sensibilities have been deeply wounded, Annis! When I heard you invite that young woman to come here to be a companion to you, I suffered an—an electrical shock from which I fear my nerves will never recover!'

Perceiving that her elderly cousin was very much upset, Annis applied herself to the task of soothing her lacerated feelings. It took time and patience to mollify Miss Farlow, and although she succeeded in convincing her that she stood in no danger of being dismissed she failed to reconcile her to Lucilla's presence in Camden Place. 'I cannot like her, cousin,' she said impressively. 'You must forgive me if I say that I am astonished that you should have offered her the hospitality of your home, for in general you have such very superior sense! Mark my words, you will live to regret it!'

'If I do, Maria, you will have the comfort of being able to say that you told me so! But what reason could I possibly have for not rescuing that child from a very awkward predicament?'

'It's my belief,' said Miss Farlow darkly, 'that the story she told you was a take-in! A very hurly-burly young female I thought her! So coming—quite brass-faced indeed! Such a want of delicacy, running away from her home, and in the company of a *young gentleman*! No doubt I am oldfashioned, but such conduct doesn't suit my sense of propriety. What is more, I am very sure dear Sir Geoffrey would disapprove quite as strongly as I do!'

'Probably more strongly,' said Annis. 'But I hardly think he could be so foolish as to call her either coming or brass-faced!'

Miss Farlow quailed under the sparkling look of anger in Annis's eyes, and embarked on a confused speech which incoherently mixed an apology with a great deal of self-justification. Annis cut her short, telling her that she expected her to treat Lucilla with civility. She spoke with most unusual severity, and when the afflicted Miss Farlow sought refuge in tears was wholly unmoved, merely recommending her to go upstairs and to unpack her trunk.

# Two

When Miss Wychwood had changed her travelling dress for one of the simple cambric gowns she wore when she meant to spend the evening by her own fireside, and had endured a scold from Miss Jurby on the subjects of wilfulness, imprudence, and what her papa would have said had he been alive, she went to tap on the door of the Pink bedchamber, and, upon being bidden to come in, found her protégée charmingly attired in sprig muslin, only slightly creased from having been packed in a portmanteau, and with her dusky curls brushed free of tangles. They clustered about her head, in the artless style known as the Sappho, which, to Miss Wychwood's appreciative eyes, was not only very becoming, but which emphasized her extreme youth. Round her neck was clasped a row of pearls. This demure necklace was the only jewellery she wore, but Miss Wychwood did not for a moment suppose that the absence of trinkets denoted poverty. The pearls were real, and just the thing for a girl newly emerged from the schoolroom. So was that sprig muslin dress, with its high waist and tiny puff sleeves, but its exquisite simplicity stamped it as the work of a high class modiste. And the shawl which Lucilla was about to drape around her shoulders was of Norwich silk, and had probably cost its purchaser every penny of fifty guineas. It was plain to be seen that Lucilla's unknown aunt had ample means and excellent taste, and grudged the expenditure of neither on the dressing of her niece. It was equally plain that such a fashionable damsel, bearing all the appearance of one born to an independence, would never find favour with Mrs Nibley.

Lucilla said apologetically that she feared her dress was sadly crumpled. 'The thing was, you see, that I haven't been in the way of packing, ma'am.'

'I shouldn't think you've ever done so before, have you?'

'Well, no! But I couldn't ask my maid to do it for me, because she would have instantly told my aunt. That,' said Lucilla bitterly, 'is the worst of servants who have known one since one was a baby!'

'Very true!' agreed Annis. 'I am afflicted with several myself and know just how you feel. Now, tell me by what name I am to present you to people!'

'I *did* think of calling myself Smith,' said Lucilla doubtfully. 'Or—or Brown, perhaps. Some very ordinary name!'

'Oh, I shouldn't choose anything too ordinary!' said Annis, shaking her head. 'It wouldn't suit you!'

'No, and I am persuaded I should come to hate it,' said Lucilla naïvely. She hesitated for a moment. 'I think I'll keep my own name, after all, on account of not being rag-mannered, which I'm afraid I was, when I wouldn't let Ninian tell you what it is. I was in dread that you might betray me to my horrid uncle, but that was because I didn't know you, or how kind you are. So I'll tell you, ma'am. It's Carleton—with an E in the middle,' she added conscientiously.

'I will take care not to reveal the E to a living soul,' promised Annis, with perfect gravity. 'Anyone could be called Carlton without an E in the middle, but the E gives distinction to the name, and that, of course, is what you wish to avoid. So now that we have settled that problem let us go down to the drawing-room and await Mr Elmore's arrival!'

'If he does arrive!' said Lucilla unhopefully. 'Not that it signifies if he doesn't, except that my conscience will suffer a severe blow, even though it wasn't my fault that he came with me. But if he gets into a hobble I shall never cease to blame myself for having left him quite stranded!'

'But why should he be stranded?' said Annis reasonably. 'We left him some eight miles short of Bath—not in the middle of a desert! Even if he can't hire a vehicle, he might easily walk the rest of the way, don't you think?'

'No,' said Lucilla, sighing. 'He wouldn't think it at all the thing. I don't care a button for such antiquated flummery, but he does. I am excessively attached to him, because I've known him all my life, but I cannot deny that he is sadly wanting in— in *dash*! In fact, he is a pudding-heart, ma'am!'

'Surely you are too severe!' objected Miss Wychwood, ushering her into the drawing-room. 'Of course, I am barely acquainted with him, but it did not seem to me that he was wanting in dash! To have aided and abetted you in your flight was not the action of a pudding-heart, you must own!'

Lucilla frowned over this, and tried, not very successfully, to explain the circumstances which had led young Mr Elmore to embark on what was probably the only adventure of his blameless career. 'He wouldn't have done it if he hadn't been sure that Lord Iverley would have thought it the right thing,' she said. 'Though I daresay Lord Iverley will blame him for not having stopped me, which is wickedly unjust, and so I shall tell him if he gives poor Ninian one of his scolds! For how could he expect Ninian to be full of pluck when he has brought him up to be a pattern-card of—of amiable compliance? Ninian always does exactly what Lord Iverley wishes him to do—even when it comes to offering for me, which he doesn't in the least want to do! And for my part I don't believe Lord Iverley would have a fatal heart-attack if Ninian refused to obey him, but Lady

Iverley does think so, and has reared Ninian to believe that it is his sacred duty not to do *anything* to put his papa out of curl. And I will say this for Ninian: he has a very kind heart, besides holding Lord Iverley in great affection, and having pretty strict notions of—of filial duty; and I daresay he would liefer do anything in the world than drive his papa into his grave.'

Surprised, Miss Wychwood said: 'But is Lord Iverley— I collect he is Ninian's father?—a very old man?'

'Oh, no, not *very* old!' replied Lucilla. 'He is the same age as *my* papa would have been, if papa hadn't died when I was just seven years old. He was killed at Corunna, and Lord Iverley— well, he wasn't Lord Iverley then, but Mr William Elmore, because *old* Lord Iverley was still alive—but, in any event, he brought my papa's sword, and his watch, and his diary, and the very last letter he had scribbled to my mama, home to England, and gave them to my mama. They say he has never been the same man since Papa died. They were bosom-bows, you see, from the time when they were both at Harrow, and even joined the same regiment, and were never parted until Papa was killed! Which I *perfectly* see is a very touching story, for I am *not* hard-hearted, whatever Aunt Clara may say! But what I do *not* see, and never shall see, is why Ninian and I must be married merely because our fathers, in the *milkiest* way, made an idiotish scheme that we should!'

'It does seem a trifle unreasonable,' admitted Miss Wychwood.

'Yes, and because, when he married my mama, Papa bought a house just beyond the gates of Chartley Place, and Ninian and I were almost brought up together, and were very good friends, nothing will persuade Lord Iverley that we were *not* made for one another! And, *most* unfortunately, Ninian has fallen in love with someone whom Lord and Lady Iverley have taken in strong dislike—though why they should have done so I can't imagine, for they never stir out of Chartley Place, and have never set eyes on her! I daresay they think her rather too old for Ninian, and I must own it does seem strange that he should be dangling after a lady at least thirty years of age, and very likely more!'

This circumstance did not seem strange to Miss Wychwood, but what seemed very strange indeed to her was that the Iverleys should be taking so serious a view of what was, to her understanding, a case of calf-love, of violent but short duration. She said, smiling a little: 'I expect it does seem strange to you, Lucilla, but it is a well-known fact that young men are very apt to fall in love with women older than themselves. I fancy the Iverleys have no need to go into high fidgets over it!'

'Oh, no, of course they haven't!' Lucilla agreed. 'Good gracious, he fell desperately in love with some girl when he was in his first year at Oxford, and even I could guess that she was *most* ineligible! Fortunately, he fell out of love with her before the Iverleys knew anything about it, so they didn't fuss and fret over it. But this time some tattling busybody wrote to tell Lord Iverley that Ninian was making up to this London-lady, so Lord Iverley taxed him with it, and Lady Iverley implored him not to—to hasten his father's end by persisting in—in his suit, and—'

'Good God!' interrupted Miss Wychwood. 'What a couple of cabbage-heads! They deserve that Ninian should marry this undesirable female out of hand!' She caught herself up on this impulsive utterance, and said: 'I shouldn't say so, but I have an unruly tongue! Forget it! Am I right in thinking that Chartley Place is somewhere to the north of Salisbury? Is that where you too live?'

'No, not now. I did live there until Mama died, three years ago, but since then I've lived at Cheltenham, with my aunt and my uncle, and the house, which belongs to me, has been leased to strangers.'

This disclosure left Miss Wychwood at a loss. The words were melancholy, but the manner in which they were uttered was not at all melancholy. She said, tentatively: 'No doubt it must have been distressing to you to see strangers in your house?'

'Oh, no, not at all!' responded Lucilla sunnily. 'They are very agreeable people and pay a most handsome rent, besides keeping the grounds in excellent order. I should be happy to live in Cheltenham if my aunt would but take me to the Assemblies, and the theatre—but she won't, because she says I am too young, and it would be improper for me to go to balls and routs and drums until I have been regularly presented! But she doesn't think me too young to be married! That,' she said, her eyes kindling wrathfully, 'is why she took me to Chartley Place!' She paused, her bosom swelling with indignation. 'Miss Wychwood!' she said explosively. 'C–could you have conceived it possible that anyone could be so—so cockle-brained as to suppose that Ninian, having formed a strong attachment to another lady, would feel the least inclination to make me an offer? Or that I would be so obliging as to accept his offer? But they did!—all of them!' She stopped, deeply flushed, and it was a minute or two before she could overcome her agitation. She managed to do so, however, and continued, in a tight voice, saying: 'I thought that if I consented to visit the Iverleys I could depend on Ninian to—to stand buff, even though he lacked the—the *spunk* to tell his father he didn't wish to marry me if I wasn't there to support him! I should have known better!'

Considerably astonished, Miss Wychwood asked: 'But am I to understand that he told his father he was willing to offer for you? If that is so, isn't it possible that—'

'It isn't so!' said Lucilla flatly. 'I don't know what he said to Lord Iverley, but to me he said that it would be unwise to provoke a quarrel, and that the best thing would be for us to *seem* to be willing to become engaged, and to trust in providence to rescue us before the knot was tied between us. But I have no faith in providence, ma'am, and I felt as though—as though I was

being tangled in a net! And the only thing I could think of to do
was to run away. You see, there isn't anyone I can appeal to since
my uncle died—and I daresay he wouldn't have been of much
use, because he always let Aunt Clara have her own way in everything! He was a great dear, but *not* a man of resolution.'

Miss Wychwood blinked. 'Is he dead, then? I beg your
pardon, but I thought you said that your uncle would very likely
come to find you, if he could be persuaded to bestir himself!'

Lucilla stared at her, and suddenly gave a crack of scornful
laughter. 'Not *that* uncle, ma'am! The other one!' she said.

'The other one? To be sure! How stupid I am to have
supposed you only had one uncle! Do, pray, tell me about your
*horrid* uncle, so that I shan't become confused again! Was your
amiable uncle his brother?'

'Oh, no! My Uncle Abel was *Mama's* brother. My Uncle
Oliver is a Carleton, and Papa's elder brother—though only
three years older!' said Lucilla, in further disparagement of
Mr Oliver Carleton. 'He and my Uncle Abel were appointed to
be my guardians, but naturally they weren't obliged to take care
of me while Mama was alive, except for managing my fortune.'

'Have you a fortune?' asked Miss Wychwood, much impressed.

'Well, I *think* I have, because Aunt Clara is for ever telling me
to beware of fortune-hunters, but it seems to me that it belongs
to my Uncle Oliver, and not to me at all, because I am not
allowed to spend it! He sends my allowance to Aunt Clara, and
she only gives me pin-money, and when I wrote to tell him that
I was old enough to buy dresses *myself*, he sent me a disagreeable answer, refusing to alter the arrangement! Whenever I have
appealed to him he always says that my aunt knows best, and
I must do as she bids me! He is the most odiously selfish person
in the world, and hasn't a particle of affection for me. Only
fancy, ma'am, he has an *enormous* house in London, and has
never asked me to visit him! Not once! And when I suggested

that he might like me to keep house for him he answered in the rudest way that he wouldn't like it at all!'

'That was certainly uncivil, but perhaps he thought you rather too young to keep house. I collect he is not married?'

'Good gracious, no!' said Lucilla. 'Which just *shows* you, doesn't it?'

'I must own that he does sound very disagreeable,' admitted Annis.

'Yes, and what is more his manners are most disobliging—in fact, he is detestably top-lofty, never takes the least trouble to behave with civility to anyone, and—and treats one with the sort of stupid indifference which makes one *long* to hit him!'

Since it was obvious that she was fast working herself into a state of considerable agitation, it was perhaps fortunate that the entrance of Miss Farlow acted as an effectual stop to any further animadversions on the character of Mr Oliver Carleton. Miss Farlow's demeanour informed her employer that she was deeply wounded, but determined to bear the slight cast upon her with Christian resignation. Nothing could have exceeded her civility to Lucilla, which was so punctilious as almost to crush that ebullient young lady; and the manner in which she listened to whatever Annis said, and instantly agreed with it, was so servile that an impartial observer might well have supposed her to be the slave of a tyrannical mistress. But just as Annis, exasperated beyond endurance by these tactics, was on the point of losing her temper, Mr Elmore was announced, creating a welcome diversion.

He was looking decidedly out of temper, and, with only a glowering glance at Lucilla, devoted himself to the task of apologizing to his hostess for presenting himself in topboots and breeches: a social solecism which plainly lacerated all his finer feelings. In vain did Miss Wychwood beg him not to give the matter a thought, and draw his attention to her own morning-dress: nothing would do for him but to explain the circumstances which had compelled him to appear before her looking, as he termed it, like a dashed shabrag. 'Owing to the haste in which I was obliged to set out on the journey I had no time to pack up my gear, ma'am,' he said. 'I can only beg your forgiveness for being so improperly dressed! And also for being, I fear, so late in coming here! I was detained by the necessity of providing myself with additional funds, what little blunt I had in my pockets having been exhausted by the time I reached Bath!'

'I *knew* it was wrong of me to have deserted you!' cried Lucilla remorsefully. 'I am so very sorry, Ninian, but why didn't you tell me you were brought to a standstill? I have *plenty* of money, and if only you had asked me for it I would have given you my purse!'

Revolted, Mr Elmore was understood to say that he was not, he thanked God, reduced to such straits as that. He had laid his watch on the shelf which was bad enough, but better than breaking the shins of his childhood's friend. These mysterious words left his listeners at a loss, so he was obliged to explain that he had pawned his watch, which he considered to be preferable to borrowing money from Lucilla. Miss Farlow said that such sentiments did him honour; but his childhood's friend said roundly that it was just the sort of nonsensical notion he *would* take into his head; and Miss Wychwood was obliged to intervene hastily to prevent a lively quarrel between them. Miss Farlow, who, whatever her opinion might be of girls who ran away from their homes and insinuated themselves into the good graces of complete strangers, had (like many elderly spinsters) a soft spot for a personable young man, encouraged him to unburden himself of his several grievances, and lavished so much sympathy on him that by the time the dinner-bell was heard he was in a fair way to forgetting the humiliating experiences he had undergone, and was able to make a hearty meal, washed down with the excellent claret with which Sir Geoffrey kept his sister provided. At which point Miss Wychwood ventured to ask him whether he meant to remain in Bath, or to return to his anxious parents.

'I must return, of course,' he replied, a worried expression in his eyes. 'For they won't know where I am, and I fear my father will be fretting himself into a fever. I should never forgive myself if he were to suffer one of his heart-attacks.'

'No, indeed!' said Miss Farlow. 'Poor gentleman! Your mama, too! One hardly knows which of them to pity most, though I suppose her case is the worse, because of having *double* the anxiety!' She saw that he was looking guilty, and said consolingly: 'But never mind! How happy they will be when they see you safe and sound! Are you their only offspring, sir?'

'Well, no: not precisely the *only* one,' he answered. 'I'm their only son, but I have three sisters, ma'am.'

'Four!' interpolated Lucilla.

'Yes, but I don't count Sapphira,' he explained. 'She's been married for years, and lives in another part of the country.'

'I collect your father doesn't enjoy good health,' said Miss Wychwood, 'which makes it of the first importance that you shouldn't leave him in suspense for a moment longer than is necessary.'

'That's just it, ma'am!' he said, turning eagerly towards her. 'His constitution was ruined in the Peninsula, for besides being twice wounded, and having a ball lodged in his shoulder, which the surgeons failed to extract, after subjecting him to hours of torture, he had several bouts of a particularly deadly fever, which one gets on the Portuguese border, and which he never perfectly recovered from. And although he doesn't complain, we—my mother and I—are pretty sure that his shoulder pains him a good deal.' He hesitated, and then said shyly: 'You see, when he is well he is the most amiable man imaginable, and—and the most indulgent father anyone could wish for, but the indifferent state of his health makes him very—very irritable, and inclined to become agitated, which is very bad for him. So—so you will understand that it is of the first importance not to do anything to put him into the hips.'

'Indeed I understand!' said Miss Wychwood, regarding him with a kindly eye. 'You must certainly go home tomorrow, and by the quickest way possible. I'll furnish you with the means to pay your shot, redeem your watch, and hire a post-chaise, and you may repay me by a draft on your bank—so don't set up your bristles!'

She smiled as she spoke, and Ninian, who had stiffened, found himself smiling back at her, and stammering that he was very much obliged to her.

Lucilla, however, was frowning. 'Yes, but—Well, I see, of course, that it's your duty to go home, but what will you say when you are asked what has become of *me*?'

Nonplussed, he stared at her, saying after a pause during which he tried in vain to think of a way out of this difficulty: 'I don't know. I mean, I shall say that I can't answer that question, because I gave you my word I wouldn't betray you.'

Lucilla's opinion of this was plainly to be read in her face. 'You had as well tell them immediately where I am, because your father will make it a matter of obedience, and you'll knuckle down, just as you always do! Oh, why, *why* didn't you do as I *begged* you? I knew something like this would be bound to happen!'

He reddened, and replied hotly: 'If it comes to that, why didn't *you* do as *I* begged? I warned you that no good would come of running away! And if you mean to blame me for escorting you when I found you wouldn't listen to a word of reason it—it is beyond everything! A pretty fellow I should be if I let a silly chit of an ignorant schoolgirl wander about the country alone!'

'I am not an ignorant schoolgirl!' cried Lucilla, as flushed as he was.

'Yes, you are! Why, you didn't even know that you have to be on the waybill to get a seat on a stage-coach! Or that the Bath coaches don't go to Amesbury! A nice fix you'd have been in if I hadn't overtaken you!'

Miss Wychwood got up from the table, saying firmly that any further discussion must be continued in the drawing-room. Miss Farlow instantly said: 'Oh, yes! So much wiser, for there is no saying when Limbury, or James, will come into this room, and one would not wish the servants to hear what you are talking about—not but what I daresay even Limbury, though a very respectable man, has been on the listen, for servants always seem to know *everything* about one, and how they should, if they don't listen at keyholes, I'm sure I don't know! Amesbury! I was never there in my life, but I am acquainted with several persons who have frequently visited it, and I fancy I know *all* about it! Stonehenge!'

On this triumphant note, she beamed upon the company, and followed Miss Wychwood out of the room. Neither of Miss Wychwood's youthful guests, both reared from birth in the strictest canons of propriety, returned any answer to this speech, but they exchanged speaking glances, and young Mr Elmore demanded of Miss Carleton, in an undervoice, what the deuce Stonehenge had to say to anything?

Having comfortably installed her guests in the drawing-room, Miss Wychwood said chattily that she had been considering their problem, and had come to the conclusion that the wisest course for Ninian to pursue would be to tell his father, his mother, and Mrs Amber the whole story of his escapade. She could not help laughing when she was confronted by two horrified faces, but said, with a good deal of authority: 'You know, my dears, there is really nothing else to be done! If the case had been different—if Lucilla had suffered ill-treatment at Mrs Amber's hands—I might have consented to keep her presence here a secret, but, as far as I can discover, she has never been ill-treated in her life!'

'Oh, no, no!' Lucilla said quickly. 'I never said that! But there is another kind of tyranny, ma'am! I can't explain what I mean, and perhaps you have never experienced it, but—but—'

'I haven't experienced it, but I do know what you mean,' Annis said. 'It is the tyranny of the weak, isn't it? The weapons being tears, reproaches, vapours, and other such unscrupulous means which are employed by gentle, helpless women like your aunt!'

'Oh, you *do* understand!' Lucilla exclaimed, her face lighting up.

'Of course I do! Try, in your turn to understand what must be *my* feelings on this occasion! I couldn't reconcile it with my conscience, Lucilla, to hide you from your aunt.' She silenced, by a raised finger, the outcry which rose to Lucilla's lips. 'No, let me finish what I have to say! I am going to write to Mrs Amber asking her if she will permit you to stay with me for a few weeks. Ninian shall take my letter with him tomorrow, and I must trust that he will assure her that I am a very respectable creature, well able to take care of you.'

'You may be sure I will, ma'am!' said Ninian enthusiastically. Doubt shook him, and his brow clouded. 'But what must I do if she won't consent? She is a very *anxious* female, you see, and almost never lets Lucy go anywhere without her, because she lives in dread of some accident befalling her, like being kidnapped, which did happen to some girl or other only last year, but not, of course, in Cheltenham, of all unlikely places!'

'Yes, and ever since Uncle Abel died she bolts all the doors and windows every evening,' corroborated Lucilla, 'and makes our butler take the silver up to bed with him, and hides her jewellery under her mattress!'

'Poor thing!' said Miss Wychwood charitably. 'If she is so nervous a good watch-dog is the thing for her!'

'She is afraid of dogs,' said Lucilla gloomily. '*And* of horses! When I was young I had a pony, and was used to ride every day of my life—oh, Ninian, do you remember what *splendid* times we had, looking for adventures, and following the Hunt, which we were not permitted to do, but the Master was a particular friend of ours, and never did more than tell us we were a couple of rapscallions, and would end up in Newgate!'

'Yes, by Jupiter!' said Ninian, kindling. 'He was a great gun! Lord, do you remember the time that pony of yours refused, and you went right over the hedge into a ploughed field? I thought we should never get the mud off your habit!'

Lucilla laughed heartily at this recollection, but her laughter soon died, and she sighed, saying in a melancholy voice that those days were long past. 'I *know* Mama would have bought a hunter for me, when I grew to be too big for dear old Punch, but Aunt Clara *utterly* refused to do so! She said she wouldn't enjoy a moment's peace of mind if she knew me to be *careering* all over the countryside, and if I was set on riding there was a very good livery-stable in Cheltenham, which provides *reliable* grooms to accompany young ladies when they wish to go for rides—on quiet old hacks! Exactly so!' she added, as Ninian uttered a derisive laugh. 'And when I appealed to my—my *insufferable* Uncle Carleton, all he did was to reply in the *vilest* of scrawls that my Aunt Clara was the best judge of what it was proper for me to do.'

'I must say, one would take him for a regular slow-top,' agreed Ninian. 'He isn't, though. It might be that he doesn't approve of females hunting.'

'A great many gentlemen don't,' said Miss Farlow. 'My own dear father would never have permitted me to hunt. Not that I wished to, even if I had been taught to ride, which I wasn't.'

There did not seem to be anything to say in answer to this, and a depressed silence fell on the company. Lucilla broke it. 'Depend upon it,' she said, 'my aunt will write to Uncle Carleton and he will order me to do as I'm bid. I don't believe there is any hope for me.'

'Oh, don't despair!' said Annis cheerfully. 'It wouldn't surprise me if your aunt were to be too thankful to learn that you are in safe hands to raise the least objection to your prolonging your visit to me. She might even be glad of a respite! And if she thinks the matter over she will surely perceive that to fetch you back immediately would give rise to just the sort of scandal-broth she must be most anxious to avoid. Ninian escorted you here because I invited you: what could be more natural? I wonder where I made your acquaintance?'

Lucilla smiled faintly at this, but it was a woebegone effort, and it took a little time to convince her that there was no other way out of her difficulties. Annis felt extremely sorry for her, since it was obvious that Mrs Amber was so morbidly conscious of the responsibility laid on her that she chafed the poor child almost to desperation by the excessive care she took of her.

Before the tea-tray was brought in, Annis took Ninian to her book-room while she there wrote the letter he was to carry to Mrs Amber, and supplied him with enough money to defray the various expenses he had incurred. She told Lucilla that she needed his help in the composition of the letter, but her real object was to discover rather more about Lucilla's flight than had so far been disclosed. She had mentally discounted much of what Lucilla had told her as the exaggeration natural to youth, but by the time Ninian had favoured her with his version of the affair she had realized that Lucilla had not exaggerated the pressure brought to bear on her, and could easily picture the effect on a sensitive girl such pressure would have. No one had ill-treated her; she had been suffocated with loving kindness, not only by her aunt, but by Lord and Lady Iverley, and by Ninian's three sisters; even Eliza, a ten-year-old, conceiving a schoolgirl passion for her, and doting on her in a very embarrassing way. Cordelia and Lavinia, both of whom Miss Wychwood judged to be two meekly insipid young women, had, apparently, told Lucilla that they looked forward to the day when they could call her sister. This, Ninian said, in a judicial way, had been a mistaken thing to have done; but it did not seem to have occurred to him that his own conduct left much to be desired. It was obvious to Miss Wychwood that his devotion to his parents was excessive; but when she asked him if he had indeed been prepared to marry Lucilla, he replied: 'No, no! That is to say—well, what I mean is—oh, I don't know, but I thought something would be bound to happen to prevent it!'

'But I collect, my dear boy,' said Miss Wychwood, 'that your parents love you very dearly, and have never denied you anything?'

'That is just it!' said Ninian eagerly. 'My—my every wish has been granted me, so—so how could I be so ungrateful as to refuse to do the only thing they have ever asked me to do? Particularly when my mother begged me, with tears in her eyes, not to shatter the one hope my father had left to him!'

This moving picture failed to impress Miss Wychwood. She said, somewhat dryly, that she was at a loss to understand why his loving parents should have set their hearts on his marriage to a girl he had no wish to marry.

'She is the daughter of Papa's dearest friend,' explained Ninian, in a reverential tone. 'When Captain Carleton bought Old Manor, it was in the hope that the two estates would be joined, in the end, by this marriage.'

'Captain Carleton, I assume, was a gentleman of substance?'

'Oh, yes! All the Carletons are full of juice!' said Ninian. 'But that has nothing to do with the case!'

Miss Wychwood thought that it probably had a great deal to do with the case, but kept this reflection to herself. After a moment, Ninian said, flushing slightly: 'My father, I daresay, has never had a mercenary thought in his head, ma'am! His only desire is to ensure my—my happiness, and he believes that because, when we were children, Lucy and I were used to play together, and—did indeed like each other very much, we should deal famously together as husband and wife. But we *shouldn't!*' declared Ninian, with unnecessary violence.

'No, I don't think you would!' agreed Miss Wychwood, amusement in her voice. 'Indeed, it has me in a puzzle to guess what made your parents think you would!'

'They believe that Lucy's wildness comes of her being young, and kept too close by Mrs Amber, and that I should be able to handle her,' said Ninian. 'But I shouldn't, ma'am! I never could keep her out of mischief, even when we were children, and—and I don't wish to be married to a headstrong girl, who thinks she knows better than I do *always*, and says I have no spirit when I try to stop her doing something outrageous! I did try to stop her running away from Chartley, but, short of taking her back by force, there was no way of doing it. And,' he added candidly, 'by the time I caught up with her she had reached a village, and she said if I so much as laid a finger on her she would scream for help, besides biting and scratching and kicking, and if it was pudding-hearted of me to have hung up my axe, very well, I'm a pudding-heart! Only think what a scandal it would have created, ma'am! She would have roused the whole place— and several of the farm-workers were already going to start work in the fields! I was obliged to knuckle down! Then she said that since they would none of them believe her when she said nothing would prevail upon her to marry me, the best way of proving it to them was by running away. And I'm bound to own that I did feel it might be a good thing to do. But when she tried to persuade me to go home, and pretend I knew nothing about her having left the house before dawn, I did *not* knuckle down! Well, what a miserable fellow I should be to let such a stupid chit jaunter about quite unprotected!'

'Is that what she did?' asked Miss Wychwood, unable to repress a note of appreciation in her voice.

'Yes, and if only I hadn't been woken up by the moonlight on my face I shouldn't have known a thing about it!' said Ninian bitterly. 'Of course I got up to pull the blinds closely together, and that's why I saw Lucy. She was making off down the avenue, and carrying a portmanteau. I wish I hadn't seen her, I don't mind owning, but since I did see her, what could I do but follow her?'

'I can't imagine!' confessed Miss Wychwood.

'No, well, you see how it was! I had to dress, of course, and then creep out of the house, to the stables, and by the time I'd harnessed a horse to my gig, and fobbed off Sowerby—he's one of our grooms, and what must he do but come out in his nightshirt to see who was stealing a horse and carriage!—Lucy was halfway to Amesbury. I guessed she must be going that way, for I naturally supposed her to be trying to go back to Cheltenham, and I am pretty sure there's a coach which goes to Marlborough from Amesbury, and Marlborough's on the post-road to Cheltenham. I thought that was as bird-witted as it could be, but it wasn't as bird-witted as her precious Bath-scheme! I said all I could to persuade her to abandon such a hare-brained notion, but it was to no purpose, so when it came to her saying that by hedge or by stile she would get to Bath, it seemed to me that the only thing to be done was to drive her there.'

He ended on a defensive note, and looked so sheepish that Miss Wychwood had no difficulty in realizing that Lucy, by far the stronger character, had, in fact, talked him into reluctant compliance. She said, however, that he had certainly done the right thing; and advised him to tell his father, without reserve, what were his sentiments on the subject of the marriage proposed to him. 'Depend upon it,' she said, 'he will hardly feel surprise now that Lucilla has made it abundantly clear what *her* sentiments are! I shouldn't wonder at it if he felt relief at being spared such a daughter-in-law!' She affixed a wafer to the letter she had inscribed, and rose from her desk, saying, as she handed the letter to him: 'There! That will, I trust, reassure Mrs Amber and may even convince her—though she sounds to me to be a remarkably foolish woman!—that her wisest course will be to give Lucilla permission to remain in my charge until she has had time to recover from all this agitation. Come, let us go back to the drawing-room! Limbury will be bringing in the tea-tray immediately.'

She led the way out of the room, and had reached the door into the drawing-room when a knock was heard on the front-door. Since she had no expectation of receiving any visitors, she supposed it to betoken nothing more important than a message, and went into the drawing-room. But a very few minutes later Limbury appeared on the threshold, and announced: 'My Lord Beckenham, ma'am, and Mr Harry Beckenham!'

# *Three*

MISS WYCHWOOD UTTERED A SMOTHERED EXCLAMATION of annoyance, but if he heard it the first of the visitors to enter the room gave no sign of having done so. He was a stockily built man, a little more than thirty years of age, with rather heavy features, and an air of considerable self-consequence. He was dressed with propriety, but it was easily to be seen that he had no modish leanings, for his neckcloth, though neatly arranged, was quite unremarkable, and the points of his shirt-collar scarcely rose above his jawbone. He first bowed, and then walked towards his hostess, as one sure of his welcome, and said, with ponderous gallantry: 'I might have guessed, when I found the sun shining over Bath this morning, that it heralded your return! And so it was, as I made it my business to discover. Dear Miss Annis, the town has been a desert without you!'

He carried the hand she held out to him to his lips, but she drew it away almost immediately, and extended it to his companion, saying, with a smile: 'Why, how is this, Harry? Have you come into Somerset on a repairing lease?'

He grinned at her. 'Shame on you, fair wit-cracker!' he retorted. 'When I have come all the way from London only to pay my respects to you—!'

She laughed. 'Palaverer! Don't try to hoax me with your flummery, for I cut my wisdoms before you were out of short coats! Miss Farlow you are both acquainted with, but I must make you known to Miss Carleton, whom I don't think you have met.' She waited until the gentlemen had made their bows, and then presented Ninian to them, and begged them to be seated.

Lord Beckenham said, with a reproving glance at his brother: 'Your vivacity carries you too far, Harry! That is not the way to speak to Miss Wychwood.'

His graceless junior paid no heed to this admonition, his attention being fully engaged by Lucilla, of whom he was taking a frankly admiring survey. He was a very elegant young gentleman, of engaging address, and fashionable appearance. His glossy brown locks were brushed into the Windswept style; the points of his collar reached his cheek-bones; his neckcloth was fearfully and wonderfully tied; he had a nice taste in waistcoats; his pantaloons were of a modish yellow; and the Hessians which encased his slim legs were so highly polished as to dazzle beholders. He looked to be the very antithesis of his brother, which indeed he was, for his character was as frivolous as his raiment, he had never showed any disposition to devote himself to his studies, and far too much disposition to squander his inheritance on revel-routs, expensive little barques of frailty, games of chance, and the adornment of his person. He also kept a string of prime hunters, and the fact that he was an accomplished horseman would never have been suspected by strangers who encountered him on the strut in Bond Street, and did not know that he had been a regular subscriber to the Heythrop since he first went up to Oxford; and, in spite of being a neck-or-nothing rider, had never yet come to grief over the stone walls of the Cotswold country, or been thrown into one of the quarries which all too often lay beyond those walls.

Lord Beckenham was torn between secret admiration of his horsemanship and disapproval of his extravagance. He read him many lectures, but never failed to rescue him from his pecuniary embarrassments, and was always glad to welcome him to Beckenham Court. He said, and quite sincerely believed, that he held his two brothers and his three sisters in great affection, but he was not a warmhearted man, and his unremitting care of their interests sprang partly from a rigid sense of duty, and partly from a patriarchal instinct. At an early age he had succeeded to his father's dignities, and had found himself the sole support of an ailing mother, and the guardian of two sisters, and his youngest brother. His elder sister was already married to an impecunious cleric, and the mother of two infants, the forerunners of what promised to be a large family, and he instantly made it his business to find eligible husbands for Mary and Caroline. Captain James Beckenham had, at that date, risen from the position of midshipman to that of a junior officer, and his promotion thereafter had been rapid. He had had the good fortune to win a considerable amount of prize money, which, added to his handsome inheritance, put him beyond the necessity of applying to his brother for any pecuniary assistance whatsoever. He rarely visited Beckenham Court, preferring to spend his time, when on shore, in all the forms of entertainment most deprecated by his lordship. Nor were Mary and Caroline very frequent visitors, so that having arranged marriages for both to very well-inlaid gentlemen Beckenham found himself with only the eldest and the youngest members of his family still tied to what Captain Beckenham sarcastically called his apron-strings. It would have been unjust to have said that he regretted their independence; but he certainly regretted the loosening of the bonds which kept them revolving round him; and, convinced of his own worthiness, never suspected that it was his deeply ingrained habit of censuring their follies, and giving them quite unwanted advice which drove them away from the Court.

He enjoyed the advantages of a large fortune. He was the owner of an imposing estate, situated between Bath and Wells, and was a frequent visitor to Bath, where he was a prime favourite amongst those residents whom Harry irreverently called the Bath Toughs. For years he had been regarded as the biggest matrimonial catch in the district, and caps past counting had been set at him. But, never, until the appearance on the Bath scene of Miss Annis Wychwood, had he shown the slightest disposition to make some lady an offer. He first encountered Annis when she was on a visit to a friend; realized, on being presented to her at one of the Assemblies, that she was the only female he had ever met who was worthy of becoming his wife; and thereafter prosecuted an unremitting assault on her defences. There were those (like Lady Wychwood) who thought that Annis would be foolish to refuse such an advantageous offer, but these provident ladies were outnumbered by those who thought it a very good joke that any man as prosy as Lord Beckenham should have set his heart on Annis Wychwood, who was as lively as he was dull.

Annis had done her best, within the dictates of propriety, to convince him that his suit was hopeless, but she had failed: partly because her recognition of his many good qualities prohibited her from treating him with Turkish brutality, and partly because he could not bring himself to believe that any female on whom he had bestowed the accolade of his approval could seriously refuse to marry him. Females were known to be capricious, and Miss Wychwood certainly enjoyed flirtations with her many admirers. This was the only fault he detected in her. It was a grave one, and every now and then he wondered whether, when under his influence, she would become more sober-minded, or whether her frivolity was incurable. But after one of these soul-searchings he would see her again, fall under the spell of her beauty, and become even more determined to add this piece of perfection to his collection of artistic treasures.

For the acquisition of pictures, and statues, and vases was his one extravagance; and since he was extremely wealthy he was able to indulge it. He employed several agents, whose business it was to inform him when and where some coveted object was coming up for sale; and frequently paid flying visits to the Continents returning usually with yet another Chinese bowl to add to his overflowing cabinets, or an Old Master to hang on his crowded walls. Miss Wychwood said that Beckenham Court was fast becoming more like a museum than a private residence; and once told her brother that she suspected his lordship of caring more for the possession of treasures which other men envied him than for the treasures themselves.

On this occasion he had come home from an expedition to The Hague, whence he had returned with a reputed Cuyp. He said he entertained doubts of the authenticity of the picture, and hoped he could persuade Miss Wychwood to drive out to Beckenham Court to see it. He described to her in exhaustive detail not only the composition of the picture, but all the circumstances which had led him to purchase it. She listened to him with half an ear, but was more interested in the comedy being enacted by the three youngest members of the party. Mr Harry Beckenham, having seated himself beside Lucilla, was making himself extremely agreeable, and she, after some initial shyness, was enjoying what Miss Wychwood guessed to be her first encounter with a personable young man who very obviously admired her, and who knew just how to set a shy damsel at her ease. On the other side of the fireplace, Mr Elmore had evidently taken Mr Beckenham in silent dislike. This might have arisen from a feeling that he was at a disadvantage beside a man not so many years his senior but possessed of far more address, and bearing all the appearance of a Man of Fashion; but as she covertly watched the trio Miss Wychwood was assailed by the sudden suspicion that Mr Elmore's hostility sprang from seeing his childhood's friend responding with the utmost readiness to Mr Beckenham's advances. This dog-in-the-manger attitude was amusing, but might easily lead to trouble. Miss Wychwood was not sorry when Lord Beckenham's meticulous adherence to the rules governing polite society led him to break up the party immediately after tea.

Nothing could more surely have confirmed her gathering belief that Lucilla had been kept in far too strict seclusion by Mrs Amber than her quite disproportionate pleasure in what had been, she confided to her hostess, her first grown-up party. 'For I don't count being civil to Aunt Clara's fusty friends, and being sent away as soon as I've said how do you do, as though I were still in the schoolroom.'

Had she no friends of her own? No—well, none of her own choosing! Aunt did encourage her to go for walks with two girls whose parents she knew, and approved, but as they were both models of propriety, and so stupid as to be dead bores, she never would do so. And when she had been invited to a picnic party, Aunt had refused to allow her to go, because she had once contracted the measles at a juvenile party. Aunt did not like al fresco parties: she said that nothing more surely made one catch severe chills than sitting on damp ground, and that the ground always was damp, even if the picnic wasn't spoilt by a sudden shower of rain, which, in her experience, it usually was.

Until her seventeenth birthday, a highly accomplished governess had had charge of her education, and had accompanied her wherever she went, if her aunt had succumbed (as Miss Wychwood gathered she frequently did) to one of her nervous headaches. She had been assisted by various teachers, hired at great expense, who instructed Lucilla in music, water-colour painting, and foreign languages. Aunt had chosen her as much for her rigid sense of propriety as for her learning, and she had never succeeded in winning her pupil's affection, or in inspiring her with a desire to become proficient in any of her studies. Oh, no! she hadn't been unkind! It was just that, for all her scholarship, she hadn't the least understanding of anything beyond the covers of her primers, and her lexicons.

These somewhat inarticulate revelations imbued Miss Wychwood with a determined resolve to introduce Lucilla into a wider circle than she had been permitted to enter. Bath was no longer the fashionable resort it had once been, but it had its Assemblies, its concerts, and its theatre, and although most of its residents were elderly, there were many who had large families. These Miss Wychwood passed under rapid review, and before she went to bed that night had made out a list of suitable persons to invite to a rout-party, at which Lucilla should be presented to Bath society. Perusing this list, her ever-ready sense of the ridiculous overcame her, and sent her chuckling up to her bedchamber. It would be the dullest and most undistinguished party she had ever given in Upper Camden Place, the preponderance of the invited guests being of immature age, and the rest being made up by their parents, all of whom were eminently respectable, and very few of whom could be depended on to lend life to the party.

On the following morning, having written her invitations and given them to her footman to deliver, she took Lucilla out to do a little shopping. She had requested Mrs Amber in her very polite letter to send Lucilla's maid to Bath, bringing with her the rest of the raiment which had been taken to Chartley Place, but since it might be several days before Mrs Amber complied with this request—if she did comply with it, which was by no means certain—some additions to the scanty wardrobe Lucilla had crammed into her portmanteau were necessary. Lucilla was delighted at the prospect of visiting the Bath shops, and became rapturous when she saw the very elegant hats, mantles, and dresses displayed in Milsom Street.

She made several purchases, pored over fashion plates, and was persuaded to bespeak an evening-dress, and a walking-habit from Miss Wychwood's modiste, who promised to have both made up for her as quickly as possible. Miss Wychwood wished to make her a present of them but this she resolutely refused, saying that as soon as she received her quarterly allowance of pin-money she would be so plump in the pocket as to be able to buy *dozens* of dresses.

After this agreeable session, Miss Wychwood took her down to the Pump Room, and was fortunate enough to encounter there Mrs Stinchcombe, a pleasant woman with whom she was well-acquainted, and who was the mother of two pretty girls, the elder of whom was just Lucilla's age, and one son, at present up at Cambridge. Both the girls were with their mother, and Miss Wychwood lost no time in introducing Lucilla to Mrs Stinchcombe, and soon had the satisfaction of seeing the three young ladies with their heads together, chattering away at a great rate, in a manner that showed that they were on the high road to forming bosom friendships. Mrs Stinchcombe was disposed to approve of any girl who enjoyed Miss Wychwood's patronage, and said, regarding the trio with an indulgent smile: 'What a set of little bagpipes, aren't they? Is Miss Carleton residing with you?'

'She has come to visit me, for what I hope may be a stay of several weeks,' replied Miss Wychwood. 'She is an orphan, and has been living in Cheltenham with her aunt, who has kept her in rather too strict seclusion. Not yet out, of course. But I think it of the first importance that girls should know how to go on in society before being pitchforked into the ton, and I trust I may have persuaded her aunt to permit her to try her wings in Bath before her presentation.'

Mrs Stinchcombe nodded. 'Very true, my dear! I have frequently observed how often girls being, as you aptly express it, *pitchforked* straight from the schoolroom into the ton, ruin their chances by excessive shyness, which leads them to be tongue-tied, or—worse!—disagreeably pert, in the effort to appear up to snuff, as the saying is! You must bring your protégée to a little party I am giving for my girls on Thursday: quite informal, I need hardly say!'

Miss Wychwood thanked her and accepted the invitation, reflecting, rather ruefully, that she was condemning herself to exactly the sort of party which she found intolerably boring. Another thought occurred to her, which she found peculiarly disconcerting: it flashed through her brain that she was dwindling into a duenna. It was a lowering reflection, but since she had not yet reached her thirtieth year, and had not noticed any diminution in the number of her admirers, she did not allow it to oppress her. And she had her reward when Lucilla came up to her, her eyes shining like stars, and said: 'Oh, Miss Wychwood, Corisande has invited me to a party on Thursday! May I go to it? *Pray* don't say I must not!'

'Perhaps, if you are *very* good, I shan't say that,' replied Miss Wychwood gravely. 'In fact, I have just this moment accepted Mrs Stinchcombe's kind invitation to us both.'

Lucilla laughed, but at once turned to thank Mrs Stinchcombe, and did it so prettily that Mrs Stinchcombe afterwards told Annis that the child's manners matched her lovely face.

All the way up the hill to Camden Place Lucilla bubbled over with delight in the promised treat, and intense pleasure in having met (thanks to her dear, dear Miss Wychwood!) anyone so charming and so truly amiable as Miss Corisande Stinchcombe. Edith Stinchcombe was excessively agreeable, too, although not yet emancipated from the schoolroom; and as for Mrs Stinchcombe, could Miss Wychwood conceive of a more indulgent or more excellent parent for any girl to have? According to the testimony of her daughters, Mama always understood exactly how one felt, and was never cross! So very unlike Aunt Clara's friends! Only fancy!—she permitted Corisande to go shopping, as long as Edith, or their brother, accompanied her, without being escorted by Edith's governess! Not that Miss Frampton was in the least like the unlamented Miss Cheeseburn, who had helped Aunt to make Lucilla's life a positive burden to her! 'Corisande says Miss Frampton is the greatest dear, and so jolly that she and Edith *like* her to go out with them! Oh, and Corisande says, ma'am, that she knows of a shop in Stall Street where one may purchase reticules at half the price they charge in Milsom Street, and she says she will take me there, if you see no objection to it!'

Miss Wychwood, responding suitably to these confidences, perceived that she was doomed to be bored for the rest of Lucilla's stay by references to What Corisande Said.

On the following evening, to their surprise, Ninian walked into the drawing-room, announcing that he had brought her traps to Lucilla, and had given them into the butler's charge. He was looking bright-eyed and decidedly belligerent; and it was obvious that he was labouring under a strong sense of ill-usage.

'Oh, Ninian!' Lucilla exclaimed. 'How very kind of you! I never expected to get them so soon! But there was no need for you to have put yourself to the fag of bringing them to me yourself!'

'Oh, yes, there was!' he retorted grimly.

'No, no, Sarah could well have brought them without an escort!'

'Well, she couldn't, because she isn't there! Such a dust as I walked into! Talk of riots and rumpuses—! And why even my mother should be thrown into a taking when they must all of them have known you hadn't been murdered, or kidnapped, because they knew I'd gone away with you, had me floored!'

'Do you mean Sarah isn't here?' cried Lucilla.

'That's exactly what I mean. She and your aunt got to dagger-drawing, because your aunt worked herself into a rare passion, and rang a regular peal over her, saying it was her fault for neglecting you, and I don't know what besides, and *she* nabbed the rust, and rubbed up all manner of old sores, and the end of it was that she packed her boxes, and flounced off in a rare tantrum!' He observed, with displeasure, that Lucilla was dancing round the room in an ecstasy of delight, and added, with asperity: 'You may think that a matter for rejoicing, but I didn't, I can tell you!'

'Oh, I do, I do!' Lucilla said, executing a neat step, and clapping her hands. 'If you knew how much I was dreading Sarah's arrival—!'

Miss Wychwood intervened at this point, to ask Ninian if he had dined. He thanked her, and said yes, he had stopped to bait on the road, and must not remain for more than a few minutes, because it was growing late, and he had not yet arranged for accommodation in Bath. 'Which is something about which I need your advice, ma'am,' he disclosed. 'The thing is—well, owing to one cause and another, I'm a trifle behind the wind at the moment! Until quarter-day, in fact! As soon as my allowance is paid I shall be tolerably well up in the stirrups again, but it won't do to be getting under the hatches, so I mean to put up at one of the cheaper hotels, and I thought you would very likely be able to direct me to a—a suitable one!'

Lucilla stopped dancing round the room, and asked, in astonishment: 'Why, do you mean to remain in Bath?'

'Yes,' replied Ninian, through gritted teeth, 'I do! *That* will show them!'

Before Lucilla could ask for enlightenment on this somewhat obscure utterance, a second, and even more timely, intervention was provided by Limbury, who came in with the tea-tray. Further discussion was suspended; and when Ninian had drunk two cups of tea, and eaten several macaroons, his seething rancour had subsided enough to enable him to give the ladies a fairly coherent account of the trials he had undergone at the hands of his loving relations. 'Would you believe it?' he demanded. 'They blamed me for the whole!'

'Oh, how unjust!' cried Lucilla indignantly.

'I should rather think so! For how the devil could I have prevented you from running away, I should like to know?'

'You couldn't. No one could!' she asserted. 'They ought to have been grateful to you for coming with me!'

'Well, that's what I thought!' he said. 'What's more, if anyone was to blame for driving you out of the house it was Them, not me!'

'Did you tell them so?' asked Lucilla eagerly.

'No, not *then*, but in the end I did, when I got into a pelter myself! That was when I found that your aunt's *prostration* was being laid at my door, if you please, instead of at yours! I don't know what *she* might have said to me, because I didn't see her— thank God! She fell into hysterics when it was discovered that you had run away, and then had strong convulsions, or spasms, or whatever she calls 'em, and was laid up in bed, with our doctor in attendance, and my mother trying to restore her with burnt feathers, and sal volatile, and smelling-salts; and my father almost pushing Sarah out of the house, because the mere thought that she was still at Chartley threw your aunt into fresh spasms! Well, I did say, *What a wet-goose!* and Papa—*Papa!*—said I had much to blame myself for! And Mama said how could I have reconciled it with my conscience to have abandoned you to a total stranger, and never would she have believed that a child of hers could have behaved so heartlessly! And when it came to Cordelia and Lavinia starting to reproach me—but I precious soon put a stop to that!—I—I lost my temper, and said Very well, if they thought it was my duty to protect her from *you*, ma'am, I'd go straight back to Bath, and stay there! And—and I'm afraid I said that *any* place would be preferable to Chartley, and even though you were a *total stranger* I was sure of a welcome in your house, which was more than I had had in my own home!'

'Oh, *well done*, Ninian!' exclaimed Lucilla enthusiastically clasping his arm, and squeezing it. 'I never dreamed you were so full of pluck!'

He coloured, but said: 'I don't think it was well done of me. I ought not to have spoken so to my father. I'm sorry for it, but I meant what I said, and I'm dashed well not going to crawl back until *he* is sorry too! Even if I starve in a ditch!'

'Oh, pray don't think of doing such a thing!' said Miss Farlow, who had been listening open-mouthed to this recital. 'So embarrassing for dear Miss Wychwood, for people would be bound to say she should have rescued you! Not that I think you would be allowed to die in a ditch in Bath—at least, I never heard of anyone doing so, because they are so strict about keeping the streets clean and tidy, and destitute persons are cared for at the Stranger's Friend Society: a most excellent institution, I believe, but I *cannot* think that your worthy parents would wish you to become an inmate there, however vexed they may be with you!'

This made Lucilla giggle, but Miss Wychwood, preserving her countenance, said: 'Very true! You must hold it as a weapon in reserve, Ninian, to use only if your father threatens to cast you off entirely. In the meantime, I suggest that you put up at the Pelican. It is in Walcot Street, and I'm told its charges are very reasonable. It isn't a fashionable hotel, but I believe it is comfortable, and provides its guests with a good, plain ordinary. And if it should be *too* plain for you, you can always dine here!' She added, with a lurking twinkle in her eyes: 'I've never dined there, but *of course* I have visited it, to see the room Dr Johnson slept in!'

'Oh!' said Ninian, all at sea. 'Yes—of course! Dr Johnson! Exactly so! Was he—was he a friend of yours, ma'am? Or—or one of your relations, perhaps?'

Lucilla gave a crow of laughter. 'Stupid! He was the *dixionary*-man, and he died years and years ago—didn't he, ma'am?'

'Oh, a *writing* cove!' said Ninian, in disparaging accents. 'Come to think of it, I *have* heard of him—but I'm not bookish, ma'am!'

'But surely, dear Mr Elmore, they must have used his Dixionary at your school?' said Miss Farlow.

'Ah, that would be it!' nodded Ninian. 'I daresay I must have seen the name on the back of some book or other, which accounts for my having had the notion that I recognized it!'

'If recognition you could call it!' murmured Miss Wychwood. 'Never mind, Ninian! We can't all of us be bookish, can we?'

'Well, I don't scruple to say that I never had the least turn for scholarship,' Ninian somewhat unnecessarily disclosed. He added a handsome rider to this statement, saying, with a beaming smile: 'And I promise you, ma'am, no one would ever suspect *you* of being bookish!'

Overwhelmed by this tribute, Miss Wychwood uttered in a shaken voice: 'How kind of you, Ninian, to say so!'

'It's very true,' said Lucilla, adding her mite. 'No one could think she was bookish, but she reads prodigiously, and even keeps books in her bedchamber!'

'How can you be so treacherous, Lucilla, as to betray me?' demanded Miss Wychwood tragically.

'Only to Ninian!' Lucilla said, regarding her rather anxiously. 'Of course I wouldn't dream of telling anyone else, but he won't say a word about it, will you, Ninian?'

'No, never!' he responded promptly.

Miss Wychwood shook a mournful head. 'If only I may not have sunk myself beneath reproach in your eyes!'

They made such haste to reassure her that her suppressed laughter escaped her, and she said: 'You absurd babies! Oh, don't look so astonished, or you will send me into fresh whoops! I know you can't think why, and if I were to explain it to you you would believe me to be all about in my head! Tell me, Ninian, did you give my letter to Mrs Amber?'

'No, because she was too ill to receive me, but my mother gave it to her.' He hesitated, and then said, with a deprecatory grin: 'She—she wasn't well enough to write to you, but she did charge my mother with a message!'

'A message to me?' Miss Wychwood asked, her brows lifting slightly.

'Well, not precisely!' he replied. His grin widened, and he gave a chuckle. 'What she said, in fact, was that she washed her hands of Lucilla!'

'She says that every time I vex her!' said Lucilla disgustedly. 'And never does she mean it! Depend upon it, she will come to fetch me back, and all my pleasure will be at an end!'

'Oh, I don't think she'll do that!' said Ninian consolingly. 'She does seem to be quite knocked-up. What's more, when my mother asked her if she was to direct one of the maids to pack up your gear and send it to you she said that if after all she had done for you you preferred a stranger to her she only trusted that you wouldn't regret it, and wish her to take you back, because she never wanted to set eyes on you again!'

Lucilla considered this, but presently shook her head, and sighed: 'I don't set the least store by that, but it does at least make it seem that she won't come to Bath immediately. It always takes her *days* to recover from her hysterical turns!'

'Yes,' he agreed. 'But perhaps I ought just to mention to you that the first thing she did, before she took to her bed, was to send off a letter to Mr Carleton. Ten to one he won't pay any heed to it, but I think I ought perhaps to warn you about it!'

'Oh, if that isn't just like her!' cried Lucilla, flushing with wrath. 'She is too ill to write to Miss Wychwood, but not too ill to write to my uncle! Oh, dear me, no! And if he means to come here, to force me to return, I can't and I won't bear it!'

'Well, don't put yourself into a stew!' recommended Miss Wychwood. 'If he does come here with any such intention he will find he has me to deal with—and that is an experience which I fancy he won't enjoy!'

# *Four*

ON THE FOLLOWING MORNING, MISS WYCHWOOD SENT her groom to Twynham Park with instructions to bring her favourite mare to Bath. He carried with him a letter to Sir Geoffrey, in which Miss Wychwood informed her brother that she had a young friend staying with her whom she wished to entertain with riding expeditions, to the various places of interest in the surrounding countryside.

When she had first set up her own establishment in Camden Place, she had brought two saddle-horses with her, assuming, rather vaguely, that she would find riding, in Bath, the everyday matter it was at Twynham. It had not taken very long to disabuse her mind of this misapprehension. At Twynham, she had been used to ride, as a matter of course, every day of her life, whether into the village, on an errand of mercy to one of her father's tenants struck down by sickness, or on a visit to a friend living in the neighbourhood; but she soon discovered that life in town— particularly in such a town as Bath, where the steep cobbled streets made equestrian traffic rare—was very different from life in the country. In Bath, one either walked, or took a chair: one could not stroll down to the stables on a sudden impulse, and order one's groom to saddle up for one. It was necessary to appoint a time for one's horse to be brought round to the house; and it was even more necessary that the groom should accompany one. Miss Wychwood found this intolerable, and frankly owned that it was one of the disadvantages of town-life. She also owned (but only to herself) that it was one of the disadvantages of being an unattached spinster; but having decided that the advantages of living under her own roof in Bath, subject to no fraternal vetoes, outweighed the disadvantages, she indulged in no vain repinings, but within a very few weeks sent her mare back to Twynham Park, where Sir Geoffrey, to his credit, kept her, exercised and groomed, for her use whenever she came to stay with him. She kept her carriage-horses in Bath, and one neatish bay hack, which, being an old and beloved friend, she could not bring herself to sell.

Seale brought the mare to Bath, but he was accompanied by Sir Geoffrey, bristling with suspicion that his sister had taken it into her wayward head to befriend some Young Person who would prove to be an adventuress. Unfortunately, he arrived in Camden Place to find only Miss Farlow at home, and when he had learnt from her the circumstances under which Annis had made Lucilla's acquaintance he became convinced that his suspicion had been correct.

'How can you have been so caper-witted?' he demanded of his sister, an hour later. 'I had not thought it possible that you could be such a noddy! Pray, what do you know about this young woman? Upon my word, Annis—'

'Heavens, what a piece of work about nothing!' interrupted Annis. 'I collect you've been talking to Maria, who is positively green with jealousy of poor Lucilla! She is a Carleton: an orphan, living, since her mother's death, with one of her aunts; and since this Mrs Amber is in indifferent health Lucilla has come to stay with me for a few weeks, as a sort of prelude to her regular come-out. Ninian Elmore escorted her here, and—'

'Elmore? Elmore? Never heard of him!' declared Sir Geoffrey.

'Very likely you might not: he's a mere child, not long down, I fancy, from Oxford. He is the son and heir of Lord Iverley—and I daresay you haven't heard of him either, for I collect that he lives retired, at Chartley Place. A Hampshire family, and, even if you haven't heard of them, perfectly respectable, I promise you!'

'Oh!' said Sir Geoffrey, slightly daunted. Chewing the cud of this information, he made a recover. 'That's all very well!' he said. 'But how do you know this girl *is* a Carleton? Not that I like the connection any the better if she is! The only one of the family I'm acquainted with is Oliver Carleton—'

'Lucilla's uncle,' interpolated Miss Wychwood.

'Well, I can tell you this!' said Sir Geoffrey. 'He's a damned unpleasant fellow! Got no manners, never scruples to give the back to anyone he don't happen to like, thinks his birth and his wealth gives him the right to ride rough-shod over men quite as well born as himself; and—in short, the sort of ugly customer I should never dream of presenting to my sister!'

'Do you mean that he is a libertine?' asked Miss Wychwood.

'Annis!' he ejaculated.

'Oh, for heaven's sake, Geoffrey—!' she said impatiently. 'I cut my wisdoms years ago! If you wouldn't dream of presenting him to me, what else can you mean?'

He glared at her. 'You seem to me to have no delicacy of mind!' he said peevishly. 'What my poor mother would say, if she could hear you expressing yourself with such unfeminine want of refinement I shudder to think of!'

'Then don't think of it!' she recommended. 'Think instead of what Papa would say! Though I daresay that would make you shudder too! Where *did* you learn to be so mealy-mouthed, Geoffrey? As for Mr Oliver Carleton, between you, you and Lucilla have inspired me with a strong desire to meet him! She has told me that he has all but one of the faults you've described to me; and you have added the one she, naturally, knows nothing about. He must be a positive monster!'

'Levity was ever your besetting sin,' he said severely. 'Let me tell you that it is not at all becoming in a female! It leads you into talking a deal of improper nonsense. A strong desire to meet a monster, indeed!'

'But I have never seen a monster!' she explained. 'Oh, well! I daresay it is nothing but a take-in, and he is much like any other man!'

'I must decline to discuss him with you. I should suppose it to be extremely unlikely that you ever will meet him, but if some unfortunate chance should bring him in your way I should be doing less than my duty if I did not warn you to have nothing to say to him, my dear sister! His reputation is *not* that of a well-conducted man. And if we are to talk of *take-ins*, what reason have you to think you are not the victim of one? I don't attempt to conceal from you that I am far from satisfied that this girl is the innocent you believe her to be. I know from Maria Farlow that she ran away from her lawful guardian, and in the company of a young man! That is not the conduct of an innocent—indeed, it is the most shocking thing I ever heard of!—and it wouldn't surprise me if she were bent on inching herself into your regard!'

'You know, Geoffrey, no one who heard you talking such skimble-skamble stuff would believe you to have any more sense than a zero! How can you be so idiotish as to pay the least heed to what Maria says? She has been convinced from the outset that Lucilla is scheming to take her place in my house-hold, but you may rest easy on that head! Lucilla is a consider-able heiress—far plumper in the pocket than I am, I daresay! She won't come into her fortune until she is of age, but she enjoys what I judge to be a pretty handsome income. Mr Carleton, who is her guardian, pays it to Mrs Amber; and it is very obvious to me that it *must* be a handsome sum, for Mrs Amber gives her what Lucilla calls *pin-money*, but which a girl in less affluent circumstances would think herself fortunate to receive as an allowance to cover the cost of all her clothing. Mrs Amber pays for every stitch the child wears—and, although she seems to be a foolish creature, I must acknowledge that her taste is impeccable. I should doubt if she ever counts the cost of anything she buys for Lucilla. None of your poplins or cheap coloured muslin for Miss Carleton!' She laughed suddenly. 'Jurby unpacked her trunk, and I may say that Lucilla has risen enormously in her estimation! She informed me, in a positively reverential voice, that Miss has everything of the best! As for her having run away with Ninian, it was no such thing: she ran away from Chartley Place, and Ninian very properly acted as her escort. Her aunt had very foolishly taken her there on a visit, and a great deal of pressure was being brought to bear on Ninian, to make her an offer, and on her to accept it. It seems that this scheme was hatched years ago between their respective fathers, who were devoted friends. Ninian believes this to be the only reason his father has for trying so hard to bring the match about, but I suspect Lucilla's fortune has a good deal to do with it. The estate she inherited from her father runs, I gather, close enough to Chartley to make its acquisition by the Elmores extremely desirable. Understandable enough, you will say, but can you conceive of anything more cocklebrained, in this day and age, than to try to force two children—for they are little more than children!—to get married when they have been on brother-and-sister terms since they were in short coats?'

He had listened to her in staring silence, and he did not immediately answer her. But after a moment or two, he pronounced in pompous accents that he was no advocate for the license granted to the modern generation. Embroidering this theme, he said: 'I hold that parents must be the best judges of such matters. They must, of necessity, know better than their children—'

'Fiddle!' said Miss Wychwood, bringing this dissertation to a summary closure. 'Did Papa arrange your marriage to Amabel?' She saw that she had discomfited him, and added, with her lovely smile: 'Trying it on too rare and thick, Geoffrey! You fell in love with Amabel, and proposed to her before Papa had ever set eyes on her! *Didn't you?*'

He flushed darkly, tried to meet the challenge in her eyes, looked away, and replied, with a sheepish grin: 'Well—yes! But,' he said, making another recover, 'I knew Papa would approve of my choice, and he did!'

'To be sure he did!' agreed Miss Wychwood affably. 'And if he had not approved of it, no doubt you would have cried off, and offered for a lady he did approve of!'

'I should have done no such thing!' he declared hotly. He met her laughing eyes, seethed impotently for a moment, and then capitulated, saying in the voice of one goaded to extremity: 'Oh, damn you, Annis! My case was—was different!'

'Of course it was!' she said, patting his hand. 'No one in the possession of his senses could have raised the least objection to your marriage to Amabel!'

His hand, turning under hers, grasped it warmly, and he said, with all the embarrassment of an inarticulate man: 'She—she is past price, Annis—isn't she?'

She nodded, dropped a light kiss on his brow, and said: 'Indeed she is! Now, in a little while you will see Lucilla for yourself: Maria is going to go with her, and Ninian, to the theatre this evening, which will leave us to enjoy a comfortable cose.'

He blinked at her. 'What, is the young man here too?'

'Yes, he is putting up at the Pelican, but he will be here to dine with us.'

'I don't understand any of it!' he complained.

'No, it's the most absurd situation,' she agreed mischievously. 'And the cream of the jest is that now no one is trying to prevail upon them to become engaged they are going on together perfectly harmoniously—except, of course, for a few breezes! Schoolroom stuff!'

She went away then, to change her walking habit for an evening gown, and when she returned she brought Lucilla with her. Lucilla was looking very pretty and very youthful, and when she curtsied, and said how-do-you-do, with her enchantingly shy smile, Sir Geoffrey's disapproving expression relaxed a little, and by the time Ninian presented himself he was regarding Lucilla indulgently, and drawing her out in a paternal way to talk to him. His sister was not surprised, for being himself a great stickler he was always predisposed to favour girls whose manners showed them to be well-taught and well-bred. He was at first a trifle stiff with Ninian, but Ninian's manners were very good too, so that by the time they rose from the dinner-table Sir Geoffrey had forgiven him for such signs of incipient dandyism as his uncomfortably high shirt-points, and his not entirely felicitous attempt to arrange his neckcloth in the style known as the Waterfall, and had decided that there was no harm in the boy: no doubt he would outgrow his desire to ape the dandy-set; and the deference he showed to his elders showed that he too had been strictly reared. Sir Geoffrey noted, with approval, that both he and Lucilla treated Annis with affectionate respect; but when the theatre-party had left the house, Annis saw that he was frowning. After waiting for a few moments, she said: 'Well, Geoffrey? Is she the sort of hurly-burly girl you expected?'

He did not answer immediately, and when he did speak it was to say, with a hard look at her from under his lowered brows: 'I wish you may not have got yourself into a scrape, Annis!'

'Why, how should I?' she asked, surprised.

'Good God, have you windmills in your head? That child you've chosen to befriend is no orphan lifted out of the gutter, but a member of a distinguished family, heiress to what I judge to be, from what she told me, a considerable fortune, and brought up by an aunt who may be as foolish as you say she is but who has lavished every care, attention, and luxury on her! What, I ask you, must be her sentiments upon this occasion? To all intents and purposes you have kidnapped the girl!'

'Oh, gammon, Geoffrey! I did no such thing!'

'Try if you can to persuade the Carletons to believe that!' he said grimly. 'They can hardly blame you for having taken her up into your carriage when you found her stranded on the road, but they must blame you—as I do!—for not having restored her to her aunt when you discovered what were the rights of the case! You had not even the excuse of believing that she had been ill-treated!'

She was shaken, but made a push to defend herself. 'Oh, no, but when she told me of the sort of pressure Mrs Amber was bringing to bear on her—and not only Mrs Amber but the Iverleys too!—I realized, which I daresay you don't, that she felt herself to be caught in a trap, and I pitied her from the bottom of my heart! If Ninian had had enough resolution to have told his father that he had no wish to marry Lucilla the case might have been different, but it seems that no member of Iverley's family dares thwart him, because they are all of them afraid that if he flies into a passion he will suffer a heart-attack, and very likely die of it. A contemptible form of tyranny, isn't it? But I fancy Ninian has begun to recognize it as such, for when he returned to Chartley, having left Lucilla in my charge, he found the whole house in an uproar, not one of his loving family, as it appears, having made the smallest attempt either to conceal the fact of Lucilla's flight from Lord Iverley, or to point out to him that since Ninian was with her it was extremely unlikely that she had run into any kind of danger. I collect that he had put himself into a rare passion, but so far from its having prostrated him he was in high force, and rattled Ninian off in fine style, without doing himself the least harm. So Ninian lost his temper, packed up his gear, and came back to Bath—to protect Lucilla from the machinations of a "complete stranger"! And I can't say I blame him! Poor boy! He had had the very deuce of a time with Lucilla, and to find himself the target for recriminations and abuse was rather too much for him. He had done his best to persuade her to go back with him to Chartley, but, short of taking her back by main force, there was no way of doing it. And I don't think he could have done that, for she would certainly have fought him tooth and nail, and nothing, you know, could revolt him more than the sort of public scene that would have created!'

'But this becomes even worse than I had supposed!' exclaimed Sir Geoffrey, deeply shocked. 'Not content with having embroiled yourself with the Carletons you have created a breach between young Elmore and his parents! It was wrong of you, Annis, very wrong! I might have guessed you would do something freakish if I permitted you to leave home! Elmore, too! I had not thought it possible that such a well-mannered lad could be guilty of the impropriety of quarrelling with his father!'

'My dear Geoffrey, you're quite out!' she replied, rather amused. 'I haven't embroiled myself with anyone, and I had nothing to do with Ninian's quarrel with Lord Iverley. Indeed, I carefully refrained from advising him not to be quite so docile a son, though I was strongly inclined to do so! To own the truth, I was astonished when I discovered that the worm had turned at last, for although he is in many respects an excellent young man I did think him lacking in pluck. I shouldn't wonder at it if this episode makes Iverley hold him in respect as well as affection. The best of it is that having accused Ninian of having "abandoned" Lucilla to a complete stranger he can't now rake him down for having come back to protect her. As for Mrs Amber, I wrote her a polite letter, explaining the circumstances of my meeting with Lucilla, and begging her to grant the child leave to stay with me for a few weeks. According to Ninian, she was enjoying a prolonged fit of spasms and hysterics, but although she has not yet done me the honour of replying to my letter she has signified consent by sending Lucilla's trunks to Bath.'

He could not be satisfied, but continued to enumerate and to discuss all the evil consequences which might result from what he termed her rash action until, in desperation, she induced him to talk instead about his children, with particular reference to little Tom's tendency to croup, and what were the best methods of dealing with it. Since he was a fond father, it was not difficult to divert his mind from matters of less importance to him, and he was still talking about his children when Lucilla and Miss Farlow came in. Lucilla was in raptures over the play she had seen. She thanked Annis over and over again for having given her such a splendid treat, and disclosed that it was the very first time she had visited a grown-up theatre. 'For I don't count the time Papa took me to Astley's, because I was only six years old, and I can only just remember it. But this I shall never forget! Oh, and Mr Beckenham was there, and he came up to our box, and made the box-attendant bring us tea and lemonade in the interval, which I thought so very kind of him! What an excessively agreeable man he is, isn't he?'

'Excessively,' said Miss Wychwood rather dryly. 'Where, by the way, is Ninian?'

'Oh, when he had handed us into the carriage he said he would walk back to the Pelican! I fancy he had a headache, for he became stupidly mumpish, and didn't seem to be enjoying the play nearly as much as I did. But perhaps he was affected by the heat in the theatre,' she added charitably.

'I'm sure it's no wonder if he was,' said Miss Farlow. 'I was quite affected by it myself, but a cup of tea soon revived me. Nothing so refreshing as tea, is there? So very obliging of Mr Beckenham! Such a gentlemanly young man!'

Sir Geoffrey uttered a sound between a snort and a laugh, and as soon as he was alone with his sister solemnly warned her not to encourage Harry Beckenham to dangle after Lucilla. 'Another of your here-and-thereians!' he said. 'I don't like the fellow, and never did. Very different from his brother!'

'I certainly shan't encourage him to dangle after Lucilla,' she replied coolly. 'But I shall be astonished if he isn't the first of many to do so!'

'I wish to my heart you may not find yourself with the devil to pay over this business!'

'Oh, don't make yourself uneasy, Geoffrey! I promise you I am well able to take care of myself.'

'No female is able to take care of herself,' he said positively. 'As for not making myself uneasy, I must point out to you that it it is you who make me uneasy! But so it has always been! You had always a love of singularity, and how you expect to get a husband when you conduct yourself in such a headstrong, skitterwitted fashion I'm sure I don't know!'

On this bitter speech he took himself off to bed. He was not alone with his sister again until the moment of his departure next morning, and then he contented himself with saying severely that he was far from easy about her, very far from easy. She smiled, and planted a farewell kiss on his cheek, stayed on her doorstep to see him mount the steps into his chaise, and then went back into the house, heaving a thankful sigh to be rid of him.

Her prophecy that Harry Beckenham would prove to be only the first of Lucilla's admirers was soon seen to be correct.

She took Lucilla to Mrs Stinchcombe's party that evening, and had the satisfaction of seeing her protégée make a hit. She took Ninian too, knowing that no hostess would cavil at having a young and personable gentleman added to her guests. Both he and Lucilla enjoyed themselves very much, although he was at first a trifle on his dignity, feeling that such a juvenile party was rather beneath his touch. But superiority soon wore off, and before the evening was half over he was joining in all the ridiculous games with which the dancing was interspersed, and earning great applause for the skill he displayed when playing span-counters.

He accepted with obvious pleasure an invitation to join a riding-party to Farley Castle, suggested to him by the elder Miss Stinchcombe. The party was to be composed of some half-a-dozen young persons, and it was proposed that after they had inspected the ancient chapel there they should partake of a nuncheon, and ride back to Bath at their leisure. 'It's a place any visitor to Bath ought to visit, because of the chapel, which is very interesting on—on account of its relics of—of mortality and antiquity!' said Miss Stinchcombe knowledgeably.

The effect of this sudden display of erudition was spoilt by her close friend, Mr Marmaduke Hilperton, who very rudely accused her of having 'got all that stuff' out of the local guide-book. Since Corisande was known to be far from bookish, this made everyone laugh, and emboldened Ninian to confess that he himself was not much of a dab at antiquities, but would dearly love to ride. He then drew Mr Hilperton aside, to ask him which of Bath's livery stables was the best; but at this point Miss Wychwood, who had strolled over to the group, intervened, saying that she could mount him on her own hack. He coloured up to the roots of his hair, stammering: 'Oh, *thank* you, ma'am! If you think I'm to be trusted not to lame your horse, or to bring him in with a sore back! I promise you I'll take the

greatest care of him! I'm *excessively* obliged to you! That is—
won't you be needing him yourself?'

'No, I have other fish to fry tomorrow, and if you are joining
this expedition I may do so with a quiet mind,' she answered,
smiling at him. 'You will see that Lucilla doesn't come to any
harm, won't you?'

'Yes, to be sure I will,' he responded promptly. 'But there's no
need for you to be anxious about her, ma'am; she's a capital little
horsewoman, I promise you!'

When she saw the cavalcade off on the following morning,
Miss Wychwood knew at once that she need have no qualms
either on Lucilla's behalf or the mare's. Lucilla had a good seat,
and light hands, and easily controlled the mare's playful friski-
ness. It seemed too that there would be no want of solicitous
escort for her, judging by the way Mr Hilperton and young
Mr Forden jostled one another in the effort to be the first to
throw her up into her saddle. Miss Wychwood watched them
clatter off, all in the best of spirits, and obviously looking
forward to a day of unrestricted pleasure—unless they regarded
Seale, and Mrs Stinchcombe's elderly groom, bringing up the
rear of the procession, as restrictions, which, indeed, they would
be if youthful high spirits prompted their charges to indulge in
any dangerous feats of horsemanship. Mrs Stinchcombe had told
Annis that Tuckenhay could be trusted to look after Corisande;
and Annis knew, from her own youthful experience, that Seale
was more than capable of dealing with Lucilla, if excitement
should lead her to show off her proficiency in the saddle to her
new friends.

She herself spent the morning first writing a long overdue
letter to an old friend, and next with her housekeeper. She was
inspecting some linen when Limbury came upstairs to inform
her that a Mr Carleton had called, and was awaiting her in the
drawing-room.

# Five

FIVE MINUTES LATER, MISS WYCHWOOD ENTERED THE
drawing-room, having paused on the way to assure herself,
by a swift, critical glance at her reflection in the long looking-glass
in her bedchamber, that she was presenting just the right picture
of herself to Lucilla's uncle. She was satisfied with what she saw.
Her gown of soft dove-gray silk, with its demi-train, and the little
lace ruff round her throat, were exactly the thing, she decided,
for a lady of consequence and mature age; but what she failed to
perceive (for she never gave it a thought) was that her beauty was
enhanced by the subdued colour of her gown. She considered gray
to be a middle-aged colour, and if it had occurred to her that her
luxuriant golden locks hardly belonged to a lady past her prime
she would undoubtedly have hunted through her wardrobe for a
suitable cap to wear over them. Not that a cap could have dimmed
the glow in her eyes, but that did not occur to her either, because
familiarity with her own beauty had bred contempt of it. She
would have preferred to have been a brunette, and was inclined to
think her golden loveliness a trifle flashy.

On entering the drawing-room, she paused for a moment on
the threshold, surveying her visitor.

He was standing before the fireplace, a powerfully built man
with dark hair, and a swarthy complexion. His brows were straight
and rather thick, and under them a pair of hard gray eyes stared at

Miss Wychwood, their expression one of mingled surprise and disapproval. To her wrath, he raised his quizzing glass, as though to appraise her more precisely.

Her own brows lifted; she moved forward, saying with chilling hauteur: 'Mr Carleton, I believe?'

He nodded, letting his glass fall, and replied curtly: 'Yes. Are you Miss Wychwood?'

She inclined her head, in a manner calculated to abash him.

'Good God!' he said.

It was so unexpected that it surprised an involuntary laugh out of her. She suppressed it quickly, and made another attempt to put him out of countenance, by extending her hand and saying, in a quelling tone: 'How do you do? You wish to see your niece, of course. I am sorry that she is not at home this morning.'

'No, I don't wish to see her, though I daresay I shall be obliged to,' he replied, briefly shaking her hand. 'I came to see you, Miss Wychwood—if you *are* Miss Wychwood?'

She looked amused at this. 'Certainly I am Miss Wychwood. You must forgive me if I ask you why you should doubt it?'

*And if that doesn't make you apologize for your incivility, nothing will!* she thought, waiting expectantly.

'Because you're by far too young, of course!' he replied, disappointing her. 'I came here in the expectation of meeting an elderly woman—or, at least, one of reasonable age!'

'Let me assure you, sir, that although I don't think myself *elderly* I am of very reasonable age!'

'Nonsense!' he said. 'You're a mere child!'

'No doubt I should be grateful for the compliment—however inelegantly expressed!'

'I wasn't complimenting you.'

'Ah, no! how stupid of me! I recall, now that you have put me so forcibly in mind of it, that my brother told me that you are famed for your incivility!'

'Did he? Who is your brother?'

'Sir Geoffrey Wychwood,' she answered stiffly.

He frowned over this, in an effort of memory. After a few minutes, he said: 'Oh yes! I fancy I've met him. Has estates in Wiltshire, hasn't he? Does he own this house as well?'

'No, I own it! Though what concern that is of yours—'

'Do you mean you live here alone?' he interrupted. 'If your brother is the man I think he is, I shouldn't have thought he would have permitted it!'

'No doubt he would not had I been "a mere child",' she retorted. 'But it so happens that I have been my own mistress for many years!'

The flash of a sardonic smile vanquished the frown in his eyes. 'Oh, that's doing it much too brown!' he objected. '*Many* years, ma'am? Five, at the most!'

'You are mistaken, Mr Carleton! I am nine-and-twenty years of age!'

He put up his glass again, and looked her over critically before saying: 'Yes, obviously I was mistaken, for which your youthful appearance is to blame. Your countenance belongs to a girl, but your assured manner has nothing to do with infantry. You will allow me to say, however, that being nine-and-twenty years old doesn't render you a fit guardian for my niece.'

'Again you are mistaken, Mr Carleton! I am neither Lucilla's guardian, nor have I the least ambition to supplant Mrs Amber in that post. I conclude, from your remarks, that you have come here from Chartley Place, where, I don't doubt, you have heard—'

'Well, that, Miss Wychwood, is where *you* are mistaken! What the devil should take me to Chartley Place? I've come from London—and damnably inconvenient it was!' His penetrating gaze searched her face; he said: 'Oh! Are we at dagger-drawing? What have I said to wind you up?'

'I am not accustomed, sir, to listen to the sort of language you use!' she replied frostily.

'Oh, is *that* all? A thousand pardons, ma'am! But your brother did warn you, didn't he?'

'Yes, and also that you don't hesitate to ride rough-shod over people you think beneath your touch!' she flashed.

He looked surprised. 'Oh, no! Only over people who bore me! Did you think I was trying to ride rough-shod over you? I wasn't. You do put me out of temper, but you don't bore me.'

'I am so much obliged to you!' she said, with ironic gratitude. 'You have relieved my mind of a great weight! Perhaps you will add to your goodness by explaining what you imagine I have done to put you out of temper? That, I must confess, has me in a puzzle! I had supposed that you had come to Bath to thank me for having befriended Lucilla: certainly not to pinch at me for having done so!'

'If that don't beat the Dutch!' he ejaculated. 'What the deuce have I to thank you for, ma'am? For aiding and abetting my niece to make a byword of herself? For dragging me into the business? For—'

'I didn't!' she broke in indignantly. 'I did what lay within my power to scotch the scandal that might have arisen from her flight from Chartley; and as for dragging you into the business, nothing, let me tell you, was further from my intention, or, indeed, my wish!'

'You must surely have known that that fool of a—that Clara Amber would write to demand that I should exercise my authority over Lucilla!'

'Yes, Ninian Elmore told us that she had done so,' she agreed, with false affability. 'But since nothing Lucilla has said about you led me to think that you had either fondness for her, or took the smallest interest in her, I had no expectation of receiving a visit from you. To own the truth, sir, my first feeling on having your name brought up to me was one of agreeable surprise. But that was before I had had the very doubtful pleasure of making your acquaintance!'

The effect of this forthright speech was not at all what she had intended, for instead of taking instant umbrage to it he laughed, and said appreciatively: 'That's milled me down, hasn't it?'

'I sincerely hope so!'

'Oh, it has! But it's not bellows to mend with me! I warn you, I shall come about again. Now, instead of sparring with me, perhaps you, in your turn, will have the goodness to explain to me why you didn't restore Lucilla to her aunt, but kept her here, dam— dashed well encouraging her in a piece of hoydenish disobedience?'

This uncomfortable echo of what Sir Geoffrey had said to her brought a slight flush into her cheeks. She did not immediately answer him, but when, looking up, she saw the challenge in his eyes, and the satirical curl of his lips, she said, frankly: 'My brother has already asked me that question. Like you, he disapproves of my action. You may both of you be right, but I set as little store by his opinion as I do by yours. When I invited Lucilla to stay with me, I did what I believed—and still believe!—to be the right thing to do.'

'Fudge!' he said roughly. 'Your only excuse could have been that you were bamboozled into thinking that she had suffered ill-treatment at her aunt's hands, and if that is what she told you she must be an unconscionable little liar! Clara Amber has petted and cosseted her ever since she took her in charge!'

'No, she didn't tell me anything of the sort, but what she did tell me made me pity her from the bottom of my heart. Little though you may think it, Mr Carleton, there is a worse tyranny than that of ill-treatment. It is the tyranny of tears, vapours, appeals to feelings of affection, and of gratitude! This tyranny Mrs Amber seems to have exercised to the full! A girl of less strength of character might have succumbed to it, but Lucilla is no weakling, and however ill-advised it was of her to have run away I can't but respect her for having had the spirit to do it!'

He said, rather contemptuously: 'An unnecessarily dramatic way of showing her spirit. I am sufficiently well acquainted with Mrs Amber to know that she would not indulge in tears and vapours if Lucilla had not offered her a good deal of provocation. I conclude that the tiresome chit has been imposing on her aunt's good-nature yet again. Mrs Amber has frequently complained of her wilfulness to me, but what else could she expect of a girl brought up with excessive indulgence? I guessed how it would be from the outset.'

'Then I wonder at it that you should have given your *ward* into her care!' exclaimed Miss Wychwood hotly. 'One would have supposed that if you had had the smallest regard for her welfare—' She stopped, aware that she had allowed her indignation to betray her into impropriety, and said: 'I beg your pardon! I have no right, of course, to censure either your conduct, or Mrs Amber's!'

'No,' he said.

Her eyes flew to his in astonishment, a startled question in them, for she was quite taken aback by this uncompromising monosyllable.

'No right at all,' he said, explaining himself.

For a perilous moment, she hovered on the brink of losing her temper, but her ever-ready sense of the absurd came to her rescue, and instead of yielding to the impulse to come to points with him she broke into sudden laughter, and said: 'How unhandsome of you to have given me such a set-down, when I had already begged your pardon!'

'How unjust of you to accuse me of giving you a set-down when all I did was to agree with you!' he retorted.

'It is to be hoped,' said Miss Wychwood, with strong feeling, 'that we are not destined to see very much more of each other,

Mr Carleton! You arouse in me an almost overmastering desire to give you the finest trimming you have ever had in your life!'

Her laughter was reflected in his eyes. 'Oh, no, you would be very unwise to do that!' he said. 'Recollect that I am famous for my incivility! I should instantly give you your own again, and since I am an ill-mannered man and you are a well-bred woman of consequence you would be bound to come off the worse from any such encounter.'

'That I can believe! Nevertheless, sir, I am determined to do what lies within my power to bring you to a sense of your obligations towards that unfortunate child. For fobbing her off on to Mrs Amber, when she was still a child, there may have been some excuse, but she is not a child now, and—'

'Permit me to correct you, ma'am!' he interrupted. 'I should undoubtedly have fobbed her off on to Mrs Amber if she had been left to my sole guardianship, but it so happens that I had no choice in the matter! My brother appointed Amber to share the guardianship with me; and it was the expressed wish of his wife that, in the event of her death, her sister should have charge of Lucilla!'

'I see,' she said, digesting this. 'But did you also delegate your authority over Lucilla's future? Were you willing to see her coerced into a distasteful marriage?'

'No, of course not!' he replied irritably. 'But as marriage doesn't come into the question I fail to see—'

'But it does!' she exclaimed, considerably astonished. 'That is why she ran away from Chartley! *Surely* you must have known what was intended? I had supposed you to be a party to the arrangement!'

He stared at her from under frowning brows. '*What* arrangement?' he demanded.

'Good gracious!' she uttered. 'Then she never told you! Oh, how—how unprincipled of her! It makes me more than ever convinced that I did the right thing when I kept Lucilla with me!'

'Very gratifying for you, ma'am! Pray gratify *me* by telling me what the devil you are talking about!'

'I have every intention of telling you, so you have no need to bite off my nose!' she snapped. 'For goodness' sake, sit down! I can't think why we are standing about in this absurd way!'

'Oh, can't you? Did you expect me to sit down before you invited me to do so? You do think me a ramshackle fellow, don't you?'

'No, I don't! I don't know anything about you!' she said crossly.

'Except that I am famed for my incivility.'

She was obliged to laugh, and to say, with engaging honesty, as she sat down: 'I am afraid it is I who have been uncivil. Pray, will you not be seated, Mr Carleton?'

'Thank you!' he responded politely, and chose a chair opposite to hers. 'And now will you be kind enough to tell me what is the meaning of this farrago of nonsense about Lucilla?'

'It isn't nonsense—though I own anyone could be pardoned for thinking so! I collect that you don't know why Mrs Amber took her on a visit to Chartley Place?'

'I didn't know she had taken her there, until I received a blotched and impassioned letter from her, written from Chartley. As for the reason, I don't think she divulged it. It seemed to me a perfectly natural thing: Lucilla's own home is in the immediate vicinity, and until her mother's death she was as much a part of Iverley's household as her own, and no doubt formed friendships with his children—particularly, as I recollect, with Iverley's son, who is the nearest to her in age.'

'Are you quite positive that she didn't tell you of the scheme she and the Iverleys hatched between them?' she demanded incredulously.

'No,' he replied. 'I am not *positive* that she didn't, but I was unable to decipher more than the first page of her letter—and that with difficulty, since she had spattered it with her tears!

The second sheet baffled me, for not only did she weep over it, but she crossed and recrossed her lines—no doubt with the amiable intention of sparing me extra expense.'

Her eyes had widened as she listened to him, but although she was shocked by his indifference she could not help being amused by it. Amusement quivered in her voice as she said: 'What an extraordinary man you are, Mr Carleton! You received a letter from your ward's aunt, written in extreme agitation, and you neither made any real effort, I am very sure, to decipher that second sheet, nor—if the blotches did indeed baffle you—to go down to Chartley to discover precisely what had happened!'

'Yes, it seemed at first as though that hideous necessity did lie before me,' he agreed. 'Fortunately, however, the following day brought me a letter from Iverley, which had the merit of being short, and legible. He informed me that Lucilla was in Bath, that her aunt was prostrate, and that if I wished to rescue my ward from the clutches of what he feared was a designing female, calling herself Miss Wychwood, I must leave for Bath immediately.'

'Well, if that is not the outside of enough!' she said wrathfully. 'Calling myself Miss Wychwood, indeed! And in what way am I supposed to have *designs* on Lucilla, pray?'

'That he didn't disclose.'

'If he knew that Lucilla was staying with me, he must have written to you after Ninian's return to Chartley, for he couldn't otherwise have known where she had gone to, or what my name is! Yes, and after Ninian had given Mrs Amber the letter I had written to her, informing her of the circumstances of my meeting with Lucilla, and begging her to grant the child permission to stay with me for a few weeks! I should be glad to know why, if she thought me a designing female, she sent Lucilla's trunks to her! What a ninnyhammer she must be! But as for Iverley! How dared he write such damaging stuff about me? If he talked like that to Ninian I'm not surprised Ninian ripped up at him!'

'Your conversation, ma'am, bears a strong resemblance to Clara Amber's letter!' he said acidly. 'Both are unintelligible! What the devil has Ninian to do with this hotch-potch?'

'He has everything to do with it! Mrs Amber and the Iverleys are determined to marry him to Lucilla! *That* is why she ran away!'

'Marry him to Lucilla?' he repeated. 'What nonsense! Are you trying to tell me the boy is in love with her? I don't believe it!'

'No, I am not trying to tell you that! He wants the match as little as she does, but dared not tell his father so for fear of bringing about one of the heart-attacks with which Iverley terrorizes his family into obeying his every whim! I don't think you can have the least notion of what the situation is at Chartley!'

'Very likely not. I haven't visited the house since my sister-in-law's death. Iverley and I don't deal together, and never did.'

'Then I'll tell you!' promised Miss Wychwood, and straight-way launched into a graphic description of the circumstances which had goaded Lucilla into precipitate flight.

He heard her in silence, but the expression on his face was discouraging, and when she came to the end of her recital he was so far from evincing either sympathy or understanding that he ejaculated, in exasperated accents: 'Oh, for God's sake, ma'am! Spare me any more of this Cheltenham tragedy! What a kick-up over something that might have been settled in a flea's leap!'

'Mr Carleton,' she said, holding her temper on a tight rein, 'I am aware that you, being a man, can scarcely be blamed for failing to appreciate the dilemma in which Lucilla found herself; but I assure you that to a girl just out of the schoolroom it must have seemed that she had walked into a trap from which the only escape was flight! Had Ninian had enough resolution to have told his father that he had no intention of making Lucilla an offer it must have brought the thing to an end. Unfortunately, his affection for his father, coupled with the belief—instilled into his head, I have no doubt at all, by his mother!—that to withstand Iverley's demands was tantamount to murdering him, overcame whatever resolution he may have had. As far as I have been able to discover, the only notion he had was to become engaged to Lucilla, and to trust in providence to prevent the subsequent marriage! The one good thing that has emerged from this escapade is that Ninian, finding, on his return to Chartley, that his fond father had worked himself into a rare passion, without suffering the slightest ill, began to see that Iverley's weak heart was little more than a weapon to hold over his household.'

'I am wholly uninterested in Ninian, or in any other young cub!' said Mr Carleton trenchantly. 'I accept—on your assurance!—that the pressure brought to bear on Lucilla was hard to withstand. What I do not accept, ma'am, is that her only remedy lay in flight! Why the devil didn't the little nod-cock write to *me?*'

She fairly gasped at this question, and it was a full minute before she was able to command her voice sufficiently to answer it with composure. 'I fancy, sir, that her previous experiences of writing to you for support had not led her to suppose that any other reply to an appeal to you for help would be forthcoming than that she must do as her aunt thought best,' she said.

She observed, with satisfaction, that she had at last succeeded in discomfiting him. He reddened, and said, in a voice of smouldering annoyance: 'Since the only *appeals* I've received from Lucilla have been concerned with matters quite outside my province—'

'Even an appeal for a horse of her own?' she interjected swiftly. 'Was that also outside your province, Mr Carleton?'

A frown entered his eyes. 'Did she ask me for one? I have no recollection of it.'

It was now her turn to be disconcerted, for she found that she could not remember whether a refusal to permit her to have a horse of her own had been one of Lucilla's accusations against him, or merely one of Mrs Amber's prohibitions against which she had not thought it worth her while to protest to her uncle. Fortunately, she was not obliged either to retract or to prevaricate, for, without waiting for a reply, he said: 'If she did, I daresay I did refuse to let her set up her own stable. I can conceive of few more foolish notions than to be keeping a horse and groom in a town—both, I have little doubt, eating their heads off!'

Having discovered the truth of this herself, she was unable to deny it, so she prudently abandoned the question, and cast back to her original accusation, saying: 'But am I not right in believing that your custom is to refer every request Lucilla has addressed to you to Mrs Amber's judgment?'

'Yes, of course you are,' he replied impatiently. 'What the devil do I know about the upbringing of schoolgirls?'

'What a miserable sop to offer your conscience!' she said.

'My conscience doesn't need a sop, ma'am!' he said harshly. 'I may be Lucilla's legal guardian, but it was never expected of me that I should be concerned in the niceties of her upbringing! Had it been suggested to me I should have had no hesitation in refusing such a charge. I've no turn for the infantry!'

'Not even for your brother's only child?' she asked. 'Don't you feel *any* affection for her?'

'No, none,' he replied. 'How should I? I scarcely know her. It's useless to expect me to become sentimental because she's my brother's child: I knew almost as little about him as I know about Lucilla, and what I did know I didn't much like. I don't mean to say that there was any harm in him: no doubt there was a great deal of good, but he had less than commonsense, and too much sensibility for my tastes. I found him a dead bore.'

'Well, I find my brother a dead bore too,' she said candidly, 'but however much we rub against each other there is a bond of affection between us. I had thought that that must always exist between brothers and sisters.'

'Possibly you know him better than I ever knew my brother. There were only three years between us, but although that's a mere nothing between adults, it constitutes a wide gulf between schoolboys. At Harrow, he formed a close, and, to my mind, a pretty mawkish friendship with young Elmore. They were both army-mad, and joined the same regiment when they left Harrow. From then on I only saw him by scraps. He married a pretty little widgeon, too: she wasn't as foolish as her sister, but she had more hair than wit, and a mouth full of the sort of pap I can't stomach. I knew, of course, when he bought Chartley Manor that the bosom-bow friendship between him and Elmore was as strong as ever, and I suppose I should have guessed that such a pair of air-dreamers would have hatched a scheme to achieve a closer relationship by marrying Elmore's heir to Charles's daughter. Though why Elmore—or Iverley, as by that time he was—should have persisted in this precious scheme after Charles's death is a matter beyond my comprehension! Unless he thinks that Lucilla's property is just the thing to round off his own estate?'

'Well, that is what I suspect,' nodded Miss Wychwood, 'but it is only right that I should tell you that Ninian says it is no such thing. He says his father has never had a mercenary thought in his head.'

'On the whole,' said Mr Carleton, with considerable acerbity, 'I should think the better of him if his motive had been mercenary! This mawkish reason for trying to marry Lucilla to his son merely because he and my brother were as thick as inkle-weavers fairly turns my stomach! I never liked the fellow, you know.'

Her eyes were alive with laughter. She said perfectly gravely, however: 'For some reason or other I had suspected as much! Is there anyone whom you *do* like, Mr Carleton?'

'Yes, you!' he answered bluntly.

'*M-me?*' she gasped, wholly taken aback.

He nodded. 'Yes—but much against my will!' he said.

That made her burst out laughing. Still gurgling, she said: 'You are quite outrageous, you know! What in the world have I said or done to make you *like* me? Of all the farradiddles I ever heard that bears off the palm!'

'Oh, no! I never flummery people. I do like you, but I'm damned if I know why! It isn't your beauty, though that is remarkable; and it certainly isn't anything you have said or done. I think it must be your quality—that certain sort of something about you!'

'It's my belief,' said Miss Wychwood, with conviction, 'that you are all about in your head!'

He laughed. 'On the contrary! But don't delude yourself into thinking that my liking for you makes me think that you are a fit person to have charge of my niece.'

'How mortifying!' she retaliated. 'What do you propose to do about that, sir?'

'Give her back into her aunt's care, of course!'

'What, take her back to Chartley Place? What an addle-brained notion to take into your head! You had as well bestow your blessing on her marriage to Ninian without more ado!'

'No, not to Chartley Place! To Cheltenham, of course!'

She shook her head. 'Oh, I don't think you'll be able to do that! The last intelligence we had of *poor* Mrs Amber was that she was prostrate, with Lady Iverley's doctor in attendance on her, and since Lucilla tells me that it takes her weeks to recover from these—these hysterical seizures I should very much doubt if she will be able to return to her own home for some time to come. Now I come to think of it, she has announced that she never wants to set eyes on Lucilla again, and although I don't set much store by that I do feel that it would be unreasonable to expect her to change her mind before she is perfectly restored to health.'

'I'll soon restore her to health!' he said savagely.

'Nonsense! You'd be more likely to terrify her into strong convulsions. And even if you did succeed you could still have Lucilla to contend with.'

'There will be no difficulty about that, I promise you!'

'Oh, I don't doubt you could bully her into going with you to Cheltenham!' she said, with maddening affability. 'What I do doubt is your ability to prevail upon her to remain there.'

He regarded her with kindling eyes. 'I should not *bully* her, ma'am!'

'Well, do you know, I think that's very wise of you,' she said, in an approving tone. 'She has a great deal of spirit, and any attempt on your part to coerce her would be bound to set up her bristles. She would run away again, and it really won't do for her to spend the next four years running away! No harm has come from her *first* flight, but if she were to make a habit of it—'

'Oh, be quiet!' he interrupted, between exasperation and amusement. 'What did you call me? Outrageous, wasn't it? What's sauce for the gander, ma'am, is also sauce for the goose!'

'That's given me my own again, hasn't it?' she said, with unabated cordiality.

A tell-tale muscle quivered at the corner of his mouth; he met her quizzing look, and quite suddenly laughed. 'Miss Wychwood,' he said, 'I lied when I said I liked you! I do *not* like you! I am very nearly sure that I dislike you excessively!'

'What can I say, dear sir, except that your sentiments are entirely reciprocated!' she responded.

He smiled appreciatively. 'Has anyone ever got the better of you in a verbal encounter?' he asked.

'No, but it must be remembered that I have not until today had much opportunity to engage in verbal encounters. The gentlemen I have previously been acquainted with have all been distinguished by propriety of manners and conduct!'

'That must have made 'em sad bores!' he commented.

She could not help thinking that that was one accusation which could not be levelled against him, but she did not say so. Instead, she suggested, rather coldly, that they should waste no more time pulling caps, but should turn their attention to a matter of much graver importance.

'If you mean what's to be done with Lucilla—' He broke off, frowning.

'Well, I do mean that. It would be useless to take her back to Mrs Amber—even if Mrs Amber were willing to receive her. It might be thought that you were the properest person to take charge of her—'

'Oh, my God, no!' he exclaimed.

'No,' she agreed. 'It would be quite ineligible. You would be obliged to hire some genteel lady to chaperon her, and I should doubt very much if you could find anyone suitable for the post. On the one hand she must have enough strength of mind to enable her to exercise some degree of control over Lucilla; on the other she must be meek enough to bear with your overbearing temper, and to obey even the most idiotish of your commands without argument.' She smiled kindly at him, and added: 'An unlikely combination, I fear, Mr Carleton!'

'I am relieved! If the unpleasant picture you have drawn is with the object of inducing me to leave my ward in your care—'

'Not at all! I shall be happy to keep her with me until some more suitable arrangement has been made, but at no time have I had the smallest intention of keeping her in my permanent charge. May I suggest to you that your immediate task must be to set about the business of launching her into Society? I am astonished that this very obvious duty should not have occurred to you.'

'Are you indeed, ma'am? Then let me tell you that I have made arrangements for my cousin, Lady Trevisian, to bring her out next year!'

'Oh, that will never do!' she said quickly. 'After having had a taste of the very mild entertainments offered in Bath at this season, you cannot expect her to sink back into the schoolroom—which is what will happen to her if you succeed in bullocking Mrs Amber into resuming her guardianship.'

'In fact, ma'am,' he said, in biting accents, 'you have made her dissatisfied—which proves how very unfit you are to have even temporary charge of any girl of her age!' He saw that his words had brought a flush into her face, and fancied that he detected a hurt expression in her eyes. It was a fleeting look only, but he said, in a milder tone: 'I daresay you may have meant it for the best, but the result of your action has been to land us in a rare mess!'

'Pray don't hide your teeth, sir! You do *not* think I meant it for the best! You've as good as accused me of trying to make mischief, and I very much resent it!'

'I haven't done any such thing! And if I had it wouldn't have been as insulting as *your* accusation, that I would *bullock* Mrs Amber!' She sniffed, which had the effect of bringing the smile back into his eyes. 'What an unexpected creature you are!' he said. 'At one moment a woman of the first consequence, at the next a hornet! No, don't scowl at me! Really I've no wish to break squares!'

'Then don't provoke me!' she said crossly. 'Why don't you ask your cousin to bring Lucilla out this year?'

'Because I've no fancy for finding myself at Point Non Plus! She wouldn't do it: her eldest daughter is to be married in May, and she has her hands full already with all the ridic— with all the preparations for the wedding! I could no more persuade her to present Lucilla at such a moment than I could *bullock* her into doing it!'

'Oh, for goodness' sake!' she exclaimed, looking daggers at him, '*must* you be so—so *naggy*?'

'Alas!' he returned mournfully. 'The temptation to rouse you to fury is too great to be resisted! You can have no notion how much your beauty is enhanced by a blush of rage, and the fire in your eyes!' He watched her close her lips tightly, and his shoulders shook. 'What, lurched, Miss Wychwood?' he mocked her.

'Oh, no, there is much I could say, but having been reared—unlike yourself!—to respect the common decencies of established etiquette I am unfortunately debarred from uttering even one of the things which spring to my mind!'

'Don't give them a thought!' he begged. 'Consider under what a disadvantage you must be if you respect the common decencies which I don't!'

'If you had an ounce of—of proper feeling you would respect them!' she told him roundly. 'You are a positive rake-shame—as my brother would say!' she added, rather hastily.

His face was alive with laughter, but he said reprovingly: 'You shock me, ma'am! What an indelicate expression for a lady of quality to use!'

'Very likely! But as for it's shocking you I shouldn't think anything could!'

'How well you understand me!' he said, much gratified.

'Oh, how can you be so abominable?' she demanded, laughing in spite of herself. 'Do, pray, stop trying to goad me into being as uncivil and as disagreeable as you are yourself, and let us consider what is to be done about Lucilla! I perfectly understand how awkward it would be for your cousin to be saddled with her at this moment, but have you no other relation who would be willing to bring her out?'

'No, none,' he replied. 'Nor can I think her come-out of such urgency. She can only just have reached her seventeenth birthday, and the last time I went to Almack's I found the place choke-full of callow schoolroom misses, and determined that *my* ward shouldn't swell their ranks!'

'I know exactly what you mean!' she said. 'Girls pitchforked into the ton without a notion of how to go on, and betrayed by their anxiety not to seem as innocent as they are into quite unbecoming simpering, titters, and—oh, you know as well as I do the sort of detestable *archness* which so many very young girls display! That is why I have made it my business to introduce Lucilla into Bath society! I think it of the first importance that a girl should learn how to conduct herself in company before being introduced into the ton. But you need have no fears that Lucilla would disgrace you! She is neither shy nor coming: indeed, her manners are very pretty, and do Mrs Amber the greatest credit! If you doubt me, come and see for yourself! I am holding a small rout-party here on Thursday, particularly in her honour, and shall be happy to welcome you to it. That is, if you are still in Bath then? But perhaps you don't mean to make any very long stay here?'

'I must obviously remain in Bath until I've settled what's to be done with Lucilla, and shall certainly come to your party. Accept my best thanks, ma'am!'

She said mischievously: 'I warn you, sir, it will be the most boring party imaginable! I have invited *all* the young persons of my acquaintance, *and* as many of their parents who don't care to allow their daughters to go unchaperoned to parties! I daresay you can never have attended any party even half as insipid!'

'I would hazard a guess, Miss Wychwood, that you have never before *given* such an insipid party!' he said shrewdly.

'No, very true!' she confessed. 'To own the truth, I laughed myself into stitches when I read over the list of my invited guests! However, I'm not giving it to please myself, but to introduce Lucilla into Bath society. I am confident that she will make a hit. She did so when I took her to an informal party the other day.'

'So I suppose the next confounded nuisance I shall have to face will be sending either love-lorn cubs, or gazetted fortune-hunters to the rightabout!'

'Oh, no!' she said sweetly. 'I don't number any fortune-hunters amongst my acquaintances! I collect, from certain things she has said, and from her extremely costly wardrobe, that she is possessed of a considerable independence?'

'Lord, yes! She's rich enough to buy an Abbey!'

'Well, in that case I need not scruple to provide her with a good abigail.'

'I thought she had one. Indeed, I'm sure of it, for I've been paying her wages for the past three years. What has become of her?'

'She quarrelled with Mrs Amber, when Lucilla's flight was discovered, and left the house in a rage,' she responded.

'*Women!*' he uttered, with loathing. 'It's of no use to expect me to engage an abigail for her: what the devil does she imagine I know about such things? Since you have usurped Mrs Amber's place, I suggest that it is for you to engage a maid!'

'Certainly!' she replied, quite unruffled.

'Where *is* Lucilla?' he demanded abruptly.

'She has ridden out to Farley Castle with a party of young friends, and I don't expect to see her back for several hours yet.'

He looked annoyed, but before he had time to speak an interruption occurred, in the person of Miss Farlow, who came into the room, with her bonnet askew, and words tripping off her tongue. 'Such a vexatious thing, dear Annis! I have been *all* over the town, trying to match that sarcenet, and, would you believe it, not even Thorne's were able to offer me anything like it! So what with this horrid wind, which has positively blown me to pieces, and—' She stopped, becoming suddenly aware of the presence of a stranger. 'Oh, I beg your pardon! I didn't know! What a sadly shocking thing of me to do, bursting in on you, which of course I should never have done if James had informed me that you had a visitor! But he never said a word about it—just relieved me of my parcels, you know, for it was he who opened the door, not our good Limbury, who I daresay was busy in the pantry, and

I desired him to give the *large* one to Mrs Wardlow, and to have the others carried up to my bedchamber, which he said he would do, and then we exchanged a few words about the way the wind *whips* at one round every corner, and how dreadfully steep the hill is, particularly when one is burdened with parcels, as, of course, I was, and which has made me quite out of breath, besides tousling me quite abominably!'

Miss Wychwood, having observed with malicious enjoyment the effect on Mr Carleton of this tangled speech, intervened at this point, saying: 'I've no sympathy to waste on you, Maria! Indeed, I think you very well served for being so foolish as to walk home, instead of calling up a chair! As for "bursting in", I am glad you did, for I wish to make Mr Carleton known to you—Lucilla's uncle, you know! Mr Carleton, Miss Farlow— my cousin, who is kind enough to reside with me.'

He favoured Miss Farlow with a brief bow, but addressed himself to his hostess, saying, with the flicker of an impish smile: 'Lending you countenance, ma'am?'

'Exactly so!' she said, refusing to rise to this bait.

'You astonish me! I hadn't supposed that any lady so advanced in years as yourself would be conscious of the need of chaper- onage! Is your name Annis? A corruption, I believe, of Agnes, but I like it! It becomes you.'

'Well!' exclaimed Miss Farlow, bristling in defence of her patroness, 'I'm sure I don't know why you should, not that I mean to say it is not a very pretty name, for I think it *very* pretty, but if it is a *corruption* it cannot be thought to *become* dear Miss Wychwood, who is not in the least corrupt, let me assure you!'

'Thank you, Maria!' said Miss Wychwood, bubbling over with ill-suppressed mirth. 'I knew I might depend on you to establish my character!'

'Indeed you may, dearest Annis!' declared Miss Farlow, much moved. She glared through starting tears at Mr Carleton, and added, with a gasp at her own temerity: 'I shall take leave to tell you, sir, that I think it *most* ungentlemanly of you to cast aspersions on Miss Wychwood!'

'No, no, Maria!' said Miss Wychwood, trying to speak with proper sobriety, 'you wrong him! I don't *think* he meant to cast aspersions on me—though I own I wouldn't be prepared to hazard any large sum on such a doubtful chance!'

'Hornet!' said Mr Carleton appreciatively.

She twinkled at him, and awoke a reluctant smile in his hard eyes. 'Let us leave my character out of the discussion! You have come to Bath—at great personal inconvenience—to see your niece, but, most unfortunately, she is not here at the moment. So what is to be done? You will scarcely wish to sit here, kicking your heels, until she returns!'

'No, by God I wouldn't! Any more, I dare swear, than you would wish me to do so!'

'No, indeed! You would be very much in my way! Perhaps it would be best if you were to dine here tonight.'

'No,' he said decisively. 'You're very obliging, ma'am, but it would be best if you brought her to dine with me, at the York House. I'm putting up there, and they seem to keep a tolerable table. I shall expect you both at seven—unless you prefer a later hour?'

'Oh, no! But pray don't depend upon my joining you! My abigail shall escort Lucilla to York House, and I feel sure I can rely on you to bring her back later in the evening.'

'That won't do at all!' he said. 'Your presence at any discussion about Lucilla's future is indispensable, believe me! I do depend upon your joining me. Don't fail me!'

With that, he took his leave, bowing slightly to Miss Farlow, but grasping Miss Wychwood's hand for a moment, and favouring her with a rueful grin.

## Six

'WELL!' UTTERED MISS FARLOW, IN ACCENTS OF STRONG reprobation, as soon as Limbury had conducted Mr Carleton out of the room. 'What a *very* uncivil person, I *must* say! To be sure, Sir Geoffrey did warn us, and I do hope, dearest Annis, that you will *not* dine with him this evening! Such impertinence to have invited you—if an invitation you could call it, though *I* never heard an invitation delivered so improperly! I quite thought you must have given him a heavy set-down, and was astonished that you did not!'

'Well, I did think of doing so,' admitted Miss Wychwood. 'But since he is, as you so rightly say, a very uncivil person, I couldn't be sure that he wouldn't retaliate in kind. I feel it is my duty to go with Lucilla, if only to prevent her coming to cuffs with him.'

'I make no secret of the fact that I don't consider you owe that girl any duty!' said Miss Farlow, trembling with indignation. 'But *I* have a duty towards *you*, and don't tell me I haven't, for I shan't listen to you! Sir Geoffrey and dear Lady Wychwood entrusted you to my care, and even if he didn't say so, he *meant* it, and Lady Wychwood did say so! Just as I was about to get into the carriage, or if it wasn't then, it was in the hall, or perhaps the morning-room, because she had a little chill coming on, and so didn't come out of the house, though she wished to, but I begged her not to do so, because the weather was most

inclement, which you *must* remember, so we said goodbye in
the hall—'

'Or perhaps in the morning-room?' interpolated Miss
Wychwood.

'It may have been: I'm not perfectly sure, but it makes no
difference! And she *distinctly* said, when she bade me goodbye,
or perhaps just after she had said goodbye: "Take care of her,
Cousin Maria!" Meaning you, of course! And I promised I
would, and so I shall!'

'Thank you, Maria, I feel sure I can depend on you to come
to my rescue if I should find myself in trouble. But at the
moment I'm not in any sort of trouble, so do, I beg of you,
put your bonnet straight, and make your hair tidy again! You
look like a birch-broom in a fit!'

'Annis!' said Miss Farlow, sinking her voice impressively. 'That
man is not a proper person for you to know!'

'Fiddle! I collect Geoffrey told you so, but what harm either
of you expect him to do I haven't the most distant guess. Do
you suspect him of having designs upon my virtue? You are
quite beside the bridge if you do! He doesn't even like me!'

Miss Farlow's modesty was so much shocked by this speech
that she uttered a faint shriek, and tottered away to her own
room, there to write an agitated letter to Sir Geoffrey Wychwood,
in which she assured him that he might depend on her to do
all that lay in her power to put an end to a most undesirable
friendship, and (in the same sentence) warned him that she
feared there was nothing she could do to stop dear Annis in one
of her headstrong moods.

When Lucilla came in, it was several minutes before Miss
Wychwood was able to break the news of her uncle's arrival to
her, so anxious was she to recount all the details of the day's
expedition. But she did at last pause for breath, and the change
that came over her countenance when she heard the dread

tidings was almost ludicrous. The sparkle was quenched instantly in her eyes, the smile vanished from her lips, she turned pale, and wrung her hands together. 'He has come to drag me away! Oh, no, no, no!'

'Don't be such a goose!' said Miss Wychwood, laughing at her. 'I don't think he has any such intention, though I fancy that may well have been his original purpose. But until I told him just what the case was he had no idea that the Iverleys and Mrs Amber were trying to bring about a match between you and Ninian. You need not be afraid that he will help them to promote that precious scheme, for he most certainly will not. He was excessively vexed—partly with them, and partly with you, for not having written to tell him of it. So when you meet him don't put him out of temper by looking black at him, and getting on your high ropes! He seems to me to be as mifty as he is uncivil, and no good purpose can be served by getting into a quarrel with him, you know.'

'I don't want to meet him!' Lucilla declared, tears starting into her eyes.

'Now you are being foolish beyond permission, my dear! Of course you must see him! I am taking you to dine with him at the York House this evening, so that we may, all three of us, discuss what's to be done with you! Oh, don't look so dismayed, you ridiculous puss! I promise I won't let him bully you!'

In spite of this assurance it was a considerable time before Lucilla could be persuaded to consent to the scheme, and although she did in the end consent it was easy to see, when she took her place beside Miss Wychwood in the carriage, that she was far from being reconciled to it. Her charming little face was downcast, her eyes were full of apprehension, and it was not difficult to guess that she stood in great awe of her formidable uncle.

He received them in a private parlour, very correctly attired in the blue coat, white waistcoat, black pantaloons, and striped silk stockings which constituted the evening-dress worn by all the Smarts at private parties. Miss Wychwood noted, with slightly reluctant approval, that while he exhibited none of the exaggerated quirks of fashion which characterized the dandy-set, his coat was very well cut, his neckcloth tied with nicety, his shirt-points decently starched, and the bosom of his shirt unadorned by a frill—an outmoded fashion still worn by many provincial beaux, and almost invariably by the older generation of Smarts to which he undoubtedly belonged.

He came forward to shake hands with Miss Wychwood, paying no immediate heed to Lucilla, following her into the parlour. 'You can't think how relieved I am to see that you haven't brought your cousin with you!' he said, by way of greeting. 'I have been cursing myself these three hours for not having made it plain to her that I was not including *her* in my invitation to *you*! I couldn't have endured an evening spent in the company of such an unconscionable gabble-monger!'

'Oh, but you did!' she told him. 'She took you in the greatest dislike, and can't be blamed for having done so, or for having uttered some pretty severe strictures on your total want of conduct. You must own, if there is any truth in you, that you were shockingly uncivil to her!'

'I can't tolerate chattering bores,' he said. 'If she took me in such dislike, I'm amazed that she permitted you to come here without her chaperonage.'

'She would certainly have stopped me if she could have done it, for she does not think you are a proper person for me to know!'

'Good God! Does she suspect me of trying to seduce you? She may be easy on that head: I never seduce ladies of quality!' He turned from her as he spoke, and put up his glass to cast a critical look over Lucilla. 'Well, niece?' he said. 'What a trouble-some chit you are! But I'm glad to see that your appearance at least is much improved since I last saw you. I thought that you were bidding fair to grow into a Homely Joan, but I was wrong: you are no longer pudding-faced, and you've lost your freckles. Accept my felicitations!'

'I was not pudding-faced!'

'Oh, believe me, you were! You hadn't lost your puppy-fat.'

Her bosom heaved with indignation, but Miss Wychwood intervened, recommending her not to rise to that, or any other fly of her uncle's casting. She added severely: 'And as for you, sir, I beg you will refrain from making any more remarks expressly designed to put Lucilla all on end, and to render me acutely uncomfortable!'

'I wouldn't do *that* for the world!' he assured her.

'Then don't be so rag-mannered!' she retorted.

'But I wasn't!' he protested. 'I didn't say Lucilla *is* pudding-faced! I said she *was*, and even complimented her on her improved looks!'

Lucilla was betrayed into a little crow of involuntary laughter, and said with engaging frankness: 'Oh, what an odiously complete hand you are, Uncle Oliver! Was I *really* such an antidote?'

'Oh, no, not an antidote! Merely a chicken that had lost its down and had too few feathers to show that it might grow into a handsome bird!'

'Well!' said Lucilla, much impressed. 'I know I'm quite *pretty*, but no one has ever said I was handsome! Do you think I am, sir, or—or are you roasting me?'

'No, I don't think you handsome, but you've no need to look so downcast! Believe me, only females admire *handsome* women: men infinitely prefer pretty ones!'

She was left to digest this, while he engaged Miss Wychwood in conversation, but suddenly interrupted this exchange of elegant civilities to ask him if he thought Miss Wychwood handsome, or pretty.

Annis, torn between amusement and embarrassment, directed an admonitory frown at her, but Mr Carleton replied without hesitation: 'Neither.'

'Well, I think,' said Lucilla, bristling in defence of her patroness, 'that she is *beautiful!*'

'Yes, so do I,' he answered.

'I am very much obliged to you both,' said Annis, recovering from the shock, 'and I shall be even more obliged to you if you will stop putting me to the blush! I haven't come to listen to empty compliments, but to discuss with you, sir, how best to provide for Lucilla until her come-out!'

'All in good time,' he said. 'We will dine first.' He added, with that glint in his eyes which she found strangely disquieting: 'Your advanced years, ma'am, have impaired your memory! I told you, not so many hours ago, that I never try to flummery people! My years are considerably more advanced than yours, but I should warn you that my memory is still quite undamaged by senility!'

'Odious, *odious* creature!' she said softly, but allowed him to hand her to the table, where two waiters had just finished setting out the first course of a well-chosen dinner.

Lucilla was inclined to pout, but was subdued by a glance from Miss Wychwood's fine eyes, and meekly took her place at her guardian's left hand. She was young enough to regard the food set before her as a matter of indifference, but she had a schoolgirl's hearty appetite, and did full justice to the first course, partaking of every dish offered her, and allowing her elders to converse without interruption. The edge of her hunger having been taken off by the time the second course was brought in she refused the green goose, and the pigeons, but made great inroads on an orange soufflé, a Celerata cream, and a basket of pastry. Nibbling a ratafia biscuit, she stole a glance at her uncle's profile. He was smiling at something Miss Wychwood had said to him, so she ventured to ask him the question uppermost in her mind. 'Uncle Oliver!' she said imperatively.

He turned his head. 'Do rid yourself of this detestable habit you've fallen into of addressing me as *Uncle* Oliver! I find it quite repellent.'

She opened her eyes at him. 'But you *are* my uncle!' she pointed out.

'Yes, but I don't wish to be reminded of it.'

'Such a dreadfully *ageing* title, isn't it?' said Miss Wychwood, with spurious sympathy.

'Exactly so!' he replied. 'Almost worse than *aunt*!'

She shook her head sadly. 'Indeed yes! Though it was being called aunt that drove me from my home.'

'Well, what *am* I to call you?' demanded Lucilla.

'Anything else you like,' he responded, in a voice devoid of interest.

'Now, that very generous permission opens a wide field to you, my dear,' said Miss Wychwood. 'It wouldn't do for you to call him *Bangster*, for that would be too impolite, but I see nothing amiss with you calling him *Captain Hackum*, which has the same meaning, but wrapped up in clean linen!'

Mr Carleton grinned, and kindly explained to his bewildered niece that these terms signified a bully. 'They are cant terms,' he further explained, 'and far too vulgar for you to use! Anyone hearing them on your lips would write you down as a brass-faced hussy, without conduct or delicacy.'

'Devil!' said Miss Wychwood, with feeling.

'Oh, you're quizzing me!' Lucilla exclaimed, slightly offended. '*Both* of you! I wish you will not! I am not a brass-faced hussy, though I daresay people would think me one if I called you merely *Oliver*! I am sure it must be most improper!'

'It would not only be improper but it would bring down instant retribution on your head!' he told her. 'I have no objection to your addressing me as Oliver, but Merely Oliver I'm damned if I'll tolerate!'

She gave a choke of laughter. 'I didn't mean that! You know I didn't! Of course, if you had a title it would be perfectly proper to call you by it, but only think what my aunt would say if she heard me calling you Oliver!'

'As it seems unlikely that she will hear it, that need not trouble you,' he said. 'If you have any qualms, allay them with the reflection that Princess Charlotte addresses all her uncles—and, for anything I know, her aunts too—by their Christian names, and even the youngest of them is older than I am!'

Lucilla had little interest in Royalty and dismissed the Princess Charlotte summarily. 'Oh, well, I daresay things are different for princesses!' she said. 'But you said that it's unlikely my aunt will ever hear me call you Oliver. W-what do you mean, Unc— *sir?*'

'I understand that she has washed her hands of you?'

'Yes!' breathed Lucilla, clasping her hands together, and keeping her eyes fixed on his face. 'And so—?'

'It behoves me, of course, to find some other female willing to take charge of you.'

Her face fell. 'But when am I to make my come-out?'

'Next year,' he replied.

'*Next* year? Oh, that's too bad of you!' she cried. 'I shall be past eighteen by then, and almost on the shelf! I want to come out *this* year!'

'I daresay, but it won't harm you to wait for another year,' he answered unfeelingly. 'In any event, you must, because Julia Trevisian, who is to present you at one of the Drawing-rooms, cannot undertake the very exhausting task of chaperoning you to all the functions to which she will see to it that you are invited, until your cousin Marianne is off her hands. Marianne is to be married in May, midway through the Season, and that would be far too late for you to make your first appearance—even if Julia were not, by that time, wholly done-up, which, from her conversation when I last saw her, I gather she expects to be.'

'Is Cousin Julia going to bring me out?' she asked, brightening perceptibly. 'Well, I must say that if you arranged that, sir, it is quite the best thing you've ever done for me! In fact, it is the *only* good thing you've ever done for me, and I am truly grateful to you!'

'Handsomely said!'

'Yes, but it doesn't settle the question of where I am to live, or what I am to do for a whole year,' she pointed out. 'And I wish to make it plain to you that nothing—*nothing!*—will prevail upon me to return to Aunt Clara! If you force me to go back, I shall run away again!'

'Not if you have a particle of commonsense,' he said dryly. He looked her over, rather sardonically smiling. 'You'll do as you are bid, my girl, for if I have any more highty-tighty behaviour from you I promise you I shan't permit you to come out next Season.'

She turned white with sheer rage, and stammered: 'You—you—'

'Enough of this folly!' interposed Miss Wychwood, in blighting accents. 'You are both talking arrant nonsense! I don't know which of you is being the more childish, but I know which of you has the least excuse for behaving like a spoilt baby!'

A tinge of colour stole into Mr Carleton's cheeks, but he shrugged, and said, with a short laugh: 'I've no patience to waste on pert and disobedient schoolgirls.'

'I *hate* you!' said Lucilla, in a low and trembling voice.

'I daresay you do.'

'Oh, for heaven's sake come out of the mops, both of you!' said Miss Wychwood, quite exasperated. 'This ridiculous quarrel has sprung up for no reason at all! There can be no question of your uncle's sending you back to Mrs Amber, Lucilla, because she has made it abundantly clear that she doesn't want you back.'

'She will change her mind,' said Lucilla despairingly. 'She frequently says she washes her hands of me, but she never does so!'

'Well, it's my belief your uncle wouldn't send you to her even if she does change her mind.' She raised a quizzical eyebrow at Mr Carleton, and said: '*Would* you, sir?'

A reluctant smile just touched his lips. 'As a matter of fact, no: I wouldn't,' he admitted. 'She seems to me to have exercised no control over Lucilla, and is demonstrably not a fit or proper person to have charge of her. So I am now faced with the unenviable task of finding another, and, it is to be hoped, a more resolute member of the family to fill her place.'

Very little of this speech gratified Lucilla, but she was so much relieved by the discovery that he had no intention of restoring her to Mrs Amber that she decided to ignore such parts of it which had grossly offended her. She said tentatively: 'Wouldn't it be possible for me to remain in my dear Miss Wychwood's charge, sir?'

'No,' he replied uncompromisingly.

She choked back an unwise retort. 'Pray tell me why not!' she begged.

'Because, in the first place, she is even less a fit and proper person to act as your guardian than is your aunt, being far too young to chaperon you, or anyone else, and wholly unrelated to you.'

'She is not too young!' cried Lucilla indignantly. 'She is quite *old*!'

'. . . and in the second place,' he continued, betraying only by a quiver of the muscles beside his mouth that he had heard this hot interjection, 'it would be the height of impropriety for me—or, indeed, you!—to impose so outrageously on her good nature.'

It was evident that this aspect had not previously occurred to Lucilla. She took a moment or two to digest it, and said, finally: 'Oh! I hadn't thought of that.' She looked imploringly at Miss Wychwood, and said: 'I wouldn't—I wouldn't for the world impose on you, ma'am, but—but should I be an imposition? *Pray* tell me!'

Throwing a fulminating glance at Mr Carleton, Miss Wychwood replied: 'No, but *one* of the objections your uncle has raised I realize to be just. I am not related to you, and it would be thought very odd if you were to be known to have been removed from Mrs Amber's care, and put into mine. Such an extraordinary change must give rise to conjecture, and a great deal of poker-talk which I am persuaded you wouldn't relish. Moreover, that sort of scandal-broth must inevitably reflect on Mrs Amber, and that, I know, you wouldn't wish to happen. For however many tiresome restrictions she has subjected you to, and however boring you found them, you must surely acknowledge that she has acted always—however mistakenly—with nothing but your welfare in mind.'

'Yes,' Lucilla agreed reluctantly. 'But not when she tried to make me accept an offer from Ninian!'

This, as Mr Carleton, cynically appreciative of this exchange, recognized to be (in his own phraseology) a leveller, did not prove to be a home-hit. Miss Wychwood rallied swiftly, and said: 'I shouldn't wonder at it if she thought she *was* promoting your welfare. Recollect, my love, that Ninian was quite your best friend when you were children! Mrs Amber may well have thought that you would find true happiness with him.'

'Are you—*you*, ma'am!—trying to persuade me to go back to Cheltenham?' Lucilla demanded, in sharp suspicion.

'Oh, no!' replied Miss Wychwood calmly. 'I don't think that would answer. What I am trying to do is to point out to you that if you, by some unlikely chance, could prevail upon your uncle to appoint me to be your guardian, in preference to any of your own relations, we should all three of us come under the gravest censure. Well, I shan't attempt to conceal that I have no wish to incur such censure; and, in your case, it would be extremely damaging, for you may depend upon it that Mrs Amber would inform every one of her friends and acquaintances—and probably your paternal relatives as well—that you were quite beyond her control, and had left her to reside with a complete stranger, which—'

'. . . would have the merit of being true!' interpolated Mr Carleton.

'Which,' pursued Miss Wychwood, ignoring this unmannerly interruption, 'would have a far more damaging effect on your future than you are yet aware of. Believe me, Lucilla, *nothing* is more fatal to a girl than to have earned (however unjustly) the reputation of being a hurly-burly female, wild to a fault, and so hot-at-hand as to be ready to tie her garter in public rather than to submit to authority.'

'That would be *very* bad, wouldn't it?' said Lucilla, forcibly struck by this masterly representation of the evils attached to her situation.

'It would indeed,' Miss Wychwood assured her. 'And it is why I am strongly of the opinion that your uncle should make arrangements for you to reside, until your come-out, with some other of your relations—preferably one who lives in London, and is in a position to introduce you into the proper ways of conducting yourself in Society before you actually enter it. *He* is the only member of your father's family with whom I am acquainted, but I should suppose that he is not the only representative of it.' She turned her head, to direct a look of bland enquiry at Mr Carleton, and said: 'Tell me, sir, has Lucilla no aunts or cousins, on your side of the family, with whom it would be quite unexceptionable for her to reside?'

'Well, there is my sister, of course,' he said thoughtfully.

'My Aunt Caroline?' said Lucilla, doubtfully. 'But isn't she a great invalid, sir?'

'Yes, being burnt to the socket is her favourite pastime,' he agreed. 'She suffers from a mysterious complaint, undiscoverable, but apparently past cure. One of its strangest symptoms is to put her quite out of frame whenever she finds herself asked to do anything she doesn't wish to do. She has been known to become prostrate at the mere thought of being obliged to attend some party which promised to be a very boring function. There's no saying that she wouldn't sink into a deep decline if I were to suggest to her that she should take charge of you, so I shan't do it. I can't have her death laid at my door.'

Lucilla giggled a little at that, but expressed her profound relief as well, saying frankly that she thought life with Lady Lambourn would be even more insupportable than life with Mrs Amber. 'Besides, I am scarcely acquainted with her,' she added, as a clincher. 'Indeed, I don't think I've seen her more than once in my life, and that was years ago, when Mama took me with her to pay a morning call on her. I was only a child, but she didn't *seem* to be invalidish. I remember that she was very pretty, and *most* elegant. To be sure, she did tell Mama that she could seldom boast of being in high health, but she didn't say it in such a way as to lead anyone to suppose that she suffered from an incurable complaint.'

'Ah, that must have been before she attained the status of widowhood!' he replied. 'Lambourn had the good sense to cock up his toes when he realized which way the wind was blowing.'

'What a vast number of enemies your tongue must have made for you!' observed Miss Wychwood. 'May I suggest that instead of casting what I strongly suspect to be unjust aspersions on your sister, you bend your mind to the question of which of your relations you judge to be the most proper to have charge of Lucilla until Lady Trevisian is at liberty to introduce her into the ton?'

'Certainly!' he responded, with the utmost cordiality. 'I shall make every effort to do so, but at this present I find myself at a stand, and must, reluctantly, beg you to continue in your self-appointed post as her chaperon.'

'In that case,' she said, getting up from the table, 'we have no more to do here, and will take our leave of you, sir. Come, Lucilla! Thank your uncle for his kind hospitality, and let us go home!'

He made no attempt to detain them, but murmured provocatively, as he put Miss Wychwood's shawl round her shoulders: 'Accept my compliments, ma'am! Were you obliged to put great force on yourself *not* to rise to that fly?'

'Oh, no, none at all!' she retorted, without an instant's hesitation. 'My father taught me many years ago never to pay the least attention to the ill-considered things uttered by rough diamonds!'

He gave a shout of laughter. 'A facer!' he acknowledged. He turned from her to flick Lucilla's cheek lightly with one careless finger. '*Au revoir*, niece!' he said, smiling quite kindly at her. 'Do, pray, strive to re-establish the family's reputation, which I have placed in such jeopardy!'

He then escorted them downstairs, and, while Miss Wychwood's carriage was called for, engaged her, with the utmost civility, in an exchange of very proper nothings. These were interrupted by the entrance from the street of a somewhat rakish looking gentleman whose lively eyes no sooner perceived Miss Wychwood than he came quickly forward, exclaiming: 'Ah, now, didn't I know fortune was going to smile on me today? Most dear lady, how do you do?'

She gave him her hand, which he instantly carried to his lips, and said: 'How do you do, Mr Kilbride? I collect you are in Bath on a visit to your grandmother. I trust she is well?'

'Oh, in a state of far too high preservation!' he said, with a comical look. 'Out of reason cross, too! It is most disheartening!'

She ignored this, and briefly introduced him to her companions. Her manner, which was slightly chilly, did not encourage him to linger, but he was apparently impervious to hints, and, after exchanging nods with Mr Carleton, with whom he was already acquainted, turned to address himself to Lucilla, which he did to such good purpose that she told Miss Wychwood, on the drive to Camden Place, that he was the most delightful and amusing man she had ever met.

'Is he?' said Miss Wychwood, with calculated indifference. 'Yes, I suppose he is amusing, but his wit is not always in good taste, and he is an incurable humbugger, which I find a little tedious. By the bye, your uncle has charged me with the task of engaging a new abigail for you, so will you go with me tomorrow morning to the Registry Office?'

'No, *has* he?' cried Lucilla, astonished. 'Yes, indeed I will, ma'am! And may we take a look in at the Pump Room? Corisande will be there, with her mama, and I told her I would ask you if I might join her.'

'Yes, certainly. And while we are in town we must buy a new pair of gloves for you, to wear at our rout-party.'

'*Evening*-gloves?' Lucilla said eagerly. 'They will be the first I have ever possessed, because my aunt *will* buy mittens for me, as if I were a mere schoolgirl! Did my uncle say I might have them as well as a new maid?'

'I didn't ask him,' replied Miss Wychwood. 'From what I have seen of him, I am tolerably certain that he would have answered in a disagreeably rusty way that he knew nothing about such matters, and I must do what I thought best.'

Lucilla gave a gurgle of laughter, and said: 'Yes, but the thing is, will he pay for them? For I know how expensive long gloves are, and—and I haven't very much of my pin-money left!'

'There is no need for you to tease yourself about that: of course he will do so!' replied Miss Wychwood, adding, with a good deal of mischievous satisfaction: 'His pride makes it a hard matter for him to be forced to permit *his* ward to reside with me, as my guest, and I take great credit to myself for having imbued him with enough respect to have prevented him from offering to pay me for taking charge of you! I shouldn't wonder at it if he tried to transfer the allowance he makes Mrs Amber to me. As for cutting up stiff at being required to meet the cost of whatever you may purchase—pooh! he is a great deal more likely to encourage you to be extravagant, for fear that if he refused to pay your bills I might do so!'

# Seven

*J*UST AS MISS WYCHWOOD AND LUCILLA WERE WALKING next morning along Upper Camden Place on their way to Gay Street, they encountered Ninian Elmore, striding towards them. It became immediately apparent that he was labouring under a strong sense of resentment, for hardly waiting to greet them he burst out with the rather unnecessary information that he was coming to visit them, adding explosively: 'What do you think has happened, ma'am?'

'I have no idea,' replied Miss Wychwood. 'Tell us!'

'I was coming to do so. You wouldn't believe it! I scarcely do myself! I mean to say, when you consider all that has taken place, and how it was *their* fault, and not mine—well, it makes me as mad as Bedlam, and so it would anyone!'

'But what *is* it?' demanded Lucilla impatiently.

'You may well ask! Not but what it will send you up into the boughs when I tell you! For of all the—'

She interrupted him, stamping her foot, and hugging her pelisse round her against the sharp wind that was blowing. 'For heaven's sake *tell* me, instead of talking in that hubble-bubble way, and keeping us standing in this detestable wind!' she almost screamed.

He glared at her, said with stiff dignity that he was just about to tell her when she had so rudely broken in on him, and, pointedly turning his shoulder towards her, addressed himself to Miss Wychwood, saying portentously: 'I have received a letter from my father, ma'am!'

'Is *that* all?' interpolated Lucilla scornfully.

'No, it is not all!' he retorted. 'But how anyone can utter more than a word with you interrupting—'

'Peace!' intervened Miss Wychwood, considerably amused. 'You cannot quarrel in the street—at least, I daresay you can, but I beg you won't! Has your father disinherited you, Ninian? And, if so, why?'

'Well, no, he hasn't done that, precisely,' he replied, 'but it wouldn't astonish me if he did do so—except that I rather fancy it isn't within his power, on account of the Settlement which was executed by my grandfather. I didn't pay much heed to it at the time, though I know that I had to sign some document or other—but he threatens to discontinue my allowance (besides repudiating any debts I may incur in Bath) if I do not instantly return to Chartley! I—I wouldn't have believed he could ever have behaved in such a manner! It has opened my eyes, I can tell you! He has always seemed to me to be the— the best of fathers, and—and the most understanding, and I don't scruple to say that *this* business has wounded me deeply! And, what's more, I'll be—dashed—if I crawl back to Chartley with my tail between my legs, as though I had done something wrong, which I have *not*!'

'It certainly seems very odd,' acknowledged Miss Wychwood. 'But perhaps there is an explanation! Will you walk with us to Gay Street, before Lucilla becomes quite frozen, and tell us why your father has issued such an ultimatum?'

He agreed to this, and, falling into step between them, disclosed that Lord Iverley (like Mrs Amber) had washed his hands of Lucilla, whose conduct had shown him that she was unworthy to be admitted into the family, being such as to convince him that she was so wholly wanting in propriety, modesty, and delicacy as to have sunk herself below reproach.

Ignoring an indignant gasp from Lucilla, he ended by saying: 'And so if you please, he forbids me to have anything more to do with her, but to return instantly to Chartley—under pain of his severest displeasure! As though the blame for her running away didn't lie at his door! Which it did! By God, Miss Wychwood, it has put me in such a rage that I have a very good mind to marry Lucilla immediately!'

Lucilla, who had listened to this speech with strong resentment, said warmly: 'He would be very well served if you did! But, for my part, I think you should ignore his letter. Because neither of us wishes to be married, and even if we did I don't think my uncle would give his consent. And I can't marry anyone without it, unless, I suppose, I eloped to the Border, which nothing would prevail upon me to do, even with someone I *wished* to marry! That *would* sink me below reproach, wouldn't it, ma'am?'

'It would indeed,' agreed Miss Wychwood. 'Besides condemning you both to a lifetime of regret!'

'Well, I know, but I didn't really mean it!' growled Ninian. 'All the same, I'd as lief be shackled to you as submit tamely to such an unreasonable order as this, and that I do mean!'

To Miss Wychwood's relief Lucilla took this in perfectly good part. She said: 'I must say, it is enough to drive anyone to desperation. It isn't even as though you had been an undutiful son, for the case has been far otherwise. And what seems to be most extraordinary is that he never kicked up such a dust when you were trying to fix your interest with that female in London, and she was by far more improper than I am, wasn't she?'

He cast her a fulminating glance. 'I'll tell you this, Lucy! It will be well for you to learn to keep your tongue between your teeth! Besides, you know nothing about it! I was not trying to fix my interest with her! A mere flirtation! Bachelor's fare!

You wouldn't understand, but you may depend upon it my father did!'

'Well, if he understood that, why doesn't he understand *this*?' Lucilla asked reasonably. 'It seems to me to be quite addle-brained!'

'It seems to *me*,' interposed Miss Wychwood, 'as though Lord Iverley wrote to you when he was in too much of a flame to consider what might be the effect of sending you such an intemperate letter, Ninian. I daresay he will be sorry for it by now; and I am very sure that it came as a shock to him when he found himself in a quarrel with you, for I fancy that had never happened before. Nor do I doubt that, however little he may acknowledge it, he knows he has been at fault in his dealings with you and Lucilla. So, having been pandered—having had his own way for a great number of years, he was naturally put into a pelter when he met with opposition—particularly from you, my dear boy! You told us yourself that you had parted from him on the worst of bad terms, and I expect he was sadly hurt—'

'Yes, I did, but I was sorry for it later, and was meaning to go back, to beg his pardon, when his letter reached me! But I shan't now! I could forgive his cutting at *me*, but the things he said about Lucy I cannot forgive—unless he withdraws them! It isn't that I approved of her running off as she did, for I didn't, but to accuse her of *wanton* behaviour, which he did, though I didn't intend to repeat that, besides having sunk herself below reproach, is unjust, and unforgiveable!'

Keeping her inevitable reflections on Lord Iverley's unwisdom to herself, Miss Wychwood responded, with soothing tact: 'You will of course do what you feel to be best, but I cannot help feeling that you ought, in common civility, to send your father an answer to his letter—and not an angry one! If you already had the intention of going back to beg his pardon—'

'I had, but I haven't that intention now!' he declared pugnaciously.

'When you've come out of the mops,' she said, smiling at him in a disarming way, 'I am persuaded that your good sense will make you perceive the propriety of offering him an apology for having expressed yourself more forcefully than was becoming. I don't think you should mention Lucilla at all, for what purpose could be served by your defending her against accusations which Lord Iverley must know very well are unjust? As for his summons to you, it would be foolish to refuse to obey it, for that, you know, would make you seem like a naughty little boy, shouting "I won't!" Far more dignified, don't you agree, to write that you will of course return presently to Chartley, but that you have several engagements in Bath in the immediate future from which it would be grossly impolite to cry off.'

Much impressed by this worldly wisdom, he exclaimed: 'By Jove, yes! That's the dandy! I *will* write to him, exactly as you suggest! I should think it must make him ashamed, besides showing him that I am not a schoolboy but a grown man, not to be ordered about but to be treated with respect! What's more, I'll send my duty to Mama, though after the things she said to me—However, whatever *they* choose to do, I hope *I* am not one to rip up grievances!'

Miss Wychwood applauded this; and as they had reached Gay Street, took leave of him, recommending him, if he had nothing better to do, to stroll down to the Pump Room, where she and Lucilla were going as soon as they had executed some business, and done a little shopping. Since her object was to prevent his writing a reply to his father's letter until his smouldering anger had had time to die down, she was glad to see that this suggestion found favour with him. When Lucilla, adding her helpful mite, told him that he would find her dear friend, Miss Corisande Stinchcombe, there, and charged him with a message for her, his clouded brow lightened perceptibly, and he went off quite happily down the hill. 'Which,' Lucilla informed

Miss Wychwood confidentially, 'I had a notion would give his thoughts another direction, because I could see yesterday that he took a marked fancy to her!'

'Then it was very well done of you,' approved Miss Wychwood. 'Which reminding him of his London-flirt was not!'

'No,' admitted Lucilla guiltily. 'I knew I had said the wrong thing as soon as the words were out of my mouth. Though why he should have taken snuff at it I haven't the least guess, for he told me all about her himself!'

Miss Wychwood was not obliged to enter into an explanation, because they had by this time mounted the flight of stairs that led to the Registry Office, recommended by Mrs Wardlow, who had engaged a highly respectable Young Person through its agency, to act as Second Housemaid in Camden Place, and was so well satisfied with the Young Person that she had no hesitation in directing her mistress to the office. Lucilla was too much overawed by the oppressive gentility of the proprietress to do more than agree with whatever Miss Wychwood suggested to her, and confided to that lady when they left the premises that the statuesque Mrs Poppleton had frightened her to death, so that she was deeply thankful her dear Miss Wychwood had been present to support her. 'And when the maids she means to send to Camden Place to be interviewed come, you *will* be there, won't you?' she said anxiously.

Reassured on this head, she tripped happily beside Miss Wychwood, and recklessly bought not one but two pairs of long kid gloves, which (she said) made her feel truly grown-up at last.

Since the Bath Season had hardly begun, the musicians who entertained the company every morning in the Pump Room during the full Season were not present, but a fair sprinkling of visitors was already in evidence. A somewhat depressingly large number of the visitors were valetudinarians, either hobbling about on sticks, being afflicted by gout or rheumatism; or elderly dyspeptics, hopefully seeking a cure for liver disorders arising from the excesses of their earlier years. There were also several dowagers, suffering from nervous disorders and from a conviction that a recital of their various ills, and the many treatments they had undergone must be of as much interest to those of their acquaintances whom they could contrive to buttonhole as they were to themselves. But as most of the confirmed invalids were attended by younger members of their families the assembly, which at first glance appeared to consist of crippled persons, stricken in years, included quite a number of young persons wholly unafflicted by the numerous ailments for which the Bath waters were considered to be an infallible remedy. For the most part, these attendants were females, but there were some exceptions, notably the fascinating Mr Kilbride, who, whenever (for financial reasons) he came to Bath on a visit to his grandmother, dutifully escorted her to the Pump Room, tenderly settled her in a chair, brought her a glass of the hot pump water, took immense pains to discover amongst the company one of her cronies, and, having inexorably led this unfortunate up to her, and seen him (or her) safely ensconced beside her, occupied himself for the rest of his stay in the Pump Room in strolling about, greeting chance acquaintances, and flirting lightheartedly with all the prettiest girls present.

Besides these seasonal visitors there were the residents, and the first of these on whom Miss Wychwood's eyes fell, as she glanced round the Pump Room, was Lord Beckenham. He was talking to a lady in a preposterous hat, trimmed with several upstanding ostrich feathers, but as soon as he perceived Miss Wychwood he excused himself and purposefully threaded his way towards her between the several groups of people which separated them. Lucilla, having located Corisande Stinchcombe, darted away in her direction, and Miss Wychwood was left to Lord Beckenham's mercy.

He greeted her with his usual punctiliousness, but almost immediately said, with a grave look, that he was excessively sorry to learn that her young friend's visit had led to a disagreeable consequence. 'I understand that Oliver Carleton has come to Bath, and that you have been obliged to receive him,' he said heavily. 'It was inevitable, of course, that he should call in Camden Place, but I trust it was to make arrangements to remove his niece from Bath?'

'Oh, no, not immediately!' replied Miss Wychwood cheerfully. 'That would certainly be a disagreeable consequence! I hope to have her company for some time yet. She is a delightful child—positively a ray of sunshine in the house!'

'I own she appeared to be an amiable girl, and I was favourably impressed by her manners,' he conceded, with a patronizing air which she found intolerable. 'The danger attached to her visit is that you may find yourself obliged to become more closely acquainted with her uncle than can be thought desirable. You will not object to my venturing to give you a hint, I know.'

'On the contrary, sir! I object very much to it,' she said, sparks of wrath in her eyes. 'I think it is a gross impertinence—to give you the word with no bark on it!—for what right have you to give me hints on how I should conduct myself? None that I have granted you!'

He looked to be a little confounded by this forthright speech, but embarked on a ponderous explanation of the purity of his intention, in which his regard for her, his hope that he might one day have the right to guide her judgment, his conviction that the warning he had uttered would meet with her brother's warm approval, and his knowledge of the world, became entangled almost beyond unravelling. He seemed to be aware of this, for he brought his speech to an end by saying: 'In short, dear Miss Annis, you are ignorant—as indeed one would wish you to be!—of how very undesirable an acquaintance for a delicately nurtured female Carleton is! Particularly for a lady of quality such as yourself! I am persuaded that your good brother would echo my sentiments on this occasion, and that there is no need for me to say more.'

She bestowed a glittering smile upon him, and said: 'No need at all, sir! In point of fact, there was no need for you to have said as much. But since you seem to be so much concerned with my welfare let me assure you that my acquaintance with Mr Carleton is unattended by any danger either to my reputation or to my virtue! He is quite the rudest man I have ever met, and I am not so ignorant as to be unaware that he is what I believe is termed a *man of the town*, but I have it on the best of authority—his own!—that he never attempts to seduce ladies of quality! So you may be easy—and I beg you will say no more on this subject!'

An amused voice spoke at her elbow. 'I expect he will, though, and you can see he is far from easy,' said Mr Carleton. He nodded at Beckenham, who was visibly swelling with hostility, and greeted him with a careless tolerance which still further exacerbated his lordship's resentment. 'How do you do?' he said. 'They tell me it was you who bought that dubious Brueghel at Christie's last month, but I daresay rumour lied!'

'I did buy it, and I do not consider it dubious!' responded his lordship, growing almost purple in the face from his effort to suppress his spleen. '*I* heard that *you* had a fancy for it, Carleton!'

'No, no! not when I had had the opportunity to inspect it more closely!' replied Mr Carleton soothingly. 'I wasn't the bidder who ran you up so high—in fact, I wasn't in the bidding at all!' Observing, with satisfaction, the effect this had on the infuriated connoisseur, he added, by way of rubbing salt into the wound: 'I don't think I was told who your unsuccessful rival was: some silly gudgeon, no doubt!'

'Do I understand you to mean that I too am a gudgeon?' demanded Lord Beckenham fiercely.

Mr Carleton put up his black brows in exaggerated surprise, and said in a bewildered voice: 'Now, what in the world can I have said to put such a notion as that into your head? It cannot have escaped your notice, my dear Beckenham, that I carefully refrained from saying "some *other* silly gudgeon"!'

'I shall take leave to tell you, Carleton, that I find your—your *wit* offensive!'

'By all means!' replied Mr Carleton. 'You have my leave to tell me anything you choose! How unjust it would be in me to refuse to grant you leave to do so when it has never occurred to me that I should ask your permission to say that I find you a dead bore, which I've been doing for years.'

'If it were not for our surroundings,' said Lord Beckenham, between his teeth, 'I should be strongly tempted to land you a facer, sir!'

'It's to be hoped you would have the strength of mind to resist temptation,' said Mr Carleton, with spurious sympathy. 'Such a very gudgeon-ish thing to do, don't you agree?'

Since Beckenham was well aware that Mr Carleton was almost as famous for his punishing skill in the boxing-ring as for his rudeness this reply infuriated him so much that, with only the briefest of bows to Miss Wychwood, he turned on his heel and walked off, his brow thunderous, and his lips tightly compressed.

'I have never been able to understand,' remarked Mr Carleton, 'why it is that so many persons find it impossible to rid themselves of such pompous bores as that fellow!'

'Perhaps,' offered Miss Wychwood, 'it is because very few persons—if any at all!—are as rude as you are!'

'Ah, no doubt that is the reason!' he nodded.

'You should be ashamed of yourself!' she told him.

'No, no, how can you say so? You don't mean to tell me you didn't wish to be rid of him!'

'Well, no,' she admitted. 'I did wish it, but that was because he vexed me to death. I was going to do the thing myself if you hadn't interrupted us! And I shouldn't have been grossly uncivil!'

'You can't be very well-acquainted with him if you imagine you would have succeeded,' he said. 'Nothing short of the *grossest* incivility has ever been known to pierce his armour of self-importance. He can empty a room quicker than any man I've ever known.'

She smiled, but said charitably: 'Poor man! One can't but feel sorry for him.'

'A waste of sympathy, believe me! He would be incredulous, I daresay, if it were disclosed to him that he was an object for pity. In his own eyes, his consequence is so great that when people smother yawns in the middle of one of his pretentious lectures *he* is sorry for *them*, because it is plain to him that they are persons of vastly inferior intellect, quite unworthy to receive instruction from him.'

Recalling very vividly the numerous occasions when she had been provoked almost to screaming point by his lordship's disquisitions, accompanied as they invariably were, by kindly but intolerable attempts to enlighten her ignorance, or to correct what his superior taste assured him were her false artistic judgments, she could not suppress a little chuckle, but she atoned for this by saying that even if his lordship were a trifle prosy he had many excellent qualities.

'I should hope he had. Everyone has *some* excellent qualities. Why, even I have! Not many, of course, but some!'

She thought it wisest to ignore this bait, and continued, as though she had not heard the interpolation, to defend Lord Beckenham's character. 'He is a man of the first respectability,' she said, in a reproving tone. 'Always well-conducted, with propriety of taste, and—and delicacy of principle. He is an affectionate brother, too, and—and altogether a very worthy man!'

'I don't think you should encourage him to make such a dead-set at you,' he said, shaking his head. 'You will have the poor fellow making you an offer, and if you don't accept it very likely he will be so broken-hearted that if he doesn't put a period to his life he will fall into a deep melancholy.'

The picture this conjured up was too much for Miss Wychwood's gravity. She choked, and broke into laughter, informing him, however, as soon as she was able to control her voice, that it ill-became him to poke fun at his betters.

'If it comes to that it doesn't become you to laugh at him!' he retorted.

'I know it doesn't,' she acknowledged. 'But I was not laughing at him, precisely, but at you for saying anything so absurd about him. Now, if you wish to talk to Lucilla—'

'I don't. Who is the young sprig at her elbow?'

She glanced across the room, to where Lucilla was the centre of an animated group. 'Ninian Elmore—if you mean the fair boy?'

He put up his glass. 'Oh, so that's Iverley's heir, is it? Not a bad-looking halfling, but too chitty-faced. Legs like cat-sticks too.' His glass swept round the group, and his face hardened. 'I see she has Kilbride dangling after her,' he said abruptly. 'Let me make it plain to you, ma'am, that that's a connection I don't wish you to encourage!'

She was nettled by his suddenly autocratic tone, but replied with characteristic honesty: 'I shall certainly not do so, Mr Carleton, rest assured! To be frank with you, I was vexed that he should have come up to me last night, so that I was obliged to introduce him to Lucilla, for although I find him an agreeable companion, I am well aware that his engaging manners, coupled as they are with considerable address and a propensity for flirting desperately with almost any pretty female, make him an unde-sirable friend for a green girl.'

He let his glass fall, and transferred his gaze to her face. 'You have a *tendre* for him, have you? I might have guessed it! *Your* affairs are no concern of mine, Miss Wychwood, but Lucilla's are very much my concern, and I give you fair warning that I don't mean to let her fall into the clutches of Kilbride or any other loose screw of his kidney!'

She replied, in a cold voice at startling variance with the flame of anger in her eyes: 'Pray enlighten my ignorance, sir! In what way does Mr Kilbride's character differ from your own?'

Any hope she might have cherished of putting him out of countenance died stillborn: he merely looked astonished, and ejac-ulated: 'Good God, do you imagine I would permit her to marry any one like myself? What a bird-witted question to have asked me! And I had begun to think you a woman of superior sense!'

She found herself without a word to say, but no answer was required of her. With the briefest of bows he turned away, leaving her to regret that she had allowed her vexation to betray her into what she realized, too late, had been an impropriety. Ladies of the first consideration did not accuse even the most hardened rake-shame of being a loose screw. She told herself that the fault lay at his door: she had caught the infection of far too plain speaking from him. But it would not do; her conscience smote her; she foresaw that she would be obliged to offer him an apology; and discovered, with some surprise, that it was more mortifying to be thought by him to be bird-witted than brassily forward.

Giving herself a mental shake, she made her way to Mrs Stinchcombe's party, and greeted that lady with her usual smiling calm. But before she had time to exchange greetings with the rest of the company she suffered a set-back. Lucilla cried impulsively: 'Oh, Miss Wychwood, do pray tell Mr

Kilbride that we shall be happy to see him at the party! I ventured to invite him, for you told me I might invite anyone I chose, and I know he is a friend of yours! Only he says he dare not come without an invitation from you!'

It was at this point that Miss Wychwood realized that taking charge of Lucilla was not likely to be the sinecure she had blithely expected it to be. It was impossible to repudiate the invitation so innocently given, but she did her best. She said: 'Certainly, if he cares to come, I shall be happy to include him.'

'I do care to come!' he said promptly, moving forward to bow over her hand. He raised his head, smiling wickedly at her, and added softly: 'Why don't you wish me to, most adored lady? Surely you must know that I am an excellent man to have at a party!'

'Oh, yes!' she said lightly. 'Amusing rattles always are! But I don't think mine is going to be the sort of party you enjoy. In fact, I fancy you would find it a very insipid one—almost a children's party!'

'Oh, in that case you can't possibly exclude me! I am at my best at children's parties, and will engage myself to organize any number of parlour games to keep your youthful guests enter-tained. Charades, for instance, or Blind Man's Buff!'

'Don't be so absurd!' she said, laughingly. 'If you come, I shall expect you to entertain the dowagers!'

'Oh, there will be no difficulty about that! I have even succeeded in entertaining my grandmother, and that, you know, calls for great skill in the art!'

'You know, you are a sad scamp!' she told him, as she moved away from him.

She found that Mr Beckenham had joined the group, and it occurred to her, as she shook hands with him, that Mr Kilbride's presence at her rout would be less marked if she invited Mr Beckenham too. He was considerably younger than Kilbride, but his easy address, and decided air of fashion made him appear to be older than his years. He was accompanied by a very dashing Tulip, whom he presented as Jonathan Hawkesbury: a friend of his who had toddled down from London to spend a few days at Beckenham Court, so Miss Wychwood promptly included him in her invitation. She did not form any very high opinion of his mental powers, but his manners were extremely polite, and his raiment so exquisite that he was bound, she thought, to lend lustre to her party. Both gentlemen accepted her invitation, Mr Hawkesbury expressing himself as being very much obliged to her, and Harry saying, with his careless grace: 'By Jove, yes! We shall be delighted to come to your party, dear Miss Annis! Will there be dancing?'

Miss Wychwood rapidly revised her plans. She had engaged a small orchestra to discourse soft music to her guests, but she now began to think that the musicians might well strike up a country dance or two, and perhaps—daring thought!—a waltz. That might shock some of the starchier dowagers, for although the waltz was becoming increasingly fashionable in London it was never danced at any of the Bath Assemblies. But it would undoubtedly raise her party from the doldrums of the dull and ordinary to the ranks of the unexpectedly modish. She said: 'Well, that will depend on circumstances! It is to be a rout-party, not a ball, but I daresay it will end as—not a ball, but an impromptu hop.'

Mr Beckenham applauded this suggestion, and added the information that his somewhat inarticulate friend sported a very pretty toe. Mr Hawkesbury disclaimed, but expressed with great gallantry the hope that he might be granted the honour of leading his hostess on to the floor. Miss Wychwood then detached herself from the group, with the intention of enlarging her party by the inclusion of Major Beverley, who had just entered the Pump Room, in attendance on his mama. He was not a dancing-man, but he was of much the same age as Denis Kilbride, and, from the circumstance of his having had the misfortune to lose an arm at the sanguinary engagement at Waterloo, was an object of awed interest to the damsels who would be present at the party. Having successfully enrolled him, she strolled round the room in search of further prey. She found two; and it suddenly occurred to her that her object was not so much to provide Lucilla with a counter-attraction, as to hide Mr Kilbride from Mr Carleton's penetrating eyes. This was so ridiculous that it made her laugh inwardly; but it was also vexing: what concern was it of his whom she chose to invite to her house? She didn't give a straw for his opinion, and wouldn't waste another thought on it.

Nothing was seen of him for the following two days, but towards evening on the third day he called in Camden Place to inform Lucilla that he had procured a well-mannered mare for her to ride. 'My groom is bringing her down, and will look after her,' he said. 'I'll tell him to come here for orders every day.'

'*Oh!*' squeaked Lucilla joyfully. '*Thank* you, sir! I am excessively obliged to you! Where does she come from? When shall I be able to ride her? What sort of a mare is she? Shall I like her?'

'I trust so. She's a gray, carries a good head, and jumps off her hocks. She comes from Lord Warrington's stables, and is accustomed to carrying a lady, but I bought her at Tattersall's, Warrington having no further use for her since his wife's death. You may ride her the day after tomorrow.'

'Oh, famous! capital!' she cried, clapping her hands. 'Was *that* why I thought you must have left Bath? Did you go all the way to London to buy me a horse of my very own? I am—I am truly grateful to you! Miss Wychwood has lent me her own favourite mare, and she is the sweetest-goer imaginable, but I don't like to be borrowing her mare, even though she says she doesn't wish to ride herself.'

'No, nor do I like it,' he said. He put up his glass, surveying through it Mr Elmore, who had risen at his entrance, but was standing bashfully in the background. 'You, I fancy, must be young Elmore,' he said. 'In which case, I have to thank you for having taken care of my niece, I believe.'

'Yes, but—but it was nothing, sir!' stammered Ninian. 'I mean, the only thing I could do was to accompany her, for I—I was unable to persuade her to return to Chartley, say what I would, which, of course, was what she should have done!'

'Heavy on hand, was she? You have my sympathy!'

Ninian grinned shyly at him. 'I should rather think she was!' he said. 'Well, she was in one of her hey-go-mad humours, you know!'

'I am thankful to say that I don't,' replied Mr Carleton caustically.

'I was not!' declared Lucilla, taking instant umbrage. 'And as for taking care of me, I was very well able to take care of myself!'

'No, you weren't!' retorted Ninian. 'You didn't even know how to get to Bath, and if I hadn't caught you—'

'If you hadn't meddled I should have hired a chaise in Amesbury,' she said grandly. 'And it wouldn't have lost a wheel, like your odious gig!'

'Oh, would you indeed? And have found yourself without a feather to fly with when you reached Bath! Don't be such a widgeon!'

Miss Wychwood, entering the room at that moment, put a stop to further hostilities, by saying in her calm way: 'How many more times am I to tell you both that I will *not* have you pulling caps in my drawing-room? How do you do, Mr Carleton?'

'Oh, Miss Wychwood, whatever do you think?' cried Lucilla eagerly. 'He has bought me a mare—a gray one, too, which is exactly what I should have chosen, because I love gray horses, don't you? And he says his own groom is to look after her, so that now you will be able to ride with us!'

'Redeeming yourself in your ward's eyes?' Miss Wychwood said quizzically, shaking hands with him.

'No: in yours, I hope!'

Startled, her eyes flew to his face, but swiftly sank again. Considerably shaken, she turned away, for there could be no mistaking the glow in his hard eyes: Mr Carleton, that noted profligate, had conceived a strange, unaccountable fancy for a maiden lady, of advanced years, who was no straw damsel, but a lady of the first consideration, and of unquestioned virtue. Her first thought, that he meant to fascinate her into accepting a *carte blanche* from him, occurred only to be dismissed: Mr Carleton might be a libertine, but he was not a fool. Perhaps he meant to get up a flirtation with her, by way of alleviating the boredom of Bath society. Hard on the heels of this thought came the realization that a flirtation with him would alleviate her own constantly growing boredom. He was so very different from any of her other flirts: in fact, she had never met anyone in the least like him.

Lucilla and Ninian were arguing about the several rides to be enjoyed outside Bath. They went into the back-drawing-room to consult the guide-book which Lucilla was almost positive she had left there. 'And if they find it,' remarked Miss Wychwood, 'they will instantly disagree on whether to go to see a Druidical monument, or a battlefield. I cannot conceive how anyone but a confirmed chucklehead could suppose that they were in the least degree suited to each other!'

'Iverley and Clara Amber are both chuckleheads,' replied Mr Carleton, dismissing them from further consideration. 'I hope you mean to join the riding-party?'

'Yes, very likely I shall. Not that I think it at all necessary to provide Lucilla with a chaperon when she goes out with Ninian!'

'No, but it is very necessary, I promise you, to provide me with a companion who won't bore me past endurance. I can think of few worse fates than to be obliged to ride bodkin between that pair of bickerers.'

Surprised, she said: 'Oh, are you going with them?'

'Not unless you go too.'

'For fear that you may have to listen to bickering?' she said, smiling a little. 'You won't! They don't quarrel when they go riding together, I'm told. Corisande Stinchcombe complained that they talked of nothing but horses, hounds, and hunting!'

'Even worse!' he said.

'You are not a hunting man, Mr Carleton?'

'On the contrary! But I do not indulge myself or bore my companions by describing the great runs I've had, the tosses I've taken, the clumsiness of one of my hunters—only saved from coming to grief over a regular rasper, be it understood, by my superior horsemanship!—or the sure-footedness of another. Such anecdotes are of no interest to anyone but the teller.'

'I am afraid that's true,' she acknowledged. 'But the impulse to boast of great runs and of clever horses is almost irresistible— even though one knows one is being listened to because the other person is only waiting for the chance to do some boasting on his own account! To which, of course, one is bound to listen, for the sake of common honesty! Don't you agree?'

'Yes: it is why I learned years ago to overcome that impulse. You yourself hunt, I believe?'

'I was used to, when I lived in the country, but I was obliged to give it up when I came to Bath,' she said, with a faint sigh.

'Why did you come to Bath?' he asked.

'Oh, for several good reasons!' she responded lightly.

'If you mean that for a set-down, Miss Wychwood, I should inform you that I am not so easily set down! *What* good reasons?'

She looked at him rather helplessly, but, after a moment, replied with a touch of asperity: 'They concern no one but myself, sir! And if you are aware that I did give you what I hoped would be a civil set-down for asking me an—an impertinent question, you will permit me to tell you that I consider you positively rag-mannered to pursue the subject!'

'Very likely, but that's no answer!'

'It's the only one I mean to give you!'

'Which leaves me to suppose that some murky secret lies in your past,' he said provocatively. 'I find that hard to believe. With another, and very different, female, I might assume that some scandal had driven you from your home—an unfortunate *affaire* with one of the local squires, for instance!'

She curled her lip at him, and said disdainfully: 'Curb your imagination, Mr Carleton! No murky secret lies behind me, and I have had no *affaires*, fortunate or otherwise!'

'I didn't think you had,' he murmured.

'This is a most improper conversation!' she said crossly.

'Yes, isn't it?' he agreed. 'Why *did* you come to live in Bath?'

'Oh, how persistent you are!' she exclaimed. 'I came to Bath because I wished to live a life of my own—not to dwindle into a mere aunt!'

'That I can well understand. But what the devil made you choose Bath, of all places?'

'I chose it because I have many friends here, and because it is within easy reach of Twynham Park.'

'Do you never regret it? Don't you find it cursed flat?'

She shrugged. 'Why, yes, sometimes I do, but so I should, I daresay, in any place where I resided all the year round.'

'Good God, is that what you do?'

'Oh, no! That was an exaggeration! I frequently visit my brother and his wife, and sometimes I go to stay with an aunt, who lives at Lyme Regis.'

'Gay to dissipation, in fact!'

She laughed. 'No, but I am past the age of wishing for dissipation.'

'Don't talk that balderdash to me!' he said sharply. 'You have left your girlhood behind—though there are moments when I doubt that!—and have not reached your prime, so let me have no more fiddle-faddle about your advanced years, my girl!'

She gave an outraged gasp, but was prevented from flinging a retort at him by Lucilla, who came back into the front half of the room, demanding support in her contention that *somewhere* on Lansdown there were the remains of a Saxon fort which King Arthur had besieged. 'Ninian says there isn't. He says there was no such person as King Arthur! He says he was just a legend! But he wasn't, was he? It is all here, in the guide-book, and I should like to know what makes Ninian think he knows more than the guide-book!'

'Oh, my God!' ejaculated Mr Carleton, and abruptly took his leave.

# Eight

ON THE FOLLOWING DAY LORD BECKENHAM CALLED IN Camden Place to offer Miss Wychwood an apology for having offended her. Since the servants were busily employed with all the preparations for the evening's rout-party, his visit was ill-timed. Limbury, or James, the footman, would have informed his lordship that Miss Wychwood was not at home; but since Limbury was heavily engaged in the pantry, assembling all the silver and the glasses which would be needed for the entertainment of some thirty guests; and James, assisted by the page-boy and two of the maidservants, was moving various pieces of furniture out of the drawing-room, the door was opened to Lord Beckenham by a very junior housemaid whose flustered attempt to deny her mistress he had no difficulty in over-bearing. He said, with a majestic condescension which awed her very much, that he fancied Miss Wychwood would grant him a few minutes of her time, and walked past her into the house. She gave back before this determined entry, excusing herself later, to Limbury, who took her severely to task, by saying that his lordship had walked through her as though she wasn't there. There seemed to be nothing for it but to usher him into the book-room at the back of the house, and to scurry away in search of her mistress. She found her, after an abortive tour of the upper floors, in the basement, conferring with her chef, so that Beckenham was left to kick his heels for a considerable time before Miss Wychwood appeared on the scene.

She was in no very good humour, and after the briefest of greetings, told him that she could spare him only a few minutes, having a great deal to do that morning, and begged that he would state his business with her without loss of time.

His answer disarmed her. He said, retaining her hand in a warm clasp: 'I know it: you are holding a party tonight, are you not? I shall not detain you longer than to beg you to forgive me for my part in what passed between us in the Pump Room the other day, and to believe that I was betrayed by my ardent concern for your welfare into uttering words which you thought *impertinent*! I can only assure you, dear Miss Annis, that they were not meant to be impertinent, and beg you to forgive me!'

Her resentment died. She said: 'Why, of course I forgive you, Beckenham! Don't waste another thought on it! We all of us say what we ought not sometimes.'

He pressed his lips to her hand. 'Too good, too gracious!' he said, in a deeply moved voice. 'I feared, when I learned from Harry that you had invited him and young Hawkesbury to your party this evening, but not me, that I had offended beyond forgiveness.'

'Nonsense!' she said. 'I didn't invite you, because it is a party for Lucilla, and will be entirely—*almost* entirely composed of girls not yet out, and their attendant brothers and swains, with a sprinkling of careful mamas and papas as well. You would be bored to death!'

'I could never be bored in your company,' he said simply.

She was at once assailed by a heartrending vision of him, left to endure a lonely evening, feeling himself to be unwanted while his brother went off with his friend for an evening's jollification, and yielded to a kindly impulse, saying: 'Why, by all means come, if you can face children and dowagers!'

The words were no sooner uttered than regretted. Too late did she recall that Beckenham was well-accustomed to being alone. It was seldom that Harry, during his infrequent visits, spent an evening at home. He said, when reproved, that Will didn't want him; and Theresa, Beckenham's eldest sister, complained that it was his habit to retire to his library after dinner, poring over the catalogue of his possessions, or rearranging his bibelots.

She said, in an unhopeful attempt to make him refuse the invitation: 'I should warn you, sir, Lucilla's uncle will be present. You might prefer not to meet him, perhaps.'

'I trust,' he said, with a smile of superior tolerance, 'that I am sufficiently in command of myself not to embarrass you by engaging in a brangle with Carleton under your roof, dear Miss Annis!'

He then, with renewed protestations of his gratitude and devotion, took his leave. She had only to rake herself down for having been betrayed into having encouraged his pretensions.

The rest of the day passed without any other incident than the arrival of Eliza Brigham, hired to be Lucilla's abigail. Annis had been prepared to encounter criticism of this pleasant-faced woman from the older members of her domestic staff, but although Jurby said cautiously that it was early days yet to judge, she added that Miss Brigham *seemed* to know her work; and Mrs Wardlow and Limbury expressed wholehearted approval of the new inmate. 'A very genteel young woman, and such as Miss is bound to like,' said Mrs Wardlow. 'Not one to put herself forward,' said Limbury, adding confidentially: 'And no fear that she'll rub against Miss Jurby, Miss Annis!'

Miss Brigham demonstrated her quality when she dressed Lucilla for the evening's party, for she not only persuaded her to wear a muslin gown of the softest shade of rose-pink instead of the rather more sophisticated yellow one which Lucilla wished to wear, but also managed to convince her that the string of beads which Lucilla had purchased that very day was not as suitable for evening wear as her pearl necklace; brushed her dusky curls till they shone, and arranged them in a simple and charming style, which drew praise from Miss Wychwood, when she came into Lucilla's room just before dinner.

She brought with her a pretty bangle, set with pearls, and clasped it round Lucilla's wrist, saying: 'That's a small gift, with my love—for your first party!'

'*Oh!*' gasped Lucilla. 'Oh, Miss Wychwood, *thank* you! Oh, how pretty it is! How *very* kind you are to me! Look, Brigham!'

'Very pretty indeed, miss. Just the thing, if I may say so,' responded Brigham, casting the eye of an expert over Miss Wychwood's attire.

She found nothing to criticize. Miss Wychwood was wearing a robe of celestial blue crepe with an open front over a white satin slip. A sapphire necklace was clasped about her neck, and a sapphire spray was set in her burnished hair. She looked, Lucilla told her in awed accents, magnificent. She laughed at this, and protested at Lucilla's choice of adjective, saying that it sounded as though she were overdressed for the occasion.

'Well—well, *beautiful!*' amended Lucilla.

'Then there are a pair of us,' said Miss Wychwood. 'Let us go downstairs to dazzle Ninian! I'm told he arrived a few minutes ago.'

They found him awaiting them in the drawing-room. He had been invited to dinner, and it was evident that he had taken immense pains over his apparel. Lucilla exclaimed admiringly: 'Oh, first-rate, Ninian! You are as fine as fivepence, I do declare! Isn't he, ma'am?'

'Yes, indeed! A veritable Pink of the Ton!' said Miss Wychwood. 'I am wholly spell-bound—particularly by the elegance of his neckcloth! How long did it take you to achieve anything so beautiful, Ninian?'

'Hours!' he replied, blushing. 'It's the Oriental, you know, and I do think I've succeeded pretty well with it. Now do, pray, stop poking bogey at me, ma'am!' He turned to pick up from the table on which he had laid them two tight posies, and presented them with awkward grace, saying: 'Pray, ma'am, do me the honour to accept of these few flowers! And this one, Lucy, is for you!'

The ladies received these tributes with becoming gratitude, Lucilla being particularly struck by her posy's being composed of pink and white hyacinths, a circumstance which made her exclaim: 'How clever of you, Ninian! Did you guess that I was going to wear my pink gown?'

'Well, no!' he confessed. 'But the girl who made the posies up for me asked what you looked like, and when I told her you were dark, and not yet out, she said that pink and white flowers would best become you. And I must say,' he added handsomely, looking her over, 'pink does become you, Lucy! I never saw you look so pretty before!'

Miss Wychwood, admiring her own posy, which was made up of spring blossoms ranging in colour from palest mauve to deep purple, realized with an inward chuckle that Ninian had probably described her to the helpful florist as a lady somewhat stricken in years. She refrained from quizzing him, and, with even greater nobility, refrained from telling him that posies, tied up with long ribbons, wound round stalks encased in silver paper, however proper for balls, were not commonly carried by ladies at rout-parties.

Some two hours later she had the satisfaction of knowing that not only was her party a success, but so too was her protégée. She received her guests with Lucilla beside her, and had nothing to blush for in Lucilla's manners. Not for the first time she handed a silent tribute to Mrs Amber, who, whatever her errors, had demonstrably instructed the child in all the rules governing polite behaviour. The wild rose colour that flushed her cheeks when she was embarrassed, and her occasional gaucheries did her no disservice in the eyes of Bath's most influential hostesses, even old Mrs Mandeville, that most rigid critic, who had already gratified Annis by appearing at the rout, saying to her: 'A nice gal, my dear. I don't know where you picked her up, or why you're sponsoring her, but if she's a Carleton I should say that she was born with a silver spoon in her mouth, and you'll have no difficulty in buckling her to an eligible gentleman!'

Mr Carleton was amongst the last to appear. Miss Wychwood had released Lucilla from her post at her side, but was herself still standing at the entrance to the drawing-room when he came leisurely up the stairs. Lord Beckenham, who, from the moment of his arrival, had been hovering solicitously about her, no sooner saw who was approaching than he withdrew immediately from her vicinity, muttering that it would be better if he and 'that fellow' didn't come face to face. His abrupt retreat did not escape Mr Carleton's hawklike eyes; he said as he bowed slightly, and carried Miss Wychwood's gloved hand to his lips: 'If looks could kill I should be stretched lifeless on the threshold! How do you do, ma'am? Accept my felicitations on being able to hold such a brilliant Assembly thus early in the Season!' He put up his glass, and through it surveyed the crowded room. 'All the rank and fashion of Bath, I collect,' he said. 'Who, in God's name, is the formidable dame in the wig and enough feathers to furnish an ostrich with plumage for two of her kind?'

'That, sir,' said Miss Wychwood, controlling a quivering lip, 'is Mrs Wendlebury, one of the leaders of Bath Society. Only Mrs Mandeville's approval is more necessary than hers for a girl making her first appearance in Bath. She has brought her widowed daughter, and her granddaughter, to my party tonight which I count amongst my triumphs!'

He lowered his glass, and directed one of his penetrating looks at her. 'I wish you will tell me why you are putting yourself to so much trouble for my tiresome niece?' he said unexpectedly.

'I don't find her tiresome,' she replied. 'Indeed, she has provided me with a great deal of amusement! When I met her, I was feeling sadly languid and bored, but that, thanks to her, is a thing of the past. Come, I must make you known to Mrs Stinchcombe! Her eldest daughter and Lucilla have struck up a great friendship, and I am persuaded she will wish to make your acquaintance.'

She led him inexorably away to where Mrs Stinchcombe was seated beside Mrs Mandeville on an elegant settee, pushed against the wall, and performed the introductions. To her surprise, Mrs Mandeville said: 'No need to present him to me, child! His mama and I were bosom-bows, and I knew him when he was in his cradle! Well, Oliver, how do you do? Are *you* that pretty child's guardian? When Annis told me that she was a Carleton, and the ward of her uncle, it did cross my mind that you might be the uncle, but it didn't seem to me to be possible!'

'It doesn't seem possible to me either, ma'am,' he said ruefully.

She cast him a shrewd glance. 'Makes you feel older than you thought you were, does it? High time you did, if all I hear about you is true! But that's no bread-and-butter of mine! I like your little niece: not fully fledged yet, but a bud of promise. Don't you agree, ma'am?'

'Yes, I do indeed,' answered Mrs Stinchcombe. 'She casts the rest into the shade.' She smiled up at Mr Carleton, and said: 'You will certainly have enough on your hands when she comes out, driving away ineligible suitors, sir!'

'You shouldn't have invited Kilbride tonight, Annis,' said Mrs Mandeville, in her forthright fashion. 'An engaging scamp, I grant you, but dangerous.'

Avoiding Mr Carleton's eyes, Annis responded with a lightness she was far from feeling: 'I'm afraid my hand was forced, ma'am!'

'In what way, Miss Wychwood?' asked Mr Carleton, more than a hint of steel in his voice.

She was obliged to look at him, read condemnation in his face, and was goaded by vexation into making him a sharp answer. 'Lucilla forced my hand, sir, by inviting him, and begging me to endorse the invitation! As he was standing beside her at the time, what could I do but say I should be happy to see him here tonight?' She saw his brows draw together, and added quickly: 'Pray don't blame her! She knew him to be a friend of mine, and I had told her she might invite whom she liked.'

'Well, it was a pity,' said Mrs Stinchcombe, 'but I don't think any harm will come of it. From what I can see, he will find it a hard matter to get up a flirtation with her! Young Elmore is playing watch-dog, and is sticking to her as close as a court plaster!'

Miss Wychwood soon found that this was true: Ninian was obviously standing guard over Lucilla, which would have been amusing had his hostess been in the mood to be amused. Whether he was protecting her from Kilbride, or from Harry Beckenham, each of whom was making her the object of his gallantry, was a moot point: Miss Wychwood could only be thankful that his jealously possessive instinct had prompted him to behave very much like a dog guarding a bone; and to derive a certain amount of satisfaction from the realization that Lucilla was showing no preference for either of these dashing blades, but was merely enjoying, quite innocently, the novel experience of being a Success.

A cold supper had been laid out in the dining-room. It was informal, but most of the very young gentlemen present had engaged the very young ladies of their choices to go down to it under their escorts, and just as Miss Wychwood, an accomplished hostess, had matched the dowagers with appropriate partners, she found herself being confronted by Lord Beckenham, begging for the honour of leading her down to supper. She felt that nothing more was wanting to set the seal on the most unenjoyable evening of any she had ever spent but there seemed to be no way of escaping this added scourge, and she was about to smile politely, and to lay her hand on his arm, when Mr Carleton, standing, unperceived, immediately behind her, said: 'Too late, Beckenham! Miss Wychwood is promised to me! Are you ready to go now, ma'am?'

She found herself in a quandary. If she repudiated this engagement a quarrel between the two men would be the inevitable outcome: Beckenham's face had already assumed an alarmingly purple hue. Anything, she decided, would be preferable to a brawl in her house! She forced a smile to her lips, and said, mendaciously, but placably: 'I'm afraid I did promise to let Mr Carleton take me down to supper, Beckenham! Will you oblige me very much by taking Maria down in my stead?'

Mr Carleton, having drawn her hand within his arm, and led her inexorably out of the room, said reproachfully, as they began to go downstairs: 'You know, that was quite unworthy of you, my child! To have fobbed your most distinguished suitor off on to your cousin will very likely have made him your enemy for life!'

'I know, but what else could I do, when she was the only lady left in the room, and you had claimed—falsely, as you well know!—that I had promised to go down with you? Heaven knows there is no one I wouldn't liefer be with!' she said bitterly.

'Come, come, that's trying it on much too rare and thick!' he told her. 'You can't gammon me into believing that you would prefer Beckenham's company to mine!'

'Well, I would!' she asserted. 'For I know very well you only wish to be with me so that you may pinch at me for having invited Denis Kilbride to my party, and I won't endure it, and so I warn you! What right have you, pray, to dictate to me on whom I invite or do not invite to my parties?'

'Lay all those bristles!' he recommended. 'You are not going to come to cuffs with me, my girl, so don't be so ready to show hackle for no reason at all! I may deplore your taste in admirers, but I don't presume to meddle in what is no concern of mine. And when I pinch at you, it won't be in public, I promise you!'

Slightly mollified, she said, in a more moderate tone: 'Well, I will own, sir, that it was no wish of mine to include Kilbride amongst my guests. Indeed, I said all I could, within the bounds of civility, to make him think he would find the party a dead bore. And when that didn't answer I invited Harry Beckenham, and his friend, and Major Beverley, and—oh, several others as well!'

'In the belief that they might cut Kilbride out, or the hope that I might not notice him amongst so many dashers?'

This hit the nail on the head with sufficient accuracy to surprise a laugh out of her. She said: 'Oh, how detestable you are! And the worst of it is that you make me detestable too, which is quite unpardonable!'

'I don't do any such thing,' he replied, a queer twisted smile hovering at the corner of his mouth. 'I don't think I could— even if I wished to.'

They had reached the foot of the stairs by this time, and were about to enter the dining-room, so that she was not obliged to answer, which was just as well, since she could think of nothing to say. She could not even decide whether he had paid her a compliment, or whether she had misunderstood him, for although the words he had spoken were certainly complimentary the tone in which he had uttered them was coldly dispassionate. He left her side as soon as they entered the dining-room, but returned in a very few minutes with various patties for her, and a glass of champagne. She was already the centre of a group, and he did not linger, but was next to be seen exchanging a few words with Lucilla, who was eating ices under the aegis of Harry Beckenham. She greeted him with acclaim, and a demand to know whether he had ever been to a more delightful party. He looked rather amused, but assured her that he hadn't. Harry said: ''Evening, sir! I've been telling your niece that Miss Wychwood is famous for the first-rate refreshments she gives her guests, but all she will eat is ices! Shall I bring you another, Miss Carleton?'

'Yes, please!' she responded promptly. 'And may I have some more lemonade? Oh, sir, should I like champagne? Mr Beckenham says I shouldn't.'

'No,' said Mr Carleton. He held out his own glass to her. 'Try it for yourself!' he bade her.

She took the glass, and sipped cautiously. The expression of distaste on her face was almost ludicrous. She gave the glass back to her uncle, saying: 'Ugh! Nasty! How *can* people drink anything so horrid? I quite thought Mr Beckenham was hoaxing me when he said I shouldn't like it, for he, and you, and even Miss Wychwood seem to like it very well.'

'Now you know that he wasn't hoaxing you.' He looked her over critically, and surprised her by saying: 'Remind me, when I return to London, to hand over to you your mother's turquoise set. Most of her jewels are not suitable for girls of your age, but I imagine the turquoises must be unexceptionable. As I recall, there is also a pearl brooch, and a matching ring. I'll send them to you.'

The unexpectedness of this took her breath away. She could only regain enough of it to thank him, but this she did so fervently that he laughed, flicked her cheek with one finger, and said: 'Ridiculous brat! There's no need to thank me: your mother's jewels are yours: I merely hold them in trust for you until you come of age—or until I judge you to be old enough to wear them.'

Mr Beckenham having come back by this time, Mr Carleton left Lucilla to his care, and returned to Miss Wychwood. She had been observing what had passed between him and his niece, and moved forward to meet him, saying in a conscience-stricken voice: 'I have been shockingly remiss! I ought to have told Lucilla not to drink champagne!'

'You ought indeed,' he said.

'Well, if you know that, I am astonished that you should have given your glass to her!' she said, with some asperity.

'Did you like your first sip of champagne?' he asked.

'No, I don't think I did.'

'Exactly so! Young Beckenham had told her she wouldn't like it, so I proved his point for him.'

'I suppose,' she said thoughtfully, 'that that was probably more to the purpose than to have forbidden her to drink it.'

'*Certainly* more to the purpose!'

She flashed a mischievous smile at him, and murmured: 'I feel it won't be long before you become an excellent guardian!'

'God forbid!'

At this moment, Denis Kilbride, disengaging himself from a group of matrons, bore down upon his hostess and said in deeply wounded accents, belied by the laughter in his eyes: 'Now, how could you have misled me so about your party, most cruel fair one? Is it possible you can have been trying to keep me away from it! I cannot believe it!'

'Dear me, no! why should I?' she returned. 'I am glad you don't find it abominably insipid, which I feared you might.'

'No party which you grace with your exquisite presence could be insipid, believe me! I have only one fault to find with this one: I cherished the hope of being permitted to bring you down to supper, only to find myself cut out by Carleton here! But for one circumstance, Carleton, I should ask you to name your friends!'

Mr Carleton was so patently uninterested and unamused by this lively nonsense that Annis was impelled to step into the breach caused by his silence. She said smilingly: 'It's to be hoped the one circumstance was the impropriety of spoiling my party!'

'Alas, no! It was mere cowardice!' he said, mournfully shaking his head. 'He is such a devilish good shot!'

Mr Carleton accorded this sally a faint, contemptuous smile, and stepped back politely to allow Major Beverley to approach Miss Wychwood. He then strolled away, and was next seen talking to Mrs Mandeville. He left the party before the dancing began, declining unequivocally to join the whist-players for whose entertainment Miss Wychwood had had two tables set up in the book-room. Nettled by this cavalier behaviour, she raised her brows, when he took leave of her, saying sarcastically: 'But dare you leave Lucilla in such dangerous company?'

'Oh, yes!' he replied. 'From what I've seen, young Beckenham and Elmore will take good care of her. And since the only *dangerous company* seems to be bent on fixing his interest with you rather than with Lucilla there's no need for me to play the careful guardian. It's not a rôle which suits me, you know. Ah—accept my thanks for an agreeable evening, ma'am!'

He bowed, and left her. She was so much infuriated that it was long before her wrath abated sufficiently to permit the suspicion to enter her head that his outrageous conduct sprang from anger at what he no doubt considered her encouragement of Denis Kilbride's familiarities. While she continued to move amongst her guests, outwardly as serene as ever, uttering smiling nothings, her brain was seething with conjecture. She had been prepared to play the game of flirtation with Mr Carleton, but it was now plain that idle flirtation was not what he had in mind. It seemed incredible that he could have fallen in love with her, but his anger could only have been roused by jealousy, and such fierce jealousy as had led him to say the most wounding things he could think of to her had nothing to do with flirtation. It clearly behoved her to set him at a distance, but even as she resolved to do this it occurred to her that perhaps he believed her to be ready to accept an offer from Denis Kilbride, and instantly it became a matter of the first importance to disabuse his mind of this misapprehension. It was in vain that she told herself it didn't matter a button what he believed: for some inscrutable reason it did matter.

The last of her guests did not leave until eleven o'clock, a late hour by Bath standards, for which the success of the impromptu hop was responsible. Several very young ladies were too shy to waltz, or perhaps too conscious of parental eyes of disapproval on them; but although the waltz was barred from both the Assembly Rooms even the starchiest and most oldfashioned of the dowagers knew that it would not be long before it penetrated these strongholds, and confined their objections to sighs and melancholy head-shakings over times past. As for the matrons with daughters to launch into society, few were to be found whose principles were so rigid as to make the spectacle of their daughters seated against the wall preferable to the shocking, but gratifying, sight of these dashing girls twirling round the room in the embrace of a succession of eligible young gentlemen.

Miss Wychwood confined her part in these mild revelries to keeping an eye on them, seeing to it that inexperienced girls unaccompanied by their mamas did not stand up more than twice with the same man, and finding partners for neglected damsels. Since nearly all the young people were well acquainted there was not much of this to be done: indeed, it was more important to take care that the impromptu dance did not develop into a romp, which, with so many very young persons who had known one another from the nursery onwards, was more than likely it would.

She was many times solicited to dance, but smilingly refused to stand up with even a gallant old friend, who might well have been her father. 'No, no, General!' she said, twinkling up at him. 'Chaperons don't dance!'

'Chaperon? *You?*' he said. 'Moonshine! I know to a day how old you are, puss, so don't talk flummery to me!'

'Next you will say that you dandled me when I was an infant!' she murmured.

'At all events, I might have done so. Now, come, Annis! You can't refuse to stand up with such an old friend as I am! Damme, I knew your father!'

'I should like very much to stand up with you, but you must excuse me! *You* may think it absurd, but I *am* being a chaperon tonight, and if I were to stand up with you how could I refuse to stand up with anyone else?'

'No difficulty about that!' he said. 'You have only to say that you stood up with me because you didn't care to offend an old man!'

'Yes, no doubt I could if you weren't well known to be the wickedest flirt in Bath!' she retorted.

This pleased him so much that he chuckled, threw out his chest a little, apostrophized her as a saucy minx, and went off to dally with all the best looking women in the room.

Miss Wychwood enjoyed dancing, but she was not tempted to take the floor on this occasion. There was no one with whom she wished to dance; but no sooner had she realized this truth than a question posed itself in her mind: if Mr Carleton, instead of leaving the party in something remarkably like a dudgeon, had stayed, and had invited her to dance a waltz with him, would she have been tempted to consent? She was forced to admit to herself that she would have been very strongly tempted, but she hoped (rather doubtfully) that she would have had enough strength of mind to have resisted temptation.

In the middle of these ruminations, Lord Beckenham came up, and sat down beside her, saying: 'May I bear you company, dear Miss Annis? I do not ask you to dance, for I know you don't mean to dance this evening. I cannot help being glad of it: it gives me the opportunity to enjoy a comfortable cose with you, and—to own the truth—I don't care for the waltz. I am aware that it is the height of à la modality, but it never seems to me to be quite the thing. You will say I am oldfashioned, I fear!'

'Quite Gothic!' she answered flatly. 'Excessively uncivil, too, when you must know that I delight in waltzing!'

'Oh, I intended no incivility!' he assured her. 'You lend distinction to everything you do!'

'For goodness' sake, Beckenham, stop throwing the hatchet at me!' she said tartly.

He gave an indulgent laugh. 'What an odd expression to hear on your lips! I myself am not familiar with modern slang, but I hear a great deal of it from Harry—more, indeed, than I like!— and I understand *throwing the hatchet* means to flatter a person, which, I promise you, I was not doing! Nor am I doing so when I tell you that I have rarely seen you look more beautiful than you do tonight.' He laughed again, and, laying his hand over hers, gave it a slight squeeze. 'There, don't eat me! Your dislike of receiving compliments is well known to me, and is what one so particularly likes in you, but my feelings overcame my prudence for once!'

She drew her hand away, saying: 'Excuse me! I see Mrs Wendlebury is about to take her leave.'

She got up, and moved across the room towards this formidable dame, and, having said goodbye to her, responded to a signal from Mrs Mandeville, and went to sit beside her.

'Well, my dear, a very pleasant party!' said Mrs Mandeville. 'I congratulate you!'

'Thank you, ma'am!' Annis said gratefully. 'From you that is praise of a high order! May I also thank you for having been kind enough to honour me with your presence tonight? I assure you I appreciate it, and can only hope you haven't been bored to death!'

'On the contrary, I've been vastly amused!' replied the old lady, with a chuckle. 'What made Carleton take himself off in a rage?'

Annis coloured faintly. 'Was he in a rage? I thought him merely bored.'

'No, no, he wasn't *bored*, my dear! It looked to me as though he and you were at outs!'

'Oh, we come to cuffs whenever we meet!' Annis said lightly.

'Yes, he makes a lot of enemies with that bitter tongue of his,' nodded Mrs Mandeville. 'Spoilt, of course! Too many caps have been set at him! My second son is a friend of his, and he told me years ago that it was no wonder he'd been soured, with half the mamas and their daughters on the scramble for him. That's the worst of coming into the world as rich as a Nabob: it ain't good for young men to be too full of juice. However, I don't despair of him, for there's nothing much amiss with him that marriage to the woman he falls in love with won't cure.'

'I haven't understood that *love* was lacking in his life, ma'am!'

'Lord, child, I'm not talking of his bits of muslin,' said Mrs Mandeville scornfully. 'It ain't *love* a man feels for the lightskirts he entertains! Myself, I'd always a soft corner for a rake, and it's my belief most women have! Mind you, I don't mean the sort of ramshackle who gives some gal a slip on the shoulder, for them I can't abide! Carleton ain't one of those sneaking rascals. Has he put you in charge of that pretty little niece of his?'

'No, no! She is merely staying with me for a short time, before going to live with one of her aunts, or cousins—I am not perfectly sure which!'

'I'm glad to hear it. You're a deal too young to be burdened with a gal of her age, my dear!'

'So Mr Carleton thinks! Only he goes further than you, ma'am, and doesn't scruple to inform me that he considers me to be quite unfit to take care of Lucilla.'

'Yes, I'm told he can be very uncivil,' nodded Mrs Mandeville.

'Uncivil! He is the rudest man I have ever met in my life!' declared Miss Wychwood roundly.

# Nine

$\mathcal{B}$Y THE TIME MISS WYCHWOOD HAD SAID GOODBYE TO
the last, lingering guests she was feeling more weary than
ever before at the end of a party. Everyone except herself (and,
presumably, Mr Carleton) seemed to have enjoyed it, which was,
she supposed some slight consolation to her for having spent a
most disagreeable evening. Lucilla was in what she considered to
be exaggerated raptures over it: she wished it might have gone on
for ever! Miss Wychwood, barely repressing a shudder, sent her
off to bed, and was about to follow her when she found Limbury
in the way, obviously awaiting an opportunity to speak to her.
She paused, looking an enquiry, and he all unwittingly set the
seal on a horrid evening by disclosing, with the smile of one bearing welcome tidings, that Sir Geoffrey had arrived in Bath, and
wished her to give him a look-in before she retired to bed.

'Sir Geoffrey?' she repeated blankly. '*Here?* Good God, what can
have happpened to bring him to Bath at this hour of the night?'

'Now, don't you fret yourself, Miss Annis!' Limbury said, in a
fatherly way. 'It's no worse than the toothache which Master Tom
has, and which my lady thinks may be an abscess, so she wishes
to take him instantly to Mr Westcott. Sir Geoffrey arrived twenty
minutes before you went down to supper, but when he saw you
was holding a rout-party he charged me not on any account to say
a word to you about it until the party was over, him being dressed

in his riding-habit, and not having brought with him his evening attire, and not wishing to attend the rout in all his dirt. Which is very understandable, of course. So I directed Jane to make up the bed in the Blue bedchamber, miss, and myself carried up supper to him, which is what I knew you would wish me to do.'

Miss Farlow, who had paused in her rather ineffective attempts to restore the drawing-room to order, to listen to this interchange, exclaimed: 'Oh, *poor* Sir Geoffrey! If only I had *known*! I would have run up immediately to make sure that he was comfortable—not that I mean to say Jane is not to be trusted, for she is a very dependable girl, but still—! Dear little Tom, too! His papa must be in *agonies*, for nothing is worse than the pain one undergoes with the toothache, particularly when an abscess forms, as well I know, for *never* shall I forget the *torture* I suffered when I—'

'It is Tom who has the toothache, not Geoffrey!' snapped Miss Wychwood, interrupting this monologue without ceremony.

'Well, I *know*, dearest, but the sight of one's child's suffering cannot but cast a fond parent into agonies!' said Miss Farlow.

'Oh, fiddle!' said Annis, and went upstairs to rap on the door of the Blue bedchamber.

She found her brother flicking over the pages of the various periodicals with which Limbury had thoughtfully provided him. A decanter of brandy stood on a small table at his elbow, and he held a glass in his hand, which, on his sister's entrance, he drained, before setting it down on the table, and rising to greet her. 'Well, Annis!' he said, planting a chaste salute upon her cheek. 'I seem to have come to visit you at an awkward moment, don't I?'

'I certainly wish you had warned me of it, so that I might have had time to prepare for your visit.'

'Oh, no need to worry about that!' he said. 'Limbury has looked after me very well. The thing was there was no time to warn you, because I was obliged to leave Twynham in a bang. I daresay Limbury will have told you what has brought me here?'

'Yes, I understand Tom has the toothache,' she replied.

'That's it,' he nodded. 'It became suddenly worse this afternoon, and we fear there may be an abscess forming at the root. Ten to one, it's no more than a gumboil, but nothing will do for Amabel but to bring him to Bath so that Westcott may see it, and judge what is best to be done.'

Something in his manner, which was much that of a man airily reciting a rehearsed speech, made her instantly suspicious. She said: 'It seems an unnecessarily long way to bring a child to have a tooth drawn. Surely you would be better advised to take him to Frome?'

'Ah, you are thinking of old Melling, but Amabel has no faith in him. We have been strongly recommended to take Tom to Westcott. It doesn't do, you know, to ignore advice from a trustworthy source. So I have ridden over ahead of Amabel, to arrange for Westcott to do whatever he thinks should be done tomorrow, and to ask you, my dear sister, if they may come to stay with you for a day or two.'

'They?' said Annis, filled with foreboding.

'Amabel and Tom,' he explained. 'And Nurse, of course, to look after the children.'

'Is Amabel bringing the baby too?' asked Miss Wychwood, in a voice of careful control.

'Yes—oh, yes! Well, Amabel cannot manage Tom by herself and she can't be expected to leave Baby without Nurse to take care of her, you know. But they won't be the least trouble to you Annis! In this great house of yours there must be room for two small children and their nurse!'

'Very true! Equally true that they won't be any trouble to me! But they will make a great deal of trouble for my servants, who are none of them accustomed to working in a house which contains a nursery to be waited on! So, if you mean to saddle me with your family, I beg you will also include the maid who waits on Nurse in the party!'

'Of course if it is inconvenient for you to receive my family—'
'It is extremely inconvenient!' she interrupted. 'You know very well that I have Lucilla Carleton staying with me, Geoffrey! I am astonished that you should expect me to entertain Amabel and your children at such a moment!'

'I must say I should have thought your own family had a greater claim on you than Miss Carleton,' he said, in an offended voice.

'You haven't any claim on me at all!' she flashed. 'Nor has Lucilla! Nor anyone! That's why I left Twynham, and came to Bath, to be my own mistress, not to be accountable to you or to anyone, for what I choose to do, and not to grow into a spinster aunt! Particularly not that! Like Miss Vernham, who is only valued for the help she gives her sister, can be depended on to look after the children whenever Mr and Mrs Vernham wish to go junketing to London! but at other times is very much in the way. She can't escape, because she hasn't a penny to fly with. But I have a great many pennies, and I *did* escape!'

'You are talking wildly!' he said. 'I should like to know what demands have ever been made of you when you lived with us!'

'Oh, none! But if one lives in another person's house one is bound to share in the tasks which arise, and who can tell how long it would have been before you and Amabel fell into the way of saying: "Oh, Annis will look after it! She has nothing else to do!"'

'I really believe your senses are disordered!' he exclaimed. 'All this scolding merely because I have ventured to ask you to shelter my wife and children for a few days! Upon my word, Annis—'

'You didn't ask me, Geoffrey! You made it impossible for me to refuse by arranging for Amabel to set out for Bath tomorrow morning, knowing that I should be forced to let them stay here.'

'Well, I was obliged to make all possible haste, when Tom was crying with pain,' he said sulkily. 'He was awake all last night, let me tell you, and here are you expecting me to write you a letter through the post, and wait for you to answer it!'

'Not at all! What I should have expected you to do, had I known anything about it, would have been to have taken Tom to Melling immediately he complained of the toothache—whatever Amabel's opinion of his skill may be! Good God, how much skill is required to pull out a milk-tooth? Why, I daresay Dr Tarporley would have whisked it out in a trice, and spared Tom his sleepless night!'

This left Sir Geoffrey with nothing to say. He looked discomfited, and sought refuge in wounded dignity. 'No doubt it will be best for me to hire a suitable lodging in the town!'

'Much best—except that it would set all the Bath quizzes' tongues wagging! I will give orders in the morning for rooms to be prepared, but I am afraid I shan't be able to entertain Amabel as I should wish: I have a great many engagements which I must keep, in addition to accompanying Lucilla when she goes out. That, since her uncle has entrusted her to my care, is, you will agree, an inescapable duty!'

On this Parthian shot, she left the room. She was still seething with anger, for her brother's demeanour and lame excuses for his descent on her had confirmed her suspicion that his real reason was an obstinate determination to prevent any intimacy between her and Oliver Carleton. Amabel was to be planted in her house as a duenna—though what Geoffrey imagined Amabel (poor little goose!) could do to prevent her doing precisely as she chose only he knew! She was too angry to consider whether what seemed to her to be unwarrantable interference might not be a clumsy but well-meaning attempt to protect her from one whom he believed to be a dangerous rake; and the sight of Miss Farlow, hovering on the threshold of her bedchamber did nothing to assuage her wrath. She had no doubt that Miss Farlow was responsible for Geoffrey's sudden arrival, and it would have afforded her great pleasure to have shaken the irritating titter out of that meddlesome old Tabby, and have boxed her ears into the bargain. Suppressing this most unladylike impulse, she said coldly: 'Well, Maria? What is it you want?'

'Oh!' said Miss Farlow, in a flutter. 'Nothing in the world, dear Annis! I was just wondering whether dear Sir Geoffrey has everything he needs! If only Limbury had told me of his arrival I should have slipped away from the party, and attended to his comfort, as I hope I need not assure you, for it is my business to provide for your visitors, is it not? And even such excellent servants as our good Limbury, you know—'

'Limbury is far more capable than you, cousin, to provide for Sir Geoffrey's needs,' interposed Miss Wychwood, putting considerable force on herself to hold her temper in check. 'If anything should be wanting, Sir Geoffrey will ring his bell! I advise you to go to bed, to recruit your strength for the task that lies before you tomorrow! I shall require you to provide for several more visitors! Goodnight!'

A night's repose restored much of Miss Wychwood's shaken equilibrium, and she was able to confront her brother over the breakfast cups with tolerable composure. She asked him, quite pleasantly, whether he wished her to provide accommodation for him during Amabel's stay, and accepted, without betraying the relief she felt, his prosy explanation of why circumstances prevented him from staying beyond the time of Amabel's arrival. This instantly made Miss Farlow break into a flood of protestations, in which (she said) she knew well dear Annis would join her. 'I am persuaded dear Lady Wychwood must need your support through the approaching ordeal!' she said. 'Such a time as it is, too, since you last came to stay in Bath, for I don't count the scrap of a visit you paid us the other day! And if you are thinking that there is no room for you, there can be no difficulty about *that*, for you and dear Lady Wychwood can be perfectly comfortable in the Green room, which can be made ready for you in a trice. You have only to say the word!'

'If he can edge one in!' said Miss Wychwood dryly.

Sir Geoffrey gave a snort of laughter, and exchanged a glance pregnant with meaning with her. As little as any man did he welcome conversation at the breakfast-table, and it was probable that he had never liked Miss Farlow less than when he came under the full fire of her inconsequent chatter.

'When am I to expect Amabel to arrive?' asked Miss Wychwood smoothly.

'Well, as to that, I can't precisely answer you,' he replied, looking harassed. 'She has the intention of starting out betimes, but with all the business of packing, and seeing to it that Nurse hasn't forgotten anything—which very likely she will, because excellent though she is in her management of the children she has no head—none at all! When we took Tom to visit his grandparents last year, we had to turn back *three* times! I can tell you it tried my patience sadly, and I was provoked into declaring that I would never undertake a journey in her company again! Or in Tom's!' he added, with a reluctant grin. 'The thing is, you know, that he is a bad traveller! Feels sick before one has gone a mile, and after that one has to be for ever pulling up, to lift him down from the chaise to be sick in the road—poor little fellow!'

This perfunctory rider made Miss Wychwood break into laughter, in which he somewhat sheepishly joined her. 'Now I know what the circumstances are which make your immediate return to Twynham quite imperative!' she said.

'Well, I hope I am not an unfeeling parent, but—well, you know how it is, Annis!'

'I can hazard a guess at all events! It has not yet been my fate to travel with a child afflicted with carriage-sickness, I thank God!'

'Oh, it quite wrings my heart to think of that sweet little boy being sick, for there is nothing more miserable!' broke in Miss Farlow. 'Not that I am myself a bad traveller, for I daresay

I could drive from one end of the country to the other without experiencing the least discomfort, but I well remember how ill my particular friend, Miss Aston, always felt, even in hackney carriages. She is dead now, poor dear soul, though not in a hackney carriage, of course.'

Judging from her brother's expression that he was on the brink of delivering himself of a hasty snub, Miss Wychwood intervened, to suggest to her garrulous companion that if she had finished her breakfast she should go to talk to Mrs Wardlow about the arrangements to be made for Lady Wychwood, her children, her nurse, her dresser, and the nurse's maid. Miss Farlow expressed the utmost willingness to do so, and instantly plunged into a minute description of the plans she had already formulated. Miss Wychwood checked her by saying: 'Later, Maria, if you please! Domestic details are not interesting to Geoffrey!'

'No, indeed! Gentlemen never take any interest in them, do they? My own dear father was always used to say—'

She was interrupted by the impetuous entrance of Lucilla, so they never learned what the late Mr Farlow was always used to say. Lucilla was full of apologies for being so late. 'I can't think how I came to oversleep, except that I wasn't called! Oh, how do you do, Sir Geoffrey! My maid told me you arrived in the middle of the party: were you too tired to join it? I wish you might have done so, for it was a truly *splendid* party, wasn't it, ma'am?'

Miss Wychwood laughed, told her to pull the bell for a fresh pot of tea, and said that she had given orders she was not to be disturbed. 'Indeed, I meant to have your breakfast carried up to you as soon as you woke,' she said.

'Oh, yes, Brigham told me so, but I am not in the least fagged, and I can't *bear* having my breakfast in bed! The crumbs get into it, and the tea gets spilt over the sheet. Besides, I am to ride my mare this morning, and how dreadful it would be if

I were late! Did my uncle tell you when he means to bring the horses round, ma'am?'

'No,' replied Miss Wychwood, aware that Sir Geoffrey had stiffened alarmingly. 'To own the truth, I had forgotten we were to ride out today. I have had other things to think of. My sister-in-law is bringing her children to stay with me, and I am not very sure when they will arrive.'

'Oh!' Lucilla said blankly. 'I didn't know. Does it mean that you can't go with us? *Pray* don't cry off, ma'am!'

His evil genius prompted Sir Geoffrey to utter unwise words. 'My dear young lady,' he said kindly, 'you must not expect my sister to jaunter off on an expedition of pleasure, leaving no one to receive Lady Wychwood!'

'No. Of course not,' Lucilla agreed politely, but in a disappointed tone.

Now, Miss Wychwood had decided, many hours before, not to ride out in Mr Carleton's company, not even to see him. She had had the intention of charging Lucilla with a formal message of regret. That, she thought, would teach him a salutary lesson. But no sooner had Sir Geoffrey spoken than her hackles rose, and she said: 'As to that, Mrs Wardlow will be only too happy to receive Amabel, and to be granted an opportunity to dote on the children, besides discussing with Amabel all the nursery details which they both find so absorbing, and in which I take no interest.' She rose as she spoke, saying: 'I must go and tell Miss Farlow what I wish her to do for me this morning.'

'You *will* ride with us?' Lucilla cried eagerly.

Miss Wychwood nodded smilingly, and left the room. She was almost immediately followed by Sir Geoffrey, who caught her up as she was about to mount the stairs. 'Annis!' he said commandingly.

She paused, and looked over her shoulder at him. 'Well, Geoffrey?'

'Come into the library! I can't talk to you here!'

'There is no need for you to talk to me anywhere. I know what you wish to say, and I have no time to waste in listening to it.'

'Annis, I must insist—'

'Good God, will you never learn wisdom?' she exclaimed.

'Wisdom! I have more of that than you, I promise you!' he said angrily. 'I will not stand by and watch my sister compromising herself!'

'Doing *what*?' she gasped, taken-aback. 'Don't be such a dummy, Geoffrey! Compromise myself indeed! By going for a morning's ride with Lucilla, her uncle, and Ninian Elmore? You must have windmills in your head!'

She began to go upstairs, but he halted her, stretching up an arm to grasp her wrist. 'Wait!' he ordered. 'I warned you to have nothing to do with Carleton, but so far from paying any heed you have positively encouraged him to pursue you! He has dined here, and you have even dined with him at his hotel—and in a private parlour! I had not thought it possible you could behave with such impropriety! Ah, you wonder, I daresay, how I should know that!'

'I know exactly how you know it,' she said, with a disdainful curl of her lip. 'I don't doubt Maria has kept you informed of everything I do! That is why you are here today, and why you have bullocked Amabel into coming to keep an eye on me! Before you accuse me of impropriety, I recommend you to consider your own conduct! I can conceive of few more improper things than to have permitted Maria to report to you on my actions, and few things more addlebrained than to have believed them when anyone but a gudgeon must have realized that they sprang from the jealousy of a very stupid woman!'

She wrenched herself free from his hold on her wrist, and went swiftly upstairs, only pausing when he said weakly that

Maria had only done what she thought to be her duty, to say dangerously: 'I would remind you, brother, that it is I who am Maria's employer, not you! I will add that I keep no disloyal servants in my house!'

Five minutes later she was giving Miss Farlow precise instructions about the shopping she wished her to undertake. As these included a command to obtain from Mrs Wardlow a list of the various items of infant diet which would be needed, Miss Farlow showed signs of taking umbrage, and said, bridling, that she fancied she was quite as well qualified as the housekeeper to decide what were the best things to give children to eat.

'Please do as you are told!' said Miss Wychwood coldly. 'You need not trouble yourself to prepare the necessary bedchambers: Mrs Wardlow and my sister will settle that between them. Now, if there is anything you wish to know that I've not told you, pray tell me what it is immediately! I am going out, and shall be away all the morning.'

'Going out?' exclaimed Miss Farlow incredulously. 'You cannot mean that you are going on this riding expedition when dear Lady Wychwood may arrive at any moment!'

If anything had been needed to strengthen Miss Wychwood's resolve, that tactless speech supplied the necessary goad. She said: 'Certainly I mean it.'

'Oh, I am persuaded Sir Geoffrey won't permit it! Dear Miss Annis—' She broke off, quailing before the fiery glance cast at her.

'Let me advise you, cousin, not to meddle in what in no way concerns you!' said Miss Wychwood. 'You have worn my patience very thin already! I shall have a good deal to say to you later, but I've no time now to waste. Will you be kind enough to send Jurby up to me?'

Considerably alarmed by this unprecedented severity, Miss Farlow became flustered, and plunged into an incoherent speech, partly apologetic, partly self-exculpatory, but she did not get very far with it, for Lucilla came running up the stairs, to inform Miss Wychwood that Mr Carleton's groom had just called with a message from his master: if it was convenient to the ladies, he would bring the horses to Camden Place at eleven o'clock.

'So I said it was convenient! That was right, wasn't it?'

'Quite right but we shall have to make haste into our riding-habits.'

Miss Farlow uttered a sound between a hen-like cluck and a moan, and wrung her hands together, which had the effect of making Annis turn on her, and to say, in an exasperated voice: 'Maria, will you have the goodness to send Jurby to me at once? Pray don't make it necessary for me to ask you a third time!'

Miss Farlow scuttled away. Lucilla, wide-eyed with surprise, asked: 'Are you vexed with her, ma'am? I never heard you speak so crossly to her before!'

'Yes, I am a trifle vexed: she is the most tiresome creature! Her tongue has been running on wheels ever since we sat down to breakfast. But never mind that! Run and change your dress!'

Lucilla, having assured her that she could scramble into her habit in the twinkling of a bedpost, darted off to her own chamber, and if (thanks to Brigham) she did not actually scramble into her habit she was ready before her hostess. By the time Miss Wychwood came downstairs, Mr Carleton and Ninian had arrived, and Lucilla was cooing over a very pretty gray mare, patting and stroking her, and feeding her with sugar lumps. Ninian, who had borrowed a well ribbed-up hack from one of his new acquaintances, was pointing out all the mare's good points to her; and Mr Carleton, who had dismounted from his chestnut, was holding his own and Miss Wychwood's bridles, and when Miss Wychwood came out of the house he handed both to his groom, making it plain that he meant to put her up into the saddle himself. She went forward, greeting him with a good deal of reserve, and without her usual delightful smile. He took her hand, and surprised her by saying quietly: 'Don't look so sternly at me! Did I offend you very much last night?'

She said, rather stiffly: 'I must suppose you meant to do so, sir.'

'Yes,' he answered. 'I did mean to. But afterwards I wished I had cut out my tongue before I said such things to you. Forgive me!'

She was not proof against this blunt apology. She had not expected it; and when she answered him her voice was a little unsteady. 'Yes—of course I forgive you! Pray say no more about it! What a—a *prime 'un* you have bought for Lucilla! You will be first-ears with her hereafter!'

She gathered her bridle, and allowed him to take her foot between his hands. He threw her up into the saddle where she quickly settled herself, while the mare danced on impatient hooves.

'Bit fresh, ma'am!' warned the groom.

'Yes, because she hasn't been out for three days, poor darling! She'll settle down when the saddle has had time to get warm to her back. Stand away, if you please! Now, steady, Bess! Steady! You can't gallop through the town!'

'By Jupiter, you're a regular out-and-outer, ma'am!' exclaimed Ninian, watching the mare's playful and unavailing attempts to unseat her. 'I'll go bail you set a splitting pace in the hunting-field!'

'That sounds as though you take me for a thruster!' she retorted. 'Have you decided which way we are to go?'

'Yes, up on to Lansdown—unless you had liefer go somewhere else, ma'am?'

'No, not at all: Lansdown let it be! Well, Lucilla? How do you like her?'

'Oh, beyond anything great!' Lucilla said ecstatically. The groom had mounted her, and she was groping for her stirrup-leather under her skirt. 'Oh, botheration!'

'Here, I'll do that for you!' Ninian said. 'Do you want it short-ened or lengthened?'

'Shortened, please. Just one hole, I think. Yes, that is exactly right! Thank you!'

He tested the girths, tightened them, told her sternly to remember that her hand was strange to the mare, and to be careful what she was about, and swung himself into his own saddle. They then set forward, Lucilla and Ninian leading the way, and Mr Carleton, following close on their heels with Miss Wychwood beside him, keeping a critical eye on his ward. He seemed soon to be satisfied that a perfect understanding between the gray mare and her rider was in a fair way to becoming established, for he withdrew his gaze from them, and turned his head to speak to Miss Wychwood, saying: 'No need to follow so closely: she seems to know how to handle strange horses.'

'Yes,' she agreed. 'Ninian assured me that I had no need to worry about her for she was a capital horsewoman.'

'She should be,' he responded. 'My brother threw her into the saddle when she was hardly out of leading-strings.'

'Yes,' she said again. 'She told me that.'

Silence fell between them. It was not broken until they had drawn clear of the town, and Ninian and Lucilla, once off the stones, were trotting some way ahead. Mr Carleton said then, in his direct fashion: 'Are you still angry with me?'

She started a little, for she had been lost in her own thoughts, and replied, with an uncertain laugh: 'Oh, no! I'm afraid I was wool-gathering!'

'If you are no longer angry with me, who, or what, has put you all on end?'

'I—I'm not all on end!' she stammered. 'Why—why should you think I am, merely because I let my thoughts wander for a minute or two?'

He appeared to give this question consideration. A slight frown drew his brows together, and a searching look between narrowed eyes, staring between his horse's ears into the middle distance, failed to provide him with an answer, for, after a short pause, he smiled wryly, and said: 'I don't know. But I do know that something has happened to put you in a passion, which you are trying to bottle up.'

'Oh, dear!' she sighed. 'Is it so obvious?'

'To me, yes,' he replied curtly. 'I wish you will tell me what has destroyed your tranquillity, but if you don't choose to do so I won't press you. What would you wish to talk about?'

She turned her head to look at him wonderingly, a smile wavering on her lips, and in her mind the thought that he was strangely incalculable. At one moment, he could be brusque, and unfeeling; and then, when he had made her blazingly angry, his mood seemed to change, and her resentment was dispelled by the sympathy, however roughly expressed, which she heard in his voice, and detected in the softened look in his eyes. Now, as she met those penetrating eyes, she saw the hint of a smile in them, and was conscious of an impulse to admit him, at least a little way, into her confidence. There was no one else to whom she could unburden herself, and she badly needed a safe confi-dant, for the more she kept her rancour to herself the greater it grew. Why she should consider Mr Carleton a safe confidant was a question it never occurred to her to ask herself: she felt it, and that was enough.

She hesitated, and after a moment he said in a matter-of-fact way: 'You had better open the budget, you know, before all that seething wrath in you forces off the lid you've clamped down on it, and scalds everything within sight.'

That made her laugh. She said: 'Like a pot of boiling water? That would be very shocking! It's true that I am out of temper, but it's no great matter. My brother arrived in Camden Place last night, to inform me that he was planting his wife, his two children, their nurse, and—I conjecture!—my sister-in-law's abigail, upon me today, for—according to himself!—a few days! Without warning, if you please! I am very fond of my sister-in-law, but it vexed me very much!'

'I imagine it might. Why are you to be subjected to this invasion?'

Her eyes kindled. 'Because he—' She stopped, realizing suddenly that it was impossible to disclose to Mr Carleton, of all people, Sir Geoffrey's true reason. 'Because Tom—my small nephew—has the toothache!' she said.

'You must think of something better than that!' he objected. 'I daresay you believe me to be a cabbage-head, but you are mistaken: I'm not! And swallow that clanker I can't!'

'I don't think anything of the sort,' she retorted. 'If you want the truth, I believe you to be a most complete hand, awake upon every suit!'

'Then you should know better than to try to tip me the double,' he said. 'Bring his entire family to Bath because Tom has the toothache? What a Banbury story!'

'Well, I must own it does sound like one, but it isn't. My sister-in-law is—is set on taking Tom to the best dentist possible, and has had Westcott recommended to her. If you think that ridiculous, so do I!'

'I think it is a damned imposition!' he said roundly. 'Oh, you are not accustomed to the language I use, are you? Accept my apologies, ma'am!'

'Willingly! You have exactly expressed my feelings! To overset all my arrangements without so much as a by your leave makes me so out of reason cross that I want to rip and tear! You need not tell me that I am building a mountain out of a molehill, for I know I am!'

'Oh, no, I shan't! You are far too well-bred to vent your wrath on Wychwood, so rip and tear at me instead!'

'Don't be so absurd! *You* are not—in this instance—the cause of my vexation!'

'Oh, don't let that weigh with you! I will confidently engage myself to offer you enough provocation to rattle me off in fine style! Don't hesitate to make use of me!'

'Mr Carleton,' she said, with a quivering lip, 'I have already requested you not to be absurd!'

'But didn't I promise to offer you provocation?'

'One of the things I most dislike in you, sir, is your disagreeable habit of *always* having an answer!' she told him, with considerable acerbity. 'And, in general,' she added, 'a rude one!'

'Come, this is much better!' he said encouragingly. 'You have already rid yourself of some of your spleen! Now tell me exactly what you think of me for having said an unjust thing to you last night, and for having, with such abominable rudeness, left your rout-party! If that doesn't rid you of the rest of your spleen, you can animadvert, more forcefully than you did in the Pump Room that day, on the obliquity of my life and character! And if that doesn't take the trick—'

She interrupted him, the colour flaming into her cheeks. 'I beg you to say no more! I should not have said—what I did say—and I regretted it as soon as the words were out of my mouth, and—and have wished to beg your pardon ever since. But somehow the opportunity to do so never arose. It has arisen now, and—and I do beg your pardon!'

He did not immediately answer her, and, stealing a glance at his face, she saw that that queer smile had twisted his mouth. He said: 'One of the things *I* most dislike in *you*, my entrancing hornet, is your unfailing ability to put me at Point Non Plus! I'm damned if I know why I like you so much!'

She was powerfully affected by these words, but made a gallant attempt to pass them off lightly. 'Indeed, I can't think why you should like me, for we have come to points whenever we have met! And I have a melancholy suspicion that we should continue to do so, however many times we were condemned to meet each other!'

'Have you?' he said, a harsh note in his voice. 'With me it is otherwise!' He saw the instinctive gesture of repulsion she made, and said, with a short, sardonic laugh: 'Oh, don't be afraid! I shall say no more until I have contrived by hedge or by stile to overcome your dislike of me! In the meantime, let us push on to overtake Lucilla and young Elmore.'

'Yes, do let us!' she said, not knowing whether to be glad or sorry for this abrupt change of subject. In an effort to bridge an awkward gap, she said, as she encouraged her mare to break into a canter: 'I must tell you that I shouldn't—I trust!—have allowed my vexation to take such strong possession of me if my cousin Maria had not chosen that most unlucky moment to talk me almost to the gates of Bedlam!'

'That doesn't surprise me at all!' he replied. 'If I were forced to endure more than five minutes of her vapid gibble-gabbling there would be nothing for it but to cut my throat! Or hers,' he added, apparently giving this alternative his consideration. 'No, I think not: the jury, not having been acquainted with her, would probably find me guilty of murder. What shocking injustices are perpetrated in the name of the law! How the case of your cousin brings that home to one! She ought, of course, to have been strangled at birth, but I daresay her parents were wanting in foresight.'

This drew a positive peal of laughter out of Miss Wychwood. She turned her head towards him, her eyes brimful of merriment, and said: 'Oh, how often I have felt the same! She is the most tactless, tedious bore imaginable! When I left Twynham, my brother prevailed on me to employ her as my companion, to lend me countenance, and I have seldom ceased to wonder at myself for having been so want-witted as to have agreed to do it! How horrid I am to say so! Poor Maria! she means so well!'

'Worse you could not say of her! Why don't you send her packing?'

She sighed and shook her head. 'I own, I am often tempted to do so, but I am afraid it isn't possible. Her father, according to what Geoffrey tells me, was sadly improvident, and left her very ill provided for, poor thing. So I couldn't turn her off, could I?'

'You might *pension* her off,' he suggested.

'And have Geoffrey plaguing my life out to hire another in her place? No, I thank you!'

'Does he do that? Do you permit him to plague you?'

'I can't prevent him! I don't permit him to dictate to me—which is why we are so frequently at outs! He is older than I am, you see, and nothing will ever disabuse his mind of its belief that I am a green and headstrong little sister whom it is his duty to guide, admonish, and protect! Which is, I acknowledge, very admirable, but as vexatious as it is misjudged, and seldom fails to send me up into the boughs!'

'Ah! I thought there was more to his descent on you than his little boy's toothache! He came, in fact, to warn you to have nothing to say to me, didn't he? Does he suspect me of having designs on your virtue? Shall I tell him that his suspicion is groundless?'

'No, certainly not!' she said emphatically. 'I am very well able to deal with Geoffrey myself. Ah, there are the children! Indulge me with a race to overtake them, Mr Carleton! I have been pining these many weeks for a good gallop!'

'Very well, but 'ware rabbit holes.'

'Pooh!' she threw at him, over her shoulder, as the mare lengthened her stride.

She had the start of him, but he overtook her, and they reached the two winning posts neck and neck, and were greeted, by Lucilla with applause, and by Ninian with mock reproach, for having, he said, set Lucilla such a bad example.

'Don't you mean a good example?' enquired Mr Carleton.

'No, sir, I don't, for how the deuce am I to stop her galloping hell-for-leather when she has seen Miss Wychwood doing it?'

'As though you could *ever* stop me if I choose to gallop!' said Lucilla scornfully. 'You couldn't catch me!'

'Oh, couldn't I? If I had my Blue Devil between my legs we'd soon see that!'

'Blue Devil would never come within *lengths of* my Lovely Lady! Oh, sir, that is the name I've given her! I thought at first that I would call her Carleton's Choice, but Ninian said he didn't think you would care for that!'

'Then I am very much obliged to him! I should *not* have cared for it!'

'Well, I meant it as a compliment!' said Lucilla, slightly aggrieved.

'Good God!' he said.

Ninian chuckled, and said: 'I told you so! I don't like Lovely Lady either: a sickly name to give a horse! But at least it's better than the other!'

'Shall we ride on to visit the Saxon fortifications, or would you prefer to remain here abusing one another?' intervened Miss Wychwood.

Thus called to order the combatants hastily begged pardon, and the whole party moved forward.

# Ten

I T WAS CONSIDERABLY PAST NOON WHEN MISS WYCHWOOD
re-entered her house, and there were unmistakable signs
that her uninvited guests had arrived, and were partaking of a
late nuncheon in the breakfast parlour. James was halfway up the
stairs, lugging, with the assistance of one of the maids, a large
trunk; the page-boy was collecting as many of the smaller articles
of luggage as he could conveniently carry; Lady Wychwood's
abigail was sharply admonishing him, and warning James to be
careful not to let the trunk fall; and Limbury had just come out of
the parlour with a tray. He was looking somewhat harassed, as well
he might, for the hall was littered with portmanteaux, valises, and
bandboxes, amongst which he was forced to pick his way. At sight
of his mistress, he looked even more harassed, and begged her to
excuse the disorder, in a voice which gave her to understand that
it was no fault of his that the luggage was still in the hall. 'The
coach in which it was packed, ma'am, arrived barely a quarter of
an hour ago, and since Nurse wanted something out of one of the
trunks, and insisted on searching for it immediately, and was unable
to recall in which of the trunks she had packed it, we have been,
as you might say, slightly impeded.' He added, in an expressionless
tone: 'It happened to be in one of the valises, ma'am.'

The abigail took up the tale, bobbing a curtsy, and saying that
she was sure she was excessively sorry that Miss should have

come home to find her house in such a pickle, which would not have happened if the second-coachman had not fallen so far behind on the road, and if Nurse had not been so foolish as to have packed at the bottom of a trunk what one would have supposed she must have known she would need on the journey.

'Well, never mind,' said Miss Wychwood. 'Are Sir Geoffrey and her ladyship eating a nuncheon, Limbury?'

Lucilla, who was looking at the impedimenta in round-eyed astonishment, whispered: 'Good gracious, ma'am! What an extraordinary amount of baggage for just a few days! One would think they had come to spend *months* with you!'

'They probably have,' replied Miss Wychwood bitterly. 'Run up and change your dress, my love! I must greet my sister-in-law, I suppose, before I do the same.'

'I will bring a fresh pot of tea for you directly, Miss Annis. Would you care for a baked egg, or a bowl of soup?'

'No, nothing, thank you: I'm not hungry!'

Limbury bowed, set his tray down on one of the trunks, and opened the door for Miss Wychwood to pass into the parlour.

Her brother, his wife, and Miss Farlow were seated at the table, but they all rose, and Amabel tottered towards her, and almost fell into her arms, saying faintly: 'Oh, Annis, dearest one, how glad I am to see you at last! How good you are to me! You cannot imagine how much I have longed for you through this dreadfully agitating time! I can't describe to you what I have been through! Now I can be comfortable again!'

'Of course you can!' said Annis, returning her fond embrace, and gently pushing her back to her chair. 'Sit down, and tell me how Tom is!'

Lady Wychwood shuddered. 'Oh, my poor, precious little son! He was so brave through it all, even though he was screaming with pain most of the night! Nothing eased it until I ventured to give him a few drops of laudanum, in a teaspoon, which did send him to sleep for a very little while, but, alas, not for long, and I dared not give him any more, for I am convinced it is unwise to dose children with laudanum. And this morning the pain was so much worse that if the trunks had not been packed, and the horses harnessed, I think I *must* have gone against Geoffrey's wishes, and taken the poor little love to Melling after all!'

Miss Wychwood cast a satirical glance at her brother. He was obviously discomposed, but he returned the glance with a defiant glare, and said, in minatory accents: 'You forget, my love, that it was you who wished Westcott to see Tom!'

'Oh, I am persuaded you were right, dear Lady Wychwood!' exclaimed Miss Farlow, for once in her life stepping opportunely into an awkward breach. 'My dear father always said that it was a false economy to consult any but the *best* medical practitioners in such cases! I daresay this Melling you speak of would have bungled the extraction, but once Westcott had coaxed dear little Tom to open his mouth he whisked the tooth out in the shake of a lamb's tail!'

'Well, that's good news, at all events!' said Miss Wychwood. 'I collect he is now relieved of his pain, for I heard no screams of anguish when I entered the house.'

'He is asleep,' said Lady Wychwood, sinking her voice as though she feared to disturb the rest of her son, tucked into a crib three floors above her. She directed a wan smile at Miss Farlow, and said: 'Cousin Maria sang lullabies to him until he dropped off. I don't think I can ever be grateful enough to her for all she has done this morning! She even accompanied us to Westcott's, and was of the greatest support to me through the ordeal. She had the strength of mind to hold Tom's hands down at the Fatal Moment, which I could not bring myself to do!'

'But where was Geoffrey at the Fatal Moment?' enquired Annis, in seeming bewilderment.

Lady Wychwood began to explain that Geoffrey had been unable to go to the dentist because he had a business engagement in the town, but he broke in on this, well-aware that his loving sister was not one to be so easily bamboozled. 'No use trying to come crab over Annis, my love!' he said, laughing. 'She's far too needle-witted! Well, you are right, Annis, and I don't mind owning that I cut my stick when I saw what a state Tom had worked himself into, kicking, and screaming, and saying he wouldn't have his tooth drawn! Well, what could *I* do in such a situation, I ask you?'

'Spanked him!' said Annis.

He grinned, and admitted that he had been strongly tempted to do so, but Amabel uttered a shocked protest, and Miss Farlow said that she knew he was only funning, and that it would have been the height of brutality to have spanked dear little Tom when he was demented with the agony he was suffering.

Annis then withdrew, saying that she must put off her riding-habit, and recommending Amabel to lie down on her bed for an hour or two, to recover from so many sleepless nights. As she left the room, she heard Miss Farlow eagerly endorsing this piece of advice, assuring dear Lady Wychwood that she had no need to be anxious about poor little Tom, and telling her that a hot brick had already been put into her bed. 'For I gave orders for that to be done before we drove to Westcott's, knowing that you would be quite exhausted, after all the trials you have been forced to undergo!'

Sir Geoffrey, following his sister out of the room, caught up with her at the head of the stairs. 'Stay a moment, Annis!' he said. 'Something I wish to consult with you about! These new vapour-baths which I hear so much about: do you agree with me that they would be of benefit to Amabel? The state of her health has been causing me grave concern—very grave concern! She insists that she is in perfectly good point, but you must have noticed how pulled she looks! It's my belief she never *has* been in high health since her confinement, and this unfortunate business of Tom's abscess has put her quite out of curl. You would be doing me a great favour if you would prevail upon her to take a course of the baths, which, I'm told, are excellent in such cases.'

She regarded him steadily, and with a disquieting smile in her eyes, which had a discomposing effect on him, but all she said was: 'I am sorry you should feel so anxious about her. She is certainly tired, and overwrought, but that was to be expected, wasn't it, after so many sleepless nights? She seemed, when I was visiting you, to be in a capital way!'

He shook his head. 'Ah, she is never one to complain of feeling out of sorts, and, I daresay, would be laid by the wall before she would admit to being fagged to death when *you* were visiting us! But so it was—not that she will own it!'

'I've no doubt she won't,' said Miss Wychwood. 'I have heard, of course, of the new baths in Abbey Street, but I know nothing about them, except that they are under the management of a Dr Wilkinson. And I cannot suppose, dear brother, that if *you* have failed to persuade Amabel to try a course of them she would yield to any persuasion of mine.'

'Oh, I think she might!' he said. 'She sets great store by your opinion, I promise you! You have great influence over her, you know.'

'Have I? Well, I should think it most impertinent to exert it in a matter of which she can be the only judge. But you may be easy! Amabel may remain with me for as long as she chooses to do so.'

'I knew I might depend on you!' he said heartily. 'You are wishful to change your dress, so I won't detain you another minute! I must make haste to be off myself, so I'll take my leave of you now. I daresay I shall be riding over to see how Amabel goes on in a day or two, but I know I can rely on you to take good care of her!'

'But surely you have brought her here so that *she* may take good care of *me*?'

He thought it prudent to ignore this, but halfway down the stairs he bethought him of something he had forgotten to tell her. He paused, and looked back at her, saying: 'Oh, by the bye, Annis! You asked me to send the nursery-maid, didn't you? There was no time for me to send a message to Amabel, so I have arranged to hire a suitable girl to wait on the nursery here.'

'You shouldn't have put yourself to the trouble of doing that,' she answered, rather touched.

'No trouble at all!' he said gallantly. 'I wouldn't for the world upset your servants! Maria has promised to attend to the matter this very day.'

He waved an airy hand, and went off down the stairs, feeling that he had done all that could have been expected of him.

By the time Miss Wychwood descended to the drawing-room he had left the house, and Amabel, as Miss Farlow informed her in an audible aside, was laid down on her bed, with the blinds drawn, and a hot brick at her feet. She would have described all the arrangements she had made for Amabel's comfort, had Miss Wychwood not checked her, and moved past her to greet Lord Beckenham, who had called to return thanks for the previous evening's party, and was making ponderous conversation to Lucilla. He kissed her hand, and told her that his intention had been to have left his card, but that hearing from Limbury that she was at home he had ventured to come in, just to see how she did.

'Miss Carleton has been telling me that you went out riding this morning. You are inexhaustible, dear Miss Annis! And now I hear that Lady Wychwood has come to stay with you, which must have meant that you were obliged to go to a great deal of trouble! I wish—indeed, we must all of us wish! that you would take more care of yourself!'

'My dear Beckenham, you speak as though I were one of these invalidish females for ever hovering on the brink of a decline! You should know better! I don't think I've suffered a day's illness since I came to Bath! As for being knocked-up by a small rout what a poor thing you must think me!' She turned to Lucilla, and said: 'My dear, did you tell me that you were going to go for a walk in the Sydney Garden with Corisande and Edith and Miss Frampton this afternoon? I had meant to have accompanied you to Laura Place, and to have had a chat with Mrs Stinchcombe, but I'm afraid I must cry off, now that Lady Wychwood has come to visit me. Oh, don't look so downcast! Brigham can go with you to Laura Place, and I will send the carriage to bring you back again in time for dinner. You will make my excuses to Mrs Stinchcombe, and explain the circumstances, won't you?'

'Oh, yes, indeed I will, ma'am!' said Lucilla, her clouded brow clearing as if by magic. 'I will run up to put on my bonnet immediately! Unless—unless there is anything you would wish me to do for you here?'

'Not a thing!' said Miss Wychwood, smiling affectionately at her. 'Say goodbye to Lord Beckenham, and be off with you, or you will keep them waiting!' When the door was shut behind Lucilla, she addressed herself to Miss Farlow, speaking with cool friendliness. 'You too should be off, Maria, if you have pledged yourself to hire a suitable maid to wait on the nursery, which I understand is the case.'

'Oh, yes! I was persuaded it was what you would wish me to do! If I had known one would be needed I would have popped into the Registry Office this morning, on my way home from Milsom Street, only if I had done so I should have been too late to welcome dear Lady Wychwood, for, as it was, I had so much shopping to do that I almost *was* too late. Not that I mean to complain! That would be a very odd thing for me to do! But so it was, and I saw a chaise drawn up outside the house just as I was passing that house with the green shutters, so I ran the rest of the way, and reached *our* house at the very moment James was helping Nurse to get down from the chaise. So I gave all my parcels to Limbury, and told him to take them down to the kitchen, and was able—though sadly out of breath!—to welcome dear Lady Wychwood, and explain to her how it came about that you were obliged to depute that agreeable task to me. And then, you know—'

'Yes, Maria, I do know, so you need not tell me any more! These details are of no possible interest to Lord Beckenham.'

'Oh, no! Gentlemen never care for domestic matters, do they? I well remember my dear father saying that I was a regular *bagpipe* when I recounted some little happening to him which I quite thought would entertain him! Well, I mustn't run on, must I? You and his lordship will be wanting to talk about the party, and although I should like very much to stay I see that it wants only two minutes to the hour, and I must tear myself away!'

Lord Beckenham showed no disposition to follow her example; he remained for more than an hour, and might have stayed for another hour had not Amabel come into the room. This gave Miss Wychwood an opportunity to get rid of him, which she did quite simply by telling him that Amabel ought to be in her bed, for she was quite worn-out, and in no fit state to have come down to the drawing-room. He said at once that he would go away, and pausing only to express his concern to Lady Wychwood, and his hope that Bath air, and the tender care which he knew well she would receive in her sister-in-law's house, would soon restore her to the enjoyment of her usual health, he did go away.

Lady Wychwood said, when she was alone with Annis: 'How devoted he is to you, dearest! You shouldn't have sent him away on my account!'

'Yes, I know you have a *tendre* for him,' said Annis, gravely shaking her head. 'I am very sorry to be so disobliging, but I feel it my duty to Geoffrey to keep such a dashing blade away from you.'

'For shame, Annis! It's very naughty of you to poke fun at the poor man! Keep him away from me indeed! How ridiculous you are!'

'No more ridiculous than you, my dear.'

Lady Wychwood's eyes flew to her face. 'Why—why what can you mean?' she faltered.

'Haven't you come here to keep Oliver Carleton away from me?' Annis asked her, a little satirical smile lilting on her lips.

Colour flooded Lady Wychwood's cheeks. 'Oh, Annis!'

Annis laughed. 'Don't sound so tragical, you goose! I'm well aware that this absurd notion is Geoffrey's, and not yours.'

'Oh, Annis, pray don't be vexed!' Lady Wychwood said imploringly. 'I would never have ventured to presume—I was perfectly sure you would never do anything imprudent! I begged Geoffrey not to meddle! Indeed, I went so far as to say that nothing would prevail on me to come to stay with you! I was never nearer falling into a quarrel with him, for I *knew* how bitterly you would resent such interference!'

'I do resent it, and wish very much you hadn't yielded to Geoffrey,' Annis replied. 'But that's past praying for, I collect! Oh, don't cry! I am not angry with *you*, love!'

Lady Wychwood wiped away her starting tears, and said, with a sob in her voice: 'But you are angry with Geoffrey, and I cannot bear you to be!'

'Well, that too is past praying for!'

'No, no, don't say so! If you knew how anxious he has been! how fond he is of you!'

'I don't doubt it. Each of us has a good deal of fondness for the other, but we are never so fond as when we are apart, as you

know well! *His* fondness doesn't lead to the smallest understanding of my character. He persists in believing me to be a sort
of bouncing, flouncing girl, with no more rumgumption than a
moonling, who is so caper-witted as to stand in constant need
of guidance, admonition, prohibition, and censure from an elder
brother who thinks himself far wiser than she is, but if you will
forgive me for saying so—very much mistakes the matter!'

These forceful words made the gentle Amabel quail, but she
tried, bravely, to defend her adored husband from his sister's
strictures. 'You wrong him, dearest! indeed, you do! He is for
ever telling people how clever you are—needle-witted, he calls
it! He is excessively proud of your wit, and your beauty, but—
but he knows—as how should he not?—that in *worldly* matters
you are not as experienced as he is, and—and his dread is that
you may be taken-in by—by a *man of the town*, which he tells
me this Mr Carleton is!'

'I wonder what it was that gave poor Geoffrey such a
dislike of Mr Carleton?' said Annis, considerably amused. 'I
would hazard a guess that he received from him, at some time
or another, one of his ruthless set-downs. I remember that
Geoffrey told me he was the rudest man in London, which I
don't find it difficult to believe! He is certainly the rudest man
*I* ever encountered!'

'Annis,' said Lady Wychwood, impressively sinking her voice,
'Geoffrey has informed me that he is a libertine!'

'Oh, no! Has he sullied your ears with *that* word?' Annis
exclaimed, her eyes and her voice brimming over with laughter.
'He didn't sully my virgin ears with it! It was what he meant,
of course, when he said that Mr Carleton was an ugly customer
whom he would not dream of presenting to me, but when
I asked him if it *was* what he meant all the answer he made was
to deplore my want of *delicacy of mind*! Well! You and I, Amabel,
cut our eye-teeth years ago, so let us, for God's sake, have the

word with no bark on it! I should be amazed if a bachelor of Mr Carleton's age had had no dealings with straw damsels, but I am still more amazed at his apparent success in that line! It must, I conjecture, be due to his wealth, for it cannot have been due to his address, for he has none! From the moment of our first meeting, he has neglected very few opportunities to be unpardonably uncivil to me, even going to the length of informing me that Maria had no need to fear he was trying to seduce me, because he had no such intention.'

'Annis!' gasped her ladyship. 'You must be funning! He *could* not have said anything so—so abominably rude to you!'

She obviously was more shocked by this evidence of Mr Carleton's crude manners than by Sir Geoffrey's allegation that he was a profligate. Miss Wychwood's eyes began to dance; but all she said was: 'Wait until you have met him!'

'I hope never to be compelled to meet him!' retorted Amabel, the picture of affronted virtue.

'But you will be bound to meet him!' Annis said reasonably. 'Recollect that his niece—and ward—is in my charge! He comes frequently to this house, to assure himself that I am not permitting her to encourage the advances of such gazetted fortune-hunters as Denis Kilbride, or to overstep the bounds of the strictest propriety. He does not, if you please, consider me a fit and proper person to have charge of Lucilla, and doesn't scruple to say so! I'm told it is always so with loose-screws: they become downright prudes where the females of their own families are concerned! I imagine that must be because they know too much about the wiles of seducers—from their own experiences! Besides, my dear, how can you possibly protect me from him if you run out of the room the instant he is ushered into it?'

Lady Wychwood could find no answer to this, except to say, weakly, that she had told Geoffrey that no good could come of his insisting on her going to stay in Camden Place.

'None at all!' agreed Annis. 'But don't let that cast you in the mops, love! I hope I have no need to assure you that I am always happy to welcome you to my house!'

'Dear, dear Annis!' uttered Lady Wychwood, powerfully affected, and wiping away a fresh flow of tears from her brimming eyes. 'Always so kind! So much kinder to me than my own sisters! Believe me, one of the wishes nearest to my heart is to see you happily married, to a man *worthy* of you!'

'Beckenham?' enquired Annis. 'I don't think I'm acquainted with anyone worthier than he is!'

'Alas, no! I wish very much that he had been able to fix his interest with you, but I know there is no chance of that: you think him a bore, and a bobbing block, and I sometimes think— are blind to all his excellent qualities.'

'Oh, no! He is stuffed with good qualities, but the melancholy truth is that however much I may respect a man's good qualities they don't inspire me with a particle of love for him! I shall either marry a man stuffed with bad qualities, or remain a spinster—which is the likeliest fate to befall me! Don't let us talk any more about my future! Tell me about yourself!'

But Lady Wychwood said that there was nothing to tell. Annis asked her whether she indeed meant to take a course of Russian vapour-baths. This made her giggle. 'Oh, no, and so I told Geoffrey!'

'Well, he depends on me to persuade you to do so! *I* told him that I should deem it an impertinence to do any such thing. Is it true that you have been out of sorts?'

'No, no! That is to say, I had a slight cold, but it was nothing! And then, of course, I had all the anxiety about Tom, which has made me look horridly hagged. I daresay that was what made Geoffrey get into one of his ways. Perhaps I might drink the waters, just—just to satisfy him! After all, that can't do me any harm!'

'Unless they make you feel as sick as I did, the only time I ever took a glass! We shall soon see! Since Lucilla came to stay with me I have visited the Pump Room almost every day, so that she can meet her new friend, who accompanies her mother to the Pump Room. I fancy you have met Mrs Stinchcombe: did she not come to dinner here when you and Geoffrey visited me last year?'

'Oh, yes! A most agreeable woman! I remember her very well, and shall be happy to renew my acquaintance with her. But this Lucilla of yours! Where is she?'

'You will see her presently. She has gone to take a walk in the Sydney Garden, with Corisande and Edith Stinchcombe. She and Corisande have become almost inseparable, for which I am truly thankful! I am extremely attached to the child, but I own I find it more than a little boring to be obliged to go everywhere with her! Chaperonage is no light task, I promise you!'

'No, indeed! I was shocked when I heard that you had taken it upon yourself to look after Miss Carleton. You are much too young to be *any* girl's duenna, no matter who she may be. Geoffrey thought you should have restored her to her aunt, and I must own I cannot but feel he was quite right. I don't mean to say that she is not an agreeable girl: Geoffrey was pleasantly surprised by her manners, which he tells me are very pretty—but what a responsibility to have assumed, dearest! I cannot like it for you.'

'Well, if she were to be with me permanently I shouldn't like it either,' admitted Miss Wychwood. 'She is a lovely little innocent, had never been in Society—what she calls "grown-up" parties—until she came to Bath, and made an instant hit! Already she has I know not how many young men dangling after her, which makes it necessary for me to keep a strict watch over her. To make matters worse, she is a considerable heiress: a sure bait for fortune-hunters! Fortunately, the Stinchcombes have a governess to whom the girls are devoted—even Lucilla likes her, having previously taken the whole race of governesses in detestation!—and so I am able to relinquish Lucilla into her care when it is a question of going for walks, or buying fripperies in the town. I only wish the Stinchcombes lived in Camden Place, but they don't! They have a house in Laura Place, so that I am obliged to provide Lucilla with an escort when she visits them. However, Mr Carleton gave me leave to engage a maid for her, who, I judge, is to be trusted to fill my place at need.'

'But, Annis, is it so necessary to chaperon girls in *Bath*? Why, even in London my sisters tell me that nowadays it is quite unremarkable to see two girls walking together without even a footman coming behind them!'

'*Two* girls, yes!' said Miss Wychwood. 'But not one girl alone, I think! Mrs Stinchcombe is an indulgent parent but I am very sure she would not permit Corisande to come up to Camden Place unattended. And in Lucilla's case—no, no! Out of the question! Mr Carleton has, however reluctantly, confided her to my care until he has made other arrangements for her, and what a *horrid fix* I should be in if I let her come to harm!'

'He had no right to lay such a charge upon you!'

'He didn't. He had no alternative but to leave her with me, having himself, as he so gracelessly told me, no turn for the infantry, and not the smallest intention of taking Lucilla into his own charge. I will allow that he has enough sense of his duty to his ward to place her in the temporary guardianship of a—a lady of unquestioned respectability, which I flatter myself I am! But it went sadly against the grain with him to do it, and I fancy nothing would afford him more satisfaction than a failure on my part to guard Lucilla from all the hazards threatening a green young heiress on her first emergence from the schoolroom!' She checked herself, and, after a moment's consideration, said: 'No!

Perhaps I am wronging him! He would certainly derive satisfaction from the knowledge that he had been right to doubt my
ability to take proper care of Lucilla; but I do him the justice
to think that he would be seriously displeased if Lucilla were to
come to harm.'

'I wish you had never met her!' sighed Lady Wychwood.

But when Annis presented Lucilla to her that evening she was
quite as pleasantly surprised as her husband had been, talked
very kindly to her, and later told Annis that it was difficult to
believe that such a sweet and pretty-behaved child could be the
ward of a man of Carleton's reputation. She was rather puzzled
by Ninian's presence at dinner, still more by the familiar terms
he stood on with Annis, her house, and her servants. He behaved
as if he had been a favoured nephew, or, at any rate, a boy who
had known Annis all his life and it was evident that he ran tame
in the house, and more often than not dined there. She
wondered if he was perhaps related to Lucilla, and when Annis
disclosed his identity she was at first incredulous, and then so
forcibly struck by the absurdity of the situation that she went
into paroxysms of laughter.

'Oh, I haven't been so much diverted since Mrs Preston's hat
was carried off by the wind, and took her wig with it!' she
gurgled. 'The end of it will be, of course, that they will marry
one another!'

'God forbid! What a cat-and-dog life they would lead!'

'I don't know that. You say they disagree on every subject, but
it didn't seem like that to me, listening to them at dinner. I think
they have a great deal in common. Only wait for a year or two,
when they will both be wiser, and see if I am not right! They
are still only a pair of bickering children, but when they are a
little older they won't bicker, any more than I bicker with my
sisters—though when we were all in the schoolroom we were
used to bicker incessantly!'

'I can't conceive of your bickering with anyone!' smiled Annis. 'As for Lucilla and Ninian, the Iverleys no longer wish for that marriage, and would—if they are to be believed—strongly oppose it. It wouldn't astonish me if Mr Carleton opposed it too, for he doesn't like Iverley.'

'Oh, that settles it!' said Lady Wychwood, laughing. 'Opposition is all that is wanting in the case!'

Annis could not help thinking that opposition from Mr Carleton would probably take a ruthless form, impossible to withstand, but she kept this reflection to herself.

She was destined, a few hours later, to be confronted by a dilemma. Lucilla, peeping into her bedchamber on her return from Laura Place, to thank her for having sent the carriage to bring her home, and to tell her how much she had enjoyed her first visit to the Sydney Garden, with its shady groves, its grottoes, labyrinths, and waterfalls, said, her eyes and cheeks aglow: 'And Mr Kilbride says that during the summer they have illuminations, and gala nights, and public breakfasts! Oh, *dear* Miss Wychwood, will you take me to a gala night? *Pray* say you will!'

'Yes, certainly I will, if your heart is set on it,' replied Miss Wychwood. 'Did Mr Kilbride tell you of the galas and the illuminations last night?'

'Oh, no! It was this afternoon, when I told him that I was going to explore the Garden with Corisande. We walked smash into him, Brigham and I, not two minutes after we left the house. He said he was coming to visit you, but he *very* obligingly turned back, to escort me to Laura Place. Wasn't that kind of him, ma'am? He was so amusing, too! He had me in whoops with the droll things he said! I do think he is a delightful creature, don't you?'

Miss Wychwood took a full minute to respond to this, covering her silence by pretending that her attention was concentrated on the pinning of a brooch to her corsage. In truth, she knew not what to say. On the one hand, she felt it to be incumbent on her to warn Lucilla against the wiles of a charming but impecunious man on the look-out for a rich wife; on the other, she neither wished to destroy Lucilla's innocence, nor—which would be worse—to arouse in the child a rebellious spirit which might, too easily, lead her to flout the authority of her elders, and to encourage Kilbride's advances.

She compromised. She said, with an indulgent little laugh: 'Kilbride's ingratiating manners and lively wit are his stock-in-trade. Pray do not you, my dear, administer to his vanity by adding yourself to the list of his victims! He is an irreclaimable here-and-thereian, and cannot see a personable female without making up to her! I long since lost count of the silly girls left languishing on his account.'

Her words brought a crease between Lucilla's brows. She said hesitantly: 'Perhaps he found that he didn't truly love any of them, ma'am?'

'Or that they were none of them as well-endowed as he had supposed!'

No sooner had she uttered these acid words than she regretted them. Lucilla's eyes flashed, and she said hotly: 'How can you say anything so—so detestable about him, ma'am? I thought he was a friend of yours!'

She ran out of the room, leaving Miss Wychwood with nothing to do but to blame herself bitterly for having been betrayed into saying precisely what she had determined not to say. She could only hope that no malicious tongue had informed Mr Carleton that his ward had been escorted through the town by a man whom he knew to be a gazetted fortune-hunter.

It was an empty hope. On the following morning, she went with Lady Wychwood and Lucilla to the Pump Room. Mrs Stinchcombe, who was seeking a cure for her rheumatism by drinking a glass of the famous water every morning, was there, with both her daughters, and Annis led Lady Wychwood up to her at once, and had the satisfaction of seeing the two ladies fall instantly into very friendly conversation. She left them together while she went across the room to procure a glass of the water from the pumper, and was wending her way back with it to Lady Wychwood's side when she saw Mr Carleton advancing purposefully towards her. She braced herself, but the first words he spoke were quite unalarming. 'Well met, Miss Wychwood!' he said cheerfully. 'Ought I to condole with you? Are you too a martyr to rheumatism?'

'No, indeed, I'm not!' she replied lightly. 'This is for my sister-in-law, not for me! What brings you here this morning, sir?'

'The hope of finding you here, of course. There is something I wish to say to you.'

Her heart sank, but she replied coolly enough: 'Well, you may do so, but first I must give this horrid drink to my sister-in-law. I should like, besides, to present you to her.' Another two steps brought her to Lady Wychwood's side, and she handed the glass to her saying: 'Here you are, my dear! I believe it should be drunk hot, so take hold of your courage and gulp it down immediately!'

Lady Wychwood eyed the potion doubtfully, but obediently took, not a gulp, but a cautious sip. She then took a larger sip, and declared that it was not by half as nasty as Annis had led her to expect.

'By which I collect you to mean that it is not as nasty as they tell me the Harrogate water is! You must let me present Mr Carleton to you: he is Lucilla's uncle, you know!'

Mr Carleton, who had exchanged a brief greeting with Mrs Stinchcombe, bowed, and said that he was happy to make her ladyship's acquaintance. He sounded indifferent rather than happy, and Lady Wychwood, somewhat coldly acknowledging his bow, was much inclined to suspect that her dear Geoffrey

had been mistaken in believing Annis stood in danger of succumbing to this libertine's fascinating arts. It did not appear to
Lady Wychwood that he had any fascinating arts at all: why, he
wasn't even a handsome man! Recalling Annis's past suitors, all
of whom had been blessed with good-looks and distinguished
manners, she began to suspect that Annis had been making
a May-game of her brother, as (regrettably) she too often did.
She could perceive nothing in Mr Carleton that could appeal to
any female as critical and fastidious as Annis, and consequently
unbent towards him, complimenting him on his charming niece,
and saying how much she liked Lucilla.

He bowed again, and said: 'You are too kind, ma'am. Are you
making a long stay in Bath?'

'Oh, no! That is to say, I hardly know, but not more than a
week or two, I think. Are *you* making a long stay, sir?'

'Like you, I hardly know. It depends on circumstances.' He
glanced round, and addressed himself to Annis, saying: 'Spare me a
moment, Miss Wychwood! I wish to consult you—about Lucilla.'

'Certainly! I am quite at your disposal,' said Annis.

He took civil but unsmiling leave of the two other ladies,
and moved apart with Miss Wychwood. No sooner were they
out of tongue-shot of her companions than he said abruptly:
'How came it about that you permitted Kilbride to escort
Lucilla through the town yesterday, ma'am? I thought I had
made my wishes plain to you!'

'My permission was not sought,' she replied frigidly. 'Mr
Kilbride met Lucilla, and her maid, on their way to Laura Place,
and turned back to accompany Lucilla.'

'It hardly seems that the maid was an adequate chaperon.'

'I don't know what you would have had her do,' she said,
nettled. 'It was not as though Kilbride were a stranger! Lucilla
greeted him with pleasure, believing him to be a friend of mine,
and I have no doubt Brigham accepted him as such.'

'In which she was justified!'

She heaved an exasperated sigh. 'Very well! he is a friend of mine, but I am as well aware as you are, Mr Carleton, that he is not a fit friend for an impressionable and quite inexperienced girl, and I shall do my best to keep him at arm's length. In future, when I am unable to accompany her myself I will send her out in the carriage! And when she objects, as object she will, I shall tell her that I am merely obeying your orders!'

'But I haven't given such an unreasonable order!' he said. 'I haven't, in fact, given any order at all.'

'You said that you thought you had made your wishes plain to me, and you might as well have said orders, instead of wishes, for that was what you meant! So detestably top-lofty that you apparently think I must obey your *wishes*, as though I had no mind or will of my own!'

'Well, where Lucilla is concerned I do think you must,' he said. 'Recollect that you took it upon yourself to assume control over her, and not, let me remind you, by any wish of mine! I said then, and I will say again, that I do not think you a fit person to have charge of her.'

'Then I suggest, sir, that you take charge of her yourself!' she said tartly.

'I might have known you would be quick to seize the opportunity to throw me in the close,' he murmured.

She was obliged to laugh. 'I collect that is a piece of pugilistic slang, and I suppose I can guess what it means! I only wish it might prove to be true! It would, I daresay, be useless to tell you that it is not at all the thing to employ cant terms when you are talking to a female!'

'Oh, quite!' he said affably.

'You know, you are perfectly abominable!' she said. 'And far less a fit and proper person to have charge of Lucilla than I am!'

'You can't think how relieved I am that you've realized *that*!' he said.

She cast up her eyes despairingly. 'I had as well level at the moon as try to get a point the better of you!'

'You are mistaken. You tipped me a settler at our very first meeting, my dear!'

'Did I?' she said, wrinkling her brow. 'I can't imagine how I contrived to do so!'

'No. I am unhappily aware of that,' he replied, with a wry smile. 'And this is not the place in which to tell you what I mean!'

Colour rushed into her cheeks, for these words had made his meaning very plain to her. She said hurriedly: 'We seem to have strayed a long way from the point, sir. We were discussing Lucilla's somewhat unfortunate meeting with Denis Kilbride. I shan't attempt to deny that I regret it, but is it, after all, such a great matter that she should have accepted his escort to Mrs Stinchcombe's house? What harm could come of it?'

'More than you think!' he answered. 'I haven't sojourned in Bath for long, but for long enough to have arrived at a pretty fair estimate of the amount of tale-pitching that goes on amongst those known, I believe, as the Bath quizzes! Kilbride's reputation is well-known to them, and I think it of the first importance that Lucilla should not be seen in his company. Tongues are wagging already, and who can say how many of the scandalmongers have friends or relations living in London whom they regale with tit-bits of the local *on dits*? Don't think that it was one of these who dropped a word of warning in my ear! It was Mrs Mandeville, with whom I dined last night!'

'Oh, heavens!' exclaimed Miss Wychwood, dismayed. 'I wouldn't for the world have Mrs Mandeville, of all people, think Lucilla to be a *coming* girl!'

'You have no need to be afraid of that. She doesn't think it, but she knows as well as I do that nothing can do a pretty

innocent more harm than to be seen to encourage the attentions of such men as Kilbride.'

'Oh, nothing! nothing!' said Miss Wychwood fervently. 'I
can assure you that I shall take good care that it doesn't happen
again!' A rather rueful smile touched her lips. She said, not
without difficulty: 'I am afraid she is not—not impervious to his
charm, and I ought perhaps to tell you that I find it very difficult to know how best to combat this. I think—no, I am *sure*
that I took a false step yesterday, when she was telling me about
his escorting her to Laura Place, and how kind and amusing
she thought him: I said—funningly,.of course!—that I had lost
count of the silly girls who had lost their hearts to him, and had
been left languishing. If I had said no more than that, it might
have given her pause, but when she replied that perhaps he
hadn't truly loved any of them I was betrayed into suggesting
that perhaps none of them had been as well-endowed as he
had believed them to be. She—she flew out at me, asked me
how I could say anything so detestable about him, and fairly ran
out of the room. Pray don't rake me down for having said
anything so ill-judged! I have been raking myself down ever
since I said it!'

'Then stop raking yourself down!' he replied. 'I am not concerned with the possibility that Lucilla might fall in love with
him: one doesn't form a lasting passion at her age, and the experience won't harm her. All that concerns me is that she should
not be beguiled into indiscretion.'

'You don't feel—it has occurred to me that *you* might
perhaps say something to Kilbride?'

'My dear girl, it is not in the least necessary that I should do
so. He may flirt with her, but he won't go beyond flirtation,
believe me! He is no coward, but he is as little anxious to risk
a meeting with me, as I am to force one on him. You may
rest assured that I shan't do so, for nothing could be more preju-

dicial to Lucilla's reputation than the scandal *that* would create!
Take that anxious frown off your face! It doesn't become you!
I perceive that Lady Wychwood is about to descend on you,
so we had better part: she clearly feels it to be her duty to come
between us! I wonder what harm she thinks I could do you in
such a public place as this?'

# Eleven

*I*N ASSUMING THAT LADY WYCHWOOD WAS COMING TOWARDS them to protect Annis, Mr Carleton wronged her. She had swallowed the glass of hot water, had enjoyed a comfortable chat with Mrs Stinchcombe, and she now wished to go back to Camden Place, to take Tom for a gentle airing in the crescent-shaped garden which lay between Upper and Lower Camden Place. Not being in the habit of indulging ridiculous fancies, the fear that Mr Carleton could do Annis a particle of bodily harm in the Pump Room never entered her head; and as for the danger of his ingratiating himself with her to her undoing, she thought this equally ridiculous. While she talked to Mrs Stinchcombe, she had contrived to watch, from the tail of her eye, the brief tête-à-tête between Annis and this reputed profligate, and she was perfectly assured that her lord had allowed his brotherly anxiety to overcome his good sense. She was going to occupy herself during the afternoon by writing a soothing letter to him, and she said, as she and Annis left the Pump Room: 'I can't for the life of me conceive, dearest, what can have made Geoffrey take such a maggot into his head as to suppose that there was the least fear of that disagreeable man's making you the object of his gallantry—if gallantry it can be called! I promise you, I mean to give him a *severe* scold, for supposing that you, of all people, could possibly develop a *tendre* for such a brusque, and extremely *ungallant* man!'

'Deplorably rag-mannered, isn't he?' agreed Annis.

'Oh, shockingly! I could see that he had made you as cross as crabs, and positively *quaked* for fear that you would fly up into the boughs, which wouldn't have astonished me, but which would have been a very improper thing to have done in the Pump Room. How unfortunate it is that you are obliged to be on terms with him! Forgive me if I say that I think the sooner he removes Lucilla from your house the better it will be for you! What was he looking so black about?'

'Denis Kilbride,' replied Miss Wychwood, calmly, but with a gleam in her eyes hard to interpret.

'Denis Kilbride?' echoed Lady Wychwood, too much surprised to notice either the gleam, or the little smile that hovered at the corners of Miss Wychwood's mouth. 'Why, what has he to say to anything?'

'Too much!' said Miss Wychwood, with a wry grimace. 'I fear he may be in a fair way towards capturing Lucilla's silly heart, and although that possibility doesn't seem to worry Mr Carleton much, what does worry him, and made him try to ring a peal over me just now, is the circumstance of Kilbride's having escorted Lucilla yesterday all the way from Camden Place to Laura Place. It was unfortunate, for several people saw them, and if you had ever lived in Bath, Amabel, you would know that it is a veritable hotbed of gossip!'

'But surely, Annis, it is perfectly permissible for a gentleman to accompany a girl through the town, in the daytime, and with her maid walking behind, as I don't doubt Lucilla's maid did!' expostulated Lady Wychwood. 'Why, it is quite the thing for a gentleman to take up some young female beside him in his curricle, or his phaeton, or whatever sporting vehicle he happens to be driving! And *without* her maid!'

'Perfectly permissible, my dear, but not if the gentleman is Denis Kilbride! At the best, he is recognized as a dangerous flirt, and at the worst, a confirmed fortune-hunter.'

'Oh, dear!' said Lady Wychwood, sadly shocked. 'I know Geoffrey didn't at all like it when Kilbride was courting you, when we were all three of us in London. He said he was a here-and-thereian; and I do recall that he once said he suspected him of hanging out for a rich wife. I didn't set much store by that, for Geoffrey does sometimes say things he doesn't really mean, when he takes anyone in dislike, and he never desired me not to receive him, or to invite him to my parties. And when, last year, he had been visiting his grandmother, and had ridden over to Twynham to pay his respects to us, Geoffrey received him with perfect complaisance.'

'By that time, Geoffrey knew that there was no fear of my succumbing to Kilbride's wiles,' said Annis, with a touch of cynicism. 'He is everywhere received, even in Bath! In part, this is due to the respect in which old Lady Kilbride is held; and in part because he is regarded as an amusing rattle, whose presence can be depended on to enliven the dullest party. For myself, though I can imagine few worse fates than to be leg-shackled to him, I like him, I invite him to my own parties, I frequently dance with him at the Assemblies. But although—in Geoffrey's opinion—I set too little store by the conventions!—I take care not to see so much of him as to give even the most censorious critic reason to say that I live in his pocket! Because I was well-acquainted with him before I came to reside in Bath, he is thought to be an old friend of mine, and as such his presence at my parties, the free-and-easy terms on which we stand are looked on with indulgence. But although I am no girl, and might be supposed to be past the age of looking for a husband, I should hesitate very much to drive with him, ride with him, or even walk with him. Not because I am not very well able to

check his familiarities, but because I know just how many malicious tongues would start to wag if I were to be seen tête-à-tête
with him! So, with the best will in the world to do so, I cannot
blame Mr Carleton for having raked me down!'

'I consider it to have been excessively impertinent of him,
and I hope you gave him a set-down!' said Lady Wychwood
roundly.

Annis made no reply to this, but it occurred to her that
giving Mr Carleton a set-down was something she had never
yet succeeded in doing. She thought that it would perhaps be as
well if she didn't discuss his character with her sister-in-law, for
she had made the disconcerting discovery that however much
she herself criticized his faults an almost overmastering impulse
to defend them arose in her when anyone else did so. So she
turned the subject by directing Lady Wychwood's attention to a
very pretty bonnet displayed in a milliner's window. The rest
of the walk was beguiled by an animated discussion of all the
latest quirks of fashion, which lasted until they reached Upper
Camden Place, and Lady Wychwood caught sight of her small
son, playing ball in the garden with Miss Farlow. This made her
exclaim: 'Oh, look! Maria has taken Tom into the garden! What
a good, kind creature she is, Annis!'

'I wish I were rid of her!' replied Annis, with considerable
feeling.

Lady Wychwood was shocked. 'Wish you were rid of her?
Oh, no, how can you say so, dearest? I am sure there was never
anyone more amiable, and obliging! You cannot be serious!'

'I am very serious. I find her a dead bore.'

Lady Wychwood thought this over for a moment, and then
said slowly: 'She isn't bookish, of course, and not *clever*, as you are.
And she does talk a great deal, I own. Geoffrey calls her a gabble-
grinder, but gentlemen, you know, don't seem to like *chatty*
females, and even he recognizes her many excellent qualities.'

'Are you trying to hoax me into thinking that you don't find her a bore?' demanded Annis incredulously.

'No, indeed! I mean, I truly don't. Oh, sometimes she does chatter rather too much, but, in general, I enjoy talking with her because she is interested in the things which don't interest you. *Little* things, such as household matters, and the children, and—and new recipes, and a host of things of that nature!' She hesitated, and then said simply: 'You see, dearest, I'm not clever, as you are! Indeed, I often wonder whether you don't find *me* a dead bore!'

Annis instantly disclaimed, and warmly enough to win a grateful smile from Lady Wychwood; but in her secret heart she knew that fond though she was of her gentle sister-in-law she did find most of her conversation insipid.

'What I like in her so much,' pursued Lady Wychwood, in a thoughtful tone, 'is the way she enters into all one's *chiefest* concerns, as one couldn't expect even Geoffrey to do, gentlemen not being able to share one's anxieties about household matters, and croup, and the red gum. And the way she busies herself with any small difficulty that arises, without having been asked to do so—which I hope I should never do! I cannot tell you what a support she was to me when I arrived here, with poor little Tom frantic with the toothache! She went with us to Mr Westcott's, and actually held Tom's hands down—which I, alas, had not the resolution to do—when he pulled out the offending tooth.'

'Sister,' said Annis, solemnly, but with wickedly dancing eyes, 'I have long wanted to make you a present of real value, and you have now shown me how I may do it! I will bestow Maria upon you!'

'How can you be so absurd?' said Lady Wychwood laughingly. 'As though I would dream of taking her away from you!'

No more was said, Tom, by this time, having seen his mother, and run to the railings to greet her. She entered the garden, and

Annis went on by herself to the house. Lucilla was spending the rest of the day with the Stinchcombes, and as Mrs Stinchcombe had promised to have her escorted back to Camden Place in time for dinner she felt herself relieved of responsibility. She could not help feeling glad of it, for not only was the entertainment of a lively seventeen-year-old a more onerous charge than she had foreseen, but what Mr Carleton had said to her had made her realize that a period of quiet reflection was her most immediate need. Unless she had been wholly mistaken in the meaning of his cryptic utterance in the Pump Room, she could not doubt that he had the intention of making her an offer of marriage. It would have been false to have said that such a notion had never before occurred to her: it had occurred, but only as a suspicion, which she had been able, without very much difficulty, to banish from her mind. Now that the suspicion had been confirmed she felt that she had been taken by surprise, and was vexed by the realization that she was shaken quite out of her calm self-possession, and was suffering all the fluttering uncertainties of a girl in her first Season. She had been for so long a single woman that it had become a habit with her to think herself beyond marriageable age, and even more beyond the age of falling in love. It was a shock to discover that this had suddenly become a question open to doubt, and that it was a matter for doubt made her out of reason cross with herself, for she ought, surely, to be old enough and wise enough to know her own mind. But the melancholy truth was that she didn't know it. She told herself, in a scolding way, that it ought to be obvious to her that Mr Carleton possessed none of the attributes (except fortune, which was of no interest to her) which could be supposed to make him an acceptable suitor to a lady who had had many suitors, nearly all of whom had been blessed with good-looks, excellent address, polished manners, and a considerable degree of charm. To none of these attributes could Mr

Carleton lay claim: it made her smile to think of setting even one of them to his credit; and as she smiled the thought darted through her mind that perhaps it was his lack of social grace which attracted her. It seemed absurd that this should be so, but it was undeniable that not the most charming of her suitors had so much as scratched her heart. She thought that if she had been left without the means to support herself she might have accepted an offer from that particular man, for she liked him very well, and felt reasonably sure that he would be an amiable husband; but when he did make her an offer she unhesitatingly declined it; and, far from regretting her decision, was thankful that her circumstances did not compel her to accept it. She had been sorry for him, because he had been desperately in love with her, and had exerted himself in every imaginable way to win her regard. The only effect her snubs had seemed to have on him had been to make him redouble his efforts to please her. She thought, recollecting his courtship, that he had been quite her most assiduous suitor; and as she remembered the attentions he had lavished on her she instantly contrasted him with Mr Carleton, and gave an involuntary chuckle. No two men could be more unlike. The one had employed every art known to him to bring his courtship to a successful conclusion; the other employed no arts at all. In fact, thought Miss Wychwood judicially, he seemed to lose no opportunity to alienate her. He was ruthlessly blunt, too often brusque to the point of incivility, paid her no extravagant compliments, and showed no disposition to go out of his way to please her. A very odd courtship—if courtship it was—and why he should have seriously disturbed her tranquillity, which, since she was too honest to deceive herself, she owned that he had done, was a problem to which she could discover no answer, the only solution which presented itself to her, that her well-regulated mind had become disordered, being wholly unacceptable to her. She wondered if she was refining too much on the few signs he had given of having fallen in love with her, whether they betokened nothing more than a wish to engage her in a flirtation. This idea no sooner occurred to her than she dismissed it: he had never tried to flirt with her, and the indifference of manner which characterized him did not belong to a man bent on idle dalliance. She thought that the best thing for her peace of mind would be for him to go back to London; and instantly realized that she did not wish him to do so. But she found herself unable to decide whether she wished to become his wife, or what she was to say if he did propose to her. She had always supposed that if ever she had the good fortune to meet the man destined to reach her heart she would recognize him immediately, but it seemed that either she had been mistaken in this belief, or that he was not that man.

It was with these tangled thoughts jostling against each other in her head that she joined Lady Wychwood and Miss Farlow to partake of a light luncheon, but she was too well-bred to allow the least sign of her mental perturbation to appear either in her face or in her manner. To invite anxious questions which she had no intention of answering would be to show a lamentable want of conduct: no woman of consideration wore her heart on her sleeve, or made her guests uncomfortable by behaving in such a way as to lead them to think she was blue-devilled, or suffering from a severe headache. So neither Lady Wychwood nor Miss Farlow suspected that she was not in spirits. She listened to their everyday chit-chat, responded to such remarks as were addressed to her, made such comments as occurred to her, all with her lovely smile which hid from them her entire lack of interest in what they were discussing. It was second-nature to her to maintain a boring conversation with the better part of her mind otherwise, but she would have been hard put to it when she rose from the table to tell an enquirer what had been the subjects under discussion.

It was Lady Wychwood's custom to retire to her own bed-chamber for an hour's repose in the early afternoon before spending the next hour with her much loved offspring; Miss Farlow, for reasons which she frequently gave at tedious length, never rested during the daytime, and brightly detailed the several tasks which awaited her. They ranged from mending a broken toy for Tom to darning a sad rent in the flounce of one of her dresses. 'How I came to tear it I cannot for the life of me conjecture!' she said. 'I haven't the smallest recollection of having caught it on anything, and I am persuaded I couldn't have done so without noticing it, and I am always careful to raise my skirt when I go upstairs so I cannot have trodden on it, for even if I did I should very likely have fallen, which I did once, when I was young and thoughtless. And I must have noticed *that*, for I daresay I should have bruised myself. Yes, and talking of bruises,' she added earnestly, 'it has me in a puzzle to know how it comes about that one can bruise oneself without having the least recollection of having done so! It seems to me to be most extraordinary that this should be so, for one would suppose it *must* have hurt one when it happened, but it is so. I well remember—'

But what it was she well remembered Miss Wychwood never knew, for she slipped away at this point, and sought refuge in her book-room, with the intention of dealing with her accounts. She did indeed make a determined effort to do so, but she made slow progress, because her mind wandered in an exasperating way which put her out of all patience with herself. Mr Carleton's swarthy countenance, and his trenchant voice kept on obtruding themselves so that she continually lost count in the middle of a column of figures, and was obliged to start adding it up again. After she had arrived at three different answers to the sum, she was so cross that she uttered in a far from ladylike manner: 'Oh, the devil fly away with you! You needn't think I like you, for I don't! I hate you!'

She bent again to her task, but ten minutes later Mr Carleton again intruded upon her, this time in person. Limbury came into the room, carefully shutting the door behind him, and informed her that Mr Carleton had called, and begged the favour of a few words with her. She was immediately torn between conflicting emotions: she did not wish to see him; there was no one whom she wished to see more. She hesitated, and Limbury said, in deprecating accents: 'Knowing that you was busy, Miss Annis, I informed him of the circumstance, and ventured to say that I doubted if you was at home to visitors. But Mr Carleton, miss, is regrettably not one to take a hint, and instead of leaving his card with me, and going away, he desired me to convey to you the tidings that he had come to see you on a matter of considerable importance. So I agreed to do so, thinking that it was on some question concerning Miss Lucilla.'

'Yes, it must be, of course,' replied Miss Wychwood, with all her usual calm. 'I will join him immediately.'

Limbury coughed in a still more deprecating manner, and disclosed that he had been obliged to leave Mr Carleton in the hall. Encountering an astonished stare from Miss Wychwood, he explained this extraordinary lapse by saying: 'I was on the point, Miss Annis, of conducting him upstairs to the drawing-room, as I hope I have no need to tell you, when he stopped me by asking me in his—his forthright way if there was any danger of his finding Miss Farlow there.' He paused, and a slight quiver disturbed the schooled impassivity of his countenance, which Miss Wychwood had no difficulty in interpreting as barely repressed sympathy for a fellow-man faced with the prospect of encountering her garrulous cousin. He continued smoothly: 'I was obliged to tell him, Miss Annis, that I believed Miss Farlow to be occupied with some stitchery there. Upon which, he desired me to carry his message to you, and said that he would await your answer in the hall. What would you wish me to tell him, miss?'

'Well, I am very busy, but no doubt you are right in thinking he has come to consult with me on some business connected with Miss Lucilla,' she replied. 'I had better see him, I suppose. Pray show him in!'

Limbury bowed and withdrew, reappearing a minute later to usher Mr Carleton into the room. Miss Wychwood rose from the chair behind her desk, and came forward, holding out her hand, and with a faint questioning lift to her brows. Nothing in her demeanour or in her voice could have given the most acute observer reason to suspect that her pulses had quickened alarmingly, and that she was feeling strangely breathless. 'For the second time today, how do you do, sir?' she said, with a faintly mocking smile. 'Have you come to issue some further instructions on how I am to treat Lucilla? Ought I to have asked your permission before permitting her to spend the day with the Stinchcombes? If that is the case, I *do* beg your pardon, and must hasten to assure you that Mrs Stinchcombe has promised to see her safely restored to me!'

'No, my sweet hornet,' he retorted, 'that is not the case! I've no wish to see her, and I don't care a straw for her present whereabouts, so don't try to stir coals, I beg of you!' He shook hands with her as he spoke, and continued to hold hers in a strong grasp for a moment or two, while his hard, penetrating eyes scanned her countenance. They narrowed as he looked, and he said quickly: 'Did I hurt you this morning? I didn't mean to! It was the fault of my unfortunate tongue: pay no heed to it!'

She drew her hand away, saying as lightly as she could: 'Good God, no! I hope I have too much sense to be hurt by the rough things you say!'

'I hope so, too,' he said. 'If my tongue is not to blame, what has happened to cast you into the doldrums?'

'What in the world makes you think I have been cast into the doldrums, Mr Carleton?' she asked, in apparent amusement, sitting down, and inviting him with a slight gesture to follow her example.

He ignored this, but stood looking down at her frowningly, in a way which she found disagreeably disconcerting. After a short pause, he said: 'I can't tell that. Suffice it that I know something or someone has thrown a damp on your spirits.'

'Well, you are mistaken,' she said. 'I am not in the doldrums, but I own I am somewhat out of temper, because I can't make my wretched accounts tally!'

His rare smile dawned. 'Let me see whether I can do so!'

'Certainly not! That would be to acknowledge defeat! I wish you will sit down, and tell me what has brought you here!'

'First, to inform you that I am returning to London tomorrow,' he replied.

Her eyes lifted swiftly to his face, and as swiftly sank again. She could only hope that they had not betrayed the dismay she felt, and said at once: 'Ah, you have come to take leave of us! Lucilla will be very sorry to have missed you. If only you had told us that you were going back to London she would certainly have stayed at home to say goodbye to you!'

'Unnecessary! I don't expect to be absent from Bath for very many days.'

'Oh! She will be glad of that, I expect.'

'Doubtful, I think! Lucilla's sentiments upon this occasion don't interest me, however. Will *you* be glad of it?'

Something between panic and indignation seized her: panic because a proposal was clearly imminent, and she was as far as ever from knowing how she was to respond to it; indignation because she was unaccustomed to dealing with sledge-hammer tactics, and strongly resented them. He was an impossible creature, and the only fit place for any female crazy enough to consider becoming his wife for as much as a second was Bedlam. Indignation made it possible for her to say, with a tiny shrug, and in a voice whose indifference matched his own: 'Why, certainly, Mr Carleton! I am sure we shall both of us be happy to see you again.'

'Oh, for God's sake—!' he uttered explosively. 'What the devil has Lucilla to do with it?'

She raised her brows. 'I imagine she has everything to do with it,' she said coldly.

He apparently managed to get the better of his spleen, for he gave a short laugh, and replied: 'No, not everything, but certainly a good deal. I am going to London to try if I can discover amongst my numerous cousins one who will be willing to take charge of her until her come-out next year.'

Her eyes flashed, colour flooded her cheeks, and she said, in a shaking voice: 'I see! To be sure, it is stupid of me to feel surprise, for you have repeatedly informed me that you consider me to be totally unfit to take care of Lucilla. Alas, I had flattered myself into thinking that your opinion of my fitness had undergone a change! But that, of course, was before you flew up into the boughs when you learned that Denis Kilbride had accompanied Lucilla to Laura Place! I perfectly understand you!'

'No, you do not understand me, and I shall be grateful to you if you will stop ripping up grievances and flinging them in my teeth!' he said savagely. 'My decision to remove Lucilla from your charge has nothing whatsoever to do with *that* episode! I don't deny that I thought, at the outset, that you were not a fit person to act as her chaperon. I thought it, and I said it, and I still think it, and I still say it, but not for the same reason! I find it intolerable that anyone as young and as beautiful as you are should set up as a duenna, behaving as though you were a dowager when you should be going to balls and assemblies for the pleasure of dancing till dawn, not to spend the night talking to the real dowagers, and keeping a watchful eye on a silly chit of a girl only a few years younger than you are yourself!'

'Lucilla is twelve years younger than I am, and I *frequently* dance the night through—'

'Don't try to humbug me, my girl!' he interrupted. 'I was cutting my wisdoms when you were sewing samplers! I know very well when dancing comes to an end at the New Assembly Rooms. Eleven o'clock!'

'Not at the Lower Rooms!' she protested. 'They—they keep it up till midnight there! Besides, there are private balls, and—and picnic parties, and—and all manner of entertainments!' She perceived by the curl of his lip that he was not impressed by this list of Bath gaieties, and said defiantly: 'And in any event if I choose to chaperon Lucilla it is quite my own concern!'

'On the contrary! It is mine!' he said.

'I acknowledge that you have the right to do as you think best for Lucilla, but you have no right to dictate to me, sir! And, what is more,' she added wrathfully, 'you need not try to ride rough-shod over me, so don't think it!'

That made him laugh. 'I am more likely to box your ears!'

She was spared the necessity of answering by the appearance on the scene of Miss Farlow, who peeped into the room at that moment, saying: 'Are you here, dear Annis? I just looked in to tell you that I am obliged to—Oh! I didn't know you had a visitor! I do trust I don't intrude! If I had had the least suspicion that you were not alone I shouldn't have dreamt of disturbing you, for it is of no consequence, only that I find myself obliged to run into the town to purchase some more thread, and so I just popped in to ask you if you happen to need anything your-self. Oh, how do you do, Mr Carleton? I daresay you are wish-ing me at Jericho so I won't stay another moment! I shall just look into the nursery before I go out, Annis, because we think poor Baby is cutting another tooth, and I mean to ask dear Lady Wychwood if she would wish me to purchase some teething-powder, though I daresay she has some by her, or, if she hasn't, you may depend upon it Nurse will have brought some from Twynham. Well! I mustn't interrupt you for another instant, must I? Of course, I shouldn't have come in if I had known that Mr Carleton was with you, no doubt to consult with you about Lucilla. So, if you are quite sure there is nothing I can do for you in Gay Street—not that I am not perfectly ready to go further, as I hope I need not assure you!'

Miss Wychwood stemmed the flow at this point by saying firmly: 'No, Maria, there is nothing you can do for me, thank you. Mr Carleton has come to talk privately to me about Lucilla's affairs, and I am afraid you *are* interrupting us! So pray go away to do your shopping without any more ado!'

She had been in a state of seething fury when Miss Farlow had come into the room, but the expression on Mr Carleton's face had turned fury into amusement. He looked as though it would have afforded him the maximum amount of pleasure to have wrung Miss Farlow's neck, and this struck Miss Wychwood as being so funny that a bubble of laughter grew in her which she had the greatest difficulty in suppressing.

The door was hardly shut behind Miss Farlow when he demanded, in the voice of one driven to the extreme limit of his patience: 'How you can endure to have that prattle-bag living with you is beyond my comprehension!'

'Well, I must confess that it is beyond mine too,' she answered, allowing her mirth to escape her.

'What the devil possessed her to come in babbling about thread and teething powder when she must have known you were not alone?'

'Rampant curiosity,' she replied. 'She must always discover whatever may be going on in the house.'

'Good God! Send her packing!' he said peremptorily.

'I wish I might! But since the world thinks that I should sink myself beneath reproach if I didn't employ a respectable female to act as my chaperon I fear I can't. It would be too brutal to dismiss her, for she *means* well, and what possible reason could I give for getting rid of her?'

'That you are about to be married!'

She was growing accustomed to his abrupt utterances, but this one came as a shock to her. She stared at him with startled eyes, and only managed to say faintly: 'Pray don't be absurd!'

'I am not being absurd. Marry me! I'll engage myself to keep you safe from all such pernicious bores as your cousin.'

'You *are* being absurd!' she declared, in a much stronger voice. 'Marry you to escape from poor Maria? I never heard anything to equal it! You must be out of your mind!'

'No—unless to be deep in love is to be out of one's mind! I am, you see. After all these years, to have found the woman I had come to think didn't exist—!' He saw that she was looking at him in considerable astonishment, and exclaimed, with a rueful crack of laughter: 'Oh, my God, what a mull I'm making of it! I deserve that you should refuse ever to speak to me again, don't I?'

'Yes,' she said candidly.

'I can't make elegant speeches. I wish I could! If I could find the words to tell you what's in my heart—!' He broke off, and took a quick turn about the room.

'Do you always find it impossible to make elegant speeches?' she asked. 'I can't bring myself to believe that, sir. You must have made many pretty speeches in your time—unless report has wronged you.'

'To the incognitas? That's a very different matter!' he said impatiently. 'A man don't form a connection with a convenient with the same feelings as he has when he forms a lasting passion for the one woman in the world he wishes to make his wife!' He came to a sudden stop in his agitated perambulation, and directed a look of fierce enquiry at her, saying incredulously:

'Good God, are you holding it against me that I have frequently had some high-flyer in keeping?'

This blunt reference to his checkered career, coupled as it was with his cool acceptance of her understanding of the meaning of such terms as he had used to describe his mistresses, pleased rather than shocked her, and certainly did him no harm in her eyes. Contrasting his attitude with her brother's, she thought it was as refreshing as it was unusual, and, insensibly, she warmed to him. The abominable Mr Carleton was not one either to credit unmarried ladies with an innocence very few of them possessed, or to subscribe to the convention that prohibited a gentleman from mentioning in their presence any subject that could bring a blush to their cheeks. She liked this, but saw no reason why she should say so. Instead, she said, with unruffled composure: 'By no means, sir! Your past life concerns no one but yourself. But if I were to accept your extremely obliging offer your future life would also concern me, and, at the risk of offending you, I must tell you that I have no ambition to marry a rake.'

He did not seem to be at all offended; rather, he seemed to be amused. He heard her out in appreciative silence, but when she came to an end, he adjured her not talk like a ninnyhammer. 'Which, dear love, I know well you are not! You should know better than to suppose I should continue in that way of life if I were married to you. I shouldn't even wish to! No man who had the inestimable good fortune to call you his wife would ever desire any other woman. If you don't know that, there is nothing I can do or say to convince you!'

She felt her cheeks growing hot, and instinctively pressed her hands to them. 'You are very obliging, sir, but—but sadly mistaken, I fear! I am not the—the paragon you seem to think me!' she stammered. 'I—I know that I am generally held to be quite pretty, but—'

'If ever I heard such a whisker!' he interjected. 'Generally held to be *quite pretty*? You are generally held to be a diamond of the first water, my girl! And don't tell me you don't know it, for I am a hard man to bridge, and I give you fair warning that you'll catch cold if you try to gammon me!'

She smiled. 'That I can well believe! Try, in your turn, to believe me when I say that I don't admire my kind of—oh, beauty, for want of a better word!'

'There isn't one,' he said. 'I have a wide experience of beauties, but during the course of a misspent career I have never set eyes on a woman as beautiful as you are.'

She tried to laugh, and said: 'It is clearly midsummer moon with you! I think you have fallen in love with my face, Mr Carleton!'

'Oh, no!' he responded, without hesitation. 'Not with your face, or with your elegant figure, or your graceful carriage, or with any of your obvious attributes! Those I certainly admire, but I didn't fall in love with any of them, any more than I fell in love with Botticelli's Venus, greatly though I admire her beauty!'

She knit her brows, in honest bewilderment. 'But you know nothing about me, Mr Carleton! How could you, on so short an acquaintance?'

'I don't know *how* I could: I only know that I do. Don't ask me *why* I love you, for I don't know that either! You may be sure, however, that I don't regard you as a valuable piece to be added to my collection!'

This acid reference to Lord Beckenham's determined courtship drew a smile from her, but she said: 'You have paid me so many extravagant compliments, that I need not scruple to tell you that yours is not the first offer I have received.'

'I imagine you must have received many.'

'Not many, but several. I refused them all, because I preferred my—my independence to marriage. I think I still do. Indeed, I am almost sure of it.'

'But not quite sure?'

'No, not quite sure,' she said, in a troubled tone. 'And when I ask myself what you could give me in exchange for my liberty, which is very dear to me, I—oh, I don't know, I don't know!'

'Nothing but my love. I have wealth, but that's of no consequence. If it were—if you were purse-pinched—I would never offer you any of my possessions as inducements. If you marry me, it must be because you wish to spend your life at my side, not for any other reason! There are many things I can give you, but I don't mean to dangle them before you, in the hope that you might be bribed into marrying me.' His eyes gleamed. 'You would send me to the rightabout in two shakes of a lamb's tail if I did, wouldn't you, my dear hornet? And I wouldn't blame you!'

'It would certainly be carrying incivility to the verge of insult!' she said, trying for a lighter note. 'There's no saying, however, that you might be able to bribe me by promising never to snap my nose off!'

He smiled, and shook his head. 'I never make empty promises!'

She could not help laughing, but she said: 'A grim warning, in fact! I begin to suspect, sir, that you already wish you hadn't made me an offer, and are now trying to frighten me into refusing it!'

'You know better!' he said. '*Could* I frighten you? I doubt it! It would be an easy matter to promise never to be out of temper, but I mean you to find me as good as my word, and the deuce is in it that I have an untoward disposition, and a hasty temper!'

'Yes, I have noticed that!'

'You could hardly have failed to!' He hesitated, and then said roughly: 'I've several times hurt you—snapping your nose off, as you say—but never without wishing that I hadn't done so. But when I'm put out my tongue utters cutting things before I can check it!'

'What an admission to make!'

'Shocking, ain't it? It cost me something to make it, but I like pound dealing, and I won't attempt to fob myself off on to you with court-promises.' She did not reply to this, and, after a moment, he said: 'Have I made you take me in dislike? Be frank with me, my dear!'

'No—oh, no!' she said. 'I too like pound dealing, and I *will* be frank with you. I don't know if you can understand—or think that I must be indulging a distempered freak—but the truth is that my mind is all chaos!' She got up jerkily, and again pressed her hands to her cheeks, saying with an uncertain little laugh: 'I beg your pardon! I must sound detestably missish!'

'I think I do understand. You have persuaded yourself into the belief that you prefer to live alone—and that, if the alternative was to live with your brother and sister-in-law, is perfectly understandable. You have grown so much accustomed to your single state that to change it seems to you unthinkable. But you are thinking of it! That's why your mind is all chaos. If you felt that to continue to live alone would be infinitely preferable to living with me, you would have refused to marry me without an instant's hesitation. Was your mind thrown into chaos when Beckenham proposed to you? Of course it wasn't! You regard him with indifference. But you don't regard me with indifference! I've taken you by surprise, and I am threatening to turn your beautifully ordered life upside-down, and you don't know whether you would like it or loathe it.'

'Yes,' she said gratefully. 'You do understand! It's true that I don't regard you with indifference, but it is such a big step to take—such an important step—that you must grant me a little time to think it over carefully before I answer you. Don't—don't press me to answer you now! Pray do not!'

'No, I won't press you,' he said, unexpectedly gentle. He took her hands, and smiled into her eyes. 'Don't look so fussed and bewildered, you absurd child! And don't turn me into a Bluebeard while I am away! I have a damnably quick temper, I have no agreeable talents, and very little regard for the proprieties, but I'm not an ogre, I assure you!' His clasp on her hands tightened; he raised them to his lips, kissed them, and released them, and went out of the room without another word.

# Twelve

*I*T WAS LONG BEFORE MISS WYCHWOOD WAS ABLE TO REGAIN some measure of composure, and longer still before she could try to unravel the tangle of her thoughts. Never before had she been confronted with any question concerned with her life which she had experienced the least difficulty in answering, and it vexed her beyond bearing that a proposal from Mr Carleton should have so disastrously overset the balance of her mind as to have made it impossible for her to consider it with the calm judgment on which she had hitherto prided herself. The hardest question which had confronted her had been whether or not to remove from Twynham, and to carve a life for herself; but when she recalled what had been her sentiments on this occasion she knew that the only difficulty which had then made her hesitate had been a natural reluctance either to offend her brother, or to wound his gentle spouse. She had never had a doubt of her own sentiments, nor of the wisdom of her ultimate decision. Nor had she experienced the slightest heart burning when she had refused the many offers of marriage which had been made to her, though several of them had been (as she remembered, with an inward but reprehensibly saucy smile) extremely flattering. Endowed as she was with beauty, an impeccable lineage, and a handsome fortune, she had taken the ton by storm in her very first Season, and might, at this moment, have been married to the heir to a dukedom had she been content to marry for the sake of a great position, and to have let love go by the board. But she had not been so content, and she had never regretted her decision to refuse the young Marquis's proposal. Geoffrey, of course, had been shocked beyond measure, and had prophesied that she would end her days an old maid. That dismal prospect had not at all dismayed her: she was very sure that, comfortably circumstanced as she was, it would be far better to remain single than to marry a man for whom she felt nothing more than a mild liking. She was still sure of it, but she was well aware that there was nothing mild about her feeling for Mr Carleton. No man had ever before held such power to sway her emotions from one extreme to another, making her feel at one moment that she hated him, and at the next that she liked him much too well for her peace of mind. It was easy enough to understand why she should so often hate him; nearly impossible to know what it was in him that made her feel that if he were to go out of it her life would become a blank. Trying to solve this mystery, she recalled that he had told her not to ask him why he loved her, because he didn't know; and she wondered if that was the meaning of love: one might fall in love with a beautiful face, but that was a fleeting emotion: something more was needed to inspire one with an enduring love, some mysterious force which forged a strong link between two kindred spirits. She was conscious of feeling such a link, and could not doubt that Mr Carleton felt it too, but why it should exist between them she was wholly unable to discover. They were for ever coming to cuffs, and surely kindred spirits didn't quarrel? Surely there ought never to be any differences of opinion between them? No sooner had she put this question to herself than she thought, involuntarily: 'How very dull it would be!' It made her laugh softly to picture herself and Mr Carleton living together in perfect agreement, and suddenly it occurred to her that it would make him laugh too—if it didn't make him say *How mawkish!* which, in all probability it would.

She had begged him not to demand an answer from her until she had had time to think the matter over; she had told him that the step he was asking her to take was too big a one to be taken without careful consideration. It was true, but even as she had said it the realization had darted into her head that it was not the nature of her sentiments which required consideration, but other and more worldly matters which would arise if she married Mr Carleton. They might be relatively unimportant, but they were, in their degree, of some importance. Foremost amongst them was the knowledge that her brother would be most violently opposed to such a marriage. He would do all that lay within his power to dissuade her from marrying a man whom he not only disliked, but of whom he unequivocally disapproved. He would not succeed, but it was possible that he might sever all connection between his household and hers; and that was a prospect she found it hard to face. She had set up for herself because she had found that he and she were continually chafing one another, but she had been careful to do so without wounding him by betraying the real cause of her removal from Twynham. They were unable to live in amity together, but they were bound by ties of family affection, and although these might be loose they existed, and she knew that it would give her great pain if they were to be broken. One could not lightly cut oneself off from one's home and one's family. And if Geoffrey did cast her off, it must inevitably redound to Mr Carleton's discredit, and that was a consequence she would find it very hard to bear.

Then there was the question of being obliged to give up her freedom, to turn her life upside-down, as he had himself said, to submit to his judgment, and how was she to know that he would not prove to be a domestic tyrant? He was certainly of an autocratic disposition. But then she remembered how well (and how unexpectedly) he had understood her jumbled thoughts, and with what sympathetic compassion he had refrained from pressing her to give him an answer, and she decided that however autocratically he might express himself he was no tyrant.

By this time she had reached the point where she was forced to own that she was in love with Mr Carleton, but for no discoverable reason. She thought, disgustedly, that she was behaving like a silly schoolgirl, and that it was a very good thing that he was going away. Probably she would find that she went on quite happily without him, in which case it would be a sure sign that she was not in love, but merely infatuated. So the wisest thing she could do would be to put him out of her mind. After which, she continued to think about him until Jurby came in to tell her severely that it wanted only ten minutes till dinner-time, and if she didn't come up to change her dress immediately she would be late. 'Which is not like you, Miss Annis! A full half-hour have I been waiting for you!'

Miss Wychwood said guiltily that she had been too busy to notice the time, thrust her accounts, on which she had done no work at all, into a drawer, and meekly went upstairs with her stern henchwoman. An attempt to dissuade Jurby from brushing her glowing locks, and pinning them up afresh, failed. 'I have my pride to consider, miss, and permit you to go down with your hair looking as though you had come backwards through a bush I will not do!' said Jurby.

So it was ten minutes after the dinner-bell had sounded before Miss Wychwood hurried down to the drawing-room, where she found her guests patiently awaiting her. She apologized, saying, with her lovely smile: 'I *do* beg your pardon, Amabel! So rag-mannered of me to have kept you waiting! I have been busy all the afternoon, and never noticed how the time was slipping by. I've been making up my accounts, and an errant shilling persisted in going astray!'

'Oh, and I interrupted you, didn't I, dear Annis?' exclaimed Miss Farlow remorsefully. 'I am sure it is no wonder that you should have lost count of your shillings! The only wonder is that you should be able to count them up at all, for *I* can never do so! I daresay it would divert you excessively if I were to tell you of the ridiculous mistakes I make in my addition. Not but what you had already been interrupted when I burst in on you, which, I hope you know me well enough to believe, I would never have done if I had known you had a visitor with you!'

'Yes, Mr Carleton called,' replied Miss Wychwood smoothly. 'Good-evening, Ninian!'

Young Mr Elmore was wearing for the first time a new and beautiful pair of Hessians which had been made for him by the first bootmaker in Bath, and he could not resist the urge to draw attention to their shining magnificence, which he did by begging his hostess to forgive him for coming to dine with her in boots. 'Which is not at all the thing, of course, but I thought you would excuse it, because I am engaged with a party of friends this evening, and it is not a *dress*-party. No ladies, I mean, or dancing, or anything of that sort!'

'*I* see!' said Miss Wychwood, twinkling at him. 'Just a few choice spirits! Well, don't get taken up by the Watch!'

He grinned, and blushed. 'No, no, nothing of that nature!' he assured her. 'Only a—a small jollification, ma'am!'

'Whatever brought my uncle here?' wondered Lucilla. 'I thought I saw you talking to him in the Pump Room, ma'am!'

'Very true: you did!' responded Miss Wychwood. 'But as he didn't then know that he would be obliged to go up to London tomorrow, for a few days, he came to inform us of it. He was sorry not to find you at home, but I promised to make his apologies to you!'

Lucilla's eyes widened in amazement. '*Well!*' she gasped. 'Whoever heard of his being so civil?' She added shrewdly, and with a mischievous look: 'If he really did say he was sorry not to find me at home, it was a great fib, for he never shows the least wish to see me, and I think it is you he always wished to see!'

'For the pleasure of picking quarrels with me, no doubt!' retorted Miss Wychwood, laughing. 'Shall we go down to dinner now, Amabel?'

Lady Wychwood had looked up quickly at Lucilla's saucy speech, as though struck by a sudden and by no means agreeable suspicion, and Annis was aware that her eyes were fixed on her face. For perhaps the only time in her life she was thankful to Miss Farlow for interrupting, even though Miss Farlow did so merely because she seldom missed an opportunity to give Lucilla a set-down. She said sharply: 'A very odd thing it would be in your uncle if he were to leave Bath without taking leave of dear Miss Wychwood, to whom he has so *much* cause to be grateful! I am sure it isn't wonderful that he should wish rather to see her than you, Miss Carleton, for gentlemen find girls only just out of the schoolroom excessively boring! Indeed, at your age I should never have expected a gentleman to *wish* to see me!'

Lucilla's eyes flashed, and she replied swiftly: 'How fortunate!'

Ninian uttered a choking sound, which he turned into a very unconvincing cough; and Lady Wychwood rose, and said with gentle dignity: 'Yes, do let us go down, dearest, or we shall be in disgrace with your cook. Cooks *always* look black if one keeps dinner waiting, and one cannot blame them, for it must be dreadfully provoking to have one's work spoilt!'

She then recounted a mildly amusing story about a French cook she had once employed, and Annis, grateful to her for bridging the awkward gap, laughed, and led her on to tell a few more anecdotes. Behind them, on the staircase, came Miss

Farlow, muttering to herself. Not much of what she said reached Annis's ears, but such overheard scraps as 'pert minx . . . grossly indulged . . . shocking manners' were enough to give her fair warning that she would be forced to listen to Miss Farlow's outraged complaints before the evening was out.

Lucilla and Ninian brought up the rear. Ninian whispered: 'You abominable little gypsy! You dashed nearly had me in whoops!'

Lucilla jerked up an impatient shoulder, saying under her breath that she didn't care; but at the foot of the stairs she caught up with Annis, who was standing aside to allow Lady Wychwood to precede her into the dining-room, and detained her by tugging a fold of her dress, and said in her ear, as Miss Farlow, in obedience to a sign from Annis, followed Lady Wychwood: 'I'm sorry! I know I ought not to have said it! Don't say I must beg her pardon, because I won't!'

Annis smiled, but held up an admonitory finger, murmuring: 'No, very well, but don't do it again!'

Lucilla followed her into the room in a chastened mood, and for the better part of the meal remained largely silent. But by the time the second course was placed on the table a chance remark made by Ninian put her in mind of something she wanted to ask Annis, and she said impetuously: 'Oh, Miss Wychwood, will you take me to the Dress Ball at the Lower Rooms on Friday?'

'Not without your uncle's permission, my dear—and I doubt very much if he would give it.'

'But he isn't here, so how can I ask him if I may go?' objected Lucilla. 'Besides, even if he was here he would be bound to say that you must be the only judge of what is proper for me to do!'

'Oh, no, not a bit of it! He keeps a stricter watch over you than you think!'

'Well, he needn't know anything about it!' said Lucilla, with something very like a pout.

'I hope you are not suggesting that I should try to conceal from him that I had allowed you to do anything of which I am very certain he would disapprove!' said Miss Wychwood. 'You must remember that he has entrusted you to my care! How very shocking it would be if I were to prove myself unworthy of his trust! You are trying to get me into a scrape, and I beg you won't!'

'No, but I don't see why I shouldn't go to the Dress Ball,' argued Lucilla. 'I have been to *several* private balls, so why may I not attend a public one?'

'I daresay it does seem rather hard to you,' said Miss Wychwood sympathetically, 'but there is a difference between the private parties you've been to and a public ball, believe me! The private parties you've attended have been informal hops, not *balls*; and have been got up for the entertainment of girls, like yourself, who are not yet out. Don't eat me! but I am afraid that if your uncle asked me if it would be proper for you to go to the Friday Dress Ball I should be obliged to say that I didn't think it would be at all the thing for a girl not yet out.'

'No, indeed!' struck in Miss Farlow. 'A very off appearance it would present! In *my* young days—'

Miss Wychwood flickered a warning glance at Lucilla, and silenced her cousin by saying: 'You sound just like my Aunt Augusta, Maria! That is what she was used to say whenever I wanted to do something she disapproved of. And I strongly suspect that it was said to her, and to you too, in *your* young days, and that you found it quite as provoking as I did!'

Miss Farlow opened her mouth to argue this point, but shut it again as she encountered a quelling look from Miss Wychwood which she dared not ignore. Lucilla was not so easily silenced, and continued to harp on the subject until Miss Wychwood lost patience, and said: 'That's enough, child! I daresay Harry Beckenham will be disappointed not to see you at the ball, but he will certainly not be surprised.'

'Yes, he will be!' Lucilla said, firing up. 'I told him I should be there, when he asked me, because I never *dreamed* you wouldn't take me—'

'Oh, do cut line!' interrupted Ninian impatiently. 'You're getting to be a regular jaw-me-dead, Lucy!'

Flushing scarlet, Lucilla prepared to give battle, but Miss Wychwood applied an effective damper by saying that if they wished to quarrel they might do so in the breakfast-parlour, but not at the dinner-table. Ninian, conscience-stricken, instantly begged pardon; but Lucilla was too angry to follow his example. However, she did not venture to pursue the quarrel, so Miss Wychwood was satisfied.

Ninian took his leave as soon as dinner came to an end; and Lucilla, having maintained what she believed to be a dignified silence, but which bore a strong resemblance to a fit of childish sulks, until she found that no one was paying the least attention to her, took herself off to bed before the tea-tray was brought in.

'Very pretty behaviour, upon my word!' said Miss Farlow, with an irritating titter. 'Of course, I knew how it would be from the moment I set eyes on her! I said at the start—'

'You have said more than enough already, Maria!' interrupted Miss Wychwood. 'I hold you entirely to blame for Lucilla's mifti-ness, and wasn't surprised that she lost her temper, and gave you a back-answer! No, don't start again, for I haven't the patience to listen to you!'

Miss Farlow began to cry, and to explain between sobs that it was her sincere affection for her dear Annis which had led her to offend her. 'Not that I meant to offend you, but to see you being imposed on is more than flesh and blood can bear!'

Perceiving that Annis was far from being mollified, Lady Wychwood intervened, and applied herself to the task of soothing Miss Farlow's injured feelings and succeeded so well that Miss Farlow soon stopped crying, accepted a cup of tea, agreed that she had a headache, and allowed herself to be persuaded to retire to bed.

'What a conjuror you are, love!' said Annis, as soon as Miss Farlow had departed. 'You can't think how grateful I am to you! I was within ames-ace of giving her such a rake down as I daresay she has never had in her life!'

'Yes, I could see you were,' replied Lady Wychwood, smiling a little. 'Of course she shouldn't have said what she did to Lucilla, but one can't help feeling sorry for her!'

'I can very easily help it!'

'No, you only say that because she vexed you. Poor Maria! She is so dreadfully jealous of Lucilla! I think she feels that Lucilla has put her nose quite out of joint, and she is one of those who wants to be held in affection—to know that she is valued. And when she thinks you value Lucilla far more highly than you value her it makes her miserably jealous, and then she says foolish things which she doesn't really mean.'

'Such as saying that Lucilla imposes on me!'

'Yes. Nonsensical, of course: Lucilla is just a spoilt child.' She paused, hesitating for a moment or two, and then said apologetically: 'Will you be cross with me if I say that I do think you have indulged her rather too much?'

'No, how should I be?' said Annis, sighing. 'I have come to realize it myself. You see, she had been kept so close by her aunt, never being allowed to go to parties, or to make friends of her own choosing, and never out of her governess's sight that I made up my mind that I would do what I could to make up for the dreary time she had had ever since her mother died. You can't think what satisfaction it gave me when I watched her huge enjoyment of things other girls think the merest commonplace amusements! I suppose I ought to have foreseen that it would go to her head a little. You'll say I ought also to have foreseen that chaperoning a high-spirited and very pretty girl is not an easy task to undertake! I have a melancholy suspicion that Mr Carleton is odiously right when he says I am not a fit person to have charge of his niece!'

'It was uncivil and ungrateful of him to have said it, but I must own that I think it was the truth. I wish very much that he would place her in somebody else's care.'

'Well, you may be easy, for that is what he is going to do. His purpose in coming here today was to inform me of it. I haven't told Lucilla. I am afraid she will violently object to being taken away from me, so I am leaving her uncle to break the news to her. If she runs away, as it is quite likely she will—indeed, she might even elope with Kilbride!—it is Mr Carleton who will bear the responsibility, and not me!'

'Oh, I hope she won't do anything so foolish!' said Lady Wychwood, in a voice of comfortable conviction. 'I understand that you don't wish to give her up, but you should reflect, dearest, that you would be bound to lose her when she comes out next spring, and the longer she lives with you the harder you would find it to part with her. So don't let yourself be thrown into gloom, will you?'

'Good God, no! I shall certainly miss her, for she is a very engaging girl, and I have become attached to her; but to tell you the truth, Amabel, I do find the task of taking care of her rather more irksome than I had thought it would be. If Mr Carleton can discover, amongst his relations, one who is not only willing to receive her into her household, but one whom Lucilla will be happy to live with until her come-out, I shall be perfectly content to relinquish the child into her charge.'

Lady Wychwood said no more, and it was not long before she went away to bed, saying that she didn't know how it was but that Bath air always made her sleepy. Annis soon followed her, but it was some time before she was able to get into bed, because while Jurby was still brushing her hair a knock on the door heralded the entrance of Lucilla, who stood hesitating on the threshold, and stammering: 'I came—I wanted to say something to you—I will come back later!'

She had obviously been crying, and little though Annis wished for any emotional scenes that day she could not bring herself to repulse the girl. She smiled, and held out her hand, saying: 'No, don't do that! Jurby has just finished making me ready for bed. Thank you, Jurby! I shan't need you any more, so I'll bid you goodnight.'

Jurby went away, sharply adjuring Lucilla not to keep Miss Annis up until all hours: 'For she's fagged to death, as anyone can see! And no wonder! Racketting all over at her age!'

'At my age?' exclaimed Annis, with a comical look of dismay. 'Jurby, you wretch, I'm not in my *dotage!* '

'You're old enough to know better than to be on the jaunter from morning till night, miss,' replied Jurby implacably. 'The next thing will be that we shall have people saying you're a regular gadabout!'

This made Miss Wychwood burst out laughing, which had the effect of sending her sternest critic out of the room, saying darkly: 'Mark my words!'

'I wonder which of her words I am to mark?' said Miss Wychwood, still laughing.

'She means that you are quite worn out with taking me about, and oh, *dear* Miss Wychwood, I never meant to wear you out!' declared Lucilla, on a convulsive sob.

'Lucilla, you goose! How *can* you be so absurd? Pray, how old do you think I am? Take care how you answer, for between you, you and Jurby have made me feel that I am dwindling into the grave, and if anyone else dares to tell me that I'm looking hagged I shall go into strong hysterics!'

But it would not do. Lucilla, having passed from the sulks into remorse and indulged in a flood of tears, was in no mood to deny herself the relief of pouring out her contrition into Miss Wychwood's unwilling ears. It was long before she could be persuaded that her momentary lapse had been quite as much Miss Farlow's fault as hers; and when she had at last been brought to accept the assurance that her regrettable, but very understandable breach of the canons of propriety in which she had been reared had not put her beyond pardon, it was only to fall into an orgy of self-blame for having been so forgetful of all she owed Miss Wychwood as to have teased her to take her to the Dress Ball, and to have behaved thereafter as though she had been born in a back-slum.

By the time Miss Wychwood had succeeded in sending her to bed in a more cheerful frame of mind, it was nearly an hour later, and she herself was feeling quite exhausted and was much inclined to crawl into bed without putting on her nightcap. That, of course, would not do at all, and she was tying the strings under her chin when another knock fell on her door, to be immediately followed by Miss Farlow, also in a lachrymose condition, and more than ordinarily garrulous. She had come, she said, to explain to her dear cousin how it had come about that she had allowed her feelings to overcome her. Annis said wearily: 'Pray don't, Maria! I am too tired to listen, and can think of nothing but my bed. It was an unfortunate contretemps, but too much has been said about it already. Let us forget it!'

But this Miss Farlow declared herself unable to do. She would not for the world keep dear Annis from her bed. 'I shan't stay above a minute,' she said, 'But I shouldn't be able to close my eyes all night if I didn't tell you what my feelings are upon this occasion!'

In fact, she stayed for twenty minutes, saying: 'Just one word more!' every time Annis tried to get rid of her; and might have stayed for twenty more minutes had Jurby not stalked in, and informed her, in forbidding accents, that it was high time she went to bed, instead of talking Miss Annis into a headache. Miss Farlow bridled, but she was no match for Jurby, and pausing only to press Annis to take a few drops of laudanum if she found herself unable to sleep, she bade her a fond goodnight and at last went away.

'There's one that has more hair than wit, and a mouthful of pap besides,' Jurby said grimly. 'It's a good thing I didn't go to bed myself, which I never meant to do, not for a moment, for I guessed she'd come fretting you to death! As though you hadn't had enough trouble this day!'

'Oh, Jurby, hush! You shouldn't speak of her like that!' said Annis weakly.

'Nor I wouldn't to anyone but you, miss, but it's coming to something, after all the years I've looked after you, if I can't speak my mind to you. Next you'll be telling me I'd no right to send her packing!'

'No, I shan't,' sighed Annis. 'I'm too thankful to you for having rescued me! I haven't had anything to *trouble* me, but from some cause or another I'm out of temper—probably because my accounts wouldn't come right!'

'And probably for quite another reason, miss!' said Jurby. 'I haven't said anything, and nor I don't mean to, for you know your own business best.' She tucked in the blankets, and began to draw the curtains round the bed. 'Which isn't to say I don't know which way the wind is blowing, for I'm not a cabbage-head, and I haven't lived next and nigh you ever since the day you came out of the nursery without getting to know you better than you think, Miss Annis! Now, you shut your eyes, and go to sleep!'

Miss Wychwood was left wondering how many members of her domestic staff also knew which way the wind was blowing; and fell asleep wishing that she did know her own business best.

The night brought no counsel, but it did restore her to something not too far removed from her usual cheerful calm, and enabled her to support with creditable equanimity the spate of conversation which enlivened (or made hideous) the breakfast-table. For this, Lucilla and Miss Farlow were responsible, Miss Farlow being determined to show that she bore Lucilla no ill-will by chatting to her in a very sprightly way, and Lucilla being anxious to atone for her pert back-answer, by responding to these amiable overtures with equal amiability and the appearance of great interest.

In the middle of one of Miss Farlow's reminiscent anecdotes, a note addressed to Lucilla was brought in by James, who told her that Mrs Stinchcombe's man had been instructed to wait for an answer. It had been written in haste by Corisande, and no sooner had Lucilla read it than she gave a squeak of delight, and turned eagerly to Miss Wychwood. 'Oh, ma'am, Corisande invites me to join a riding-party to Badminton! May I do so? *Pray* don't say I mustn't! I won't tease you—but I want to visit Badminton above all places, and Mrs Stinchcombe sees no objection to the scheme, and it is *such* a fine day—'

'Stop, stop!' begged Miss Wychwood, laughing at her. 'Who am I to object to what Mrs Stinchcombe approves of? Of course you may go, goose! Who is to be of your party?'

Lucilla jumped up, and ran round the table to embrace her. 'Oh, *thank* you, dear, dear Miss Wychwood!' she said ecstatically. 'And will you send someone down to the stables to desire them to bring Lovely Lady up to the house immediately? Corisande writes that if I am permitted to join the party they will pick me up here, on the way, you know! It is Mr Beckenham's party, and Corisande says there will be no more than six of us: just her, and me, and Miss Tenbury, and Ninian, and Mr Hawkesbury! Besides Mr Beckenham himself, of course.'

'Unexceptionable!' said Miss Wychwood, with becoming gravity.

'I made sure you would say so! And I think Mr Beckenham is one of the most obliging people imaginable! Only fancy, ma'am! He arranged this expedition merely because he heard me telling someone in the Pump Room yesterday—I forgot who it was, and it doesn't signify!—that I had *not* visited Badminton, but hoped very much to do so. And the best of it is,' she added exultantly, 'that he will be able to take us inside the house, even if this doesn't chance to be a day when it is open to visitors, because he has frequently been staying there, being a friend of Lord Worcester's, Corisande says!'

She then sped away to hurry into her riding-habit, and before she reappeared Ninian arrived in Camden Place, and, leaving James to take charge of his borrowed hack, came in to tell Miss Wychwood that although he did not above half wish to join Mr Beckenham's party he had consented to do so because he thought it his duty to see that Lucilla came to no harm. 'Which I thought you would wish to be assured of, ma'am!' he said grandly.

It was difficult to imagine what possible harm could threaten Lucilla in such elegant company, but Miss Wychwood thanked him, said that she could now be easy, and that she hoped he would contrive to derive *some* enjoyment from the expedition. She was perfectly aware that he regarded Harry Beckenham with a jealous eye; and guessed, shrewdly, that seeing Lucilla came to no harm was his excuse for accepting an invitation too tempting to be refused. The guess became a certainty when he said, in an off-hand way: 'Oh, well, yes! I daresay I shall! I own, *I should* like to get a glimpse of the Heythrop country! And it isn't everyone who gets the chance to see the house in *a private* way, so it would be a pity to miss it. I believe it is very well worth a visit!'

Miss Wychwood agreed to this, without the glimmer of a smile to betray her amusement at the instant picture this airy speech conjured up of young Mr Elmore's dazzling his family and his acquaintances with casual references to the elegance and the various amenities of a ducal seat, which he had happened to visit, quite privately, of course, during his sojourn at Bath.

She saw the party off, a few minutes later, confident that Mr Carleton in his most censorious mood would be hard put to it to find fault with her for having done so. And if he did find fault with her, she would take great pleasure in reminding him that when he had so abruptly left her rout-party he had said that since Ninian and Harry Beckenham were taking good care of Lucilla there was no need for him to keep an eye on her.

The rest of the morning passed without incident, but shortly after Lady Wychwood had retired for her customary rest, Miss Wychwood, again wrestling with accounts in her book-room, received a most unexpected visitor.

'A Lady Iverley has called to see you, miss,' said Limbury, proffering a salver, on which lay a visiting-card. 'I understand she is Mr Elmore's respected parent, so I have conducted her to the drawing-room, feeling that you would not wish me to say you was not at home.'

'Lady Iverley?' exclaimed Miss Wychwood. 'What in the world—No, of course I don't wish you to tell her I'm not at home! I will come up directly!'

She thrust her accounts aside, satisfied herself, by a brief glance at the antique mirror which hung above the fireplace that her hair was perfectly tidy, and mounted the stairs to the drawing-room.

Here she was confronted by a willowy lady dressed in a cling-ing robe of lavender silk, and a heavily veiled hat. The gown had a demi-train, a shawl drooped from Lady Iverley's shoulders, and a reticule from her hand. Even the ostrich plumes in her hat drooped, and there was a strong suggestion of drooping in her carriage.

Miss Wychwood came towards her, saying, with a friendly smile: 'Lady Iverley? How do you do?'

Lady Iverley put back her veil, and revealed to her hostess the face of a haggard beauty, dominated by a pair of huge, deeply sunken eyes. 'Are you Miss Wychwood?' she asked, anxiously staring at Annis.

'Yes, ma'am,' replied Annis. 'And you, I fancy, are Ninian's mama. I am very happy to make your acquaintance.'

'I knew it!' declared her ladyship throbbingly. 'Alas, alas!'

'I beg your pardon?' said Annis, considerably startled.

'You are so beautiful!' said Lady Iverley, covering her face with her gloved hands.

An alarming suspicion that she was entertaining a lunatic crossed Miss Wychwood's mind. She said, in what she hoped was a soothing voice: 'I am afraid you are not quite well, ma'am; pray won't you be seated? Can I do anything for you? A—a glass of water, perhaps, or—or some tea?'

Lady Iverley reared up her head, and straightened her sagging shoulders. Her hands fell, her eyes flashed, and she uttered, in impassioned accents: 'Yes, Miss Wychwood! You may give me back my son!'

'*Give you back your son?*' said Miss Wychwood blankly.

'You cannot be expected to enter into a mother's feelings, but surely, surely you cannot be so heartless as to remain deaf to her pleadings!'

Miss Wychwood now realized that she was not entertaining a lunatic, but a lady of exaggerated sensibility, and a marked predilection for melodrama. She had never any sympathy for persons who indulged in such ridiculous displays: she considered Lady Iverley to be both stupid and lacking in conduct; but she tried to conceal her contempt, and said kindly: 'I collect that you are labouring under a misapprehension, ma'am. Let me hasten to assure you that Ninian isn't in Bath on my account! Do you imagine him to be in love with me? He would stare to hear you say so! Good God, he regards me in the light of an aunt!'

'Do you take me for a fool?' demanded her ladyship. 'If I had not seen you, I might have been deceived into believing you, but I have seen you, and it is very plain to me that you have ensnared him with your fatal beauty!'

'Oh, fiddle!' said Miss Wychwood, exasperated. 'Ensnared him, indeed! I make all allowances for a parent's partiality, but of what interest do you imagine a green boy of Ninian's age can possibly be to me? As for his having fallen a victim to my *fatal beauty*, as you choose to call it, such a notion has never, I am very sure, entered his head! Now, do, pray, sit down, and try to calm yourself!'

Lady Iverley sank into a chair, but shook her head, and said mournfully: 'I don't accuse you of *wantonly* ensnaring him. Perhaps you didn't realize how susceptible he is.'

'On the contrary!' said Miss Wychwood, laughing. 'I think him very susceptible—but not to the charms of a woman of my age! At the moment I believe him to be dangling after the daughter of one of my closest friends, but there's no saying that by tomorrow he won't be fancying himself in love with some other girl. I think it will be some few years yet before he outgrows the youthful gallantries which he is now enjoying.'

Lady Iverley looked to be unconvinced, but the calm good sense of what had been said had had its effect, and she said far less dramatically: 'Are you telling me that he has cut himself off from his home and his family for the sake of a girl he never laid eyes on until he came to Bath? It isn't possible!'

'No, of course it isn't! Nor do I believe that he has the slightest intention of cutting himself off! Forgive me if I say that if you, and his father, had not set up his bristles by raking him down—really very unjustly!—when he returned to you, he would in all probability be with you today.'

Lady Iverley paid little heed to this, but said tragically: 'I would never have believed he would have behaved so undutifully! He was always such a good, affectionate boy, so considerate, and so devoted to us both! And he hadn't any excuse for leaving us, for his papa granted him *every* indulgence, and never uttered a word of censure when he was obliged to settle his debts! I am persuaded he has fallen under an evil influence.'

'My dear ma'am, it's no such thing! He is merely enjoying a spell of freedom! He is extremely attached to his father, and to you too, of course, but perhaps you have kept him in lamb's wool for rather too long.' She smiled. 'I think he and Lucilla are suffering from the same complaint! Too much anxious care, and too little liberty!'

'Do not speak to me of that wicked girl!' begged Lady Iverley, shuddering. 'I was never so deceived in anyone! And if it is *her* influence which has made my deluded child turn against us I shall not be surprised. A girl who could bring her poor aunt to death's door would be capable of anything!'

'Indeed? I had no notion that things were as serious as that!' said Miss Wychwood, with a satirical smile.

'I fancy you do not understand what it means to have shattered nerves, Miss Wychwood.'

'No, I am happy to say that I don't. But we must trust that the damage done to Mrs Amber's nerves won't prove to be past mending. I daresay she will feel very much better when she is assured that there is no danger of having Lucilla restored to her care.'

'How can you be so unfeeling?' said Lady Iverley, gazing reproachfully at her. 'Have you no sympathy for the agonizing anxiety suffered by Mrs Amber, knowing that the niece to whose well-being she has devoted her life has left her to live with a stranger?'

'I am afraid I haven't, ma'am. To own the truth, I feel that if Mrs Amber had been so excessively anxious she would have come to Bath to discover for herself whether or not I was a proper person to take care of Lucilla.'

'I see that it is useless to say any more to you, Miss Wychwood,' replied Lady Iverley, rising to her feet. 'I shall only beg you to prove your sincerity by sending Ninian back to me.'

'I am sorry to be disobliging,' said Miss Wychwood, 'but I shall do nothing of the sort! A most impertinent piece of meddling that would be! Ninian's concerns are no bread-and-butter of mine. May I suggest that you speak to him yourself? And I think you would be wise not to mention this visit to him, for he would, I am certain, very much resent your having discussed his business with anyone other than his father!'

# Thirteen

HE RIDING-PARTY DID NOT RETURN UNTIL CLOSE ON SIX o'clock, by which time Miss Farlow was begging Miss Wychwood to prepare herself to meet the news of a disaster's having befallen the company, and saying that she had known how it would be from the start, if dear Annis permitted Lucilla to go off with a set of heedless young people. As two middle-aged and far from heedless grooms had accompanied the party, this description of it was singularly inept; but when Lady Wychwood placidly reminded her of this circumstance she only shook her head and demanded of what use two grooms could be? She was very sure that dear Annis must be excessively anxious, however bravely she tried to hide it.

Miss Wychwood was not at all anxious; she was not even surprised, for she had never expected to see Lucilla as early as had been promised, and had, in fact, told her chef as soon as she had seen the party off, not to serve dinner until a later hour than was usual. 'For you may depend upon it they will find so much to interest them at Badminton that they will never notice the time!' she said.

She was perfectly right, of course. Just after seven o'clock, Lucilla and Ninian burst into the drawing-room, both full of apologies, and disjointed attempts to describe the glories of Badminton, and the splendid time they had had, which had included—only fancy!—a delicious cold nuncheon, especially provided by his Grace's housekeeper for their delectation. Nothing had ever been like it!

It seemed that careless Harry Beckenham had gone to considerable trouble to ensure the success of the expedition. 'I must own,' said Ninian honestly, 'I didn't expect him to have done the thing in such bang-up style! He actually sent a message to Badminton yesterday, warning the housekeeper that it was very likely he would be bringing a few friends to visit the house today! Or perhaps he wrote to the steward, for it was the steward who led us over the place, and told us all about everything. And I must say it was amazingly interesting!'

'Oh, I never enjoyed anything as much in all my life!' said Lucilla, with an ecstatic sigh. 'Corisande and I were in raptures, and neither of us had a notion how late it was until Miss Tenbury chanced to catch sight of a clock in one of the saloons, and drew our attention to it. And so we were obliged to hurry away immediately, and I do hope, ma'am, that you aren't vexed!'

'Not in the least!' Miss Wychwood assured her. 'I am famous for my foresight, and had set dinner back before you were all out of sight!'

Ninian then disclosed that (if she did not think him very uncivil) he had accepted an invitation from Harry Beckenham to join him and Mr Hawkesbury at the White Hart for dinner. 'Oh, and he told me to present his compliments to you, ma'am, and to explain why he was unable to come in to beg you, in person, to forgive him for having made us all so late! The thing is, you see, that he was obliged to escort Miss Stinchcombe and Miss Tenbury to their homes. He said that he knew you would understand.'

Miss Wychwood said that she perfectly understood, and that she would have thought Ninian quite muttonheaded if he had refused Mr Beckenham's invitation. What she did not tell him was that she was considerably relieved to learn that he would not be dining in Camden Place that evening. The foresight for which she had said she was famous had several hours earlier warned her that an awkward situation might arise, if it came to Lady Iverley's ears that Ninian, according to his usual custom, had dined with her, instead of hastening to his doting parent's side. It seemed improbable that he would return to the Pelican before going to the White Hart, since he would think it unnecessary to change his riding clothes for evening attire—indeed, quite improper for him to do so, when he knew that it was impossible for his host, or the amiable Mr Hawkesbury, to change their raiment. That meant that whatever message Lady Iverley might have left for him at the Pelican he would not receive until an advanced hour of the evening, which was, she acknowledged, regrettable, but not as regrettable as it would have been if Lady Iverley had been able to lay the blame of his failure to respond instantly to the summons at her door. So she sped Ninian on his way, adjured Lucilla to make haste to put off her riding-habit, and left whatever tomorrow's problems might be to take care of themselves.

On the following morning, Lucilla, who was eager to discuss the previous day's entertainment with Corisande, volunteered to accompany Lady Wychwood to the Pump Room. Annis excused herself from going with them, for she felt reasonably certain that she would receive a visit from Ninian. Nor was she mistaken; but it was nearly midday before he arrived on the doorstep, hot and out of breath from having walked at breakneck speed up the steep hill from the Christopher. She received him in the book-room, because it seemed likely that her sister-in-law and Lucilla would return at any minute; and he said impetuously as he crossed the threshold: 'Oh, I am so glad to find you at home, ma'am! I was afraid you might have gone down to the Pump Room, where I couldn't have talked privately to you! And that I must do!'

'Then it is as well that I didn't go to the Pump Room this morning,' she replied. 'Sit down, and tell me all about it!'

He did sit down, and dragged his handkerchief from his pocket to wipe the sweat from his brow. Recovering his breath, he said in a tight, rigidly controlled voice: 'I've come to take my leave of you, ma'am!'

'Have you decided to go back to Chartley?' she asked. 'We shall miss you, but I think perhaps you should go back.'

'I suppose so,' he said dejectedly. 'I said at first—but I see it won't do! It seems that my father is quite knocked-up, and—and all through my having left Chartley in a huff, though I wrote to him, just as I told you I should, so why he should have taken it into his head that I meant never to return I can't conceive! It makes me afraid that he must be in very, very queer stirrups, and—and I could never forgive myself if—if anything happened to him! There seems to be nothing for it but for me to go back. You see, my mother arrived here yesterday morning, Miss Wychwood. She is putting up at the Christopher.'

'I see,' she replied sympathetically.

'And my sister Cordelia as well,' he added, on a gloomy note. 'If she *had* to bring one of my sisters with her she might at least have brought Lavinia, for she has *some* sense, and she ain't a watering-pot, and she don't wind me up anything like as often as Cordelia does! I can tell you, ma'am, it made me as mad as fire when the silly wet-goose flung her arms round my neck before I could stop her, and wept all over me!'

'I—I expect it did!' said Miss Wychwood, a trifle unsteadily.

'Well, of course it did, and it would have made any man feel just as I did! I told Mama *perfectly* politely! that it was enough to make me jump on the Bristol coach, and ship aboard the first packet bound for America, or anywhere else that the Bristol boats sail to, because I had rather live in the *Antipodes* than have Cordelia hanging round my neck, and dashed well ruining my neck-tie, besides calling me her beloved brother, which was the biggest hum I ever heard, for she don't like me any better than I like her! So then Cordelia asked me, as though she had been acting in some tragedy or another, if I wished to drive my sainted parents into their graves! Well, that did make me lose my temper, and I told her to her head that I had come to talk to Mama, and not to listen to fustian rubbish from *her*!'

Miss Wychwood, hugely enjoying this recital, perceived that the eldest Miss Elmore was a daughter after Lady Iverley's heart. She also perceived that his sojourn in Bath had done Ninian (to her way of thinking) a great deal of good; and she hoped that Lady Iverley had realized that he was no longer the adored and dutiful son who did as he was bid, but a young gentleman who had crossed the threshold of adolescence, and had become a man.

Apparently she had. She had sent Cordelia out of the room. According to Ninian, she had done this because she had recognized the justice of his complaint; Miss Wychwood thought that she had done it because she had been frightened. But this she did not say. She merely said: 'Oh, dear! What a sad ending to the day!'

'I should rather think it was!' said Ninian fervently. 'Except that it wasn't the end of the day, but the beginning of it! Of *this* day, I mean! Well, I didn't get back to the Pelican till past midnight, so I didn't see the note my mother wrote me until then, when it was far too late to visit her, even if I hadn't been—' He stopped, in a good deal of embarrassment.

'Foxed?' suggested Miss Wychwood helpfully.

He grinned at her. 'No, no, not *foxed*, ma'am! Just a little bit on the go! If you know what I mean!'

'Oh, I know exactly what you mean!' she assured him, the smile dancing in her eyes. 'You had been dipping rather deep, but you were not too bosky to perceive the unwisdom of presenting yourself to your mama until you had slept off your potations! Have I that right?'

He burst out laughing. 'Yes, by Jupiter you have! You're a great gun, ma'am! Well, I went up to bed, but I told the boots to wake me not a moment later than eight this morning, which he did, and though I must say I felt pretty devilish at first, a cup of strong coffee more or less set me to rights, and I went off to the Christopher.' He paused; the laughter vanished from his voice, a frown descended on to his brow, and his mouth hardened. It was a full minute before he spoke again, and when he did speak it was with a little difficulty. He said: 'Do you think it chicken-hearted of me to have knuckled down, Miss Wychwood?'

'By no means! You owe a duty to your father, remember!'

'Yes, I know. But I have begun to wonder if he is so very ill as Mama believes him to be. Or even if she does believe it, or if she says it to compel me to go home, and stay at home, because she is—well, much more deeply attached to me than to my sisters!'

'I daresay she might *exaggerate* a little, but from what you have told me I collect that Lord Iverley's constitution was seriously impaired by his service in the Peninsula.'

'Yes, it was: there can be no doubt about that!' said Ninian, brightening. He thought it over for a moment, and then said: 'And he did have a bad heart-attack some years ago. But—but Mama seems to live in dread of his having another, which might prove fatal, if he is put into a passion, or if one doesn't do exactly as he bids one!'

'That is very natural, Ninian.'

'Yes, but it isn't true! He was in the devil of a passion when Lucy ran away, and I helped her to do it; and when I lost my temper, and we quarrelled, and I said I should go straight back to Bath, he flew into such a rage that he *shook* with anger, and could hardly speak. But he didn't suffer a heart-attack!

What's more, he went *on* being in a rage, for it was several days later that he wrote me that thundering scold, so that it is absurd to expect me to believe that he was exhausted. But when I tried to point this out to Mama, all she would say was that she couldn't blame me for turning against my parents because she knew well that I had fallen under an evil influence! I couldn't think what had put such a crackbrained notion into her head! It took me an age to get it out of her, but she did tell me in the end, and what do you think it was? *Your* influence, ma'am! Lord, I nearly laughed myself into stitches! Well, did you ever hear of anything so ridiculous?'

'Never!' said Miss Wychwood. 'I trust you were able to convince her that she was mistaken?'

'Yes, but it was deuced hard work! Someone seems to have told her that you were the most beautiful woman in Bath—described you pretty thoroughly to her, too, for she talked of your eyes, and your hair, and your figure as though she had actually seen you! So I said Yes, you were very beautiful, and very clever too, and I'm dashed if she didn't accuse me of having *fallen a victim to your beauty!*'

'I can almost hear her saying it!' murmured Miss Wychwood appreciatively.

'I daresay it would have made you laugh, but it didn't make me laugh, though I suppose it was funny. The thing was that it made me very angry, and I told Mama that it was a great piece of impertinence to talk in that outrageous style about a lady whom everyone holds in respect, and who has been as kind to me as though I had been her nephew. Which you have been, ma'am, and I couldn't leave Bath without telling you how very grateful I am to you for all the things you've done to make my stay in Bath so agreeable! Letting me run tame in your house, inviting me to go with you and Lucy to the theatre, making me known to your friends—oh, hosts of things!'

'My dear boy, I wish you won't talk nonsense!' she protested. 'It is I who am grateful to you! Indeed, I have made shameless use of you, and am wondering what I should have done without you, to take Lucilla about, and to stand guard over her! And another thing I wish you won't do is to talk as though we were never to meet again! I hope you will often visit Bath, and promise you will always be a welcome guest in Camden Place.'

'Th–thank you, ma'am!' he stammered, blushing. 'I mean to be a frequent visitor, I can tell you! I have made it plain to Mama that if I go home with her today it must be on the strict understanding that I am at liberty to come and go as I choose, and without having to coax Papa into giving his consent every time I wish to do something he doesn't approve of!'

'Ah, that was very wise of you!' she said. 'I daresay he may not like it at first, but depend upon it he will very soon grow accustomed to having a sensible man for his son and not a mere boy!'

'Do you think he will, ma'am?' he asked, rather doubtfully.

'I am very sure of it,' she smiled, getting up. 'You will take some nuncheon with us before you go, will you not?'

'Oh, thank you, ma'am, but no! I mustn't stay. My mother is anxious to reach Chartley today, because she fears my father will be fretting over the chance that she may have met with an accident. Which is very possible, for she *never* goes away without him. It would be much wiser, of course, if we postponed our departure until tomorrow morning, but when I suggested this to her, I saw at once that it would not do. I don't mean that she tried to—to *persuade* me—in fact, she said I must be the only judge of what was best—but I could see that she wouldn't get a wink of sleep tonight for worrying about Papa, so even if we don't reach Chartley before *midnight* it will be better for her to go home today than to be worrying herself into a fever. And it don't really signify if we do have to drive after dark, because it won't *be* dark, the moon being at the full, and no fear that I can see of the sky's becoming overcast.' He added imploringly, as though he had detected in Miss Wychwood's expression what were her feelings on the subject: 'You see, ma'am, Mama is not robust, and her disposition is nervous, and—and I know what trials she has to undergo—and—and—'

'You love her very much,' supplied Miss Wychwood, patting his flushed cheek, and smiling at him warmly. 'She is a fortunate woman! Now you will wish to say goodbye to Lucilla, so we will go up to the drawing-room. I think I heard her come in, with my sister, a minute or two ago.'

'Yes—well, I must do so, though ten to one she will abuse me for not having any resolution!' he said resentfully.

However, Lucilla behaved with perfect propriety. She exclaimed, when he told her that he was obliged to return to Chartley: 'Oh, no, Ninian! Must you do so? Pray don't go away!' but when he explained the circumstances she made no further demur, but looked thoughtful, and said that she supposed he would be obliged to go. It was not until he had left the house that, emerging from a brown study, she said earnestly to Miss Wychwood: 'It makes me almost *glad* I am an orphan, ma'am!'

Lady Wychwood uttered a slightly shocked protest, and said: 'Good gracious, child, whatever can you mean?'

'The way the Iverleys bullock Ninian into doing what they want him to do in—in an infamous way!' Lucilla explained. 'Lady Iverley appeals to his *better self*, and the pity of it is that he *has* a better self! I quite see that it is very creditable to have a better self but it does make him rather milky.'

'Oh, no! I should never say he was milky,' responded Miss Wychwood. 'You must remember that he is very much attached to his mama, and is, I believe, fully aware of the anxious life she leads. I rather fancy she is inclined to cling to him—'

'Yes, indeed she does, and in the most *cloying* way!' said Lucilla. 'So do Cordelia and Lavinia! I wonder that he can bear it! I could not.'

'No, but you haven't a better nature, have you?' said Miss Wychwood, quizzing her.

Lucilla laughed, but said: 'Very true! And thank goodness I haven't, for it must be excessively uncomfortable!'

Miss Wychwood was amused, but Lady Wychwood shook her head over it, and later told her sister-in-law that she thought the remark a melancholy illustration of the evils attached to growing up without a mother.

'Well, they could scarcely be worse than the evils of growing up with such a mother as Lady Iverley!' said Annis caustically.

Ninian's absence was felt to have created a sad gap in the household; and even outside the household a surprising number of people told Annis how sorry they were that he had left Bath, and how much they hoped it would not be long before he revisited the town. He seemed to have made many friends, which circumstance increased Annis's respect for him: very few young men would have sacrificed their pleasures to so lachrymose and unreasonable a parent as Lady Iverley. She hoped that he was not moped to death at Chartley, but feared that he must be finding life very flat.

However, some few days later she received a letter from him, and gathered from its closely written pages that although he thought wistfully of Bath and its inhabitants conditions at Chartley had improved. He had had a long talk with his father, the outcome of which was that he was now occupying himself with the management of the estate, and spent the better part of his time going about with the bailiff. Miss Wychwood would stare if she knew how much he was learning. His quarrel with Lord Iverley had been quite made up. He had found his lordship looking dragged and weary, but was happy to say that he was plucking up wonderfully, and had even said that if Ninian wished to invite any of his friends to visit him he should be glad to welcome them to Chartley.

Miss Wychwood concluded that his lordship had learnt a valuable lesson, and that there was no need to worry about Ninian's future.

There was no need to worry about anything, of course: Lucilla was well, and behaving with great docility; little Tom's toothache was remembered by no one but his mama and Nurse; Miss Farlow had won Nurse's approval and had begun to spend a large part of the days either in the nursery or taking Tom for walks; and if Mr Carleton had thought better of his intention to return to Bath it was a very good thing, for they went on perfectly happily without him.

But when, one morning, she received a letter from him her heart jumped, and she hardly dared to break the seal, for fear that she might read that he had indeed changed his mind.

It did not seem as though he had done so, but although it was a relief to know that he still meant to come back his letter was not really very satisfactory. Mr Carleton had written it in haste, and merely to inform her that he had been obliged to postpone his return. He was much occupied with some tiresome business which made it necessary for him to visit his estates. He was on the point of setting out on the journey, and begged her to excuse his sending only a short scrawl to apprise her of his immediate intentions. He had no time for more, but remained hers, as ever, Oliver Carleton.

Not a model of the epistolary art; still less the letter of a man in love, she thought. The only part of it which encouraged to hope that he did still love her was its ending. But very likely he signed all his letters *Yours, as ever,* and it would be nonsensical to read more into these simple words than mere friendliness.

She found herself in low spirits, and tried very hard to shake off this silly fit of the dismals, and not to allow herself to think about Mr Carleton, or his letter, or how much she was missing him. She thought that even if she didn't succeed in carrying out this admirable resolution she had at least succeeded in hiding her depression from Lady Wychwood, but soon discovered that she was mistaken. 'I wish you will tell me, dearest, what is making you so—so down pin,' said her ladyship coaxingly.

'Why, nothing! Do I seem to be down pin? I wasn't aware of it—except wet streets, dripping trees, and nothing else to be seen but umbrellas and puddles always does put me into the hips. I hate being shut up in the house, you know!'

'Well, it is sad that the weather should have turned off, but you were never used to care a straw for the weather. How often have I begged you not to venture out, when it was raining pitchforks and shovels! But you never paid any heed! You said you liked to feel the rain on your face.'

'Oh, that was in the country, Amabel! It is a very different matter in town, where one can't tie a shawl round one's head, find a pair of stout list shoes and go for a tramp! You wouldn't have me make such a figure of myself in Bath!'

'Of course not,' said Lady Wychwood quietly, and bent her head again over the robe she was making for her infant daughter.

'The truth is, I expect, that I need occupation,' offered Annis. 'Now, if only I didn't find sewing a dead bore, or if I had Lucilla's talent for water-colour drawing—have you seen any of her sketches? They are infinitely superior to the generality of young-lady-drawings!'

'Oh, I don't think sewing or sketching would answer the purpose! They don't divert one's mind, do they? I don't know about sketching, for I was never at all fond of it, but I should think it is much the same as sewing, and that I find doesn't divert one's mind in the least—in fact, quite the reverse!'

'I think I shall embark on a course of serious reading,' said Annis, bent on leading Lady Wychwood down a less dangerous conversational avenue.

'Well, dearest, I daresay that might answer the purpose, but you have been sitting with a book open in front of you for the past twenty minutes, and I could not but notice that you haven't yet turned the page,' replied Lady Wychwood. She looked up, and smiled faintly at Annis. 'I don't mean to tease you with prying questions, so I'll say no more. Only that I hope so much that you won't do anything you might live to regret. I couldn't bear you to be made unhappy, my dear one. Tell me, do you think I have made this bodice large enough for Baby?'

# Fourteen

HE WEATHER REMAINED UNSETTLED FOR SEVERAL DAYS, and it became obvious that the various al fresco entertainments which had been planned by Corisande and her many friends would have to be postponed. This was naturally a disappointment to Lucilla; and after a very short space of time, even Lady Wychwood's patience wore thin, and upon Lucilla's asking, for the twentieth time, if she didn't think the sky was growing lighter, and if it might not still be possible for the morrow's party at the Sydney Garden to take place, she addressed mild but measured words of reproof to her, saying: 'Dear child, the weather won't improve because you keep running to the window, and asking us if we don't believe it to be clearing up. Neither my sister nor I have the least notion whether it will be a fine day tomorrow, so of what use is it to expect us to answer you? You would do much better to stop pressing your nose against the window every few minutes and to occupy yourself with your drawing, or your music, instead.' She smiled kindly, and added: 'You know, my dear, however fond people may be of you they will soon begin to think you a sad bore if you fall into the way of harping on every little thing that puts you out, as though you were still only a spoilt baby.'

Lucilla reddened, and it seemed for a moment as though she was going to retort; but after a moment's inward struggle she said, in a subdued voice: 'I'm sorry, ma'am!' and ran out of the room.

It was soon seen that Lady Wychwood's words had gone home, for although Lucilla frequently cast wistful glances at the rain-drops chasing one another down the window-panes she only now and then complained of the perversity of the weather, and really made a praiseworthy effort to bear her disappointment with cheerful composure.

Just as the weather at last showed signs of improvement, Miss Farlow created a most unwelcome diversion by succumbing to an attack of influenza. She dragged herself about the house, wrapped in a shawl, saying that she had contracted a slight cold in the head, and not until she fainted one morning when she got out of bed could she be induced either to remain in bed or to allow Annis to send for the doctor. There was nothing the matter with her; she was a trifle out of sorts, but would very soon be better; it was quite unnecessary for dear Annis to send for Dr Tidmarsh, not that she knew anything against him, for she was sure he was very amiable and gentleman-like, but dear papa hadn't believed in doctors; and, besides, very strange behaviour it would be for her to fall ill when the house was full of guests, and it was her duty to remain on her feet, even if it killed her. However, she was clearly feverish, and in spite of being flushed, and complaining of feeling too hot, she shivered convulsively; so Annis took matters into her own hands, and dispatched the page-boy with a message for Dr Tidmarsh. By the time he arrived, Miss Farlow was feeling so poorly that instead of repulsing him she greeted him as a saviour, wept bitterly, and described to him, with a wealth of detail, every one of her many symptoms. She ended by imploring him not to say that she had scarlet fever.

'No, no, ma'am!' he said soothingly. 'Merely a touch of influenza! I shall send you a saline draught, and you will very soon be more comfortable. I'll look in tomorrow, to see how you go on. Meanwhile, you must stay quietly in your bed, and do as Miss Wychwood bids you.'

He then went out of the room with Annis, told her that there was no reason for her to be anxious, gave her some instructions, and, when he took his leave, looked rather narrowly at her, and said: 'Now, don't wear yourself out, ma'am, will you? You don't look to be in such good point as when I saw you last: I suspect you have been trotting too hard!'

When Annis returned to the sick-room, she found Miss Farlow in a state of tearful agitation, the reason for this fresh flow of tears being her fear that poor little Tom might have taken the disease from her, for which she would never, never forgive herself.

'My dear Maria, it will be time enough to cry about it if he *does* contract influenza, which very likely he won't,' said Annis cheerfully. 'Betty will be bringing you some lemonade directly, and perhaps when you have drunk a little of it you will be able to go to sleep.'

But it soon became plain that Miss Farlow was not going to be an easy patient. She begged Miss Wychwood not to give her a thought, but to go away and on no account to feel she must stay at her side, because she had everything she wanted, and she couldn't bear to be giving her so much trouble; but if Miss Wychwood absented herself for more than half-an-hour she fell into sad woe, because this showed her that nobody cared what became of her, least of all her dear Annis.

Lady Wychwood and Lucilla were both anxious to share the task of nursing Miss Farlow, but Annis would not permit either of them to go into the sick-room. Lucilla looked decidedly relieved, for she had never nursed anyone in her life, and was secretly scared that she might do the wrong things; and Lady Wychwood, when it was pointed out to her that she had her children to consider and owed it to them not to expose herself to the risk of infection, agreed reluctantly to stay away from Poor Maria. 'But you must promise me to take care of yourself, Annis! You must let Jurby help you, and you mustn't linger in the room, or approach Maria too closely! How shocking it would be if *you* were to become ill!'

'Very shocking—and very surprising too!' said Annis. 'You know I am never ill! You can't have forgotten all the occasions when an epidemic cold has laid everyone at Twynham low, except Nurse and me! If you will look after Lucilla for me I shall be very much obliged to you!'

Jurby, when asked if she would help to nurse Miss Farlow, said that Miss Annis might leave it entirely to her, and not bother her head any more; but as she apparently believed that Miss Farlow had contracted influenza on purpose to set them all by the ears Annis took care always to be at hand when she stalked into the room to measure out a dose of medicine, wash Miss Farlow's face and hands, or shake up her pillows. Jurby disliked Miss Farlow, thought that she could be better if she wished, and in general behaved as if she had been a gaoler in charge of a trou-blesome prisoner. Miss Wychwood remonstrated with her in vain. 'I've no patience with her, miss, making such a rout about nothing more than the influenza! Anyone would think she was in a confirmed consumption to hear the way she talks about her aches and ills! What's more, Miss Annis, it puts me all on end when she says she don't want you to be troubled with her, or to sit with her, and the next minute wonders what's become of you, and why you haven't been next or nigh her for hours!'

'Oh, Jurby, pray hush!' begged Miss Wychwood. 'I know she—she is being tiresome, but one must remember that influenza does make people feel very ill so that it is no wonder she should be in—in rather bad skin! But you won't have to bear with her for much longer, I hope: Dr Tidmarsh has told me that he sees no reason why she should not get up out of her bed for a little while tomorrow, and I think it will vastly improve her spirits if she does so, because it is what she has been wanting to do from the outset.'

Jurby gave a snort of disbelief, and said darkly: 'That's what she *says*, Miss Annis, but it's my belief we shan't see her out of her bed for a sennight!'

But in this prophecy she wronged Miss Farlow. Permitted to sit up in an armchair for an hour or two on the following day, her spirits revived; she began to enumerate all the tasks which she had been obliged to leave undone; and announced her conviction that by the next day she would be stout enough to resume all her duties; so that Miss Wychwood had difficulty in dissuading her from setting to work immediately on the careful darning of a damaged sheet. Fortunately, she discovered herself to be so sadly weakened by her brief but severe attack that after the exertion of dressing her hair she was glad to sit quietly in her armchair, with one shawl round her shoulders and another spread over her legs, and to engage in no more strenuous occupation than that of reading the Court News in the *Morning Post*.

However, she was certainly on the mend, and Miss Wychwood, in spite of feeling unaccountably exhausted, was looking forward to a period of calm when she received from Jurby, as that stern handmaid drew back the curtains from round her bed on the following morning, the sinister tidings that Nurse wished to have Dr Tidmarsh summoned to take a look at Master Tom.

Thus rudely awakened, Miss Wychwood sat up with a jerk, and said in horrified accents: 'Oh, Jurby, *no*! You can't mean that *he* has got the influenza?'

'There isn't a doubt of it, miss,' said Jurby implacably. 'Nurse suspicioned he was sickening for it last night, but she had the sense to take the baby's crib into the dressing-room, so we must hope the poor little innocent won't have caught the infection from Master Tom.'

'Indeed we must!' said Annis, flinging back the blankets, and sliding out of bed. 'Help me to dress quickly, Jurby! I must send a message to Dr Tidmarsh at once, and warn Wardlow to lay in a stock of lemons, and some more pearl barley, and chickens for broth, and—oh, I don't know, but no doubt she will!'

'You may be sure she will, miss; and as for the doctor, her lady-ship sent down a message to him the instant Nurse told her Master Tom was taken ill. Of course,' she added gloomily, as she handed her stockings to Miss Wychwood, 'the next thing we shall know is that her ladyship has caught the infection. Then we *shall* be in the suds!'

'Oh, pray don't say so, Jurby!' begged Miss Wychwood.

'I shouldn't be doing my duty by you, miss, if I didn't warn you. In my experience, if you get one trouble coming on you which you didn't expect you may look to get two more.'

Miss Wychwood might smile at this oracular pronounce-ment, but it was in a mood of considerable dismay that she went down, some minutes later, to the breakfast-parlour. Here she found Lady Wychwood eating bread-and-butter, with her infant daughter in her lap, and Lucilla watching this domestic picture with a kind of awed fascination. Miss Wychwood, knowing how anxious her sister-in-law was inclined to be whenever anything ailed her children, was much relieved to see her looking so calm. She said, as she bent to kiss her: 'I am so sorry, Amabel, to hear that Tom is now a victim of this horrid influenza!'

'Yes, it is most unfortunate,' agreed her ladyship, sighing faintly. 'But not unexpected! I thought he would be bound to take it from Maria, for she had been playing with him the very day she began to feel unwell. But Nurse doesn't think it will prove to be a bad attack, and I am persuaded I may have complete faith in Dr Tidmarsh. I formed the opinion, when I was talking to him the other day, that he is a *perfectly* competent person, which, of course, one would expect a *Bath* doctor to be. The worst of it is,' she added, her eyes filling with tears, and her lips trembling a little, 'that I must not take care of Tom myself. Whenever he has been ill he has always called for *Mama*, and *never* have I left him for more than a minute! However, I do see that it's my duty to keep Baby out of the way of the infection, and I don't mean to be silly about it. I have talked it over with Nurse, and we are agreed that she is to look after Tom, and I am to have sole charge of Baby. Which I shall like very much, shan't I, my precious?'

Miss Susan Wychwood, who had been chortling to herself, responded to this by uttering a series of unintelligible remarks, which her mama interpreted as signifying agreement; and blew several bubbles.

'*What* a clever girl!' said Lady Wychwood, in a voice of doting fondness.

When the doctor arrived, he confirmed Nurse's diagnosis; warned Lady Wychwood that Tom was unlikely to make such a quick recovery as Miss Farlow's had been; and told her that she must not worry if he was still inclined to be feverish at the end of a sennight, because it was often so with obstreperous little boys whom it was almost impossible to keep quietly in their beds, since the instant their aches and pains subsided it was one person's work—or, perhaps it would be more accurate to say *two* persons' work, to prevent them from bouncing about, and even getting out of bed the instant one took one's eye off them. 'I have two little rascals of my own, my lady!' he told her, with ill-concealed pride. 'Just such bits of quicksilver as your boy is, so you may believe I don't speak without personal experience!' He then told her that she was very wise to preserve her baby from any risk of infection; complimented her on Miss Susan Wychwood's sturdy limbs and powerful lungs; and went off leaving her to inform

Annis that he was quite the most agreeable and sympathetic doctor she had ever known.

On Miss Farlow the news that Tom was ill acted like a tonic. She did indeed burst into tears, and say that she would never dare to look dear Lady Wychwood in the face again, but this threatened relapse into gloom was not of long duration. An opportunity to prove herself to be of real value had presented itself, and she seized it. She cast off her shawls, dressed herself, and emerged from her bedchamber, rather shakily, but determined to share with Nurse the task of keeping Tom quiescent. Nurse accepted her services graciously. 'For there is no denying, Miss Jurby,' said Nurse, 'that though she may be a hubble-bubble female with a tongue that runs like a fiddlestick, she does know how to handle children, and will sit for hours telling them fairy-tales, and the like, which makes it possible for me to get a bit of rest.'

It began to seem as though Jurby's bleak prophecy was going to be falsified, but two days later Betty, the young housemaid who had waited on Miss Farlow throughout her indisposition, also took to her bed, a circumstance of which Jurby informed her mistress with somewhat heartless satisfaction. 'Which all goes to show how right I was, miss!' she said, opening the doors of the big wardrobe which housed Miss Wychwood's dresses. 'I told you troubles come in threes, and if it's only Betty who's got this dratted influenza there's no harm done. Now, will you wear your blue cambric today, or shall I put out the French muslin, with the striped spencer?'

'Jurby,' said Miss Wychwood, in an uncertain voice, 'I think— I am afraid—that I too have the influenza!'

Jurby turned quickly. Miss Wychwood was sitting on the edge of her bed, still wearing her nightgown, and although the rainy spell had given way to a hot, sunny day she was shivering so violently that the teeth chattered in her head. Jurby took one look at her, and then cast the French muslin aside, and hurried towards her, muttering: 'Oh, my goodness me! I might have known this would happen!' She grasped Miss Wychwood's hands, and instantly thrust her back into bed. 'And there you'll stay, Miss Annis!' she said, in a threatening tone. 'It's to be hoped you've nothing worse the matter with you than influenza!'

'Oh, no, I don't think so!' Annis said faintly. 'It came on me during the night. I woke up, feeling as though I had been beaten all over with cudgels, and with such a headache—! I hoped it would pass off, if I kept my eyes shut, but it didn't, and I feel quite dreadfully ill. Don't tell her ladyship!'

'Now, don't start fretting and fussing, Miss Annis!' said Jurby, laying a hand on Miss Wychwood's brow. 'I'm bound to tell her ladyship that you're out of curl today, and mean to stay in bed, but I won't let her come into the room, I promise you!'

'Don't let Miss Lucilla come near me either!'

'The only person who'll come into this room is the doctor!' said Jurby grimly, stumping over to the window and drawing the blinds across it. 'Do you lie quiet now till I come back, and don't get into the high fidgets, fancying the house will fall down just because you're knocked up with all the trouble you've had, and mean to recruit your strength by staying in bed today, because it won't!' She sprinkled lavender-water lavishly over the pillow, drenched a handkerchief with it, which she tenderly wiped across Miss Wychwood's burning forehead, assured her that she would be as right as a trivet before the cat had time to lick her ear, and hurried away, first to send the page-boy scurrying down the hill with an urgent message for Dr Tidmarsh, and then to inform Lady Wychwood, who had not yet left her room, that Miss Annis was laid up, and that she had sent for the doctor. 'I don't doubt it's nothing worse than the influenza, my lady, but she's in a raging fever!' she said bluntly.

Lady Wychwood started up instinctively, saying: 'I'll come at once!'

'No, that you won't, my lady!' said Jurby, barring her passage to the door. 'There's nothing you can do for her, and you've got the baby to consider. Miss Annis has laid it on me not to let you, or Miss Lucilla, come near her. Very agitated she is, for fear you should insist on seeing her and get ill in consequence. If you don't want her to get into a stew, which I'm sure you don't, you'll do as she asks you.'

'Alas, I *must*!' said Lady Wychwood, much distressed. 'Why, oh, *why* didn't I send the children home with Nurse the instant Miss Farlow took ill? Why didn't I persuade Miss Annis to go to bed yesterday, and send for Dr Tidmarsh immediately? I could see she wasn't quite well, but I never dreamed she was sickening for anything, because she is so very rarely ill! I might have guessed, though! *Fool* that I was!'

'Well, my lady, I don't see that it would have done a bit of good if the doctor had come to see her yesterday, because if she had the influenza on her there was nothing he nor anyone else could have done to drive it off. And as for not guessing she was ill, I don't see that you've any call to blame yourself, for *I* didn't guess it, and—if you'll pardon me for saying so, my lady!— there's no one who knows her as well as I do! I knew she wasn't in very plump currant but I thought she was out of sorts, on account of having to dance attendance on Miss Farlow, on top of—' She checked herself, and ended her sentence by saying, at her most forbidding: 'Other things!'

They looked at one another. After a moment, Lady Wychwood said simply: 'I know.' She then turned away to pick up her rings from the dressing-table, and said, as she slid them on to her fingers: 'Give her my dear love, Jurby, and tell her that she mustn't worry about the house, or about Miss Lucilla, because she knows she can trust me to see that everything goes on just as it ought. And tell her that I shan't attempt to see her until Dr Tidmarsh says it is safe for me to do so.'

'Thank you, my lady! You can be sure I will! It will do her good to have *that* worry at least taken off her mind!' said Jurby, with real gratitude. She lingered, on the pretext of picking up a hairpin, and said: 'I shall take the liberty of saying, my lady—being as I have been Miss Annis's personal maid since she came out of the nursery—that I can't help hoping that Mr Carleton will make some other arrangement for Miss Lucilla. Not that I have anything against her, for I am sure she is a sweetly behaved young lady, but I have always felt that Miss Annis was taking too much on her shoulders when she adopted her, as one might say. Particularly now, when Miss Annis is ill, and will be in a tender state, I daresay, for some weeks. I suppose you don't know when Mr Carleton means to return to Bath? Or if he has gone away for good?'

'No,' answered Lady Wychwood. 'I am afraid I don't know, Jurby.'

Nothing more was said between them, but much that was unspoken was understood.

Dr Tidmarsh, when he arrived less than an hour later, spent much longer with Miss Wychwood than he had found it necessary to spend either with Miss Farlow or with Tom, and when he came downstairs again, he told Lady Wychwood that while Miss Wychwood was suffering from no more serious disorder than influenza the attack was a severe one. He had found her pulse tumultuous; she was extremely feverish; and although he was confident that the medicine he had prescribed for her would soon reduce the fever, he warned her ladyship that it was possible—even, he was sorry to say, probable—that she might become a trifle delirious as the day wore on. 'I tell you this, my lady, because I don't wish you to be alarmed if she should wander a little in her mind. I assure you there is no cause for alarm! I hope that she will sleep, but if she should be restless you may give her a few drops of laudanum. Rather, I should say, her maid may do so, for you will, I trust, abide by your wise determination to stay out of the way of infection. I must add that the fear that you, or Miss Carleton, should run the slightest risk of taking influenza from her is preying on her mind, which is very undesirable, as I am persuaded you must recognize. In short, I consider it to be of the first importance that she should be kept as quiet as may be possible. The fewer people to enter her room the better it will be for her, while she is so feverish.'

'No one shall enter it without your permission, doctor,' said Lady Wychwood.

She was agreeably surprised, when she reported the doctor's words to Lucilla, to see a look of chagrin in Lucilla's face, for she had been inclined to think that for all her engaging ways and pretty manners she wanted heart. She had certainly not expected tears to spring to Lucilla's eyes when she was told that she must not enter Miss Wychwood's room until all danger of infection was over, and she was a good deal touched when Lucilla said forlornly: 'May I not nurse her, ma'am?'

'No, my dear, I am afraid not. Jurby is going to nurse her.'

'Oh, yes, but I could help her, couldn't I? I promise I would do just as she bade me, and even if she doesn't think I'm old enough to nurse people I could at least sit with Miss Wychwood while Jurby rests, or goes down to eat her dinner, couldn't I? I can't bear it if I am not allowed to do *anything*, because I do love her so much, and she does *everything* for me!'

Lady Wychwood was moved to put an arm round her, and to give her a slight hug. 'I know how hard it is for you, dear child,' she said sympathetically. 'I'm in the same case, you know. I would give anything to be able to look after my sister, but I must not.'

'But you have your baby to look after, ma'am, which makes it quite different!' Lucilla said urgently. 'I haven't got a baby, or *anyone* who would be a penny the worse for it if I caught influenza!'

'I can tell you of *one* who would be the worse for it, and that is my sister,' said Lady Wychwood. 'Jurby tells me that she is in a great worry about us, and has made Jurby promise not to permit either of us to go near her. I know you wouldn't wish to distress her—and to tell you the truth I think she is feeling too poorly even to *wish* to see anyone but Jurby. Wait until she is rather better! The instant Dr Tidmarsh tells us that she is no longer infectious I promise you shan't be kept out of her room. As for sitting with her now, she isn't ill enough to make it necessary for someone to be always with her, you know. Indeed, from what I know of her, I am very sure she would find it very irksome never to be left alone!'

Lucilla heaved a doleful sigh, but submitted, saying humbly that she didn't mean to be troublesome. Lady Wychwood then had the happy notion that she might like to go out with Mrs Wardlow, who had shopping to do, and buy some flowers to put in Miss Wychwood's room. The suggestion took well. Lucilla's face brightened, and she exclaimed: 'Oh, yes! I should like that of all things, ma'am! Thank you!' But when Lady Wychwood further suggested that she should write a note to Corisande to ask her to ride with her on the following morning, she shook her head, and said decidedly that nothing would prevail upon her to go pleasuring while Miss Wychwood was ill.

It was not to be expected that Miss Farlow would submit as meekly to the doctor's decree, and nor did she. Hardly had Lucilla tripped out with the housekeeper than she subjected Lady Wychwood to an extremely trying half-hour, during which she complained passionately of Jurby's insolence in daring to shut her out of Annis's room; declared her intention of taking care of Annis herself, whatever the doctor said; delivered herself of a moving but muddled speech in support of her claims to be the only proper person to have charge of the sick-room, in which she several times begged Lady Wychwood to agree that whatever *anyone* said blood was thicker than water; and ended an agitated monologue by pointing out, in triumph, that it was of no use for her ladyship to talk of the danger of infection, because she had already had the influenza.

It was some little time before Lady Wychwood was able to bring her to reason, and a great deal of tact was necessary; but she managed it at last, and without wounding Miss Farlow's sensibilities. She said that she did not know how she and Nurse were to go on, if Maria felt she must devote herself to Annis. That was quite enough. Miss Farlow, in a gush of affection, said that she was ready to do anything in the world to ease the burdens under which she knew well dear, dear Lady Wychwood was labouring, and went off, happy in the knowledge that her services were indispensable.

Unlike Tom, or Miss Farlow, Miss Wychwood was a very good patient. She obeyed the doctor's directions, swallowed the nastiest of drugs without protest; made few demands, and still fewer complaints; and resolutely refrained from tossing and turning in what she knew to be an unavailing attempt to get into a more comfortable position. As Dr Tidmarsh had prophesied, her fever mounted, and though it was too much to say that she became delirious, her mind did wander a little, and once she started out of an uneasy doze, exclaiming: 'Oh, why doesn't he come?' in an anguished voice; but she almost immediately came to herself, and after staring for a moment in bewilderment at Jurby's face, bent over her, she murmured: 'Oh, it's you, Jurby! I thought—I must have been dreaming, I suppose.'

Jurby saw no reason to report this incident to Lady Wychwood.

The fever began to abate on the second day, but it still remained high enough to make Dr Tidmarsh shake his head; and it was not until the third day that it burnt itself out, and did not recur. Miss Wychwood emerged from this shattering attack so much exhausted that for the next twenty-four hours she had no energy to do more than swallow, with an effort, a little liquid nourishment, or to rouse herself to take more than a vague interest in whatever events were taking place in her household. For the most part of the day she slept, conscious of a feeling of profound relief that her bones were no longer being racked, and that the Catherine wheel in her head was no longer making her life hideous.

The fourth day saw the arrival in Camden Place of Sir Geoffrey. He had borne with equanimity the news, conveyed to him by his dutiful wife, that Miss Farlow was in bed with influenza; a second letter, informing him that Tom had caught the infection disturbed him a little, but not enough to make him disregard Amabel's assurance that there was not the smallest need for him to be anxious; but the third letter (though she still begged him not to come to Bath), containing the news that Annis too had succumbed to the prevailing epidemic, set him on the road to Bath within an hour of his receiving it. He couldn't remember any occasion since her childhood when Annis had contracted anything more serious than a slight cold in the head, and it seemed to him that if she could fall ill there was no saying when his Amabel would also be laid low.

Lady Wychwood received him with mixed feelings. On the one hand she was overjoyed to have his strong arms round her again; on the other, she could not help feeling that his presence in the house would be an added burden in an establishment already over-burdened by three invalids, one of whom was the second housemaid. She was a devoted wife, but she knew well that he did not shine in a sick-room: in fact, he was more of a liability than an asset, for, enjoying excellent health himself he had very little experience of illness, and either caused the invalid to suffer a relapse by talking in heartily invigorating tones; or (if warned that the invalid was extremely weak) by tiptoeing into the room, addressing the patient in an awed and hushed voice, and bearing all the appearance of a man who had come to take a last farewell of one past hope of recovery.

He was considerably relieved to find that his Amabel, instead of being on a bed of sickness, was looking remarkably well, but he could not like it that she had been tied to a cradle ever since Tom had developed influenza. He thought it extraordinary that there should be no one in the household able to look after a mere infant, and could not be convinced that Amabel was neither tired nor bored. She laughed at him, and said: 'No, no, of course I'm not! Do you realize, my love, that it is the first time I have ever had Baby all to myself? Except for being unable to go to Tom, and being very anxious about Annis, I have enjoyed every minute, and shall be sorry to give her back to Nurse tomorrow. Dr Tidmarsh considers it to be perfectly safe now, but I am keeping Baby with me for one more night, for she is cutting another tooth, and is rather fretful, and I want Nurse to have a peaceful night before she takes charge of her again. You shall see Tom presently: he is laid down for his rest at the moment. Say something kind to Maria, won't you? She has been most helpful, looking after Tom.'

'Yes, very well, but tell me about Annis! I was never more shocked in my life than when I read that she was in such very queer stirrups! I could hardly believe my eyes, for I don't recall that I've ever known her to *collapse* before. It must have been a pretty violent catching?'

At this moment they were interrupted by Miss Susan Wychwood, who had been laid down to sleep on the sofa in the back drawing-room, and who now awoke, querulously demanding attention. Lady Wychwood glided into this half of the room, and was just about to pick Miss Susan up when Miss Farlow came hurrying in, and begged to be allowed to take the little darling. 'For I saw Sir Geoffrey drive up, and so, of course, I knew he would wish to talk to you, which is why I have been on the listen, thinking that very likely Baby would wake—Oh, how do you do, Cousin Geoffrey? Such a happiness to have you with us again, though I feel you will be quite alarmed, when you see our dear Annis—if Jurby permits you to see her!' She gave vent to a shrill titter. 'I daresay it will astonish you to know that Jurby has become the Queen of Camden Place: none of us dares to move hand or foot without her leave! Even I have not been permitted to see dear Annis until today! I promise you, I was excessively diverted, but I couldn't help pitying poor Annis, compelled to accept the services of her abigail when those of a blood-relation would have been more acceptable. However I made no demur, because I knew that, tyrant though she is, I could depend upon Jurby to take almost as good care of her mistress as I should have done, besides that there was dear Lady Wychwood to be thought of, so worn-down as she was, which made me realize that *her* need of me was greater than Annis's!'

She began to rock the infant in her arms, and Sir Geoffrey, who had listened to her with growing disfavour, beat a retreat, almost dragging his wife with him. As they mounted the stairs he said: 'Upon my word, Amabel, I begin to wish I hadn't prevailed upon Annis to engage that woman! But I don't remember that she talked us silly when she and Annis have visited us!'

'No, dear, but at home you never saw very much of her. That is what I dislike about town houses: however commodious they may be one can never get away from the other people living in the house! And goodnatured and obliging though poor Maria is I own I have frequently been forced to shut myself into my bedchamber to escape from her. I think,' she added reflectively, 'if ever she came to live at Twynham I should give her a sitting-room of her own.'

'Came to live at Twynham?' he ejaculated. 'You don't mean that Annis means to turn her off?'

'Oh, no! But one never knows what circumstances might arise to make her chaperonage unnecessary. Annis might be married, for instance.'

He laughed at this, and said, with comfortable conviction: 'Not she! Why, she's nine-and-twenty, and a confirmed old maid!'

She said nothing, but he apparently turned her words over in his mind, for he asked her, a few minutes later, if that fellow Carleton was still in Bath.

'He went to London some ten days ago,' she replied. 'His niece, however, is still here, so I imagine he must mean to return.'

'Ay, you wrote to me that she was here, and I wish to my heart she were not! Mind you, she's a taking little thing, and I don't wish to say a word against her, but I've never approved of Annis's conduct over that business, and I never shall!'

'Mr Carleton doesn't approve of it either. He says Annis is not a fit person to take charge of Lucilla.'

'Damned impudence!' growled Sir Geoffrey. 'Not but what she ain't a fit person, and so I've said all along!'

'No, I am persuaded you are right,' she agreed. 'But I fancy— indeed, I *know*—that Mr Carleton has every intention of removing her from Annis's charge. That is why he has gone to London. You must not mention this, Geoffrey, for Lucilla knows nothing about it, and Annis told me in confidence.'

'You told me in the first letter you wrote after I left you here that you thought there was no danger of Annis's losing her heart to him. The Lord only knows why so many women do lose their hearts to him, for a more disagreeable, top-lofty fellow I wish I may never meet!'

'I own I don't like him, but I think he could make himself very agreeable to anyone he wished to please.'

'Good God, you don't mean to tell me he's been making up to Annis?' he exclaimed, in patent horror.

'You wouldn't think so, but—I don't know, Geoffrey! He doesn't flirt with her, and he seems to say detestably uncivil things to her, but if he isn't trying to fix his interests with her, I cannot help wondering why he has remained in Bath for so long.'

'Does she *like* him?' he demanded.

'I don't know that either,' she confessed. 'One wouldn't think so, because they seem to rip up at each other every time they meet; but I have lately suspected that Annis is not as indifferent to him as she would have me believe.'

'You must be mistaken! Annis, of all people, to have a *tendre* for a fellow like Carleton? It isn't possible! Why, they call him the rudest man in London! I am not surprised that he should be trying to attach her: he is notorious for his philandering, and I was very uneasy as soon as I discovered that Lucilla was his niece, for it seemed likely that he would come here, and Annis is a devilish goodlooking woman! But that *she* should be in love with *him*—no, no Amabel, you *must* be mistaken!'

'Perhaps I am, dearest. But if I am not—if she accepts an offer from him—we must learn to like him!'

'*Like him?*' echoed Sir Geoffrey, in a stupefied voice. 'I can tell you this, Amabel: nothing will ever prevail upon me to consent to such a marriage!'

'But Geoffrey—!' she expostulated. 'Your consent isn't needed! Annis isn't a minor! If she decides to marry Mr Carleton she will do so, and you will be obliged to accept him with a good grace—unless you wish to become estranged from her, which I am very sure you don't.'

He looked to be somewhat disconcerted, but said: 'If she chooses to marry Carleton, she will have to bear the consequences. But I shall warn her most solemnly that they may be more disagreeable than she foresees!'

'You will do as you think proper, dearest, but you must promise me that you won't mention this matter to her until she herself speaks of it. Recollect that it is all conjecture at present! And on no account must you say anything to distress her! But when you see her you won't wish to!'

He was not to see her, however, until the following day, a visit from Miss Farlow having left her with a headache, and a disinclination to receive any more visitors. Once the doctor had said that there was no longer any danger of infection to be feared, Lady Wychwood had found it to be impossible to exclude Miss Farlow from her room, for Annis had asked to see Lucilla, and Miss Farlow had, most unfortunately, encountered Lucilla coming out of the sick-room. A painful scene had been the outcome, for, accused of having gone slyly in to see Miss Wychwood when Jurby's back had been turned, Lucilla said indignantly that she had done nothing of the sort: Miss Wychwood had asked for her, and as for Jurby's back having been turned, Jurby had been in the room and was still there. This sent Miss Farlow scurrying away in search of Lady Wychwood, demanding hysterically to know why Lucilla had been permitted to see Miss Wychwood while *she*, her own cousin, was kept out. The end of it was that Lady Wychwood, feeling that there was a certain amount of justification for Miss Farlow's threatened attack of the vapours, had said that no one was trying to keep her away from Annis: of course she might visit her! She added that she knew Maria might be trusted not to stay with her too long, or to talk too much. Miss Farlow, still convulsively sobbing, had replied that she hoped she knew better than to talk too much to persons in dear Annis's tender condition. So too did Lady Wychwood, but she doubted it, and put an end to the visit twenty minutes after Miss Farlow had entered the room, by which time Annis looked as if she was in danger of suffering a relapse.

'I think I must turn you out now, Maria,' Lady Wychwood said, smiling kindly. 'The doctor said only a quarter of an hour, you know!'

'Oh, yes, indeed! So right of him! Poor Annis is sadly pulled! I declare I was quite shocked to find her so pale and unlike herself, but, as I have been telling her, we shall soon have her to rights again. Now I shall leave her, and she must try to go to sleep, must she not? I will just draw the blinds across the window, for nothing is more disagreeable than having the light glaring at one. Not that it is not very pleasant to see the sun again after so many dull days, and they say that it is very beneficial, though I myself rather doubt that. I remember my dear mama saying that it was injurious to the female complexion, and she never went out into the open air without a veil over her face. Well, I must leave you now, dear Annis, but you may be sure I shall be always popping in to see how you go on!'

'Amabel,' said Miss Wychwood faintly, as Miss Farlow at last got herself out of the room, 'if you love me, murder our dear cousin! The first thing she said when she came in was that she wasn't going to talk to me, and she hasn't ceased talking from that moment to this.'

'I am so sorry, dearest, but there was no way of keeping her out without giving grave offence,' responded Lady Wychwood, drawing the blinds back. 'I shan't let her visit you again today, so you may be easy.'

Miss Farlow succeeded in exasperating Sir Geoffrey at the dinner-table, first by uttering a series of singularly foolish observations, and then by trying to argue with Lady Wychwood. As dinner came to an end, she got up, saying: 'Now you must excuse me, if you please! I am going up to sit with our dear invalid for a little while.'

'No, Maria,' said Lady Wychwood, 'Annis is extremely tired, and must have no more visitors today.'

'Oh,' said Miss Farlow, with an angry little titter, 'I do not rank myself as a visitor, Lady Wychwood! *You* have several times gone into Annis's room, and *some* might think *I* had a better claim to do so, being a *blood* relation! Not that I mean to say that you are not a *welcome* visitor, for I am sure she must always be pleased to see you!'

Sir Geoffrey took instant umbrage at this, told her sharply that Lady Wychwood must be the only judge of who should, and who should not be permitted to visit Annis; and added, for good measure, that if she took his advice she would not allow her to go near Annis again, since he had no doubt that it was her ceaseless bibble-babbling that had tired her.

Realizing that she had gone too far, Miss Farlow hastened to say that she had no intention of casting the least slight on dear Lady Wychwood, but she was unable to resist the temptation to add, with another of her irritating titters: 'But as for my visit having tired dear Annis, I venture to suggest that it was Lucilla who did the mischief! A great mistake, if I may say so, to have permitted her to visit—'

'Shall we go up to the drawing-room?' interposed Lady Wychwood, in a voice of quiet authority. 'I think you are rather tired yourself, Maria. Perhaps you would prefer to retire to bed. We must not forget that it is only a very few days since you too were ill.'

Finally quelled, Miss Farlow did retire, but in so reluctant and lingering a way that she was still within tongue-shot when Sir Geoffrey said: 'Well done, Amabel! Lord, what a gabster! Ay, and worse! The idea of her having the brass to say that it was Lucilla who exhausted Annis! A bigger piece of spite I never heard! More likely your visit did my sister a great deal of good, my dear!'

'Of course it did,' said Lady Wychwood. 'Don't look so downcast, child! You must surely be aware that poor Maria is eaten up with jealousy. And allowances must be made for people who are convalescent from the influenza: it often makes them cantankersome! Pray let us put her out of our minds! I was wondering whether it would entertain you to play a game of backgammon with Sir Geoffrey until Limbury brings in the tea-tray?'

But hardly had the board been set out than it had to be put away again, for a late caller arrived, in the person of Lord Beckenham. He had come to enquire after Miss Wychwood. He had only that very afternoon heard of her indisposition, for he had been obliged to visit the Metropolis at the beginning of the week. He explained at somewhat tedious length that he had stopped to eat his dinner at the Ship before continuing his journey, why he had done so, how he had come by the distressing news, and how he had been unable to wait until the next day before coming to discover how Miss Wychwood was going on. He did not know what she, and her ladyship, must have been thinking of him for not having called days ago.

He stayed to drink tea with them, and by the time he left Sir Geoffrey was heartily sick of him, and, having seen him off the premises, informed his wife that if he had to listen to any more forty-jawed persons that day he would go straight off to bed.

# Fifteen

Miss Wychwood, next morning, declared herself to be so much better as to be in a capital way. Jurby did not think that she looked to be in a capital way at all, and strenuously opposed her determination to get up. 'I *must* get up!' said Miss Wychwood, rather crossly. 'How am I ever to be myself again, if you keep me in bed, which of all things I most detest? Besides, my brother is coming to see me this morning, and I will *not* allow him to find me languishing in my bed, looking as if I were on the point of cocking up my toes!'

'We'll see what the doctor says, miss!' said Jurby.

But when Dr Tidmarsh came to visit his patient, just as her almost untouched breakfast had been removed, he annoyed Jurby by saying that it would do Miss Wychwood good to leave her bed for an hour or two, and lie on the sofa. 'I don't think she should dress herself, but her pulse has been normal now since yesterday, and it won't harm her to slip on a dressing-gown, and sit up for a little while.'

'Heaven bless you, doctor!' said Miss Wychwood.

'Ah, that sounds more like yourself, ma'am!' he said laughingly.

'Begging your pardon, sir,' said Jurby, 'Miss Wychwood is not at all like herself! And it is my duty to inform you, sir, that she swallowed only three spoonfuls of the pork jelly she had for her dinner last night, and has had nothing for her breakfast but some tea, and a few scraps of toast!'

'Well, well, we must tempt her appetite, mustn't we? I have no objection to her having a little chicken, say, or even a slice of boiled lamb, if she should fancy it.'

'The truth is that I don't fancy anything,' confessed Annis. 'I have quite lost my appetite! But I will try to eat some chicken, I promise!'

'That's right!' he said. 'Spoken like the sensible woman I know you to be, ma'am!'

Miss Wychwood might be a sensible woman, but the attack of influenza had left her feeling much more like one of the foolish, tearful creatures whom she profoundly despised, for ever lying on sofas, with smelling-salts clutched in their feeble hands, and always dependent on some stronger character to advise and support them. She had heard that influenza often left its victims subject to deep dejection, and she now knew that this was true. Never before had she been so blue-devilled that she felt it was a pity she had ever been born, or that it was too much trouble to try to rouse herself from her listless depression. She told herself that this contemptible state really did arise from her late illness; and that to lie in bed, with nothing better to do than to think how weak and miserable she felt, was merely to encourage her blue-devils. So she refused to yield to the temptation to remain in bed, but got up presently, found that her legs had become inexplicably wayward ('as though the bones had been taken out of them!' she told Jurby, trying to laugh), and was glad to accept the support of Jurby's strong arm on her somewhat tottery progress to her dressing-table. A glance at her reflection in the mirror did nothing to improve her spirits. 'Heavens, Jurby!' she exclaimed. 'What a fright I am! I have a good mind to send you out to buy a pot of rouge for me!'

'Well, I wouldn't buy you any such thing, Miss Annis! Nor you don't look a fright. Just a trifle hagged, which is only to be expected after such a nasty turn as you've had. When I've given your hair a good brushing, and pinned it up under the pretty lace cap you bought only last week, you won't know yourself!'

'I don't know myself now,' said Miss Wychwood. 'Oh, well! I suppose it doesn't signify: Sir Geoffrey never notices whether one is looking one's best or one's worst—but I do wish I had asked you to paper my hair last night!'

'Well, your hair don't signify either, miss, for I shall tuck it into your cap,' replied her unsympathetic handmaid. 'And it's such a warm day there's no reason why you shouldn't wear that lovely dressing-gown you had made for you, and haven't worn above two or three times—the satin one, with the blue posies embroidered all over it, and the lace fichu. That will make you feel much more like yourself, won't it?'

'I hope so, but I doubt it,' said Miss Wychwood.

However, when she had been arrayed in the expensive dressing-gown, and had herself tied the strings of the lace cap under her chin, she admitted that she didn't look *quite* such a mean bit.

Sir Geoffrey was admitted shortly after eleven o'clock, and so far from not noticing that she was not looking her best he was so much shocked by her white face, and heavy eyes that he forgot the injunctions laid upon him and ejaculated: 'Good God, Annis! Dashed if I've ever seen you look so knocked-up! Poor old lady, what a devil of a time you've been having! And when I think that it was that infernal bagpipe who gave it you I could—Well, never mind!' he added, belatedly remembering his instructions. 'No use working ourselves up! Now, I'll tell you what Amabel and I wish you to do, and that is to come to Twynham as soon as you're well enough to travel, and pay us a long visit. How would that be?'

'Delightful! Thank you: how kind of you both! But tell me, how do you find Tom?'

He never needed much encouragement to talk about his children, and spent the rest of his brief stay thus innocuously employed. When he got up to go, he kissed her cheek, gave her an encouraging pat on the shoulder, and said: 'There, no one can accuse *me* of having stayed too long, or talked you to death, can they?'

'Certainly not! It has done me a great deal of good to have a chat with you, and I hope you'll give me a look in later on.'

'Ay, to be sure I will! Ah, is that you, Jurby? Come to turn me out, have you? What a dragon you are! Well, Annis, be a good girl, and see how fast you can get back into high force! I am going to take Amabel for an airing now: just a gentle walk, you know; but I'll look in on you when we come back.'

He then went off, and Jurby removed one of the cushions which was propping her mistress up, and adjured her to close her eyes, and have a nap before her nuncheon was brought up to her.

Lady Wychwood, having reluctantly handed her daughter over to Nurse, was very well pleased to go for an ambling walk with Sir Geoffrey, and not sorry when Lucilla refused an invitation to accompany them. She set off in the direction of the London Road, leaning on her husband's arm, and saying: 'How agreeable it is to be with you again, dearest! Now we can have a comfortable cose, without poor Maria's breaking in on us!'

'Yes, that's what I thought, when I coaxed you to come for a walk with me,' he said. 'Devilish good notion of mine, wasn't it?'

But he would not have thought it a good notion had he known that little more than ten minutes later Mr Carleton would be seeking admittance to Miss Wychwood's house.

Limbury, opening the door to Mr Carleton, said that Miss Wychwood was not at home to visitors. Miss Wychwood, he said, had been unwell, and had not yet left her room.

'So I have already been informed,' said Mr Carleton. 'Take my card up to her, if you please!'

Limbury received the card from him, and said, with a slight bow: 'I will have it conveyed to Miss's room, sir.'

'Well, don't keep me standing on the doorstep!' said Mr Carleton impatiently.

Limbury, an excellent butler, found himself at a loss, for he had never before encountered a morning caller of Mr Carleton's calibre. Vulgar persons he could deal with; no other of Miss Wychwood's friends would have demanded admittance when told that Miss Wychwood was not at home; and Sir Geoffrey, who disliked Mr Carleton, as Limbury was well aware, would certainly wish him to be excluded.

'I regret, sir, that it is not possible for you to see Miss Wychwood. Today is the first time she has been well enough to sit up for an hour or two, and her maid informs me that she had hardly enough strength to walk across the floor to the sofa. So I am persuaded you will understand that you cannot see her today.'

'No, I shan't,' said Mr Carleton, rudely brushing past him into the hall. 'Shut the door! Now take my card up to your mistress immediately, and tell her that I wish to see her!'

Limbury was affronted by Mr Carleton's unceremonious entrance, and he by no means relished being given peremptory commands. He was about to reply with freezing dignity when a suspicion entered his head (he described it later to Mrs Wardlow as a blinding light) that he was confronting a man who was violently in love. To gentlemen in that condition much had to be forgiven, so he forgave Mr Carleton, and said in the fatherly way he spoke to Master Tom: 'Now, you know I can't do that, sir! I'll tell Miss you called, but you can't expect to see her when she has only just got up out of her bed!'

'I not only expect to see her, but I am going to see her!' replied Mr Carleton.

Fortunately for Limbury, he was rescued from his predicament by the appearance on the scene of Jurby, who came down the stairs, dropped the hint of a curtsy, and said: 'Were you wishful to see Miss Annis, sir?'

'Not only wishful, but determined to see her! Are you her abigail?'

'Yes, sir, I am.'

'Good! I have heard her speak of you, and I think your name is Jurby, and that you have been with Miss Wychwood for many years. Am I right?'

'I have been with her ever since she was a child, sir.'

'Good again! You must know her very well, and can tell me whether it will harm her to see me.'

'I don't think it would *harm* her, sir, but I cannot take it upon myself to say whether she will be willing to receive you.'

'Ask her!'

She seemed to consider him dispassionately for a moment; and then said: 'Certainly, sir. If you will be pleased to wait in the drawing-room, I will do so.'

She turned and went majestically up the stairs again; and Limbury, recovering from the shock of seeing the most formidable member of the household yield without a sign of disapproval to Mr Carleton's outrageous demand, conducted him to the drawing-room. He was immensely interested in this unprecedented situation, and his enjoyment of it was no longer marred by fear of Sir Geoffrey's wrath, because if Sir Geoffrey came the ugly he could now foist the blame of Mr Carleton's intrusion on to Jurby.

Mr Carleton had not long to wait before Jurby came into the drawing-room, saying: 'Miss Annis will be happy to receive you, sir. Please to come with me!' She conducted him up the second pair of stairs, and paused on the landing, and said: 'I must warn you, sir, that Miss Annis is by no means fully restored to health.

You will find her very pulled by the fever, and I hope you won't agitate her.'

'I hope so too,' he replied.

She seemed to be satisfied with this reply, for she opened the door into Miss Wychwood's bedroom, and ushered him in, saying in a voice wholly devoid of interest: 'Mr Carleton, miss.'

She stayed, holding the door open, for a few moments, because when she had carried the news of Mr Carleton's arrival to her mistress Miss Wychwood had behaved in an extremely agitated way, and had seemed not to know whether she wished to see him or not. She had started up from her recumbent position, uttering distractedly: 'Mr Carleton? Oh, no, I cannot—Jurby, are you hoaxing me? Is he indeed here? Oh, why must he come back just when I am so hagged and miserably unwell? I won't see him! He is the most detestable—Oh, whatever am I to do?'

'Well, miss, if you wish me to send him away, I'll try my best to do it, but from the looks of him it's likely he'll order me to get out of the way, and come charging up the stairs, and the next thing you'll know he'll be knocking at your door—if he don't walk in without knocking, which wouldn't surprise me!'

Miss Wychwood gave an uncertain laugh. '*Odious* man! Take this horrid shawl away! If I *must* see him, I will *not* do so lying on the sofa as though I were dying of a deep decline!'

So, when Mr Carleton entered, he found Miss Wychwood seated at one end of the sofa, the train of her dressing-gown lying in soft folds at her feet and her glorious hair hidden under a lace cap. She had managed to regain a measure of composure, and said, in a tolerably steady voice: 'How do you do? You must forgive me for receiving you like this: Jurby will have told you, I daresay, that I have been unwell, and am not yet permitted to leave my room.'

As she spoke, she tried to rise, but her knees shook so much that she was obliged to clutch at the arm of the sofa to save herself from falling. But even as she tottered Mr Carleton, crossing the room in two strides, caught her in his arms, and held her close, breast to breast, and fiercely kissed her.

'Oh!' gasped Miss Wychwood, making a feeble attempt to thrust him off. 'How *dare* you? Let me go at once!'

'You'd tumble over if I did,' he said, and kissed her again.

'No, no, you must not! Oh, what an abominable person you are! I wish I had never met you!' declared Miss Wychwood, abandoning the unequal struggle to free herself, and subsiding limply within his powerful arms, and shedding tears into his shoulder.

At this point, Jurby, smiling dourly, withdrew, apparently feeling that Mr Carleton was very well able to deal with Miss Wychwood without her assistance.

'Don't cry, my precious wet-goose!' said Mr Carleton, planting a third kiss under Miss Wychwood's ear, which, as her head was resting on his shoulder, was the only place available to him.

A watery chuckle showed that Miss Wychwood's sense of humour had survived the ravages of influenza. 'I am not a wet-goose!'

'You can't expect me to believe you if you don't stop crying at once!' he said severely. He swept her off her feet as he spoke, and set her down again on the sofa, himself sitting beside her, taking her hands in his, and pressing a kiss into each pink palm. 'Poor Honey!' he said. 'What a wretched time you've been having, haven't you?'

'Yes, but it is very unhandsome of you to call me a poor Honey!' she said, trying for a rallying note. 'You had as well tell me that I've become a positive antidote! My glass has told me so already, so it won't come as a shock to me!'

'Your glass lies. I see no change in you, except that you are paler than I like, and are wearing a cap, which I've not known you to do before.' He surveyed it critically. 'Very fetching!' he approved. 'But I think I prefer to see your guinea-curls. Will you feel obliged to wear caps when we are married?'

'But—*are* we going to be married?' she said.

'Well, of course we are! You don't suppose I'm offering you a *carte blanche*, do you?'

That made her laugh. 'I shouldn't be surprised if you were, for you are quite abominable, you know!'

'Wouldn't you be surprised?' he demanded.

Her eyes sank before the hard, questioning look in his. She said: 'You needn't glare at me! I only meant it for a joke! Of course it would surprise me!'

'Unamusing! Are you afraid I should be unfaithful to you? Is that why you said "*are* we to be married?" as though you still had doubts?'

'No, I'm not afraid of that. After all, if you did become unfaithful I should only have myself to blame, shouldn't I?'

The hard look vanished; he smiled. 'I don't think you would find many people to agree that *you* were to blame for *my* sins!'

'Anyone with a particle of commonsense would agree with me, because if you were to set up a mistress it would be because you had become bored with me.'

'Oh, if that's the case we need not worry! But you do still have doubts, don't you?'

'Not when you are with me,' she said shyly. 'Only when I'm alone, and think of all the difficulties—what a very big step it would be—how much my brother would dislike it—I wonder if perhaps it wouldn't be a mistake to marry you. And then I think that it would be a much greater mistake *not* to marry you, and I end by not knowing *what* I want to do! Mr Carleton, are you *sure* you want to marry me, and—and that I'm not a mere passing fancy?'

'What you are trying to ask me is whether I am sure we shall be happy, isn't it?'

'Yes, I suppose that is what I mean,' she sighed.

'Well, I can't answer you. How can I be *sure* that we shall be happy when neither of us has had any experience of marriage? All I can tell you is that I am perfectly sure I want to marry you, and equally sure that you are not a "mere passing fancy" of mine—what a damned silly question to ask me! If I had ever been such a shuttlehead as to have asked one of my passing fancies to marry me, I shouldn't be a bachelor today!—and there are two other things I am *sure* of! One is that I have never cared for any of the charmers with whom I've had agreeable connections as I care for you; and another is that I have never in my life wanted anything more than I want to win you for my *own*—to love, and to cherish, and to guard—Oh, damn it, Annis, how can I make you believe that I love you with my whole heart and body, and mind?' He broke off, and said sharply: 'What have I said to make you cry? Tell me!'

'Nothing! I d–don't know why I began to cry. I think it must be because I'm so happy, and I've been feeling so dreadfully miserable!' she replied, wiping her tears away, and trying to smile.

Mr Carleton took her back into his arms. 'You're thoroughly knocked-up, sweetheart. *Damn* that woman for having foisted her influenza on to you! Kiss me!'

'I won't!' said Miss Wychwood, between tears and laughter. 'It would be a most improper thing for me to do, and you have *no* right to fling orders at me as though I were one of your bits of muslin, and I won't submit to being ridden over rough-shod!'

'Hornet!' said Mr Carleton, and put an end to further recrimin-ations by fastening his lips to hers.

Not the most daring of her previous suitors had ventured even to slide an arm round her waist, for although she enjoyed light-hearted flirtation, she never gave her flirts any cause to think she would welcome more intimate approaches. She had supposed that she must have a cold, celibate disposition, for she had always found the mere thought of being kissed, and (as she phrased it) mauled by any gentleman of her acquaintance shudderingly distasteful. She had once confessed this to Amabel, and had privately thought Amabel's response to be so foolishly sentimental as to be unworthy of consideration. Amabel had said: 'When you fall in love, dearest, you won't find it at all distasteful, I promise you.' And sweet, silly little Amabel had been right! When Mr Carleton had caught Miss Wychwood into his arms, and had so ruthlessly kissed her, she had not found it at all distasteful; and when he did it again it seemed the most natural thing in the world to return his embrace. He felt the responsive quiver that ran through her, and his arms tightened round her, just as some one knocked on the door. Miss Wychwood tore herself free, uttering: 'Take care! This may well be my sister, or Maria!'

It was neither. The youngest of her three housemaids came in, bearing a jug and a glass on a tray. At sight of Mr Carleton this damsel stopped on the threshold, and stood goggling at him, with her eyes starting from their sockets.

'What the devil do you want?' demanded Mr Carleton, pardonably annoyed.

'Please, sir, I don't want anything!' said the intruder, trembling with terror. 'I didn't know Miss had a visitor! Mrs Wardlow told me to bring the fresh barley-water up to Miss, being as Betty is sick!'

'*Barley-water?*' ejaculated Mr Carleton, in revolted accents. 'Good God! No wonder that you are in low spirits if that's what they give you to drink!'

'It has lemon in it, sir!' offered the maid.

'So much the worse! Take it away, and tell Limbury to send up some Burgundy! *My* orders!'

'Yes, sir, b-but what will I say to Mrs Wardlow, if you p-please, sir?'

Miss Wychwood intervened. 'You need say nothing to her, Lizzy. Just set the barley-water on that table, and desire Limbury to send up a bottle of Burgundy for Mr Carleton. And when it comes *you* will drink it,' she informed her visitor, as soon as Lizzy had scurried away. '*I* don't want it!'

'You may think you don't, but it is exactly what you do want!' he retorted. 'Next they will be bringing you a bowl of gruel!'

'Oh, no!' said Miss Wychwood demurely. 'Dr Tidmarsh says that I may have a little chicken now that I am so much better. Or even a slice of boiled mutton.'

'That ought to tempt you!' he said sardonically.

She smiled. 'Well, to tell you the truth, I haven't any appetite, so it doesn't much signify what they bring me to eat!'

'Oh, how much I wish I had you under my own roof!'

'So that you could bullock me into eating my dinner, Mr Carleton? I shouldn't like that at all!' she said, shaking her head.

'If you don't stop calling me *Mr Carleton*, my girl, we shall very soon find ourselves at dagger-drawing!'

'Oh, that terrifies me into obedience—Oliver! What a shocking thing it would be if we were to fall out!'

He smiled, and raised her hand to his lips. 'Shocking indeed! And so unprecedented!'

'It's all very well for you to kiss my hand,' said Miss Wychwood austerely, 'but what you *ought* to do is to promise that you will never quarrel with me again! But as I have known ever since I made your acquaintance that you haven't the least notion of conducting yourself with elegance or propriety, I imagine it is ridiculous of me to expect that of you!'

'Quite ridiculous! I never promise what I know I can't perform!

'*Odious* creature!'

He grinned at her. 'Should I be less odious if I humbugged you with court-promises? Of course we shall quarrel, for I have a naggy temper, and you, I thank God, are not one of those meek women who say yes and amen to everything! Which reminds me that I have hit on a solution to the problem of what to do with Lucilla to which I do expect you to say yes and amen!'

'But when we are married she will naturally live with us!'

'Oh, no, she will not!' he said. 'If you imagine, my loved one, that I am prepared to stand by complacently while my bride devotes herself to my niece, rid yourself of that idiotic notion! Think for a moment! Do you really wish to include a third person—and one who must be chaperoned wherever she goes!—into our household? If you do, I do not! I want a *wife*, not a chaperon for my niece!' He took her hands, and held them in a compelling grasp. 'A companion, Annis! Someone who may say, if I suggest to her that we should jaunt over to Paris, that she doesn't feel inclined to go to Paris, but who won't say: "But how can I leave Lucilla?" Do you understand what I mean?'

'Oh, my dear, of course I do! I don't wish to include a third person in our household, and I must own that fond though I am of Lucilla I do find that the task of looking after her is heavier than I had supposed it would be. But how unkind it would be to send her to live with someone else, for no fault of hers, but merely because we didn't wish to be bothered with her! If she knew, and liked, any of her paternal aunts, or cousins, the case would be different, but she doesn't, and thanks to that miserable aunt the only friends the poor child has are those she has made here, in Bath!'

'Yes, exactly so! What do you say to giving her into Mrs Stinchcombe's charge until it is time for her to make her comeout?'

Miss Wychwood sat up with a jerk. 'Oliver! Of course it would be the very thing for her, and what she would like best, I am very sure. But would Mrs Stinchcombe be willing to take her?'

'Perfectly willing. In fact, it was settled between us this morning! I came here straight from Laura Place. It was Mrs Stinchcombe who told me that you had been ill, and—Oh, lord, *now* what?'

But the timid tap on the door merely heralded the reappearance of Lizzy, who came in carrying a silver salver, on which stood a decanter, two of Miss Wychwood's best Waterford wineglasses, and a wooden biscuit tub with a silver lid. Mr Carleton, perceiving that the decanter was in imminent danger of sliding off the salver, got up quickly, and went to take the tray into his own hands, saying: 'That's a good girl! Run along now!'

'Yes, sir! Thank you, sir!' said Lizzy, and slid out of the room in a manner strongly suggestive of one escaping from a tiger's cage.

Miss Wychwood, observing with some surprise her cherished Waterford glasses, said: 'What in the world possessed Limbury to send up the best glasses? I only use them for parties! I collect you frightened him out of his wits, just as you frightened poor Lizzy!'

'No such thing!' said Mr Carleton, pouring Burgundy into one of the best glasses. 'Limbury is doing justice to this occasion. Good butlers are always awake upon every suit! Here you are, love: see if my prescription doesn't pluck you up!'

Miss Wychwood took the glass, but refused to drink the Burgundy unless Mr Carleton joined her. So he poured out a glass for himself, and was just raising it to toast her when Miss Farlow burst into the room, powerfully agitated, stopped dead on the threshold, and exclaimed: '*Well!*'

Miss Wychwood was startled into spilling some of the Burgundy. She set her glass down, and tried to rub away the stains from the skirt of her gown with her handkerchief, saying crossly: 'Really, Maria, it is too bad of you! *Look* what you have made me do! What do you want?'

'I am here, Annis, to preserve you from the consequences of your own folly!' said Miss Farlow. 'How *could* you receive a member of the Male Sex in your bedchamber, and in your *dressing-gown*? Sir, I must request you to leave immediately!'

'You don't mean to tell me that's a dressing-gown?' interrupted Mr Carleton, a dangerous gleam in his eyes. 'Well, it's by far the most elegant one I've ever been privileged to see, and I suppose I must have seen scores of 'em in my time—paid for them too!'

'For goodness' sake, Oliver—!' Miss Wychwood said, in an imploring whisper.

Trembling with outraged propriety, Miss Farlow uttered a terrible indictment of Mr Carleton's manners, morals, and shameless disregard of the rules of conduct governing any man venturing to call himself a *gentleman*. A shattering retort rose to his lips, but he bit it back, because he saw that Miss Wychwood was by no means enjoying this encounter, and merely said: 'Well, now that you have convinced me, ma'am, that I am so far sunk in moral turpitude as to be past praying for, may I suggest that you withdraw from this scene of vice?'

'Nothing,' declared Miss Farlow, 'will prevail upon me to leave this room while you remain in it, sir! I do not know by what means you forced yourself into it—'

'Oh, do, pray, Maria, stop talking such fustian nonsense, and go away!' begged Miss Wychwood. 'Mr Carleton did not force his way into my room! He came at my invitation, and if I have to listen to any more ranting from you I shall go into strong hysterics!'

'Sir Geoffrey entrusted you to my care, Annis, and never shall it be said of me that I betrayed the confidence he reposed in me! Since Jurby has been so unmindful of her duty—not that that surprises me, for I have always considered that you permitted her *far* too much license, so that she has grown to be so big in her own esteem that—'

'Oh, cut line, woman!' said Mr Carleton, striding to the door, and opening it. 'Miss Wychwood has asked you to go away, and

I have every intention of seeing to it that you do go away! Don't keep me waiting!'

'And leave my sacred charge unprotected? Never!' declared Miss Farlow heroically.

'Oh, for God's sake—!' snapped Mr Carleton, at the end of his patience. 'What the devil do you suppose I'm going to do to her? Rape her? I will give you thirty seconds to leave this room, and if you are not on the other side of the door by that time I shall eject you forcibly!'

'Brute!' ejaculated Miss Farlow, bursting into tears. 'Offering violence to a defenceless female! Only wait until Sir Geoffrey knows of this!'

He paid no heed, but kept his eyes on his watch. Miss Farlow hesitated between heroism and fright. He shut his watch with a snap, restored it to his pocket, and advanced purposefully towards her. Miss Farlow's courage failed. She uttered a shriek, and ran out of the room.

Mr Carleton shut the door, and applied himself to the more agreeable task of soothing Miss Wychwood's lacerated nerves, in which he succeeded so well that in a very short space of time her racing pulses had steadied to a normal rate, and she not only allowed herself to be coaxed to swallow the rest of the Burgundy in her glass, but even to nibble a biscuit.

Miss Farlow's state was less happy. The intelligence, conveyed to her by Jurby, who was hovering on the landing, that Miss Wychwood had a visitor with her, and did not wish to be disturbed, had aroused all her smouldering jealousy. She had told Jurby that she had had no business to introduce a visitor into Miss Wychwood's room, and was unwise enough to say: 'You should have asked leave to do so from me, or from her ladyship! Who is this visitor?'

'One that will do her more good than you ever will, miss!' had said Jurby, goaded into retort. 'It is Mr Carleton!'

Miss Farlow had been at first incredulous, and then sincerely shocked. In her chaste mind, every man—except, of course, doctors, fathers, and brothers—figured as a potential menace to a maiden's virtue. Even had it been Lord Beckenham who was closeted with Miss Wychwood she would have felt it to be her duty to have pointed out to him the impropriety of his visiting a lady in her bedchamber, who was wearing nothing but a dressing-gown over her nightdress. But Lord Beckenham—such a perfect gentleman!—would never have dreamt of compromising a lady in such a scandalous fashion. As for Annis, not only tolerating, but actually *encouraging* Mr Carleton in his nefarious conduct, she could only suppose that her poor dear cousin had taken leave of her senses. Since she (a defenceless female) had been unable to prevail upon this Brute to withdraw from Miss Wychwood's room, there was only one thing to be done, and that was to pour the whole story into Sir Geoffrey's ears the instant he returned from his walk with Lady Wychwood. With this intention, she hurried downstairs, mentally rehearsing her rôle in the forthcoming drama, and working herself up into a hysterical state. She encountered Sir Geoffrey just as he was about to enter the drawing-room.

He and Lady Wychwood had returned to the house some minutes earlier. Fortunately for Lady Wychwood, she had gone up immediately to the nursery, to assure herself that Tom had taken no harm from his first expedition, since his illness, into the garden, so she was spared the horrid news Miss Farlow was only too anxious to recount to her.

Sir Geoffrey was not so fortunate. Having regaled himself with a glass of sherry, he mounted the stairs to the first floor, and was instantly assailed by Miss Farlow, who came stumbling down the stairs, uttering in a hysterical voice: 'Cousin Geoffrey! Oh, Cousin Geoffrey! Thank God you are come!'

Sir Geoffrey eyed her with disfavour. He was unaccustomed to females who flew into distempered freaks, and he had already

taken Miss Farlow in dislike. He said: 'What the deuce is the
matter with you, Maria?'

'Oh, nothing, nothing—except that I have never been so
shocked in my life! It is Annis! You must go up to her room
immediately!'

'Eh?' said Sir Geoffrey, startled. 'Annis? Why, what's amiss
with her?'

'I do not know how to tell you! If it were not my duty to
do so, I could not bring myself to disclose to you what will curl
your liver!' said Miss Farlow, extracting the last ounce of drama
from the situation.

Sir Geoffrey was incensed. 'For God's sake, Maria, stop talking
as if you were taking part in a Cheltenham tragedy, and tell
me what has put you into this taking! Curl my liver indeed!
Without any more ado, answer me this!—Is there anything
wrong with my sister?'

'Everything!' declared Miss Farlow, clinging to the most
important rôle of her life.

'Balderdash!' said Sir Geoffrey. 'It's my belief you're getting
to be queer in your attic, Maria! Never mind my liver! *What has
happened to my sister?*'

'That Man,' disclosed Miss Farlow, 'has been closeted with
her since you and dear Lady Wychwood left the house! And he
is still with her! Had I known that he had forced his way into
the house, and that Jurby was so lost to all sense of her duty as
to admit him into Annis's bedchamber—but no doubt he
bribed her to do it!—I should have summoned James to cast
him out of the house! But I was with Tom, in the garden, and
I knew nothing until I came in, and was just about to pop into
Annis's room, when Jurby stopped me, saying that Annis was
engaged. "Engaged?" I said. "She has a visitor with her, and she
don't wish to be disturbed," she said. You may depend upon it
that I insisted on her telling me who had come to visit Annis

without so much as a by your leave! And then Jurby told me that it was That Man!'

'*What* man?' demanded Sir Geoffrey.

'Mr Carleton!' said Miss Farlow, shuddering.

'Carleton? What the devil is he doing in my sister's room?'

'Carousing!' said Miss Farlow, reaching her grand climax.

It fell sadly flat. Sir Geoffrey said testily: 'I wish to God you wouldn't talk such nonsense, Maria! Next I suppose you'll tell me my sister was *carousing* too!'

'Alas, yes!'

'It seems to me that it's you who have been carousing!' said Sir Geoffrey severely. 'You had best go and sleep it off!'

With this he went on up the stairs to the second floor, paying no heed whatsoever to the protests, the assurances that she never touched strong liquor; or the impassioned entreaties to listen to her, which Miss Farlow addressed to him.

He entered Miss Wychwood's room without ceremony, and was confronted by the spectacle of his sister seated beside Mr Carleton on the sofa, supported by his arm, and with her head on his shoulder.

'Upon my word!' he ejaculated thunderously. 'What the devil does this mean?'

'Oh, pray don't shout!' said Miss Wychwood, straightening herself.

Mr Carleton rose. 'How do you do, Wychwood? I've been waiting for you! I imagine you must know what the devil it means, but before we go into that, *I* want to know what the devil *you* mean by planting that atrocious woman on your sister! Never in the whole of my existence have I encountered any one who talked more infernal twaddle, or who had less notion of how to look after sick persons! She burst in on us, just as I had succeeded in getting Annis to drink a glass of Burgundy—which, if I may say so, will do her far more good than barley-water! See to it that she has a glass with her dinner, will you?—and had the damned impudence to say that nothing would prevail upon her to leave the room while I remained in it! I can only assume that she thought Annis was in danger of being raped! If I hadn't threatened to throw her out, she'd be here still, upsetting Annis with all her ravings and rantings, and I-will-not permit her, or anyone else, to upset Annis!'

Sir Geoffrey disliked Mr Carleton, but he found himself so much in sympathy with him that instead of requesting him, with cold dignity, to leave the house, which he had meant to do, he said: 'I didn't plant her on Annis! All I did was to *suggest* to Annis that she would be a suitable person to act as her companion!'

'*Suitable*?' interpolated Mr Carleton scathingly.

Sir Geoffrey glared at him, but being a just man he felt himself obliged to say: 'No, of course she's not suitable, but I didn't know *then* that she was such an infernal gabster, and I didn't know until today that she's touched in her upper works! I shall certainly take care she don't come near Annis again—though what right you have to interfere I'm quite at a loss to understand! What's more, I'll thank you to leave *me* to look after my sister!'

'That,' said Mr Carleton, 'brings us back to the start of our conversation. Your sister, Wychwood, has done me the honour to accept my hand in marriage. That's what the devil this means, and it also explains the right I have to concern myself with her welfare!'

'Well, I won't have it!' said Sir Geoffrey. 'I refuse to give my consent to a marriage of which I utterly disapprove!'

'Oh, Geoffrey, don't! *Pray* don't get into a quarrel!' begged Miss Wychwood, pressing her hands against her throbbing temples. 'You are making my head ache again, *both* of you! I am very sorry to displease you, Geoffrey, but I am not a silly schoolgirl, and I haven't decided to marry Oliver on an impulse! And as for giving your consent, your consent isn't necessary! I'm not under age, I'm not your ward, and never was your ward, and there is nothing you can do to stop me marrying Oliver!'

'We'll see to that!' he said ominously. 'Let me make it plain to you—'

'No, don't try to do that!' intervened Mr Carleton. 'She's far too exhausted to talk any more! Make it plain to me instead! I suggest we go down to the book-room, and discuss the matter in private. We shall do much better without female interference, you know!'

This made Miss Wychwood lift her head from between her hands, and say indignantly: 'This has nothing to do with Geoffrey! And if you think I am going to sit meekly here while you and he—'

'Come, come!' said Mr Carleton. 'Where is your sense of decorum? Your brother, very properly, wishes to discover what my circumstances are, what settlement I mean to make on you—'

'No, I do not!' interrupted Sir Geoffrey angrily. 'Everyone knows you're swimming in lard, and settlements don't come into it, because if I have anything to say to it there will be no marriage!'

'You have nothing to say to it, Geoffrey, and no right to meddle in my affairs!'

'Oh, that's going too far!' said Mr Carleton. 'He may not have the right to *meddle*, but he has every right to try to dissuade you from making what he believes would be a disastrous marriage. A poor sort of brother he would be if he didn't!'

Taken aback, Sir Geoffrey blinked at him. 'Well—well, I'm glad that you at least realize that!' he said lamely.

'Well, I do not realize it!' struck in Miss Wychwood.

'Of course you don't!' said Mr Carleton soothingly. 'In another moment you'll be saying that the marriage has nothing to do with me either, my lovely wet-goose! So we will postpone this discussion until tomorrow. Oh, no! don't look daggers at me! I never come to cuffs with females who are too knocked-up to be a match for me!'

She gave a choke of laughter. 'Oh, how detestable you are!' she sighed.

'That sounds more like you,' he approved. He bent over her, and kissed her. 'You are worn out, and must go back to bed, my sweet. Promise me you won't get up again today!'

'I doubt if I could,' she said ruefully. 'But if you and Geoffrey mean to quarrel over me—'

'It takes two to make a quarrel. I can't answer for Wychwood, but I have no intention of quarrelling, so you may be easy on that head!'

'*Easy?* When you spend your life quarrelling, and being disagreeable to people for no reason at all? I am not in the least easy!'

'Hornet!' he said, and went out of the room, thrusting Sir Geoffrey before him. 'I don't think much of your strategy, Wychwood,' he said, as they began to descend the stairs. 'Abusing me won't answer your purpose: it will merely set up her bristles.'

Sir Geoffrey said stiffly: 'I must make it plain to you, Carleton, that the thought of my sister's marriage to a man of your reputation is—is wholly repugnant to me!'

'You've done so already.'

'Well, I have no wish to offend you, but I don't consider you a fit and proper person to be my sister's husband!'

'Oh, that doesn't offend me! I have every sympathy with you, and should feel just as you do, if I were in your place.'

'Well, upon my word!' gasped Sir Geoffrey. 'You are the most extraordinary fellow I've ever met in all my life!'

'No, am I?' said Mr Carleton, grinning at him. 'Because I agree with you?'

'If you agree with me I wonder that you should have proposed to Annis!'

'Ah, that's a different matter!'

'Well, I think it only right to warn you that I think it is my duty—distasteful though it is to speak of such things to delicately nurtured females—to tell Annis frankly *why* I consider you to be unfit to be her husband!'

Mr Carleton gave a crack of laughter. 'Lord, Wychwood, don't be such a gudgeon!' he said. 'She knows all about my reputation! Tell her anything you like, but don't do so today, will you? I don't want her to be upset again, and she would be. Goodbye! My regards to Lady Wychwood!'

A nod, and he was gone, leaving Sir Geoffrey at a loss to know what to make of him. He went gloomily up to the drawing-room, and when Lady Wychwood joined him a little later, disclosed to her that she had been right in her forecast, adding, with a heavy sigh, that he didn't know what was to be done to prevent the match.

'I'm afraid there's nothing to be done, dearest. I know it isn't what you like. It isn't what I like for her either, but when I saw the *difference* in her! I have just come from her room, and though she is tired, she looks much better, and so happy that I knew it would be useless, and even *wrong* to try to make her cry off! So we must make the best of it, and *pray* that he won't continue in his—his present way of life!'

Sir Geoffrey shook his head. 'A man don't change his habits,' he said. 'I don't believe in reformed rakes, Amabel.'

'I don't mean to set up my opinion against your judgement, for naturally you must know best, but has it occurred to you, dearest, that although we have heard a great deal about his mistresses, and the shameless way he flaunts them abroad, and the money he squanders on them, we have never heard of his attaching himself particularly to any girl of quality? Indeed, I believe Annis is the only woman to whom he has offered marriage, though lures past counting have been thrown out to him, because even the highest sticklers think that his wealth is enough to make him acceptable. So don't you think, Geoffrey, that perhaps he never *truly* loved anyone until he met Annis? Which makes me feel that they were *destined* for each other, for it has been the same with her. I don't mean, of course, *exactly* the same, but only think of the offers she has received, and refused! Such brilliant ones, too! Never, until she met Mr Carleton, has she been in love! Not even with Lord Sedgeley, though one would have said he was the very man for her! You will think me fanciful, I daresay, but it seems to me as if—as if each of them has been waiting for the other for years, and when they at last met they— they fell in love, as though it had been ordained that they should!'

Sir Geoffrey, listening to this speech in frowning silence, was secretly impressed by it, but all he said was: 'Well, you may be right, my love, but I do think that you're being fanciful! All I can say is that if you *are* right, I wish to God they never had met!'

'It is very natural that you should,' responded the perfect wife. 'But don't let us talk about it any more until you have had time to weigh the matter in your mind! Mrs Wardlow asked me this morning if she should instruct the chef to send up baked eggs for our nuncheon, and, knowing how partial you are to baked eggs, I said it was the very thing. So let us go down to the breakfast-parlour now, before the eggs grow cold!'

Sir Geoffrey got up, but before he had reached the door stopped in his tracks like a jibbing horse, and said: 'Is Maria there? Because if she is nothing would prevail upon me—'

'No, no, dearest!' Lady Wychwood hastened to assure him. 'Mrs Wardlow and I have put her to bed, and I have compelled her to drink a glass of laudanum and water, as a sedative, you understand. She fell into a fit of the vapours when you went up to see Annis, and what it was that you said to her to overset her so completely, I haven't a notion, for you cannot possibly have accused her of being *inebriated*, which is what she said you did! But I am sorry to say that when Maria becomes hysterical, one cannot place the least dependence on the ridiculous things she says. She even said that Mr Carleton offered her *violence*!'

'No, did he?' exclaimed Sir Geoffrey, brightening perceptibly. 'Well, damme if I don't think he's not by half as black as he's been painted! But mind this, Amabel! I may not have the power to stop him marrying my sister, but if he thinks he's going to foist Maria on to us, he will very soon learn that he is mistaken! And so I shall tell him!'

'Yes, dearest,' said Lady Wychwood, gently propelling him towards the door. 'You will of course do what you think is right, but do, pray, come and eat your baked egg before it is quite spoilt!'

# Charity
# Girl

# One

$\mathcal{A}$S FAR AS IT WAS POSSIBLE FOR AN ELDERLY GENTLEMAN suffering from dyspepsia and a particularly violent attack of gout to take pleasure in anything but the alleviation of his various pains the Earl of Wroxton was enjoying himself. He was engaged on the agreeable task of delivering himself of a diatribe on the shortcomings of his heir. To the uninitiated his strictures must have seemed unjust, for Viscount Desford bore the appearance of a son of whom any father must have been proud. In addition to a goodlooking countenance, and a lithe, athletic figure, he had the easy manners which sprang as much from an innate amiability as from his breeding. He had also a considerable store of patience, and a sense of humour which showed itself in the smile which lurked in his eyes, and which was thought by a great many persons to be irresistible. His father was not of their number: when a victim of gout, he thought it exasperating.

The month was July, but the weather was so far from sultry that the Earl had caused a fire to be kindled in his library. On either side of the hearth he and his heir were seated, the Earl with one heavily bandaged foot on a stool, and his heir (having discreetly edged his chair away from the warmth of the smouldering logs) at his graceful ease opposite him. The Viscount was wearing the coat, the buckskin breeches, and the topboots which were the correct morning-attire for any gentleman sojourning in the country, but a certain elegance, deriving from the cut of his coat, and the arrangement of his neckcloth, gave his father an excuse for apostrophizing him as a damned dandy. To which he responded, in mild protest: 'No, no, sir! The dandy-set would be shocked to hear you say so!'

'I collect,' said his father, glaring at him, 'that you call yourself a Corinthian!'

'To own the truth, sir,' said the Viscount apologetically, 'I don't call myself anything!' He waited for a moment, watching with as much sympathy as amusement the champing of his parent's jaws, and then said coaxingly: 'Now, come, Papa! What have I done to earn such a trimming from you?'

'What have you done to earn praise from me?' instantly countered the Earl. 'Nothing! You're a skitterbrain, sir! A slibber-slabber here-and-thereian, with no more thought for what you owe your name than some rubbishing commoner! A damned scattergood—and you've no need to remind me that you're not dependent on *me* for the money you waste on your horses, and your betting, and your bits of muslin, for I'm well aware of it, and what I said at the time, and say now, and always shall say is that it was just like your great-aunt to leave her fortune to you, and exactly what might have been expected of such a shuttlehead as she was! As well have handed you a carte blanche to commit every sort of—of extravagant folly! But on that head,' said his lordship inaccurately, but with perfect sincerity, 'I shall say nothing! She was your mother's aunt and *that* circumstance seals my lips.'

He paused, throwing a challenging glance at his heir, but the Viscount merely said, with becoming meekness : 'Just so, Papa!'

'Had she stipulated that her fortune was to be used for the support of your wife and family I should have thought it a very proper bequest,' announced his lordship, adding, however: 'Not that I was not at that time, and at this present, able and willing to increase your allowance to enable you to meet the added expenses consequent on your entry into the married state.'

He paused again, and the Viscount, feeling that some comment was expected, said politely that he was much obliged to him.

'Oh, no, you're not!' said his lordship grimly. 'And, what's more, you won't be until you provide me with a grandson, no matter how fast your great-aunt's fortune burns in your pockets! Upon my word, a pretty set of children I have!' he said, suddenly enlarging his scope. 'Not one of you cares a straw for the Family! At my age I might have expected to have had a score of grandchildren to gladden my last years! But have I? No! Not one!'

'In fact you have three,' replied the Viscount disconcertingly. 'Not that it has ever seemed to me that they gladdened you precisely, but I do feel it to be only just to Griselda that her offspring should be mentioned!'

'Girls!' snapped the Earl, sweeping them aside with a contemptuous gesture. 'I take no account of them! Besides, they're Broxbourne brats! What I want is sons, Ashley! *Carring-tons,* to succeed to our Name, and our Honours, and our Tradition!'

'But scarcely a score of them!' protested the Viscount. 'One must be reasonable, sir, and even if I had obliged you by marrying when I was twenty, and my unfortunate wife had presented me with twins every year, you must still have been at least two short of your expectation—setting aside the probability that there would have been several girls amongst such a bevy of grandchildren.'

This attempt to win his parent out of his ill-humour might have succeeded (for the Earl was fond of the ridiculous) had not a sudden twinge in his afflicted foot caused him to wince, and to utter in a menacing voice: 'Don't be impertinent, sir! I would remind you that you—I thank God!—are not my only son!'

'No,' agreed the Viscount, with unruffled cordiality. 'And while I can't but feel that Simon is too young to be setting up his nursery I have great hopes that Horace may oblige you—when the Occupation ends, as, from all accounts, it will do in the not too far distant future—and he returns to us.'

'Horace!' uttered his lordship. 'I may think myself fortunate if he doesn't come home with some French hussy on his arm!'

'Oh, I don't think that very likely!' said the Viscount. 'He is not at all partial to foreigners, sir, and quite as mindful of what is due to the Family as you are.'

'I shan't be alive to see it,' said the Earl, seeking refuge in decrepitude, but slightly damaging his effect by adding an acrimonious rider: 'Much any of you will care!'

The Viscount laughed, but with a good deal of affection. 'No, no, Papa!' he said. 'Don't try to pitch the fork to me! I haven't been on the town for nine years—and intimately acquainted with you for *twenty*-nine years!—without learning when a man is trying to come crab over me! Good God, sir, you're all skin and whipcord—saving only a tendency to gout, which you may easily overcome by *not* drinking the best part of two bottles of port at a sitting—and you'll hold for a long trig! Long enough, I've little doubt, to rake down a son of mine as you're raking me down today!'

The Earl could not help being gratified to know that his heir considered him to be in very good condition, but he thought it proper to say austerely that he neither understood nor approved of the cant expressions so deplorably in use amongst the young men of the day. He toyed for a moment with the impulse to inform the Viscount, in forthright terms, that when he desired his opinion of his drinking habits he would ask him for it, but discarded this notion, because he knew that no dependence could be placed on Ashley's receiving a snub in filial silence, and he had no wish to embark on an argument in which he stood on very unreliable ground. Instead, he said: 'A son of yours? I want no base-born brats, I thank you, Desford—though I daresay you have a score—any number of them!' he amended hastily.

'Not to my knowledge, sir,' said the Viscount.

'I'm glad to hear it! But if you had agreed to the marriage I planned for you a son of yours might have been sitting on my knee at this moment!'

'I hesitate to contradict you, sir, but I find myself quite unable to believe that any grandchild attempting—at this moment—to sit on your knee would have met with anything but a severe rebuff.'

The Earl acknowledged this hit by giving a bark of laughter, but said: 'Oh, well, there's no need for you to take me up so literally! The thing is that you behaved very badly when you refused to make Henrietta Silverdale an offer! Never did I think to meet with such ingratitude, Desford! Anyone would have supposed that I had chosen a bride for you whom you disliked, or with whom you were unacquainted—which, I may tell you, was not an uncommon thing to happen in *my day*! Instead of that, I chose for you a girl with whom you had been closely acquainted all your life, and to whom I believed you to be sincerely attached. I might have looked much higher, but all I desired was your happiness! And what has been my reward? Tell me that!'

'Oh, for God's sake, sir!' exclaimed the Viscount, for the first time showing impatience. 'Must you hark back to what happened nine years ago? Can't you believe that Hetta had no more wish to marry me than I had to marry her?'

'No—and if you mean to tell me you were not attached to her you may as well spare your breath!'

'Of course I was attached to her—as though she had been my sister! I still am: we are the best of good friends, but a man don't wish to marry his sister, however fond he may be of her! The truth of the matter is, Papa, that you and Sir John hatched the scheme between you—though how the pair of you could be such gudgeons as to suppose that to rear us almost as though we *had* been brother and sister would further this precious scheme is something that has me in a puzzle to this day! No, no, don't rattle me off for calling you a gudgeon! Recollect that I did say it has me in a puzzle!'

'Ay, you've a soft tongue, and think to turn me up sweet with it!' growled his father.

'Alas, I know well I can't!' said the Viscount ruefully. 'But I wish you will tell me, sir, why you, who didn't become riveted until you were past thirty, were so determined to see me leg-shackled before I had even attained my majority?'

'To keep you out of mischief!' replied the Earl, with more promptitude than wisdom.

'Oho!' said the Viscount, quizzing him wickedly. 'So that was it, was it? Well, I've long suspected that you were not—in your day—such a pattern of rectitude as you would have us believe!'

'Pattern of rectitude! Of course I was no such thing!' said the Earl, repulsing the suggestion with loathing.

'Of course you weren't!' said the Viscount, laughing at him.

'No! I sowed my wild oats just as any youngster must, but I never consorted with rake-shames!'

This announcement put a quick end to the Viscount's laughter. He directed a searching look at his father from under suddenly frowning brows, and demanded: 'What's this? If it is to my address, you'll permit me to tell you that you've been misin-formed, sir!'

'No, no!' replied his lordship testily. 'I'm talking of Simon, muttonhead!'

'Simon! Why, what the devil has he been doing to provoke you?'

'Don't tell me you aren't very well aware that he's for ever on the spree with a set of rascally scrubs, knocking up disgraceful larks, committing every sort of extravagant folly, creating riot and rumpus—'

'Well, I do tell you so, sir!' said the Viscount, interrupting this wholesale indictment without ceremony. 'I don't see much of him, but you may depend upon it that I should hear of it fast enough if he'd got into the sort of company you're describing! Good God, anyone to hear you would suppose Simon had joined the Beggars' Club, or ended up each night either in the Finish, or in a Round-house! I daresay you wouldn't care for the set he runs with—I don't care for them myself, but that's because I'm nine-and-twenty, not three-and-twenty, and have outgrown the restiness of my salad days. But they're not *rascally*, and they're certainly not *scrubs*! Coming it much too strong, Father, believe me!'

'It's a pity you *don't* see much of him!' countered the Earl. 'I should have known better than to think you might make it your business to do so!'

'Well, yes, I think you should!' replied the Viscount frankly.

'I take it,' said the Earl, visibly controlling his temper, 'that I should be wasting my breath if I asked you to take the young wastrel in hand!'

'You would indeed, Papa! Lord, what heed do you think he would pay to me?'

'Oh, well,' replied his lordship grudgingly, 'for all your faults you're good ton, you're a member of the Four-horse Club, and—thanks to my training!—a pretty accomplished fencer. They tell me that the younger men are inclined to follow your lead, so there's no saying but what you might have more influence over him than I have.'

'If you had had any brothers, Papa,' said the Viscount, smiling, 'you would know that the junior members of the fraternity are very much more likely to run directly counter to what their eldest brother advises than to follow his lead, even if he were a far more notable sportsman than I am! I am sorry to disoblige you, but I must firmly decline to meddle in Simon's career. I don't think there's the least need for anyone to do so, but if you do think so it's for you to curb his activities, not me!'

'How the devil can I curb them?' demanded his father explosively. 'He's a curst care-for-nobody, and although you may consider me a gudgeon I promise you I'm not such a gudgeon as to stop his allowance! A pretty thing it would be if he got himself rolled-up and I were forced to rescue him from some sponging-house! Not but what it would do him good to be locked up!'

'You know, sir, you are taking much too gloomy a view of young Simon's prospects! I wish you won't tease yourself over him—even if he *has* put you all on end!'

'I might have known *you* wouldn't tease yourself!' said the Earl, assailed by another stab of pain. 'You're all alike! Why I've been saddled with a pack of selfish, worthless, ungrateful brats I shall never know! Your mother spoilt you to death, of course, and I was fool enough to let her do it! As for you, damme if you're not the worst of the bunch! I wash my hands of you, and the sooner you take yourself off the better pleased I shall be! I don't know what brought you down here, but if it was to see me you might have spared yourself the pains! I don't want to see your face again!'

The Viscount got up, saying with perfect affability: 'Well, in that case I'll remove it from your sight, sir! I won't ask you for your blessing, for your sense of propriety would compel you to bestow it on me, and I'm sure it would choke you to utter the words! I won't even offer to shake hands with you—but that's to save myself a wounding snub!'

'Jackanapes!' said his parent, thrusting out his hand.

The Viscount took it in his, dropped a respectful kiss on it, and said: 'Take care of yourself, Papa! Goodbye!'

The Earl watched him cross the room to the door, and, as he opened it, said, in the voice of a man goaded beyond endurance: 'I suppose you came home because you wanted something!'

'I did!' replied the Viscount, throwing him a look brimful of mockery over his shoulder. 'I wanted to see Mama!'

He then withdrew in good order, firmly closing the door on the explosion of wrath which greeted this parting shot.

When he reached the hall of the house he found that the butler was there, and encountered such a glance of mournful sympathy from this aged and privileged retainer that he broke into a chuckle, saying: 'You're looking your last at me, Pedmore! My father has cast me out! He says I'm a worthless skitterbrain, and a jackanapes, besides a number of other things which I can't at the moment remember. Would you have believed he could be so unfeeling?'

The butler clicked his tongue disapprovingly, and shook his head. Sighing deeply, he replied: 'It's the gout, my lord. It always makes him mifty!'

'Mifty!' said the Viscount. 'What you mean is that it sets him at dagger-drawing with anyone unwise enough to cross his path, you old humbugger!'

'It would not become me to agree with your lordship, so I shall hold my peace,' said Pedmore severely. 'And, if I may venture to proffer a word of advice—being as I have known your honoured parent for many years longer than you have, my lord—I would respectfully beg you not to set any store by anything he may say when he's in the gout, for he doesn't mean it—not if it's you! And if you was to take snuff he'd be regularly blue devilled—he would indeed, my lord, whatever he may have said to you!'

'Bless you, Pedmore, do you think I don't know it?' said the Viscount, smiling affectionately at him. 'You must think I'm a lunkhead! Where shall I find my mother?'

'In her drawing-room, my lord.'

The Viscount nodded, and ran lightly up the broad stairway. His mother greeted his entrance to her sanctum with a warm smile, and a hand held out to him. 'Come in, dearest!' she said. 'Have you been having a *dreadful* peal rung over you?'

He kissed her hand. 'Lord, yes!' he said cheerfully. 'He rattled me off in famous style! In fact, he has informed me that he doesn't wish to see my face again.'

'Oh, dear! But he doesn't mean it, you know. Yes, of course you do: you always understand things without having to have them explained to you, don't you?'

'Do I? It seems very unlikely! And I don't think it can be true, for both you and old Pedmore seem to believe that I must need reassurance! I don't, but I claim no extraordinary powers of understanding for that! No one who was not a confirmed sapskull could suppose—being intimately acquainted with Papa!—that his violent attacks spring from anything but colic and gout! I feared the worst when I saw him partake so lavishly of the curried crab at dinner last night; and my fears were confirmed when he embarked on the second bottle of port. Pray don't think me captious, Mama, but ought he to regale himself quite so unwisely?'

'No,' replied Lady Wroxton. 'It is very bad for him, but it is quite useless to remonstrate with him, for it only puts him out of temper to be offered the wholesome dishes Dr Chettle prescribes, when he has expressed a desire for something *most* indigestible, and you know what he is, Ashley, when he is thwarted! And when he flies into one of his odd rages!'

'I know!' said the Viscount, smiling.

'It is even worse for him when he does that, because he becomes exhausted, and then falls into a fit of dejection, and says that he is burnt to the socket, and has nothing to do but to wind up his accounts. And it is quite as bad for the household, for even Pedmore, who is so *very* devoted to us, doesn't like to have things thrown at him—particularly when it chances to be mutton-broth.'

'As bad as that?' said the Viscount, considerably startled.

'Oh, not always!' his mother assured him, in a comfortable voice. 'And he is in general very sorry afterwards, and tries to make amends for having behaved with so little moderation. I daresay he will be a trifle twitty tonight, but I have the greatest hope that tomorrow he will be content to eat a panada, or a boiled chicken. So you have no need to look so concerned, dearest: very likely it will be several weeks before he indulges himself again with his favourite dishes.'

'I am concerned for you, Mama, far more than I am for him! I don't know how you are able to bear your life! *I* could not!'

'No, I don't suppose you could,' she responded, looking at him in tolerant amusement. 'You weren't acquainted with him when he was young, and naturally you were never in love with him. But I was, and I remember how gay, and handsome, and dashing he used to be, and how very happy we were. And we still love one another, Ashley.'

He was frowning a little, and asked abruptly: 'Does he subject you to that sort of Turkish treatment, Mama?'

'Oh, no, never! To be sure, he does sometimes scold me, but he has *never* thrown anything at me—not even when I ventured to suggest that he should add some rhubarb and water to his port, which is an excellent remedy for a deranged stomach, you know, but he would have none of it. In fact, it put him into a regular flame.'

'I'm not surprised!' said the Viscount, laughing at her. 'You almost deserved to have it thrown at you, I think!'

'Yes, that's what he said, but he didn't throw it at me. He burst out laughing, just as you did. What made him suddenly so vexed, dearest? Did you say something to make him pucker up? I know you haven't *done* anything to displease him, for he was delighted to see you. Indeed, that is why we had the dressed crab, and he made Pedmore bring up the best port.'

'Good God, in my honour, was it? Of course, I dared not tell him so, but I'm not at all fond of port, and I had to drink the deuce of a lot of it. As for what vexed him, it was certainly nothing I said, for not an unwise word passed my lips! I can only suppose that the crab and the port were responsible.' He paused, thinking of what had passed in the library, the frown returning to his brow. He turned his eyes towards his mother, and said slowly: 'And yet—Mama, what made him hark back, after all this time, to the match he tried to make between Hetta and me, when I was twenty?'

'Oh, did he do so? How unfortunate!'

'But why did he, Mama? He hasn't spoken of it for years!'

'No, and that is what one particularly likes about him. He has a shockingly quick temper, but he never sinks into the mops, or rubs up old sores. The thing is, I fear, that it has all been brought back to his mind because he has been told that at last dear Henrietta seems likely to contract a very eligible alliance.'

'Good God!' exclaimed the Viscount. 'You don't mean it! Who's the suitor?'

'I shouldn't think you know him, for he has only lately come into Hertfordshire, and I fancy he very rarely goes to London. He is old Mr Bourne's cousin, and inherited Marley House from him. According to Lady Draycott, he is an excellent person, of the first respectability, a thousand agreeable talents, and most distinguished manners. I haven't met him myself, but I do hope something may come of it, for I have the greatest regard for Henrietta, and have always wished to see her comfortably established. And, if Lady Draycott is to be believed, this Mr—Mr Nethersole—no, not Nethersole, but some name like that— seems to be just the man for her.'

'He sounds to me like a dashed dull dog!' said the Viscount.

'Yes, but persons of uniform virtues always do sound dull, Ashley. It seems to me such an odd circumstance! However, we must remember that Lady Draycott is not wholly to be relied on, and I daresay she has exaggerated. She thinks everyone she likes a pattern-saint, and everyone she doesn't like a rascal.' Her eyes twinkled. 'Well, she says *you* are a man of character, and *very* well conducted!'

'Much obliged to her!' said the Viscount. 'To think she should judge me so well!'

She laughed. 'Yes, indeed! It is a striking example of the advantage of having engaging manners. What a sad reflection it is that to have powers of captivation should be of much more practical use than worthiness!' She leaned forward to pinch his chin, her eyes full of loving mockery. 'You can't bamboozle me, you rogue! You *are* a here-and-thereian, you know, exactly as I am persuaded Papa told you! I wish you might form a tendre for some very nice girl, and settle down with her! Never mind! I don't mean to tease you!'

She withdrew her hand, but he caught it, and held it, saying, with a searching look: 'Do you, Mama? Did you, perhaps, wish me to offer for Hetta, nine years ago? Would you have liked her to have been your daughter-in-law?'

'What a very odd notion you have of me, my love! I hope I am not such a pea-goose as to have wished you to marry any girl for whom you had formed no lasting passion! To be sure, I have a great regard for Hetta, but I daresay you would not have suited. In any event, that has been past history for years, and nothing is such a sad bore as to be recalling it! I promise you, I shall welcome the bride you do choose at last with as much pleasure as I shall attend Hetta's wedding to the man *of her* choice.'

'What, to the pattern-card whose name you can't remember? Are the Silverdales at Inglehurst? I haven't seen Hetta in town for weeks, but from what she told me when we met at the

Castlereaghs' ball I had supposed that she must by now have
been fixed at Worthing, poor girl!'

'Lady Silverdale,' said his mother, in an expressionless voice,
'finding that the only lodging she could tolerate in Worthing
was not available this summer, has recollected that the sea-air
always makes her bilious, and has chosen to retire to Inglehurst
rather than to seek a lodging at some other resort.'

'What an abominable woman she is!' said the Viscount cheerfully. 'Oh, well! I daresay Hetta will be better off with her
pattern-card! I'll drop in at Inglehurst tomorrow, on my way
back to London, and try to discover what this fellow, Nether-
what's-it, is really like!'

Slightly taken aback, Lady Wroxton said, in mild expostulation:
'My dear boy, you cannot, surely, question Hetta about him?'

'Lord, yes! of course I can!' said the Viscount. 'There are no
secrets between Hetta and me, Mama, any more than there are
between Griselda and me—in fact,' he added, subjecting this
confident assertion to consideration, 'far fewer!'

# Two

VISCOUNT DESFORD LEFT HIS ANCESTRAL HOME ON THE following morning without seeking another interview with his father. Since the Earl rarely left his bedchamber before noon, this was not difficult. The Viscount partook of an excellent breakfast in solitary state; ran upstairs to bid his mother a fond farewell, issued a few final directions to his valet, who was to follow him into Hampshire with his baggage, and mounted into his curricle as the stable clock began to strike eleven. By the time the echoes of its last stroke had died he was out of sight of the house, bowling down the long avenue that led to the main gates.

The pace at which he drove his mettlesome horses might have alarmed persons of less iron nerve than the middle-aged groom who sat beside him; but Stebbing, who had served him ever since his boyhood, had a disposition which matched his square, severe countenance, and sat with his arms folded across his chest, and an expression on his face of complete unconcern. As little as he betrayed alarm did he betray his pride in the out-and-outer whom he had taught to ride his first pony, and who had become, as well as an accomplished fencer, a first-rate dragsman. Only in the company of his intimates did he say, over a heavy wet, that, taking him in harness and out, no man could do more with his horses than my Lord Desford could.

The curricle which Desford was driving was not precisely a racing curricle, but it had been built to his own design by Hatchett, of Longacre, so lightly that it was very easy on his horses, and capable (if drawn by the sort of blood cattle his lordship kept in his stables) of covering long distances in an incredibly short space of time. In general, Desford drove with a pair only under the pole, but if he set out on a long journey he had a team harnessed to the carriage, demonstrating (so said his ribald cronies) that he was bang up to the knocker. He was driving a team of splendid grays on this occasion, and if they were not the sixteen-mile an hour tits so frequently advertised for sale in the columns of the Morning Post they reached the Viscount's immediate destination considerably before noon, and without having once been allowed to break out of a fast trot.

Inglehurst Place was a very respectable estate owned, until his death some years previously, by a lifelong friend of Lord Wroxton's. Its present owner, Sir Charles Silverdale, had inherited it from his father when still at Harrow, and he had not yet come into his majority, or (according to those who shook sad heads over his rackety ways) shown the least desire to assume the responsibilities attached to his inheritance. His fortune was controlled by his trustees, but since neither of these two gentlemen whose lives had been devoted to the Law had any but a superficial understanding of country matters the management of the estate was shared by Sir Charles's bailiff, and his sister, Miss Henrietta Silverdale.

The butler, a very stately personage, accorded the Viscount a bow, and said that he regretted to be obliged to inform him that her ladyship, having passed an indifferent night, had not yet come downstairs, and so could not receive him.

'Come down from your high ropes, Grimshaw!' said the Viscount. 'You know dashed well I haven't come to visit her ladyship! Is Miss Silverdale at home?'

Grimshaw unbent sufficiently to say that he thought Miss would be found in the garden, but his expression, as he watched Desford stride off round the corner of the house, was one of gloomy disapproval.

The Viscount found Miss Silverdale in the rose-garden, attended by two gentlemen, one of whom was known to him, and the other a stranger. She greeted him with unaffected pleasure, exclaiming: 'Des!' and stretching out her hands to him. 'I had supposed you to be in Brighton! What brings you into Hertfordshire?'

The Viscount took her hands, but kissed her cheek, and said: 'Filial piety, Hetta! How do you do my dear? Not that I need ask! I can see you're in high force!' He nodded and smiled at the younger of the two gentlemen present, and looked enquiringly at the other.

'I don't think you are acquainted with Mr Nethercott, are you, Des?' said Henrietta. 'Mr Nethercott, you must let me make you known to Lord Desford, who is almost my foster-brother!'

The two men shook hands, each swiftly weighing the other up. Cary Nethercott was rather older than Desford, but lacked the Viscount's air of easy assurance. His manners, though perfectly well-bred, held a good deal of shy reserve. He was taller and more thick-set than Desford; and while he was dressed with propriety there was no suggestion about him of the man of fashion: his coat was made of Bath cloth, but only a clodpole could have supposed it to have come from the hands of Weston, or Nugee. He had a well-formed person, regular features, and if his habitual expression was grave it was also kindly, and his rare smile held a good deal of sweetness.

'No, I fancy we've never met,' said Desford. 'You have only lately come into the district, haven't you? My mother was speaking of you yesterday: said you were old Mr Bourne's heir.'

'Yes, I am,' replied Cary. 'It seems very strange that I should be, because I scarcely knew him!'

'All the better for you!' said Desford. 'The most crotchety old rumstick I ever met in my life! Lord, Hetta, will you ever forget the dust he kicked up when he found us trespassing on his land?'

'No, indeed!' she said, laughing. 'And we weren't doing the least harm! I do hope, Mr Nethercott, that *you* won't fly into a rage if I should stray on to the sacred ground of Marley House!'

'You may be very sure I won't!' he said, smiling warmly at her.

At this point, young Mr Beckenham's evil genius prompted him to embark on a tangled speech. He said throatily: 'For my part, I can promise Miss Silverdale that if ever she should stray on to *my* land I should think it hallowed ground thereafter! At least, what I mean is I should if it *were* my land, but that's of no consequence, because it will be, when my father dies—not that I wish him to die!—and, in any event, he would be as happy as I should be to welcome you to Foxshot, if there were the least chance of your *straying* on to our land! I only wish Foxshot had been situated within walking distance of Inglehurst!'

He then perceived that Cary Nethercott was looking very much amused, and subsided into blushful silence.

'Well said!' approved the Viscount, patting him on the shoulder. 'If you're not very much obliged to him, Hetta, you should be!'

'Of course I am!' said Henrietta, smiling kindly upon her youthful admirer. 'And if Foxshot were not fifteen miles distant I expect I *should* stray on to it!'

'In the meantime,' quietly interposed Cary Nethercott, 'I believe it is time we both took our leave, and allowed Miss Silverdale to enjoy a comfortable cose with his lordship.'

Mr Beckenham could not gainsay it; and although Henrietta said merrily that she and his lordship were more likely to come to cuffs than to indulge in a comfortable cose she made no attempt to deter the departure. Mr Beckenham reverently kissed her hand, but his older and less demonstrative rival merely shook it, begging her to convey his compliments to her mama.

He then bade the Viscount goodbye, expressing a conventional hope that he might have the pleasure of meeting him again, and took himself off.

'Well,' said the Viscount, critically watching his withdrawal, 'he's better than I looked for! But I don't think it will do, Hetta: he ain't the man for you!'

Miss Silverdale had very fine eyes. They were, indeed, her only claim to beauty, for her mouth was held to be too large, her high-bridged nose too aquiline, and her hair of an undistinguished brown; but her eyes dominated her face, and were responsible for the generally accepted dictum that she had a great deal of countenance. Their colour was unremarkable, being of that indeterminate colour which passes for gray, but they were subject to changes seldom to be seen in the more admired blue, or brown eyes. If she was bored, they looked to be almost lightless, but as soon as her interest was roused they darkened, and glowed; they could sparkle in anger; or, more frequently, in amusement; and they were at all times reflective of her moods. As she turned them now upon the Viscount, they held surprise, a hint of anger, and a good deal of laughter. She said: 'Do you think so indeed? Well, if you're right what a fortunate circumstance it is that he hasn't made me an offer! Who knows but what, at my age, I might have accepted it?'

'Don't hide your teeth with me, Hetta! It's as plain as a pikestaff that he *will* make you an offer! I daresay he's a very worthy man, and I can see he has good, easy manners, but he wouldn't do for you! Take my word for it!'

'What a dog in the manger you are, Ashley!' she exclaimed, between indignation and amusement. 'You don't want me yourself, but you can't endure the thought that I might marry another man!'

'Nothing of the sort!' said the Viscount. 'I may not wish to marry you—and don't try to hoax me into believing that you've been wearing the willow for me these nine years, because there's nothing amiss with my memory, and I remember as clearly as if it was yesterday how you begged me *not* to offer for you, when that abominable plot was hatched between your father and mine!—but I'm devilish fond of you, and I'd be happy to see you married to a man who was up to your weight. The thing is that Nethercott ain't! You'd be bored with him before the end of your honeymoon, Hetta!'

'You can't think how much obliged to you I am, Des, for having my interests so much at heart!' she said, with immense, if spurious, earnestness. 'But it is possible, you know just faintly possible!—that I am a better judge of what will suit me than you are! Since your memory is so good there can be no need to remind you that I am not a silly schoolgirl, but in my twenty-sixth year—'

'No need at all,' he interrupted, with one of his disarming smiles. 'You will be twenty-six on the 15th of January next, and I know already what I mean to give you on that occasion. How could you think I would forget your birthday, best of my friends?'

'You are quite atrocious, you know,' she informed him, in a resigned voice. 'However I should miss you very much if we ceased to be the best of friends, for there's no denying that it is a great comfort to be able to turn to you for advice whenever I find myself in a hobble—which, to do you justice, you've never failed to give me. So do, pray, let us leave this nonsensical argument about poor Mr Nethercott before we find ourselves at outs! You said it was filial piety which brought you home: I do hope this doesn't mean that Lord Wroxton is ill?'

'Not unless rage has caused him to fall into an apoplectic fit,' he responded. 'We parted on the worst of bad terms last night— in fact, he said he never wanted to see my face again—but Mama and Pedmore have assured me that he didn't mean it, and

I believe them. Provided I don't make the mistake of intruding my phiz upon him too soon, I daresay he will be quite pleased to see it again. Of course, it was quite cockleheaded of me to have let him see it twice in less than two months!'

She laughed. 'From which I collect that he is in the gout again! Poor Lord Wroxton! But what made him rip up at you? Has some tattle-box been carrying tales about you to him?'

'Certainly not!' he replied austerely. 'There are no tales to carry!'

'What, have you cast off the dasher I saw you with at Vauxhall a month ago?' enquired Miss Silverdale, artlessly surprised.

'No, she cast me off!' he retorted. 'A lovely little barque of frailty, wasn't she? But much too expensive, unfortunately!'

'Oh, that's too bad!' she said sympathetically. 'And haven't you found another to take her place? But you will, Des, you will!'

'One of these days you will be found strangled—very likely by me!' the Viscount warned her. 'Pray, what business has a delicately nurtured female to know anything about such things?'

'Ah, that's one of the advantages of having outgrown one's girlhood!' she said. 'One need no longer pretend to be an innocent!'

The Viscount had been lounging beside her on a rustic seat, but this utterance startled him into straightening himself with a jerk, and exclaiming: 'For God's sake, Hetta—! Is that how you talk to people?'

Her eyes twinkled mischievously; she said, on a choke of laughter: 'No, no, only to you, Des! That's another of the ways in which you are a comfort to me! Of course, I do talk pretty freely to Charlie, but he's only my younger brother, not my elder brother! Does Griselda never talk frankly to you?'

'I can't remember that she ever did, but I had only just come down from Oxford when she got herself hitched to Broxbourne, and I don't see much of her nowadays.' He gave a sudden chuckle. 'Would you believe it, Hetta? My father suddenly ripped up an old grievance which I had thought dead and buried years ago, and raked me down in thundering style for not having coaxed you to marry me!'

'Oh, good God!' she cried. '*Still?* Why didn't you tell him that we didn't *wish* to marry one another?'

'I did, but he didn't believe me. To be sure, I didn't tell him that we knew all about the plot he and your father had so inexpertly hatched, and had decided what we must do about it. Believe me, my dear, that would never do!'

'No,' she agreed. 'And it wouldn't do for Mama either! I did tell Papa, and he perfectly understood our feelings, and never once reproached me. But Mama never ceases to do so! I do wish you would do something to give her a disgust of you, instead of making yourself agreeable to her! Every time she meets you she complains of my ingratitude until I could scream, and begs me not to blame her when I find myself at my last prayers. According to her, you are everything that is most desirable, and I must be all about in my head! What she might say of you if you were not heir to an Earldom I haven't asked her!' Her little spurt of temper subsided; she gave a rueful laugh, and said: 'Oh, dear, how very improper of me to talk like that about her! Let me assure you that I do *not* do so to anyone but you! And how shocking it is that I should be glad she is feeling not quite the thing today, and doesn't mean to leave her room! I do hope Grimshaw can be trusted not to tell her you have been here!'

'Well, it may be shocking, but I don't scruple to tell you that I was even more glad to learn that she wasn't receiving visitors!' said the Viscount candidly. 'She makes me feel I'm some sort of a heartless loose-screw, for she's got a way of sighing, and smiling sadly and reproachfully at me when I accord her the common decencies of civility.' He drew out his watch, and said: 'I must be off, Hetta. I'm on my way to Hazelfield, and my aunt won't like it if I arrive at midnight.'

Henrietta rose from the seat, and accompanied him towards the house. 'Oh, are you going to visit your Aunt Emborough? Pray give her my kind regards!'

'I will,' he promised. 'And do you—if Grimshaw should have disclosed my presence here!—say all that is proper to your mama! My compliments, and my—er—regret that I should have paid her a morning visit when she was indisposed!' He bestowed a fraternal hug upon her, kissed her cheek, and said: 'Goodbye, my dear! Don't do anything gooseish, will you?'

'No, and don't you do anything gooseish either!' she retorted.

'What, under my Aunt Sophronia's eye? I shouldn't dare!' he tossed at her over his shoulder, as he strode off towards the stableyard.

# Three

$\mathcal{L}$ADY EMBOROUGH WAS LORD WROXTON'S SOLE surviving sister. In appearance they were much alike, but although persons of nervous disposition thought that the resemblance was very much more than skin-deep they were misled by her loud voice and downright manners. She was certainly inclined to manage the affairs of anyone weak-minded enough to submit to her autocracy, but she was inspired quite as much by a conviction that such persons were incapable of managing their own affairs as by her belief in her own infalli-bility, and she never bore anyone the least malice for withstand-ing her. She was thought by some to be odiously overbearing, but not by those who had sought her help in a moment of need. Under her rough manners she had a warm heart, and an inex-haustible store of kindness. Her husband was a quiet man of few words who for the most part allowed her to rule the house-hold as she chose, a circumstance which frequently led the uninitiated to think that he was henpecked. But those more intimately acquainted with her knew that her lord could check her with no more than a look, and an almost imperceptible shake of his head. She took these silent reproofs in perfectly good part, often saying, with a goodnatured laugh: 'Oh, there is Emborough frowning me down, so not another word will I utter on the subject!'

She greeted her nephew characteristically, saying: 'So here you are at last, Desford! You're late—and don't tell me one of your horses lost a shoe, or you broke a trace, because I shan't believe any of your farradiddles!'

'Now, don't bullock poor Des, Mama!' her eldest son, a stalwart young man who bore all the appearance of a country squire, admonished her.

'Much he cares!' she said, laughing heartily.

'Of course I don't!' Desford said, kissing her hand. 'Do you take me for a rabbit-sucker, ma'am? None of my horses lost a shoe, and I did not break a trace, or suffer any accident whatsoever, and if you mean to tell me I've kept you waiting for dinner I shan't, of course, be so disrespectful as to accuse *you* of telling farradiddles, but I shall think it! The thing was I called at Inglehurst on my way, and stayed chatting to Hetta for rather longer than I had intended. She told me to give you her kind regards, by the way.'

'Inglehurst! Why, have you come from Wolversham?' she exclaimed. 'I had supposed you to have been in London still! How's your father?'

'In the gout!'

She gave a snort. 'I daresay! And no one but himself to blame! It would do him good to have me living at Wolversham: your mother's too easy with him!'

The violent altercations which had taken place between Lord Wroxton and his sister when last she had descended upon Wolversham still lived vividly in the Viscount's memory, and he barely repressed a shudder. Fortunately, he was not obliged to answer his aunt, for she switched abruptly to another subject, and demanded to be told what he meant by instructing his postilions to lodge at the Blue Boar. 'I'll have you know, Desford, I'm not one of these modern hostesses who tell their guests they won't house any other of their servants than their valets! Such nipcheese ways won't do for me: shabby-genteel *I* call 'em! Your groom and your postboys will be lodged with our own, and I want no argument about it.'

'Very well, ma'am,' said the Viscount obediently, 'you shall have none!'

'Now, that's what I like in you!' said his aunt, regarding him with warm approval. 'You never disgust me with flowery commonplaces! By the by, if you were expecting to find the house full of smarts you'll be disappointed: we have only the Montsales staying here, and young Ross, and his sister. However, I daresay you won't care for that if you get good sport on the river, which Ned assures me you will. Then there's racing at Winchester, and—'

She was interrupted by Lord Emborough, who had entered the room in the middle of this speech, and who said humourously: 'Don't overwhelm him with the treats you have in store, my love! How do you do, Desford? If you can be dragged away from the trout, you must come and look at my young stock tomorrow and tell me how you like the best yearling I've bred yet! He's out of my mare, Creeping Polly, by Whiffler, and I shall own myself surprised if I haven't got a winner in him.'

This pronouncement instantly drew the five gentlemen present into an exclusively male conversation, during the course of which Mr Edward Emborough loudly seconded his father's opinion; Mr Gilbert Emborough, his junior by a year, said that although the colt had great bone and substance he couldn't rid himself of the conviction that the animal was just a *leetle* straight-shouldered; Mr Mortimer Redgrave, who had entered the room in Lord Emborough's wake, and was the elder of that gentleman's two sons-in-law, said that for his part he never wanted to see a more promising young 'un; and Mr Christian Emborough, in his first year at Oxford, who had been reverently observing the exquisite cut of his cousin's coat, said that he would be interested to hear what he thought of the colt, 'because Des is much more knowing about horses than Ned and Gil are—even if he doesn't boast about it!' Having delivered himself of this snub to his seniors, he relapsed into blushful silence. The Viscount, not having seen the colt, volunteered no opinion, but engaged instead in general stable-talk with his host. Lady Emborough allowed the gentlemen to enjoy themselves in their own way for quite a quarter of an hour before intervening, with a reminder to her sons and nephew that if they didn't rig themselves out for dinner at once they would get nothing but scraps to eat, since she did not mean to wait for them. Upon which the male company dispersed, young Mr Christian Emborough confiding to his cousin, as he went up the broad stairway beside him, that he happened to know that a couple of ducklings and a plump leveret were to form the main dishes for the second course. The Viscount agreed that it would be a shocking thing if these succulent dishes should be spoilt; and young Mr Emborough, taking his courage in his hands, ventured to ask him if he had tied his neckcloth in the style known as the Oriental. To which the Viscount responded gravely: 'No, it's called the Mathematical Tie. Would you like me to teach you how to achieve it?'

'Oh, by Jupiter, wouldn't I just?' exclaimed Christian, the ready colour flooding his cheeks in gratification.

'Well, I will, then,' promised Desford. 'But not just at this moment, if those ducks are not to be over-roasted!'

'Oh, no, no! Whenever it is perfectly convenient to you!' Christian stammered.

He then went off to his own bedchamber, more than ever convinced that Des was a bang-up fellow, not by half as top-lofty as his own brothers; and filled with an agreeable vision of stunning these censorious seniors by appearing before them in a neckcloth which they must instantly recognize as being slap up to the mark.

When the Viscount went back to the drawing-room, he found that the party was rather larger than his aunt had led him to expect, for besides the persons she had mentioned, it included Miss Montsale; both the married daughters of the house, with their spouses; a rather nebulous female of uncertain age, in whom he vaguely recognized one of Lady Emborough's indigent cousins; and the Honourable Rachel Emborough, who was the eldest of the family, and seemed to be destined to fill the rôles of universal confidant, companion of her parents, wise and reliable sister of her brothers and sisters, and beloved aunt of their off-spring. She had no pretensions to beauty, but her unaffected manners, her cheerfulness, and the kindness that sprang from a warm heart made her a general favourite. And finally, because Lady Emborough had discovered almost at the last moment that her numbers were uneven, the Honourable Clara Emborough had also been included. This damsel, who had not yet attained her seventeenth birthday, was not considered to have emerged from the schoolroom but, as her mama told the Viscount: 'It don't do girls any harm to attend a few parties before one brings 'em out in the regular way. Teaches 'em how to go on in Society, and accustoms 'em to talking to strangers! Of course I wouldn't let her appear at formal parties until I've presented her! And I can depend on Rachel to keep an eye on her!'

The Viscount, who had been watching Rachel check, in the gentlest way, Miss Clara's mounting exuberance, intervene to give her brothers' thoughts a fresh direction when an argument which sprang up between them threatened to become acrimonious, and attend unobtrusively to the comfort of the guests, said impulsively: 'What a good girl Rachel is, ma'am!'

'Yes, she's as good as wheat,' agreed Lady Emborough, in a somewhat gloomy voice. 'But she ain't a girl, Desford: she's older than you are! And no one has ever offered for her! Heaven knows I shouldn't know what to do without her, but I *can't* be glad to see her dwindling into an old maid! It ain't that the men don't like her: they do, but they don't fall in love with her. She's like Hetta Silverdale—except that Hetta's a very well-looking girl, and my poor Rachel—well, there can be no denying that she's something of a Homely Joan! But each of them would make any man an excellent wife—a much better wife than my Theresa there, who is so full of whims and crotchets that I never expected her to go off at all, far less to attach such a good bargain as John Thimbleby!'

Aware that Mr Thimbleby was seated well within earshot, the Viscount shot an involuntary glance at him. He was relieved to see a most appreciative twinkle in this gentleman's eye, and to receive from him something suspiciously like a wink. He was thus able to reply to his aunt with perfect equanimity: 'Very true, ma'am! But there is no accounting for tastes, you know! However, you're out when you say that Hetta has no suitors! I could name you at least four very eligible *partis* whom she might have had for the lifting of a finger. Indeed, when I saw her this morning I found her entertaining two more of them! Perhaps neither she nor my cousin Rachel wishes to become a mere wife!'

'Gammon!' said her ladyship crudely. 'Show me the female who doesn't hope for marriage, and I'll show you a lunatic past praying for! Yes, and if you wish to know what *I* think—not that I suppose you do!—you're a shuttlehead not to have married Hetta when I daresay she was yours for the asking!'

The Viscount was annoyed, and betrayed it by a slight contraction of his brows, and the careful civility with which he said: 'You are mistaken, my dear aunt: Hetta was never mine for the asking. Neither of us has ever wished for a closer relationship than that of the friendship we have always enjoyed—and, I trust, may always enjoy!'

As little as Lady Emborough resented the quiet checks her husband imposed upon her exuberance did she resent a deserved snub. She replied, laughing: 'That's the hammer! Quite right to give me a set-down, for what you do is no business of mine! Emborough is for ever scolding me for being too wide in the mouth! But, wit-cracking apart, Desford, isn't it time you were thinking of matrimony? I don't mean Hetta, for if you don't fancy each other there's nothing to be said about *that*, but with Horace still in France, and Simon, from all I hear, sowing even more wild oats than your father did, in his day, I can't but feel that you do owe it to your father to give him a grandson or two—legitimate ones, I mean!'

This made the Viscount burst out laughing, and effectually banished his vexation. 'Aunt Sophronia,' he said, 'you are quite abominable! Did anyone ever tell you so? But you are right, for all that, as I've lately been brought to realize. It is clearly time that I brought my delightfully untrammelled life to an end. The only difficulty is that I have yet to meet any female who will both meet with Papa's approval, and inspire me with the smallest desire to become riveted to her for life!'

'You are a great deal too nice in your requirements,' she told him severely; but added, after a moment's reflection: 'Not but what I don't wish any of my children to marry anyone for whom they don't feel a decided preference. When I was a girl, you know, most of us married to oblige our parents. Why, even my bosom-bow in those days did so, though she positively disliked the man to whom her parents betrothed her! And a vilely unhappy marriage it was! But your grandfather, my dear Ashley, having himself been forced to contract an affiance which was *far* from happy, was resolute in his determination that none of *his* children should find themselves in a similar situation. And nothing, you will agree, could have been more felicitous than the result of his liberality of mind! To be sure, there were only three of us, and your Aunt Jane died before you were born, but when I married Emborough, and Everard married your dear mama, no one could have been more delighted than your grandfather!'

'I am sorry he died before I was out of short coats,' Desford remarked. 'I have no memory of him, but from all I have heard about him from you, and from Mama, I wish that I had had the privilege of knowing him.'

'Yes, you'd have liked him,' she nodded. 'What's more, he'd have liked you! And if your father hadn't waited until he was more than thirty before he got married to your mama you *would* have known him! And why Wroxton should glump at you for doing exactly what he did himself is something I don't understand, or wish to understand! There, you be off to play billiards with your cousins, and the Montsale girl, before I get to be as cross as crabs, which they say I always do when I talk about your father!'

He was very ready to obey her, and she did not again revert to the subject. He stayed for a week in Hampshire, and passed his time very pleasurably. After the exigencies of the Season, with its ceaseless breakfasts, balls, routs, race-parties at Ascot, opera-parties, convivial gatherings at Cribb's Parlour, evenings spent at Watier's, not to mention the numerous picnics, and al fresco entertainments ranging from quite ordinary parties to some, given by ambitious hostesses, so daringly original that they were talked of for at least three days, the lazy, unexacting life at Hazelfield exactly suited his humour. If one visited the Em-boroughs there was no need to fear that every moment of every day would have been planned, or that you would be dragged to explore some ruin or local beauty spot when all you wished to do was to go for a strolling walk with some other like-minded members of the party. Lady Emborough never made elaborate plans for the entertainment of her guests. She merely fed them very well, and saw to it that whatever facilities were necessary to enable them to engage in such sports or exercises as they favoured were always at hand; and if any amusement, such as a race-meeting, happened to be taking place she informed them that carriages were ready to take them to it, but if anyone felt disinclined to go racing he had only to say so, and need not fear that she would be offended.

She adhered strictly to this admirable course when she disclosed to Desford that she had promised to attend a party on the last night of his visit, taking with her her two elder sons, as many of her daughters as she thought proper, and any of the guests she would no doubt have staying with her at Hazelfield and who did not despise quite a small, country ball. 'I shall be obliged to go,' she said, in the resigned voice of one who did not expect to derive any pleasure from the offered festivity. 'And Emma and Mortimer mean to go too. Theresa has cried off, but that won't surprise Lady Bugle, for she knows very well that Theresa is increasing. The Montsales don't wish to go either, and there's no reason why they should when I *must* go, and can chaperon Mary for them. Ned and Gil mean to go, but Christian don't: he hasn't started to dangle after pretty girls yet. And if you don't fancy it, Desford, there's no reason why you shouldn't remain here, and play whist with the Montsales and John Thimbleby! In fact, I strongly advise you to do so, because it's my belief you'll think the Bugles' party a dead bore.'

'Think it a dead bore when that glorious creature will be present?' ejaculated Mr Gilbert Emborough, who had entered the room in time to hear the last part of this speech. 'Nothing could be a bore when *she* is there!'

'Come, this is most promising!' said Desford. 'Who is this glorious *she*? Am I acquainted with her?'

'No, you ain't *acquainted* with her,' replied Gilbert, 'but you have seen her! What's more, you were much struck—well, anyone would be!—and you asked Ned who she was.'

'What, the ravishing girl I saw at the races?' exclaimed Desford. 'My dear aunt, of course I will go with you to this ball!

The most exquisite piece of nature I've seen in a twelvemonth! I hoped Ned might present me to her, and very unhandsome I thought it of him that he didn't do so.'

Gilbert gave a crack of laughter. 'Afraid you'd cut him out! See if I don't roast him for it!'

'But who is she?' demanded the Viscount. 'I didn't properly hear what Ned said, when I asked him that question, for at that moment we were joined by some friends of his, and by the time we had parted from them the next race was about to start, and I thought no more about the Beauty.'

'Shame!' said his cousin, grinning at him.

'Her name is Lucasta,' said Lady Emborough. 'She's the eldest daughter of Sir Thomas Bugle: he has five of 'em, and four sons. Certainly a very handsome girl, and I daresay she may make a good marriage, for she has all the men in raptures. But if her portion is above five thousand pounds I shall own myself astonished. Sir Thomas's fortune is no more than genteel, and he hasn't the least notion of trying to sconce the reckoning.'

'Poor Lucasta!' said the Viscount lightly.

'You may well say so! Her mama brought her out in the spring, and there was never anything so unfortunate! Would you believe it?—within three days of her being presented at Court Sir Thomas received an express letter from Dr Cromer, informing him that *old* Lady Bugle had been suddenly taken ill! So, of course, they were obliged to post home in a great hurry, because she *was* very old, and even though one knew she was as tough as whitleather there is always the chance that such persons will be perfectly stout one day, and dead the next. Not that she did die the next day: she lasted for more than two months, which naturally made it impossible for her mama to take Lucasta to balls and assemblies until they are out of black gloves. This dance Lady Bugle has got up is to be quite a small affair. She gives it in honour of Stonor Bugle's engagement to the elder Miss

Windle. A good enough girl in her way, but it's not an alliance I should welcome for one of *my* sons!'

'I should think not indeed!' said Gilbert. 'Why, she's down-right knocker-faced!'

Lady Emborough called him sharply to order for so rudely exaggerating Miss Windle's appearance; but when, on the following evening, the Viscount was presented to the lady he could not feel that Gilbert had been unjust. But he felt also that her homeliness would not have struck him so forcibly had not Lady Bugle caused her to stand side by side with Lucasta Bugle, to receive the guests.

Lucasta was certainly something quite out of the ordinary way, for besides a countenance of classic beauty her figure was good, and her teeth, when she smiled, were seen to be very even, and as white as whalebone. She had luxuriant hair, which only jealous rivals stigmatized as gingery: it was, in fact, the colour of ripening corn; and her proud mama had frequently been known, when accepting compliments on her burnished curls, to whisper confidentially that they had never to be papered. She seemed to have acquired habits of easy intercourse, in spite of the abrupt curtailment of her first season, for she betrayed none of the signs of shyness which so often made it difficult for their partners at a ball to talk to girls who had only just emerged from the school-room. Her manners were assured; she had a fund of social chit-chat at her tongue's end; she was all delight and cordiality towards her mama's guests; she was animated, and laughed a great deal; and seemed to be an expert in the art of light-hearted flirtation.

The Viscount had the honour of standing up with her for the dance that was forming when the Emborough party arrived, and since he was more expert in this art than she was he grati-fied her by responding in the most obliging way to the encour-agement he received to pay her just the sort of compliments he judged likely to be the most acceptable. His cousin Edward, indignantly observing the progress he was making into the Beauty's good graces, and the arch, laughing looks which she threw at him, was torn between envy of his address, and cynical reflections on the advantages attached to being the heir to an Earldom. For these he took himself severely to task, telling himself, with dogged loyalty, that the divine Lucasta was merely trying to put a stranger at his ease. But when Gilbert, who had never contrived to grow higher in the Beauty's esteem than had his elder brother, encountered him for a fleeting moment, and said, with a malicious wink: 'Des is devilish taken with her, ain't he?' he was unable to disagree. All he could think of to say was that he was sure it was no wonder. But when he saw his divinity waltzing, a little later in the evening, with Desford, he would, had he not been a very goodnatured young man, have taken his cousin in violent dislike. The waltz was still considered by old-fashioned persons to be an improper dance, and was seldom played at country assemblies. One or two dashing hostesses had caused it to be played, but Ned, having painstakingly mastered the steps, had found that he had wasted his time: Lucasta never waltzed.

He had not expected that it would figure amongst the country dances and the boulangers offered to the company in the Bugles' establishment, but Lady Bugle, hopeful that Lady Emborough would bring to her little party her tonnish nephew, had warned the musicians to be prepared to strike up for one, and had told Lucasta that if the Viscount did happen to ask her to dance it with him she might do so.

'For there can be no objection to your doing so *here*, my love, amongst our particular friends. In London, of course, the case would be different—until, as I need scarcely remind you, you have been approved by the Patronesses of Almacks; but I should be excessively mortified if any of our guests thought it a dowdy party, and if dear Lady Emborough does bring Lord Desford to it you may depend upon it that he will expect to hear waltzes played, for he is quite one of the Pinks of the Ton, you know!'

Lord Desford did ask her, saying, as he led her off the floor at the end of the country dance, that he hoped she would stand up with him again, and adding, with his attractive smile: 'Dare I ask you to waltz with me? Or do you frown on the waltz in Hampshire? I wonder if my aunt does? How stupid it was of me not to have asked her! Now, don't, I do beg of you, Miss Bugle, tell me that I've committed a social solecism!'

She laughed, and said: 'No, indeed you have not! *I do* waltz, but whether Mama will permit me to do so in public is another matter!'

'Then I shall instantly ask Mama's permission to waltz with you!' he said.

This having been granted, he was presently seen twirling round the room with an arm lightly encircling Lucasta's trim waist: a spectacle which Lady Bugle regarded with complacency, but which was watched by the Viscount's two cousins, and by several other young gentlemen equally enamoured of the Beauty, with no pleasure at all.

After this, the Viscount did his duty by Miss Windle, and Miss Montsale, and then asked his cousin Emma to stand up with him.

'For heaven's sake, Ashley, don't ask me to dance, but take me out of this insufferably hot room!' replied Mrs Redgrave, who had inherited much of her mother's forthrightness.

'With the greatest pleasure on earth, cousin!' he replied, offering his arm. 'I've been uneasily aware for the past half-hour that my shirt-points are beginning to wilt! We will walk over to the doorway, as though we wished to exchange a word with Mortimer, and slip out of the room while the next set is forming. I daresay no one will notice our absence.'

'I don't care a rush if they do notice it!' declared Mrs Redgrave, vigorously fanning herself. 'People have no business to hold assemblies on such a sultry night as this! They might at least have opened a window!'

'Oh, they never do!' said Desford. 'Surely you must know, Emma, that it is only imprudent *young* people who open windows on even the hottest of nights! Thereby causing their elders to suffer all the ills which, I am assured, arise from sitting in a draught, and exposing themselves to even worse dangers. Mortimer, why are you not doing your duty like a man, instead of lounging there and holding up your nose at the company?'

'I wasn't!' said Mr Redgrave indignantly. 'The thing is that it's a dashed sight too hot for dancing—and no one thinks anything of it when we old married men don't choose to dance!'

'Quoth the graybeard!' murmured Desford.

'Be quiet, wretch!' Emma admonished him. 'I won't have poor Mortimer roasted! Recollect that although he is not so very many years older than you he is *much* fatter!'

'There's an archwife for you!' said Mr Redgrave. 'If you take my advice, Des, you'll steer wide of parson's mousetrap!'

'Thank you, I mean to! The melancholy sight of you living under the cat's foot is enough to make any man beware!'

Mr Redgrave grinned, but said that Des had hit the nail on the head, adding that he had grown to be a regular Jerry-sneak. Emma knew very well that this inelegant expression signified a henpecked husband, but said with dignity that she didn't understand cant terms. She then said, as both gentlemen laughed, that they were a couple of horrid rudesbys.

'To be sure we are!' cordially agreed her life's companion. 'You know, if you mean to take part in this dance, the pair of you, you'd best join the set before it's too late!'

But when he learned that so far from joining the set they were going in search of a little fresh air he instantly said, with considerable aplomb, that having watched Des desperately flirting with Miss Bugle he was dashed well going to see to it that he didn't get the chance to make up to Emma too.

So the three of them passed through the wide double-doors which stood open into the hall. Several people were gathered there, in small groups, most of the ladies fanning themselves, and the gentlemen surreptitiously wiping their heated brows; but Mrs Redgrave had the advantage over them in knowing the geography of the house, and she led her two cavaliers past the stairway to the back of the hall, and through a door which gave access to the gardens. The air was rather more oppressive than it had been during the day, but in comparison to the conditions within the house it was refreshing enough to cause Mr Redgrave to draw a deep breath, and let it go in a vulgar: 'Phew!' He then expressed a wistful desire for a cigarillo, but as his wife recognized this as a mere attempt to hoax her into begging him not to do anything so improper as to light a cigarillo at a ball she paid no attention to it, but tucked her hand in his arm, and strolled on to the lawn. The moon was at the full, but was every now and then hidden by clouds drifting across the sky. Summer lightning flickered, and Mr Redgrave said that he wouldn't be surprised if they were in for a storm. A few minutes later a distant rumble made Emma think that perhaps it was time they returned to the ballroom. Her disposition was in general calm, but she had a nervous dread of thunderstorms. Any of her brothers would have scoffed at her fears, but her husband and her cousin were more understanding, and neither scoffed nor tried to convince her that the storm was not imminent.

When they re-entered the house there was no one in the hall, but just as Mr Redgrave softly shut the door into the garden Stonor Bugle came out of the ballroom, and exclaimed: 'So there you are! I've been looking for you all over!'

'Oh, dear!' said Emma guiltily. 'I hoped no one would notice it if I slipped away for a few minutes! It is *such* a hot night, isn't it?'

He laughed heartily at this. 'Ay! Devilish, ain't it? I only wish *I* could sherry off into the garden, but I can't, you know! My mother would comb my hair with a joint-stool if I did! The thing is that old Mrs Barling has been asking for you, ma'am: says she hasn't seen you since time out of mind, and has been peering round the room after you ever since someone told her you was here.'

'Oh—! Dear Mrs Barling! I'll come at once!' Emma said, and went back into the ballroom, bearing her reluctant spouse with her.

Stonor followed them, but the Viscount lingered in the hall to adjust his neckcloth, having caught sight of himself in a mirror that hung beside the double-doors into the drawing-room. He was not a dandy; he would have repudiated without hesitation Lady Bugle's assertion that he was a Pink of the Ton; but he was undeniably one of the Smarts, and the glimpse of himself in wilting shirt-points, and a slightly disarranged neck-cloth came as a disagreeable shock to him. There was little he could do to restore their starched rigidity to the points of his shirt-collar, but a few deft touches were all that was needed to repair the folds of his neckcloth. Having bestowed these upon it, he turned away, gave his shirt-bands a judicious twitch or two, and was just about to go back into the ballroom when a feeling that he was not alone, as he had supposed himself to be, made him look up, and cast a swift glance round the hall. No one was in sight, but when he raised his eyes towards the upper floor he found that he was being watched by a pair of wondering, innocent eyes which were set in a charming little face, framed by the bannisters through which its owner was look-ing. He smiled, guessing that it belonged to one of the younger daughters of the house: possibly a member of the schoolroom-party, but more probably one of the nursery-children, and said, as he saw that she was about to run away in evident alarm: 'Oh, don't run away! I promise I won't eat you—or tell tales of you to your mama!'

The big eyes widened, in mingled fear and doubt. 'You couldn't!' said the lady. 'I haven't got a mama! She's been dead for years! I don't think I have a papa either, though that is by no means a certain thing! Oh, don't come up! *Pray* don't come up, sir! They would be so vexed!'

He had mounted half-way up the first flight of stairs, but he paused at this urgent entreaty, saying, between amusement and curiosity: 'No mama? But are you not one of Sir Thomas's daughters?'

'Oh, no!' she replied, still in that hushed, scared voice. 'I'm not related to him, because being married to my aunt does *not* make him a true uncle—does it?'

'No, no!' he assured her. 'It makes him nothing more than an uncle-in-law. But even so I find it hard to believe that he would be cross with you for peeping through those bannisters at the ladies in their smart ball-dresses, and the gentlemen trying to straighten their neckcloths!'

'It isn't *him*!' she said, with an apprehensive look over his head towards the drawing-room. 'It's Aunt Bugle, and Lucasta! Oh, pray, sir, go away, before anyone sees you on the stairs, and asks you what you are doing there! You would be obliged to say that you had been talking to me, and that would get me into trouble again!'

His amusement grew, and also his curiosity. 'Well, no one is going to see me on the stairs, because I am coming up to further my acquaintance with you, you engaging elf! Oh, don't look so scared! Recollect that I've promised I won't eat you! And talking of eating,' he added, remembering his own childhood, 'shall I bring you some of the tarts and jellies I've seen laid out for supper? I shall say I want them for my cousin, so you needn't be afraid that anyone will know you ate them!'

She had seemed to be on the point of scrambling to her feet, and beating a hasty retreat, but these words checked her. She stared at him for a moment, and then gave a soft little chuckle, and said: 'No, thank you, sir! I had supper hours ago, with Oenone, and Corinna—and Miss Mudford, of course—and my aunt directed the cook to set aside some of the tarts and cakes for the schoolroom supper. So I am not at all hungry. In fact, I'm never hungry, because my aunt doesn't *starve* me! But I am very much obliged to you for being so kind—which I thought you were, the instant you looked up, and smiled at me!'

'Ah, so you are one of the schoolroom-girls, are you?' he said, mounting the rest of the stairs till he stood at the head of the first flight, on the upper hall. 'Then I owe you an apology, for I took you for one of the nursery-babies!' He broke off, for she was on her feet, and although the only light illuminating the scene came from the candles burning in the chandelier that hung in the hall below there was enough to show him that she was considerably older than he had supposed.

She smiled shyly up at him, and said: 'People nearly always do. It is because I'm such a wretched little dab of a creature, and a severe mortification to me—particularly when I'm amongst my cousins, who are all so tall that I feel a mere squab beside them! At least Lucasta and Oenone and Corinna are tall, and Dianeme is very well grown, so I expect she will be too. Perenna is only just out of leading-strings, so one can't tell about her yet.'

Slightly stunned, he said faintly: 'Are you sure you have your cousins' names correctly? Did you say *Dianeme*? And *Perenna*?'

'Yes,' she answered, with another of her soft chuckles. 'You see, when she was very young my aunt was much addicted to poetry, and her papa had a library crammed with old books. That's how she came upon the poems of Robert Herrick. She has the book to this day, and she showed it to me once, when I ventured to ask her why my cousins have such peculiar names. She said she thought them so pretty, and not commonplace, like Maria, and Eliza, and Jane. She wished very much to call Lucasta Electra, but thought it more prudent to name her after her godmama, from whom Lucasta has Expectations. Though I shouldn't think, myself, that anything will come of it,' she added, in a reflective tone, 'because she's as cantankersome as *old* Lady Bugle was used to be, and she doesn't seem to me even to like Lucasta, or to admire her beauty, which one must own to be unjust, for Lucasta always behaves to her most obligingly, and it must be acknowledged that she *is* beautiful!'

'Very true!' he agreed, his voice grave, but his eyes full of laughter. 'And are—er—Oenone and Corinna beautiful too? They should be, with such names as those!'

'Well,' she said temperately, '*old* Lady Bugle was for ever telling my aunt that neither of them has beauty enough to figure in London, but I think they are both very pretty, though not, of course, to compare with Lucasta. And as for their names—' She choked on a smothered giggle, and a mischievous gleam shone in her eyes. She raised them to his face, and confided: 'Oenone doesn't dislike hers, but Corinna perfectly detests hers, because Stonor discovered the poem called *Corinna's Going a Maying*, and read it to the other boys, so that they instantly took to calling her Sweet Slug-a-bed, and shouting to her outside her door in the morning to Get up, get up for shame, which put her in such a flame that she actually tried to come to cuffs with her papa for having allowed my aunt to saddle her with such a silly, outmoded name. Which was improper, of course, but one can't but sympathize with her.'

'No, indeed! And what was her papa's reply to this very just rebuke?' he enquired, much entertained by this artless recital.

'Oh, he merely said that she might think herself fortunate that she hadn't been christened Sappho, and that if it hadn't been for him she would have been. It doesn't sound to me any worse than Corinna, but I believe there was a Greek person of that name who wasn't at all the thing. Oh, *pray* don't laugh so loud, sir!'

He had uttered an involuntary crack of laughter, but he checked it, and begged pardon. He had by this time had time to assimilate the details of her dress and person, and had realized that her figure was elegant, and that her dress had been adapted rather unskilfully from one originally made for a much bigger girl. He also realized, being pretty well experienced in such matters, that it was a trifle dowdy, and that her soft brown ringlets had not enjoyed the ministrations of a hairdresser. It was the fashion for ladies to have their locks cropped and curled, or twisted into high Grecian knots from which carefully brushed and pomaded clusters of curls fell over their ears; but this child's hair fell loosely from a ribbon tied round her head, several strands escaping from it, which gave her a somewhat dishevelled appearance.

Desford said abruptly: 'How old are you, my child? Sixteen? Seventeen?'

'Oh, no, I am much older than that!' she replied. 'I'm as old as Lucasta—all but a few weeks!'

'Then why are you not downstairs, dancing with the rest of them?' he demanded. 'You must surely be out!'

'No, I'm not,' she said. 'I don't suppose I ever shall be, either. Unless my papa turns out not to be dead, and comes home to take care of me himself. But I don't think that at all likely, and even if he did come home it wouldn't be of the least use, because he seems never to have sixpence to scratch with. I am afraid he is not a very respectable person. My aunt says he was obliged to go abroad on account of being monstrously in debt.' She sighed, and said wistfully: 'I know that one ought not to criticize one's father, but I can't help feeling that it was just a *little* thoughtless of him to abandon me.'

'Do you mean that he left you in your aunt's charge?' he asked, his brows drawing together. 'He can't have *abandoned* you!'

'Well, he did,' she said. 'And it was horridly uncomfortable, I can tell you, sir! I was still at school, in Bath, you see—and I must own that Papa did pay the bills, when he was in funds, and Miss Fletching was very kind, and she never told me that he had stopped doing so until she was obliged to realize that he wasn't going to remember that he owed her for a whole year. She disclosed to me afterwards that for a long time she expected to get a letter from him, or even a visit, for he did sometimes come down to see me. And it seems he had never been very punctual in paying Miss Fletching, so that she was quite in the habit of waiting. And I fancy she had a tendre for him, because she was for ever saying what a handsome man he was, and how particularly affable, and what distinguished manners he had. She was fond of me, too: she said it was because I had lived with her for such a long time, which I had, for Papa placed me in the school when my mama died, and I was only eight years old then, and lived at school all the year round.'

'You poor child!' he exclaimed.

'Oh, no!' she assured him. 'In the holidays my friends amongst the day-boarders often invited me to their parties, or took me with them on expeditions, and Miss Fletching several times took me to the theatre. I was perfectly happy—indeed, I don't suppose I shall ever be so happy again. But naturally I couldn't remain there for ever, so Miss Fletching was obliged to write to my grandfather. But it so happens that he had disowned Papa years and years before, and he wrote very uncivilly to Miss Fletching, saying that he wanted to know nothing about his ramshackle son's brats, and recommending her to apply to my mama's relations. Which—is how I come to be here.'

She ended on a forlorn note, which made Desford say gently: 'But you're not happy here, are you?'

She shook her head, but said, with a valiant attempt to smile: 'Not very happy, sir. But I do try to be, because I know I am very much obliged to Aunt Bugle for—for giving me a home, when she held Papa in the utmost aversion, and had had a terrible quarrel with my mama when Mama eloped with him, and never forgave her. Which makes it my duty to be grateful to her, don't you think?'

'Who is your father?' he demanded, not answering this question. 'What is his name? And what is your name?'

'Steane,' she replied. 'Papa is Wilfred Steane, and I am Cherry Steane.'

'Well, you have a very pretty name, Miss Steane!' he said, smiling down at her. 'But—Steane? Are you related to old— to Lord Nettlecombe?'

'Yes, he's my grandfather,' she said. 'Are you acquainted with him, sir?'

'No, I haven't that honour,' he replied rather dryly. 'I have, however, met your Uncle Jonas, and as I've been credibly informed that he closely resembles his father I am strongly of the opinion, my child, that you are better off with your aunt than you would be with your grandfather! But why should we waste our time talking about either of them? You have told me your name, but it occurs to me that you don't know mine! It is—'

'Oh, I know who you are!' she said. 'You are Lord Desford! I knew that when I saw you waltzing with Lucasta. That's why I was looking through the bannisters: you can see this end of the drawing-room from here, you know. I saw you first when you came down the country dance, but I couldn't be positive it was you until I caught a glimpse of you waltzing with Lucasta.'

'And then you were positive?' he said, in some amusement. 'Why?'

'Oh, because I heard Aunt Bugle tell Lucasta she might waltz if *you* invited her to!' she replied blithely. Then her expression changed swiftly, as some faint sound in the shadows behind her came to her ears, and the wary, frightened look returned to her face. She whispered: 'I mustn't stay! That was a board creaking! Please, oh, please go away, and *pray* take care no one sees you going down the stairs!'

She was gone on the words, as noiseless as a ghost; and the Viscount, having assured himself that the coast was clear, walked calmly down the stairs, and went back into the ballroom.

# *Four*

≈⚮≈

EIZING ON THE EXCUSE OFFERED BY HER DAUGHTER'S FEAR of being driven back to Hazelfield through a thunderstorm, Lady Emborough carried her party off immediately after supper. Lady Bugle was regretful, but since she was even more frightened of lightning than was Emma she fully sympathized with her alarms, and made no effort to delay the departure, prophesying, when she heard that a storm was brewing, that a great many others would also leave early: certainly all those faced with a drive of more than half-an-hour.

The Redgraves took up Edward and Gilbert in their carriage, and Desford occupied the fourth seat in the Emborough landaulet, sitting beside his uncle, and confronting Lady Emborough and Miss Montsale. For the first few minutes the ladies discussed the ball, but presently Miss Montsale said that although she had been prepared to find that Miss Bugle fell short of the enthusiastic descriptions furnished by Ned and Gil she had no sooner set eyes on her than she felt that they had underrated her beauty rather than exaggerated it. 'Such great, sparkling eyes!' she said. 'Such a lovely complexion, and such glorious hair! Oh, I thought she was one of the most beautiful creatures I've ever seen! Did not you, Lord Desford?'

He was not, like his uncle, drowsing, but he was obviously abstracted, and she had to repeat her question to recall him from

whatever thoughts were occupying his mind. He said: 'I beg
pardon! I wasn't attending! Miss Bugle? Oh, yes, undoubtedly!
A dazzling piece of nature!'

'And not just in the common style!'

'By no means!'

'What do you think, Desford? Will she take?' asked Lady
Emborough.

'Lord, yes!'

'Well, I hope she will. I don't like her mother above half, but
I do sincerely pity her, for it's no laughing matter to have five
daughters to establish creditably when one hasn't a large enough
fortune to grease the wheels,' she said bluntly. 'There's one that
ought to be brought out next Season, and so she would be if old
Lady Bugle hadn't chosen to die at the most inconvenient time
she could! Lucasta might have been engaged by now, which
would have made it possible for the next one—I can't remember her name! they all have the most outlandish names!—to
have been allowed to try her wings at that little affair tonight,
and to have been brought out during the Little Season, this
autumn. Not what one would choose, of course, but what's to
be done, when the girl is turned seventeen already, and her elder
sister has scarcely been seen yet, much less turned-off? And
before that unfortunate woman has time to make a recover
she'll have the third girl ready for her come-out!'

'Tell me, ma'am!' interposed Desford. 'What do you know
about Lady Bugle's niece? Have you met her?'

'Why, have *you* met her?' she asked, considerably surprised.

'Yes, I met her tonight,' he answered. 'But pray don't divulge
that to her aunt! She was peeping through the bannisters
to watch as much as she could see of the dancing, and I
happened to catch sight of her. I thought her one of the children at first, but discovered that she is—all but a few weeks!—
as old as her cousin Lucasta. A pretty child, with big, scared

eyes, a tangle of brown hair, and a deplorably outmoded and ill-fitting gown.'

Lady Emborough tried hard to see his face, but it was too dark inside the carriage for her to distinguish more than its outlines. She said: 'Yes, I think I have seen her once. I must own, it astonishes me to learn that she is as old as Lucasta, for—like you!—I thought her a schoolroom miss! A poor little dab of a girl, isn't she? Well, she's the daughter of Lady Bugle's only sister, who ran off with that ne'er-do-well son of old Nettlecombe's. Before your time, but I remember what a scandal it was! Lady Bugle was obliged to take this girl under her roof—oh, a little over a year ago! I forget the rights of it, but I know that I thought it very charitable of her to have done so, when she told me about it.'

'Oh, was that how it was?' he said, in an indifferent tone.

'Charitable?' said Miss Montsale. 'Why, yes—if the charity was not used as a cloak to cover more mercenary aims!'

'Good God, Mary, what in the world do you mean?' demanded Lady Emborough.

'Oh, nothing, dear ma'am, against Lady Bugle! How could I, when I never met her before tonight? But I have so often seen—as I am persuaded you too must have seen!—the—the indigent female who has been received into the household of one of her more affluent relations, as an act of charity, and has been turned into a drudge!'

'And has been expected to be grateful for it!' struck in the Viscount.

'If,' said Lady Emborough awfully, 'these remarks refer to my cousin Cordelia's position at Hazelfield—'

'Oh, no, no, no!' Miss Montsale assured her laughingly. 'Of course they don't! Lord Desford, *could* anyone suppose Miss Pembury to be a downtrodden drudge?'

'Certainly not!' he responded promptly. 'No one, that is to say, who had been privileged to hear her giving handsome set-downs to my aunt! But you are very right, Miss Montsale: I too have seen just what you have described, and I suspect that the child I met tonight may be an example of that sort of charity.'

No more was said, for by this time the carriage had drawn up before the imposing portals of Hazelfield House. The ladies were handed down from it; Lord Emborough was roused by his nephew from his gentle slumber; and his sons, springing down from the Redgrave carriage, which drew up a minute later, were indignantly calling upon their pusillanimous sister to own that the storm was still miles distant, and that it had been a great shame to have dragged them away from the ball when (according to them) it had scarcely begun.

Lord Emborough, on entering his house, presented all the appearance of a gentleman no more than half awake, but when he walked into my lady's bedchamber, an hour later, he had emerged from his drowsy mists, and so obviously wished to engage her in private conversation that she dismissed her abigail, who was in the act of fitting a nightcap over her iron-grey locks, and said, as this excellent female curtsied herself out of the room: 'Now we can be comfortable, and talk about the party—which I have for long thought to be the best thing about parties, even the finest of 'em! Which the lord knows this wasn't! An insipid evening, wasn't it?'

'It was indeed,' he agreed, disposing himself in a cushioned chair, and yawning. 'I have never known, my love, why my old friend—as good a man as ever stepped when we were up at Oxford together!—should have chosen to marry—I won't say a smatterer, but a mere miss, which was what we all thought her!'

'Well,' said Lady Emborough tolerantly, 'I do not say that she is a woman of the first consideration, but it must be acknowledged that she has been a good wife to Sir Thomas, and is an excellent mother. And even you, Emborough, must also acknowledge that Sir Thomas's sense is not superior!'

'No,' he agreed, with a melancholy sigh. He then fell silent, but said, after a few moments, somewhat acidly: 'I am excessively glad, my dear, that I have never been mortified by the spectacle of *my* wife throwing a daughter at the head of an eligible *parti* in what I can only describe as a positively shocking way!'

'Certainly not!' responded his lady, with unruffled calm. 'I hope I have too much rumgumption to do anything so bird-witted. But it must be remembered, my lord, that I have not been cursed with an improvident husband, and five daughters! I promise you, I do most sincerely feel for Lady Bugle, little though I may like her, and perfectly sympathize with her anxiety to achieve a good match for Lucasta as soon as may be possible.'

He directed a worried look at her. 'Did it seem to you that Desford was strongly attracted to that girl, my love?'

'Not in the least,' she replied unhesitatingly.

'Well, I hope you may be right,' he said. 'It seemed to me that he treated her with very flattering distinction! And it wouldn't do, you know!'

'Of course it wouldn't do, and he knows that as well as we do! Lord, my dear sir, can you suppose that a personable man of birth and fortune who has been on the town for years, and has had I don't know how many girls on the catch for him, don't recognize a lure in no more than the shake of a lambstail? If the mother's odious toadying didn't disgust him, you may depend upon it the coming manners Lucasta assumed did!'

'One would have thought so, but he appeared to me to be quite blatantly flirting with her!'

'To be sure he was!' said her ladyship. 'But in my judgment he was very much more interested in Lucasta's little cousin!'

'Good God!' ejaculated Emborough. 'Do you mean that scamp's child?—*Wilfred Steane's* daughter?'

His wife burst out laughing, for the look of dismay on his face was comical. 'Yes, but there's no need for you to be on the

GEORGETTE HEYER

fidgets, I promise you! Recollect that Desford leaves us tomorrow! It is in the highest degree unlikely that he will ever see
the girl again; and for my part I wouldn't wager a groat on the
chance that he won't have forgotten all about her by the time
he reaches London!'

If this was a somewhat exaggerated statement, it is probable
that had not Chance intervened Miss Cherry Steane would not
have lived for long in the Viscount's memory. But Chance did
intervene, and on the very next day.

Since Hazelfield was situated within a few miles of Alton,
and he was bound for London, he did not take leave of his hosts
until he had consumed a leisurely breakfast. The threatened
storm had burst (according to Emma's account) directly over
the house in the small hours, but after a violent downpour the
weather had cleared, and the Viscount set out on his journey
with every expectation of covering the distance in bright sunlight, and of reaching his destination in excellent time to change
his dress, and to stroll from his house in Arlington Street to
White's Club, where he meant to dine.

At Alton, he joined the post-road to Southampton, and was
soon driving through Farnham. It was when he was a few miles
beyond this town that Fate took a hand in his affairs.

A female figure, wearing a round bonnet and a gray cloak, plod-
ding ahead, with a slightly dilapidated portmanteau in her grasp,
did not attract his attention, but just as his horses drew abreast of
her she turned her head, looking up at him, and disclosed the
child-like countenance of Miss Cherry Steane. Considerably startled, he uttered an exclamation, and reined in his horses.

'Why, what's amiss, my lord?' demanded Stebbing, even
more startled.

The Viscount, slewing round to obtain a second view of Miss
Steane, found that the fleeting glance he had cast down at her as
his curricle swept past had not deceived him: Miss Steane it most

certainly was. He thrust the reins into Stebbing's hands, saying briefly: 'Hold 'em! I know that lady!' He then jumped lightly down on to the road, and strode back to meet Miss Steane.

She greeted him with frank delight, and said, in a voice of passionate thanksgiving: 'I *thought* it was you, sir! Oh, I am so glad! If you are going to London, would you—would you be so *very* kind as to take me up in your carriage?'

He took the portmanteau from her, and set it down. 'What, to London? Why?'

'I've run away,' she explained, with a confiding smile.

'That, my child, is obvious!' he said. 'But it won't do, you know! How could I possibly aid and abet you to leave the protection of your aunt?'

Her face fell ludicrously; it seemed for a moment that she was going to burst into tears, but she overcame the impulse, swallowing resolutely, and saying in a prim, forlorn little voice: 'C-couldn't you, sir? I beg your pardon! I thought—I thought— But it's of no consequence!'

'Will you tell me why you have run away?' he suggested gently.

'I couldn't bear it! You don't *know*!' she said, in a stifled tone.

'No, but I wish you will tell me. I think something must have happened since we talked together last night. Did someone hear you, and tell your aunt?' She nodded, biting her lips. 'And she perhaps gave you a scold?'

'Oh, yes! But that's not it! I don't care for mere scolds, but she said such things—and Lucasta too—and all in front of Corinna—and Corinna told the others—' Her voice failed on a sob, and she was quite unable to continue.

He waited until she had in some degree recovered her composure. He thought he had seldom seen a more pathetic picture. Not only was her countenance woebegone, but her shoes and the hem of the duffle cloak which she wore were sadly muddied; several strands of her unruly hair had escaped from the confinement of the round, schoolgirl's bonnet, and strayed across her flushed features; and beads of sweat glistened on her forehead. She looked to be hot, tired, and despairing. For the first of these three ills the duffle cloak was certainly responsible; for the second it was no wonder that she should be tired if she had trudged all the way from her home, carrying a cumbrous portmanteau; but the despair was not to be accounted for so easily: nothing she had said to him on the previous evening had prepared him to find her flying from the security of the only home she seemed to have.

She succeeded in mastering her agitation, and even managed to summon up a gallant, if unconvincing, smile. 'I beg your pardon!' she uttered. 'It was only because you look so kind, sir, and—and talked to me last night—But it was wrong of me to ask you to take me up in your carriage. Pray don't regard it! My—my affairs are not your concern, and I shall do very well by myself!'

He ignored the hand she was resolutely holding out to him, but picked up her portmanteau, and said: 'We cannot stand talking in the road! I don't promise to take you to London, but at least I'll take you to Farnborough! As I remember, there is a tolerable inn there, where I can procure some refreshment for you, and where we can continue this conversation at our ease. Come along!'

She hung back, searching his face with her wide, scared eyes. 'You won't compel me to return to Maplewood, will you?'

'No, I won't do that. What right have I to compel you to do anything? Though it is undoubtedly what I ought to do!'

She seemed to be satisfied with this reply, for she said no more, but went obediently beside him to where his curricle stood. The expression on Stebbing's face when he realized that his master was going to hand into the curricle a Young Person whose unattended state and dowdy raiment clearly denoted that she was not a female of consequence spoke volumes; but he relinquished the reins to the Viscount, without a word, and climbed up into the groom's seat between the springs.

Miss Steane, sinking back against the squabs, uttered a sigh of relief. 'Oh, how comfortable this is!' she said thankfully.

'Have you trudged all the way from Maplewood?'

'No, no! I was so fortunate as to have been given a lift to Froyle, in a tax-cart, so I have only been obliged to walk for six or seven miles, and I shouldn't regard that in the least if I weren't burdened with this portmanteau. And I must own I wish my pelisse wasn't quite worn out, so that I might have worn it instead of this dreadful cloak.'

'It is certainly not the thing for such a warm day,' he agreed.

'No, but I thought I should wear it, in case it comes on to rain, or I felt chilly when the sun goes down.'

'When the sun goes down—! You absurd child, you are surely not meaning to continue walking till nightfall?'

'No—at least—Well, I thought I should have been able to travel on the stage-coach, but—but when it reached Alton it was cram-full, and of course I hadn't booked a seat, so I wasn't on the way-bill, and the guard wouldn't take me up. And even if there had been room I found that I hadn't quite enough money to pay for the fare. But I daresay I shall be able to get a lift on a carrier's wagon: they will often take people up, you know, and for no more than a shilling or two. And if I don't I shall go on for as long as I can, and then find a lodging for the night in some respectable farmhouse.'

The Viscount's reflections on the sort of reception she was likely to meet at a respectable farmhouse he kept to himself, merely asking her where she proposed to lodge when she did reach London.

'I am going to my grandfather,' she replied, a hint of defiance in her voice.

'Indeed! May I ask if he knows it?'

'Well—well, not yet!' she confessed.

He drew an audible breath, and said rather grimly: 'Yes, well, we will postpone further discussion until we get to Farnborough, when I must hope to be able to convince you that this scheme of yours won't do, my child!'

'You won't convince me!' she said, betraying signs of agitation. 'Oh, pray don't try, sir! It is the only thing I *can* do! You don't understand!'

'Then you shall explain it to me,' he said cheerfully.

She said no more, but groped in the folds of her cloak for the pocket which held her handkerchief. He was afraid that she was going to cry, and suffered a moment's dismay. He was not chicken-hearted, but he found himself quite unable to face with equanimity the prospect of driving a lady in floods of tears along a busy post-road. However, she bravely suppressed all but one small sob, and did no more than blow her nose. He was moved to say, for her encouragement: 'Good girl!' glancing down at her as he spoke, and smiling.

Of necessity it was a very brief glance, but as he turned his head back again to watch the road he caught a glimpse of the wavering, would-be valiant smile which answered his, and it wrung his heart.

In a few minutes Farnborough was reached, and he had drawn up in front of the Ship. Not many persons patronized this small post-house, so the landlord, who came out to welcome a recognizable member of the Quality, was saddened, but not surprised, when the Viscount, handing Miss Steane into his care, told him that they had stopped only to bait. 'Anyone in the coffee-room?' he asked.

'No, sir, no one—not at the moment! But if your honour would wish to partake of refreshment in the private parlour—'

'No, the coffee-room will do very well. Some lemonade for the lady, and cold meat—cakes—fruit—whatever you have! And a tankard of beer for myself, if you please!' He looked down at Miss Steane, and said: 'Go in, my dear: I'll be with you in a moment.'

He watched her enter the inn, and turned to issue a few instructions to Stebbing, standing at the wheelers' heads. Stebbing received these with a wooden: 'Very good, my lord,' but the Viscount had taken barely two steps towards the door into the inn before his feelings overcame him, and he said, explosively: ' My lord!'

'Well?' said the Viscount, over his shoulder.

'It ain't my place to speak,' said Stebbing, with careful restraint, 'but being as I've known your lordship ever since you was a little lad, which I taught to ride your first pony—ah, *and* pulled you out of scrapes! and being that—'

'You needn't go on!' interrupted Desford, quizzing him. 'I know just what you are trying to say! I must take care I don't fall into yet another scrape, mustn't I?'

'Yes, my lord, and I hope you will—though it don't look to me, the way things is shaping, that you will!'

But Desford only laughed, and went into the inn. The mistress of the establishment had taken Miss Steane upstairs, and when she presently joined his lordship in the coffee-room she had washed her face, tidied her unruly hair, and was carrying her cloak over her arm. She looked much more presentable, but the round dress of faded pink cambric which she wore was rather crumpled, besides being muddied round the hem, and in no way became her. She was looking very grave, but when she saw the chicken, and the tongue, and the raspberries on the table her eyes brightened perceptibly, and she said gratefully: 'Oh, thank you, sir! I am very much obliged to you! I ran away before breakfast, and you can't think how hungry I am!'

She then sat down at the table, and proceeded to make a hearty meal. Desford, who was not at all hungry, sat watching her, his tankard in his hand, thinking that for all her nineteen years she was very little removed from childhood. While she ate he forbore to question her, but when she came to the end of her nuncheon, and said that she now felt much better, he said: 'Do you feel sufficiently restored to tell me all about it? I wish you will!'

Her brightened eyes clouded, but after a slight hesitation she said: 'If I tell you why I've run away, will you take me to London, sir?'

He laughed. 'I am making no rash promises—except to carry you straight back to Maplewood if you *don't* tell me!'

She said with quaint dignity, but as though she had a lump in her throat: 'I cannot believe that you would do anything so—so unhandsome!'

'No, I am sure you cannot,' he said sympathetically. 'But you must consider my position, you know! Recollect that all I know at this present is that although you told me last night that you were not very happy I am persuaded you had no intention then of running away. Yet today I come upon you, in a good deal of distress, having apparently reached a sudden decision to leave your aunt. Did you perhaps have a quarrel with her, fly up into the boughs, and run away without giving yourself time to consider whether she had really been unkind enough to warrant your taking such an extreme course? Or whether she too had lost her temper, and had said much more than she meant?'

She looked forlornly at him, and gave her head a shake. 'We didn't quarrel. I didn't even quarrel with Corinna. Or with Lucasta. And it wasn't such a sudden decision. I've wished desperately—oh, almost from the moment my aunt took me to Maplewood!—to escape. Only whenever I ventured to ask my aunt if she would help me to find a situation where I could earn my own bread she always scolded me for being ungrateful, and—and said I should soon wish myself back at Maplewood, because I was fit for nothing but a—a menial position.' She paused, and, after a moment or two, said rather hopelessly: 'I can't explain it to you. I daresay you wouldn't understand if

I could, because you have never been so poor that you were obliged to hang on anyone's sleeve, and try to be grateful for a worn-out ribbon, or a scrap of torn lace which one of your cousins gave you, instead of throwing it away.'

'No,' he replied. 'But you are mistaken when you say that I don't understand. I have seen all too many of such cases as you describe, and have sincerely pitied the victims of this so-called charity, who are expected to give unremitting service to show their gratitude for—' He broke off, for she had winced, and turned away her face. 'What have I said to upset you?' he asked. 'Believe me, I had no intention of doing so!'

'Oh, no!' she said, in a stifled voice. 'I beg your pardon! It was stupid of me to care for it, but that word brought it all back to me, like—like a stab! Lucasta said I was well-named, and my aunt s-said: "Very true, my love!" and that in future I should be called Charity, to keep me in mind of the fact that that is what I am—a charity girl!'

'What a griffin!' he exclaimed disdainfully. 'But she won't call you Charity, you know! Depend upon it, she wouldn't wish people to think her spiteful!'

'They wouldn't. Because it *is* my name!' she disclosed tragically. 'I know I told you it was Cherry, but it wasn't a fubbery, sir, to say that, because I have always been called Cherry.'

'I see. Do you know, I like Charity better than Cherry? I think it is a very pretty name.'

'You wouldn't think so if it was your name, and *true!*'

'I suppose I shouldn't,' he admitted. 'But what did you do to bring down all this ill-will upon your head?'

'Corinna was on the listen last night, when we talked together on the stairs,' she said. 'She is the most odious, humbugging little cat imaginable, and if you think I shouldn't say such a thing of her I am sorry, but it is true! I was used to think her the most amiable of my cousins, and—and my friend! And even though

I did know that she was a shocking fibster, and not in the least above carrying tales against Oenone to my aunt, I never dreamed she would do the same by me! Well—well, there was some excuse for her trying for revenge against Oenone, because Oenone is a very disagreeable girl, and for ever picking out grievances, and trying to set my aunt against her sisters. But—' Her eyes filled with tears, which she made haste to brush away—'she—she had no cause to do me a mischief! But—but she twisted everything I said to you, sir, m-making it seem quite different from what I *did* say! She even said that you wouldn't have come upstairs if I hadn't th-thrown out lures to you! Which I didn't! I *didn't!*'

'On the contrary! You begged me not to come upstairs!' he said, smiling.

'Yes, and so I told them, but neither my aunt nor Lucasta would believe me. They—they accused me of being a— a designing little squirrel, and my aunt read me a scold about g-girls like me ending up in the Magdalen: and when I asked her what the Magdalen is, she said that if I continued to make sheep's eyes at every man that crossed my path I should very soon discover what it is. But I don't, I *don't!*' she said vehemently. 'It wasn't my fault that you came up to talk to me last night, and it wasn't my fault that Sir John Thorley took me up in his chaise and so very kindly drove me back to Maplewood, the day he overtook me walking back from the village in the rain; and it wasn't my fault that Mr Rainham came over to talk to me when I brought Dianeme and Tom down to the drawing-room one evening! I did *not* put myself forward! I sat down, just as my aunt bade me, in a chair against the wall, and made not the least push to keep him beside me! I *promise* you I didn't, sir!' Her tears brimmed over, but she brushed them away, and said: 'It was nothing but kindness on their parts, and to say that I lured either of them away from Lucasta is wickedly unjust!'

Since he had himself succumbed to the unconscious appeal of her big eyes, and had been moved to compassion by her forlorn aspect, he could readily understand the feelings that had prompted two gentlemen, whom he guessed to be admirers of Lucasta, to pay her a little attention. He thought, with a sardonic curl of his lips, that Lady Bugle was no wiser than a wet-goose; and wondered how many of Lucasta's court would have paid any attention to her little cousin had Cherry been suitably attired, and treated by Lady Bugle with the affection that lady showed towards Lucasta. Not many, he guessed, for, although she had an innocent charm, she was no more than a candle to the sun of Lucasta's beauty; and if she had been happy she would have roused no chivalrous emotions in any male breast. These reflections, however, he kept to himself, setting himself instead to the task of soothing her agitation, prior to doing what lay within his power to convince her that a return to her house of bondage would be preferable to her present scheme.

With the first of these objects in view, he encouraged her to unburden herself of her wrongs, thinking that to be allowed to pour out her troubles would sensibly allay whatever feelings of hurt and injustice had overset her. He suspected that these might have been exaggerated in her mind by what had obviously been a pulling of caps; but by the time she had been induced to describe what her life had been at Maplewood there was no hint of a smile in his eyes, and no scepticism in his mind.

For she did not answer his questions willingly, and she seemed always to be able to find excuses for the many unkindnesses she had received at Maplewood. Nor did she resent the demands that had been made on her: she felt it was only right that she should repay her aunt's generosity by performing whatever services were required of her; but when she said simply: 'I would do anything if only she would love me a little, and just *once* say thank you!' he thought he had never heard a sadder utterance.

It was obvious that Lady Bugle had seen in her not an orphaned niece to be cherished, but a household slave, to be made to fetch and carry all day long, to wait not only on her aunt but on her cousins as well, and to mind the two eldest nursery children whenever Nurse desired her to do so. He suspected that if she had been less docile and less easily dismayed she would have fared better at Maplewood: he had been standing close enough to Lady Bugle on the previous evening to observe her when she approached her husband, and said something pretty sharp to him under her breath. He had not heard what she had said, but that she had issued an order was patent, for Sir Thomas had at first expostulated, and then gone off to do her bidding, and Desford had written her down then and there as one of those overbearing females who would tyrannize over anyone too meek or too scared to withstand her. It had at first surprised him to learn that his brief meeting with Cherry had brought down on her head such a venomous scold, but the more he studied the sweet little face before him the less surprised did he feel that the ambitious mother and daughter should have been so furious to learn that he had been sufficiently attracted by Cherry to have gone upstairs to talk to her. Lucasta was a Beauty, but Cherry was by far the more taking.

While she told her story, at least half of his brain was occupied in trying to think what to do for her. It had not taken long to make him abandon his original intention of restoring her to her aunt, and he wasted no eloquence on attempting to persuade her to agree to such a course. A fleeting notion of placing her in Lady Emborough's care no sooner occurred to him than he banished it; and when he suggested that she should return to Miss Fletching she shook her head, saying that nothing would prevail upon her to make any more demands on that lady's kindness.

'Don't you think you might be very useful to her?' he coaxed. 'As a teacher, perhaps?'

'No,' she replied. Suddenly her eyes lost their despairing look, and danced mischievously. She giggled, and said: 'I shouldn't be in the least useful, and certainly not as a teacher! I am not at all bookish, and although I do *know* how to play on the pianoforte I don't play at all well! I have no aptitude for languages, either, or for painting, and my sums are always wrong. So you see —!'

It was certainly daunting. He could not help laughing, but he said: 'Well, now that you've told me all the things you can't do, tell me what you can do!'

The cloud descended again on her brow. She said: 'Nothing— nothing of a genteel nature. My aunt says I am only fitted to perform menial tasks, and I suppose that is true. But while I have been at Maplewood I have learnt a great deal about housekeeping, and I know I can take care of sick old ladies, because when old Lady Bugle became too ill to leave her bed there were days when she wouldn't let anyone enter her room except me. And I think she liked me, because though she pinched at me a good deal—she was nearly always as cross as crabs, poor old lady— she never ripped up at me as she did at my aunt, and Lucasta, and Oenone, or accuse me of wishing her dead. So I thought that I could very likely be a comfort to my grandfather. I believe he lives quite alone, except for the servants, which must be excessively melancholy for him. Don't you think so, sir?'

'I should certainly find it so, but your grandfather is said to be a—a confirmed recluse. I have never met him, but if the stories that are told about him are true he is not a very amiable person. After all, you told me yourself that he had written a very disobliging reply to Miss Fletching's letter, didn't you?'

'Yes, but I don't think she asked him to take charge of me,' she argued. 'She wanted him to pay the money Papa owed her, and

I shouldn't wonder at it if she set up his back, for I know, from
what Papa has said to me, that he is shockingly dutch-fisted.'

'Did your aunt pay her?' he interrupted.

She shook her head, flushing a little. 'No. She too said that
she wasn't responsible, but because of blood being thicker than
water she—she would relieve Miss Fletching by taking me
away to live with her. So—so no one has paid for me—yet! But
I mean to save every penny I can earn, and I shall pay her!' Her
chin lifted, and she said: 'If my grandfather—if I can see him,
and explain to him how it is—surely he won't refuse to let me
stay with him at least until I've found a suitable situation?'

The Viscount could not think this likely. No matter how ill-
disposed and eccentric Lord Nettlecombe might be, he could
scarcely turn away a destitute granddaughter who had no other
shelter in London than his house. The probability was that he
would take a fancy to her, and if that happened her future would
be assured. And if he was such a shabster as to turn her away, he
would find he had to deal with my Lord Desford, who would
cast aside the deference to his elders so carefully drilled into him
from his earliest days, and would counsel the old muckworm in
explicit terms to think well before he behaved in so scaly a
fashion as must alienate even the few friends he had, once the
story became known, as he, Desford, would make it his business
to see that it did.

He did not favour Cherry with these reflections, but got up
abruptly, and said: 'Very well! I will take you to London!'

She sprang to her feet, caught his hand, and kissed it before
he could prevent her. 'Oh, thank you, sir!' she cried, gratitude
throbbing in her voice, and making her eyes shine through the
sudden tears of relief which filled them. 'Thank you, thank you,
*thank* you!'

Considerably embarrassed, he drew his hand away, and gave
her a pat on the shoulder with it, saying: 'Draw bridle, you fool-

ish child! Wait until we see how your grandfather receives you before you fly into raptures! If he doesn't receive you, you will have nothing to thank me for, you know!'

He then went away to pay his shot, telling her that he would bring his curricle to the door in a few minutes, and so cut short any further expressions of her gratitude.

But he had still to run the gauntlet of his devoted servitor's disapproval. When he informed Stebbing that he was driving Miss Steane to London, that worthy found himself wholly unable to receive this news in a manner befitting his station, but said forthrightly: 'My lord, I beg and implore you not to do no such thing! You'll find yourself in the briars, as sure as check, and it's me as will get the blame for it when his lordship comes to hear of it!'

'Don't be such a gudgeon!' said the Viscount impatiently. 'His lordship won't come to hear of it—and if he did the only thing he would blame you for is making such a piece of work about nothing! Do you imagine I'm abducting the child?'

'More likely she's abducting you, my lord!' muttered Stebbing.

The Viscount's eyes hardened; he said coldly: 'I allow you a good deal of licence, Stebbing, but that remark goes far beyond the line of what I will permit!'

'My lord,' said Stebbing doggedly, 'if I spoke too free, I ask your pardon! But I've served you faithfully ever since you was pleased to accept of me as your personal groom, and I couldn't look myself in the face if I didn't make a push to stop you doing something so caper-witted as to carry off this young pers— lady!—the way you're meaning to! You can turn me off, my lord, but I must and will tell you to your head that *I* never seen a young lady which would go off with a gentleman like this Miss Steane is willing to go off with you!'

'Doesn't it suit your sense of propriety? Well, you must bear in mind that you will be sitting behind us, and I give you leave to intervene to protect Miss Steane's virtue from any improper advances I might make to her!' Perceiving that Stebbing was deeply troubled, he relented, and said, laughingly: 'There's no need for you to be so hot in the spur, you old pudding-head! All I've engaged myself to do is to convey Miss Steane to her grandfather's house. And if you weren't a pudding-head you would know that her willingness to go with me to London springs from innocence, and not, as you seem to think, from a want of delicacy! Good God, what would you have me to do in this situation? Abandon her to become the prey of the first rake-shame she encounters on the road? A pretty fellow you must think me!'

'No, my lord, I don't think no such thing! But what I do think is that you should take her back where she came from!'

'She won't go, and I have no right to force her to do so.' A gleam of humour shot into his eyes; he added: 'And even if I had the right I'd be damned if I'd do it! Lord, Stebbing, would *you* drive a girl who was crying her eyes out, in an open carriage?' He laughed, and said: 'You know you wouldn't! Put to the horses, and don't spill any more time sermonizing!'

'Very good, my lord. But I shall take leave to say—asking your pardon for making so bold as to open my budget!—that I never seen you—no, not when you was in the heyday of blood, and kicking up all kinds of conflabberation!—so bedoozled as what you are now! And if you don't end up in the basket—and me with you!—you can call me a Jack Adams, my lord!'

'I'm much obliged to you! I will!' retorted the Viscount.

# Five

THE VISCOUNT DREW UP HIS SWEATING TEAM TWO–AND–a-half hours later in Albemarle Street, having driven his horses in a spanking style that in anyone but a top-sawyer, which he was, would have been extremely dangerous. Even Stebbing, who had good reason to know that he could drive to an inch, clutched the edge of his seat three times: twice when, on a narrow stretch of the road, he sprang his horses to give the go-by to a slower vehicle, and once when he feather-edged a blind corner without checking; but it was only when they reached the outskirts of London that he allowed himself to utter a gruff warning, saying: 'Easy over the pimples, my lord, I do beg of you!'

'What do you take me for?' the Viscount tossed over his shoulder. 'A spoon?'

Stebbing returned no answer to this, for while he secretly considered his master to be a first-rate fiddler nothing would have induced him to say so, except when boasting of the Viscount's excellence amongst certain of his cronies at the Horse and Groom. He rarely praised the Viscount's skill to his face; and never when Desford stood in his black books.

Miss Steane, whose spirits had soared from the instant Desford had said that he would convey her to London, enjoyed the journey hugely. She confided to him, with what he thought engaging ingenuousness, that she had never before been driven in a curricle. A gig had hitherto been her only experience of open carriages, and although her cousin Stonor possessed a curricle it was a very shabby affair compared with the Viscount's lightly built and graceful carriage. She thought well of his horses too, and told him so, for which commendation he thanked her with a gravity only very slightly impaired by the quiver of laughter in his voice. They were, in fact, perfectly matched grays, and he had paid so long a price for them as would have confirmed his father (if he had known it) in his belief that his heir was a scattergood.

'You can't think what a high treat this is for me, sir!' she said gaily. 'Everything is new! You see, I have never travelled at all since my Papa carried me to Bath, and I don't remember very much about that journey. Besides, we went in a closed coach, and that is *not* the way to see the countryside. This is beyond anything great!'

She chatted away in this artless style, interested in all that met her wondering gaze, continually craning her neck to obtain a better view of a particularly bright garden, or a picturesque cottage, fleetingly seen down a side lane. Such of her conversation as was not concerned with the passing scene was devoted to an earnest discussion with Desford on what ought to be her approach to her grandfather. But when they reached London she became rather silent, a circumstance which made Desford say quizzingly: 'Tired, little bagpipe? Not far to go now!'

She smiled, and shook her head: 'No, not tired. Has my tongue been running on like a fiddlestick? I beg your pardon! Why didn't you tell me to button my lip? I must have been a sad bore to you.'

'On the contrary! I found your conversation most refreshing. Why have you shut up shop? Are you in a worry about your grandfather?'

'A little,' she confessed. 'I didn't know that London is so big, and—and so noisy, and I cannot help wondering what to do if my grandfather refuses to see me. I wish I had some acquaintance here!'

'Don't fret!' he said reassuringly. 'It is in the highest degree unlikely that he will. And if he does I promise I won't desert you! Depend upon it, we shall hit upon some scheme for your relief!'

He spoke lightly, for the more he considered the matter the more convinced did he become that however eccentric Lord Nettlecombe might be he could scarcely be so lost to all sense of propriety as to cast upon the world a granddaughter whose childlike innocence must be obvious to anyone but an incurable lobcock. But when he drew up his weary team outside Lord Nettlecombe's town residence in Albemarle Street such optimistic reflections suffered a severe set-back. Every window of the house was shuttered, and the knocker was off the door: his lordship's eccentricity had not led him to remain in London during the summer months.

'Would your lordship wish me to ring the bell?' enquired Stebbing, in Cassandra-like accents.

'Yes: do so!' the Viscount said curtly.

By this time Miss Steane had had time to assimilate the significance of the closed shutters, and panic seized her. She gripped her hands tightly together in her lap, in a brave attempt to remain calm; and after a few minutes, during which Stebbing vigorously pulled the bell, said, in a voice of would-be carelessness: 'It seems that the house has been shut up, d-doesn't it, sir?'

'It does indeed! But I daresay there may be someone left in charge from whom we can discover your grandfather's direction. Try the basement, Stebbing!'

'Begging your lordship's pardon, I don't hardly know how I can do so, being as the area-gate is chained and padlocked.' He observed, not without a certain satisfaction, that the Viscount, momentarily at least, was at a non-plus, and relented sufficiently to say that he would enquire at the neighbouring houses. But as one of these had been hired for the summer months by a family whom Stebbing disdainfully described as Proper Mushrooms, and who had no knowledge of Lord Nettlecombe; and the other by an elderly couple whose porter said, with a sniff, that he had seen the old hunks drive off about a week ago, but had no notion where he was going. 'My master and mistress don't have nothing to do with him, nor don't any of us in this house have nothing to do with his servants,' he stated loftily.

When Stebbing returned to the curricle to report these discouraging tidings, Miss Steane uttered in an anguished whisper: 'Oh, what shall I do, what shall I do?'

'Shall I ask at any of the other houses, my lord?'

But the Viscount had had time to think, and he replied: 'No. We have wasted enough time, and wherever his lordship may be we can scarcely hope to reach him today. Up with you!' He then turned his attention to his agitated passenger, and said with a cheerfulness he was far from feeling: 'Now, why are you shaking like a blancmanger, little pea-goose? To be sure, this mischance has cast a slight rub in our way, but the case isn't desperate, you know!' He set his horses in motion as he spoke, turning them round, and added, with a rueful laugh: 'Of course, if we discover that he is drinking the waters in Bath we *shall* be made to look blank, shan't we?'

She paid no heed to this, but repeated: 'What shall I do? What *can* I do? Sir, I—I haven't very much money!'

This disclosure was blurted out, and ended in a sob. He replied matter-of-factly: 'What you can do, Cherry, is to stop fretting and fuming, and to leave it to me to find a way out of this bumble-bath. I promise you I will, so pluck up!'

'I can't pluck up!' she uttered. 'You don't understand! It doesn't curl *your* liver to find yourself alone in this dreadful city,

with only a few shillings in your purse, and not knowing where
to go, or—Oh, how can you be so unfeeling as to laugh?'

'My dear, I can't help but laugh! Where *did* you pick up that
expression?'

'Oh, I don't know, and what does it signify?' she exclaimed.
'Where are you taking me? Do you know where there is a
Registry Office? I must set about finding a situation immediately! But I shall be obliged to put up for the night—oh, dear,
perhaps for several nights, because even if I found a situation at
once it can't be supposed that I should be wanted instantly!
Unless someone was wanted in a bang, because of some accident, or illness, perhaps, and then—'

'You are forgetting that you would be obliged to provide
yourself with a recommendation,' he interpolated dampingly.

'Well, I am persuaded Miss Fletching would give me one!'

'No doubt she would, but may I remind you that it will take
time to procure one from her?'

She was daunted, but made a quick recover. 'Very true! But
you could recommend me, couldn't you, sir?'

'No,' he replied unequivocally.

Her bosom swelled. 'I never thought you would be so
disobliging!'

He smiled. 'I'm not being disobliging. Believe me, nothing
could more certainly prejudice your chances of obtaining an
eligible situation than a recommendation from me—or any
other single man of my age!'

'Oh!' she said, digesting this. A blast on a coach-horn made
her flinch, and she said fervently: 'How can you bear to live in
this odious place, where everything is noise, and bustle, and
the streets so full of coaches and carriages and carts that—
Oh, pray take care, sir! I *know* we shall collide with something—Oh, look at that carriage, coming out of that street
over there!'

'Shut your eyes!' he advised her, amused by her evident want of faith in his ability to avoid accident.

'No!' she said resolutely. 'I must learn to accustom myself! Is it always so crowded in London, sir?'

'I am afraid it is often very much more crowded,' he said apologetically. 'In fact, it is at the moment very empty!'

'And people choose to live here!' she shuddered.

He had turned back into Piccadilly some few minutes earlier, and now checked his horses for the turn into Arlington Street. 'Yes. I am one of those very odd people, and I am taking you now to my house, so that you can rest and refresh before we continue our journey.'

She said uneasily: 'I think I ought not to go to your house, sir. I may be a pea-goose but I do know that it is not the thing for females to visit gentlemen's houses, and—and—'

'No, it is a trifle irregular,' he agreed, 'but before we go any further there are certain arrangements I must make, and you would scarcely wish to wait in the street, would you? So the best thing I can do is to hand you over to my housekeeper for half an hour. I shall tell her that my aunt Emborough placed you in my charge, and that I am taking you to your home, in Hertfordshire.'

She asked nervously: 'Where—where *are* you taking me, if you please, sir?'

'Into Hertfordshire. I am going to ask an old and dear friend of mine to take care of you until I've found your grandfather. Her name is Miss Henrietta Silverdale, and she lives with her mother at a place called Inglehurst. Don't look so scared! I am pretty sure you will like her, and entirely sure that she will be very kind to you.'

The curricle had come to a standstill outside one of the smaller houses on the east side of the street, and Stebbing had climbed down, and had gone to the horses' heads. Miss Steane whispered: 'It was wrong of me to run away, wasn't it? I know it now, because everything has gone amiss, and—and I have only you to turn to for help in this scrape. But indeed, indeed, sir, I would never have asked you to carry me to London if I had known how it would be!'

He laid his hand over her tightly clenched ones, and said gently: 'You are tired, my child, and the world looks black, doesn't it? I can only say to you: *Trust me!* Haven't I told you that I won't abandon you?'

Her hands twisted under his, and clasped it convulsively. She said: 'I never meant to be such a charge on you! Oh, pray believe me!'

'Oh, I know you didn't! What *you* don't know is that I don't regard this adventure as a charge: I regard it as a challenge, and am determined to run your grandfather to earth if I have to go to all the watering-places in the land in search of him!' He saw that his butler had opened the door, and was coming towards the curricle, and disengaged his hand, saying: 'Ah, here's Aldham! Good-day to you, Aldham! Has Tain arrived yet?'

'Just an hour since, my lord,' replied Aldham, beaming fondly upon him, but casting a doubtful glance at his companion. He had known the Viscount since Desford's cradle-days, having been employed at that time as page-boy at Wolversham, from which lowly position he had graduated by slow degrees to that of First Footman, and thence, in one longed-for leap, to the honourable post of butler to his young lordship; and he knew quite as much about him as did Stebbing, and rather more than did Tain, his lordship's excellent valet, who was the only member of the little household in Arlington Street not born and bred at Wolversham. He could have named (had he not been the soul of discretion) every fair Cyprian with whom his volatile master had enjoyed amatory adventures, from the straw damsel who had caught his first, callow fancy, to the high flyer who had almost ruined him; and he had frequently officiated at far from respectable parties in Arlington Street. But he had never known the Viscount to drive up to the door, in broad daylight, with an unattended Young Female sitting beside him. His first impression, that the Viscount had brought home with him a country lightskirt, was dispelled by a second, covert look at Miss Steane: for one thing, she was no lightskirt; and for another the Viscount never seemed to take to very young females. To Aldham's experienced eye she was more like a girl just broken out of the schoolroom—though what the Viscount was doing with any such was a problem beyond his power to solve.

But when he had been favoured with a glib explanation of her presence in the curricle he accepted it without even mental reservation. It was just like my Lady Emborough, he thought, to saddle my lord with a chit of a girl, with instructions to conduct her to her home in Hertfordshire, just as though it had been on the way from Hazelfield to London. And very much embarrassed the young lady was, by the looks of her! So he received her with a fatherly smile, and ushered her into the narrow hall of the house, saying that he would fetch up Mrs Aldham directly to wait upon her.

The Viscount lingered on the flagway to exchange words with the second of his chief mentors and well-wishers, the expression on whose face, compound of sorrow and censure, caused him to say: 'Yes, you've no need to look at me like that— as though I didn't know as well as you do that this is a rare case of pickles!'

'My lord,' said Stebbing very earnestly, 'when I heard you tell Miss you was going to take her into Hertfordshire I was that comfumbuscated I pretty near fell off my seat, because it looked to me like you was going to take her to Wolversham!'

'No, I did think of doing so, but it wouldn't answer,' replied the Viscount.

'No, my lord—as I would have taken the liberty of telling your lordship! As I beg leave to do now, for I wouldn't be able to sleep easy in my bed if I didn't, and it don't signify if you choose to turn me off, because—'

'Of course it doesn't signify! You wouldn't go!' retorted the Viscount.

The corners of Stebbing's grim mouth twitched involuntarily, but he refused to be beguiled. He said: 'My lord, I've known you do some hey-go-mad things in your time, but you've never till this day done anything so cockle-brained as to make me think you must be short of a sheet! Which I do! My lord, you're never going to take Miss to Inglehurst!'

'But I am,' asserted the Viscount. 'Unless you can suggest where else I can take her?' He paused, regarding his henchman with mockery in his eyes. 'You can't, can you?'

'You hadn't ought to have brought her to London at all!' muttered Stebbing.

'Very likely not, but it's a waste of time to lay that in my dish now! I did bring her to London, and must now abide the consequence. Even you must own that to abandon her here would be the action of a damned ugly customer—which I am not, however hey-go-mad you may think me!' He saw that Stebbing was deeply troubled, and smiled, dropping a hand on his shoulder, and slightly shaking him. 'Stubble it, you old rumstick! To whom else should I turn for help in this hobble than to Miss Hetta? Bless her, she's never yet failed me! Good God, *you* should know how often we've rescued one another from scrapes!'

'When you was children!' Stebbing said. 'That was different, my lord!'

'Not a bit of it! Stable the grays now, and tell the postilions I shall be needing them to carry me to Inglehurst within the hour. I'll take my own chaise, but I shall have to hire horses:

Ockley can be depended on to choose the right type, but warn him that I mean to return tonight. That's all!'

He gave Stebbing no opportunity to utter any further protests, but turned on his heel, and went quickly into his house. Stebbing was left to address his embittered remarks to the weary gray at whose head he was standing before climbing into the curricle and driving it away.

# Six

*I*T WAS PAST SEVEN O'CLOCK WHEN THE VISCOUNT'S beautifully sprung chaise reached Inglehurst, for although the journey had taken no more than three hours to accomplish he had not left Arlington Street until after four. Miss Steane, revived as much by the kindly and uncritical attitude of Mrs Aldham (yet another of those born on my Lord Wroxton's wide estates) as by the tea with which she had been regaled, set forth in a tolerably cheerful mood, suppressing as well as she could the inevitable shrinking of a shy girl, who, realizing too late her imprudence, found herself without any other course open to her than to submit to her protector's decree, and to allow him to thrust her into a household which consisted of a widow and her daughter who were wholly unknown to her. She could only hope that they would not resent her intrusion, or think her sunk beneath reproach for having behaved in a manner which she was fast becoming convinced was improper to the point of being unpardonable. Had she been able to think of an alternative to the Viscount's plan she believed she would have embraced it thankfully, even had it been the offer of a post as cook-maid, but no alternative had presented itself to her, and the thought of being stranded in London, with only a few shillings in her purse, and not even the merest acquaintance to seek out in all that terrifying city, was not one she could face.

Something of what was in her mind the Viscount guessed, for although London held no terrors for him, and he had never been stranded anywhere with his pockets to let, neither his consequence nor his wealth had made him blind to the troubles that beset persons less comfortably circumstanced. He might be careless, and frequently rackety, but no one in dire straits had ever appealed to him for help in vain. His friends, and he had many friends, said of him that he was a great gun—true as touch—a right one; and even his severest critics found nothing worse to say of him than that it was high time he brought his carryings on to an end, and settled down. His father did indeed heap opprobrious epithets on him, but anyone unwise enough to utter the mildest criticism of his heir to my lord met with very short shrift. The Viscount was well aware of this; but while he did not doubt his father's affection for him he was far too familiar with the Earl's deep prejudices to introduce Miss Steane into his household. My lord was a rigid stickler, and it was useless to suppose that he would feel any sympathy with a young female who had behaved in a way which he would undoubtedly condemn as brass-faced. My lord's views on propriety were clearly defined: male aberrations were pardonable; the smallest deviation from the rules governing the behaviour of females was inexcusable. He had placed no checks upon his sons, regarding (except when colic or gout had exacerbated his temper) their follies and amatory adventures with cynical amusement, but his daughter had never been allowed, until her marriage, to take a step beyond the gardens without a footman in attendance; and whenever she had gone on a visit to an approved friend or relative she had travelled in my lord's carriage, accompanied not only by her footman and her maid but by a couple of outriders as well.

So the Viscount, not entertaining for more than a very few seconds the notion of conveying his protégée to Wolversham, had, in almost the same length of time, decided to place her in

Miss Silverdale's care until he should have run her grandfather to earth, and compelled him to honour his obligations. The only flaw to this scheme which he could perceive was the objection which Miss Silverdale's mama might—and probably would—raise against it; but he had a comfortable belief in Miss Silverdale's ability to bring her hypochondriacal parent round her thumb, and was thus able to set out for Inglehurst without fear of meeting with a rebuff.

However, he did feel that it might be prudent to warn Cherry that Lady Silverdale enjoyed indifferent health, and consequently indulged in rather odd humours, which found expression in fits of the blue-devils, a tendency to fancy herself ill-used, and a marked predilection for enacting what he called Cheltenham tragedies.

She listened to him attentively, and, to his surprise, seemed to derive encouragement from this somewhat daunting description of her prospective hostess. She said, with all the wisdom of one versed in the idiosyncrasies of invalids: 'Then perhaps I can be of use in the house! Even Aunt Bugle says I am good at looking after invalids, and although I don't wish to puff myself off I think that is perfectly true. In fact, I have been wondering if I shouldn't seek for a post as attendant to an old, cantankersome lady: I daresay you know the sort of old lady I mean, sir!'

Lively memories of the tyranny exercised by his paternal grandmother over her family and her dependants crossed his mind, and he replied rather grimly: 'I do, and can only trust that you will not be obliged to seek any such post!'

'Well,' she said seriously, 'I own that it's disagreeable to be pinched at for everything one does, but one must remember how much more disagreeable it must be to be old, and unable to do things for oneself. And also,' she added reflectively, 'if a twitty old lady takes a fancy to one, one becomes valuable to her family. My aunt, and my cousins, were never so kind to me as during the months before poor old Lady Bugle died. Why, my aunt even said that she didn't know how they would go on without me!'

She sounded so much gratified by this tribute that Desford bit back the caustic comment that sprang to the tip of his tongue, and merely said that Lady Silverdale was neither old nor dying; and although she would (in his opinion) wear down the patience of a saint it would be unjust to call her twitty.

When they reached their destination, they were received by Grimshaw, who showed no pleasure at sight of one who had run free at Inglehurst ever since he had been old enough to bestride a pony, but said dampingly that if my lady had known his lordship meant to visit her she would no doubt have set dinner back to suit his convenience. As it was, he regretted to be obliged to inform his lordship that my lady and Miss Henrietta had already retired to the drawing-room.

Too well-accustomed to the butler's habitual air of disparaging gloom to be either surprised or offended the Viscount said: 'Yes, I guessed how it would be, but I daresay her ladyship will forgive me. Be a good fellow, Grimshaw, and drop the word in Miss Hetta's ear that I want to see her privately! I'll wait in the library.'

Grimshaw might be proof against the Viscount's smile but he was not proof against the lure of a golden coin slid into his hand. He did not demean himself by so much as a glance at it, but his experienced fingers informed him that it was a guinea, so he bowed in a stately way, and went off to perform the errand, not allowing himself to show his disapproval of Miss Steane by more than one look of outraged surprise.

The Viscount then led Miss Steane to a small saloon, and ushered her into it, telling her to sit down, like a good girl, and wait for him to bring Miss Silverdale to her. After that he withdrew to the library at the back of the hall, where, after a few minutes, he was joined by Miss Silverdale, who came in, saying in a rallying tone: 'Now, what's all this, Des? What brings you here so unexpectedly? And why the mystery?'

He took her hands, and held them: 'Hetta, I'm in a scrape!'

She burst out laughing. 'I might have known it! And I am to rescue you from it?'

'And you are to rescue me from it,' he corroborated, the smile dancing in his eyes.

'What an unconscionable rogue you are!' she remarked, drawing her hands away, and disposing herself on a sofa. 'I can't conceive how I am to rescue you from the sort of scrapes you fall into, but sit down, and make a clean breast of it!'

He did so, telling his story without reservation. Her eyes widened a little, but she heard him in silence, until he reached the end of it, saying: 'I would have taken her to Wolversham, but you know what my father is, Hetta! So there was nothing for it but to bring her to you!'

Then, at last, she spoke, shattering his confidence. 'But I don't think I can, Ashley!'

He stared incredulously. 'But, Hetta—!'

'You can't have considered!' she said. 'If I know what your father is you should know just as well what my mother is! Her opinion of your Cherry's exploit wouldn't differ from his by so much as a hair's breadth!'

'Oh, I know that!' he said. 'I shan't tell her the true story, stoopid! All I have to do is to say that my Aunt Emborough placed her in my charge, with instructions to deliver her into old Nettlecombe's hands, but owing to his having misread the date—or the letter informing him of it having gone astray—or some such thing—he is still out of town, so that I was at my wits' end to know what to do with the child.'

'And what,' she enquired conversationally, 'will you say when she asks you why you didn't rather place her in your mother's care?'

He took a minute or two to find an answer to this poser, but finally produced, with considerable aplomb: 'When I was at Wolversham, little more than a sennight since, I found my father quite out of curl, and Mama in too much of a worry about him to be troubled with a guest.'

She drew an audible breath. 'You are not only a rogue, Des, but a Banbury man as well!'

He laughed: 'No, no, how can you say so? There's a great deal of truth in that part of the story, and you can scarcely expect me to tell your mother that if I were to walk in with Cherry on my arm my poor misguided Papa would instantly leap to the conclusion that I had not only fallen in love with her, but had brought her home in the hope that she would captivate him into bestowing his blessing on precisely the sort of match he most abominates. I daresay she might captivate him, for she's a taking little thing, but hardly to that point!'

'Is she very pretty?' asked Miss Silverdale, keeping her fine eyes on his face.

'Yes, very, I think—even when dressed in cast-off garments which don't become her, and with her hair in a tangle! Enormous eyes in a heart-shaped face, a mouth clearly made for kissing, and a great deal of innocent charm. Not in your style, but I fancy you'll see what I mean when I present her to you. When I first saw her she looked to me to be scared out of her wits—which, half the time, she is, thanks to the Turkish treatment she has endured in her aunt's house—but when she isn't frightened she chatters away in the most engaging fashion, and has the merriest twinkle in her eyes. I think you will like her, Hetta, and I'm pretty sure your mother will. From what I gather she has a positive genius for waiting on—er—elderly invalids!' He paused, scanning her face. It was inscrutable, so, after a moment, he said coaxingly: 'Come, now, Hetta! You can't fail me! Good God, I've depended on you all my life! Yes, and if it comes to that, so have you depended on me—and have I ever failed you?'

A gleam of humour shone in her eyes. 'You may have rescued me from scrapes when we were children,' she said, 'but I haven't been in a scrape for years!'

'No, but Charlie has!' he retorted. 'You can't deny that I've frequently rescued him, just because you begged me to!'

'Well, no,' she acknowledged. 'And I can't deny, either, that you have several times given me excellent advice on the management of the estate, but the thing which makes it so very awkward for me to do what you ask this time is that Charlie is at home! And if Miss Steane is so pretty, and so charming, he is bound to fall in love with her, for you know how often he tumbles into love!'

'Yes, and I also know how often he tumbles out of love! When I last saw him he was dangling after a lovely man-trap— thirty if she's a day, and widowed a bare twelvemonth ago!'

'Mrs Cumbertrees,' she nodded. 'But she has been a thing of the past for weeks, Des!'

'Then he is probably at the feet of some other dasher years older than he is himself. You may take it from me, Hetta, that there's no need for you to be in a worry over the chance that he might take a fancy to Cherry: halflings rarely become nutty upon girls of their own age. In any event, she won't be here long enough for Charlie to form a lasting passion for her! What's he doing here, by the way? I thought he was going to Ireland, with a couple of choice spirits, in search of horses?'

'He was, but he had the misfortune to overturn his new high-perch phaeton three days ago, and broke his head, and his arm, and two of his ribs,' said Miss Silverdale, in the voice of one inured to such misfortunes.

'Hunting the squirrel?' asked Desford, with mild interest.

'Very likely, though of course he doesn't say so. He is still confined to his bed, for he was pretty knocked-up, but I don't expect Mama will be able to prevail upon him to remain there for very much longer. He is already fretting to get up, which was why Mama was glad to see Simon drive up—Oh, good heavens! I quite forgot to tell you! I think you would wish to know that Simon has been dining with us, and is now sitting with Charlie! At least, he was when I came away from the drawing-room, but I daresay Mama has drawn him away by this time, for she said that she would only permit him to stay with Charlie for twenty minutes.'

'Oh, my God!' ejaculated the Viscount, in accents of the liveliest dismay.

She could not help laughing, but she said severely: 'If a stranger heard you, Des, he couldn't be blamed for thinking that you held your little brother in the most unnatural dislike!'

'Well, there aren't any strangers present, and you know well enough that I don't hold him in dislike,' said the Viscount impenitently. 'But if ever there was a leaky rattle—! I shall be obliged to see him, I suppose, but if he don't make me grease him handsomely in the fist to keep his tongue about this affair I don't know young Simon!'

She cried shame on him, but in the event he was seen to know his graceless brother better than she did; for when he had talked her into making Cherry's acquaintance, and judging for herself how innocent, and how much to be pitied she was, and had accompanied her to the Green saloon, the unwelcome sight of the Honourable Simon Carrington making himself agreeable to Miss Steane confronted him, and he had no difficulty in interpreting the sparkling look of mischief with which the Honour-able Simon greeted him.

He ignored it, and presented Cherry to Miss Silverdale, saying easily: 'I must warn you, Hetta, that I've brought this foolish child to you very much against her will! I strongly suspect that she fears I am handing her over to a dragon!'

Cherry, who had risen quickly to her feet, blushed and stammered, as she dropped a slight curtsy: 'Oh, no, no! In—in-*deed* I d-don't, ma'am!'

'Well, if she does think it I shall hold you entirely to blame, Desford,' said Miss Silverdale, moving forward, with her hand held out to Cherry, and a smile on her lips. 'A pretty picture you must have drawn of me! How do you do, Miss Steane? Desford has been telling me of your adventures, and how you have been quite thrown out by finding that your grandfather is out of town. I can well imagine what your feelings must have been! But I expect Desford will find him very soon, and in the meantime I hope we can make you comfortable at Inglehurst.'

Cherry lifted her big eyes, brimming with grateful tears, to Henrietta's face, and whispered : 'Thank you! I am so *sorry*—!'

The Viscount, having watched this interchange with satisfaction, transferred his attention to his brother, and demanded, with revulsion: 'For God's sake, Simon, what kind of a rig is that?'

Henrietta said laughingly, over her shoulder: 'Didn't I tell you, Simon, that Des would utterly condemn it?'

Young Mr Carrington, a very dashing blade, was indeed wearing a startling habit, and the fact that he had the height and the figure to adopt any extravagant mode without appearing grotesque did nothing to recommend the style he had chosen to adopt to his elder brother. He was a goodlooking young man, full of effervescent liveliness, and as ready to laugh at himself as at his fellow-men. His eyes laughed now, as he said solemnly: 'This, Des, is the highest kick of fashion, as you would know if you were as dapper-dog as you think you are!' He thrust one foot forward as he spoke, and indicated with a sweep of his hand the voluminous garments which clothed his nether limbs. 'The Petersham trousers, my boy!'

'I am aware!' said the Viscount. He raised his quizzing-glass, and through it surveyed his brother from his heels to the inordinately high points of his shirt-collar. These were rivalled by the height of his coat collar, which rose steeply behind his head, and by the gathered and hugely padded shoulders of his coat. The sleeves of his coat were embellished with a number of buttons, those nearest to his wrists being left unbuttoned in a negligent style; and he wore round his neck a very large striped neckcloth. The Viscount, having taken in all these enormities, shuddered, and let his glass fall, saying: 'Have you had the infernal brass to sit down to dine with Lady Silverdale in that rig, jackanapes?'

'But, Des, she begged me to do so!' said Simon, deeply injured. 'She liked my beautiful new clothes, didn't she, Hetta?'

'I rather think she was stunned by them,' Henrietta replied. 'And by the time she had recovered from the shock you had flummeried her into inviting you to dine with us—playing off more cajolery than I've been privileged to see in a twelvemonth!'

'Oh, come, come!' instantly protested Simon. 'It isn't as long as that since you saw me last!'

She laughed, but turned from him to Cherry, who had been listening to this badinage with an appreciative twinkle in her eyes. Miss Silverdale perceived that Desford had spoken no less than the truth when he had described her as a taking little thing, and wondered, with an inexplicable sinking of the heart, if he was more captivated by her than he perhaps knew. Recognizing the tiny pang she felt as the envy of one who was neither little nor taking—besides being past the first blush of youth—of one who was young, and pretty, and little, and very taking indeed, she sternly repressed such ignoble thoughts, smiled at Cherry, and held out her hand, saying: 'I must introduce you to my mother, but I am very sure you would wish to put off your bonnet and cloak first, so I shall take you up to my room, while Desford explains to my mother how it comes about that we are to have the pleasure of entertaining you for a little while. You will find Mama in the drawing-room, Des!'

He nodded, and would have followed her out of the saloon immediately had not Simon detained him, with a demand to know whether he meant to spend the night at Wolversham. 'No, I am returning to London,' he replied. 'But I want a word with you before I leave, so don't you go home until we've had a talk!'

'I'll be bound you do!' said Simon, grinning impishly at him. 'I won't go!'

The Viscount threw him a speaking glance, and went off to try his own powers of flummery on Lady Silverdale.

He found her engaged, in a somewhat languid fashion, in embroidering an altar cloth, but she pushed the frame aside when he entered the room, and held out a plump hand to him, and saying, in a sweet, failing voice: 'Dear Ashley!'

He kissed her hand, retained it in his own for a minute, and set about the task of cajoling her by paying her a compliment. 'Dear Lady Silverdale!' he said. 'Don't think me abominably saucy!—How is it that you contrive to look younger and prettier every time I see you?'

If she had had the forethought to have provided herself with a fan she would undoubtedly have rapped his knuckles with it, but as it was she was obliged to content herself with giving him a playful slap, and saying archly: 'Flatterer!'

'Oh, no!' he returned. 'I never flatter!'

'Oh, what a farradiddle!' she said.

He denied it, and she accepted this with a complacency born of the knowledge that she had been, in her heyday, a remarkably pretty girl. Time, and a life of determined indolence, had considerably impaired her figure, but she was generally held to have great remains of beauty; and she had discovered that a *fraise*, or little ruff, admirably concealed a tendency to develop a double chin. A mild attachment to the late Sir John

Silverdale had grown, during the years of her widowhood, to proportions which would have astonished that gentleman, and would not have outlived an offer for her hand made by another suitor of birth and fortune. None had come forward to woo the widow, so as much affection as she could spare from herself she had bestowed upon her only son. Such persons who were not intimately acquainted with her believed her to be passionately devoted to her children, which, indeed, she herself believed, but those who had the opportunity to observe her at close quarters were not deceived by her caressing manner: they knew that although she might fairly be said to dote on Charles she had only a tepid affection for Henrietta.

The Viscount was of their number, and he lost no time in enquiring solicitously into the state of Charlie's health, and listening with an air of concern to the description given him of the various injuries Charlie had suffered, of the shock the accident had been to his nerves, and of how serious the repercussions might be if he were not kept perfectly quiet until such time as dear Dr Foston pronounced him to be well enough to leave his room. Since few things interested her more than the ills that could attack the human body, and she was one of those who believed that physical disorders lent distinction to those who fell victims to them, the recital took time in the telling, and was further prolonged by an account of the spasms and palpitations she had herself endured ever since she had seen her son's battered body borne into the house on a stretcher. 'I fell down instantly in a swoon, for I thought him dead!' she said impressively. 'Indeed, they thought *I* was dead, for it was an age before they were able to revive me, and then, you know, I was so much agitated that I couldn't believe dear Hetta was speaking the truth when she assured me Charlie wasn't dead, but in a deep concussion. I've been very poorly ever since, and Dr Foston has been obliged to give me a cordial, besides valerian for my nerves, which are sadly shattered, as you may suppose.'

He replied suitably; and after expressing his admiration for the wonderful spirit she showed in bearing up under so prostrating an experience, at last ventured to broach his errand to her. He did it very well, but it was no easy task to gain her consent to his proposal. It was rendered all the more difficult when he disclosed that Cherry was Lord Nettlecombe's grand-daughter. She exclaimed at once that she wished to have nothing to do with any member of *that* family. He replied frankly: 'I don't blame you, ma'am: who *does* wish to have anything to do with them? But I think your kind heart must be touched by this unfortunate child's plight! If her father isn't dead, he has certainly abandoned her—and without a feather to fly with! She has lately been living with some maternal relations, who haven't used her at all well. So very ill, in fact, that she formed the resolve to claim her grandfather's protection, until such time as she can find employment in some genteel household. So, as I was staying at Hazelfield at the time, my aunt desired me to carry her to London with me, and see her safely deposited in old Nettlecombe's charge. You may conceive of my dismay when we arrived in Albemarle Street to find the house shut up, and none of the neighbours able to give me his lordship's direction! What to do with the girl had me at a stand, until I remembered you, ma'am!'

She interrupted him, demanding: 'Is it possible that she is *Wilfred Steane's* daughter?'

'Yes, poor child! As good as orphaned, even if he should chance to be alive!'

'Desford!' she uttered, groping for her vinaigrette, 'I little thought that you, of all people, would be so wanting in conduct as to bring that—that *Creature's* child to Inglehurst! And how your aunt could—but I always thought poor dear Sophronia strangely freakish! But how she could have supposed that *I* should be willing to befriend the girl—'

'Oh, she didn't, ma'am!' he interposed. 'All she asked me to do was to take Cherry to her grandfather. It was I—knowing you much better than my aunt does!—who realized that if there was one person on whom I could depend to shelter this unfortunate girl that person is yourself!' He smiled at her, and added: 'Are you trying to hoax me into believing that you are hardhearted enough to repulse her? You won't succeed: I know you too well!'

She plucked uncertainly at the fringe of the silk shawl she wore, eyeing him with resentment. Before she had made up her mind what to say to make him remove Cherry without impairing the vision he had of the saintliness of her own disposition the door opened, and Henrietta came in, leading Miss Steane by the hand.

'Mama, here is poor little Cherry, who has been having a horridly uncomfortable time, as I collect Desford will have told you. She is quite worn down by her troubles, but she *would* have me bring her to you before I tuck her into bed. Now, my dear, you can see for yourself that my mother is no more a dragon than I am!'

'So pleased!' said Lady Silverdale, in a faint voice, and favouring Cherry with a very slight inclination of her head. 'Hetta, my love, my cordial!'

Quite dismayed, Cherry whispered: 'I should not have come! Oh, I *knew* I should not! I beg your pardon, ma'am!'

Lady Silverdale was a selfish but not an unfeeling woman, and this stricken speech, coupled as it was with a face pale with weariness, considerably mollified her. It was clearly impossible to cast this miserable little girl out of the house, so although she maintained the attitude of one on the brink of sinking into a swoon, and continued to speak in a faint, long-suffering voice, she said: 'Oh, not at all! You must forgive me if I leave it to my daughter to show you to your bedroom: I have been very unwell, and my medical attendant warns me that I must avoid all unnecessary exertion. So unfortunate that you should have come to visit us at just this moment! But my daughter will look after you. Pray tell me if there is anything you would wish for! A glass of hot milk, perhaps, before you retire to bed.'

'I fancy, ma'am, that she needs something more substantial than a glass of milk,' said the Viscount, perceiving that Cherry was looking quite crushed, and most improperly flickering a wink at her.

'Well, of course she does!' said Henrietta. 'She is going to have supper as soon as I've tucked her into her bed.'

'Oh, thank you!' said Cherry gratefully. 'I don't feel I deserve to be given such a treat, but I would very much like it! Aunt Bugle never allowed me to have—'

She broke off in consternation, for these words had had a startling effect on her hostess. At one moment leaning limply back in her chair, and sniffing at her vinaigrette, she suddenly abandoned this moribund pose, sat bolt upright, and said sharply: '*Who* did you say?'

'M-my Aunt Bugle, ma'am,' faltered Cherry.

Lady Silverdale's bosom swelled visibly. '*That* woman!' she pronounced awfully. 'Do you mean to tell me she is your aunt, child?'

'Yes, ma'am,' said Cherry, trembling.

'Are you acquainted with her, Mama?'

'We were brought out in the same season!' disclosed Lady Silverdale dramatically. 'I beg you will not speak to me of Amelia Bugle! A bouncing, flouncing young female, setting her cap at every single gentleman that crossed her path, and fancying herself to be a beauty, which she was not, for she had a deplorable figure, and a particularly ugly nose, and as for the pretentious airs she gave herself when she caught Bugle, and took to thinking herself the pink of gentility, I laugh whenever I remember them!'

Laughter did not appear to be her predominant emotion, though she did utter a Ha! of withering sarcasm. Henrietta, briefly meeting Desford's dancing eyes, said, with a quivering lip: 'We collect, Mama, that she wasn't one of your bosom-bows!'

'Certainly not! But I remained on common civility terms with her until she had the effrontery to thrust herself before me in a doorway, saying, like the self-important mushroom she was, that she fancied she must take precedence since her husband's baronetcy was an older creation than Silverdale's! After that, of course, I never did more than bow to her, or felt the smallest interest in her. Come and sit down beside me, my dear child, and tell me all about her! I am persuaded she used you shamefully, for I recall that she was never used to waste a particle of politeness on people she considered to be beneath her. You did very right to leave her!'

She patted the place beside her on the sofa invitingly, and Cherry, swiftly recovering from her astonishment, smiled shyly, dropped a little curtsy, and accepted the invitation. The curtsy pleased Lady Silverdale; she was moved to press Cherry's hand, and to say: 'Poor child! There! You will not meet with Turkish treatment in *this* house! Is it true that That Woman has *five* daughters?'

Perceiving that her volatile parent was now wholly engrossed by the dreadful fate that had overcome her old rival, Henrietta seized the opportunity thus afforded her to exchange a few words with the Viscount. 'Nothing could be more fortunate, could it?' she said, in an undervoice. 'I wonder what That Woman really did to make Mama take her in such dislike?'

'Yes, so do I!' he returned. 'I depend on you to discover the answer! Clearly, her want of delicacy in claiming precedence in that doorway can only have been the culminating impertinence!'

'I should suppose that they must have been rival beauties,' said Henrietta. 'But never mind that! We will keep Cherry with us until you have found her grandfather, but what would you have me tell her to do? Should she not write a civil letter to Lady Bugle, informing her that she is at present residing at Inglehurst? I cannot think it right that she should leave her without a word! Lady Bugle cannot be so monstrous as to feel no anxiety about her!'

'No,' he agreed reluctantly. 'At the same time—Hetta, tell her to write that she has gone to visit her grandfather! Dash it, I must be able to discover where he is in a very few days, and if she mentions Inglehurst she must surely connect me with the business, which will lead her to make enquiries of my Aunt Emborough, and then I *shall* be in the suds!'

'Couldn't you write to Lady Emborough, explaining it all to her?' she suggested.

'No, Hetta, I could not!' he replied. 'She doesn't like Lady Bugle, but she don't want to quarrel with her, and she wouldn't thank me for embroiling her in this mingle-mangle!'

'Very true! I hadn't considered that. It shall be as you wish. Do you mean to rack up here for the night, or are you going to Wolversham with Simon?'

'Neither: I'm going back to London. You can picture me tomorrow, scouring the town to find somebody able to give me Nettlecombe's direction—and in all probability wasting my time! Ah, well! It will be a lesson to me, won't it, not to rescue damsels in distress?'

'Not to venture to cross quagmires without making sure you don't go in over shoes, over boots, at all events!' she said, laughing at him.

'Or at least without making sure that Hetta is there to pull me out!' he amended. He took her hand, and kissed it. 'Thank you, my best of friends. I am eternally obliged to you!'

'Oh, fiddle! If you are to drive back to London this evening you had better take leave of your damsel now, because I mean to put her to bed immediately: she's so tired she can scarcely keep her eyes open! I've instructed Grimshaw to set out a supper for you, and you'll find Simon waiting to bear you company.'

'Bless you!' he said, and turned from her to bid his protégée farewell.

She got up quickly when she saw him coming towards the sofa, and he saw that she was indeed looking very tired. It was with an effort that she smiled at him, and tried to thank him for his kindness. He cut her short, patted her hand, and adjured her, in avuncular style, to be a good girl. He then promised Lady Silverdale that he would come to take his leave of her as soon as he had eaten his supper, and went off to the dining-room.

Here he found his brother seated sideways at the table, with one elbow resting on it, his long legs, in their preposterous Petersham trousers, stretched out before him, and the brandy decanter beside him. Grimshaw, wearing the expression of one whose finer feelings were grossly offended, bowed the Viscount to his chair and regretted that the dishes laid out before him were of a meagre nature, the lobster and the chickens having been consumed at dinner. Also, he added, in an expressionless voice, the almond cheesecakes, which Mr Simon had been pleased to esteem.

'What he means is that I finished the dish,' said Simon. 'Devilish good they were too! I wish you will take that Friday-face away, Grimshaw! You've been wearing it the whole evening, and it's giving me a fit of the dismals!'

'I daresay your new rig don't take his fancy,' said the Viscount, helping himself to some pickled salmon. 'And who shall blame him? It makes you look like a coxcomb. Wouldn't you agree with me, Grimshaw?'

'I should prefer to say, my lord, that it is not a mode which commends itself to me. Nor, if I may be pardoned for putting forward my opinion, one befitting a young gentleman of rank.'

'Well, you're out there!' retorted Simon. 'It's the very latest style, and it was Petersham who started it!'

'My Lord Petersham, sir,' said Grimshaw, unmoved, 'is well known to be an Eccentric Gentleman, and frequently appears in a style that one can only call rather of the rstest.'

'And besides which,' said Desford, as Grimshaw withdrew from the room, 'Petersham is a good fifteen years older than you are, and he don't look like a macaroni-merchant whatever he wears.'

'Take care, brother!' Simon warned him. 'A little more to that tune and you will find yourself done to a cow's thumb!'

Desford laughed, and surveyed the various dishes before him through his glass. 'Shall I? No, really, Simon, those trousers are the outside of enough! However, I didn't come to discuss your clothes: I've something more important to say to you.'

'Well, now you put me in mind of it I've something important to say too! It's a lucky chance I dined here tonight. Lend me a monkey, Des, will you?'

'No,' responded Desford bluntly. 'Or a groat, if it comes to that.'

'Quite right!' said Simon approvingly. 'One should never encourage young men to break shins! Just make me a present of it, and not a word about this bud of promise you're jauntering about with shall pass my lips!'

'What a stretch-halter you are!' remarked Desford, embarking on a raised pie. 'Why do you want a monkey? Considering it isn't a month since the last quarterday it ought to be high tide with you.'

'Unfortunately,' said Simon, 'the last quarter's allowance was, so to say, bespoke!'

'And my father called *me* a scattergood!'

'That's nothing to what he'll call you, my boy, if he gets wind of your little charmer!'

Desford paid no heed to this sally, but directed a searching look at his brother, and asked: 'I collect you've been having some deep doings: not let yourself be hooked into any of the Greeking establishments, have you?'

Simon smiled ruefully. 'Only once, Des. I may be said to have bought my experience dearly.'

'Physicked you, did they? Well, it happens to us all. Is that what brought you home? Wouldn't my father frank you?'

'To own the truth, dear boy, I haven't dared to broach the matter, though that *is* what brought me home. It hasn't yet seemed to me the moment to raise ticklish subjects. His mood is far from benign!'

'No wonder, if he saw you in that rig! What a fool you are, Simon! You might have known it would set him all on end!'

'No, no, how can you suppose me to be so wanting in tact? I clothed myself with the utmost propriety of taste. I even sought to gratify him by wearing knee-breeches for dinner, but knee-breeches have no chance of success against gout. I may add that having been obliged to listen to him cutting at me, you, and even Horace for over an hour this afternoon I seized the opportunity to escape, and very handsomely offered to bear Mama's letter to Lady Silverdale in place of the groom she had meant to send with it. She felt it behoved her to write to enquire after Charlie. Did Hetta tell you that the silly cawker has knocked himself up?'

Desford nodded. 'Oh, yes! How bad is he?'

'Well, he looks as sick as a horse, but they seem to think he's going on pretty prosperously. Now, about that monkey, Des!'

'I'll give you a cheque on Drummond's—on one condition!'

Simon laughed. 'I won't breathe a word, Des!'

'Oh, I know that, codling! My condition is that you throw those clothes away!'

'It will be a sacrifice,' said Simon mournfully, 'but I'll do it. What's more, if there's any little thing you think I might be able to do for you in your present very odd situation I'll do that too.'

'Much obliged to you!' said Desford, rather amused, but touched as well. 'There isn't anything—unless you chance to know where old Nettlecombe has loped off to?'

'Nettlecombe? What the devil do you want with that old screw?' demanded Simon, in considerable astonishment.

'My bud of promise, as you call her, is his granddaughter, and I've charged myself with the task of delivering her into his care. Only when we reached London we found he had gone out of town, and shut up his house. That's why I brought her here.'

'Good God, is she a Steane?'

'Yes: Wilfred Steane's only child.'

'And who the deuce may he be?'

'Oh, the black sheep of the family! Before your time! Before mine too, if it comes to that, but I remember all the talk that went on about him, and in particular the things Papa said of him, and every other Steane he had ever heard of! Which is why I don't want him to get wind of Cherry!'

'Is that the girl's name?' asked Simon. 'Queer sort of a name to give a girl!'

'No, her name is Charity, but she prefers to be called Cherry. I met her when I was staying at Hazelfield. I don't propose to take you into the circumstances which led me to bring her to London in search of her grandfather, but you may believe I was pretty well forced to do so. She was living with her maternal aunt, and being so shabbily treated that she ran away. I met her trying to walk to London, and since nothing would prevail upon her to let me take her back to her aunt what else could I do but take her up?'

'A regular Galahad, ain't you?' grinned Simon.

'No, I am not! If I'd dreamed I should be dipped in the wing over the business I wouldn't have done it!'

'You would,' said Simon. 'Think I don't know you? What, by the way, did the black sheep do to cause a scandal?'

'According to my father, just about everything, short of murder! Nettlecombe cast him off when he eloped with Cherry's mother, but what forced him to fly abroad was being found out in Greeking transactions. Took to drinking young 'uns into a proper state for plucking, and then fuzzed the cards.'

Simon opened his eyes very wide. 'Nice fellow!' he commented. 'What has become of him?'

'Nobody seems to know, but since nothing has been heard of him for some years he is generally thought to be dead.'

'Well, it's to be hoped he is,' said Simon. 'If you don't mind my saying so, dear boy, the sooner you palm the girl off on to her grandfather the better it will be. You haven't a tendre for her, have you?'

'Oh, for God's sake—!' Desford exclaimed. 'Of course I haven't!'

'Beg pardon!' murmured Simon. 'Only wondered!'

# Seven

$\mathcal{B}$EFORE THE BROTHERS PARTED THAT EVENING SIMON had tucked into his pocket the Viscount's cheque, and had asked him in a soft, mischievous voice if he meant to go to Newmarket, for the July Meeting. The Viscount answered that he had meant to go, but now saw little hope of it. 'Ten to one I shall still be hunting for Nettlecombe,' he said. 'But if you are going I rather fancy I can put you on to a sure thing: Mopsqueezer. Old Jerry Tawton earwigged me at Tatt's last week, and he's in general a safe man at the corner.'

Simon gripped his hand, smiling warmly at him, and said: 'Thank you, Des. Dash it, you *are a* trump!'

Slightly surprised, Desford responded: 'What, for passing on Jerry's tip? Don't be such a gudgeon!'

'No, not for that, and not even for this,' said Simon, patting his pocket. 'For not reading me any elder-brotherly jobations!'

'Much heed you would pay to them if I did!'

'Oh, you never know! I might!' Simon said lightly. He picked up his hat, and set it at a rakish angle on his fair locks. He hesitated for a moment, and then said: 'I shall go back to London tomorrow, and shall be fixed there until I go to Newmarket. So, if you do find yourself in a hobble, and think I might be able to help, come round to my lodgings, and—and I'll do my best for you!' He added, returning to his insouciant manner: 'You've no notion how nacky my best is! Goodbye, dear boy!'

The Viscount left Inglehurst some twenty minutes later relieved of at least one of his worries. Lady Silverdale, thanks largely to her dislike of Lady Bugle, and in some measure to Cherry's modest demeanour, seemed inclined to look favourably upon her uninvited guest. It was perhaps fortunate that she did not think Cherry more than passably pretty. 'Poor child!' she said. 'Such a pity that she should be a little dab of a thing, and dress so dowdily! Hetta, my love, it would be only kind, I think, to make her rather more presentable; and I have been wondering whether, if you gave her that green cambric which we decided was not the colour for you, she might make herself a dress. Just a simple round dress, you know! And she must have her hair cropped, for I cannot endure untidy heads.'

Henrietta being very willing to encourage her parent in these charitable schemes, the Viscount took his leave of both ladies, and went away feeling that, at least for the present, her hostess would treat Cherry kindly.

When he left the house Cherry was sunk in profound slumber, from which the noise of his chaise-wheels under her window, and the trampling of hooves on the gravel, did not even disturb her dreams. She was so tired after the exertions and the agitations of the day that she hardly stirred until one of the housemaids came in to draw back the curtains round her bed, expressing, as Cherry opened her drowsy eyes and stretched like a kitten, the hope that she had slept well, and informing her that it was a beautiful morning. In proof of this statement she drew back the window-blinds, making Cherry blink at the sudden blaze of sunlight that flooded the room. Cherry sat up with a jerk, remembering all the events of the previous day, and asked to be told what time it was. Upon hearing that it was eight o'clock, she gave a gasp of dismay, and exclaimed: 'Oh, goodness!

Then I must have slept for twelve hours! However did I come to do such a thing?'

The housemaid, perceiving that she was about to scramble out of bed, told her that there was no need for her to hurry herself, since my lady never came downstairs to breakfast, and Miss Hetta had given orders that she was not to be disturbed until eight o'clock. She then set a burnished brass can of hot water down beside the little corner washstand, begged Miss to ring the bell if there was anything else she required, and went away, pausing in the doorway to say that breakfast would be served in the parlour at ten o'clock.

Cherry was left to take stock of her surroundings. She had been too much exhausted when Hetta had put her to bed to pay much heed to them, the only things which had impressed themselves on her having been very soft pillows, and the most comfortable bed in which it had ever been her lot to lie; but now, hugging her knees, she stared about her in awe and wonderment. She thought it the most elegant bedchamber imaginable, and would have been amazed had she known that Lady Silverdale was most dissatisfied with the hangings, which she said had faded so much that they now looked detestably shabby. Her ladyship had also detected a slight stain on the carpet, where some careless guest had spilt some lotion. But Cherry did not notice this, or that the hangings were faded. Miss Fletching's Seminary for Young Ladies had been furnished neatly but austerely; and at Maplewood Cherry had shared a room with Corinna and Dianeme, who were not considered by their mama to be old enough to justify the expenditure of any more money on them than was strictly necessary. Consequently, their room was furnished with a heterogeneous collection of chairs and cupboards which had either been judged too shabby for the rooms where they had originally stood, or bought dog-cheap in a saleroom. And even Aunt Bugle's bed was not hung with curtains of silk damask, thought Cherry, almost fearfully stroking them.

She slid out of bed, and made a discovery: someone had not only unpacked her portmanteau, but had also ironed the creases out of the two dresses she had brought with her. This seemed to her such a dizzy height of luxury that she almost supposed herself to be still asleep and dreaming.

When she entered the breakfast-parlour, conducted to it by Grimshaw at his most stately, she found Henrietta making the tea, and was greeted by her in so kind and friendly a way that she lost the terror with which Grimshaw had inspired her, and said impulsively: 'I think I was so stupid last night that I didn't tell you how very, very grateful I am to you, and to Lady Silverdale, for being so excessively kind to me! Indeed, I don't know how to thank you enough!'

'Nonsense!' said Henrietta, smiling at her. 'I lost count of the times you thanked me last night! I think it was the last thing you said, when I blew out the candle, but as you were three parts asleep I might be mistaken!'

By the time they rose from the table Henrietta had succeeded in charming Cherry out of her nervous shyness, and had won enough of her confidence to make her feel sincerely sorry for her. It was plain that she had not been encouraged to confide in her aunt; and although she spoke affectionately of Miss Fletching Henrietta did not think that their relationship had been closer than that of kind and just mistress, and grateful pupil. Cherry answered her questions with a good deal of reserve, and seemed at first to expect to be snubbed; but when she realized that she stood in no such danger she became very much more natural, and chatted away as easily as she had done on her journey to London. But much persuasion was needed to prevail upon her to accept the length of green cambric, and when she did at last yield, it was on condition that she should be allowed to pay for it—not with money, but with service. 'I have been used to being employed,' she assured Henrietta. 'So *pray*, Miss Silverdale, tell me what you would wish me to do!'

'But I don't wish you to do anything!' objected Henrietta. 'You are our guest, Cherry, not a hired servant!'

'No,' said Cherry, flushing, and lifting her determined chin. 'It is only your kindness which makes you say that, and—and it gives me such a warm *feel* in my heart that I couldn't be happy if you didn't permit me to make myself useful here. I can see, of course, that you have a great many servants, but there must be hundreds of things I could do for you, and for Lady Silverdale, that perhaps you would not ask the servants to do! Running errands—fetching things—searching for things you have mislaid—darning holes in your stockings—oh, all the things which I daresay you do for yourselves, and think a dead bore!'

Since Henrietta had yet to discover anything her parent would hesitate to ask her servants to do for her she could not help laughing, but she naturally did not tell Cherry why she laughed. All she said was: 'Well, I'll do my best to oblige you, but I think it only right to warn you that if you encourage me to shuffle off every dull task it is my duty to perform you will rapidly turn me into the most indolent, selfish creature imaginable!'

'No. That I know I *couldn't* do!' said Cherry, mistily smiling at her.

She spent most of the morning happily engaged in cutting out the green cambric, and tacking the pieces together. In this she had the expert assistance of Miss Hephzibah Cardle, my lady's own dresser, whose spinsterish form and acidulated countenance could have led no one to suppose that she combined a rare talent for turning her mistress out complete to the last feather with a jealous adoration of that singularly unappreciative lady. Her services to Miss Steane were proffered with extreme reluctance, and would not have been proffered at all if her ladyship had not

commanded her to do what she could to give Miss Steane a
new touch. Professional pride overcame less admirable feelings,
and even led her (to save my lady the expense of sending for her
own hairdresser, she said) to trim Miss Steane's unruly locks into
a more manageable, and very much more becoming style, which
won for her one of my lady's rare encomiums. But although
nothing could have been more prettily expressed than Cherry's
gratitude for her kind offices she could not like her. She found
only one sympathizer in the household: Mrs Honeybourne, the
stout and goodnatured housekeeper, might declare that Miss was
a sweet young lady; the maids and the two footmen, and even
the cross-grained head-gardener smiled indulgently upon her,
but Grimshaw regarded her with dislike and suspicion. He and
Miss Cardle were convinced that she was an artful humbugger,
bent on insinuating herself into my lady's and Miss Hetta's good
graces by palavering them, and playing off all manner of cajol-
eries. 'If you was to ask me for my opinion, Miss Cardle,' he said
portentously, 'I should feel myself bound to say that I consider
she is cutting a wheedle. And what I think of my Lord Desford's
conduct in foisting her on to my lady is something I wouldn't
demean myself by divulging.'

Happily for Cherry's peace of mind the punctilious civility
with which both these ill-wishers treated her precluded her from
realizing how bitterly they resented her presence at Inglehurst.
Within three days of her arrival she had lost her apprehensive
look, and was unfolding shy petals in the warmth of a hitherto
unknown approval. To be greeted with a smile, when she entered
a room; to be addressed as 'dear child' by Lady Silverdale; to be
fondly scolded by that lady for running an unnecessary errand;
to be encouraged by Miss Silverdale to roam about the grounds at
will; and to be treated as though she had been an invited guest,
and not the unwanted incubus she felt herself to be, were such
hitherto unexperienced circumstances that she was passionately

anxious to repay her kind hostesses by every means that lay within her power. It did not take her more than a day to realize that there was little she could do for Henrietta, but much she could do for Lady Silverdale; and since she had never previously encountered Lady Silverdale's like she did not for a moment suspect that that lady's plaintive voice and caressing manner concealed a selfishness and a determination to have her own way far more ruthless than the cruder methods employed by Aunt Bugle. Where Lady Bugle would have imperiously commanded her to go in search of something she had mislaid, and reward her, when she brought the object to her, by wondering what in the world had taken her so long to find it, Lady Silverdale would initiate the search by saying, at the outset: 'Oh dear, how stupid of me! I've lost my embroidery-scissors! Now, where can I have left them? No, no, dear child! Why should *you* suffer for *my* carelessness?' And when Cherry, after an exhaustive search, found the missing scissors, and presented them, Lady Silverdale would say: 'Oh, Cherry, you dear child! You shouldn't have troubled yourself!'

It was small wonder that she should blossom under such treatment, and think no task too laborious or too irksome to be performed for so amiable a benefactress. She had never been so happy in her life; and Henrietta, realizing this, forbore to intervene. She did, however, drop a gentle hint in Cherry's ear that Lady Silverdale's disposition was a trifle uncertain, and depended largely on how she happened to be feeling, the state of the weather, or the shortcomings of her domestic staff. It was by no means unknown for her to take sudden dislikes to persons whom she had previously, and just as suddenly, taken into the warmest favour; and while such capricious fits seldom lasted for very long they made life extremely uncomfortable for their victim.

Cherry listened to this, and nodded wisely, saying that old Lady Bugle had been subject to just such distempered freaks. 'Only her crotchets were worse, because she wasn't at all kind, or amiable, even at her best, which dear Lady Silverdale *is*! Indeed, I think she and you are the kindest people I have ever met!'

This was said with a glowing look. Henrietta could only hope that her parent's sunny mood would outlast Cherry's visit.

It was three days before Sir Charles Silverdale was allowed to leave his bedchamber, and it was plain to his mother and his sister that he was much more shaken by his accident than he would admit. He insisted on coming downstairs but when, leaning heavily on his valet, he reached the library he was only too glad to stretch himself out on the sofa, and even to drink the cordial his mama pressed upon him. He was a handsome youth, but his features were too often marred by his expression, which was inclined to be petulant, and even, when he could not have his own way, or anything went amiss, sullen. In temperament, as in looks, he was very like his mother; but owing to the circumstance of his having been bereft of a father at an early age, and grossly indulged by his doting mama, all the faults which he had inherited from her were exaggerated. He had a good deal of charm; an ease of manner which made him generally an acceptable guest; and a reckless daring which won him the admiration of a number of like-minded young gentlemen. His servants liked him, for although he was quite as exacting as his mother, and very much more selfish, he had inherited her genius for making his most outrageous demands appear to be the merest requests; and because he always thanked them, with the sweetest of smiles, expressed contrition for any outburst of temper, and gave them leave of absence whenever he foresaw no need of their services, he was thought to be very goodnatured. His hare-brained exploits were regarded by them with indulgence, as being the natural conduct to be expected of any high-spirited young gentleman; and his carelessness was excused on the score of his youth. Only his sister, whose natural fondness for him did not prevent her from recognizing his faults, had said once, when exasperated by some example of churlishness, that since he seemed to have a number of friends it was to be supposed that he reserved his bad temper for his family, conducting himself with propriety everywhere that lay beyond the bounds of his home; and since this caustic comment had drawn down upon her the instant wrath and longlasting reproaches of her mother, she had never repeated the offence.

She had looked forward to her brother's emergence from his sickroom with misgiving, knowing his susceptibility, and well-aware that the smallest tendency on his part to flirt with Cherry would transform Lady Silverdale, in the twinkling of a bedpost, from a benevolent protectress into an inveterate enemy. But she discovered that Desford had been right: the dashing Mrs Cumbertrees might be a thing of the past, but Sir Charles's taste still ran to ladies of opulent charms and vast experience. He had no interest in ingénues, and his only comment, on meeting Cherry, must have allayed any alarm felt by his anxious parent. In fact, she felt none, and quite agreed with him when he said: 'What a snippety thing she is, Mama! A regular go-by-the-ground! I wonder Des should have troubled himself with her.'

Mr Cary Nethercott wondered too, but, being a simple, straightforward man, he accepted what was indeed the true explanation without question, and without difficulty. 'One can only honour his lordship for his conduct in such a difficult situation,' he said, adding with a faint smile: 'And hope that one would have had the strength of mind to have behaved in the same way, had one been in his place!'

'I expect you would have!' Henrietta returned, smiling. 'It was a very sad case, you know—sadder than the poor child revealed to Desford, I am afraid. Only a monster could have left her to her fate!'

He agreed, but said gravely: 'But what is to become of her? So young, and so friendless—for *you* cannot continue to be responsible for her—or, I don't doubt, Lord Desford expect it of you.'

'No, of course he doesn't. He has merely left her at Inglehurst while he discovers her grandfather's whereabouts. Though whether Lord Nettlecombe will be willing to receive her into his household I can't but think extremely doubtful.'

'I am not acquainted with his lordship—except by reputation.'

'Nor am I, but if only half the tales told of him are true he must be the most disagreeable, clutchfisted old man imaginable! I can but hope that he may be moved by Cherry's plight—even take a fancy to her, which wouldn't be wonderful, for there is something very attaching about her, and she has the sweetest of dispositions.'

'She is certainly a very taking little thing,' he concurred. 'One doesn't like to think of her becoming a slave to such a purse-leech as Lord Nettlecombe is said to be.' He paused, frowning, and tapping his finger on the table. 'What does she mean to do if Nettlecombe doesn't acknowledge her?' he asked abruptly. 'Has she considered that possibility?'

'Oh, yes! She has the intention—the very firm intention!— of seeking a post in some genteel household.'

His frown deepened. 'What kind of a post? As governess? She must be too young to fill such a position!'

'Not only too young, but quite unqualified for it,' said Henrietta. 'She thinks she could instruct children just out of the nursery, but I hope I may have convinced her that such a situation would be no improvement on the conditions she endured in her aunt's establishment. The other notion she has is to seek employment with an elderly invalid. She says—and I believe her!—that although she is not bookish she does know how to deal with what she calls cantankersome old ladies. Well, my own mama may not be old, and God forbid I should call her cantankersome, but it must be owned that—that she has odd humours! I daresay you know what I mean?' He bowed, looking gravely at her. 'Yes. Well, I can only say that I have never known anyone who knew better how to keep her pleased and happy!'

'Other than yourself!' he suggested.

'Oh, good God, no!' she said, laughing. 'I'm no hand at it, I promise you! I haven't enough patience! But Cherry has. And she has more sympathy than I fear I shall ever have with hypochondriacs! Does that shock you? Forget I said it!'

He shook his head. 'Nothing you did me the honour to confide to me could shock me,' he said simply. 'What shocks me is knowing that you are aware of the imaginary nature of Lady Silverdale's aches and ills. Forgive me if I am expressing myself badly! I'm not ready of tongue, and find it hard to put my thoughts into words! But it has always seemed to me that you believed her to be in failing health, in which case your devotion to her was a natural thing, making it an impertinence for anyone to pity you, or—or to presume to think of rescuing you!'

He stopped, reddening, as he perceived in her expressive eyes as much amusement as surprise. When she spoke, her words acted on him like a douche of cold water, for she said, on a quiver of laughter: 'Well, so I would suppose, sir! Good God, is it possible that you think me an object for pity, or that I need to be rescued? What a very odd notion you must have of me—and, indeed, of my poor mama! She may sometimes be tiresome, but I assure you she is as much attached to me as I am to her. I am perfectly happy, you know!'

'Forgive me!' he muttered. 'I said too much!'

'Why, of course!' she said, smiling at him. 'The truth is that you are too romantical, my friend, and should have lived when gentlemen of your cut used to ride out to rescue some damsel in distress. What a vast number of them there seem to have been, by the way! While as for the dragons and giants and ogres who held the damsels in thrall, when you consider how many of them were slain by the rescuing knights, you must be forced to the conclusion that the country was positively infested with them!'

He could not help laughing, but he shook his head, saying: 'You are always so humoursome, Miss Hetta, that one can't but be diverted by your jokes. Are you *never* serious?'

'Well, not for very long at a time!' she replied. 'I fear I am like Beatrice, and was born to speak all mirth and no matter! But come, we were discussing little Cherry's situation, not mine! She really is a damsel in distress!'

'Hers is indeed a hard case,' he said heavily.

'Yes, but I have every hope that it won't be long before she receives an offer!'

'From Lord Desford?' he interrupted, watching her face closely.

'From Desford?' she exclaimed involuntarily. 'Good God, no! At least, I most sincerely hope not! It would never do!'

'Why do you say that? If he has fallen in love with her—'

'My dear sir, I daresay Desford must be the last man to forget what he owes to his name, and his family! What in the world do you imagine Lord Wroxton would say to such a match?'

'Do you mean to say that Lord Desford will marry to oblige his father?' he demanded.

'No, but I am very sure he won't marry to disoblige him!' she said. 'When I said that I hoped it wouldn't be long before she received an offer I meant that if we can but introduce her into some household where she will be expected to help to entertain the visitors I have little doubt that she *will* receive an offer—perhaps several offers!—from perfectly respectable suitors, to whom her father's reputation won't signify a button.'

'You must permit me to say, Miss Hetta, that her father's reputation ought not to signify to any man who loved her!'

'Yes, that is all very well,' she said impatiently, 'but you cannot expect a Carrington to ally himself to a Steane! It isn't even as if they were of the true nobility! Lord Nettlecombe is only the second baron, you know, and his father, from all I have heard, was a very rough diamond.'

'A man need not be contemptible because he was a rough diamond.'

'Very true!' she retorted. 'He might be an admirable person! But unless I have been quite misinformed he was certainly not that! There is bad blood in the Steanes, Mr Nethercott, and although it hasn't come out in Cherry, who knows but what it might show itself in her children?'

'If these are your sentiments, Miss Hetta, I must wonder at it that you dared to expose your brother to the risk of falling in love with her!' he said, in a quizzing tone, but with a grave look.

She responded lightly: 'Yes, and I must own that I had the strongest misgivings! But Desford said that there was no need for me to tease myself over that, because it wouldn't happen. He says that boys of Charlie's age seldom fall in love with girls no older than they are themselves, but languish at the feet of dashing man-traps. And he was perfectly right, as he by far too often is!—Charlie thinks poor Cherry a very mean bit! Which is a good thing, of course, but I do trust that by the time he is old enough to think of settling down he will have outgrown his taste for dashing man-traps!'

'Is that Lord Desford's opinion?' asked Mr Nethercott, unable to keep a sardonic note out of his voice.

It passed her by. She said, wrinkling her brow: 'I don't think I ever asked him, but I'm very sure it would be, because, now you put me in mind of it, I recall that the first females he ever dangled after were years older than he was himself, and not at all the sort of women anyone but a confirmed noddicock would have dreamt of asking to marry him. And that, you know, Desford never was, even in his most ramshackle days!'

Her eyes lit with reminiscent amusement as she spoke, but a glance at Mr Nethercott's face informed her that he did not share her amusement, so she very wisely brought their tête-à-tête to an end, by getting up from her chair, and inviting him to go with her to the library, where Charlie, still confined largely to the sofa, would be delighted to enjoy a comfortable cose with him.

# Eight

$\mathcal{I}$N THE MEANTIME THE VISCOUNT WAS BEING AFFORDED ample opportunity to regret his chivalry. He spent the day following his return to Arlington Street in a number of abortive attempts to discover Lord Nettlecombe's whereabouts, even (though with extreme reluctance) going to the length of overcoming his strong dislike of Mr Jonas Steane, and calling at his house in Upper Grosvenor Street. But Mr Steane, like his father, had gone out of town; and although he had not left his house entirely empty the ancient caretaker who was at last induced to respond to the summons of a bell pulled with enough vigour to have broken the wires, and to a crescendo of knocks, was unable to give Desford any more precise information than that Mr Steane had taken his family to Scarborough. No, he disremembered that he had ever been told the exact direction of his lodgings: all he knew was that the servants had been given a fortnight's holiday, but would be back again at the end of the following week, with orders to give the house a proper cleanup before the family returned to it. No, he hadn't never heard that Lord Nettlecombe had gone off to Scarborough too, but if anyone was to ask him he'd be bound to say he didn't think he had, being as he was at outs with Mr Steane. Finally, with the praiseworthy intention of assisting the Viscount, he said that he wouldn't wonder at it if Mr Steane's lawyer knew where he was to be found; but as he was unable to furnish Desford with the lawyer's name, misdoubting that no one had ever told him what it was, being that it wasn't no concern of his, the suggestion that Desford should seek him out was not as helpful as he plainly believed it to be.

It was at the end of a singularly unrewarding day, when the Viscount sat down to dine in solitary state in his own house, that his deeply sympathetic butler, distressed by his master's sad lack of appetite, and extremely harassed expression, racked his own brains, and was suddenly inspired to present him with the most promising advice of any that had yet been proffered. He said, as he refilled the Viscount's glass: 'Has it occurred to your lordship that Lord Nettlecombe may have retired to his country seat for the summer months?'

The Viscount, who had been lost in gloomy consideration of the difficulties which confronted him, looked up quickly, and ejaculated: 'Good God, what a fool I am! I'd forgotten he had one!'

'Yes, my lord,' said Aldham, placing a cheesecake before him. 'I have only a few minutes ago remembered it myself. So while you were partaking of your first course I took the liberty of consulting the *Index to the House of Lords*, which I recalled having seen on your lordship's bookshelves, and although this volume is ten years old I fancy the information it contains may still be relied upon. It states that Lord Nettlecombe's country seat is situated in the County of Kent, not far from Staplehurst. One cannot suppose that it will be difficult to find, for it is known as Nettlecombe Manor.'

'Thank you!' said the Viscount warmly. 'I am very much obliged to you! Indeed, I don't know where I should be without you! I'll post off to Staplehurst tomorrow morning!'

He did so, demanding his breakfast at an unfashionably early hour, so that his chaise had gone beyond the stones before such members of the ton who still remained in London had emerged from their bedchambers. His postilions had no difficulty at all in locating Nettlecombe Manor, for a few miles before Staplehurst was reached a signpost pointed the way to the house. It was approached by a narrow lane, bordered by high, straggling hedges, and with grass growing between the wheel-ruts. This did not hold out much promise that my Lord Nettlecombe's house would justify the description of it as a 'Country seat', but it was found to be, if not a mansion, quite a large house, set in a small park, and approached by a short carriage-drive, which led from a pretty little lodge, and showed signs of having undergone extensive weeding operations. When the chaise drew up before the main entrance, and the Viscount jumped lightly down from it, he saw that the house was being repaired, a circumstance which, as he later said acidly, should have been enough to inform him that whoever was residing in the house he was not Lord Nettlecombe.

This was soon proved to be the case. My lord had hired the house to a retired merchant, whose wife, he informed Desford, had been mad after what he called a grand Country Place for years. 'Mind you, my lord,' he said, with a fat chuckle, 'what *she* set her heart on was a swapping big house, like Chatsworth, or some such, but I told her to her head that ducal mansions was above my touch, even if his grace was wishful to hire it, which, so far as I am aware of, he ain't. All to one, it took pretty nigh on two years before we found this place, and I was so sick and tired of jumbling and jolting all over the country to look at houses that wasn't one of them what we wanted, nor what they was puffed off to be by the agents, that when I saw this place I'd have hired it, even if I hadn't taken a fancy to it, which I own I did. Of course I saw in no more than a pig's whisper that there was a lot wanted doing to it, but, lord, I said to myself, it'll give me something to do when I retire from my business, and if I don't have anything to do it's likely I'll get to be as blue as megrim. What's more, I was able to drive a bargain with his lordship's man of business, though not,' he added, with a darkling look, 'as good a one as I'd have driven if I'd known what I know now about the house! Well, if you're one of his lordship's friends, sir, I wouldn't wish to say anything unbecoming, but you wouldn't credit the way everything's been let go to rack and ruin!'

'I'm not one of his friends, and I do credit it!' Desford said promptly, before Mr Tugsley could continue his discourse. 'I have a—a matter of business to discuss with him, and hoped I might find him here when I called at his London house, and discovered that he had gone out of town. If you know where he is to be found I should be very much obliged to you if you would furnish me with his direction.'

'Well, that I can't do, but I *can* tell you his lawyer's name, *and* his direction, so if you'll do us the honour to step into the next room, which Mrs T. calls the Green Saloon, but which to my way of thinking is just a parlour, and partake of a morsel of refreshment, I'll go and see if I can't find it for you.'

The Viscount thanked him, but would have declined the offer of hospitality had he not perceived that Mr Tugsley's feelings would be hurt by a refusal. He never willingly wounded the susceptibilities of his social inferiors, so he accompanied his host into the adjoining room, bowed to Mrs Tugsley just as though (as she later informed her husband) she had been a duchess, and even endured, with an air of courteous interest, twenty minutes of her somewhat overpowering conversation, during which time he drank a glass of wine, and ate a peach. The table was loaded with dishes, but he contrived to refuse them all without giving offence, saying (with perfect truth) that although he couldn't resist the peach, he never ate a nuncheon.

It was plain that Mrs Tugsley had social ambitions, and her efforts to impress him led her to ape what she supposed to be the manners of the haut ton, and to interlard her conversation with the names of a number of titled persons, generally describing them as 'such a sweet creature!' or 'a perfect gentleman', and trying to convey the impression that she was well-acquainted with them. The Viscount responded with easy civility, and allowed no trace either of disgust or boredom to appear in his demeanour, but he was thankful when Mr Tugsley returned, bearing a slip of paper on which he had transcribed the name and direction of Lord Nettlecombe's lawyer. This he handed to Desford, recommending him not to let the old huckster burn him. Mrs Tugsley begged him not to talk in such a vulgar way, and wondered (with a minatory frown at him) whatever his lordship must be thinking of him. But Desford laughed, and said that he was much obliged to Mr Tugsley for the warning, adding that if Lord Nettlecombe's man of business was as hardfisted as he was himself he must be a very neat article indeed.

He parted from the Tugsleys at long last on the best of good terms, and neither of them suspected that he had been chafing to get away from Nettlecombe Manor for the greater part of an hour. There could be little hope of his reaching London before Mr Crick had shut up his office, and, since the following day would be Sunday, none at all of his being able to consult Mr Crick until Monday.

In the event it was not until Monday afternoon that he interviewed Mr Crick, for when he drove to that practitioner's office early in the morning it was to be met by the intelligence that Mr Crick had been summoned to attend another of his clients. The apologetic clerk who informed Desford of this circumstance was unable to say when he would return to his office, but he did not think it would be before noon. He asked, with another of his deprecatory bows, if my lord would wish him to desire Mr Crick to call in Arlington Street, to learn his pleasure; but the Viscount, to whom it would not have occurred to visit his own, and his father's, man of business, unhesitatingly refused this offer, saying that the matter on which he wished to see Mr Crick was merely to discover from him the present whereabouts of Lord Nettlecombe. 'And that,' he added, with his pleasant smile, 'I daresay *you* may be able to tell me!'

But it was immediately apparent that this information the clerk was either unable or unwilling to disclose, so there was nothing for it but to withdraw, leaving his card, and saying that he would return later in the day.

'Which,' said Stebbing, as he resumed his place beside the Viscount in the tilbury, 'will give this Crick plenty of time to play least-in-sight.'

'I wish to God you'd come out of the sullens!' retorted Desford, in some exasperation. 'You've been glumping ever since we left Hazelfield, and I'm sick of it! Why the devil should he want to play least-in-sight?'

'That's more than I can tell, my lord, but what the both of us knows is that he's my Lord Nettlecombe's man of business, and if my lord ain't cut his stick I'm a bag-pudding! Which I ain't!'

'You may not be a bag-pudding, but you're one of the worst surly-boots it has ever been my ill-fortune to encounter!' said Desford roundly. 'I know very well what made you turn knaggy, but what I do not know is what business it is of yours if I choose to lend my aid to Miss Steane, or to any one else!'

Chastened by the Viscount's most unusual severity, Stebbing muttered an apology, but since the Viscount cut short his subsequent stumbling attempt to excuse himself by saying curtly: 'Very well, but don't let it happen again!' he did not venture to speak again until Arlington Street was reached, when, as he received the reins from his master, he asked with unprecedented humility at what hour my lord wished his tilbury to be brought to the door for his second visit to the City.

'I shan't need it again: I'll take a hack,' replied Desford.

'Very good, my lord,' said Stebbing woodenly. 'It is just as your lordship pleases, of course. Though if you prefer to drive yourself, you could take young Upton with you, in my place.'

Neither this speech, nor his expression, could have led any uninitiated person to suppose that he passionately desired to be reconciled with his master, but the Viscount was not uninitiated, and he relented, well-aware that Stebbing's gruffness and frequent attempts to scold and bully him sprang from a very real regard for him; and that to take the under-groom in his place would be to wound him to the heart. So, after eyeing him sternly for a moment, he laughed, and said: 'Don't try to play off your tricks on me, you old humbugger! Think I don't know you? Bring it round at two o'clock!'

Stebbing was so much relieved by this sure sign that the Viscount was no longer angry with him that when he again took his place beside him in the tilbury he comported himself with such anxious civility that the Viscount, if he had not known that such unnatural subservience was unlikely to last for long, would have adjured him to abandon it. In fact, it showed signs of deserting him when the Viscount handed the reins to him outside the grimy building in which Mr Crick had his office, saying that he expected to be with him again in a very few minutes. He then said that he was sure he hoped his lordship would find Mr Crick, and demanded to know what his lordship was meaning to do if he didn't find him. But the Viscount only laughed, and walked into the building.

The clerk bowed him into Mr Crick's room, where he was received by that practitioner with the greatest civility. Mr Crick begged him to be seated; he apologized for having been absent from his office that morning; but he did not furnish him with Lord Nettlecombe's direction. He said that he was fully conversant with my lord's affairs, and did not doubt that if my Lord Desford would condescend to divulge the nature of the business he wished to discuss with my lord he would be able to deal with it.

'What I wish to discuss with him is not a business matter,' said the Viscount. 'It is private, and personal, and can only be answered by himself.'

He spoke perfectly pleasantly, but there was an underlying note of determination in his voice which did not escape Mr Crick, and appeared to discompose him. He coughed genteelly, and murmured: 'Quite! Exactly so! Naturally I understand . . . But I assure your lordship that you need have no hesitation in disclosing it to me. A delicate matter, I apprehend? You might not be aware—perhaps I should tell you that my client honours me with his entire confidence.'

'Yes?' said the Viscount politely.

Mr Crick fidgeted with the pounce-box, straightened a sheet of paper, and finally said: 'He is—er—quite a *character*, my lord, if I may so put it!'

'I'm not—yet!—acquainted with him, but I have always understood him to be a deuced odd fish,' agreed the Viscount.

Mr Crick uttered a little titter, but said it wouldn't become him to agree, though he was bound to own that Lord Nettlecombe had some rather odd ways. 'He has become quite a recluse, you know, and almost never receives anyone, except Mr Jonas Steane—and not even him at present.' He sighed, and shook his head. 'I regret to say that he and Mr Steane had a difference of opinion a few weeks ago, which resulted in his lordship's going off to Harrowgate, and leaving me with instructions to deal with any matters that might arise during his absence. He stated in—in what I may call unequivocal terms that he did not wish to see Mr Steane, or, in fact, *anyone*, or to receive any communications whatsoever—even from me!'

'Good God, he must be short of a sheet!' exclaimed the Viscount.

'No, no, my lord!' Mr Crick said hastily. 'That is, not if you mean to say that he's *deranged*, which, I collect, *is* your meaning! He has a—a somewhat untoward disposition, and has what I venture to say are some rather odd humours, but he is very shrewd—oh, very shrewd indeed!—in all worldly matters! Extremely long-headed, or, as he would say himself, *up to all the rigs*!' He tittered again, but, as the Viscount remained unresponsive to this evidence of Lord Nettlecombe's humour, changed the titter into a cough, and said, with a confidential drop of his voice: 'His—his eccentricities derive, I believe, from the unfortunate circumstances of his *private* life, which has not, alas, been a happy one! It would be improper in me to expatiate on this subject, but I need not scruple to tell your lordship (for it is common knowledge) that his marriage was not attended by that degree of connubial bliss which one has so frequently known to soften a somewhat harsh disposition. And the very unsteady character of his younger son was a source of great pain to him—oh, *very* great pain! One had hoped that he would find consolation in Mr Jonas Steane, but, unfortunately, he did not care for Mr Jonas's wife, so that his relationship with Mr Jonas has sometimes been a trifle strained, though there has never been any serious quarrel between them, until—But more I must not say on that head!'

'My dear sir,' interrupted the Viscount, who had been growing perceptibly impatient during this monologue, 'do, pray, let me make it plain to you that I am not concerned with Lord Nettlecombe's marital troubles, or with his quarrels with his sons! All I wish to know is where, in Harrowgate, he is to be found!'

'Oh dear, oh dear, did I say that he was in Harrowgate?' asked Mr Crick, looking dismayed.

'You did, so you may just as well give me his exact direction,' said the Viscount. 'That will save me the trouble of enquiring for him at every hotel, inn, or lodging-house in the place, which, I promise you, I shall do, if you persist in withholding his direction!'

'My lord, I don't know his direction!'

The Viscount's brows drew together. He said incredulously: 'You don't know it? How is this possible? You have told me that you are wholly in his confidence!'

'Yes, yes, I am!' averred Mr Crick, apparently on the verge of bursting into tears. 'That is to say, I know why he has chosen to go away, but he would not tell me where he meant to stay, because he said he didn't wish to be troubled with any business while he was away. He did me the honour to say that he was confident I could settle any matter that might come up without referring it to him. May I venture to suggest to your lordship that you should wait until he returns to London—which, according to my information, he will do next month—'

'Why, certainly!' said the Viscount affably, rising from his chair, and picking up his hat and gloves. 'You may suggest anything you please, Mr Crick! I am sorry you are unable to furnish me with Lord Nettlecombe's direction, and I won't waste any more of your time. Oh, no! pray don't trouble to escort me to the door! I can very well find the way out!'

But this Mr Crick would by no means permit him to do. He darted across the room to hold open the door for his distinguished visitor, bowing even more deeply than his clerk had done, and followed him down the dusty stairs, begging first his pardon and then his understanding of the delicacy of his own position as the trusted confidant of a noble client. The Viscount reassured him on both heads, but left him looking more harassed than ever. His last words, as Desford was about to mount into his tilbury, were that he hoped nothing he had said had given a wrong impression! Lord Nettlecombe had gone to try what the Harrowgate Chalybeate would do for his gout.

'Don't tease yourself!' Desford said, over his shoulder. 'I won't disclose to his lordship that it was you who let slip the information that he had gone to Harrowgate!'

He then took his seat in the tilbury, recovered the reins from Stebbing, and drove off at a brisk trot, saying abruptly: 'Didn't my father go to Harrowgate once—oh, years ago, when he was first troubled by the gout! I was still up at Oxford, I think.'

Stebbing took a minute or two to answer this, frowning in an effort of memory. Finally he said: 'Yes, my lord, he did. But, according to what I remember, he came home within a sennight, not liking the place. Unless it was Leamington he took against.' His frown deepened, but cleared after another few moments, and he said: 'No, it wasn't Leamington, my lord—though the waters never did him any good. It was Harrowgate right enough. And those waters didn't do him any good neither—not but what there's no saying that they wouldn't have done him good if he'd drunk more than one glass, which tasted so bad it made him sick.'

The Viscount grinned appreciatively. 'Poor Papa! Who shall blame him for going home? Did he take you there?'

'Me, my lord?' said Stebbing, shocked. 'Lor', no! In them days I was only one of the under-grooms!'

'I suppose you must have been. What a pity! I hoped you might know the place, for I don't. Oh, well, we'd best stop at Hatchards, and I'll see if I can come by a guide-book there!'

'My lord, you're never going to go all that way just to find Miss's grandpa?' exclaimed Stebbing. 'Which—if you'll pardon the liberty!—don't seem to be a grandpa as anyone would be wishful to find!'

'Very likely not—indeed, almost certainly not!—but I've pledged my word to Miss Steane that I will find him, and—damn it, my blood's up, and I will *not* be beaten!'

'But, my lord,' expostulated Stebbing, 'it'll take you four or five days to get there! It's above two hundred miles away: that I *do* know, for when my lord and her ladyship went there, they were five days on the road, and Mr Rudford, which was his lordship's valet at that time, always held to it that it was that which set up his lordship's back so that he wouldn't have liked the place no matter what!'

'Good God, you don't imagine, do you, that I mean to go in the family travelling-carriage? What with four people in the carriage, the coachman, and I'll go bail a couple of footmen outside, and a coach following, chuck-full of baggage, besides the rest of my father's retinue, I'm astonished they weren't a sennight on the road! I shall travel in my chaise, of course, taking Tain, and one portmanteau only, and changing horses as often as need be, and I promise you I shan't be more than three days on the road. No, don't pull that long face! If I can post to Doncaster in two days, which you know well I have frequently done, I can certainly reach Harrowgate in three days—possibly less!'

'Yes, my lord, and possibly more, if you was to have an accident,' said Stebbing. 'Or find yourself with a stumbler in the team, or maybe a limper!'

'Or founder in a snowdrift,' agreed the Viscount.

'That,' said Stebbing coldly, 'I didn't say, nor wouldn't, not being such a cabbage-head as to look for snowdrifts at this time o'year. But if you was to drop the high toby, who's to say you won't find yourself foundering in a regular hasty-pudding?'

'Who indeed? I'll bear it in mind, and take care to stick to the post-road,' promised his lordship.

Stebbing sniffed, but refrained from further speech.

Desford was unable to find a guide-book of Harrowgate at Hatchard's shop, but he was offered a fat little volume, which announced itself to be a Guide to All the Watering and Sea-bathing Places, and contained, besides some tasteful Views, numerous maps, town-plans, and itineraries. He bore this off for perusal that evening, hoping to discover in the chapter

devoted to the amenities of Harrowgate a list of the hotels and
lodgings there. But although almost a dozen inns received
favourable notice neither High nor Low Harrowgate appeared
to boast of any establishment comparable to the hotels to be
found at more fashionable watering-places; nor was any lodging-
house mentioned. As he read what the unknown author had to
say about the place, and pictured his father there, he was torn
between appreciative amusement, and a strong wish that he himself were not obliged to go there. The very first paragraph was
daunting, for it stated that because Harrowgate possessed 'in
a superior degree' neither the attraction of being fashionable,
nor beauty of scenery, it was chiefly resorted to by valetudinarians. No doubt feeling that he had been rather too severe, the
author bestowed some temperate praise on the situation of High
Harrowgate, which he described as exceedingly pleasant, and
commanding an extensive prospect of the distant country. But as,
in the very next paragraph, he referred to the 'dreary common'
on which both High and Low Harrowgate were built, and to 'the
barren wolds of Yorkshire', it seemed safe to assume that the place
had not taken his fancy. Which, thought Desford, flicking over
the pages which dealt with the qualities and virtues of the wells,
and reading the passage headed Customs and Accommodations,
was not to be wondered at. He could almost feel the hairs rising
on his scalp when he read that one of the advantages enjoyed by
visitors to Harrowgate was that the narrow circle of their amusements drew them into 'something like family parties'; but when
he read that the presence of the ladies sitting at the same board as
the gentlemen excluded any rudeness or indelicacy, he began to
chuckle; and when, on the next page, he learned that one of the
advantages of mixing freely with the ladies was the sobriety it
ensured—to which the author acidly added that to this the waters
contributed 'not a little', he laughed so much that it was several
moments before his vision was sufficiently clear to enable him

to read any more. However, he did read more, and although he found no mention of a pump room, he did learn that there was an Assembly Room, and a Master of Ceremonies, who presided over the public balls; a theatre; two libraries; a billiard-room; and a morning lounge in one of the new buildings, called the Promenade; which made it seem probable that he would experience no very great difficulty in discovering where he could find Lord Nettlecombe.

But what he found very difficult to understand was why Lord Nettlecombe, who, so far from enjoying the company of his fellow men and women, had for years spurned even his oldest acquaintances, should have elected suddenly to spend the summer months where, according to the author of the Guide, repasts (served in the long rooms of the various inns) were 'seasoned by social conversation'; and where 'both sexes vied with each other in the art of being mutually agreeable'. It was possible, of course, that the circumstance of the expenses of living and lodging being moderate might have attracted his cheese-paring lordship; but this advantage must surely have been off-set by the cost of so long a journey. The Viscount, as he took his candle up to bed, wondered if Nettlecombe had travelled north on the common stage, but abandoned this notion, feeling that the old screw could not be such a shocking lickpenny as that. He might, with perfect propriety, have travelled on the Mail coach, but although this was much cheaper than hiring a private chaise it was by no means dog-cheap, particularly when two places would have to be booked. Lord Nettlecombe might not travel in the rather outmoded state favoured by Lord Wroxton, but it was inconceivable to Desford that he could have gone away on a protracted visit without taking his valet with him. The thought of his high and imposing father's regal progress to Harrowgate, and his very brief stay there, made Desford begin to chuckle again. He must remember, he told himself, to ask Poor Dear Papa, at a suitable moment, for his opinion of Harrowgate.

Tain, his own extremely accomplished valet, had received without a blink the news that his lively young master meant to leave almost at crack of dawn for an unfashionable resort in Yorkshire; and when further told that he must pack whatever was strictly necessary into one portmanteau, he merely said: 'Certainly, my lord. For how many days does your lordship mean to stay in Harrowgate?'

'Oh, not above two or three!' replied Desford. 'I shan't be attending any evening-parties, so don't pack any ball-toggery.'

'Then one portmanteau will be quite sufficient for your lordship's needs,' said Tain calmly. 'Your dressing-case may go inside the chaise, and I shall not pack your Hessians, or any of your town-coats. I fancy they would be quite ineligible for wear in Those Parts.'

That was all he had to say about the projected expedition, either then or later; and Desford, who had had several years' experience of his competence, never so much as thought of asking him whether he had packed enough shirts and neck-cloths, and had found room for a change of outer raiment.

For his part, Tain showed not the smallest surprise at what he might have thought to be a very queer start, or betrayed by look or word that he was well aware of the Viscount's purpose in going post-haste to Harrowgate, when his intention had been to attend the races at Newmarket. He had not yet seen Miss Steane, but he knew all about her meeting with the Viscount, for he stood on very friendly terms with both the Aldhams, and had contrived, without showing a vulgar curiosity unbecoming to a man of his consequence, to discover from them quite as much as they knew, and many of Mrs Aldham's conjectures on the probable outcome of the adventure. On these he withheld judgment, feeling that he knew my lord far more intimately than they did, and having yet to see in him any of the signs of a gentleman who had fallen head over ears in love. He did not discuss the matter with Stebbing, not so much because it would have been beneath a gentleman's gentleman to hob-nob with a groom, but because he was as jealous of Stebbing as Stebbing was of him.

Before he went to bed, the Viscount wrote a brief letter to Miss Silverdale, informing her that he was off to Harrowgate, where he was reliably informed Nettlecombe was to be found, but hoped to be back again in not much more than a sennight's time, when he would come to Inglehurst immediately, to tell her how his mission had prospered, *or,* he added, *if it has not prospered, to discuss with you what were best to do next for that unfortunate child. I should think myself the biggest rascal unhung to have foisted her on to you, my best of friends, if I were not persuaded that she must have made you like her.*

This missive he gave to Aldham on the following morning, telling him to send it by express post to Inglehurst. He then climbed into his chaise, and set forward on the long journey into Yorkshire.

# Nine

HE VISCOUNT SUFFERED NO DELAYS ON HIS JOURNEY, and might have reached Harrowgate at the end of the second day had it not occurred to him that to arrive without warning at a watering-place in the height of its season would probably entail a prolonged search for accommodation, and that the late evening was scarcely the time to prosecute this. So he spent the second night at the King's Arms, in Leeds, leaving himself with only some twenty more miles to cover. He was an extremely healthy young man, and since he spent a great part of his time in all the more energetic forms of sport it was hard to tire him out, but two very long days in a post-chaise had made him feel as weary as he was bored. The chaise was his own, and very well-sprung, but it was also very lightly built, which, while it made for speed, meant that it bounded over the inequalities of the road in a manner not at all conducive to repose. Midway through the second day he remarked to Tain that he wished he could exchange places with one of the postboys. Quite shocked, Tain said incredulously: 'Exchange places with a *post-boy*, my lord?'

'Yes, for he at least has something to do. Though I daresay I shouldn't care to be obliged to wear a leg-iron,' he added reflectively.

'No, my lord,' said Tain, primly. 'Certainly not! A very unbecoming thing for any gentleman to do!'

'Also uncomfortable, don't you think?' suggested Desford, gently quizzing him.

'I have never worn one, my lord, so I cannot take it upon myself to venture an opinion,' replied Tain, in chilly accents.

'I must remember to ask my own wheel-boy,' said Desford provocatively.

But Tain, refusing to be drawn, merely said: 'Certainly, my lord,' leaving Desford to regret that it was he and not Stebbing who was sitting beside him. Stebbing would undoubtedly have entered with enthusiasm into a discussion, embellishing it with some entertaining anecdotes illustrative of the advantages and disadvantages attached to a postilion's career.

However, the regret vanished when the Viscount remembered how valuable Tain's services became from the instant that he climbed down from the chaise, and entered whatever posting-house his employer had chosen to honour with his patronage on this or any other journey. In some mysterious way known only to himself he could transform the most unpromising bedchamber into an inviting one in no more than a flea's leap, as the saying was; to lay out a change of raiment for his master; to make such arrangements for his comfort as Desford would not have thought it necessary to command, if left to manage for himself; to press out the creases in his coat; to launder his neckcloth and his shirt; to procure extra candles; and to overawe the domestic staff into bringing up hot water to my lord's room without delay as soon as he himself demanded it. Stebbing might be a more amusing companion during a tedious journey, but none of Tain's arts was known to him, as the Viscount realized, and acknowledged, when, as Tain drew the curtains round his bed that evening, he murmured: 'Thank you! I only wish may have ensured your own comfort half as well as you have ensured mine!'

He did not reach Harrowgate until shortly before noon on the following morning, because although he had had the intention of setting forward on the last few miles of his journey at eight o'clock Tain had quite deliberately refrained from rousing him until an hour later, saying mendaciously, but with complete sangfroid, that he had misunderstood his instructions. What he did not say was that when he had softly entered the room at six o'clock he had found the Viscount sunk in a profound sleep from which he had not had the heart to rouse him. He guessed, judging by his own experience, that my lord had spent the first part of the night under the lingering impression that he was still bowling and bounding and swaying over the road, and had only slept in uneasy snatches until overcome by exhaustion. As this guess was correct, and Desford was still feeling both sleepy and battered, the excuse was received with a prodigious yawn, accompanied by nothing more alarming than a sceptical glance, and a rather thickly uttered: 'Oh, well—!'

Revived by an excellent breakfast, Desford shook off his unaccustomed lassitude, and resumed his journey. It was a day of bright sunshine, with just enough wind blowing off the moors to make it invigorating, and under these conditions he saw Harrowgate at its best, and was much inclined to think that his anonymous Guide had maligned the place. The Low Town did not attract him, but the situation of High Harrowgate, which lay nearly a mile beyond it, was as pleasant as the Guide had grudgingly described. On a clear day—and this was a very clear day— York Minster could be seen in the distance, with the Hambleton hills beyond; and to the west the mountains of Craven. Besides the race course, the theatre, and the principal Chalybeate, High Harrowgate possessed a large green, which was one of its most agreeable features, and round which three of its chief hotels stood, a great many shops, and what bore all the appearance of being a fashionable library. 'Come now!' exclaimed Desford cheerfully, as the chaise drew up at the Dragon. 'I don't consider this a dreary place at all, do you, Tain?'

'Your lordship has not yet seen it in bad weather,' responded Tain unencouragingly. 'I should not myself choose to sojourn here on a dull day, when the prospect would no doubt be shrouded in mist.'

Neither the Dragon nor the Granby had a room to spare, but the Viscount was more fortunate at the Queen's, where, after a hurried colloquy with his spouse, conducted in an urgent whisper, the landlord was happy to inform his lordship that he had just one room vacant—indeed, one of his best rooms, looking out on to the green, which he was only able to offer because the gentleman who had booked it had unaccountably failed to honour his contract. He then escorted Desford upstairs to inspect it, and, on its being approved, bowed himself out, and hurried downstairs again, first to order a couple of menials to carry up the gentleman's baggage to No. 7, and then to inform his flustered wife that if Mr Fritwell *should* happen to show his front Jack (the hope of his house) would have to give up his room to him, and bed down over the stables. Upon her venturing to expostulate he silenced her by saying that if she thought he was going to turn away a well-breeched swell, travelling in a chaise-and-four, and attended by his valet, merely to avoid offending old Mr Fritwell, who was more inclined to argue over the reckoning than to drop his blunt freely, she was the more mistaken.

Little though he knew it, the Viscount was indebted to Tain's entrance upon the scene, bearing his dressing-case, for the landlord's decision to sacrifice old Mr Fritwell. The landlord was sharp enough to recognize after one look at his lordship that a member of the Quality had walked into the inn, and—after a second, shrewd, glance at the cut of his lordship's coat, the intricate folds of his neckcloth, and the gloss on his top-boots—no

country squire, but a London buck of the first head; but it was
Tain's arrival which clinched the matter. Unknown ladies and
gentlemen travelling without their personal servants found it hard
to obtain accommodation at any of the best inns in Harrowgate,
valets and abigails apparently being regarded by the landlords as
insurances against the possibility of being choused out of their
due reckonings.

The Viscount had not thought it necessary to acquaint the
landlord either with his name or his rank, but this was a foolish
omission speedily rectified by Tain, far better versed in such
matters than his master. Instead of following immediately in the
Viscount's wake, he awaited the landlord's return at the foot of
the stairs, and proceeded with quelling civility to make known
to him my lord's requirements. By the time he had reached the
stage of warning the landlord not, on any account, to permit
the Boots to lay a finger on my lord's footwear, he had succeeded in so much enlarging his master's consequence that it
would not have been surprising if the landlord had believed
himself to be entertaining, if not a Royal prince, at least a Serene
Highness.

As a result of these competent, if top-lofty, tactics, he was able
to inform the Viscount, when he presently rejoined him in No.
7, that he had ventured to bespeak a private parlour for him, and
to arrange with the landlord for his dinner to be served there.
The Viscount, who was standing by the window, watching the
various persons passing below, replied absently: 'Have you? I
thought it not worth while to ask for one since I don't expect
to be here above a couple of nights, but I daresay you're right.
You know, Tain, the place *is* full of valetudinarians! I've never
seen so many people hobbling along on sticks in my life!'

'Exactly so, my lord!' said Tain, beginning swiftly to unpack
the contents of the dressing-case. 'I have myself seen three of
them enter this house, one of them being an elderly lady of what

one must call a garrulous disposition. I formed the opinion that if she were to subject your lordship to a description of her sufferings and of the cure which she is undergoing you would be hard put to it to maintain even the appearance of civility.'

'Then you were certainly right to procure a private parlour for me,' said the Viscount, laughing.

Leaving Tain to unpack his portmanteau, he sallied forth to continue his search for Lord Nettlecombe. He had already enquired for him at the Dragon and the Granby, without meeting with anything but blank looks, and head-shakings, so, as the Chalybeate, under its imposing dome, lay on the opposite side of the green he thought he might as well make that his first port of call. If Lord Nettlecombe had come to Harrowgate for his health's sake it seemed likely that he must by now have become a familiar figure there. But none of the attendants seemed to have heard of his lordship, the most helpful amongst them being unable to do more than suggest that he should be sought at the Tewit Well, which was the second of the two Chalybeates, situated half-a-mile to the west of the principal one.

Desford strode off, glad to be able to stretch his legs after having been cooped up for so many hours, but although he enjoyed a brisk walk it ended in another rebuff, accompanied by a recommendation to try the Sulphur Wells, at Lower Harrowgate, and the information that although the Lower town was a mile distant by road it was no more than half-a-mile away if approached 'over the stile'. But as the directions given to him on how to reach the stile were as vague as such directions too often are, Desford decided to enquire at the inns and boarding-houses in High Harrowgate, before extending his search to the Lower town.

He very soon discovered that although Harrowgate was described by the Guide as consisting of two scattered villages this was another of that anonymous author's misleading statements:

no village that Desford had yet seen contained so many inns and boarding-houses as High Harrowgate. At none of those he visited was he able to obtain any news of his quarry, and by the time a church clock struck the hour of six, at which unfashionable time dinner was served at all the best inns, he was tired, hungry, and exasperated, and thankfully abandoned, for that day, his fruitless search.

When he reached the Queen he was considerably surprised by the respect with which he was greeted, the porter bowing him in, a waiter hurrying forward to discover whether he would take a glass of sherry before he went upstairs to his parlour, and the landlord breaking off a conversation with a less favoured guest to conduct him to the stairs, informing him on the way that dinner—which he trusted would meet with his approval—should be served immediately, and that he had taken it upon himself to bring up a bottle of his best burgundy from the cellar, and one of a very tolerable claret, in case my lord should prefer the lighter wine.

The reason for these embarrassingly obsequious attentions was soon made plain to the Viscount. Tain, relieving him of his hat and gloves, said that he had ventured to order a neat, plain dinner for him, consisting of a Cressy soup, removed with a fillet of veal, some glazed sweetbreads, and a few petit pâtés, to be followed by a second course of which prawns, peas, and a gooseberry tart were the principal dishes. 'I took the precaution, my lord,' he said, 'of looking at the bill of fare, and saw that it was just as I had feared: a mere ordinary, and not at all what you are accustomed to. So I ordered what I believe you will like.'

'Well, I am certainly hungry, but I couldn't eat the half of it!' Desford declared.

However, when he sat down to table he found that he was hungrier than he had supposed, and he ate rather more than half of what was set before him. The claret, though not of the first growth, was better than the landlord's somewhat slighting description of it had led him to expect; and the brandy with which he rounded off the repast was a true Cognac. Under its benign influence he began to take a more hopeful view of his immediate prospects, and to consider what his next move should be. He decided that the best thing he could do would be to visit first the Sulphur Well, and next, if he failed to come by any intelligence of Lord Nettlecombe's whereabouts there, to discover the names and directions of the doctors practising in Harrowgate.

The experiences of the first wearing day he had spent in his search for Nettlecombe prevented him from feeling either surprise or any marked degree of disappointment when his enquiries at the Sulphur Well were productive of nothing more than regretful headshakes; but he was a trifle daunted when presented with a list of the Harrowgate doctors: he had not thought that so many medical men were to be found in so small a spa. He betook himself to the Crown, to study the list over a fortifying tankard of Home Brewed; and, having crossed off from it those who advertised themselves as Surgeons, and consulted a plan of both High and Low Harrowgate, which he had had the forethought to buy that morning, set out on foot to visit the first of the Lower town's practitioners which figured on the list. Neither this member of the Faculty, nor the next on his list, numbered Lord Nettlecombe amongst his patients, but just as the Viscount was contemplating with disgust the prospect of spending the rest of the day in what he was fast coming to believe was an abortive search, fortune at last smiled upon him: Dr Easton, third on the list, not only knew where Nettlecombe was lodging, but had actually been summoned to attend him, when his lordship had suffered a severe attack of colic. 'As far as I am aware,' he said, austerely regarding Desford over the top of his spectacles, 'his lordship has not removed from that lodging, but since he has not again sought my services I do not claim him as a patient. I will go further! Should he again request my attendance upon him I should have no hesitation in recommending him to consult some other physician more willing than I am, perhaps, to being told that his diagnosis is false, and to having his prescription spurned!'

Resisting an absurd but strong impulse to offer Dr Easton an apology for Nettlecombe's rudeness, Desford took his leave, saying that he was much obliged to him, and assuring him, with a disarming smile, that he had all his sympathy.

It transpired that Nettlecombe's lodging was in one of the larger boarding-houses in the Lower town. It had an air of somewhat gloomy respectability, and was presided over by an angular lady whose appearance carried the suggestion that she must be in mourning for a near relation, since she wore a bombasine dress of sombre hue, without frills, or lace, or even a ribbon to lighten its sobriety. Her cap was of starched cambric, tied tightly beneath her chin; and as much of her hair as was allowed to be seen was iron-gray, and smoothed into bands as severe as her expression. She put Desford forcibly in mind of the dame in the village that lay beyond Wolversham who terrified the rural children into good behaviour and the rudiments of learning; and he would not have been in the least surprised to have seen a birch-rod on the high desk behind which she stood.

She was talking to an elderly couple, whose decorous bearing and prim voices exactly matched their surroundings, when Desford entered the house, but she broke off the conversation to direct a piercing look of appraisal at him, which made him feel that at any moment she would tell him that his neckcloth was crooked, or demand to know if he had washed his hands before venturing into her presence. His lips twitched, and his eyes began to dance, upon which her countenance relaxed, and, excusing herself to the elderly couple, she came towards him, saying, with a slight bow: 'Yes, sir? What may I have the honour to do for you? If it is accommodation you are seeking, I regret I have none to offer: my house is always fully booked for the season.'

'No, I don't want accommodation,' he replied. 'But I believe you have Lord Nettlecombe staying here. Is that so?'

Her face hardened again; she said grimly: 'Yes, sir, it *is* so!'

It was apparent that the presence of Lord Nettlecombe in her house afforded her no gratification, and that Desford's enquiry had caused whatever good opinion she had formed of himself to wither at birth. When he requested her to have his card taken to my lord she gave a small, contemptuous sniff, and without deigning to reply, turned away to call sharply to a waiter just about to enter the long room: 'George! Conduct this gentleman to Lord Nettlecombe's parlour!'

She then favoured the Viscount with a haughty inclination of her head, and resumed her conversation with the elderly couple.

Amused, but also a trifle ruffled by this cavalier treatment, Desford was on the verge of telling her that when he had handed her his card he had intended it to be taken to Lord Nettlecombe, not laid on her desk, when it occurred to him that perhaps it would be as well not to give his lordship the opportunity to refuse to see him, so he suppressed the impulse to give this ridiculously uppish creature a set-down, and followed the waiter up the stairs, and along a corridor. The waiter, whose air of profound gloom argued a life of intolerable slavery, but was probably due to the pain of flat feet, stopped outside a door at the end of the corridor, and asked what name he should say, and, upon learning it, opened the door, and repeated it in a raised, indifferent voice.

'Eh? What's that?' demanded Lord Nettlecombe wrathfully. 'I won't see him! What the devil do you mean by bringing people up here without my leave? Tell him to go away!'

'I fear you will be obliged to do that yourself, sir,' said Desford, shutting the door upon the waiter, and coming forward. 'Pray accept my apologies for not sending up my card! It was my intention to have done so, but the formidable lady below-stairs thought otherwise.'

'That damned pigeon-fancier!' ejaculated his lordship fiercely. 'She had the curst impudence to try to diddle me! But I'm no pigeon for her plucking, and so I told her! Gull-catcher! Slip-gibbet! Nail!' He broke off suddenly. 'What do you want?' he snarled.

'A few words with you, sir,' said the Viscount coolly.

'Well, I don't want to talk to you! I don't want to talk to anyone! If your name's Desford you must be old Wroxton's son, and he's no friend of mine, I'll have you know!'

'Oh, I do know it!' responded the Viscount, laying his hat, his gloves, and his malacca cane down on the table.

This indication that he meant to prolong his visit infuriated Nettlecombe so much that he said, in a kind of scream: 'Don't do that! Go away! Do you want to send me off the hooks? I'm a sick man! Worn to the bone with all the worry and trouble I've had! Burnt to the socket, damn it! I won't have strangers thrust in on me, I tell you!'

'I'm sorry you are in such indifferent health,' said Desford politely, 'I will try not to tax your strength, but I have a duty to discharge which closely concerns you, and I believe—'

'If you've come from my son Jonas you've wasted your time!' interrupted Nettlecombe, his pale eyes sharp with suspicion.

'I have not,' said Desford, his calm voice in marked contrast to Nettlecombe's shrill accents. 'I have come on behalf of your granddaughter.'

'That's a damned quibble!' instantly exclaimed his lordship. 'Jonas may take care of his brats himself, and so you may tell him! I wash my hands of the whole brood!'

'I am not speaking of Mr Jonas Steane's daughters, sir, but of your younger son's only child.'

My lord's bony hands clenched the arms of his chair convulsively. 'I have no younger son!'

'From what I have been able to discover I fear that that may be true,' said Desford.

'Ha! Dead, is he? And a good thing if he is!' said Nettlecombe viciously. 'He's been dead to me for years, and if you think I'll have anything to do with any child of his you're mistaken!'

'I do think it, and I am persuaded that I'm not mistaken, sir. When you have heard in what a desperate situation she has been left I cannot believe that you will refuse to help her. Her mother died when she was a child, and her father placed her in a school in Bath. Until a few years ago, he paid the necessary fees, though not always, I fancy, very punctually, and from time to time he visited her. But the payments and the visits ceased—'

'I know all this!' interrupted Nettlecombe. 'The woman wrote to me! Demanded that *I* should pay for the girl! A damned insolent letter I thought it, too! I told her to apply to the girl's maternal relations, for she wouldn't get a groat out of me!'

'She obeyed you, sir, she applied to Lady Bugle, but I don't think she got a groat out of her either,' said Desford dryly. ' Lady Bugle, perceiving an opportunity to provide herself with an unpaid servant, took Miss Steane to her home in Hampshire, under an odious pretence of charity, for which she demanded a slavish gratitude, and unending service, not only for herself, but for every other member of her large family. Miss Steane's disposition is compliant and affectionate: she had every wish in the world to repay her aunt for having given her a home, and uncomplainingly performed every task set before her, from hemming sheets, or running errands for her cousins, to taking charge of the nursery-children. And I daresay she would still be doing so, perfectly happily, had her aunt treated her with kindness. But she did not, and the poor child became so unhappy that she ran away, with the intention of appealing to you, sir, for protection.'

Nettlecombe, who had listened to this speech with a scowl on his brow, punctuating it with muttered comments, and fidgeting restlessly in his chair, burst out angrily: 'It's no concern of mine! I warned that scoundrelly son of mine how it would be if he didn't mend his ways. He made his bed, and he must lie on it!'

'But it is not he who is lying on it,' said the Viscount. 'It is his daughter who is the innocent victim of her father's misdeeds.'

'You should read your Bible, young man!' retorted Nettlecombe on a note of triumph. 'The sins of the fathers shall be visited on the children! What about *that*, eh?'

A pungent reply sprang to the Viscount's lips, but it remained unuttered, for at that moment the door opened, and a middle-aged and buxom woman sailed into the room, saying in far from refined accents: 'Well, this *is* a surprise, to be sure! When that old Tabby downstairs, which has the impudence to call herself *Mrs* Nunny, just as though a rabbit-pole like she is ever had a husband, told me my lord had a gentleman visiting him you could have knocked me down with a feather, for in general he don't receive, not being in very high force. Though we shall soon have him quite rumtitum again, shan't we, my lord?'

My lord responded to this sprightly prophecy with a growl. As for Desford, the newcomer's surprise was as nothing to his, for she spoke as though she were well-acquainted with him, and he knew that he had never before seen her. He wondered who the devil she could be. Her manner towards Nettlecombe suggested that she might be a nurse, hired to attend him during recuperation from some illness but a stunned look at the lavishly plumed and high-crowned bonnet set upon her brassy curls rapidly put that idea to flight. No nurse wearing such an exaggeratedly fashionable bonnet would ever have been allowed to cross the threshold of a sick-room; nor would she have dreamt of arraying herself (even if she could have afforded to do so) in a purple gown with a demi-train, and trimmed with knots of ribbon.

His blank astonishment must have shown itself in his face, for she simpered, and said archly: 'I have the advantage of you, haven't I? You don't know who I am, but I know who *you* are, because I've seen your card. So my lord don't have to tell me.'

Thus put pointedly in mind of his social obligations Lord Nettlecombe said sourly: 'Lord Desford—Lady Nettlecombe. And you've no need to look like that!' he added, as Desford blinked incredulously at him. 'My marriage doesn't have to meet with your approval!'

'Certainly not!' said Desford, recovering himself. 'Pray accept my felicitations, sir! Lady Nettlecombe, your servant!'

He bowed, and finding that she was extending her hand to him took it in his, and (since she clearly expected it) raised it briefly to his lips.

'However did you find us out, my lord?' she asked. 'Such pains did we take to keep it secret that we'd gone off on our honeymoon! Not that I'm not very happy to make your acquaintance, for I'm sure we couldn't have wished for a more amiable bride-guest, neither of us!'

'Don't talk such fiddle-faddle, Maria!' said Nettlecombe irascibly. 'He's not a bride-guest! He didn't know we were married when he forced his way in here! All he wants to do is to foist Wilfred's brat on to me, and I won't have her!'

'You are mistaken, sir!' said the Viscount icily. 'I have not the smallest wish to see Miss Steane in a house where she is not welcome! My purpose in coming to visit you is to inform you that she—your granddaughter, let me remind you!—is entirely destitute! Had I not been with her when she found your house shut up she must have been in a desperate case, for she has no acquaintance in London, no one in the world to turn to but yourself! What might have become of her I leave to your imagination!'

'She had no business to run away from her aunt's house!' Nettlecombe said angrily. 'Most unbecoming! Hoydenish behaviour! Not that I should have expected anything better from a daughter of that rake-shame I refuse to call my son!' He turned towards his bride. 'It's Wilfred's brat he's talking about, Maria: you remember how vexed I was when some brass-faced schoolkeeper wrote to demand that I—*I!*—should pay for the girl's schooling? Well, now, if you please—' He broke off, his gaze suddenly riveted to the shawl she was wearing draped across her elbows. 'That's new!' he said, stabbing an accusing finger at it. 'Where did it come from?'

'I've just purchased it,' she answered boldly. She still smiled, but her smile was at variance with the determined jut of her chin, and the martial gleam in her eyes. 'And don't try to bamboozle me into thinking you didn't give me leave to buy myself a new shawl, because you did, and this very morning, what's more!'

'But it's *silk!*' he moaned.

'Norwich silk,' she said, smoothing it complacently. 'Now, don't fly into a miff, my lord! You wouldn't wish for me to be seen about in a cheap shawl, such as anyone could wear, not when I'm your wife!'

There was nothing in his expression to encourage her in this belief; and as he complained mournfully that if she meant to squander his money on finery he would soon be ruined, and added a reproachful rider to the effect that he had expected his marriage to be an economy, Desford very soon found himself the sole, and wholly disregarded, witness to a matrimonial squabble. From the various things that were said, he gathered, without much surprise, that Lord Nettlecombe had married his housekeeper. Why he had done so did not emerge; the reason was to be revealed to him later. But it was plain that in the rôle of housekeeper my lord's bride had proved herself to be as big a save-all as he was himself; and that once she had him firmly hooked she had lapsed a little from her former economical habits. And, watching her, as she contended with her lord, always with that firm smile on her lips and that dangerous gleam in her eyes, he thought that it would not be long before my lord would be living under the cat's foot, as the saying was. For a moment he wondered whether it might be possible to enlist her support, but only for a moment: my Lady Nettlecombe was concerned only with her own support. There was not a trace of womanly compassion in her eyes, and no softness beneath her determined smile.

The quarrel ended as abruptly as it had begun, my lady suddenly recollecting Desford's presence, and exclaiming: 'Oh, whatever must Lord Desford be thinking of us, coming to cuffs like a couple of children over no more than a barley-straw? You must excuse us, my lord! Well, they do say that the first year of marriage is difficult, don't they, and I'm sure my First and I had many a tiff, but no more than lovers' quarrels, like this little breeze me and my Second has just had!' She leaned forward to fondle her Second's unresponsive hand as she spoke, and adjured him, in sugared accents, not to put himself into a fuss over a mere shawl.

'I don't give a rush for what Desford thinks of me!' declared Nettlecombe, two hectic spots of colour burning in his cheeks. 'Cocky young busy-head! Meddling in my affairs!'

'Oh, no!' Desford interposed. 'Merely bringing your affairs to your notice, sir!'

Nettlecombe glared at him. 'Wilfred's daughter is no affair of mine! It seems to me she's *your* affair, young man! Ay, and it seems to me there's something very havey-cavey about this! How did you come to be with her when she called at my house? Tell me that! It's my belief you ran off with her from her aunt's house, and now you're trying to be rid of her! Well, you're blowing at a cold coal! No man has ever contrived to put the change on *me*!'

Desford turned white with anger, and for an instant such an ugly look blazed in his eyes that Nettlecombe shrank back in his chair, and his spouse rushed forward, and dramatically commanded the Viscount to remember her lord's age and infirmities. It was unnecessary. The Viscount had already regained control over his temper, and although he was still pale with wrath, he was able to say in a level voice: 'I do not forget it, ma'am. His lordship's infirmities seem to have affected his brain, and God forbid I should call a lunatic to account! If I allowed myself to follow my own inclinations I should leave this house immediately, but I am not here for any purpose of my own, but solely on behalf of an unfortunate child, who has no one but him to turn to, and so must suffer him to insult me with what patience I can muster!'

Nettlecombe, who had been scared out of his ungovernable fury, muttered something that might have been an apology, and added, in a querulous tone: 'Well, it *does* sound havey-cavey to me—and so it would to anyone!'

'It is not, however. I did not *run off* with Miss Steane from her aunt's house. Even if I were such a loose screw as to run off with any girl, you can hardly suppose that I could possibly do so after barely half-an-hour's conversation with her! I encountered her, the day after my one meeting with her, trudging along the post-road to London, quite unattended, and carrying a heavy portmanteau. I pulled up my horses, of course, and tried to discover what had led her to take such an imprudent—indeed, such an improper step! I shall not weary you with what she was induced to tell me: I will merely say that she was in great distress, and by far too young and inexperienced to have the least idea of what might be the disastrous consequences of her rashness. Her one thought was to reach *you*, sir—believing in her innocence that you would help her! Since you haven't hesitated to throw the grossest of insults at my head, I need not scruple to tell you that I didn't share her belief! I did what I could to persuade her to let me drive her back to her aunt's house, but I failed. She begged me instead to take her to London. We reached your house in the late afternoon, by which time I had seen enough of her to make me feel that no one, least of all a grandparent, could be hardhearted enough to turn her from his door. And in spite of the intemperate things you have said I still think that had you been at home, and had seen her, you must have taken pity on her. But you were not at home—which was almost as big a facer for me as it was for her! In the circumstances, I thought the best thing I could do was to take her to a very old friend of mine, and leave her in her charge until I could discover your whereabouts, and put her case before you. I trust I have now done so to your satisfaction.'

'There's only one thing she can do. She must return to her aunt,' said Nettlecombe. '*She* took the girl away from school, so it's *her* responsibility to look after her, not mine!'

'That's just what I was thinking!' nodded the lady.

'It is a waste of time to think it, ma'am: she won't go. I daresay she would liefer hire herself out as a cook-maid!'

'Well, and why shouldn't she?' demanded her ladyship, bristling. 'I'm sure it's a very respectable calling, and there's plenty of chances for her to rise higher, if she has her wits about her, and gives satisfaction!'

'What have you to say to that, sir?' asked the Viscount. 'Could you stomach the knowledge that your granddaughter was earning her bread as a servant?'

Nettlecombe uttered a brutal laugh. 'Why not? I *married* one!'

This declaration not unnaturally took Desford's breath away. He found himself bereft of words; but on my lady it had quite another effect. She rounded on Nettlecombe, and said in a trembling voice: 'I was never a servant of yours, and well you know it! I was your lady-housekeeper, and I'll thank you to remember it! The idea of you casting nasty aspersions at me! Don't you dare do so never no more, or you'll hear some home-speaking from me, my lord, and so I warn you!'

He looked a little ashamed, and more than a little apprehensive, and said hastily: 'There, don't take a pet, Maria! I didn't mean it! The thing is that Desford has nettled me into such a flame that I hardly know what I'm saying. Not but what— However, let it rest! I'll give you a new bonnet!'

This offer led to an instant reconciliation, my lady even going so far as to embrace him, exclaiming: '*That's* more like my dear old Nettle!'

'Yes, but I'll go with you to choose it, mind!' said his lordship warily. 'And as for Wilfred's brat, if you think you can palaver me into taking her into my house, Desford, I'll tell you once and for all I won't do it!'

'I don't think it. What I beg leave to suggest to you, sir, is that you should make her an allowance: enough to enable her to maintain herself respectably. Not a fortune, but an independence.'

But this proposal made Nettlecombe's eyes start alarmingly in their sockets, with as much incredulity as dismay. He said in a choked voice: 'Squander my money on that little gypsy? Do you take me for a cabbage-head?'

He received prompt support from his bride, who advised him strongly not to let himself be choused out of his blunt. She added, with great frankness, that for her part she had no notion of raking and scraping to save his blunt for him only to see it thrown away on a hurly-burly girl who had no claim on him. 'It's bad enough for you to be obliged to grease Jonas's wheels,' she said, 'and when I think of the way he's behaved to me, trying to get you to turn me off, let alone coming the nob over me, it turns me downright queasy to think of him, and that niffy-naffy wife of his, living as high as coach-horses at *our* expense!'

The Viscount picked up his hat and gloves, and said contemptuously: 'Very well, sir. If money means more to you than reputation there is nothing further to be said, and I'll take my leave of you.'

'It does!' snapped Nettlecombe. 'I care nothing for what anyone says of me—never have cared! And the sooner you take yourself off the better pleased I shall be!'

But the Viscount's words had made the bride look sharply at him, a shade of uneasiness in her face. She said, in a blustering manner: 'I'm sure there's no reason why anyone should blame my lord! No one ever blamed him for disowning the girl's father, and he was his son!'

The Viscount, who had not missed that swift, faint look of uneasiness, replied, slightly raising his brows: 'Well, that is not quite true, ma'am. It was acknowledged that he had been given great provocation, but a number of people considered that he had acted in a—let us say, in a way that was unbecoming in one who was not only a father, but a man of rank.'

'Balderdash!' ejaculated Nettlecombe, flushing. 'How do *you* know what anyone thought? You were in the schoolroom!'

'You must have forgotten, sir, that my father was one of those who did blame you,' said the Viscount gently. 'And—er—made no secret of his disapproval!'

As Lord Wroxton's disapproval had found expression in giving Nettlecombe the cut direct in full view of some dozen members of the ton, it was not surprising that the angry flush on Nettlecombe's face deepened to a purple hue. He snarled: 'Much I cared for Wroxton's opinion!' but his fingers curled themselves into claws, and he glared at Desford as though he would have liked to fix those claws round his throat.

'Furthermore,' pursued Desford relentlessly, 'whatever excuses might be found for your treatment of your son, none can be found for your behaviour towards his orphaned daughter, who is innocent of any fault, but is to become not only the victim of her father's improvidence but also of her grandfather's rancour!'

'Let 'em say what they choose! I don't care a button *what* they say!'

'They won't know anything about it!' said my lady. 'My lord don't go about much nowadays, so—' She stopped, staring at Desford, who was smiling in a very disquieting way.

'Oh, yes, they will know, ma'am!' he said. 'I pledge you my word the story will be all over town within a sennight!'

'Jackanapes! Rush-buckler!' Nettlecombe spat at him.

But at this point my lady quickly intervened, begging him not to fret himself into a fever. 'It won't do to act hasty!' she urged. 'You may not care for what people say of you, but it's my belief it's me as will be blamed! Even your friends have behaved very stiff to me, and I don't doubt but what they'd say it was my doing you wouldn't have anything to do with this girl, and that won't suit *me*, my lord, and no amount of argufying will make me say different!'

'And it won't suit me to waste my money on the girl! Next you'll be telling me it's my duty to buy her an annuity!'

'No, I shan't. It isn't to be expected that you should, nor that you should pay her an allowance, for who's to say when you might find it inconvenient to be obliged to shell out the ready—pay the allowance, I mean? I don't hold with allowances: it makes anyone fidgety to have a thing like that coming due every quarter. No, I've got a better notion in my noddle—better for the girl too! What she wants, poor little thing, is a home, and that's what you *can* give her, and without being purse-pinched. So why don't you write to her, and offer to take her into the family? I'll see to it she don't worrit you, and she won't worrit me either. In fact, the more I think of it the more I feel I should *like* to have her. She'll be company for me.'

'Take Wilfred's brat into the family?' he repeated, almost stunned.

She patted his hand. 'Well, my lord here is in the right of it when he says it ain't her fault she's Wilfred's brat. I declare I feel downright sorry for her! And if it's expense you're thinking of, Nettle, I shouldn't wonder at it if she turned out to be an economy, because it wouldn't be an extra mouth to feed, for you know I paid off Betty before we left London, thinking it was a sinful waste of money to keep a girl just to mend the linen, and wash the chandeliers, and the best china, and lend old Lattiford a hand with the silver, and that. Mind you, it's a bigger waste of money keeping a butler that's as old and infirm as what he is, but you'd have to pension him off if you sent him packing, so while he *can* work it's best for us to keep him.'

Nettlecombe, who had listened to her in gathering exasperation, said explosively: 'No, I tell you! I won't have her in my house!'

'Allow me to set your mind at rest!' said Desford. 'You will most certainly not have her in your house, sir! I didn't help her to escape from one slavery only to pitchfork her into another!'

He strode towards the door, ignoring a plea from my lady to wait. She followed him into the corridor, begging him not to take her lord's tetchiness amiss, and assuring him that he might rely on her to bring him round. 'The thing is,' she said earnestly, 'that he's out of sorts, poor dear gentleman, and no wonder, with all the kick-up there's been, thinking he was going to lose me, because that shabster, Jonas, had the impudence to set it about that I was setting my cap at him, which I never did, nor thought of! All I thought of was to make him comfortable, which I promise you I did! What's more, I was the most saving house-keeper he'd ever had! But when that Jonas took to saying I was a man-trap, and warning his pa against me—*well*! I was obliged to tell his lordship I must leave at the term, because I've got my good name to think about, haven't I? So his lordship made me an Offer, which is all the good Master Jonas got out of trying to be rid of me!' She ended on a triumphant note, but as the Viscount was wholly unresponsive, tightened her hold on his sleeve, and said ingratiatingly: 'And as for making his granddaughter a *slave*, you quite mistook my meaning, my lord! I'm sure I wouldn't ask her to do anything I wouldn't do myself— yes, and have done, times out of mind! Not that I was born to it, mind you! Oh, dear me, no! I often think my poor father would have turned in his grave if he'd lived to see the straits I was reduced to, him having been cheated out of his inheritance, like he was, and my First losing his fortune, and leaving me without a souse, which is why I was forced to earn my own bread as best I could. No one knows better than me what it means to step down from one's rightful station, so if you was thinking Miss Steane would be a *servant* in her grandpa's house you're quite beside the bridge, my lord! She'll have a good home, and not be asked to do anything any genteel girl wouldn't be expected to do to help her ma!'

'You are wasting your breath, ma'am,' he replied, inexorably removing her hand from his sleeve, and continuing his progress towards the stairs.

Baffled, she delivered a Parthian shot. 'At any hand,' she said shrilly, 'you can't say it was me that wouldn't offer the girl a home!'

# Ten

OR SEVERAL MINUTES AFTER HE LEFT LORD NETTLECOMBE'S lodging the Viscount seethed with anger, but by the time he was half-way to the High town this had diminished, and the comical side of the late interview struck him, so forcibly that the sparkling look of wrath in his eyes vanished, and the hardened lines about his mouth relaxed. As he recalled some of the things which had been said he began to chuckle; and when he pictured the scenes which must have goaded Nettlecombe to marry the most economical housekeeper he had ever employed he found that he was within ames-ace of positively liking the vulgar creature.

He wished very much that there was someone with him to share the joke: Hetta, for instance, whose sense of the ridiculous was as lively as his own. He would tell her all about it, of course, but recounting an absurd experience was not the same as sharing it. It was to be hoped she didn't make the mistake of marrying that prosy fellow whom he had found dangling after her at Inglehurst, for he wouldn't suit her at all: he was just the kind of slow-top to ask her in a puzzled voice what she meant when she made a joke. Come to think of it, none of Hetta's suitors—and, lord, how many of them there had been!—had ever seemed to him worthy of her: queer that such an intelligent girl should be unable to recognize at a glance men who were quite beneath her touch! Recalling her numerous suitors he could not bring to mind one whom he had liked. There had been several dead bores amongst them; at least two bladders, who never stopped gabbing; and any number of men who were, in his opinion, very poor sticks indeed.

These reflections had led his mind away from the immediate problem confronting him, but the recollection of it soon recurred, and put an end to any desire in him to laugh at the failure of his mission, or to speculate on the strange vagaries of females. A less determined man might have felt that he had been tipped a settler, and have thrown his towel into the ring, but the Viscount had a streak of strong determination running through his easy-going nature, and he had no intention of being beaten on this, or any other, suit. He had certainly suffered a set-back, so what he must now do was to think of some other way of providing for Cherry's future well-being. None immediately occurred to him. He wondered what she was doing, whether she was happy at Inglehurst, or whether she was too anxious to be happy; and realized with a slight sense of shock that it was now nine days since he had left her there.

Had he but known it, Cherry was blissfully happy, and only now and then thought about her future. She had fitted into her surroundings as though she had lived at Inglehurst all her life; and she seemed to take as much pleasure in making herself useful to her hostesses as in the small parties Lady Silverdale gave to her neighbours. Indeed, Henrietta thought that she took more, for her disposition was retiring, and her shyness tied her tongue, so that when she was seated at the dinner-table beside a stranger her conversation was inclined to be monosyllabic. Henrietta ascribed this to Lady Bugle's treatment. She had relegated the poor child to the background, and had so systematically impressed upon her that she was far less important than her cousins, and must never put herself forward as though she thought herself their equal, that it had become second nature to her. Henrietta hoped that she would overcome her almost morbid shrinking from strangers for such excessive shyness was, in her view, a handicap to any penniless female obliged to make her own way in the world. It was unfortunate, too, that she was noticeably more ill-at-ease with the various young gentlemen who visited the house than with their fathers. However, once she became acquainted with them she grew less self-conscious, and chatted to them quite naturally. With Sir Charles, and young Mr Beckenham, she was soon on friendly terms; but she treated Tom Ellerdine, who showed a disposition to make her the object of his youthful gallantry, with marked reserve. Henrietta could not help feeling that it was a pity.

Lady Silverdale did not agree. 'For my part,' she said, 'I think her a very pretty-behaved girl. I own, my love, it quite astonishes me that she is not in the least pert, or *coming*, as so many girls are nowadays, for one never expected a Steane to be so well-conducted, and her mama was not at all the thing. Not that I ever knew her, because she eloped with Wilfred Steane out of the schoolroom, you know, which shows the most shocking want of delicacy, and just what one would expect in any sister of that Bugle woman!'

'Dear Mama, I am perfectly ready to join you in abusing Lady Bugle, but that is going too far!' expostulated Henrietta laughingly. 'She is a horrid creature, but I'm persuaded that she is quite boringly respectable!'

'Good gracious, Hetta, how you do take one up!' Lady Silverdale complained. 'You know very well what I mean! She's an excessively underbred woman, and that, you will allow, dear little Cherry is not! I think it remarkable that she shouldn't be, for we all know what the Steanes are like, and although I never heard anything said against the Wissets they did *not* move in the first circles. I believe old Mr Wisset was an attorney, or some-

thing of the sort. And when you consider that Cherry has had
no other home than her aunt's house it has me in a puzzle to
know how she came by her pretty, modest manners. She certainly cannot have learnt them from Amelia Bugle!'

'No, I fancy she must have learnt them from Miss Fletching,'
said Henrietta. 'From what Cherry has told me, she must be
an excellent woman—and it is to Mr Wilfred Steane's credit
that he placed Cherry in her school, even if he did forget to
pay the bills!'

'Well, it may be so,' acknowledged Lady Silverdale, reluctant
to perceive any saving grace in Mr Wilfred Steane's character,
'but for my part I should rather suppose that he chose the first
school that hit his eye. And I am much inclined to think that
Cherry's manners spring from her disposition—so very amiable
and obliging, and with such delicacy of principle!—than from
any lesson Miss Fletching could have taught her. You know,
dearest, how very rarely I take a fancy to anyone, but I own I
have taken a strong fancy to Cherry, and shall miss her sadly
when she leaves us. Indeed, if Nettlecombe refuses to adopt her,
which wouldn't surprise me in the least, because he was always
known to be as close as wax, and has become positively *freakish*
of late years—I have a very good mind to keep her here!'

Henrietta, who knew well, not how rarely her mama took
fancies to people, but how frequently she did, and how inevitably
she discovered that she had been mistaken in the character of her
latest protégée, was startled into exclaiming: 'Handsomely over
the bricks, Mama, I do beg of you! You have only known Cherry
for a sennight!'

'I have known her for nine days,' replied her ladyship, with
dignity. 'And I must request you, Hetta, not to employ vulgar
slang when you are talking to me! Or to anyone, for it is not at
all becoming in you! I have not the remotest conjecture what
*handsomely over the bricks* may signify, but I collect that you have

heard Charlie say it, and I must tell you that you are very ill-advised to copy the things young men say.'

'Oh, don't blame Charlie, ma'am!' Henrietta said, her eyes alight with laughter. 'It is what Desford says, when he thinks I am about to do something rash! But I should not have said it to you, and I beg your pardon! In—in unexceptionable language, I hope that you will consider carefully before you come to any decision about Cherry.'

'Naturally I shall do so,' said Lady Silverdale. 'You may be sure of *that*!'

Henrietta was anything but sure of it, but she said no more, knowing that few things were more likely to goad Lady Silverdale into precipitate action than opposition from herself. Upon reflection she realized that she ought to have been prepared for the announcement which had startled her into uttering the slang phrase which had offended her mama's chaste ears for she had watched Cherry winning more and more approval, and had several times heard Lady Silverdale say that she couldn't conceive how she had ever contrived to exist without 'our sweet little sunbeam'. Well, there was nothing surprising in that: still less was it surprising that Lady Silverdale should be enjoying Cherry's visit, for Cherry was always ready to do whatever her kind hostess wished, and happily ran errands, unravelled tangled embroidery silks, went for tediously slow walks with her round the gardens, accompanied her on sedate drives in her landaulette, read aloud to her, and listened with unfeigned interest to her store of very dull anecdotes. These duties had hitherto fallen to Henrietta's lot, and although she had performed them cheerfully they had bored her very much, and none of them more than listening to reminiscences which had been told her many times before, and reading aloud absurdly romantic and adventurous novels, for which form of literature Lady Silverdale had an incurable passion. But three days after Cherry's arrival at Inglehurst Henrietta contracted a slight cold, which made her throat too sore for reading aloud, and she had suggested that Cherry might take her place until she had recovered from her trifling indisposition. She had apologized to Cherry for saddling her with a task which she feared she would think abominably dull, but Cherry had said that indeed she wouldn't think it dull, and the wonder was that she didn't. At least, it seemed wonderful at the outset, but it was soon brought home to Henrietta that Cherry's literary taste exactly matched Lady Silverdale's. Never having been permitted by Miss Fletching to read novels, she was instantly entranced by the specimen Henrietta gave her, entering into all the hapless heroine's alarms, adoring the hero, hating the villain, uncritically accepting every extravagance of the plot, and eagerly discussing with Lady Silverdale how the story would end. Almost as absorbing did she find the *Mirror of Fashion,* a monthly periodical to which Lady Silverdale subscribed, and was ready to pore over it for as long as Lady Silverdale pleased. It had to be admitted that with all the advantages of a pretty face, engaging manners, and sweetness of disposition, one attribute had been denied her: she was regrettably lacking in intellect. Henrietta thought that when the ingenuousness of youth left her she would be as foolish as Lady Silverdale (though probably not as indolent), and a sad bore to any man of superior sense, for she was interested only in trivialities and domestic matters, and had very little understanding of wider issues. To Henrietta, who possessed considerable force of mind, this made her no more companionable than a small child would have been, but it suited Lady Silverdale admirably, and would possibly suit some other elderly and rather silly lady just as well. But what a bleak prospect for an affectionate girl, crying out to be loved and cherished! Henrietta sighed over it, but could see no other solution to the problem of her future, if Nettlecombe refused to acknowledge her. The realization that her mother had taken it into her head to keep Cherry with her seriously dismayed her. No dependence could be placed on Lady Silverdale's continuing to dote on the girl: at any moment she might take her in dislike; and even if she did not do that she would almost certainly find her an irksome burden when the family removed to London, which they always did in the spring, and she became engaged in too many social activities to have the smallest need of any other attendant than her dresser. In London, Cherry would inevitably be regarded as that tiresome Extra Female, the bane of all hostesses, and could count herself fortunate if the sudden indisposition of one of the invited ladies led to her inclusion in some of her ladyship's dinner-parties. To suppose that Lady Silverdale's matchmaking instincts would prompt her to find a suitable husband for Cherry was to indulge fancy far beyond the bounds of probability: they were concentrated on her daughter, whose obstinate spinsterhood constituted almost the only flaw in her otherwise carefree existence. In a year or two she would no doubt be seeking a bride for her adored son, but at no time would she think it incumbent upon her to find a mate for Cherry.

The thought of her brother caused Henrietta to feel a twinge of uneasiness. It had not occurred to Lady Silverdale that he might seek distraction in his enforced stay at Inglehurst by pursuing an à suivie flirtation with Cherry, but Henrietta laboured under no delusions about him, and she knew that he had begun to look far more favourably upon Cherry than when he had first seen her. He no longer spoke contemptuously of her as a snippety-thing, but had described her to at least two of Lady Silverdale's morning visitors as a taking little puss. Henrietta did not for a moment suppose that he had any serious intention in mind; and she had a shrewd suspicion that Cherry's friendly manner towards him rose from a very proper wish to avoid offending the susceptibilities of his mother and sister, and not at all from a desire to encourage his advances. She had at first been very shy of him, but that, naturally, had worn off, as she became better acquainted with him, and it was not many days before she was able to take him very much for granted, behaving towards him with little more ceremony than she would have used towards an elder brother. She fetched and carried for him, and sought to divert him by playing cribbage and backgammon and draughts with him, or even such infantile games as span-counters, in which his superior skill was counterbalanced by his inability to use his right hand. She did these things because she was sorry for him, and anxious to help his mother and sister to keep him amused; but although she enjoyed playing such games and was young enough to be intent on proving herself a match for him, Henrietta did not think that she liked him very much. That made Henrietta sigh again. Not that she wanted Cherry to fall a victim to Charlie's lures, but she did wish that Cherry were not so indifferent to every young man she met, for her indifference, coupled as it was with a tongue-tied shyness, did not make her appear to advantage. The only men with whom she was natural and at ease were nearly all of them old enough to have fathered her; or, if not quite so middle-aged, too old to be considered as possible suitors, at all events. She certainly liked Desford, but although in years he was only ten years her senior, in experience he was at least twenty years older; and Henrietta believed (and hoped) that she regarded him in the light of a protector, not as a possible suitor. Cary Nethercott, and Sir James Radcliffe had also won her liking, but both these kindly gentlemen were in their thirties, which was probably why she didn't retire into her shell when they came to Inglehurst, but chatted away to them in the most natural style imaginable. She even told Mr Nethercott all about the lurid romance she was reading to Lady Silverdale, when she was seated beside him at dinner one evening. Henrietta heard her doing it, and was moved to silent admiration of the good-nature which made him listen with apparent interest to the tangled story that was being described to him.

As for Charlie, she had little doubt that if some dashing beauty were to come within his ken he would have no thoughts to spare for Cherry. Unfortunately, there were no dashing beauties living in the vicinity, and very few unattached young females of any description. Whether it was unfortunate that his particular cronies, none of whom hailed from Hertfordshire, were either disporting themselves at Brighton, or had retired to their parental homes in distant parts of the country, to recover from the ravages to their constitutions and purses caused by too many sprees, jollifications, and revel-routs, was a moot point. Lady Silverdale was for ever saying that if only two or three of his friends lived within visiting-distance they could have ridden over to entertain him; and she even went so far as to suggest to him that he should invite one of them to spend a week or two at Inglehurst. He spurned the notion, saying ungraciously that his friends would think it curst flat to be stuck down in the country with nothing to do all day, and nothing to enliven the evenings but short whist, or half-guinea commerce. Having uttered this disagreeable speech, he found that his sister had raised her eyes from her book and was steadily regarding him from under lifted brows. He coloured, and begged his mother's pardon, saying: 'I didn't mean to be uncivil, ma'am, but you don't understand how it is! I mean—oh, dash it, how could it be possible to invite anyone to visit me when I can't ride, or drive, or play billiards, or—or *anything?*'

Lady Silverdale saw the force of this argument; but as she continued to regret it for the next twenty minutes Henrietta could hardly blame Charlie for dragging himself up from the sofa, and walking out of the room.

She was sorry for him, but she had suspected long since that his haggard appearance and slow recovery from his injuries were due not so much to his accident, but to the dissipated life he had been leading, in the company of those choice spirits who, in her private opinion, belonged to a fast, rackety set, and were rapidly ruining his character. The suspicion had been confirmed by the Squire, who had visited him two days after his accident, and had told her bluntly that it was just as well that the young ram-stam *had* knocked himself up. He was one of Charlie's trustees, and had been intimately acquainted with both him and his sister all their lives, and he saw no need to mince his words. He said that what Charlie wanted was a long repairing lease. 'Been going the pace, m'dear: only have to look at him to know that! I warned your mother he was too callow to be let loose on the town, but all she would do was to talk gibble-gabble about not keeping him tied to her apron-strings, and having complete confidence in him, and a lot more to that tune. "All very well," I told her, "if the boy's father were alive, or he had elder brothers, or a *male* guardian, to tell him how he should go on, and warn him against the things no female knows anything about, but—" Oh, well! No use crying over spilt milk, so I'll say no more. Though how your father, as shrewd a man as ever I knew, could have allowed her ladyship to bamboozle him into appointing her to be Charlie's guardian—Well, well, my tongue runs away with me, but you're a sensible girl, Hetta, and you won't take it amiss! We must hope that this latest bit of folly will have taught Charlie a lesson!' He refreshed himself with a pinch of snuff, and added, in a heartening tone: 'No reason why he shouldn't turn out to be as good a man as his father! Most codlings take time to find their feet, y'know, Hetta! Best thing for him would be to get himself buckled to a nice girl! He's been philandering after dashing women of fashion, but there's no harm in that! He don't have petticoat affairs with straw damsels, and you may take it from me that's true, for I've had my eye on him, ever since he set up for himself in London!'

'What can I do, Sir John?' she asked straitly.

'Can't do anything!' he answered, restoring his snuff-box to the capacious pocket of his riding-coat. 'Just try what you can to keep him amused, so that he don't run off before he's in better point than he is now!'

With this piece of advice she had to be satisfied, but she found it almost impossible to follow. The only things that amused Charlie were the country-sports which he was debarred from pursuing, and almost every variety of gaming. To do him justice, he enjoyed, for their own sake, such games as offered a challenge to his skill, but Henrietta, who played a good game at chess, had so little card-sense that it bored him to play with her. Cherry, on the other hand, had neither the desire nor the ability to master the intricacies of chess, but she possessed a certain quickness which enabled her to grasp the rules and the objects of any card game he taught her, and to play well enough to make him declare that it wouldn't be long before she became a dashed dangerous opponent.

'Such a good thing, dearest!' Lady Silverdale confided to her daughter. 'At last we have hit upon something that keeps him tolerably well entertained! Gentlemen, you know, always like to *instruct* one, but they are much inclined to be vexed when people like you and me, my love, show no aptitude, or, at any hand, don't instantly comprehend what they tell us. What a fortunate circumstance it is that dear little Cherry has a turn for cards! I declare I am positively grateful to Desford for having brought her to me!'

But two days later Cherry's star suffered a temporary eclipse, when the most longstanding of Lady Silverdale's cicisbeos was so ill-advised as to beg her to bestow on him one of the roses she was carrying into the house. With playful gallantry he insisted that she should put it into his buttonhole with her own fair hands, saying that it would smell the sweeter. Since she regarded him in the light of a grandparent, which indeed he was, she complied with his requests, but could not help giggling a little at the fulsome compliment he had paid her. Lady Silverdale, on the other hand, was not amused; and for an anxious moment Henrietta feared that Cherry's popularity had already come to an end. Happily, Lady Silverdale's faithful admirer had the wit to say (after one look at her stiffening countenance) that he was glad Cherry had gone into the house, because he never knew what to say to chits of her age, adding, as he sat down again on the rustic seat beside my lady: 'Now we can be comfortable together, my lady!' This mollified her so much that instead of scolding Cherry she merely warned her not to encourage strange gentlemen to flirt with her. But even this mild reproof made startled tears spring to Cherry's eyes as she exclaimed in trembling accents: 'Oh, no, no! Indeed I didn't! I thought he was being kind to me because you had asked him to be, ma'am!' She added imploringly, as the tears coursed down her face: 'Don't be vexed with me! Pray don't be vexed with me, dear, dear Lady Silverdale! I can't bear you to be displeased with me, for I wouldn't displease you for the world, after all your goodness to me!'

Much touched by this speech, Lady Silverdale melted completely, to the extent of shedding a few tears herself; and within the hour told her dresser, when that jealous spinster uttered a sly criticism of Cherry, that she was a nasty, ill-natured creature, and if she ever again dared to speak of Miss Steane as *That* Miss Steane she would find herself turned off without a character. Upon which, Cardle too burst into tears, but as this display of sensibility was accompanied by lamentations that her own virtues should go unrecognized, and a pious hope that my lady would learn before it was too late who were her real friends, Lady Silverdale was easily able to refrain from succumbing to her own tendency to become lachrymose upon the smallest provocation. She accepted an apology from Cardle, but with chilly dignity; and immediately went off to tell Henrietta that Cardle was growing to be intolerably bumptious, and that if it weren't for the circumstances of her being such an excellent dresser she would be much inclined to get rid of her. Henrietta knew, of course, that nothing would prevail upon her to put this threat into execution, but her mother's account of the painful scene which had taken place, made her heart sink. Nothing, she thought, could have more surely increased Cardle's jealousy of one whom she persisted in believing to be her rival. She embarked on the task of peace-making, soothing her ruffled parent by agreeing that Cardle was detestably uppish, but saying that she was so devoted to her mistress that she resented it if even Mama's own daughter dared to perform any service for her which she regarded as her sole prerogative. 'Do, pray, say something kind to her, Mama, when she puts you to bed tonight! She'll cry herself to sleep, if she thinks you are still angry with her!'

These tactics succeeded very well with Lady Silverdale, but Henrietta failed to induce any softening of Cardle's heart towards Cherry. Not even a casual reference to the probability that Cherry's visit would soon come to an end had the least effect on Cardle. 'And the sooner the better, miss!' she said tartly. '*One* thing's certain! The day my lady invites her to *live* here is the day I leave this house! I pity you, Miss Hetta, having your nose put out of joint by that designing little hussy, and being taken in by her coaxing ways, every bit as much as my poor deluded mistress is! And it's no good telling me I've got no business to say she's a designing hussy, which I wouldn't have presumed to do if you hadn't opened the subject, for I know what I know, and I hope and pray you won't regret your kindness to her!'

Henrietta went down to dinner fervently hoping, for her part, that Desford's return from Harrowgate would not be long delayed.

In fact, it was delayed for longer than the Viscount had antici-
pated, for his journey south was not attended by the good fortune
which had made his northward journey so speedy. A series of
mishaps befell him, the most serious of which, the loss of a tyre,
kept him kicking his heels for a day and a half, this accident
occurring on the first day out from Harrowgate, which happened
to be a Saturday, midway between Chesterfield and Mansfield. By
the time the chaise bumped its way into Mansfield it was too late
for the necessary repair to be effected, and on the Sunday the
premises of both the wheelwright and the black-smith were
found to be closed: the one because its owner was a stern opposer
of Sunday Travel; the other because the smith had gone off to
spend the day with his married sister. It was not until Monday
morning was merging into Monday afternoon that a new tyre
was fitted to the wheel, and the Viscount was able to proceed on
his way. And then (proving to him his belief that his luck had run
out) one of his wheelers went dead lame, so that his progress to
the next post-house more nearly resembled a funeral cortège than
the swift journey of a gentleman of wealth and fashion. What
with this, and several minor hindrances, it was four days before he
reached Dunstable, where he decided to put up for the night,
since there were still almost thirty miles to cover to Inglehurst,
and he had no wish to arrive there long after the dinner-hour.

So it was not until a fortnight after he had deposited Cherry
at Inglehurst that Henrietta, a little before noon, was at last gratified by having him ushered into her presence. Grimshaw
announced him, in a sepulchral voice, and she started up out of
her chair in front of the writing-desk, exclaiming impulsively:
'Oh, Des, I am so thankful you've come at last!'

'Good God, Hetta, what's amiss?' he demanded, brought up
short in his advance across the room.

'Nothing!—that is to say, I *hope* nothing, but I am much
afraid that things are beginning to go amiss.' He had taken her

hands in his, and kissed them both, and was still holding them in his strong clasp, but she gently drew them away, and said, scanning his face: 'Your errand hasn't prospered, has it?'

He shook his head. 'No. Nettlecombe has become an April-gentleman!'

Her eyes widened. '*Married?*' she asked incredulously.

'That's it: leg-shackled to his housekeeper—oh, I beg her pardon! his *lady*-housekeeper!'

'Ah!' she said, with a twinkle of perfect comprehension. 'No doubt she told you so herself!'

He grinned at her. 'No, she told Nettlecombe, when *he* told me that he had married his cook. She said she would thank him to remember it, too, and I don't doubt he will. Oh, Hetta, you can't think how much I longed for you to be present at that interview! You must have laughed yourself into stitches!'

She moved to the sofa, and sat down, patting the place beside her. 'Tell me!' she invited.

He did tell her, and she appreciated the story just as he had known she would. But he ended on a sober note, when, having described the final scene, in the corridor, he paused for an instant, before saying abruptly: 'Hetta, I *could* not thrust that unfortunate child into such a household!'

'No,' she agreed, her own brow as troubled as his. 'Only—Des, what is to be done with her? Mama said, a week ago, that if Nettlecombe repudiated her she had a good mind to keep her here, but—it wouldn't do—I *know* it wouldn't do! It is always the same when Mama takes a violent fancy to anyone! At first she thinks the new treasure perfect, and then she begins to perceive faults in her—and even when they are quite trivial faults she exaggerates them in her mind, and—which is worse!—remembers them, and adds them on to the next error her wretched favourite falls into!'

'Good God, has it come to that? Poor Cherry!'

'No, no, not yet!' she assured him. 'But she has begun to criticize her—oh, not unkindly! merely noticing little innocent
habits, or tricks of speech, and saying that she wishes Cherry
would rid herself of them. And that odious woman of hers is so
jealous of Cherry that she never loses an opportunity to drop
poison into Mama's ears. So far, she hasn't succeeded in turning
Mama against poor Cherry, but I own to you, Des, that I can't
persuade myself that—'

'Don't tease yourself!' he interrupted. 'There can be no question of Cherry's remaining here! I never for a moment had such
a solution to the problem in my mind. I had hoped to have
left her with you only for a very few days, but I didn't discover
Nettlecombe's whereabouts until Monday of last week, and even
when I did discover that he had gone to Harrowgate I couldn't
induce his man of business to divulge his exact direction, and was
obliged to spend the better part of two days scouring the town
for him.'

'Oh, poor Des! No wonder you are looking so tired!'

'Am I? Well, if I am it's only because I had the most devilish
journey up from Yorkshire,' he said cheerfully. 'No sooner did
we get over one check than we fell into another, which is why
I'm so late showing my front, as Horace would say. However,
I've had time to decide what I had best do for Cherry—and
that's the most urgent matter I want you to consider, my best
of friends!'

The door opened. 'Mr Nethercott!' announced Grimshaw.

Cary Nethercott trod into the room, but checked at sight of
the Viscount, and said: 'I beg pardon! Grimshaw must have misunderstood me! I enquired for Lady Silverdale, and he ushered
me into this room, where—where I can only trust that I am not
intruding, Miss Hetta!'

'Not at all,' she responded, rising, and shaking hands with
him. 'You have already met Lord Desford, haven't you?'

The gentlemen exchanged bows. Mr Nethercott said pains-takingly that he had indeed had that pleasure, and the Viscount said nothing at all. Mr Nethercott then explained he had ridden over to bring Lady Silverdale his copy of the last number of the *New Monthly Magazine*, which contained an interesting article which he had mentioned to her ladyship on the occasion of his last visit, and which she had expressed a desire to read.

'How very kind of you!' said Henrietta. 'She has gone for a stroll in the shrubbery, with Miss Steane.'

'Oh, then I will take it to her myself!' he said, his cheeks slightly reddening. 'I shall hope to see you again presently, Miss Hetta!' He then said: 'Your servant, sir!' and bowed himself out of the room.

The Viscount, who had been eyeing him with disfavour, hardly waited for the door to be shut before demanding: 'Does that fellow *live* at Inglehurst, Hetta?'

'No,' replied Henrietta calmly. 'He lives at Marley House.'

'Well, he seems to be here every time *I* come to visit you!' said the Viscount irritably.

She wrinkled her brow, and, after apparently cudgelling her memory, said, with a wholly spurious air of innocence: 'But had you met him before you came to visit us on your way to Hazelfield?'

The Viscount ignored this home-question, and said: 'I wonder which of us he thought he was hoaxing with his gammon about the *New Monthly*? Lord, what a fimble-famble!' He did not resume his seat, but glanced frowningly down at Henrietta, and said, with unaccustomed asperity: 'I can't conceive why you—No, never mind! What were we saying when that fellow interrupted us?'

'You were about to tell me what you have decided will be the best thing to do for Cherry,' she replied. 'The most urgent question to be considered—or, rather, which you wish me to consider.'

'Yes, so I was. There are other things I should wish to talk about, but until I've provided for her Cherry must be my only concern.'

'Provided for her?' she repeated, her eyes lifting quickly to his face.

'Yes, of course. What else can I do but try to establish her comfortably? It was no doing of mine when she ran away from Maplewood, but when I drove her to London I became responsible for her: there's no getting away from that, Hetta! Good God, what a shabster I should be if I abandoned her now!'

'Very true. What scheme have you in mind?' she asked. 'I have thought that—that marriage is the only answer to the problem, only—her parentage, and her want of fortune must stand in the way—don't you think?'

He nodded, but said: 'Not in the way of a man who fell in love with her, and had no need of a rich wife. But that's for the future: my concern is for the immediate present. I'm going to Bath, to try if I can persuade Miss Fletching to help Cherry. Has she spoken to you about her? She was at Miss Fletching's school, and talked to me about her on the way to London, saying how kind she had been.'

'Yes, indeed she has, and most affectionately, but when I suggested to her that she might return to that school, as a teacher, rather than hire herself out as a companion, she said Miss Fletching would have offered her that position if she had had enough learning, or enough skill on the pianoforte to teach music. Only she hadn't. And I am afraid, Des, that that is true. Her only skill is in stitchery. She has the most amiable disposition in the world, but she is not at all bookish, you know. If Miss Fletching were to offer to take her I am very sure she would refuse, because she feels herself to be under a heavy obligation to her already.'

'I know she does. And if I were to pay Miss Fletching the debt that is owing to her—'

'No, Desford!' Henrietta said stringently. 'You mustn't do that! She is by far too proud to countenance such a thing!'

'Not, surely, if she supposed I had prevailed upon Nettlecombe to tip over the dibs!'

'If she believed you she would write to thank him.'

'I should tell her that he had paid Miss Fletching on condition that she neither wrote to him nor attempted to see him ever again. It is exactly what he *would* say, too!'

She smiled, but shook her head. 'It won't do. Only consider what an uncomfortable situation she would be in if ever it became known that you had paid Miss Fletching to give her a home! You must consider your own situation as well: you would compromise yourself as much as Cherry. You know what all the tattle-boxes would say! And it is useless to suppose that the secret wouldn't leak out, because you may depend upon it that it would.'

The smile was reflected in his eyes, but he said ruefully: 'I've wondered about that. I hoped you would tell me I was being absurd—but I had a pretty shrewd notion you wouldn't! You're right, of course. So I shall lay the whole case before Miss Fletching, and ask her if she knows of anyone residing in Bath who would be glad to employ Cherry. There must be scores of elderly invalids there: whenever I've visited the place it has always seemed to me to teem with decrepit old ladies! And if she must seek such a post I think Bath would be the best place for her. She would have Miss Fletching to turn to, and I know she has other acquaintances in the town whom she would be able to visit.'

The tiny crease vanished from between her brows; she exclaimed: 'Yes, that would be the very thing for her! But not, Des, if *you* recommend her to a prospective employer!'

'I thought it wouldn't be long before you made me stand the roast, my sweet wit-cracker,' he observed appreciatively. 'How fortunate it is that you should have warned me—such a slow-top as I am!'

She laughed. 'No, no, not a *slow-top*, Ashley! But dreadfully imprudent when you take one of your quixotic notions into your head!'

'Lord, Hetta, you must have windmills in your own head! I've never done such a thing in my life! Now, stop funning! If I'm to post off to Bath tomorrow, I've precious little time to waste—and, all things considered, I fancy it will be as well if I leave from here before Cherry comes in. I should be obliged to tell her what I mean to do, and if she didn't try to stop me, but liked the scheme, I don't wish to raise what might prove to be a false hope.'

'But she's bound to know that you've been here!' protested Henrietta. 'What am I to say to her, pray?'

'Tell her that I called here, but was unable to stay more than a few minutes, because I have an urgent appointment in London, and only broke my journey to tell her that although I couldn't bring old Nettlecombe up to scratch I haven't abandoned her, but—but have now hit upon a fresh plan for her relief. Which I didn't disclose to you, for fear it might not come to anything!'

'Banbury man!'

'No. I do fear it may come to nothing! By the by, has Lady Bugle tried to make her return to Maplewood?'

'No—and that puts me in mind of something I must tell you! Lady Bugle doesn't know where she is, because when I suggested to Cherry that she should write to her she became so much agitated that I let the matter drop. But I should warn you that although Lady Bugle doesn't know she's here she does know that you had something to do with her flight. And that brings me to another thing I must tell you. Lord and Lady Wroxton know she is at Inglehurst.'

'Oh, my God!' he ejaculated. 'As though I hadn't enough to deal with! Who was the tale-pitcher who carried that news to Wolversham?'

'My dear Ashley, you cannot, surely, have forgotten how inevitably the smallest piece of news flies round the county! Steward's gossip, but in this case it reached Wolversham by way of one of the chambermaids, who is the daughter of our head groom. Lady Wroxton gave her leave to come to Inglehurst, on the occasion of her parents' silver wedding—and *so* you can wish for no further explanation!'

He was regarding her intently. 'That's not the whole story, is it?'

'No, not quite. Lord and Lady Wroxton visited us two days ago.'

'If my father undertook a drive of sixteen miles, either his gout has spent itself, or he must have supposed me to be on the verge of disgracing him!' interjected the Viscount.

'Well, he was walking with a stick, but I think he *is* much improved in health,' said Henrietta, forgiving this rude interruption for the sake of the balm it applied to her sorely troubled heart. 'They came to enquire after Charlie—at least, that was what Lord Wroxton told Mama—but their real purpose, I am very sure, was to discover the truth of the story they had heard. I didn't have much conversation with Lord Wroxton, but your mama made an excuse to take me apart, and she asked me, without any roundaboutation, to tell her if it was true that you had brought Cherry here, and, if so, why you had done so. She said that I need not scruple to open my budget to her, because she was very sure that you had a good reason for having done so. Des, I do like your mama so much!'

'Yes, so do I,' he agreed cordially. 'She's a right one! What did you tell her?'

'I told her the truth, exactly as you told it to me. And she then disclosed to me that she had received a letter from your aunt

Emborough, saying that Lady Bugle had called upon her, demanding to know what *you* had done with Cherry. It seems that one of her daughters—I can't recall her name, but I know it was most extraordinary—'

'They all have extraordinary names—all five of 'em!'

'Good gracious! Well, this one seems to have been on the listen when you talked to Cherry, that night at the ball; and when it was discovered that Cherry had run away, she put it into Lady Bugle's head that she had gone off with you! How Lady Bugle can have believed such a nonsensical story I can't conceive, but apparently she did, and at once drove over to Hazelfield to demand of Lady Emborough what were your intentions! Lady Emborough wrote to your mama that she had laughed to scorn the idea that you had had anything to do with Cherry's flight, and had assured Lady Bugle that so far from stealing Cherry away from Maplewood at dawn you had been eating breakfast at Hazelfield at ten o'clock. But she also wrote that she was burning to know whether you *had* had anything to do with Cherry's escape, because she recalled that it had seemed to her that you were much more interested in Cherry than in her cousin, who is a singularly beautiful girl.'

'Lucasta,' he nodded. 'I was, but never mind that! My aunt wrote to my mother, you say. She hasn't divulged any of this to my father, has she?'

'No, and your mother hasn't shown him her letter. But it was he who first heard the local tittle-tattle, and I have a very shrewd notion that it was he who insisted on coming to visit us, to discover how true it was. Or, rather, that your mama should do so! You know what he is, Des!'

'None better! He would think it beneath him to betray the least interest in the exploits of his sons—to anyone, of course, but the sons themselves!'

'Exactly so!' she said, with a twinkle. 'Most fortunately, this visit was paid when Mama was feeling particularly pleased with

Cherry, for having found a lace flounce which was thought to have been thrown away years ago, so I am quite certain she must have spoken of her to Lord Wroxton with the warmest approbation!'

'Did he see Cherry?'

'Yes, certainly he did—but whether he liked her or not I don't know! He was perfectly civil to her, at all events.'

'That's nothing to judge by,' said Desford. 'He would be, even if he had taken her in dislike. Well, there's nothing for it: I shall have to sleep at Wolversham tonight, which means a further delay. I'm sorry for it, Hetta, but you see how I'm fixed, don't you? I don't ask you if you are willing to keep Cherry here for a few more days, because I know what your answer would be. Bless you, my dear!' He possessed himself of her hands, and again kissed them, and with no more words took his departure.

# Eleven

THE VISCOUNT'S RECEPTION AT WOLVERSHAM WAS unexpectedly benign. It did not surprise him that Pedmore should greet him with a beaming smile, and say, as he relieved him of his hat and his gloves: 'Well, my lord, this is a pleasant surprise!' because he knew that Pedmore held him, and both his brothers, in deep affection; but he smiled a little wryly when Pedmore said: 'His lordship *will* be pleased to see you, sir! My lady is taking her afternoon rest, but you will find his lordship in the library. Will you be making a long stay, my lord?'

'No: only one night,' the Viscount replied. 'Will you give orders for the housing of the post-boys? But of course you will!'

'Of *course* I will, my lord!' said Pedmore fondly.

The Viscount, having assured himself, by a swift glance at the Chippendale mirror which hung in the hall, that the folds of his neckcloth had not become disarranged, or his shining locks ruffled—two possibilities certain to incur censure from his father—trod resolutely towards the double-doors which opened into the library. He paused for a moment before entering the room, bracing himself to face what he felt sure (in spite of Pedmore's encouraging words) would be a pretty sulphurous reception; but when Lord Wroxton looked up from the journal he was perusing to see who had come into the room he said nothing more alarming than: 'Ha! Is that you, Desford? Glad to see you, my boy!'

Admirably overcoming his astonishment, the Viscount crossed the floor to the wing-chair in which my lord was sitting, dutifully kissed the hand which was held out to him, and said, with his attractive smile: 'Thank you, sir! For my part, *I* am very glad to see *you*, with your foot out of cotton at last! Are you in as plump currant as you look to be?'

'Oh, I'm in pretty good point!' said his lordship boastfully. 'The last time I saw you you said I was all skin and whipcord, jackanapes, but damme if you didn't nick the nick! It'll be a long trig before you step into my shoes!'

'So I should hope!' retorted the Viscount. 'Don't try to bamboozle *me* into thinking you're in your dotage, and are likely to stick your spoon in the wall at any moment, because I know to a day how old you are, sir!'

The Earl, apostrophizing him as an impudent whipster, told him that if he thought he could talk in such an improper style to his father he would very soon learn how mistaken he was; but he was secretly rather pleased, as he always was (except when his temper was exacerbated by gout) when any of his sons showed themselves to be full of what he called proper spunk. So, having, for form's sake, read the Viscount a brief scold, he bade him sit down, and tell him what he had been doing since he was last at Wolversham.

'That's what I've come to do,' said the Viscount. 'And since I've no more liking for beating about the bush than you have, sir, I'll tell you at once that I've driven over from Inglehurst, where I learned of your visit there.'

'I thought as much!' said the Earl. 'Come to beg me to help you out of this scrape you've got yourself into, have you?'

'No, nothing of that sort,' responded Desford. 'Merely to give you a round tale, which—since I understand you learned by way of the backstairs of Cherry Steane's presence at Inglehurst, and that it was I who took here there—I'm tolerably certain you haven't yet heard.'

'I'm well aware of that!' said his father, his eyes kindling. 'And before you say any more, Desford, let me tell you that I set no store by servants' gossip—least of all when it concerns any of my sons!'

The Viscount smiled at him. 'Of course you don't, sir. But it did send you to Inglehurst to discover what I *had* been doing to give rise to such gossip, didn't it? I don't blame you: it must have seemed to you that I was up to my chin in some devilish havey-cavey doings. Hetta could have told you why I placed Cherry in her care, but she says you didn't ask her any questions at all.'

'Do you imagine that I would ask her, or anyone else, prying questions about my sons?' demanded the Earl, bristling. 'Upon my word, Desford, if that's the opinion you hold of me you have gone your length!'

'I know you far too well, Papa, to hold any such opinion,' replied the Viscount imperturbably. 'For which reason I've thought it best to open the whole budget to you myself.'

'Then cut line and do so!' commanded his father sternly.

Thus encouraged, Desford disclosed to him, in unvarnished terms, the history of the past two weeks. The Earl listened to him in silence, and with a frown drawing his brows together over his hard, piercing eyes. It did not relax when the Viscount came to the end of his recital, but all he said was: 'In the briars, aren't you?'

'I may be in the briars,' retorted Desford, 'but I'm not at Point Non-Plus, sir, believe me!'

The Earl grunted. 'What do you mean to do if this school-dame you talk about don't come up to scratch?'

'Try a fresh cast!'

The Earl grunted again, and his frown deepened. After a long pause, during which he bore all the appearance of being engaged in a struggle with himself, he said, as though the words were being forced out of him: 'You're of age, you're independent of me, you can please yourself, but—I beg of you, Desford, don't think yourself obliged, in honour, to marry the girl!'

The Viscount said gently: 'I don't think it, sir, for I have in no way compromised her. But I do think that I am bound, in honour, to befriend her.'

His father nodded, but said, in sudden exasperation: 'I wish to God you had left Sophronia's house an hour earlier!'

'Well,' said Desford, with a twisted smile, 'between ourselves, sir, so do I! At least—No, I don't wish it, when I think of what might have befallen that pretty, foolish child if I hadn't overtaken her on the road. But I certainly wish I hadn't accepted my aunt's invitation to stay at Hazelfield!'

'No good ever yet came from crying over spilt milk, so we'll leave that! You've got yourself into a rare bumble-bath, but it might have been worse.' He pulled his snuff-box out of his pocket, and helped himself to a pinch. He then said abruptly: 'I've met the girl. I don't scruple to own to you that I went over to Inglehurst for that purpose, and I'm glad I did, for I saw at a glance that she isn't the sort of highflyer *you* dangle after.'

Desford laughed. 'Pray, sir, how do you know what sort of highflyers I dangle after?'

'I know more than you think, my boy!' said his lordship, grimly pleased with himself. 'When I first heard of this business, I was afraid you'd lost your head over the girl, and meant to become riveted to her. You wouldn't have taken a lightskirt to the Silverdales. And if you were meaning to become a tenant-for-life you wouldn't have brought her here, for you know well I'd do my utmost to prevent your marrying into *that* family! Another possibility was that she'd snared you—Yes, yes, I know you've plenty of rumgumption, but wiser men than you have been trapped by designing females! To tell you the truth, I was prepared to buy her off; but I cut my wisdoms before you were born, and it didn't take me more than a couple of minutes to realize that she was nothing but a schoolroom miss—pretty enough, but not your style of female, and damned shy into the bargain! So now, Desford, perhaps you'll have the goodness to tell me why you didn't bring her here, instead of planting her on Lady Silverdale?'

The Viscount, who had foreseen that this question would sooner or later be shot at him, flung up a hand, in the gesture of a fencer acknowledging a hit, and said, with a comical look of guilt: 'Peccavi, Papa! I didn't dare to!'

His father gave a crack of laughter, which he instantly suppressed, saying: 'I suppose I must consider it *some* comfort that in spite of your faults you are at least honest! I collect you dared not bring her here for fear that I might be so lost to all sense of propriety as to have driven the pair of you out of the house. Much obliged to you, Desford!'

'Papa, how *can* you rip up at me so unkindly?' said Desford reproachfully. 'I thought nothing of the sort—as well you know!—but I did think that it would make you as cross as crabs if I saddled you and Mama with Wilfred Steane's daughter. If you tell me that I was wrong, I have nothing to do but to beg your pardon for having so wickedly misjudged you—but *was* I wrong, sir?'

The Earl eyed him in fulminating silence for several minutes, but at last replied, in the voice of one driven into the last ditch: 'No, damn you!'

'If I'm honest,' said Desford, smiling at him, 'it's an inherited virtue, sir!'

'Mawworm!' said his lordship, concealing under this opprobrious word his gratification. 'Don't think you can flummery *me*!' He then palliated his severity by saying, after a reflective moment: 'Well, well, I don't mean to pinch at you, so we'll say no more on *that* head! All I will say is that if you find yourself at the end of your rope over this business come to me! I may be outdated, and gout-ridden, but I still know one point more than the devil!'

'Several points more than the devil, sir!' said Desford. 'I should most certainly come to you if I reached the end of my rope.'

His lordship nodded, apparently satisfied, for the next thing he said was: 'To think of old Nettlecombe's having fallen into parson's mousetrap at his time of life! Did you say that he'd married his housekeeper?'

Thus it came about that when Lady Wroxton entered the library half-an-hour later she found father and son on the best of good terms. Indeed, the first sound she heard when she opened the door was a shout of laughter from Desford, to whom his father was describing, in highly coloured terms, what had been his own experiences in Harrowgate. She was not very much surprised, for she had considerable faith in Desford's ability to deal with his father, and she knew that however violently her lord might deny the imputation, Desford was the son nearest to his heart.

My lord greeted her genially, saying: 'Ah, here you are, my lady! Now, come in, and tell Desford if I wasn't poisoned by those stinking waters at Harrowgate!'

'Well, they certainly made you extremely sick,' she said. 'But you only drank a very small quantity, you know, and there's no saying that they wouldn't have done you good if only we could have prevailed upon you to persevere.' As she spoke, she warmly embraced Desford, who had risen at her entrance, and had crossed the floor towards her, to put his arms round her in a breath-taking hug. She kissed him, but pinched his chin as well, saying, as she looked lovingly up into his handsome face: 'So now you've turned into a knight-errant, I hear! What next will you do, dearest?'

He laughed, but my lord said that he forbade her to give the boy a scold. 'He has made a clean breast of the affair to me, my love, and I have said all that was necessary, so there's an end to it! No one,' he added, with absolute conviction, 'can say that I am one to ride grub!'

'No, my dear,' she said gravely, but with Desford's smile lurking in her eyes. She let Desford lead her to a chair, and gave his hand a little squeeze before she let it go, and said: 'I had a comfortable cose with Hetta, Ashley, and I collect, from what she told me, that your protégée is a very amiable and well-conducted girl, which, I own, surprised me, and makes me think her mama must have had more delicacy of principle than one would have supposed—recalling the circumstances of her marriage—for Wilfred Steane had no principles at all. It seems that Lady Silverdale has taken a great fancy to her, and is much inclined to invite her to stay at Inglehurst, but Hetta thinks it will not answer.'

'I know she does, ma'am, and I agree with her.'

'A pity,' she said, in her calm way. 'However, I daresay Hetta is right. So what do you mean to do with the poor little creature?'

He told her what his plan was, and she accepted it, merely saying that if any other recommendation of Cherry to a possible employer than Miss Fletching's was needed, she would be very happy to supply it. After that no more was said on the subject, my lord demanding to know what she thought of old Nettlecombe's being trapped into marriage by his housekeeper, and bidding Desford tell her all about his Harrowgate adventures.

Nothing occurred to mar the harmony of the evening, and when his lordship said goodnight to Desford outside his bedroom, he was in perfect charity with him, partly because he was so much relieved to know that his heir was not contemplating matrimony with the daughter of a man whom he had no hesitation in saying was the greatest rascal he had ever known, and partly because he had succeeded in winning two out of the three rubbers of picquet he had played with him.

Before he left for London on the following day Desford was able to have some private conversation with his mother, while Lord Wroxton was engaged with his bailiff. She took him to see the improvements she had made in the rose-garden, and as they strolled down the walks together he asked her, lifting a quizzical eyebrow at her, whether he had her to thank for the welcome accorded to him by his father.

'No, no, Ashley! I didn't utter a word in your defence!' she assured him. 'Indeed, I said I would never have believed it of you, and was never more shocked in my life!'

'What a *very* sure card you are, Mama!' he said appreciatively. 'In fact, I did owe my pardon to you!'

She smiled, but shook her head. 'You may always be sure of his pardon, my dear, however much you may have vexed him. But perhaps you might not have won it as quickly if I had been so gooseish as to have tried to plead your cause, for nothing, you know, makes Papa more obstinate than opposition, and he *was* very angry. You'll own that he can scarcely be blamed! The intelligence that his eldest son had apparently formed a close connection with a member of a family which he holds in the greatest contempt came as a severe shock to him.'

He nodded, grimacing. 'Yes, I knew he would fly up into the boughs if he heard that I was having any dealings whatsoever with a Steane, which was why I hoped he never *would* hear of it. Do you wonder why I took her to Hetta, instead of bringing her here? It wasn't that I doubted *your* understanding of the case, I promise you! But his I did! Recollect, too, Mama, that I was already in his black books! He told me, on the occasion of my last visit, that he didn't wish to see my face again, and, from what Simon told me, when I ran smash into him at Inglehurst on the day I took Cherry there, his temper had not improved!'

'Alas, no!' she sighed. 'Poor Simon! I was so sorry for him, and he bore it all so patiently! But I was sorry for Papa too, because whenever he rakes any of you down, and says things he doesn't in the least mean, he is always thrown into gloom afterwards, and wishes he hadn't been so mifty. Not, of course, that he would admit it—though he did say after your last visit, dearest, that if you supposed he meant it when he told you he never wanted to see your face again you must be a bigger mutton-head than he had thought possible. He assured me that there was no occasion for me to worry about it, since he hadn't a doubt you'd come back very shortly—not that *he* cared a rush how long you stayed away! So you must never think that he doesn't hold you in affection!'

He burst out laughing. 'Proof positive, Mama!'

'Well, of course it is! You know his way, Ashley! He would think it shocking weakness to betray to any of you how dearly he loves you! But I must say that nothing could have been more unfortunate than that you and Simon should have chanced to pay us visits at just that time. He was sadly out of frame, you know, not only because his gout was paining him so much, but because the new medicine which had been prescribed for him didn't suit his constitution at all. I'm bound to say that it did do his gout good, which was why he persevered with it, but it had a very lowering effect on him, so that I was glad when our good doctor substituted for it a diet-drink of dock-roots, which suits him much better.' She smiled, and said: 'But seeing you, and having made his peace with you, will have done him more good than all the medicines in the world.'

He glanced quickly down at her. 'Is that a hint to me that it's my duty to make Wolversham my headquarters, ma'am? I have a great regard for my father—indeed, I think few men have a better father!—but I couldn't live with him!'

'Well, I don't think he could live with you either,' she replied composedly. 'You would be certain to rub against each other, for you are both so dreadfully determined! You have only to go on in just the same way, giving us a look-in every now and then, and as long as you don't give him cause to suspect you of being on the brink of an imprudent marriage he will be very well pleased with you!'

'He need never fear, ma'am, that I could ever be so lost to all sense of what I owe not only to him, but to my name as well, as to do anything that would make him regard me as a—oh, as a broken feather in the Carrington wing!'

She smiled a little at that. 'No, my dear: I am very sure he need not! And if you *had* wished to marry Miss Steane he would have tried to make the best of it, however disappointed he would have been, for he didn't dislike her, and he certainly didn't think her a *designing* girl. Indeed, he told me that he found it hard to believe she was Wilfred Steane's child! And, you know, dearest, even if he had taken her in the most violent dislike, and you had married her in the teeth of his opposition, he wouldn't have disowned you! No matter *what* any of you did, or *how* angry he was, that is something which he would never do, for it is wholly against his principles.'

'Yes, I know it is,' Desford agreed, a smile of affectionate amusement warming his eyes. 'We all do—and it is what makes it quite impossible for any of us to do anything which we know would wound him to the heart! And it is also what makes him such an excellent parent! Horry nicked the nick when he told me, once, that, for his part, Papa (in one of his tantrums) was at liberty to lay anything he liked to his dish, because he could be depended on, in the last resort, to stand buff in defence of his sons!'

'Ah, you do know that, Ashley!' Lady Wroxton said, giving his arm an eloquent squeeze.

'Of course I do, Mama!' he said reassuringly. 'But what a funny one he is! At one moment he can say that Wilfred Steane deserved to be disowned, and at the next give the cut direct to Nettlecombe for having done it!'

'For shame!' said Lady Wroxton, but with a quivering lip. 'How dare you speak so improperly? You have quite misunderstood the matter! Naturally Papa said that, because it was perfectly true; but, in his opinion, Lord Nettlecombe behaved in a manner unworthy of a father, and that was true too! So there was nothing inconsistent in his having condemned both of them, and I will *not* permit you to call him a funny one!'

'Now that you have explained the matter to me, Mama, I perceive that I was quite beside the bridge to have done so,' he replied.

She was not deceived by his air of grave remorse, but said, with an involuntary chuckle: '*Quite* beside it, wicked, odious, impertinent boy that you are!' She paused, and removed her hand from his arm to nip off a withered rose from one of the standards. 'By the by, do you remember my telling you about Mr Cary Nethercott? Old Mr Bourne's nephew, I mean, who lately came into the property?'

'Yes. Why?'

'Oh, merely that I met him, when Papa and I drove over to Inglehurst! I never had, you know, so—'

'Met him at Inglehurst, did you? I suppose he called there to give Lady Silverdale some journal to read! Or had he another excuse?'

Startled by the sardonic note in his voice, she shot a quick glance at him, before answering with her usual calm: 'My dear, how should I know? He was there when we arrived, sitting on the terrace with Hetta and Miss Steane, so what excuse he may have made for his visit I haven't a notion—if he made any! I formed the impression that he stands on such friendly terms with the Silverdales that he is free to drop in at Inglehurst whenever he chooses.'

'Runs tame there, does he? How Hetta can tolerate such a prosy fellow I shall never know!'

'Oh, you've met him then?' she said.

'I should rather think I have! I trip over him every time I go to Inglehurst!'

'And you don't like him? I thought him a pleasant, well-conducted man.'

'Well, I think him a dead bore!' said Desford.

She returned an indifferent answer, and almost immediately turned the subject, repressing, with a strong effort, a burning desire to pursue it.

The Viscount set out for London after partaking of a light luncheon, sped on his way by a recommendation from his father to post off to Bath first thing next day, and not to lie abed till all hours ('as you lazy young scamps like to do!'), because the sooner he finished with 'this business' the better it would be for all concerned in it.

'For once, sir, I am in complete agreement with you!' returned the Viscount, a laugh in his eyes. 'So much so that I shall sleep at Speenhamland tonight!'

'Oh, you will, will you? At the Pelican, no doubt!' said his lordship, with awful sarcasm.

'But of course, Papa! Where else should one put up on the Bath road?'

'I might have guessed you would choose the most expensive house in the country to honour with your patronage!' said the Earl. 'When *I* was your age, Desford, I couldn't have stood the nonsense, let me tell you! But I had no bird-witted great-aunt to leave her fortune to me! Oh, well, it's no concern of mine how you waste the ready, but don't come to *me* when you find yourself in Dun Territory!'

'No, no, you'd disown me, wouldn't you, sir? I shouldn't dare!' said the Viscount, audaciously quizzing him.

'Be off with you, wastrel!' commanded his austere parent.

But when the Viscount's chaise had disappeared from sight he turned to nod at his wife, and to say: 'This business has done him a deal of good, my lady! I own that I was a trifle put out when I first got wind of it, but there was never the least need for you to think he'd been caught by some designing hussy!'

'No, my dear,' meekly agreed his life's companion.

'Of course it was no such thing! Not but what it was a lunk-headed thing to have done—However, I shall say no more on that head! The thing is that for the first time in his life he has a wolf by the ears, and he ain't running shy! He's ready to stand buff, and, damme, I'm proud of him! Sound as a roast, my lady! Now, if only he would settle down—form an attachment to some eligible female—I'd hand Hartleigh over to him!'

'An excellent scheme!' said Lady Wroxton. 'How delightful it will be, my love, to see Ashley where you and I lived until your father deceased!'

'Ay, but when?' responded his lordship gloomily. 'That is the question, Maria!'

'Not so very long, I fancy!' said Lady Wroxton, with a smoth-ered laugh.

# Twelve

WHILE THE VISCOUNT WAS IMPATIENTLY AWAITING THE fashioning of a tyre to fit the wheel of his chaise, his youngest brother had been half-way back to London from Newmarket, with one of his chief cronies seated beside him in his curricle. Both gentlemen were in excellent spirits, having enjoyed a most profitable sojourn at Newmarket. Mr Carrington, in fact, was appreciably plumper in the pocket than his friend, for when, having boldly wagered his all on the Viscount's tip, and watched Mopsqueezer gallop home a length ahead of his closest rival, he had seen that a horse named Brother Benefactor was running in the last race he had instantly, ignoring the earnest pleas of his well-wishers not to be such a gudgeon, backed this animal to the tune of a hundred pounds. As it won by a head at the handsome price of ten-to-one, he left the course in high fettle, and with his pockets bulging with rolls of soft, one of which was considerably diminished at the end of the evening which he spent in entertaining several of his intimates to a sumptuous dinner at the White Hart.

Having a hard head and a resilient constitution, he arose on the following day feeling (as he himself expressed it) only a trifle off the hinges, and in unimpaired good spirits. The same could not have been said of his companion, whose appearance caused Simon to exclaim: 'Lord, Philip, you look as blue as a razor!'

'I've got a devilish headache!' replied the sufferer, eyeing him with loathing.

'That's all right, old fellow!' said Simon encouragingly. 'You'll be in a capital way as soon as you get out into the fresh air! Nothing like a drive on a fine, windy day to pluck a man up!'

Mr Harbledon vouchsafed no other response to this than a sound between a groan and a snarl. He climbed into the curricle, winced when it moved forward with a jerk, and for the next hour gave no other signs of life than moans when the curricle bounced over a bad stretch of ground, and one impassioned request to Simon to refrain from singing. Happily, his headache began to go off during the second hour, and by the time Simon pulled in his pair at the Green Man, in Harlow, he was so far restored as to be able to take more than an academic interest in the bill of fare, and even to discuss with the waiter the rival merits of a neck of venison and a dish of ox rumps, served with cabbage and a Spanish sauce.

Simon reached his lodging in Bury Street midway through the afternoon on the following day. Since neither he nor Mr Harbledon was pressed for time they had tacitly agreed to recruit nature by remaining in bed until an advanced hour. They had then eaten a leisurely and substantial breakfast, so that by the time they left the Green Man it was past noon. Still full of fraternal gratitude, Simon strolled round to Arlington Street, on the chance that he might find Desford at home. He was not much surprised when Aldham, who opened the door to him, said that his lordship was not in at the moment; but when he learned, in answer to a further enquiry, that his lordship had not yet returned from Harrowgate, he opened his eyes in astonishment, and ejaculated: '*Harrowgate?*'

'Yes, sir. So I believe,' said Aldham.

Simon was not wanting in intelligence, and it did not take him more than a very few moments to realize what must have made his brother go off on such a long and tedious journey. He uttered an involuntary choke of laughter, but after eyeing Aldham speculatively decided that it would be useless to try to coax any further information out of him. Besides, for anything he knew, Aldham might not have been taken into Desford's confidence. So he contented himself with leaving a message for his brother, saying: 'Oh, well, when he comes home tell him I shall be in London until the end of the week!'

'Certainly I will, Mr Simon!' said Aldham, much relieved to be rescued from the horns of a dilemma. He regarded Simon with indulgent fondness, having known him from the cradle, but he knew that Simon was inclined to be a rattlecap; and since he had learnt from Pedmore that one of the first duties incumbent upon a butler was to be unfailingly discreet, and never, on any account, to blab about his master's activities, he would have been hard put to it to answer any more searching questions without either betraying the Viscount, or offending Mr Simon.

Simon was engaged to join a party of friends at Brighton, and might well have gone there in advance of the rest of the party if he had not recollected that rooms at the Ship had been booked from the Saturday of that week. Only a greenhead would suppose that there was the smallest chance of obtaining any but the shabbiest of lodgings in Brighton, at the height of the season, if he had not booked accommodation there; so he was obliged to resign himself to several days spent in kicking his heels in London, which, in July, more nearly resembled a desert, to any member of the ton, than a fashionable metropolis. Not that London had nothing to offer for the entertainment of out of season visitors: it had several things, and Simon was considering, two days after his call in Arlington Street, whether the evening would be more amusingly spent at the Surrey Theatre, or at the Cockpit Royal, when the retired gentleman's gentleman who owned the house in Bury Street, and ministered to the three gentlemen at present lodging there, entered the room and presented him with a visiting-card, saying succinctly: 'Gentleman to see you, sir.'

The card bore, in florid script, an imposing legend: *Baron Monte Toscana*. Simon took one look at it, and handed it back. 'Never heard of the fellow!' he said. 'Tell him I'm not at home!'

A mellifluous voice spoke from the doorway. 'I must beg a thousand pardons!' it said. 'Too late did I realize that I had inadvertently presented this good man with the wrong card! Have I the honour of addressing Mr Simon Carrington? But I need not ask! You bear a marked resemblance to your father—who, I do trust, still enjoys good health?'

Considerably taken aback, Simon said: 'Yes, I'm Simon Carrington, sir, but—but I fear you have the advantage of me!'

'Naturally!' said his visitor, smiling benignly at him. 'I daresay you never saw me before in your life—in fact, I am quite sure of it, for until this moment you have been but a name to me.' He paused to wave a dismissive hand at the retired gentleman's gentleman, saying graciously: 'Thank you, my good man! That will be all!'

'The name, sir, is Diddlebury—if you have no objection!' said his good man, in a voice which clearly showed his contempt for Mr Carrington's visitor.

'None at all, my man! A very good name, in its way!' said the visitor graciously.

Diddlebury, having looked in vain for a sign from Mr Carrington, reluctantly withdrew from the room.

'And now,' said the visitor, 'it behoves me to repair the foolish mistake I made, when I gave the wrong card to that fellow!' He drew out a fat card-case as he spoke, and searched in it, while Simon stared at him in amazement.

He was a middle-aged man, dressed in clothes as florid as his countenance. When the highest kick of fashion was a severity of style which banished from every Tulip's wardrobe all the frilled evening shirts which had been the rage only six months before, not to mention such enormities as flowered waistcoats, brightly coloured coats, or any other jewelry than a ring and a tie-pin, he was wearing a tightly fitting coat of rich purple; a shirt whose starched frill made him look like a pouter pigeon; and a richly embroidered waistcoat. A somewhat ornate quizzing-glass hung round his neck; a number of seals and fobs dangled from his waist; a flashing tie-pin was stuck into the folds of his cravat; and several rings embellished his fingers. He had probably been a handsome man in his youth, for his features were good, but the unmistakable signs of dissipation had impaired his complexion, set pouches beneath his eyes, and rendered the eyes themselves a trifle bloodshot.

'Ah, here we have it!' he said, selecting a card from his case. However, having taken the precaution of inspecting it through his quizzing-glass, he said: 'No, that's not it! Can it be that I forgot—No! Here it is at last!'

Fascinated, Simon said: 'Do you—do you carry different cards, sir?'

'Certainly! I find it convenient to use one card here, and another there, for you must know that I am domiciled abroad, and spend much of my time in travel. But this card,' he said, handing it to Simon with a flourish, 'bears my true name, and will doubtless explain to you why I have sought you out!'

Simon took the card, and glanced at it with scant interest. But the name inscribed on it made him gasp: '*Wilfred Steane?* Then you *aren't* dead!'

'No, Mr Carrington, I am *not* dead,' said Mr Steane, disposing himself in a chair, 'I am very much alive. I may say that I am wholly at a loss to understand why anyone should have supposed me to have shuffled off this mortal coil. In the words of the poet. Shakespeare, I fancy.'

'Yes, I know that,' said Simon. 'But I'm dashed if I know why you shouldn't understand why you was thought to have stuck your spoon in the wall! What else could anyone think when nothing was heard of you for years?'

'Was it to be supposed, young man, that if I had done any such thing I should have neglected to inform my only child of the circumstance? Not to mention the Creature in whose charge I left her!' demanded Mr Steane, in throbbing accents of reproach.

'You couldn't have,' said Simon prosaically.

'I should have made arrangements,' said Mr Steane vaguely. 'In fact, I had made arrangements. But let that pass! I am not here to bandy idle words with you. I am here to discover where your brother is lying concealed, Mr Carrington!'

Simon's hackles began to rise. 'I have two brothers, sir, and neither of them is lying concealed!'

'I refer to your brother Desford. My concern is not with your other brother, of whose existence I was unaware. I must own that until this morning I was unaware of your existence too.' He heaved a deep sigh, and sadly shook his head. 'One grows out of touch! *Eheu fugaces, Postume, Postume*—! No doubt you can supply the rest of that moving passage.'

'Well, of course I can! Anyone could!'

'*Labuntur anni,*' murmured Mr Steane. 'How true! Alas, how true! Although you, standing as you do on the threshold of life, cannot be expected to appreciate it. How well I remember the heedless, carefree days of my own youth, when—'

'Forgive me, sir!' said Simon, ruthlessly interrupting this rhetorical digression, 'but you're wandering from the point! I collect that you wish me to tell you where my brother Desford is to be found. If I knew, I'd be happy to tell you, because he'd be devilish glad to see you, but I don't know! What I do know is that he is not *lying concealed* anywhere! And also,' he added, with

rising colour, and stammering a little, 'Th-that there's no reason
why he should be! And, what's more, I'll thank you not to make
such—such false accusations against him!'

'All alike, you Carringtons!' said Mr Steane mournfully 'How
vividly the past is recalled to my remembrance by your words!
Your esteemed father, now—'

'We'll leave my father out of this discussion!' snapped Simon,
by this time thoroughly incensed.

'Willingly, willingly, my dear boy! It is no pleasure to me to
recollect how grievously he misjudged me. How little allowance
he made for youth's indiscretions, how little he understood the
straits to which a young man could be reduced by the harsh
conduct of a parent who was—to put the matter in vulgar
terms—a hog-grubber! I will go further: a flea-mint!'

'Well, you're out there!' retorted Simon. 'I don't know much
about what you did in your youth, sir, but I do know that my father
gave yours the cut direct when he heard he'd disowned you!'

'Did he so?' said Mr Steane, much interested. 'Then I have
wronged him! I would I might have been present on the occasion! It would have supplied balm to my sorely wounded heart.
But how, I ask myself, could I have guessed it? When I disclose
to you that to me also he gave the cut direct you will realize that
it was impossible for me to have done so.'

'I daresay, but I shall be obliged to you, sir, if you will cut line,
and tell me what your purpose is in coming to visit me! I've
already told you that I don't know where Desford is, and I can
only advise you to await his return to London! He has a house
in Arlington Street, and his servants are—are in hourly expectation of his return to it!'

'That he resides in Arlington Street I know,' said Mr Steane.
'Upon my arrival from Bath, I instantly made it my business to
discover his direction—an easy task, his lordship being such a
distinguished member of Society.'

'Of course it was an easy task!' said Simon scornfully. 'All you had to do was to consult a Street Directory!'

Mr Steane dismissed this with a lofty wave of his hand. 'Be that as it may,' he said, obscurely but with great dignity, 'I did discover it, and instantly repaired to the inhospitable portals of his residence. These were opened to me by an individual whom I assumed to be his lordship's butler. He, like you, Mr Carrington, disclaimed all knowledge of his master's whereabouts. He was— not to put too fine a point upon it—strangely reticent. Very strangely reticent! I am neither a noddicock nor a souse-crown, young man—in fact, I am one who is up to every move on the board, ill though it becomes me to puff myself off! And I perceived, in the twinkling of a bedpost, that he was under orders to fob me off!'

'Well, if that's what you perceived it's time you bought a pair of spectacles!' replied Simon rudely. 'How could Desford have given him any such orders when he thought you were dead? And, damn it, why the devil *should* he have done so? I daresay there's no one he would liefer meet than yourself! Yes, and if you care to leave me *your* direction I promise you I'll give it to my brother the instant I know where he is to be found! All I know at this present is that he went off to Harrowgate, early last week!'

Mr Steane appeared to subject this information to profound consideration. After an appreciable pause, he shook his head, and said with an indulgent smile: 'It pains me to cast a doubt upon your veracity—and I would not wish you to think that I am insensible to the virtue of Loyalty! I assure you, young man, that I honour your noble determination to protect your brother, however much I may deplore his unworthiness. I will go further! If the interests of my beloved child were not so tragically involved, I should applaud it. But what, I ask myself, should take Lord Desford to Harrowgate? No doubt a salubrious resort, and one, as I recall, much patronized by persons afflicted with gout, scurvy, and paralytic debilities. But if you wish to persuade me that Desford, who cannot, by my reckoning, be above thirty years of age, suffers from any of these distressing diseases, you are—in vulgar parlance—doing it rather too brown.'

'No, he don't suffer from those diseases! He don't suffer from any diseases, and he didn't go to Harrowgate for his health. Unless I'm much mistaken, he went there on what ought to be *your* business, Mr Steane! When I last saw him he was on the point of setting out to search for your father!'

'Tut, tut, my boy!' said Mr Steane reprovingly. 'Too rare and thick altogether! I have never had any business in Harrowgate. Or, in point of fact, in any of the watering-places of its kind: they offer no scope at all to a man of my genius. As for my father, I have cut my connection with him. He has been as one dead to me for many years.'

'Desford is searching for him to claim his protection for his granddaughter—your daughter, sir, whom you left destitute!' said Simon furiously. 'Or is she too as one dead to you?'

'That I should have lived to hear such words addressed to me!' ejaculated Mr Steane, pressing a hand to his heart, and casting up his eyes. 'My only child—my beloved child—the only relative I have in the world! And do not, I beg of you, speak to me of my erstwhile brother! I have not sunk so low as to claim relationship to that snivel-nose!' he added, descending abruptly from his histrionic heights. However, he rapidly recovered himself, and said: 'I demand of you, young man, is not my presence in London proof of my devotion to the sole pledge left to me by my adored partner in the marital state?' Overcome by these reflections, he buried his face in his hand-kerchief, and became to all appearances bowed with grief.

'No, it ain't!' said Simon bluntly. 'Anyone would think you'd plunged into a burning house, or some such thing!'

Affronted, Mr Steane raised his head, and said, with a good deal of feeling: 'If you imagine that plunging into a burning house is a riskier thing to do than to come boldly into this city, you are much mistaken! Why did I shake its dust from my feet do you suppose? Why did I choose to go into exile, leaving my be-loved child—temporarily, of course—in the care of a female who had cozened me into believing her to be worthy of my trust?'

'I hardly like to say, sir!' promptly replied Simon. 'But since you ask me I should think it was because the tipstaffs were after you!'

'Worse!' said Mr Steane tragically. 'I do not propose to recount the circumstances which led to my ruin. Suffice it to say that from the hour of my birth misfortune has dogged my every step. My youth was blighted by a gripe-fisted parent, and a scaly scrub of a brother, who had not the common decency to cock up his toes when his life was despaired of! Not only did he rise up from what I confidently expected to be his death-bed, but less than a year later he fathered a son! That, young man, was the final straw!'

'Did—did you raise the recruits on a post obit bond?' asked Simon, awed.

'Naturally! Do not be misled into thinking that because I am not, I thank God, a muckworm, I am a lobcock! It was not in my father's power to cut me out of the Succession. If Jonas died, leaving a pack of daughters, I must, in due course, have inherited title, fortune, and all. Pardon me! The thought unmans me!' He disappeared once more into his handkerchief, emerging, after a few moments to say: 'I shall not say that I was shattered. It was a blow that would indeed have crushed me had I been a pudding-heart, but I am not a pudding-heart: I have ever borne my reverses with becoming fortitude, and have seldom failed to make a recover. In this crisis, did I flinch? did I despair? No, Mr Carrington! I girded up my loins, as did—well, I forget who it was, but it's no matter!—and I did make a recover! You see in me, today, one who by his own exertions has raised himself from low tide to high water.'

'Then why the deuce don't you settle your debts?' asked Simon sceptically.

Shocked by this suggestion, Mr Steane exclaimed: 'Waste the ready on my creditors? I am not such a spill-good as *that*, I hope! Nor, let me tell you, as unmindful of my duty to my child! I had no other purpose in returning to the land of my birth than to succour her. Conceive what were my feelings when I arrived in Bath, yearning to clasp her in my arms, only to discover that the Creature to whom I had entrusted her had cast her off! Delivered her, in fact, into the hands of one of my bitterest enemies! And why? Because, if you please, in the midst of my struggles to bring myself about I had been obliged to defer the payment of her bills! Could she not have reposed as much confidence in my integrity as I had reposed in hers? Did she doubt that as soon as it became possible for me to do so I should have discharged my debt to her in full? Her only reply to these home-questions was a flood of tears.' He paused, directing a challenging stare at Simon; but as Desford had divulged only the bare outlines of the circumstances which had led him to befriend Cherry, Simon had no comment to offer. So Mr Steane continued his narrative. 'I repaired instantly to Amelia Bugle's country residence. It cost me a severe struggle to do so, but I mastered my repugnance: my parental feelings overcame all other considerations. And what was my reward? To be informed, Mr Carrington, that my innocent child had been ravished from the safety of her maternal relative's home by none other than my Lord Desford!'

'If that's what Lady Bugle told you, she was lying in her teeth!' Simon said. 'He did no such thing! Lady Bugle treated Miss Steane so abominably that she ran away—meaning to seek refuge with her grandfather! All Desford did was to take her up in his curricle, when he overtook her trudging up to London!'

Mr Steane smiled pitifully at him. 'Is that his story? My poor boy, it grieves me to be obliged to destroy your faith in your brother, but—'

'It needn't, for you won't do it!' interjected Simon, at white heat. 'And I'll thank you not to call me your boy!'

'Young man,' said Mr Steane sternly, 'remember that you are speaking to one who is old enough to be your father!'

'And do you remember, sir, that you are speaking of one who is my brother!' Simon countered.

'Believe me,' said Mr Steane earnestly, 'I enter most sincerely into your feelings! I was never, I regret to say, blessed with a brother for whom I cherished the smallest partiality, but I can appreciate—'

'Partiality be damned!' interrupted Simon. 'Ask anyone who knows him whether Desford is the sort of loose screw to *ravish* a chit of a girl away from her home! You'll get the same answer you've had from me!'

Mr Steane heaved another of his gusty sighs. 'Alas, you force me to divulge to you, Mr Carrington, that I fear my unhappy child fell willingly into his arms! It rends me to the heart to be obliged to tell you this—and I need hardly describe to you how grievous a blow to me it was to learn that she had, in her innocence, succumbed to the lure of a libertine possessed of a handsome face, and engaging address. Not to mention the advantages of birth and fortune. I am led to believe that Lord Desford *is* possessed of these attributes?'

Revolted by this description of his eldest brother, Simon repudiated it, saying shortly: 'No, he ain't! He's well-enough, I daresay—never thought about it, myself!—but as for an *engaging address*—! Lord, it makes him sound like a simpering, inching macaroni merchant! I'll have you know, sir, that Desford is a gentleman! What's more, your daughter didn't fall into his arms, because he never held them out to her! Not that I mean to say she would have done so if he had, for *I* am not one to cast asper-sions on another man's close relations! And *also*, Mr Steane, if you *weren't* old enough to be my father I'd dashed well plant you a facer for having the infernal brass to call Desford a libertine!'

Mr Steane, listening to this heated speech with unimpaired equanimity, said compassionately, at the end of it: 'I perceive that he has you in a string, and deeply do I pity you! You remind me so much of what I was in my youth! Hot-headed, perhaps, but replete with generous impulses, misplaced loyalties, and a touch-ing faith in the virtue of those whom you have been taught to revere! Sad, inexpressibly sad is it that it should have fallen to my lot to shatter that simple faith!'

'What the devil—?' demanded Simon explosively. 'If you think that I was taught to revere Desford—or that I do revere him!—you're fair and far off, Mr Steane! Of course I don't! But—but—he's a damned good brother, and—and though I dare-say he may have his faults he ain't a rabshackle—and that you may depend on!'

'Would that I could!' said Mr Steane regretfully. 'Alas that I cannot! Are you ignorant, my poor young man, of the way of life your brother has pursued since he made his come-out, and—I am compelled to say—is still pursuing?'

Simon stared at him, wrath and incredulity in his eyes. The flush that had risen to his face when he had found him-self compelled to violate every canon of decent reticence by upholding Desford's virtue darkened perceptibly. In a voice stiff with pride, he said: 'My good sir, if, by those—those oppro-brious words you mean to say that my brother has ever, at any time, or in any way, conducted himself in a manner unbefitting a man of honour, I take leave to tell you that you have either been grossly misinformed, or—or you are a damned liar!' He paused, his jaw dangerously outthrust, but as Mr Steane evinced no desire to pick up the gage so belligerently flung down, but continued to sit at his ease, blandly regarding him, he said haughtily: 'I collect, sir, that when you speak of my brother's *way of life*, you refer to certain—certain connections he has had, from time to time, with members of the muslin company. But if you mean to tell me that you suspect him of seducing innocent females, or—or of littering the town with his butter-prints, you may spare your breath! As for the suggestion that he lured your daughter to elope with him—Good God, if it were not so damned insulting I could laugh myself into whoops at it! If he had fallen so desperately in love as to have done anything so kennel-raked, why the devil should he be doing his utmost to give her into her grandfaher's keeping? Answer me that, if you can!'

Mr Steane shuddered eloquently, and replied in a manner worthy of a Kemble or a Kean: 'If he has indeed done so, my dread is that he has wearied of her, and is seeking to fob her off!'

'What, in less than two days?' said Simon jeeringly. 'A likely story!'

'My dear young greenhead,' said Mr Steane, with a touch of asperity, 'one can discover that a female is a dead bore in less than two *hours*! Not that I believe this Banbury story of his having gone off to Harrowgate in search of my father! It's a bag of moonshine! The more I think about it the greater becomes my conviction that he has abducted my innocent child, and bamboozled everyone into believing that he only did so because he thought she would be happier with her grandfather than with her aunt. Now, I don't doubt she may have been unhappy in that archwife's house, but if your precious brother thought she would be happier in my father's house he might be no better than a blubber-head, which I know very well he isn't! No, no, my boy! *You* may swallow that Canterbury tale, but don't expect me to! The plain truth is that he's bent on ruining my poor little Cherry, thinking that she has no one to protect her. He will discover his mistake! Her father will see her righted! Ay! even if he—her father, I mean, or, in a word, myself!—has to publish the story of his infamy to the world! If he has the smallest claim to be a man of honour he can do no less than marry her!'

'You've taken the wrong sow by the ear, sir!' said Simon, looking at him from between suddenly narrowed eyelids. 'I'm happy to be able to inform you that your daughter's reputation is unblemished! So far from being bent on ruining her, my brother was bent on ensuring that no scandal should attach to her name! And I am even happier to inform you that she is residing, thanks to Desford's forethought, in an extremely respectable household!'

It would have been too much to have said that Mr Steane's countenance betrayed chagrin, but the bland smile certainly faded from his lips, and although his voice retained its smooth-ness its tone was somewhat flattened when he replied to what Simon, who had formed a pretty accurate idea of his character, believed to be an unwelcome piece of information. Simon began to feel a little uneasy, and to wish that he knew where Desford was to be found. Dash it all, it was Desford's business to deal with Mr Steane, not his! Desford would be well-served if he disclosed Cherry's exact whereabouts to this old countercox-comb, and washed his hands of the whole affair.

'And where,' enquired Mr Steane, 'is this respectable house-hold situated?'

'Oh, in Hertfordshire!' said Simon carelessly.

'In Hertfordshire!' said Mr Steane, sitting up with a jerk. 'Can it be that I have wronged Lord Desford? Has he made her an offer? Do not be afraid to confide in me! To be sure, he should have obtained my permission to address himself to Cherry, but I am prepared to pardon that irregularity. Indeed, if he supposed

me to be dead his informality must be thought excusable.'
He wagged a finger at Simon, and said archly: 'No need to be
discreet with me, my boy! I assure you I shall raise no objection
to the match—provided, of course, that Lord Desford and I
reach agreement over the Settlement, which I have no doubt we
shall do. Ah, you are wondering how I have guessed that the
respectable household to which you referred can be none other
than Wolversham! I have never had the pleasure of visiting the
house, but I have an excellent memory, and as soon as you spoke
of Hertfordshire I recalled, in a flash, that Wolversham is in
Hertfordshire. A fine old place, I believe: I shall look forward to
seeing it.'

Momentarily stunned, Simon pulled himself together, and
lost no time in dispelling the illusion which was obviously
working powerfully on Mr Steane's mind. 'Good God, no!' he
said. 'Of course he hasn't taken her to Wolversham! He wouldn't
dare! You must know as well as I do, sir, how my father regards
you—well, you've told me yourself that he gave you the cut
direct, so I needn't scruple to say that nothing would ever
prevail upon him to give his consent to Desford's marriage to
Miss Steane! Not that there's the least likelihood of his being
asked to do so, because there ain't! Desford has *not* made her an
offer, because, for one thing, he ain't in love with her; for
another, there's no reason why he should; and for a third—well,
never mind that!'

He had the satisfaction of seeing Mr Steane's radiant smile
fade from his face, but it was short lived. A calculating look came
into that gentleman's eyes, and his next words almost made the
hair rise on Simon's scalp. 'I fancy, young man,' said Mr Steane,
'that you will find you are mistaken. Yes. Very much mistaken!
I can well believe that your honoured parent will not favour the
match, but I venture to say that I believe he would favour still
less an action of breach of promise brought against his heir.'

'Breach of promise?' ejaculated Simon. 'You'd catch cold at that, Mr Steane! Desford never made your daughter an offer of marriage!'

'How do you know that?' asked Mr Steane. 'Were you present when he stole her out of her aunt's house?'

'No, I was not! But he told me how it came about that he was befriending Miss Steane—'

He stopped, for a slow smile had crept over Mr Steane's face, and he was shaking his head. 'It is easy to see that you can have little knowledge of the law, young man. What your brother may have told you is not evidence. If it were admitted—which I can assure you it wouldn't be!—it could scarcely outweigh my unfortunate child's evidence!'

'Do you mean to say,' gasped Simon, 'that you think your daughter is the kind of girl who would stand up in a court of law, and commit perjury? Your memory isn't as good as you suppose, if that's what you think! Why, she's no more than a chit of a schoolgirl that hasn't cut her eye-teeth!'

'Ah!' said Mr Steane, putting Simon forcibly in mind of a cat confronted with a saucer of cream. 'I collect, Mr Carrington, that you have met my little Cherry?'

'Yes, I've met her! And if she had accepted an offer from Desford, why, pray, didn't she tell me so?'

'So you have met her!' said Mr Steane thoughtfully. 'No doubt in Lord Desford's company? Very significant! Ve-ry significant! One is led to suppose that he meant, at that time, to espouse her, for why, otherwise, should he have made her known to you?'

'He didn't! What I mean is,' said Simon, becoming momently more harassed, 'I met her at—in the house to which he took her, and Desford didn't know I was there! I mean, he didn't expect me to be there, and she wasn't in his company when I met her! I mean, he didn't know I was there! She was alone, in one of the saloons, waiting for

Desford to explain the circumstances to Miss—to the lady in whose charge he placed her!'

'This,' said Mr Steane, in a stricken voice, 'is worse than I feared! Unhappy youth, has Lord Desford placed her in a *fancy-house?*'

'A fancy—No, of course he hasn't!' said Simon indignantly. 'He took her to an old friend's house—a *very* respectable house, I'll have you know!'

'It doesn't sound like it to me,' said Mr Steane simply.

'Oh, for God's sake, stop measuring twigs!' exclaimed Simon, quite exasperated. 'You're talking the most idiotic hornswoggle I've been obliged to listen to in all my life! And I'll be damned if I'll listen to any more of it! Go back to my brother's house, and leave your card there—one that bears your true name!—and inform his butler where you are to be found! I promise you he will seek you out directly, for nothing could please him more than to know that Miss Steane's father is alive, and able to take charge of her. Though whether he will be pleased when he discovers what sort of a fellow you are is another matter!'

This savage rider failed to ruffle Mr Steane's serenity. 'I venture to say that he would be very far from pleased—if he did seek me out—for he would recognize in me an avenging parent. A Nemesis, young man! It is inexpressibly painful to me to doubt your veracity, but I am forced against my will to say that I do not believe you. In fact, it has been borne in upon me that you lie as fast as a dog can trot, Mr Carrington. Or even faster! What a shocking thing that your revered parent—always such a high stickler—should have one son who is a profligate, and another—if you will pardon the expression!—a gull-catcher! And not even an expert in that delicate art!'

Simon strode across the room to the door, and wrenched it open. 'Out!' he said.

Mr Steane continued to smile at him. 'Certainly, certainly, if you insist!' he said affably. 'But consider! Is it quite wise of you to insist? You have not thought fit to disclose my unfortunate child's whereabouts to me, so there is no other course open to me than to repair to Wolversham, and to lay the facts of this distressing affair before your dear father. A course which I cannot feel that you would wish me to pursue, Mr Carrington.'

He was right. Inwardly seething, Simon was obliged to choke down his rage, and to search wildly in his brain for a way of escape from what he recognized as a dilemma. Not having seen Desford since he had parted from him at Inglehurst, he was in ignorance of Desford's meeting with his father, and on one point his determination was fixed: not through his agency was Lord Wroxton going to hear of the scrape Desford had got himself into. Lord Wroxton could be depended on to stand buff, but he would be furious with Desford for having, in the first place, befriended Cherry Steane, and in the second place for having made it necessary for him to treat with her father, or even to receive such a sneaking rascal in his house. If ever a flashy clever-shins meant mischief, Simon thought, this one did! And who knew what mischief he might be able to work, except Desford himself? Simon did not for a moment believe that Des had made Cherry an offer of marriage, but if Cherry, prompted by her father, asserted that he had done so a rare case of pickles it would be! Considering the Honourable Wilfred Steane with narrowed eyes, Simon thought that while his object might be to achieve a brilliant match for his daughter it was far more probable that his real aim was pecuniary gain. Would my Lord Wroxton tip over the hush-money to keep his proud name free from the sort of shabby scandal with which it might well be smirched? Yes, Simon thought, he would! *Damn* Des for going off the lord knew where at just such a moment! If this cunning fox were to be kept away from Wolversham, there was nothing for it but to disclose to him that so far from having been dumped in a fancy-house Cherry had been placed in the care of a lady of unimpeachable respectability. He was extremely reluctant to furnish Mr Steane with her precise direction, for not only had he an extremely vivid notion of what Lady Silverdale's feelings would be if that genteel hedge-bird presented himself at Inglehurst, but for anything he knew Desford might by this time have removed Cherry to some other asylum. The obvious way out of the dilemma was to persuade Mr Steane to await Desford's return to London: dash it all, it was he who had taken the wretched girl under his protection, and it was for him to decide whether or not to hand her over to her disreputable parent! But, whatever he did it was all Lombard Street to an eggshell that he would not, once he had set eyes on Mr Steane, present him to the Silverdale ladies.

The problem seemed to be insoluble, but just as Mr Steane said, in a voice of unctuous triumph: 'Well, young man?' a brilliant idea shot into Simon's head. He said, shrugging his shoulders: 'Oh, very well! If you won't take my word for it that your daughter is in safe hands, I shall be compelled to give you her direction, I suppose! Mind, I'm strongly tempted to urge you to visit my father—lord, what a settler he'd tip you!—but he ain't in very plump currant at the moment, and it wouldn't do him any good to fly into one of his pelters. It wouldn't do you any good either, because he wouldn't believe a word of your story. More likely to have you kicked out of the house! If you ever succeeded in entering it, which I'll go bail you wouldn't! He ain't receiving anyone but his family, and his closest friends, until he's in better cue, and you had as well go rabbit-hunting with a dead ferret as try to get past his butler! However, my mother wouldn't like it above half if there was to be a brawl, so I will inform you that when Desford found that your father was gone out of town he escorted Miss Steane to Inglehurst—which is Lady Silverdale's country house! She, let me further inform you, moves in the first circles, and is as starched-up as my father! So rid your mind of anxiety, Mr Steane!'

He ended on a confident note, for he had not failed to perceive a change in Mr Steane's expression, and was happy to know that he had succeeded in piercing his armour of self-satisfaction. He still smiled, but with tightened lips; and his pouched eyes had lost their look of tolerant amusement. But when he spoke it was as silkily as ever. He said: 'I wonder what I can have said to make you take me for a looby? I assure you, my guileless young friend, you are making a sad mistake! I am, in common parlance, up to all the rigs! Do, pray, explain to me how it came about that a starched-up lady of the first consideration—I am not acquainted with her, but I take your word for that!—welcomed to her house a girl who was brought to her by your brother—unattended by an abigail, too!'

'If your memory is as good as you would have me believe it is, you must surely recall that I told you Desford had taken your daughter to the house of an *old friend*!'

'My memory, Mr Carrington, is excellent, for I also recall that when, not so many minutes past, you hovered on the brink of uttering the name of the female into those hands your brother had delivered my innocent child you uttered a single, betraying word! Not *Lady*, young man, but *Miss*!'

'Very likely I did,' replied Simon coolly. 'Miss Silverdale, in fact. My brother's thoughts naturally flew to her when he was at his wits' end to know what to do with Miss Steane, rather than to her mother. You see, he is betrothed to her!'

'*What?*' gasped Mr Steane, for the first time shaken off his balance. 'I don't believe it!'

Simon raised his brows. 'Don't believe it?' he repeated, in a puzzled voice. 'Why don't you believe it?'

Mr Steane made a gallant attempt to recover his poise, but the announcement had been so unexpected that all he could think of to say was: 'Profligate though he may be, I cannot believe that Lord Desford is so lost to all sense of propriety—of common decency!—as to take a girl he had seduced from her home to the lady to whom he had become affianced, and to claim her protection for that girl!'

'I should think not indeed!' responded Simon readily. 'Of course he did no such thing! What's more, Miss Silverdale is far too well acquainted with him to suspect him of it! What you mean, sir, is that you don't wish to believe it, because no one but a barndoor savage could suppose that even the biggest rogue unhung would do such a thing!'

But Mr Steane's agile brain had been working. He stabbed a forefinger at Simon, and demanded: 'And why, young man, did you not inform me at the outset of this circumstance?'

'Because,' replied Simon, 'owing to my father's being in a tender state still, and to Lady Silverdale's wish to give a dress-party in honour of the betrothal at which he could not be present without knocking himself up, it has been agreed that no announcement of the engagement should be made until he is quite stout again. *We*, of course, know of it, and so, I daresay, do Desford's cronies, but as far as the scaff and ruff of society are concerned it is a secret. So I beg you won't spread it about, Mr Steane! A fine trimming my brother would give me if he knew I'd betrayed his confidence!'

Mr Steane rose to his feet, saying: 'I shall not conceal from you, young man, that I am by no means satisfied. It has already been made plain to me that you are—not to wrap the matter up in clean linen!—an accomplished fibster. Reluctant though I may be—indeed I *am*!—to bring a blush of embarrassment to any delicately nurtured female's cheeks—I perceive that it is my duty, as a parent, to discover from Miss Silverdale the truth of this shocking affair. Not to mention, of course, my ardent desire to clasp my child to my bosom again! If you will be so good,

Mr Carrington, as to inform me as to the precise locality of Miss Silverdale's abode, I will relieve you of my presence!'

'Oh, it's in Hertfordshire!' said Simon carelessly. 'Ask anyone in Ware the way to Inglehurst: they'll tell you!' He added, as Mr Steane picked up his hat: 'But you'd be better advised to await my brother's return! I daresay Lady Silverdale may consent to receive you if you go to Inglehurst under his wing, but she's devilish high in the instep, I warn you, and the chances are that if you go alone you won't get over the doorstep!'

'You are insolent, my good boy,' replied Mr Steane loftily. 'You are also foolish beyond permission. How, pray, does it come about that this model of propriety has—according to your story— received my daughter into her distinguished household?'

'Why, because she was sorry for her, of course!' said Simon. 'Just as anyone would be for a girl who had been deserted by her sole surviving parent, and cast destitute upon the world!'

Mr Steane, casting upon him a look of ineffable disdain, stalked wordlessly out of the room.

Young Mr Carrington, wasting no more than two minutes over a self-congratulatory review of his encounter with as sly a rogue as had ever, as yet, tried to tap him on the shoulder, realized that if his masterly (if far from truthful) handling of the situation were not to be overset it behoved him to make all possible speed to Inglehurst, to warn Hetta of the ordeal in store for her, and to inform her that he had recklessly betrothed her to Desford.

He was shrewd enough to feel pretty confident that Mr Steane, in spite of his air of opulence and his boast that he had raised himself from low tide to high water, was not quite so flush in the pocket as he pretended to be. It was unlikely that he would go to the expense of hiring a post-chaise and four to carry him to Inglehurst. If he hired a chaise at all, it would be a chaise and pair, but it was more probable, Simon thought, that he would travel to Ware on the Mail, or even a stage-coach, and hire a carriage there to carry him to Inglehurst. At the same time, it would not do to make too sure of this. Young Mr Carrington, that promising spring of fashion, saw that Adventure was beckoning to him, and responded to the invitation with the alacrity of a schoolboy. In less than half-an-hour he had shed his elegant pantaloons for a pair of riding-breeches; dragged off his natty Hessians; thrust his feet into his riding-boots, and hauled them up over his calves; exchanged his town-coat, with its long tails and buckram-wadded shoulders, for one more suitable for a gentleman about to take part in equestrian exercise; snatched a low-crowned beaver from his wardrobe, and a pair of gloves from a drawer in his dressing-table; a whip from the what-not littered with a heterogeneous assortment of his possessions; and was bounding down the stairs. His arrival on the doorstep coincided with the appearance, round the corner of the street, of his groom, leading the goodlooking hack on which young Mr Carrington frequently lionized in the park, and accompanied by the page-boy who had been sent to summon him.

A word to his groom, a shilling tossed to the page, and he was off almost before his feet had found the stirrups. But in spite of his delightful sense of urgency, and of being (as he himself would have phrased it) prime for a lark, young Mr Carrington had so far outgrown the heedless impulses of his schooldays as to defer his dash into Hertfordshire until he should have called, for the second time, at his brother's house in Arlington Street.

Aldham, hurrying up from the basement to answer an imperative summons conveyed by a tug at the bell which set it jangling so noisily and insistently that Mrs Aldham very nearly suffered a spasm, was pardonably incensed when he discovered that it was only Mr Simon, trying to bring the house down over their heads. 'Well, for goodness' sake, sir!' he said indignantly. 'Anyone would think you was that Bonaparty, escaped off St Helena! And don't you try to bring that horse into the house, Mr Simon, for that I will not permit you to do!'

Simon, who, in default of finding any loafer in the street, had been obliged to lead his hack on to the flagway, to the foot of the few shallow steps which led up to the door of the house, retorted: 'I don't want to bring him into the house! All I want is to know where his lordship is! *Do you know?*'

'No, Mr Simon, I do not know!'

'Oh, don't be so damned discreet!' said Simon explosively. 'This is important, man!'

'Mr Simon, I promise and swear that I'm telling you the truth! All his lordship said, when he went off, was that he didn't expect to be gone above a day or two, but he didn't tell me where he was going to, and it wasn't my place to ask him!'

'But—he has returned from Harrowgate, has he?' Simon said, frowning. 'Did you give him my message?'

'Yes, sir, I gave it to him in your very words,' Aldham assured him. ' "Tell him I shall be in London till the end of the week," you said. And so I did, but his lordship only said to tell you, if you should come enquiring for him again, that he would give you a look-in when he came back. Which, Mr Simon, we are expecting him to do at any moment, Mrs Aldham being poised, as you might say, over the kitchen-stove, with a pigeon pie ready to be popped into the oven, and a couple of collops—'

'The devil fly away with the collops!' interrupted Simon wrathfully. 'Where's his lordship's man? Where's Stebbing?'

'His lordship gave Tain leave of absence, sir, him having taken a chill on the way back from Harrowgate; and Stebbing's gone with him—with my lord, I mean—being that my lord has gone off in his curricle this time, and not travelling post.'

'In his curricle? Then he can't have gone far from London! If he should return today, tell him—No. Here, hold my horse, Aldham! I'll scribble a note for his lordship!'

With these words he thrust his bridle into Aldham's hands, and strode into the house, leaving that devoted but long suffering retainer to cast his eyes up in a mute appeal to heaven to grant him patience. It was wholly beneath his dignity to hold even his master's horse, but he accepted the charge without demur, and upon Simon's emergence from the house a bare three minutes later he went so far as to offer him a leg-up, and to chuckle when Simon vaingloriously refused this assistance.

'Pooh!' said Simon. 'Do you take me for a cripple? Here, take this note, and see you give it to my brother the instant he arrives!'

'I will, Mr Simon,' promised Aldham. 'Now hold a minute while I tighten the girths! If I'm not taking a liberty, where might you be bound for, sir?'

'Oh, only to Inglehurst!' answered Simon airily. 'Thank you: that's the dandy!' He then favoured Aldham with a smile, and a wave of his hand, and rode off at a brisk trot towards Piccadilly.

'And in which sort the wind is,' Aldham said, when recounting this episode to his wife, 'I know no more than you do, my dearie! Though that's not to say I haven't got my suspicions! And one thing I *will* say for Mr Simon! For all his carryings-on he's not one to cut his stick when my lord's in trouble, which I'm much afraid he may be!'

# Thirteen

IMON, KNOWING THE COUNTRY IN THE MIDST OF WHICH his birthplace was situated like the back of his hand, reached Inglehurst shortly after three o'clock that afternoon, and turned in at the lodge-gates hard on the heels of a landaulette, displaying on its panels the lozenge-shield proclaiming the widowhood of its owner, and drawn, at a sedate trot, by a pair of well-matched but sluggish bays. Uncertain of the identity of its solitary occupant (for she was holding up a parasol to protect her complexion from the strong sunlight), he kept at a discreet distance in the rear, until it drew up below the terrace of the house, and he saw, as she shut her parasol, and alighted from the carriage, that the unknown lady was not, as he had feared, Lady Silverdale, but her daughter. He then urged his tired mount forward, and called out, as Henrietta was on the point of walking up the broad, shallow steps to the house: 'Hetta, Hetta! Stay a minute! I want to speak to you!'

She paused, quickly turning her head, and exclaimed: 'Simon! Good God, what in the world are you doing here? I had supposed you to be in Brighton! Have you ridden over from Wolversham?'

'No, I've come from London,' he replied, dismounting, and handing his bridle to one of the footmen who had jumped down from his perch at the back of the landaulette. With a brief request to the man to give the horse into the head groom's charge, he turned, and grasped the hand Hetta was holding out to him, saying in an urgent undervoice: 'Something very important to say to you! Must see you in private!'

She looked a little startled. 'Oh, what is it, Simon? If it's bad news, pray don't try to break it gently to me! Your parents? Desford? Some accident has befallen one of them?'

'No, no, it ain't that!' he assured her. 'I've come to warn you, because it is bad news—devilish bad news! Wilfred Steane is on his way here!'

'*Wilfred Steane?*' she exclaimed. 'But I thought he was dead!'

'Well, he ain't,' said Simon. 'He's very much alive! Came to visit me this morning.'

'Oh, what a horrid creature you are! Trying to frighten me out of my skin, with your talk of bad news! I don't call *that* bad news!'

'You will when you've seen him,' said Simon. 'He's a shocking fellow!'

'Oh, dear, how unfortunate!' she said, quite dismayed.

'You may well say so! I'll tell you what passed between us, but not here! Won't do for any of the servants to overhear us.'

'No, indeed! Come into the house! You can wait for me in the Green saloon. I won't be above a couple of minutes, but I must show myself to Mama! I've been sitting with poor Mrs Mitcham all the morning, and you know what Mama is! If I venture to go more than five miles from home she is convinced that some dreadful fate will overtake me! Either I shall be robbed by highwaymen, or that there will be some accident to the carriage in which I shall be hideously hurt! It is too absurd, but it's useless to argue with her. I expect I shall find her in high fidgets, for I've been absent for nearly five hours!'

She hurried up the steps, the folds of the delicate primrose muslin dress she was wearing gathered in one hand; and when she reached the terrace she saw that Grimshaw was waiting to receive her in the open doorway, an expression on his face of portentous gloom. 'Thank God you have come home, Miss Hetta!' he said earnestly.

'Well, of course I've come home!' she replied, with a touch of impatience. 'I haven't been to the North Pole! I have been, as you very well know, a distance of no more than twelve miles, and since I had my mother's coachman to drive me there, and both her footmen to protect me from any eccentric highwaymen who *might* have chanced to fall upon the carriage, and to rescue me if those showy slugs had bolted, and overturned us, you cannot have been under the smallest apprehension that any disaster had befallen me!'

'No, miss, I was under no such apprehension. It is her ladyship's state which makes me thankful to see you back. She has suffered a terrible shock, and, I regret to say, is in great affliction.'

'Good heavens, is my mother ill? Has there been some accident?' she cried.

'Not, so to say, an *accident*, Miss Hetta,' replied Grimshaw, heaving a deep sigh, and casting a reproachful look at her. 'But when the terrible news was conveyed to her ladyship she felt a very severe spasm and went into strong hysterics.'

'But *what* news?' demanded Henrietta, in considerable alarm.

'I regret to be obliged to inform you, miss,' said Grimshaw, in a tone of ghoulish satisfaction, 'that we have every reason to fear that Sir Charles has eloped with Miss Steane.'

'Oh, my God!' muttered Simon, at Henrietta's elbow. 'Now we *are* in the basket!'

'Fiddle!' she snapped. 'How dare you talk such moonshine, Grimshaw? Who had the spiteful impudence to tell such a ridiculous story to her ladyship? Was it you, or was it Cardle? I can believe it of either of you, for you have both tried, from the moment Miss Steane set foot inside this house, to make her ladyship believe that she was an odious schemer! But it is you and Cardle who are the odious schemers! I don't wish to hear another word from you—though I promise you *you* will hear a great many words from Sir Charles when I tell him of this piece of wicked mischief-making! I am going to my mother now, but I am expecting a visit from Miss Steane's father, Mr Wilfred Steane. When he arrives, you will show him into the library, and advise me of it.'

Before this blaze of wrath, as alarming as it was unprecedented, Grimshaw quailed. 'Yes, Miss Hetta!' he said hastily. 'Her ladyship is laid down on the sofa in the drawing-room, miss! Being a little restored by some drops of laudanum. It wasn't me that broke it to her that Sir Charles was gone off with Miss Steane, and I'm sure *I* wouldn't have said anything about it until you was come home—'

'That will do!' said Henrietta superbly.

'Yes, miss!' said Grimshaw, almost cringing. 'I will show Mr Steane into the library, exactly as you say, miss!'

'Or the Baron Monte Toscano!' interpolated Simon.

Henrietta had started in the direction of the drawing-room, but she checked at this, and looked over her shoulder, saying quickly: 'No, no, Simon! I can't receive strangers at such a moment!'

'Same man!' he explained, in an undervoice. 'Explain it to you later! But for the lord's sake, Hetta, don't see him until you've first seen me! Something dashed important to warn you about!'

She looked bewildered, but promised she would join him in the Green saloon as soon as might be possible.

The scene that met her eyes when she entered the drawing-room bore eloquent testimony to Lady Silverdale's attack of the vapours. Her ladyship lay moaning softly on the sofa; Cardle was waving smelling-salts under her nose with one hand, and with the other dabbing her brow with a handkerchief drenched in vinegar; and on the table beside the sofa was a collection of bottles, ranging from laudanum and tincture of Valerian-root, to Hungary Water and Godfrey's Cordial.

'Thank God you are come home at last, Miss Hetta!' cried Cardle dramatically. 'See what that wicked creature has done to her ladyship!'

'Oh, Hetta!' quavered Lady Silverdale, opening her eyes, and holding out a limp hand.

'Yes, Mama, I'm here,' said Henrietta soothingly. She took the limp hand, and patted it, and said coldly: 'You may go, Cardle.'

'Nothing,' announced Cardle, bridling, 'shall induce me to leave my beloved mistress!'

'Your mistress doesn't need you while she has me to look after her,' said Henrietta. 'This show of devotion would be more affecting if you had not quite deliberately thrown her into such agitation! I'll speak to you later: for the present, you will please leave me to be private with her ladyship.'

'That I should have lived to hear such words addressed to me!' uttered Cardle, clasping her hands to her spare bosom, and casting up her eyes to the ceiling. 'I that have served her blessed ladyship faithfully all these years!'

'Yes, yes, but go away now!' said her blessed ladyship, reviving sufficiently to push away the vinegar-soaked handkerchief. 'I don't want this nasty-smelling stuff! You know I don't like it! Oh, Hetta, thank you, dearest!' she added, receiving from her thoughtful daughter a fresh handkerchief, sprinkled with lavender-water, and sniffing it. 'So refreshing! You see, Cardle, that Miss Hetta knows just what to do to make me better, so you needn't scruple to leave me in her care! And take away the vinegar, and the laudanum, and *all* those bottles, except the asafoetida drops, in case I should feel another spasm coming upon me! And give me my smelling-salts, please! And perhaps you should leave the cinnamon water, but *not* Godfrey's Cordial, which I am persuaded doesn't suit my constitution. And don't, I beg of you, Cardle, start sobbing, for my nerves are shattered, and I find myself in a very agitated state, and nothing upsets me more than to have people crying over me!'

At the end of this speech, which had increased in vigour surprising in a lady who had, at the start of it, presented the appearance of one who was almost beyond human aid, Cardle saw nothing for it but to withdraw, which she did, with the utmost reluctance, and with many shuddering sighs indicative of her wounded sensibilities. When she had gathered up the rejected remedies, she went with bowed shoulders to the door, turning as she reached it to bestow a last pitiful look at her mistress, and one of venomous dislike at Henrietta.

'Well, now,' said Henrietta cheerfully, 'we can be comfortable together, Mama!'

'I shall never again know a moment's comfort!' said Lady Silverdale, relapsing slightly. 'Oh, Hetta, you don't know what has happened!'

'No, I don't,' agreed Henrietta, sitting down beside her mother, and casting her very becoming hat of satin-straw on to a near-by chair. 'Grimshaw told me a ridiculous Banbury story, not one word of which am I such a goose as to believe, so do, pray, Mama, tell me what really happened here today!'

'Alas, it is no Banbury story! Charlie has run off with that wretched girl Desford persuaded me to house for him! I shall never forgive him, never! Heaven knows it was much against my will that I consented to take her, for I didn't like her. There was always something about her that seemed to me to show a want of conduct. Those inching manners, you know, were beyond the line of being pleasing. You must recall my saying so to you, several times!'

'No, I don't recall that,' said Henrietta dryly. 'It doesn't signify, however. What does signify is this nonsensical notion that Charlie has run off with Cherry Steane. It is too absurd, Mama! Cherry doesn't like him any better than she likes any young man!'

'That was just her artfulness! Exactly what one might have expected of Wilfred Steane's daughter! I see *now* that she was all the time determined to get a husband. There can be no doubt that she first set her cap at Desford, only he, being up to snuff (more shame to him!), no sooner saw what her game was than he got rid of her—at *my* expense! Hetta, when you refused to marry Desford you had a fortunate escape! I own, I was disappointed at the time, however little you may have guessed it, but I have lived to be thankful that you are not today the wife of such an unprincipled rake! You would have been miserable, dearest! And if ever I reproached you for refusing his offer I tell you now that nothing would prevail upon me to consent to your union with him!'

'As the question doesn't arise,' said Henrietta calmly, 'must we waste time in discussing Desford's morals?'

'Certainly not!' said Lady Silverdale. '*I* have no wish to discuss them! I don't wish ever to see him again, or even to waste a thought on him! In fact, if he has the effrontery to show his face here, Grimshaw will have instructions to refuse him admittance! Foisting that wretched girl on to me—*throwing* her in poor Charlie's way—coaxing you into believing his glib tale—!'

Knowing that no purpose would be served by entering into argument with her fuming parent, Henrietta sat in unresponsive silence until Lady Silverdale had talked herself out of breath She then said: 'What makes you suppose, ma'am, that Charlie has eloped with Cherry?'

'He did it in a tantrum, of course!'

Henrietta looked amused. 'I shouldn't have thought that even such a skip-brain as Charlie would elope because he was in a tantrum—and with a girl for whom he has never shown a sign of partiality, too!'

'He's not a skip-brain!' said Lady Silverdale, firing up. 'And as for not showing partiality, with my own eyes I saw him, not an hour after you had left the house, Hetta, *hugging and kissing her*!'

'Hugging her? Pray, how did he contrive to do that, with one arm in a sling, and two broken ribs?' asked Henrietta sceptically.

'He had his left arm round her, of course, and he *did* kiss her, for I came into the room just as he was doing it! And, what is more, Hetta, she made no effort to push him away from her!'

'You should be grateful to her for that, ma'am! Considering it was only yesterday that Dr Foston was shaking his head, and warning us that Charlie must take the greatest care, because though one of the broken ribs is mending the other is causing him to feel anxious, I think Cherry showed remarkable restraint not to struggle with him! I don't doubt that she was terrified of what might be the result of pushing him away.'

'How can you be so blind, Henrietta, as to let yourself be taken-in in this foolish way?' demanded Lady Silverdale. '*I* noticed many days ago that she was a flirt—indeed, I felt obliged to warn her not to encourage gentlemen to make up to her!— and Cardle tells me—'

'I wish to hear nothing of what Cardle tells you, ma'am!' Henrietta said, rather hotly. 'It is of no consequence whatsoever! She resented Cherry from the start, and hasn't ceased to try to set you against the poor child!'

'Cardle is devoted to me,' said Lady Silverdale. '*She* at least has my interests at heart!'

Henrietta started to speak, checked herself, and, after a momentary pause, said: 'What happened when you surprised Charlie kissing Cherry?'

'He released her immediately, and if ever guilt was plain to be seen in anyone's face it was in Cherry's! She was in too much confusion to be able to speak. She stammered something, turning as red as fire, and ran out of the room. And you are not to suppose, Hetta, that I didn't give Charlie a scold! I scolded him extremely severely, for whatever you may say, I do *not* ignore his faults. Not that I think it *was* his fault, but he should not have allowed himself to be led into impropriety.'

'So then he flew into one of his stupid rages, and was probably very rude to you,' nodded Henrietta.

'Yes, he was!' said Lady Silverdale, with feeling. 'He actually told me—*shouted* at me!—to "stubble it!" And when I asked him if he wanted to break my heart, he walked out of the room, and slammed the door in a way he must *know is* excessively bad for my nerves!'

'Well, I think that was more improper than to have kissed Cherry,' said Henrietta, her mouth suitably grave, but an irrepressible twinkle in her eyes. 'I expect he will be sorry now, and be ready to beg your pardon, so don't be distressed about it, Mama!'

'He has *gone!*' said Lady Silverdale tragically.

'Nonsense! I daresay he flung himself out of the house in a miff, but he will be back as soon as he has recovered his temper, depend upon it!'

'Alas, you do not know all! Cherry has gone too!' disclosed Lady Silverdale, recruiting her forces with the vinaigrette. 'And if you imagine, Hetta, that I said anything to drive her out of the house in that highty-tighty fashion, you are much mistaken! Naturally I was obliged to read her a lecture, exactly as I should to you, if you ever conducted yourself with such a want of delicacy, which, thank God, you never would do!'

'And what did she say, ma'am, in answer to this gentle scold?'

'Oh, she said it hadn't been her fault, and that Charlie had taken her by surprise, and a great deal more to that wheedling tune! So I told her—perfectly kindly—that no gentleman kisses a girl unless he has received encouragement to do so; and I warned her of what might well befall her if she didn't learn to behave with more propriety. Then I said (because she began to cry) that I wasn't angry with her, and should do my best to forget the incident, and I told her to go up to her bedchamber until she was more composed.'

'Unfortunate girl!' ejaculated Henrietta. 'How *could* you, Mama? When she has been so grateful to you, and so good to you! Telling her such a—such a *plumper*, too! And she's such a goose that I expect she believed no gentleman kisses a girl unless she encourages him, and has run off to cry her eyes out! Now I shall have to go in search of her!'

Lady Silverdale was so much incensed that she bounced up from her moribund position, and sat bolt upright. 'You are as unnatural as your brother!' she declared, in a trembling voice. 'Is it nothing to you that your mother should have spent the day in an agony of anxiety? Oh, no! All you care for is that miserable little wretch you've made into a bosom-piece! As for going in search of her, she has already been searched for, and neither she nor Charlie is on the premises! And, what is more, Cardle saw her running down the backstairs not twenty minutes after I sent her to her room, and she was wearing her bonnet and shawl, *and* the nankeen boots I procured for her! And you call *that* gratitude!'

Henrietta was frowning slightly. 'She must have gone for a walk beyond our grounds, then. Foolish of her, but if she was as upset as I collect she was, she was probably bent on finding a retreat where she wouldn't be looked for. Or perhaps of seeking relief from her feelings in exercise: it's what I should do in like circumstances!'

'Wait!' commanded Lady Silverdale. 'A little later, a closed vehicle was seen to be drawn up a few yards beyond the farm-gate, and one of the undergardeners saw Charlie come out into the lane, *with his hat pulled down over his eyes*, so that he shouldn't be recognized, of course, but James did recognize him, because he was wearing that olive-green coat, which I *cannot* like, and it is perfectly true, Hetta: he *was* wearing it today! And he looked round to be sure no one was following him, and then climbed up into the carriage. So James was in a puzzle to know what to do, because *all* the servants know that Dr Foston has expressly forbidden Charlie to ride, *or* to drive, for at least another week, and he was afraid Charlie would do himself an injury. So he made up his mind to come up to the house, and try whether he could get a word in Pyworthy's ear—not that that would have been of any use, because Charlie has Pyworthy in a string! I'm sure I am glad to think Charlie's valet is so devoted to him, but there's reason in all things, and when it comes to pretending to *me* that he doesn't know where Charlie is, or what he's doing, as he does, over and over again—well, I think it the outside of enough!'

'Mama,' said Henrietta, with determined patience, 'Simon Carrington is waiting for me, with an urgent message, in the Green saloon, so do, pray, tell me—'

'I am telling you, but if you keep interrupting me I may as well hold my peace,' replied Lady Silverdale, in an offended voice. 'And as for Simon Carrington, I forbid you to invite him to dine here, Hetta! I don't accuse him of aiding and abetting Desford, though it wouldn't surprise me if he is, but I don't wish to set eyes on *any* Carrington!'

'Very well, ma'am. Did James tell Pyworthy that Cherry was in that carriage?'

'He didn't see Pyworthy,' said Lady Silverdale stiffly. 'He saw Grimshaw!'

'And told him that?'

'No, but he knew there was *someone* in the carriage, for the door was opened from inside it, and he saw Charlie laughing, and saying something, and who else could it have been than—'

'And on this you, and Cardle, and Grimshaw have fabricated the most fantastic Canterbury tale I ever heard! The romances you are so fond of reading, ma'am, are nothing to it!'

'But, Hetta, it is not a Canterbury tale! Where could Charlie have been going to, in that secret way, except to—'

'For heaven's sake, Mama, don't say Gretna Green!' begged Henrietta, torn between exasperation and amusement. 'Without as much as one cloak-bag between the pair of them! My guess is that Charlie has gone off on some expedition he knows you'd disapprove of; and if he does himself an injury he will be well-served! What is more important is to discover what has become of Cherry! For how long has she been missing?'

'Hours! Both of them!' asserted her ladyship. And how you can be so heartless as to say that Cherry is more important than your only brother—'

'I don't believe he'll come to any harm,' said Henrietta impatiently. 'Dr Foston only said that because he knows him too well to think that he would be prudent unless he were frightened into it! But I do fear that Cherry may have met with some accident, and I am going to send out a search-party, to look for her!'

She rose quickly, but was startled by a little scream from her mother. '*Charlie!*' uttered Lady Silverdale, and sank back against the sofa cushions with one plump hand pressed to her heart.

Sir Charles came impetuously into the room. It was evident from his expression, and from his stammering utterance, that so far from having recovered his temper he was in a towering rage. 'I sh-should like to know, m-ma'am, what the dev—*deuce*—you mean by s-setting the servants to spy on me? By God, I think it beats the Dutch! Don't you frown at me, Hetta! I'll say what I dashed well choose! It's coming to something when a man can't move two steps out of his house without being followed, and spied on by his own servants, and being scolded by his butler for daring to go out without informing the whole household why he was going out, and where he was going, and when he would come back! There's no bearing it, and so I warn you, ma'am!'

'Unhappy boy!' said his mother dramatically. '*Where is Cherry?*'

'How the deuce should I know? And if you mean to give me any more jobations, I'm off! All that grand fussation just because I snatched a kiss! Anyone would think I'd tried to rape the girl!'

'Charles! If you have no respect for *my* sensibility, have you none for your sister's?'

'Well, I'm sorry,' he said sulkily. 'But it's enough to make a man go off on the ear when such a riot is kicked up over a mere trifle!'

'I know well that you were not to blame,' said Lady Silverdale, dabbing at her eyes. 'You shouldn't have done it, for you are old enough to know better, but I've no doubt you never would have done it had she not invited you to! So we shall say no more about it!'

He flushed darkly. 'Oh, yes, we shall say more about it!' he said furiously. 'She did not invite me to kiss her! As a matter of fact, she threatened to box my ears if I didn't let her go, silly little wet-goose! So don't you ring a peal over her, ma'am, because I won't have her blamed for what she couldn't help!'

'Charlie,' interposed Henrietta quietly, 'between them, Cardle and Grimshaw put it into my mother's head that you had eloped with Cherry, so you cannot be surprised to find her in a great deal of agitation! So do try to moderate your language!'

'Eloped with her?' he gasped. 'Next you'll say you thought I was on my way to the Border! In a hired hack, and with a girl I don't even like above half! If you mean to tell me *you* thought anything so addle-brained, you must have rats in the garret, Hetta, and that's all there is to it!'

'Oh, no, I didn't!' she assured him. 'But if you don't know where she may be I must send the grooms and the gardeners out to search for her immediately.'

'If she was not in that carriage, who was?' suddenly demanded Lady Silverdale. 'Do not ask me to believe that it was one of your friends, for I should hope none of them would visit you in that sly fashion! There is some mystery about this, and I am feeling very uneasy. I can feel my palpitations coming on already. Charlie, do not be afraid to confide in me! Have you got into a scrape?'

He drew an audible breath, and said, as one goaded beyond endurance: 'Much chance I've had of getting into a scrape since I've been tied by the heels here! If you must know, it was Pyworthy in the hack, and I went off with him to watch a mill! And if you want me to tell you why I sent him to hire a hack, and bring it round to the farm-gate, it was because I knew dashed well what kind of a bobbery there would be if you got wind of it, ma'am!'

Henrietta gave a low chuckle. 'I guessed as much!' she said, picking up her hat, and going to the door. 'I'll leave you to make your peace with Mama.'

'Yes, but if you mean to set the men scouring the country-side, I wish you won't!' he said uneasily. 'Dash it, she can't have come to any harm, and we don't want to set people talking!'

'Unfortunately, finding Cherry is a matter of considerable urgency,' she replied sweetly. 'I have good reason to believe that her father is coming here to claim her, and is likely to arrive at any moment. Perhaps you would like to relieve me of the task of telling him that she can't be found?'

'No, I dashed well shouldn't!' he said fervently. 'Hetta, are you bamming me? How do you know he's coming here? Good God, I thought he was dead!'

'Well, he isn't. And I know he is coming here, because Simon Carrington rode out from London to warn me of it!'

Lady Silverdale, recovering from the stupefaction which had caused her jaw to drop and her eyes to start alarmingly, shrieked after her daughter's retreating form: 'Don't dare to bring him in here, Hetta! I can't and I won't meet him. Cherry is your responsibility, not mine!'

'Don't fall into a twitter, Mama!' Henrietta said. 'I haven't the smallest intention of bringing him in here!'

# Fourteen

ENRIETTA FOUND THAT GRIMSHAW WAS HOVERING IN the wide corridor which led from the hall to the drawing-room, and at once gave him the necessary directions for an organized search for Miss Steane. He received these in a manner which showed her that the cumulative effects of having received a rating from herself and of being rattled off, probably in a most intemperate language, by his raging young master, had been so salutary as to render him, temporarily at least, all eagerness to oblige. He tried to detain her by excusing his own share in the day's evil happenings, but as he very meanly cast all the blame on to Cardle she had little compunction in cutting short his protestations. She then went quickly to the Green saloon, where she found Simon pacing round the room in a fret of impatience.

'Good God, Hetta, I thought you was never coming!' he exclaimed. 'I've been feeling like a cat on a hot bakestone!'

'You look like one!' she told him. 'I came as soon as I could, but my mother was in such a taking—'

'What, has Charlie indeed eloped with Miss Steane?' he demanded incredulously. 'What a hare-brained thing to do!'

'No, of course he hasn't! He came in a few minutes ago. He went off to watch a prize-fight, and stole out of the house so that my mother should know nothing about it. That's no matter! But what is more serious is that Cherry has been missing for several hours, and since my mother, egged on by her woman, and by Grimshaw, had it firmly fixed in her head that she had run off with Charlie no one has made the least push to find her. I've told Grimshaw to send the men out immediately to search for her, and can only trust that they do find her before her father arrives.'

He blinked at her. 'Yes, but—Did she steal out of the house too? What I mean is, queer sort of thing to do, isn't it? Not telling anyone she was going out. Come to think of it, it ain't the thing for a girl of her age to jaunter off without leave! I know Griselda never did so—in fact, I'm pretty sure my mother never allowed her to go out walking beyond the grounds without someone to bear her company, even if it was only her abigail.'

'Oh, no, nor did mine! But the case is a little different Simon! You won't repeat this, but it seems that there was a—a slight rumpus this morning, owing to my mother's having found Charlie trying to flirt with Cherry, and—and refining a great deal too much upon it! And I am afraid that what she said to Cherry upset the child so much that she ran out of the house, to—to walk off her agitation, and may have lost her way, or—or met with some accident!'

'Dash it, Hetta, this ain't the wilds of Yorkshire!' objected Simon. 'If she lost her way, anyone could have set her right! And I can't for the life of me see what sort of an accident she could have met with! Sounds to me as though she's run away. Seems to make a habit of it!'

'Oh, Simon, surely she could not be so idiotish?' Henrietta said.

'Well, I don't know,' he said dubiously. 'Of course, I wasn't talking to her above twenty minutes, but she didn't seem to me a needle-witted girl by any means.'

'No,' she sighed. 'She is a dear little creature, but sadly gooseish.'

'Good thing if you were rid of her,' he said. 'Good thing for Des too! If it weren't for this curst father of hers, I'd say let her go! But we shall find ourselves in the briars if he sails in expecting to clasp her to his fat bosom—yes, that's the way he talks! At least, he didn't say "fat": that's a what-do-you-call it by me!—and you are obliged to tell him she's run away, and can't be found!'

'*I* shall certainly be in the briars, but why you should be I can't conceive!' she replied, with some asperity. 'And it would not be a good thing if she ran away from us under any circumstances whatever! Des entrusted her to my care, and if you think it would be a good thing if I betrayed his confidence so dismally you must be all about in your head!'

'No, no!' he said hastily. 'What I meant to say was, not quite such a *bad* thing! The fact of the matter is, Hetta, that this ramshackle fellow is a pretty ugly customer, and it's as plain as a pack-saddle that what he means to do is to force Des to marry the girl—or, if that fails, to bleed him for the damage done to her reputation!'

'Des didn't damage her reputation!' she cried.

'No, I know he didn't, and so I told the old shagbag! But the thing is I can't prove he didn't, because all I know is what Des told me. And that ain't evidence, as Mr Lickpenny Steane took care to inform me! Confound Des, going off the lord only knows where, and leaving me to cope with this case of pickles! Ten to one I shall make a rare mess of it! The devil of it is, Hetta, that no one knows where he is, so I can't—'

'He is in Bath,' she interrupted. 'He came here on his way back from Harrowgate, and had formed the intention of visiting the lady who owns a school in Bath, where Cherry was educated, you know, to beg her help in finding a genteel situation for Cherry—Nettlecombe not having come up to scratch.'

'In Bath? But that's where Steane went to! And then came up to London—no, I rather think he said he went first to the Bugles' place! He must have missed running into Des, for he certainly hadn't seen him when he came to call on me. In fact, he came to discover from me where Des was. Yes, and that puts me in mind of something that went clean out of my head in the hurry I was in! Dashed if I didn't forget to ask Aldham what the dickens he meant by sending Steane round to me! Because it must have been Aldham, when Steane was badgering him to say where Des was! Fobbing the fellow off on to me! Jupiter, if I don't give him a tongue-banger when I get back to London!' He paused, and then said, in a milder tone: 'Oh, well! I daresay it was all for the best! At least I was able to head him! Now, you listen to me, Hetta! I wouldn't have sent him here if I could have avoided it!'

'But, Simon, surely you must have done so?' she protested. 'He may be a disreputable person, but he is Cherry's father, and none of us has any right to hide her from him!'

'Well, I wouldn't do it,' he said frankly. 'But, then, she don't hit my fancy. But I've a strong notion Des will do everything in his power to keep her out of Steane's hands—once he's taken the fellow's measure, which he will do, in a pig's whisper! Trouble with Des is that he's too chivalrous by half! Not but what I daresay if I'd been such a sapskull as to have picked the girl up and promised to take care of her I might feel a trifle queasy at handing her over to Steane.'

'You know, Simon,' she said, 'for some reason or other, the suspicion that you don't like Mr Steane has taken strong possession of my mind! But apart from his ambitious scheme to win a rich and titled husband for her—which, I own, gives one no very good idea of his character, but which might, after all, spring from a wish to do his utmost to ensure for her the sort of life any father must wish for his daughter, and which, from anything I have heard of him, he is not himself in the position to provide for her—apart from this, is there any reason why he shouldn't be allowed to take her into his own care? I can't but feel that in coming to find her he does show that he holds her in considerable affection.' She stopped, wrinkling her brow. 'Though it does seem odd of him to have left her for such a long time without a word, or a sign. However, there may be some reason for that!'

'He was probably in gaol,' said Simon. 'For anything I know, he may practise all kinds of roguery, but I fancy his chief business is fuzzing, cogging, and sleeving. And I should think,' he added, 'that he'd be pretty good at drinking young 'uns into a proper state for plucking! A Captain Sharp, Hetta!' he said seeing that she was looking bewildered. 'Sort of fellow who carries a bale of flat-size aces in his pocket, and knows how to fuzz the cards!'

'Good God! Do you mean he is a cheating gamester?' she gasped. 'You cannot possibly know that, Simon!'

'Oh, can't I just?' he retorted. 'You *must* think I'm a slow-top! What else could I think of a fellow that carries half-a-dozen visiting-cards in his pocket-book, all of 'em with different names, and says that places like Bath and Harrowgate offer no scope for a man of his genius? Of course they don't! There's no deep play in the watering-places where people go for their health! And if you think Des will be ready to give her up to a rascal that will drag her all over Europe with him, rubbing shoulders with all the rags and tags of society, you can't know Des as well as I thought you did!'

'No, no, indeed he wouldn't be!' she said, very much shocked. 'But, surely, if that is the kind of life Mr Steane leads, he cannot wish to be saddled with Cherry? Why should he?'

'I don't know, and I don't mean to waste my time trying to hit upon the reason. What I want you to understand, Hetta, is that he means mischief, and dangerous mischief, what's more! When I saw what his game was, and realized what a deuced unpleasant scandal he could start, if he accused Des of seducing that tiresome girl, promising to marry her, and then tipping her the double, I told him that so far from doing any of those things Des had placed her in the care of some old friends of ours, and had himself posted off to find her grandfather. He pretended that he didn't believe it. He even had the curst insolence to say— Well, never mind that! So I was forced to tell him that the girl was residing with Lady Silverdale, who was a widow, moving in the first circles, and as starched-up as my father! I meant it for the best, Hetta, but it gave him the chance to land me a heavy facer. He asked me how it came about that such a lady had consented to receive into her house a girl brought to her by a man of Desford's reputation—oh, yes! I was forgetting that piece of lying insolence! Des, you'll be interested to learn, is a rake and a libertine!—without her maid, or any other attendant!' He broke off suddenly, and jerked up his head, listening to the sound of an approaching carriage. 'Oh, my God, here he is!' he said. Two strides took him to the window, and while Henrietta waited in some anxiety, he stood watching the chaise-and-pair until it drew up below the terrace. He then uttered a groan, and said: 'Ay, it's Steane all right and tight!'

'I was never nearer in my life to playing least-in-sight!' confessed Henrietta. 'What am I to say to him, Simon? I promise you I am in a perfect quake!'

'No need for you to be in a quake!' answered Simon, in a heartening tone. 'But there's just one thing I must mention!'

'Yes, there is need! I've *lost* Cherry! And if she isn't found— Oh, I do wish Desford were here!'

'For the lord's sake, Hetta, don't *you* get in a stew!' begged Simon, alarmed. 'And as for Des—You know, I've been thinking about him, and it's my belief he will be here! If he went to Bath, we know he reached the place *behind* Steane, don't we?'

'Do we?' she said distractedly.

'Of course we do! Steane didn't meet him there, and the schooldame, whatever her name may be, didn't tell him she had seen him. All she told him was that Lady Bugle had fetched Cherry away, and had taken her to live with her. I wish you will take a damper, Hetta! If you mean to fly into the twitters we *shall* be bowled out!'

This severity had its effect. She said: 'No, no, I promise you I won't! But I find my mind is less strong than I believed it to be—in fact, it is all chaos! Oh, heavens, that is Grimshaw's step! In another moment Mr Steane will be upon us!'

'No, he won't. Grimshaw will show him into the library, and it won't hurt him to kick his heels there for a while. Never mind him, just mind me! If Des visited Miss Thingummy *after* she'd seen Steane, what would he do? Drive back to London as fast as he could, of course!'

'Unless he followed Steane to Maplewood,' she said doubtfully.

'No,' said Simon, shaking his head. 'I own I did think of that myself, but the more I consider the matter the more I feel he wouldn't have done any such thing. Well, do but put yourself in his shoes, Hetta! He knew that Cherry wasn't living with her aunt, and he must have known that the Bugles wouldn't have encouraged that old court-card to linger in their house! I daresay he didn't know that Lady Bugle had told Steane that *he* had "ravished" her away, but he must have thought the chances were that Steane would have left that place before he could reach it.'

She had been regarding him intently, trying to get her thoughts into order, but at this she said quickly: 'He did know that! Lady Emborough wrote to your mama, telling her that she had received a visit from Lady Bugle, demanding to know what Des had done with her niece, and I informed Des of it!'

'That settles it, then!' said Simon. 'Des would have returned to London immediately! And when he reached Arlington Street

Aldham gave him the letter I scribbled—there can be no doubt about that!—and as soon as he had read it it's Carlton House to a Charley's shelter that he set out instantly to join me here. I shouldn't wonder at it if he were to arrive at any minute!'

He was interrupted by Grimshaw, who came in to announce Mr Steane's arrival, but when Grimshaw had withdrawn, he said: 'There's just one more thing I must warn you about, Hetta! Well, as a matter of fact, it's why I rode out here as fast as I could! Steane thinks you're betrothed to Des.'

Henrietta had been tidying her ruffled hair in front of the mirror, but at this she turned, showing Simon a startled face. 'Thinks I'm betrothed to Des? Why should he think anything of the sort?'

'Well,' said Simon, a trifle conscience-stricken, 'I told him you were!'

'Simon!' she uttered wrathfully. 'How could you have told him so when you must know there isn't a word of truth in it?'

'It was the only thing I could hit upon to account for Lady Silverdale's having received Cherry, under such dashed havey-cavey circumstances,' he explained. 'And also it seemed to me the surest way of sending him to grass, if it came to an action for breach of promise. Well, it stands to reason that if Des was betrothed to you he wouldn't have offered another female marriage, or brought her to visit you!'

'I think it was an infamous thing to have done!' she said, those expressive eyes of hers flaming with anger.

'No, no!' he assured her. 'Only thing I could do! I promise you Desford won't care a straw!'

'Desford!' she said chokingly. 'And what about me, pray?'

'Hang it all!' he protested. 'Why should you care either? Ten to one it won't leak out, because unless I'm much mistaken Steane don't mean to stay in England a day longer than he need. Besides, I told him the engagement hadn't been announced yet—I said that was on account of my father's health, by the by: not stout enough yet for dress-parties—so if he does blab it abroad you have only to deny it, or cry off, if you prefer.'

'Oh, how abominable you are! I'll never forgive you for this!' she told him, an indignant flush reddening her cheeks.

'Well, never mind that!' he said, in a consolatory tone. 'If I'd guessed you might object to it, I wouldn't have done it, but I did do it, and there's nothing for it but to stick to it. You must see that, Hetta!'

'I don't!' she snapped.

'Do you mean to say that you're going to tell Steane you ain't engaged to Des?' he gasped. 'Of all the shabby things to do! I wouldn't have believed it of you! I thought you was too much of a right one to run away just when poor old Des most needs your help! Turning missish at such a moment! Dashed well stabbing him in the back!'

'Oh, be quiet!' she said crossly. 'If this horrible creature is rag-mannered enough to ask me, I shan't deny it. But what I *shall* do, Mr Simon Carrington, is to give you your own again!'

'That's the hammer!' he said encouragingly. 'I knew I could depend on you! Always said you were as sound as a trout! Now, you go and hold up your nose at that oily old rascal—and take care you don't let him guess I'm here, for it won't do if he realizes I came to warn you!'

With these kindly words, he patted her on the shoulder, and held open the door for her, meeting the scathing glance she threw at him with eyes brimming with laughter.

He then shut the door again, and retired to the broad window-seat to await the arrival of his brother. He had no doubt that Desford would arrive; the only doubt it was possible for one of his sanguine temperament to entertain was whether Desford would reach Inglehurst in time to deal with Mr Wilfred Steane before poor Hetta had been driven into the last ditch.

But the longer he pondered over the question the more convinced did he become that Desford would arrive in time to take the management of what (damn it all!) were his affairs, not his brother's, or Hetta's, into his own hands. It wouldn't be like Des not to make all haste to their rescue, he decided.

And his confidence was justified. Twenty minutes after Henrietta had joined Mr Steane in the library a postchaise-and-four swept round the bend in the avenue, and brought young Mr Carrington to his feet. So sure was he that its passenger was Desford that he did not wait to watch the steps being let down, but went hastily out into the hall, and intercepted Grimshaw, who was treading majestically across it towards the door. 'No need for you to trouble yourself!' he said. 'It's only my brother! I'll let him in!'

Grimshaw looked at once surprised and disapproving, but he bowed, and went back to his own quarters, reflecting that Mr Simon always was a regrettably harum-scarum young man, much too prone to brush aside the ordinary conventions of Polite Society.

Simon went bounding down the steps just as Desford alighted from the chaise, and called out: 'Lord, am I glad to see you, Des! You old slip-gibbet!'

'I'll be bound you are,' said the Viscount, receiving this unflattering appellation, and the playful punch to his ribs which accompanied it, as marks of affection, which, indeed, they were. 'I'm much obliged to you, bantling: no reason why you should be called upon to enter into this imbroglio!'

'Oh, gammon!' said Simon. 'A pretty fellow I should be to have given you the bag! And a rare hank you'd be in if I had, let me tell you!' He lowered his voice, and said seriously: 'It's worse than you know, Des.'

'Good God, is it?' He nodded to his head postilion, saying briefly: 'I don't know how long I shall be: probably an hour or two. We shall spend the night at Wolversham.' He turned back to Simon, as the chaise moved on towards the stables, and asked: 'Has Steane arrived yet?'

'Yes, about half-an-hour ago. He's with Hetta, in the library.'

'Then I had best lose no time in joining them.'

'Oh, yes, you had, dear boy!' said Simon, acquiring a firm grip on his arm. 'What you had best do is to listen to what I have to tell you, if you don't wish to make mice feet of the business! We'll take a little stroll along the terrace, as far as that damned uncomfortable stone seat, where we shan't be overheard.'

'If you're going to tell me that Steane is a fat rascal, I know it already. I visited Miss Fletching the day after Steane had been there, bullocking her until the poor lady succumbed to an attack of the vapours. I don't know what upset her most: the thundering scold she got from him, or the discovery that he had grown very fat. From what she said to me, I'd no difficulty in gathering that he hasn't altered since the days when he was obliged to fly the country. What's his lay? Card-sharping?'

'Undoubtedly, I should think, though I daresay he ain't particular. Any form of flat-catching, from the looks of him! His present lay, my boy, is to compel you to marry his precious daughter!'

The Viscount burst out laughing. 'Well, he'll be queered on that suit!'

'If I were you, Des, I wouldn't be too sure of that,' said Simon.

'My dear lad, I am quite certain of it! I met her for the first time at a ball the Bugles gave, and had a conversation with her; on the following day I encountered her on my way to London, took her up into my curricle, and conveyed her first to London, and then brought her here, since when I haven't laid eyes on her. So if Steane has any notion of accusing me of having seduced her the sooner he rids himself of it the better it will be for him.' He saw that Simon was looking unusually grave, and said, in a little amusement: 'I'm not shamming it, you know!'

'Well, of course I know it! But this fellow could make nasty mischief. What if he set it about that you stole Cherry away from her aunt's house, under a promise to marry her?'

'Good God, is he as bad as that?'

Simon nodded. 'I daresay you could disprove a charge of having made off with her, and kept her until you was tired of her—'

'What, in one day? Doing it too brown, Simon!'

'The point is can you prove it was only one day? I shouldn't think that Bugle woman would support you: she's already told Steane you ravished Cherry out of the house. Seems one of her daughters overheard what you and Cherry were saying, on the night of that ball.'

'Well, she didn't overhear me trying to persuade Cherry to run off with me. And considering upwards of half-a-dozen people saw me leave Hazelfield some time after breakfast on the following morning, and the Silverdales took charge of Cherry that same evening, I don't think that cock will fight!'

'No, very likely not, but you wouldn't want such an on-dit to be running round the town, would you? You know what all the tattlemongers would say : No smoke without fire! and the lord knows there are enough of them on the town!' He grinned, watching the kindling of the Viscount's eyes, and the hardening of the lines about his mouth. 'Never mind looking like bull-beef, Des! *Would* you want that?'

The Viscount did not answer for a moment, but sat frowning down at his own finger-nails. He had turned his closed hand over, and seemed to find the row of well-kept nails interesting. But presently he straightened his fingers, and looked up, meeting Simon's eyes. 'No, I wouldn't,' he replied. He smiled faintly 'But I hardly think he will attempt anything of that sort. For one thing, it would be to lay himself open to reprisal; and for another, he must surely know that he is in extremely ill-odour here. No one for whose opinion I care a button would believe a word he said.'

'What about your enemies?'

'I haven't any!'

'Why, you old windy-wallets!' exclaimed Simon indignantly. 'Talk of ringing one's own bell—!'

The Viscount laughed. 'No, no, how can you say so?'

'Let me tell you, Des, that this is no laughing matter!' said Simon severely. 'I don't say you couldn't beat him all to sticks if he accuses you of having seduced Cherry, for very likely you could—though I don't think you'd enjoy it. But you wouldn't find it as easy to fight an action for breach of promise!'

'Why not? For that to succeed Cherry's testimony would be needed, and he won't get that.'

'Anyone would take you for a mooncalf!' said Simon, quite exasperated. 'Next you'll say he's welcome to try it! Well, if you've no objection to setting yourself up as a subject for steward's room gossip, what do you imagine the parents would feel about it?'

'But, Simon, how could he possibly bring such an action without support from Cherry?'

'He could start one, couldn't he? What do they call it? File a suit? Because he knows you'd pay through the nose to stop him!'

'I'm damned if I would!'

'And what about my father? Ay, that's another pair of sleeves, ain't it? *He* would! I sent that old hedge-bird here because he threatened to go to Wolversham, and hoax my father with his lying story! And the next thing was that he had the infernal brass to ask me how it came about that Lady Silverdale had been persuaded to receive Cherry at the hands of such a libertine as you are, brother! So I said that you were betrothed to Hetta!'

'You said *what*?' Desford demanded, taken aback.

'Well, I thought there was nothing for it but to go the whole pile,' explained Simon. 'It seemed to me to be the best thing I could say, because if he believed it he was bound to see that it turned his scheme to accuse you of having promised to marry

Cherry into a case of crabs. Which he did see! Never saw a man
look so blue in my life! But if you don't like it I'm sorry, but
considering you and Hetta have been as thick as inkle-weavers
for the lord knows how many years, I didn't think you'd care a
straw for it!'

'I don't,' said Desford, a queer little smile hovering round his
mouth. 'But my father already knows the true story! I told it
him myself, on my way back from Harrowgate.'

'Told him—Des, you didn't!' uttered Simon, turning pale with
dismay. 'How *could* you have done anything so blubber-headed?'

There was a good deal of amusement in the Viscount's eyes,
but he answered meekly: 'Well, as he had already got wind of the
business, and had driven over here with Mama to discover what
sort of a girl I had apparently become entangled with, it seemed
to be the only thing I could do.'

'Lord!' said Simon, with an eloquent shiver. 'You've got more
bottom than I have, Des! Did he come the ugly?'

'Not at all! You should know him better than to think he
would, when any of us three were in the suds! Oh, he read me
one of his scolds, but he told me to come to him if I found myself
at the end of my rope! Mind you, he'd met Cherry by that time,
and knew at a glance that she wasn't a designing harpy!'

'So I might have spared myself the trouble of heading him
away from Wolversham!' said Simon wrathfully. 'Upon my word,
Des—'

'Oh, no! I'm grateful to you for having done so! He wouldn't
have believed Steane's story, but it's more than likely that he
would have paid him handsomely to keep his mouth shut, and
I'm damned if I'll allow Steane to put the screw on him! He
told me himself that when he came here it was with the intention of buying Cherry off, if he found that she was a designing
harpy. Never mind that! Did you come here to warn Hetta that
she is engaged to me?'

'Yes, of course! I had to!'

'And how did she take it?'

'I'm bound to own that she flew up into the boughs, which surprised me. What I mean is, not like her to turn missish all at once! However, I pointed out to her that if the story were to leak out she could either deny it, or cry off, so she mended her temper, and promised she'd stand buff. No need to fear she may run shy! I'll say this for Hetta: she may be a trifle freakish now and then, but she's a right one at heart!'

'Yes, the pick of the basket!' Desford said, getting up. 'And the sooner I go to her rescue—'

'Stay a moment, Des! They are all in an uproar, because that troublesome girl seems to have loped off!'

'Cherry? Good God, why?'

'Oh, Hetta thinks it was because Lady Silverdale found Charlie kissing her, and gave her a scold! She also thinks Cherry may have met with an accident, and she's sent off most of the men to search for her. The devil of it is, of course, that if they don't find her Steane will be sure to cut up rough. Very likely he'll accuse the Silverdales of having ill-used her!'

'Oh, my God, as though we weren't in bad enough loaf already!' groaned the Viscount, striding away towards the door into the house.

'Hi, wait!' Simon called, suddenly bethinking himself of something, and jumping up from the seat. He thrust a hand into his pocket, pulled out a package, and hurried after his brother. 'Here you are, old chap!' he said, holding it out, with a shy smile. 'Very much obliged to you!'

'But what is it?'

'A roll of soft, you gudgeon! The monkey you lent me!'

'Chuff it!' recommended the Viscount. 'I told you at the time that I wasn't going to let you break *my* shins! Did Mopsqueezer win?'

'I should rather think he did! What's more, there was a horse entered for the last race, called Brother Benefactor, so I put all my winnings on him, and he came home at ten-to-one! Bound to, of course!'

The Viscount gave a shout of laughter. 'Lord, what a cockle-headed thing to do! No, stop pushing that roll at me! I don't want it! You may be said to have earned it, what's more!' He laid a hand on Simon's shoulder, and gave him a little shake. 'You must have been having the devil of a time in the bumble-broth I brewed! Thank you, bantling!'

'Oh, fudge!' Simon said, deeply flushing. 'I wish you would take it! I'm fairly swimming in lard, you know!'

'You won't be, by the time you return from Brighton!' retorted the Viscount.

# Fifteen

WHEN HENRIETTA ENTERED THE LIBRARY, NOTHING IN her face or in her bearing betrayed her inward misgivings. She came in with her graceful, unhurried step, and looked across the room at her visitor, her brows faintly raised; and said, not uncivilly, but with a suggestion of high-bred reserve in her manner: 'Mr Steane?' She watched him execute a flourishing bow, and moved forward to a straight chair by the table in the middle of the room, saying, as she sat down on it: 'Pray, will you not be seated? Am I right in supposing you to be poor Cherry's father?'

'Yes, ma'am, you are indeed right!' he answered. 'Her sole surviving parent, separated from her by a cruel fate for too long, alas, and tortured by anxiety!'

She raised her brows rather higher, and said, in a polite, discouraging voice: 'Indeed?' She had the satisfaction of seeing that she had slightly discomfited him, and continued, with strengthened assurance: 'I regret, sir, that my mother—er—finds herself unable to receive you. She is a trifle indisposed today.'

'I shall not dream of intruding upon her,' he said graciously. 'My sole desire—I may say, my burning desire!—is to clasp my beloved child to my heart again. For this did I steel myself to revisit the land of my birth, with its poignant memories of my late, adored helpmate: inexpressibly painful to a man of sensibility, I assure you, Miss Silverdale! I presume I do have the honour of addressing Miss Silverdale?'

'Yes, I am Miss Silverdale,' she replied. 'It is unfortunate that you did not warn us of your intention to visit us today, for it so happens that Cherry is not, at the moment, here. She went out walking some time ago, and is not yet returned. However, I daresay you will not have long to wait before being—reunited with her.'

'Every moment that withholds her from me is an hour! You must pardon the natural impatience of a father, ma'am! I can scarcely bear to wait five minutes to see with my own eyes that she is safe and well.'

'She was perfectly safe and well when I last saw her,' said Henrietta calmly, 'but as she went out some hours ago I own I am a little uneasy, and have sent some of our servants to search for her, in case she may have met with an accident, or lost her way.'

He instantly assumed an expression of horror, and demanded in a shocked tone: 'Do you tell me, ma'am, that she was actually permitted to go out unattended? I had not thought such a thing to have been possible!'

'It was certainly imprudent,' she said, maintaining her air of calm. 'Had I been at home at the time I should have told her that she must take one of the footmen, or one of the maids, but I drove out myself quite early this morning, to visit an invalid, and so knew nothing about it, until I returned, an hour ago.'

'Had I known to what dangers, to what neglect, my tender, innocent child was being exposed—!' he groaned. 'But how could I have known? How could I have guessed that the woman to whose care I committed her would prove herself to be utterly unworthy of my trust, and would cast her on the world, careless into what hands she might fall?'

'Well, she didn't. She gave her into her aunt's hands. And I can't but feel, sir, that if you had kept her informed of your

whereabouts she would have written to you, to tell you that
Lady Bugle had taken Cherry to live with her.'

'I shall not weary you, ma'am, with an account of the circumstances which obliged me to withhold my direction from
Miss Fletching,' he said loftily. 'I am a man of many affairs, and
they take me all over Europe. In fact, I rarely know from one
day to the next *where* they will take me, or for how long. I
believed my child to be safe and happy in Miss Fletching's
charge. Never for an instant did I entertain the thought that she
would hand her over to one who has ever been—after my
father and my brother—my worst enemy! She has much to
answer for, and she shall answer for it! As I have told her!'

'Forgive me!' said Henrietta, 'but have not you more to answer
for than Miss Fletching, sir? It seems strangely unnatural for a
father—particularly such an affectionate father as yourself!—to
leave his daughter for so long without a word that she was forced
to mourn him as dead!'

Mr Steane dismissed this with a wave of his hand. 'If I had been
dead she would have been informed of it,' he said. 'It was quite
unnecessary for me to write to her. I will go further: it would
have been folly to have done so, for who knows but what she
might have wished to leave school, and join me abroad? I was not,
at that time, in a position to provide her with a settled home.'

'Oh!' said Henrietta. 'Are you now in that position, sir?'

'Certainly!' he replied. 'That is to say, as settled as one can ever
hope to be. But of what use is it to dwell upon what might have
been? I must resolutely banish the temptation to take the poor
child away. I must deny myself the solace of her company. I must
resign myself to loneliness. My duty is inescapable: I must see
her righted in the eyes of the world!'

'Good gracious, has she ever been wronged?' Henrietta said,
opening her eyes at him. 'If you are talking of her having run
away from her aunt, you must let me tell you that you are

making a mountain out of a molehill, Mr Steane! To be sure, it was rather a hurly-burly thing to do, and might have led her into dangerous trouble; but since, as good luck would have it, Lord Desford overtook her on the road, and brought her here, no harm has come of it.'

He heaved a deep sigh, that verged on a moan, and covered his eyes with one fat hand. 'Alas that it should fall to my lot to destroy your belief in Lord Desford's integrity!'

'Oh, you won't do that!' she said brightly. 'So pray don't fall into the dismals!'

He let his hand drop, and said, with a touch of asperity: 'That may be the story Lord Desford told you, ma'am, but—'

'It is. And it is also the story Cherry told me,' interpolated Henrietta.

'Instructed, I have no doubt at all, by his lordship! It is not the story I heard from Amelia Bugle! Far from it indeed! Very far from it! She told me that although she had been unable to discover when it was that Desford first met Cherry, it was certainly before the night of the ball at her house, when one of her daughters was a witness of his secret assignation with her, and in the course of which the elopement must have been planned.'

'What nonsense!' said Henrietta contemptuously. 'Elopement, indeed! I wonder you should have let yourself be bamboozled by such a ridiculous tale, sir! It's easy enough to see why she told it, of course: she was scared that you might discover that it was her abominable treatment that drove Cherry to run away! But that is the plain truth! As for Lord Desford's part in the business, you may think yourself very much obliged to him, for if he had not taken her up in his curricle, heaven knows what might have happened to her! I may add that as soon as he had established her in my mother's care he left immediately to find Lord Nettlecombe! He ran him to earth at Harrowgate—and any other man would have abandoned the search when he discovered that he would be obliged to travel more than two hundred miles to reach his lordship!'

Mr Steane shook his head at her, a sad, pitying smile curling his lips. 'That,' he sighed, 'is the tale Desford's young brother tried to hoax me with. I do not for a moment mean to suggest that *you* are trying to hoax me, Miss Silverdale, for it is plain to me that you too have been hoaxed. For how is it possible that Lord Desford— a man who has been on the town I know not how many years— should have supposed that my father would have contemplated for as much as a moment such a journey? *You* may not be aware that he is as scaly a snudge as was ever born, but Lord Desford must surely know it! Why, he has scarcely stirred out of Albemarle Street for years past! If he did find that his health demanded a change of air, the farthest he would have gone from London would have been Tunbridge Wells. Though I rather fancy,' he added, con- sidering the matter, 'that he would have retired to Nettlecombe Manor. Lodgings in watering-places, you know, are never to be had dog-cheap. As for the cost of travelling to Harrowgate—no, no, ma'am! That is doing it much too brown, believe me!'

'Nevertheless, he did go to Harrowgate, and is there at this moment. Perhaps his bride persuaded him to undertake the expense of the journey,' said Henrietta, with a wonderful air of innocence.

'His what?' ejaculated Mr Steane, starting upright in his chair, and staring at her very hard.

'Oh, didn't you know that he was lately married?' she said. 'Desford didn't know either, until he was introduced to the lady. I understand she was used to be his housekeeper. Not, I fear, the pink of gentility, but I feel, don't you, that it was very sensible of him to marry someone whom he can trust to look after him, and to manage his household exactly as he likes!'

She had introduced this new topic in the hope of diverting Mr Steane from the real object of his visit, and the gambit succeeded to admiration, though not in the way she had expected. Instead of going into a passion, he burst into a guffaw, slapping his thigh, and gasping: 'By God, that's the best joke I've heard in years! Caught in parson's mousetrap, is he? Damme if I don't write to felicitate him! That'll sting him on the raw! Why, he cast me off for eloping with Jane Wisset, and though I don't say she was of the first rank she wasn't a housekeeper!' He went off into another guffaw, which ended in a wheezing cough; and as soon as he was able to fetch his breath again, invited Henrietta to describe his stepmother to him. She was unable to do this, but she did regale him with some of the things Desford had told her. He was particularly delighted by the quarrel between the newly married couple which had sprung up over the silk shawl, and again slapped his thigh, declaring that it served the old hunks right. He then said, wistfully, that he wished he could have seen his brother's face when the news had been broken to him. He began to chuckle, but another thought occurred to him, and brought a cloud to his brow. 'The worst of it is he can't cut Jonas out of the inheritance,' he said gloomily. 'Still,' he added after brooding over this reflection for a few moments, and speaking in a more hopeful tone: 'I shouldn't wonder at it if this housekeeper makes the old muckworm bleed freely, so the chances are Jonas won't come into as big a fortune as he expected to.' He favoured Henrietta with a bland smile, and said: 'One should always try to look on the bright side. It has ever been my rule. You would be astonished, I daresay, how often the worst disasters do have a brighter aspect.'

She was as much diverted as she was shocked by this simple revelation of Mr Steane's character, and felt herself unable to do more than murmur an affirmative. Any hope that she might have entertained of Mr Steane's forgetting his daughter's predicament in the contemplation of his brother's rage and chagrin were dispelled by his next words. 'Well, well!' he said. 'Little did

I think that I should enjoy such an excellent joke today! But it will not do, Miss Silverdale! Jokes are out of place at such a time, when my breast is racked with anxiety. I accept that Lord Desford did go to Harrowgate; and I can only say that if he was such a dummy as to think he could fob my unfortunate child off on to her grandfather he has been like a woodcock, justly slain by its own treachery. Or words to that effect. My memory fails me, but I know a woodcock comes into it.'

What she might have been goaded to retort remained unspoken, for at this moment the Viscount came into the room. The thought that flashed into her mind was that he might have been designed to form a contrast to Wilfred Steane. There were fewer than twenty years between them, and it was easy to see that Steane had been a handsome man in his youth. But his good looks had been ruined by dissipation; and his figure spoke just as surely as his face of a life of indolence and over-indulgence. Nor were these faults remedied by his manner, or his dress. In both he favoured a florid style, which made him appear, in Henrietta's critical eyes, disastrously like a demi-beau playing off the airs of an exquisite. Desford, on the other hand, was complete to a shade, she thought. He had a handsome countenance; a lithe, athletic figure; and if the plain coat of blue super fine which he wore had had a label stitched to it bearing the name of Weston it could not have proclaimed the name of its maker more surely than did its superb cut. His air was distinguished; his manners very easy, and unaffected; and while there was no suggestion of the Pink, or the Bond Street Spark, about his trim person it was generally agreed in tonnish circles that his quiet elegance was the Real thing.

He shut the door, and advanced towards Henrietta, who had exclaimed thankfully: 'Desford!'

'Hetta, my love!' he responded, smiling at her, and kissing her hand. He stood holding it in a warm clasp for a minute, as he said:

'Had you despaired of me? I think you must have, and I do beg your pardon! I had hoped to have been with you before this.'

She returned the pressure of his fingers, and then drew her hand away, saying playfully: 'Well, at all events, you've arrived in time to make the acquaintance of Cherry's father, who isn't dead, after all! You must allow me to make you known to each other: Mr Wilfred Steane, Lord Desford!'

The Viscount turned, and raised his quizzing-glass, and through it surveyed Mr Steane, not for very long, but with daunting effect. Henrietta was forced to bite her lip quite savagely to suppress the laughter that bubbled up in her. It was so very unlike Des to do anything so odiously top-lofty! 'Oh,' he said. He bowed slightly. 'I am happy to make your acquaintance, sir.'

'I would I might say the same!' returned Mr Steane. 'Alas that we should meet, sir, under such unhappy circumstances!'

The Viscount looked surprised. 'I beg your pardon?'

'Lord Desford, I have much to say to you, but it would be better that I should speak privately to you!'

'Oh, I have no secrets from Miss Silverdale!' said Desford.

'My respect for a lady's delicate sensibilities has hitherto sealed my lips,' said Steane reprovingly. 'Far be it from me to ask a question that might bring a blush to female cheeks! But I have such a question to put to you, my lord!'

'Then by all means do put it to me!' invited Desford. 'Never mind Miss Silverdale's sensibilities! I daresay they aren't by half as delicate as you suppose—in fact, I'm quite sure they are not! You don't wish to retire, do you, Hetta?'

'Certainly not! I have not the remotest intention of doing so, either. I cut my eye-teeth many years ago, Mr Steane, and if what you have already said to me failed to bring a blush to my cheeks it is not very likely that whatever you are about to say will succeed in doing so! Pray ask Lord Desford any question you choose!'

Mr Steane appeared to be grieved by this response, for he sighed, and shook his head, and murmured: 'Modern manners! It was not so in my young days! But so be it! Lord Desford, are you betrothed to Miss Silverdale?'

'Well, I certainly hope I am!' replied the Viscount, turning his laughing eyes towards Henrietta. 'But what in the world has that to say to anything? I might add—do forgive me!—what in the world has it to do with you, sir?'

Mr Steane was not really surprised. He had known from the moment Desford had entered the room, and had exchanged smiles with Henrietta, that a strong attachment existed between them. But he was much incensed, and said, far from urbanely: 'Then I wonder at your shamelessness, sir, in luring my child away from the protection of her aunt's home with false promises of marriage! As for your effrontery in bringing her to your affianced wife—'

'Don't you think,' suggested the Viscount, 'that foolhardiness would be a better word? Or shall we come down from these impassioned heights? I don't know what you hope to achieve by mouthing such fustian rubbish, for I am persuaded you cannot possibly be so bacon-brained as to suppose that I am guilty of any of these crimes. The mere circumstance of my having placed Cherry in Miss Silverdale's care must absolve me from the two other charges you have laid at my door, but if you wish me to deny them categorically I'll willingly do so! So far from luring Cherry from Maplewood, when I found her trudging up to London I did my possible to persuade her to return to her aunt. I did not offer her marriage, or, perhaps I should add, a carte blanche! Finally, I brought her to Miss Silverdale because, for reasons which must be even better known to you than they are to me, my father would have taken strong exception to her presence under his roof!'

'Be that as it may,' said Mr Steane, struggling against the odds, 'you cannot—if there is any truth in you, which I am much inclined to doubt!—deny that you have placed her in a very equivocal situation!'

'I can and do deny it!' replied the Viscount.

'A man of honour,' persisted Mr Steane, with the doggedness of despair, 'would have restored her to her aunt!'

'That may be your notion of honour, but it isn't mine,' said the Viscount. 'To have forced her into my curricle, and then to have driven her back to a house where she had been so wretchedly unhappy that she fled from it, preferring to seek some means, however menial, of earning her bread to enduring any more unkindness from her aunt and her cousins, would have been an act of wicked cruelty! Moreover, I hadn't a shadow of right to do it! She begged me to carry her to her grandfather's house in London, hoping that he might allow her to remain there, and convinced that if he refused to do that he would at least house her until she had established herself in some suitable situation.'

'Well, if you thought he'd do any such thing, either you don't know the old snudge, or you're a gudgeon!' said Mr Steane. 'And from what I can see of you it's my belief you're the slyest thing in nature! Up to every move on the board!'

'Oh, not quite that!' said Desford. 'Only to your moves, Steane!'

'You remind me very much of your father,' said Mr Steane, eyeing him with considerable dislike.

'Thank you!' said Desford, bowing.

'Also that young cub of a brother of yours! Both of a hair! No respect for your seniors! A pair of stiff-rumped, bumptious bouncers! Don't think you can put the change on me, Desford, trying to hoax me with your Banbury stories, because you can't!'

'Oh, I shouldn't dream of doing so!' instantly replied his lordship. 'I never compete against experts!'

Henrietta said apologetically: 'Pray forgive me, but are you not straying a little away from the point at issue? Whether Desford was a gudgeon to think that Lord Nettlecombe would receive Cherry, or whether he thought what any man must have thought, doesn't seem to me to have any bearing on the case. He did drive her to London, only to find Lord Nettlecombe's house shut up. He then brought her to me. What, Mr Steane, do you suggest he should rather have done?'

'Thrown in the close!' murmured the Viscount irrepressibly.

'I must decline to enter into argument with you, ma'am,' said Steane, with immense dignity. 'I never argue with females. I will merely say that in accosting my daughter on the highway, coaxing her to climb into his curricle, and driving off with her his lordship behaved with great impropriety—if no worse! And since he abandoned her here—if she *is* here, which I gravely doubt!— what has he done to redress the injury her reputation has suffered at his hands? He would have me think that he sought my father out in the belief that he would take the child to his bosom—'

'Not a bit of it!' interrupted Desford. 'I hoped I could shame him into making her an allowance, that's all!'

'Well, if that's what you hoped you *must* be a gudgeon!' said Mr Steane frankly. 'Not that you did, of course! What you hoped was to be able to fob her off on to the old man, and you wouldn't have cared if he'd offered to engage her as a cook-maid as long as you were rid of her!'

'Some such offer was made,' said Desford. 'Not, indeed, by your father, but by your stepmother. I refused it.'

'Yes, it's all very well to say that, but how should I know if you're speaking the truth? All I know is that I return to England to find that my poor little girl has been tossed about amongst a set of unscrupulous persons, cast adrift in a harsh world—'

'Take a damper!' said the Viscount. 'None of that is true, as well you know! The unscrupulous person who cast her adrift is yourself; so let us have less of this theatrical bombast! You wish to know what I have done to redress the injury to her reputation she has suffered at my hands, and my answer is, Nothing—

because her reputation has suffered no injury either at my hands, or at anyone else's! But when I found that your father had gone out of town, the lord only knew where, and that Cherry had nowhere to go, not one acquaintance in London, and only a shilling or two in her purse, I realized that little though I might like it I must hold myself responsible for her. With your arrival, my responsibility has come to an end. But before I knew that you were not dead, but actually in this country, I drove down to Bath, to take counsel of Miss Fletching. I was a day behind you, Mr Steane. Miss Fletching most sincerely pities Cherry, and is, I think, very fond of her. She offers her a home, until she can hear of a situation which Cherry might like. She has one in her eye already, with an invalid lady whom she describes as very charming and gentle, but all depends upon her present companion, who is torn between her duty to her lately widowed parent, and her wish to remain with her kind mistress.'

'Oh, Des, it would be the very thing for Cherry!' Henrietta cried.

'What!' ejaculated Mr Steane, powerfully affected. 'The very thing for my beloved child to become a paid dependant? Over my dead body!' He buried his face in his handkerchief, but emerged from it for a moment to direct a look of wounded reproach at Desford, and to say in a broken voice: 'That I should have lived to hear my heart's last treasure so insulted!' He disappeared again into the handkerchief, but re-emerged to say bitterly: 'Shabby, my Lord Desford, that's what I call it!'

Desford's lips quivered, and his eyes met Henrietta's, which were brimful of the same appreciative amusement that had put to flight his growing exasperation. The look held, and in each pair of eyes was a warmth behind the laughter.

Mr Steane's voice intruded upon this interlude. 'And where,' he demanded, '*is* my little Charity? Answer that, one of you, before you make plans to degrade her!'

'Well, I am afraid we can't answer it just at this moment!' said Henrietta guiltily. 'Desford, you will think me dreadfully careless, but while I was visiting an old friend this morning, Cherry went out for a walk, and—and hasn't yet come back!'

'Mislaid her, have you? I learned from—Grimshaw—that she's missing, but I don't doubt she has done nothing more dangerous than lose her way, and will soon be back.'

'If she has not been spirited away,' said Mr Steane darkly. 'My mind is full of foreboding. I wonder if I shall ever see her again?'

'Yes, and immediately!' said Henrietta, hurrying across the room to the door. 'That's her voice! Heavens, what a relief!'

She opened the door as she spoke. 'Oh, Cherry, you *naughty* child! Where in the world—' She broke off abruptly, for a surprising sight met her eyes. Cherry was being carried towards the staircase by Mr Cary Nethercott, her bonnet hanging by its ribbon over one arm, a mutilated boot clutched in one hand, and the other gripping the collar of Mr Nethercott's rough shooting-jacket.

'Dear, dear Miss Silverdale, don't be vexed with me!' she begged. 'I know it was stupid of me to run out, but indeed I didn't mean to make you anxious! Only I lost my way, and couldn't find it, and at last I was so dreadfully tired that I made up my mind to ask the first person I met to show me how to get back to Inglehurst. But it was ages before I saw a single soul, and then it was a horrid man in a gig, who—who looked at me in *such* a way that—that I said it was of no consequence, and walked on as fast as I could. And then he called after me, and started to get down from the gig, and I ran for my life, into the woods, and, oh, Miss Silverdale, I tore my dress on the brambles, besides catching my foot in a horrid, trailing root, or branch, or something, and falling into a bed of nettles! And when I tried to get up I couldn't, because it hurt me so much that I thought I was going to faint.'

'Well, what a chapter of accidents!' said Henrietta. She saw that one of Cherry's ankles was heavily bandaged, and exclaimed: 'Oh, dear, dear, I collect you sprained your ankle! Poor Cherry!' She smiled at Cary Nethercott. 'Was she in your woods? Was that how you found her? How kind of you to have brought her home! I am very much obliged to you!'

'Yes, that was how it was,' he answered. 'I took my gun out, hoping to get a wood-pigeon or two, but instead I got a far prettier bird, as you see, Miss Hetta! Unfortunately I had no knife on me, so I thought it best to carry Cherry to my own house immediately, so that I could cut the boot off, and tell my housekeeper to apply cold poultices, to take down the swelling. I sent my man off to fetch Foston, fearing, you know, that there might be a broken bone, but he assured me that it was only a very bad sprain. You will say that I should have brought her back to you as soon as Foston had bound up her foot and ankle, but she was so much exhausted by the pain of having it inspected by Foston that I thought it best that she should rest until the pain had gone off.'

'You can't think how much it hurt, dear Miss Silverdale! But Mr Nethercott held my hand tightly all the time, and so I was able to bear it.'

'What a perfectly horrid day you've had!' said Henrietta. 'I'm so sorry, my dear: none of it would have happened if I hadn't been absent!'

'Oh, no, no, no!' Cherry said, her eyes and cheeks glowing, and a seraphic smile trembling on her mouth. 'It has been the happiest day of my whole life! Oh, Miss Silverdale, Mr Nethercott has asked me to marry him! Please, please say I may!'

'Good God!—I mean, you have no need to ask my permission, you goose! I have nothing to do but to wish you both very happy, which you may be sure I do, with all my heart! But there is someone here who has come especially to see you, and whom

I am persuaded you will be very glad to meet again. Bring her into the library, Mr Nethercott, and put her on the sofa, so that she can keep her foot up.'

'Who,' demanded Mr Steane of the Viscount, 'is this fellow who presumes to offer for my daughter without so much as a by your leave?'

'Cary Nethercott. An excellent fellow!' replied the Viscount enthusiastically.

He moved over to the sofa, and arranged the cushions on it, just as Cary Nethercott bore Cherry tenderly into the room. She exclaimed: 'Lord Desford! Indeed I'm glad to meet him again, Miss Silverdale, for I owe everything to him! How do you do, sir? I have wanted so much to thank you for having brought me here, and I never did, you know!'

He smiled, but said: 'Miss Silverdale didn't mean that you would be glad to meet *me* again, Cherry. Look, do you recognize that gentleman?'

She turned her head, and for the first time caught sight of Mr Steane. She stared at him blankly for an instant, and then gave a tiny gasp, and said: '*Papa?*'

'My child!' uttered Mr Steane. 'At last I may clasp you to my bosom again!' This, however, he was unable to do, since she had been set down on the sofa, and the corset he wore made it impossible for him to stoop so low. He compromised by putting an arm round her shoulders, and kissing her brow. 'My little Charity!' he said fondly.

'I thought you were dead, Papa!' she said wonderingly. 'I'm so happy to know you aren't! But why did you never write to me, or to poor Miss Fletching?'

'Do not speak to me of that woman!' he commanded, side-stepping this home-question. 'Never would I have left you in her charge had I known how shamefully she would betray my trust, my poor child!'

'Oh, *no*, Papa!' she cried distressfully. 'How can you say so, when she was so kind to me, and kept me at the school for nothing?'

'She delivered you up to Amelia Bugle, and that I can never forgive!' declared Mr Steane.

'But, Papa, you make it sound as if I wasn't willing to go with my aunt, but I promise you I was! I wanted to have a *home* *so* much. You don't know how much!' She found that Mr Nethercott, standing behind the head of the sofa, had dropped a hand on her shoulder, and she nursed it gratefully to her cheek, tears on the ends of her eyelashes. She winked them away, and continued to address her father, with a good deal of urgency: 'So, pray, Papa, don't go away again without paying her what she is owed!'

'Had I found you as I left you, happy in her care, I would have paid and overpaid her, but I did not so find you! I found you, after an unceasing search which was attended by such pangs of anxiety as only a father can know, being buffeted about the world, and not one penny will I pay her!' said Mr Steane resolutely.

'In other words,' said Desford, 'you mean to tip her the double!'

'Papa, you *cannot* behave so shabbily! You *must* not!' Cherry cried, in considerable agitation.

'I think, my love,' said Mr Nethercott, 'that you had best leave me to deal with this matter.'

'But it isn't right that you should deal with it!' she said indignantly. 'It isn't your debt! It's Papa's!'

'I do not acknowledge it,' stated Mr Steane majestically. 'She may consider herself fortunate that I have decided not to bring an action against her for gross neglect of her duty. That is my last word!'

'In that case,' said Mr Nethercott matter-of-factly, 'I will carry Cherry upstairs. You must realize, I am persuaded, sir, that she has had a very exhausting day, and has been quite knocked-up by it. Miss Hetta, will you conduct me to her bedchamber, if you please?'

'Indeed, I will!' Henrietta replied. 'No, no, don't argue, Cherry! Mr Nethercott is perfectly right, and I am going to put you to bed directly. You shall have your dinner sent up to you,—and your Papa may visit you tomorrow!'

'How kind you are! How *very* kind you are, Miss Silverdale!' Cherry sighed. 'I own I *am* feeling rather fagged, so—so if you won't think it very uncivil of me, Papa, I believe I will go to bed! Oh, Lord Desford, in case I don't see you again, goodbye, and thank you a thousand, thousand times for all you've done for me!'

He took the hand she stretched out to him, and kissed it, saying in a rallying voice: 'But you will be constantly seeing me, you little pea-goose! We are to be neighbours!'

'As to that,' said Mr Steane haughtily, 'I have by no means decided to give my consent to this marriage. I shall require Mr Nethercott to satisfy me as to his ability to support my daughter in a manner befitting her breeding.'

Mr Nethercott, already in the doorway with his fair burden, paused to say with unruffled composure that he would do himself the honour of laying before his prospective father-in-law all the relevant facts concerning his birth, fortune, and situation in life as soon as he had carried Cherry up to her room. He then continued on his purposeful way, preceded by Henrietta, and telling his betrothed, very kindly, to hush, when she attempted to argue that her marriage had nothing whatsoever to do with her father.

The Viscount shut the door, and strolled back to his chair, regarding Mr Steane with a pronounced twinkle in his eyes. 'You are to be congratulated, Mr Steane,' he said. 'Your daughter is making a very creditable marriage, and you need never suffer pangs of anxiety about her again.'

'There is that, of course,' acknowledged Mr Steane heavily. 'But when I think of the plans I have been making for years— I should have known better! All my life, Desford, I have been quite the dregs of my family as to luck. It disheartens a man! There's no denying that!' He turned his jaundiced gaze upon the Viscount, and added: 'Not that you know anything about it! You seem to me to have the devil's own luck! Well, consider what has happened this day! You wouldn't have braced it through if this fellow, Nethercott, hadn't dropped out of the sky like a honey-fall for you!'

'Oh, yes, I should!' said the Viscount. 'Not to use words with the bark on them, your intention was to bludgeon me into marrying Cherry, but you chose the wrong man, Steane: there was never the least hope of buttoning that scheme up!'

'I abandoned all thought of your marrying Cherry when I learned of your betrothal,' Mr Steane replied. 'Never shall it be said of me that I wrecked the happiness of an innocent female— however deluded she may be! But I fancy, my lord, you'd have come down handsomely to keep this scandalous business quiet! Or, at any hand, that stiff-necked father of yours would!'

'From what I know of my stiff-necked father, Mr Steane, I think he would have been far more likely to have driven you out of the country.'

'Well, it's a waste of time to discuss the matter!' said Mr Steane irritably.

'Of course it is! Consider instead how much cause you have to be thankful that your only daughter has had the good fortune to become attached to a man who will certainly make her an admirable husband!'

'My only daughter! She's another disappointment! There's no end to them. I had hopes of her when she was a child: seemed to be a bright, coming little thing. She could have been very useful to me.'

'In what way?' asked Desford curiously.

'Oh, many ways!' said Mr Steane. 'I hoped she might act as hostess in the establishment I have set up in Paris, but I saw at a glance that she's too like her mother. Pretty enough, but not up to snuff. Wouldn't know how to go on at all. A pity! Sheer waste of my time and blunt to have come to England.'

Since he seemed to be slipping rapidly into a maudlin frame of mind, the Viscount was relieved to see Mr Nethercott come back into the room. He was accompanied by Henrietta, and it was immediately plain to the Viscount that it was she who had prompted him to suggest to Mr Steane that it would be more convenient to discuss such matters as Settlements at Marley House.

'I think that an excellent notion!' she said warmly. 'You will wish to inspect Cherry's future home, I expect, Mr Steane. And if you care to visit her tomorrow, Mr Nethercott has been kind enough to say that he will be happy to put you up for the night!'

'I am obliged to you, sir,' said Mr Steane, reverting to his grand manner. 'I shall be happy to avail myself of your hospitality—but without prejudice, understand!' He then took a punctilious leave of Henrietta, bowed stiffly to the Viscount, and allowed himself to be ushered out of the room by the impassive Mr Nethercott.

'You unprincipled woman!' said the Viscount, when the door was fairly shut behind the departing visitors. 'You should be ashamed of yourself! Saddling the unfortunate man with that old rumstick!'

'Oh, did you guess it was my doing?' she said, breaking into pent-up laughter.

'Guess!' he said scornfully. 'I knew it the instant you came in looking as demure as a nun's hen!'

'Oh, no, did I? But I had to get rid of him, Des, or Mama would have taken to her bed! What with thinking Charlie had eloped with Cherry, and then hearing that Wilfred Steane was on his way to visit us, she's been having spasms, and vapours, and every sort of ache and ill, and is now in the worst of ill-humours! I shall have to go to her, or she will fall utterly into the hips. But before I do go, tell me what you feel about this astonishing betrothal! Will it do, or is he too old for her? I've noticed that she seems to prefer old men, but—'

'Never mind what I think! What do you think, Hetta?'

'How can I say? I think she is so amiable, and sweet-tempered, that she will be happy, as long as he is kind to her. As for him, he seems to be extremely fond of her, so perhaps he won't find her a trifle boring.'

'Fond of her! He must be nutty on her to be willing to marry her now that he's seen her father!'

She laughed. 'You know, Des, I didn't think he could be as bad as people say, but he's worse! If he weren't such a funny one I couldn't have borne to sit there listening to him! But when I was discussing her prospects with Mr Nethercott one day, he said that her parentage ought not to weigh against her in the mind of a man who fell in love with her. So I daresay he won't think her father worth a moment's consideration!'

'Hetta, tell me the truth! Has it hurt you?' he asked bluntly.

'Good God, no! Though it has sadly lowered my crest, I own! I was vain enough to think that he came here to visit me, not Cherry!'

'When I first met him, dangling after you, none of us had ever heard of Cherry,' he reminded her.

'I might have known you'd roast me for having been cut out by Cherry! What an odious creature you are, Des!' she said affably. 'By the by, do you and Simon mean to spend the night at Wolversham? I wish I might invite you both to dine with us, but I daren't! Mama has taken you in the most violent dislike, for having foisted Cherry on to us, and she never wants to see the face of a Carrington again! So for the present I must say goodbye to you!'

'Just a moment before you do that!' he said. 'You and I, my pippin, have still something to discuss!'

He spoke lightly, but the smile had vanished from his eyes, which were fixed on her face with a look in them that made her feel, for the first time in all their dealings, as shy as a schoolgirl. She said hurriedly: 'Oh, you refer, I collect, to that nonsensical story Simon made up about us! I must say I was excessively vexed with him, but I don't think any harm will come of it! Simon says that if it does leak out that we are secretly engaged we have only to deny it, or for one or other of us to cry off.' He returned no answer, and when she ventured to steal a look at him she found that he was still watching her intently. In an attempt to relieve what, for some inscrutable reason, she felt to be an embarrassing situation, she said, with a very creditable assumption of her usual liveliness: 'If it comes to that, I collect the task of crying off will be mine! I can never understand why it is thought very improper for a gentleman to cry off an engagement, but no such thing if the lady does it!'

'No,' he agreed, but not as if he had been attending to her. 'I give you fair warning, Hetta, that if it does come to that the task *will* be yours, for I have not the most remote intention— or desire—to cry off.' He paused for an instant, trying to read her face, but when she lifted her eyes, as though compelled, to his, his mouth twisted, and he said in a voice she had never heard before: 'But you shan't! I won't let you! Oh, Hetta, my dear pippin, I've been such a fool! I've loved you all my life, and never knew how much until I thought I was going to lose you! Don't say it's too late!'

A tiny smile wavered on her lips. She said simply: 'No, Des. N-not if you really mean it!'

'I never meant anything more in my life!' he said, and went to her, holding out his arms. She walked straight into them, and they closed tightly round her. 'My best of friends!' he said huskily, and kissed her.

This idyll was interrupted by Lady Silverdale, who came into the room, saying in the voice of one who had passed the limits of her endurance: 'I do think, Hetta, that you might have come to tell me—' She broke off, and exclaimed in scandalized accents:

'Hen-ri-etta!' Then, as Desford looked quickly round, and she perceived who it was who was embracing her daughter, her note changed. 'Desford!' she cried joyfully. 'Oh, my dear, dear boy! Oh, how happy this makes me! Hetta, my darling child! Now I don't care *what* happens!'

'But, Mama!' objected Hetta, wickedly quizzing her. 'You told me that nothing would prevail upon you to give your consent to my marrying Des! Why, you even congratulated me on my fortunate escape from such a fate!'

'Nonsense, Hetta!' said Lady Silverdale, very properly dismissing this untimely reminiscence. 'It has been the one wish of my life! I have always been excessively fond of him, and, what's more, I have never wavered from my conviction that he is just the man for you!'

'Thank you, ma'am!' said Desford, raising her hand to his lips. 'I *hope* I may be just the man for Hetta, but all I *know* is that she is just the woman for me!'

'Dear Ashley! Very prettily said!' she approved. 'It is what one so particularly likes in you! To be sure, I was not quite pleased with you when you brought Wilfred Steane's child here, but that's not of the smallest consequence *now*! But I must say, Hetta, it was as much as I could do to say what was proper when she told me, just now, that she had accepted an offer from Mr Nethercott. It seemed to me that there was to be no end to the gentlemen she steals from you! First it was Desford; then it was Charlie—not, of course, that he is one of your suitors, but the *principle is* the same—and now it's Mr Nethercott! Well, she's welcome to him, for I never thought him worthy of you, never! Desford, you will stay to dine with us, of course. Hetta, run and warn Ufford—No, I'll see him myself, and Charlie must talk to Grimshaw about champagne. Bless you, my dear ones!' With these words she went away to confer with the cook, her gait at startling variance from the tottering steps which had brought her into the room a few minutes earlier.

The lovers then resumed their previous occupation, only to be almost immediately interrupted by Simon, who strolled in, checked on the threshold in surprise at the sight which met his eyes, and burst into a shout of laughter. Reproved in no uncertain terms by his elder brother, he was quite unrepentant. 'Oh, isn't there anything to laugh at!' he said, kissing Hetta's cheek, and painfully wringing the Viscount's hand. 'Here's the pair of you, smelling of April and May ever since I can remember, and it ain't until *I* put it into your heads that it occurs to either of you to stop huffling and get spliced! Well, I told you you didn't know how nacky my best was, Des, but you know now!'

He then took his leave of them, declining an invitation to join the dinner-party on the score of its being imperative that he should be in London before it became too dark to see his way. 'I'm off to Brighton in the morning,' he explained. 'But if you should get into any more scrapes, Des, just send me word, and I'll post straight back to rescue you!'

# About the Author

*A*uthor of over fifty books, Georgette Heyer is one of the best-known and best-loved of all historical novelists, making the Regency period her own. Her first novel, *The Black Moth*, published in 1921, was written at the age of fifteen to amuse her convalescent brother; her last was *My Lord John*. Although most famous for her historical novels, she also wrote twelve detective stories. Georgette Heyer died in 1974 at the age of seventy-one.